RITA MAE BROWN

THREE MRS. MURPHY MYSTERIES

Wish You Were Here

—

Rest in Pieces

—

Murder at Monticello

Wish You Were Here

Rest in Pieces

Murder at Monticello

RITA MAE BROWN

& SNEAKY PIE BROWN

Illustrations by Wendy Wray

THREE MRS. MURPHY MYSTERIES IN ONE VOLUME

WINGS BOOKS • NEW YORK

Note on *Murder at Monticello*: During colonial times there were fewer people inhabiting the great state of Virginia and therefore fewer family names. Many of those early names are with us today, and to be true to the time, I have used them here.

Thomas Jefferson's grandson, James Madison Randolph, had no children, so "his branch" of the Randolph family used for this novel is entirely fictitious, as are the present-day characters and all events of the novel.

Originally published in three separate volumes by Bantam Books under the titles:

Wish You Were Here, copyright © 1990 by American Artists, Inc.

Rest in Pieces, copyright © 1992 by American Artists, Inc.
Illustrations copyright © 1992 by Wendy Wray

Murder at Monticello, copyright © 1994 by American Artists, Inc.

This edition contains the complete and unabridged texts of the original editions.

This 2003 edition is published by Wings Books®, an imprint of Random House Value Publishing, a division of Random House, Inc., New York, by arrangement with Bantam Dell Publishing Group, a division of Random House, Inc.

Wings Books® and colophon are trademarks of Random House, Inc.

Random House
New York • Toronto • London • Sydney • Auckland
www.randomhouse.com

Printed and bound in the United States of America.

A catalog record for this title is available from the Library of Congress.

ISBN 0-517-22223-X

10 9 8 7 6 5 4 3 2

Contents

Wish You Were Here

1

Rest in Pieces

245

Murder at Monticello

545

Wish You Were Here

Dedicated to the memory of
Sally Mead
Director of the Charlottesville-Albemarle
Society for the Prevention of Cruelty to Animals

Acknowledgments

Gordon Reistrup helped me type and proofread, and Carolyn Lee Dow brought me lots of catnip. I couldn't have written this book without them.

Cast of Characters

Mary Minor Haristeen (Harry), the young postmistress of Crozet, whose curiosity almost kills the cat and herself

Mrs. Murphy, Harry's gray tiger cat, who bears an uncanny resemblance to authoress Sneaky Pie and who is wonderfully intelligent!

Tee Tucker, Harry's Welsh corgi, Mrs. Murphy's friend and confidant; a buoyant soul

Pharamond Haristeen (Fair), veterinarian, being divorced by Harry and confused by life

Boom Boom Craycroft, a high-society knockout who carries a secret torch

Kelly Craycroft, Boom Boom's husband

Mrs. George Hogendobber (Miranda), a widow who thumps her own Bible!

Bob Berryman, misunderstood by his wife, Linda

Ozzie, Berryman's Australian shepherd

Market Shiflett, owner of Shiflett's Market, next to the post office

Pewter, Market's fat gray cat, who, when need be, can be pulled away from the food bowl

Susan Tucker, Harry's best friend, who doesn't take life too seriously until her neighbors get murdered

Ned Tucker, a lawyer and Susan's husband

Jim Sanburne, mayor of Crozet

Big Marilyn Sanburne (Mim), queen of Crozet and an awful snob

Little Marilyn Sanburne, daughter of Mim, and not as dumb as she appears

Josiah Dewitt, a witty antiques dealer sought out by Big Marilyn and her cronies

Maude Bly Modena, a smart transplanted Yankee

Rick Shaw, Albemarle sheriff

Cynthia Cooper, police officer

Hayden McIntire, town doctor

Rob Collier, mail driver

Paddy, Mrs. Murphy's ex-husband, a saucy tom

Author's Note

Mother is in the stable mucking out stalls, a chore she richly deserves. I've got the typewriter all to myself, so I can tell you the truth. I would have kept silent, but that fat toad Pewter pushed her way onto the cover of *Starting from Scratch*. She took full credit for writing the book. Granted, Pewter's ego is in a gaseous state, ever-expanding, but that act of feline self-advertisement was more than I could bear.

Let me set the record straight. I am seven years old and for the duration of my life I have assisted Mother in writing her books. I never minded that she failed to mention the extent of my contribution. Humans are like that, and since they're such frail creatures (can you call fingernails claws?), I let it go. Humans are one thing. Cats are another, and Pewter, one year my junior, is not the literary lion she is pretending to be.

You don't have to believe me. Let me prove it to you. I am starting a kitty crime series. Pewter has nothing to do with it. I will, however, make her a minor character to keep peace in the house. This is my own work, every word.

I refuse to divulge whether this novel is a *roman à clef*. I will say only that I bear a strong resemblance to Mrs. Murphy.

Yours truly,
SNEAKY PIE

1

Mary Minor Haristeen, Harry to her friends, trotted along the railroad track. Following at her heels were Mrs. Murphy, her wise and willful tiger cat, and Tee Tucker, her Welsh corgi. Had you asked the cat and the dog they would have told you that Harry belonged to them, not vice versa, but there was no doubt that Harry belonged to the little town of Crozet, Virginia. At thirty-three she was the youngest postmistress Crozet had ever had, but then no one else really wanted the job.

Crozet nestles in the haunches of the Blue Ridge Mountains. The town proper consists of Railroad Avenue, which parallels the Chesapeake & Ohio Railroad track, and a street intersecting it called the Whitehall Road. Ten miles to the east reposes the rich and powerful small city of Charlottesville, which, like a golden fungus, is spreading east, west, north, and south. Harry liked Charlottesville just fine. It was the developers she didn't much like, and she prayed nightly they'd continue to think of Crozet and its three thousand inhabitants as a dinky little whistle stop on the route west and ignore it.

A gray clapboard building with white trim, next to the rail depot, housed the post office. Next to that was a tiny grocery store and a butcher shop run by "Market" Shiflett. Everyone appreciated this convenience because you could pick up your milk, mail, and gossip in one central location.

Harry unlocked the door and stepped inside just as the huge

railroad clock chimed seven beats for 7:00 A.M. Mrs. Murphy scooted under her feet and Tucker entered at a more leisurely pace.

An empty mail bin invited Mrs. Murphy. She hopped in. Tucker complained that she couldn't jump in.

"Tucker, hush. Mrs. Murphy will be out in a minute—won't you?" Harry leaned over the bin.

Mrs. Murphy stared right back up at her and said, "*Fat chance. Let Tucker bitch. She stole my catnip sockie this morning.*"

All Harry heard was a meow.

The corgi heard every word. "*You're a real shit, Mrs. Murphy. You've got a million of those socks.*"

Mrs. Murphy put her paws on the edge of the bin and peeped over. "*So what. I didn't say you could play with any of them.*"

"Stop that, Tucker." Harry thought the dog was growling for no reason at all.

A horn beeped outside. Rob Collier, driving the huge mail truck, was delivering the morning mail. He'd return at four that afternoon for pickup.

"You're early," Harry called to him.

"Figured I'd cut you a break." Rob smiled. "Because in exactly one hour Mrs. Hogendobber will be standing outside this door huffing and puffing for her mail." He dumped two big duffel bags on the front step and went back to the truck. Harry carried them inside.

"Hey, I'd have done that for you."

"I know," Harry said. "I need the exercise."

Tucker appeared in the doorway.

"Hello, Tucker," Rob greeted the dog. Tucker wagged her tail. "Well, neither rain nor sleet nor snow, et cetera." Rob slid behind the wheel.

"It's seventy-nine degrees at seven, Rob. I wouldn't worry about the sleet if I were you."

He smiled and drove off.

Harry opened the first bag. Mrs. Hogendobber's mail was on the top, neatly bound with a thick rubber band. Rob, if he had the time, put Mrs. Hogendobber's mail in a pile down at the main post office in Charlottesville. Harry slipped the handful of mail into the mail slot. She then began sorting through the rest of the stuff: bills, enough mail-order catalogues to provide clothing for every man, woman, and child in the United States, and of course personal letters and postcards.

Courtney Shiflett, Market's fourteen-year-old daughter, received a postcard from Sally McIntire, away at camp. Kelly Craycroft, the handsome, rich paving contractor, was the recipient of a shiny postcard from Paris. It was a photo of a beautiful angel with wings. Harry flipped it over. It was Oscar Wilde's tombstone in the Père Lachaise cemetery. On the back was the message "Wish you were here." No signature. The handwriting was computer script, like signatures on letters from your congressperson. Harry sighed and slipped it into Kelly's box. It must be heaven to be in Paris.

Snowcapped Alps majestically covered a postcard addressed to Harry from her lifelong friend Lindsay Astrove.

Dear Harry—

Arrived in Zurich. No gnomes in sight. Good flight. Very tired. Will write some more later.

Best,

LINDSAY

It must be heaven to be in Zurich.

Bob Berryman, the largest stock trailer dealer in the South, got a registered letter from the IRS. Harry gingerly put it in his box.

Harry's best friend, Susan Tucker, received a large package from James River Traders, probably those discounted cotton sweaters she'd ordered. Susan, prudent, waited for the sales. Susan was the "mother" of Tee Tucker, named Tee because Susan gave her to Harry on the seventh tee at the Farmington Country Club. Mrs. Murphy, two years the dog's senior, was not amused, but she came to accept it.

A Gary Larsen postcard attracted Harry's attention. Harry turned it over. It was addressed to Fair Haristeen, her soon-to-be-ex-husband, but not soon enough. "Hang in there, buddy" was the message from Stafford Sanburne. Harry jammed the postcard in Fair's box.

Crozet was still small enough that people felt compelled to take sides during a divorce. Perhaps even New York City was that small. At any rate, Harry reeled from fury to sorrow on a daily basis as she watched former friends choose sides, and most were choosing Fair.

After all, she had left him, thereby outraging other women in Albemarle County stuck in a miserable marriage but lacking the guts to go. That was a lot of women.

"Thank God they didn't have children," clucked many tongues behind Harry's back and to her face. Harry agreed with them. With children the goddamned divorce would take a year. Without, the limbo lasted only six months and she was two down.

By the time the clock struck eight the two duffel bags were folded over, the boxes filled, the old pine plank floor swept clean.

Mrs. George Hogendobber, an evangelical Protestant, picked up her mail punctually at 8:00 A.M. each morning except Sunday, when she was evangeling and the post office was closed. She fretted a great deal over evolution. She was determined to prove that humans were not descended from apes but, rather, created in God's own image.

Mrs. Murphy fervently hoped that Mrs. Hogendobber would prove her case, because linking man and ape was an insult to the ape. Of course, the good woman would die of shock to discover that God was a cat and therefore humans were off the board entirely.

That large Christian frame was lurching itself up the stairs. She pushed open the door with her characteristic vigor.

"Morning, Harry."

"Morning, Mrs. Hogendobber. Did you have a good weekend?"

"Apart from a splendid service at the Holy Light Church, no." She yanked out her mail. "Josiah DeWitt stopped by as I came home and gave me his sales pitch to part with Mother's Louis XVI bed, canopies and all. And on the Sabbath. The man is a servant of Mammon."

"Yes—but he knows good stuff when he sees it." Harry flattered her.

"H-m-m, Louis this and Louis that. Too many Louis's over there in France. Came to a bad end, too, every one of them. I don't think the French have produced anyone of note since Napoleon."

"What about Claudius Crozet?"

This stopped Mrs. Hogendobber for a moment. "Believe you're right. Created one of the engineering wonders of the nineteenth century. I stand corrected. But that's the only one since Napoleon."

The town of Crozet was named for this same Claudius Crozet, born on December 31, 1789. Trained as an engineer, he fought with the French in Russia and was captured on the hideous retreat from Moscow. So charmed was his Russian captor that he promptly removed Claudius to his huge estate and set him up with books and engineering tools. Claudius performed services for his captor until Frenchmen were allowed to return home. They say the Russian, a prince of the blood, rewarded the young captain with jewels, gold, and silver.

Joining Napoleon's second run at power proved dangerous, and Crozet immigrated to America. If he had a fortune, he carefully concealed it and lived off his salary. His greatest feat was cutting four railroad tunnels through the Blue Ridge Mountains, a task begun in 1850 and completed eight years later.

The first tunnel was west of Crozet: the Greenwood tunnel, 536 feet, and sealed after 1944, when a new tunnel was completed. Over the eastern portal of the Greenwood tunnel, carved in stone, is the legend: C. CROZET, CHIEF ENGINEER; E. T. D. MYERS, RESIDENT ENGINEER; JOHN KELLY, CONTRACTOR. A.D. 1852.

The second tunnel, Brooksville, 864 feet, was also sealed after 1944. This was a treacherous tunnel because the rock proved soft and unreliable.

The third tunnel was the Little Rock, 100 feet long and still in use by the C & O.

The fourth was the Blue Ridge, a long 4,723 feet.

Unused tracks ran to the sealed tunnels. They built things to last in the nineteenth century, for none of the rails had ever warped.

Crozet was reputed to have hidden his fortune in one of the tunnels. This story was taken seriously enough by the C & O Railroad that they carefully inspected the discontinued tunnels before sealing them after World War II. No treasure was ever found.

Mrs. Hogendobber left immediately after being corrected. She passed Ned Tucker, Susan's husband, on his way in. They exchanged pleasantries. Tee Tucker, barking merrily, rushed out to greet Ned. Mrs. Murphy climbed out of the mail bin and jumped onto the counter. She liked Ned. Everyone did.

He winked at Harry. "Well, have you been born again?"

"No, and I wasn't born yesterday either." She laughed.

"Mrs. H. was unusually terse this morning." He grabbed a huge handful of mail, most of it for the law office of Sanburne, Tucker, and Anderson.

"Count your blessings," Harry said.

"I do, every day." Ned smiled. Escaping a tirade of salvation on this hot July morning was just one blessing and Ned was a happy enough man to know there'd be many more. He stooped to rub Tucker's ears.

"You can rub mine, too," Mrs. Murphy pleaded.

"He likes me better than you." Tucker relished being the center of attention.

"Don't you love the sounds they make?" Ned kept scratching. "Sometimes I think they're almost human."

"Can you believe that?" Mrs. Murphy licked her front paws. Being human, the very thought! Humans lacked claws, fur, and their senses were dismal. Why, she could hear a doodlebug burrow in the sand. Furthermore, she understood everything humans said in their guttural way. They rarely understood her or other animals, much less one another. To get a reaction out of even Harry, who she confessed she did love, she had to resort to extravagant behavior.

"Yeah, I don't know what I'd do without my kids. Speaking of which, how're yours?"

Ned's eyes darted for a moment. "Harry, I'm beginning to think that sending Brookie to private school was a mistake. She's twelve going on twenty, and a perfect little snob too. Susan wants her to return to St. Elizabeth's in the fall but I say we yank her out of there and pack her back to public middle school with her brother. There she has to learn how to get along with all different kinds of people. Her grades fell and that's when Susan decided she was going to St. Elizabeth's. We went through public school, we learned, and we turned out all right."

"It's a tough call, Ned. They weren't selling drugs in the bathroom when you were in school."

"They were by the time we got to Crozet High. You had the good sense to ignore it."

"No, I didn't have the money to buy the stuff. Had I been one of those rich little subdivision kids—like today—who's to say?" Harry shrugged.

Ned sighed. "I'd hate to be a child now."

"Me too."

Bob Berryman interrupted. "Hey!" Ozzie, his hyper Australian shepherd, tagged at his heels.

"Hey, Berryman." Harry and Ned both called back to him out of politeness. Berryman's personality hovered on simmer and often flamed up to boil.

Mrs. Murphy and Tucker said hello to Ozzie.

"Hotter than the hinges of hell." Berryman sauntered over to his box and withdrew the mail, including the registered letter slip. "Shit, Harry, gimme a pen." She handed him a leaky ballpoint. He signed the slip and glared at the IRS notice. "The world is going to hell in a handbasket and the goddamned IRS controls the nation! I'd kill every one of those sons of bitches given half the chance!"

Ned walked out of the post office waving goodbye.

Berryman gulped some air, forced a smile, and calmed himself by petting Mrs. Murphy, who liked him although most humans found him brusque. "Well, I've got worms to turn and eggs to lay." He pushed off.

Bob's booted feet clomped on the first step as he closed the front door. As she didn't hear a second footfall, Harry glanced up from her stamp pads.

Walking toward Bob was Kelly Craycroft. His chestnut hair, gleaming in the light, looked like burnished bronze. Kelly, an affable man, wasn't smiling.

Wagging his tail, Ozzie stood next to Bob. Bob still didn't move. Kelly arrived at the bottom step. He waited a moment, said something to Bob which Harry couldn't hear, and then moved up to the second step, whereupon Bob pushed him down the steps.

Furious, his face darkening, Kelly scrambled to his feet. "You asshole!"

Harry heard that loud and clear.

Bob, without replying, sauntered down the steps, but Kelly, not a man to be trifled with, grabbed Bob's shoulder.

"You listen to me and you listen good!" Kelly shouted.

Harry wanted to move out from behind the counter. Good manners got the better of her. It would be too obvious. Instead she strained every fiber to hear what was being said. Tucker and Mrs. Murphy, hardly worried about how they'd look to others, bumped into each other as they ran to the door.

This time Bob raised his voice. "Take your hand off my shoulder."

Kelly squeezed harder and Bob balled up his fist, hitting him in the stomach.

Kelly doubled over but caught his breath. Staying low, he lunged, grabbing Bob's legs and throwing him to the pavement.

Ozzie, moving like a streak, sank his teeth into Kelly's left leg. Kelly hollered and let go of Bob, who jumped up.

"No" was all Bob had to say to Ozzie, and the dog immediately obeyed. Kelly stayed on the ground. He pulled up his pants leg. Ozzie's bite had broken the skin. A trickle of blood ran into his sock.

Bob said something; his voice was low. The color ran out of Kelly's face.

Bob walked over to his truck, got in, started the motor, and pulled out as Kelly staggered to his feet.

Jolted by the sight of blood, Harry shelved any concern about manners. She opened the door, hurrying over to Kelly.

"Better put some ice on that. Come on, I've got some in the refrigerator."

Kelly, still dazed, didn't reply immediately.

"Kelly?"

"Oh—yeah."

Harry led him into the post office. She dumped the ice out of the tray onto a paper towel.

Kelly was reading his postcard when she handed him the ice. He sat down on the bench, rolled up his pants leg, and winced when the cold first touched his leg. He stuck his mail in his back pocket.

"Want me to call Doc?" Harry offered.

"No." Kelly half smiled. "Pretty embarrassing, huh?"

"No more embarrassing than my divorce."

That made Kelly laugh. He relaxed a bit. "Hey, Mary Minor Haristeen, there is no such thing as a good divorce. Even if both parties start out with the best of intentions, when the lawyers get into it, the whole process turns to shit."

"God, I hope not."

"Trust me. It gets worse before it gets better." Kelly removed the ice. The bleeding had stopped.

"Keep it on a little longer," Harry advised. "It will prevent swelling."

Kelly replaced the makeshift ice pack. "It's none of my business, but you should have ditched Fair Haristeen years ago. You kept hanging in there trying to make it work. All you did was waste time. You cast your pearls before swine."

Harry wasn't quite ready to hear her husband referred to as swine, but Kelly was right: She should have gotten out earlier. "We all learn at our own rates of speed."

He nodded. "True enough. It took me this long to realize that Bob Berryman, ex–football hero of Crozet High, is a damned wimp. I mean, pushing me down the steps, for chrissake. Because of a bill. Accusing me of overcharging him for a driveway. I've been in business for myself for twelve years now and no one's accused me of overcharging."

"It could have been worse." Harry smiled.

"Oh, yeah?" Kelly glanced up quizzically.

"Could have been Josiah DeWitt."

"You got that right." Kelly rolled down his pants leg. He tossed the paper towel in the trash, said, "Harry, hang in there," and left the post office.

She watched him move more slowly than usual and then she returned to her tasks.

Harry was re-inking her stamp pads and cleaning the clogged ink out of the letters on the rubber stamps. She'd gotten to the point where she had maroon ink on her forehead as well as all over her fingers when Big Marilyn Sanburne, "Mim," marched in. Marilyn belonged to that steel-jawed set of women who were honorary men. She was called Big Marilyn or Mim to distinguish her from her daughter, Little Marilyn. At fifty-four she retained a cold beauty that turned heads. Burdened with immense hours of leisure, she stuck her finger in every civic pie, and her undeniable energy sent other volunteers to the bar or into fits.

"Mrs. Haristeen"—Mim observed the mess—"have you committed a murder?"

"No—just thinking about it." Harry slyly smiled.

"First on my list is the State Planning Commission. They'll never put a western bypass through this country. I'll fight to my last breath! I'd like to hire an F-14 and bomb them over there in Richmond."

"You'll have plenty of volunteers to help you, me included." Harry wiped, but the ink was stubborn.

Mim enjoyed the opportunity to lord it over someone, anyone. Jim Sanburne, her husband, had started out life on a dirt farm, and fought and scratched his way to about sixty million dollars. Despite Jim's wealth, Mim knew she had married beneath her and she was a woman who needed external proof of her social status. She needed her name in the Social Register. Jim thought it foolish. Her marriage was a constant trial. It was to Jim, too. He ran his empire, ran Crozet because he was mayor, but he couldn't run Mim.

"Well, have you reconsidered your divorce?" Mim sounded like a teacher.

"No." Harry blushed from anger.

"Fair's no better or worse than any other man. Put a paper bag over their heads and they're all the same. It's the bank account that's important. A woman alone has trouble, you know."

Harry wanted to say, "Yes, with snobs like you," but she shut up.

"Do you have gloves?"

"Why?"

"To help me carry in Little Marilyn's wedding invitations. I don't want to befoul them. Tiffany stationery, dear."

"Wait a minute, here." Harry rooted around.

"*You put them next to the bin,*" Tucker informed her.

"I'll take you to the bathroom in a minute, Tucker," Harry told the dog.

"*I'll knock them on the floor. See if she gets it.*" Mrs. Murphy nimbly trotted the length of the counter, carefully sidestepping the ink and stamps, and with one gorgeous leap landed on the shelf, where she pushed off the gloves.

"The cat knocked your gloves off the shelf."

Harry turned as the gloves hit the floor. "So she has. She must know what we're saying." Harry smiled, then followed Big Marilyn out to her copen-blue Volvo.

"*Sometimes I wonder why I put up with her,*" Mrs. Murphy complained.

"*Don't start. You'd be lost without Harry.*"

"*She is good-hearted, I will admit, but Lord, she's slow.*"

"*They all are,*" Tucker agreed.

Harry and Mim returned carrying two cardboard boxes filled with pale cream invitations.

"Well, Harry, you will know who is invited and who isn't before anyone else."

"I usually do."

"You, of course, are invited, despite your current, uh, problem. Little Marilyn adores you."

Little Marilyn did no such thing but no one dared not invite

Harry, because it would be so rude. She really did know every guest list in town. Because she knew everything and everybody, it was shrewd to keep on Harry's good side. Big Marilyn considered her a "resource person."

"Everything is divided up by zip code and tied." Mim tapped the counter. "And don't pick them up without your gloves on, Harry. You're never going to get that ink off your fingers."

"Promise."

"I'll leave it to you, then."

No sooner had she relieved Harry of her presence than Josiah DeWitt appeared, tipping his hat and chatting outside to Mim for a moment. He wore white pants and a white shirt and a snappy boater on his head, the very image of summer. He pushed open the door, touched the brim of his hat, and smiled broadly at the postmistress.

"I have affixed yet another date with the wellborn Mrs. Sanburne. Tea at the club." His eyes twinkled. "I don't mind that she gossips. I mind that she does it so badly."

"Josiah—" Harry never knew what he would say next. She slapped his hand as he reached into one of the wedding invitation boxes. "Government property now."

"That government governs best which governs least, and this one has its tentacles into every aspect of life, every aspect. Terrifying. Why, they even want to tell us what to do in bed." He grinned. "Ah, but I forgot you wear a halo on that subject now that you're separated. Of course, you wouldn't want to be accused of adultery in your divorce proceeding, so I shall assume yours is virtue by necessity."

"And lack of opportunity."

"Don't despair, Harry, don't despair. Anyway, you got a great nickname out of ten years of marriage . . . although Mary suits you now, because of the halo."

"You're awful sometimes."

"Rely on it." Josiah flipped through his mail and moaned, "Ned has given me the compliment of an invoice. Lawyers get a cut of everything, don't they?"

"Kelly Craycroft calls you Moldy Money." Harry liked Josiah because she could devil him. Some people you could and others you couldn't. "Don't you want to know why he calls you Moldy Money?"

"I already know. He says I've got the first dollar I ever made and it's moldering in my wallet. I prefer to think that capital, that offspring of business, is respected by myself and squandered by others, Kelly Craycroft in particular. I mean, how many paving contractors do you know who drive a Ferrari Mondial? And here, of all places." He shook his head.

Harry had to agree that owning a Ferrari, much less driving one, was on the tacky side. That's what people did in big cities to impress strangers. "He's got the money—I guess he can spend it the way he chooses."

"There's no such thing as a poor paving contractor, so perhaps you're right. Still"—his voice lowered—"so hopelessly flashy. At least Jim Sanburne drives a pickup." He absentmindedly slapped his mail on his thigh. "You will tell me, of course, who is and who isn't invited to Child Marilyn's wedding. I especially want to know if Stafford is invited."

"We all want to know that."

"What's your bet?"

"That he isn't."

"A safe bet. They were so close as children, too. Really devoted, that brother and sister. A pity. Well, I'm off. See you tomorrow."

Through the glass door Harry watched Susan Tucker and Josiah engage in animated conversation. So animated that when finished, Susan leaped up the three stairs in a single bound and flung open the door.

"Well! Josiah just told me you've got Little Marilyn's wedding invitations."

"I haven't looked."

"But you will and no time like the present." Susan opened the door by the counter and came around behind it.

"You can't touch that." Harry removed her gloves as Tucker joyfully jumped on Susan, who hugged and kissed her. Mrs. Murphy watched from her shelf. Tucker was laying it on pretty thick.

"Wonderful doggie. Beautiful doggie. Gimme a kiss." Susan saw Harry's hands. "Well, you can't touch the envelopes either, so for the next fifteen minutes I'll do your job."

"Do it in the back room, Susan. If anyone sees you we're both in trouble. Stafford will be in the one-double-oh zip codes and I think he's in one-double-oh two three, west of Central Park."

Susan called over her shoulder on her way to the back room: "If you can't live on the East Side of Manhattan, stay home."

"The West Side's really nice now."

"It's not here. Can you believe it?" Susan hollered from the back room.

"Sure, I believe it. What'd you expect?"

Susan came out and put the box under the counter. "Her own son. She's got to forgive him sometime."

"Forgiveness isn't a part of Big Marilyn Sanburne's vocabulary, especially when it impinges on her exalted social standing."

"This isn't the 1940's. Blacks and whites do marry now and the miscegenation laws are off the books."

"How many mixed marriages do you know in Crozet?"

"None, but there are a few in Albemarle County. I mean, this is so silly. Stafford's been married for six years now and Brenda is a stunning woman. A good one, too, I think."

"Are you going to have lunch with me? You're the only one left who will."

"It just seems that way because you're oversensitive right now. Come on, you'd better get out of here before someone else zooms through the door. You know how crazy Mondays are."

"Okay, I'm ready. My relief pitcher just pulled in." Harry smiled. It was nice having old Dr. Larry Johnson to cover the post office from 12:00 to 1:00 so she could take a lunch hour. It was also handy when she had errands to run during business hours. All she had to do was give him a call.

Dr. Johnson held the door for Harry, Susan, and the animals.

"Thank you, Dr. Johnson. How are you today?" Harry appreciated his gentlemanly gesture.

"I'm doing just fine, thank you."

"Good afternoon, Doctor," Susan said as Mrs. Murphy and Tucker greeted him with a chorus of purrs and yips.

"Hi, Susan. Good afternoon, Mrs. Murphy. And to you, too, Tee Tucker." Dr. Johnson reached down to pet Harry's buddies. "Where are you ladies headed?"

"We're just trotting up to Crozet Pizza for subs. Thanks for holding down the fort."

"My pleasure, as always. Have a good lunch," the retired doctor called after them.

Harry, Susan, Mrs. Murphy, and Tucker strolled down the shimmering sidewalk. The heat felt like a thick, moist wall. They waved at Market and Courtney Shiflett, working in the grocery store. Pewter, Market's chubby gray cat, indulged in a flagrant display of her private parts right there in the front window. On seeing Mrs. Murphy and Tucker, she said hello. They called back to her and walked on.

"*I can't believe she's let herself go to pot like that,*" Mrs. Murphy whispered to Tucker. "*All those meat tidbits Market feeds her. Girl has no restraint.*"

"*Doesn't get much exercise either. Not like you.*"

Mrs. Murphy accepted the compliment. She had kept her figure just in case the right tom came along. Everyone, including Tucker, thought she was still in love with her first husband, Paddy, but Mrs. Murphy was certain she was over him. Over in capital letters. Paddy wore a tuxedo, oozed charm, and resented any accusation of usefulness. Worse, he ran off with a silver Maine coon cat and then had the nerve to come back thinking Mrs. Murphy would be glad to see him after the escapade. Not only was she not glad, she nearly scratched his eye out. Paddy sported a scar over his left eye from the fight.

Harry and Susan ordered huge subs at Crozet Pizza. They stayed inside to eat them, luxuriating in the air conditioning. Mrs. Murphy sat in a chair and Tucker rested under Harry's chair.

Harry bit into her sandwich and half the filling shot out the other end. "Damn."

"That's the purpose of a submarine sandwich. To make us look foolish." Susan giggled.

Maude Bly Modena came in at that moment. She started to walk over to takeout, then saw Harry and Susan. She ambled over for a polite exchange. "Use a knife and fork. What'd you do to your hands?"

"I was cleaning stamps."

"I, for one, don't care if my first class is blurred. Better than having you look like Lady Macbeth."

"I'll keep it in mind," Harry replied.

"I'd stay and chew the fat, ladies, but I've got to get back to the shop."

Maude Bly Modena had moved to Crozet from New York five years ago. She opened a packing store—cartons, plastic peanuts, papers, the works—and the store was a smash. An old railroad lorry sat in the front yard and she would put floral displays and the daily store discounts on the lorry. She knew how to attract customers and she herself was attractive, in her late thirties. At Christmastime there were lines to get into her store. She was a sharp businesswoman and friendly, to boot, which was a necessity in these parts. In time the residents forgave her that unfortunate accent.

Maude waved goodbye as she passed the picture window. Harry and Susan waved in return.

"I keep thinking Maude will find Mr. Right. She's so attractive."

"Mr. Wrong's more like it."

"Sour grapes."

"Am I like that, Susan? I hope not. I mean, I could rattle off the names of bitter divorced women and we'd be here all afternoon. I don't want to join that club."

Susan patted Harry's hand. "You're too sensitive, as I've said before. You'll cycle through all kinds of emotions. For lack of a better term, sour grapes is one of them. I'm sorry if I hurt your feelings."

Harry squirmed in her seat. "I feel as if there's no coating on my nerve endings." She settled in her chair. "You're right about Maude.

She's got a lot going for her. There ought to be someone out there for her. Someone who would appreciate her—and her business success too."

Susan's eyes danced. "Maybe she's got a lover."

"No way. You can't burp in your kitchen but what everyone knows it. No way." Harry shook her head.

"I wonder." Susan poured herself more Tab. "Remember Terrance Newton? We all thought we knew Terrance."

Harry thought about that. "Well, we were teenagers. I mean, if we had been adults, maybe we'd have picked up on something. The vibes."

"An insurance executive we all know goes home, shoots his wife and himself. My recollection is the adults were shocked. No one picked up on anything. If you can keep up your facade, people accept that. Very few people look beneath the surface."

Harry sighed. "Maybe everyone's too busy."

"Or too self-centered." Susan drummed the table with her fingers. "What I'm getting at is that maybe we don't know one another as well as we think we do. It's a small-town illusion—thinking we know each other."

Harry quietly played with her sub. "You know me. I think I know you."

"That's different. We're best friends." Susan polished off her sandwich and grabbed her brownie. "Imagine being Stafford Sanburne and not being invited to your sister's wedding."

"That was a leap."

"Like I said, we're best friends. I don't have to think in sequence around you." Susan laughed.

"Stafford sent Fair a postcard. 'Hang in there, buddy.' Come to think of it, that's what Kelly said to me. Hey, you missed it. Kelly Craycroft and Bob Berryman had a fight, fists and all."

"You wait until now to tell me!"

"So much else has been going on, it slipped my mind. Kelly said it was about a paving bill. Bob thinks he overcharged him."

"Bob Berryman may not be Mr. Charm but that doesn't sound like him, to fight over a bill."

"Hey, like I said, maybe we don't really know one another."

Harry picked tomatoes out of her sandwich. They were the cul-prits; she was sure the meat, cheese, and pickles would stay inside without those slimy tomatoes. She slapped the bread back together as Mrs. Murphy reached across the plate to hook a piece of roast beef. "Mrs. Murphy, that will do." Harry used her commanding mother voice. It would work at the Pentagon. Mrs. Murphy with-drew her paw.

"Maybe we should rejoice that Little Marilyn's made a match at last," Susan said.

"You don't think that Little Marilyn bagged Fitz-Gilbert Hamilton by herself, do you?"

Susan considered this. "She's got her mother's beauty."

"And is cold as a wedge."

"No, she isn't. She's quiet and shy."

"Susan, you've liked her since we were kids and I never could stand Little Marilyn. She's such a momma's baby."

"You drove your mother wild."

"I did not."

"Oh, yeah, how about the time you put your lace underpants over her license plate and she drove around the whole day not knowing why everyone was honking at her and laughing."

"That." Harry remembered. She missed her mother terribly. Grace Minor had died unexpectedly of a heart attack four years earlier, and Cliff, her husband, followed within the year. He couldn't make a go of it without Grace and he admitted as much on his deathbed. They were not rich people by any means but they left Harry a lovely clapboard house two miles west of town at the foot of Little Yellow Mountain and they also left a small trust fund, which paid for taxes on the house and pin money. A house without a mortgage is a wonderful inheritance, and Harry and Fair were happy to move from their rented house on Myrtle Street. Of course, when Harry asked Fair to leave, he complained bitterly that he had always hated living in her parents' house.

"Fitz-Gilbert Hamilton is ugly as sin, but he's never going to need food stamps and he's a Richmond lawyer of much repute—at least that's what Ned says."

"Too much fuss over this marriage. You marry in haste and repent in leisure."

"Don't be sour." Susan's eyes shot upward.

"The happiest day of my life was when I married Pharamond Haristeen and the next happiest day of my life was when I threw him out. He's full of shit and he's not going to get any sympathy from me. God, Susan, he's running all over town, the picture of the wounded male. He has dinner every night with a different couple. I heard that Mim Sanburne offered her maid to do his laundry for him. I can't believe it."

Susan sighed. "He seems to relish being a victim."

"Well, I sure don't." Harry practically spat. "The only thing worse than being a veterinarian's wife is being a doctor's wife."

"That's not why you want to divorce him."

"No, I guess not. I don't want to talk about this."

"You started it."

"Did I?" Harry seemed surprised. "I didn't mean to. . . . I'd like to forget the whole thing. We were talking about Little Marilyn Sanburne."

"We were. Little Marilyn will be deeply hurt if Stafford doesn't show up, and Mim will die if he does—her event-of-the-year marriage marred by the arrival of her black daughter-in-law. Life would be much simpler if Mim would overcome her plantation mentality." Susan drummed the table again.

"Yeah, but then she'd have to join the human race. I mean, she's emotionally impotent and wants to extend her affliction universally. If she changed her thinking she might have to feel something, you know? She might have to admit that she was wrong and that she's wounded her children, wounded and scarred them."

Susan sat silent for a moment, viewing the remnants of the once-huge sub. "Yeah—here, Tucker."

"*Hey, hey, what about me?*" Mrs. Murphy yelled.

"Oh, here, you big baby." Harry shoved over her plate. She was full.

Mrs. Murphy ate what was left except for the tomatoes. As a kitten, she once ate a tomato and vowed never again.

Harry strolled back to the post office, and the rest of the day ran on course. Market dropped by some knucklebones. Courtney picked up the mail while her dad talked.

After work Harry walked back home. She liked the two-mile walk in the mornings and afternoons. Good exercise for her and the cat and the dog. Once home, she washed her old Superman-blue truck, then weeded her garden. She cleaned out the refrigerator after that and before she knew it, it was time to go to bed.

She read a bit, Mrs. Murphy curled up by her side with Tucker snoring at the end of the bed. She turned out her light, as did the other residents of Crozet ensconced behind their high hedges, blinds, and shutters.

It was the end of another day, peaceful and perfect in its way. Had Harry known what tomorrow would bring, she might have savored the day even more.

2

Mrs. Murphy performed a somersault while chasing a grasshopper. She never could resist wigglies, as she called them. Tucker, uninterested in bugs, cast a keen eye for squirrels foolish enough to scamper down Railroad Avenue. The old tank watch, her father's, on Harry's wrist read 6:30 A.M. and the heat rose off the tracks. It was a real July Virginia day, the kind that compelled weathermen and weatherwomen on television to blare that it would be hot, humid, and hazy with no relief in sight. They then counseled the viewer to drink plenty of liquids. Cut to a commercial for, surprise, a soft drink.

Harry reflected on her childhood. At thirty-three she wasn't that old but then again she wasn't that young. She thought the times had become more ruthlessly commercial. Even funeral directors advertised. Their next gimmick would be a Miss Dead America contest to see who could do the best work on the departed. Something had happened to America within Harry's life span, something she couldn't quite put her finger on, but something she could feel, sharply. There was no contest between God and the golden calf. Money was God, these days. Little pieces of green paper with dead people's pictures on them were worshipped. People no longer killed for love. They killed for money.

How odd to be alive in a time of spiritual famine. She watched the cat and dog playing tag and wondered how her kind had ever drifted so far away from animal existence, that sheer delight in the moment.

Harry did not consider herself a philosophical woman, but lately she had turned her mind to deeper thoughts, not just to the purpose of her own life but to the purpose of human life in general. She wouldn't even tell Susan what zigzagged through her head these days, because it was so disturbing and sad. Sometimes she thought she was mourning her lost youth and that was at the bottom of this. Maybe the upheaval of the divorce forced her inward. Or maybe it really was the times, the cheapness and crass consumerism of American life.

Mrs. George Hogendobber, at least, had values over and above her bank account, but Mrs. Hogendobber vainly clung to a belief system that had lost its power. Right-wing Christianity could compel those frightened and narrow-minded souls who needed absolute answers but it couldn't capture those who needed a vision of the future here on earth. Heaven was all very fine but you had to die to get there. Harry wasn't afraid to die but she wouldn't refuse to live either. She wondered what it must have been like to live when Christianity was new, vital, and exciting—before it had been corrupted by collusion with the state. That meant she would have had to have lived before the second century A.D., and as enticing as the idea might be, she wasn't sure she could exist without her truck. Did this mean she'd sell her soul for wheels? She knew she wouldn't sell her soul for a buck, but machines, money, and madness were tied together somehow and Harry knew she wasn't wise enough to untangle the Gordian knot of modern life.

She became postmistress in order to hide from that modern life. Majoring in art history at Smith College on a scholarship had left her splendidly unprepared for the future, so she came home upon graduation and worked as an exercise rider in a big stable. When old George Hogendobber died, she applied for the post office job and won it. Odd, that Mrs. Hogendobber had had a good marriage and that Harry was engaged in hand-to-hand combat with the opposite sex. She wondered if Mrs. Hogendobber knew something she didn't or if George had simply surrendered all hope of individuality and that was why the marriage had worked. Harry had no regrets about her job, small though it might seem to others, but she did have regrets about her marriage.

"Mom's pensive this morning." Mrs. Murphy brushed up against Tucker. "Divorce stuff, I guess. Humans sure make it hard on themselves."

Tucker flicked her ears forward and then back. "Yeah, they seem to worry a lot."

"I'll say. They worry about things that are years away and may never happen."

"I think it's because they can't smell. Miss a lot of information."

Mrs. Murphy nodded in agreement and then added, "Walking on two legs. Screws up their backs and then it affects their minds. I'm sure that's the source of it."

"I never thought of that." Tucker saw the mail driver. "Hey, I'll race you to Rob."

Tucker cheated and tore out before Mrs. Murphy could reply. Furious, Mrs. Murphy shot off her powerful hindquarters and stayed low over the ground.

"Girls, girls, you come back here."

The girls believed in selective hearing and Tucker made it to the mail truck before Mrs. Murphy, but the little tiger jumped into the vehicle.

"I won!"

"You did not," Tucker argued.

"Hello, Mrs. Murphy. Hello, Tucker." Rob was pleased at the greeting he'd received.

Harry, panting, caught up with the cat and the dog. "Hi, Rob. What you got for me this morning?"

"The usual. Two bags." He rattled around in the truck. "Here's a package from Turnbull and Asser that Josiah DeWitt has to sign and pay for." Rob pointed out the sum on the front.

Harry whistled. "One hundred and one dollars duty. Must be a mess of shirts in there. Josiah has to have the best."

"I was reading somewhere, don't remember where, that the

mark-up in the antiques business can be four hundred percent. Guess he can afford those shirts."

"Try to get him to pay for anything else." Harry smiled.

Boom Boom Craycroft, Kelly's pampered wife, drove east, heading toward Charlottesville. Boom Boom owned a new BMW convertible with the license plate BOOMBMW. She waved and Harry and Rob waved back.

Rob gazed after her. Boom Boom was a pretty woman, dark and sultry. He came back to earth. "Today I'll carry the bags in, miss. You can save women's liberation for tomorrow."

Harry smiled. "Okay, Rob, butch it up. I love a man with muscles."

He laughed and hauled both bags over his shoulders as Harry unlocked the door.

After Rob left, Harry sorted the mail in a half hour. Tuesdays were light. She settled herself in the back room and made a cup of good coffee. Tucker and Mrs. Murphy played with the folded duffel bag and by the time Harry emerged from the back room, Mrs. George Hogendobber was standing at the front door and the duffel was moving suspiciously. Harry didn't have the time to pull Mrs. Murphy out. She unlocked the front door and as Mrs. Hogendobber came in, Mrs. Murphy shot out of the bag like a steel ball in a pinball machine.

"*Catch me if you can!*" she called to Tucker.

The corgi ran around in circles as Mrs. Murphy jumped on a shelf, then to the counter, ran the length of the counter at top speed, hit the wall with all four feet and shoved off the wall with a half turn, ran the length of the counter, and did the same maneuver in the opposite direction. She then flew off the counter, ran between Mrs. Hogendobber's legs, Tucker in hot pursuit, jumped back on the counter, and then sat still as a statue as she laughed at Tucker.

Mrs. Hogendobber gasped, "That cat's mental!"

Harry, astonished at the display of feline acrobatics, swallowed and replied, "Just one of her fits—you know how they are."

"I don't like cats myself." Mrs. H. drew herself up to her full height, which was considerable. She had the girth to match. "Too independent."

Yes, many people say that, Harry thought to herself, and all of them are fascists. This was a cherished assumption she would neither divulge nor purge.

"I forgot to tell you to watch Diane Bish Sunday night on cable. Such an accomplished organist. Why they even show her feet, and last Sunday she wore silver slippers."

"I don't have cable."

"Oh, well, move into town. You shouldn't be out there at Yellow Mountain alone, anyway." Mrs. Hogendobber whispered, "I hear Mim dumped off the wedding invitations yesterday."

"Two boxes full."

"Did she invite Stafford?" This sounded innocent.

"I don't know."

"Oh." Mrs. Hogendobber couldn't hide her disappointment.

Josiah came in. "Hello, ladies." He focused on Mrs. Hogendobber. "I want that bed." He frowned a mock frown.

Mrs. Hogendobber was not endowed with much humor. "I'm not prepared to sell."

Fair came in, followed by Susan. Greetings were exchanged. Harry was tense. Mrs. Hogendobber seized the opportunity to slip away from the determined Josiah. Across the street Hayden McIntire, the town physician, parked his car.

Josiah observed him and sighed, "Ah, my child-ridden neighbor." Hayden had fathered many children.

Fair quietly opened his box and pulled out the mail. He wanted to slip away, and Harry, not using the best judgment, called him back.

"Wait a minute."

"I've got a call. Cut tendon." His hand was on the doorknob.

"Dammit, Fair. Where's my check?" Harry blurted out from frustration.

They had signed a settlement agreement whereby Fair was to pay $1,000 a month to Harry until the divorce, when their joint assets would be equally divided. While not a wealthy couple, the two had worked hard during their marriage and the division of spoils would most certainly benefit Harry, who earned far less than Fair. Fortunately, Fair considered the house rightfully Harry's and so that was not contested.

She felt he was jerking her around with the money. Typical Fair. If she didn't do it, it didn't get done. All he could concentrate on was his equine practice.

For Fair's part, he thought Harry was being her usual nagging self. She'd get the goddamned check when he got around to it.

Fair blushed. "Oh, that, well, I'll get it off today."

"Why not write it now?"

"I've got a call, Harry!"

"You're ten days late, Fair. Do I have to call Ned Tucker? I mean, all that does is cost me lawyer's fees and escalate hostilities."

"Hey," he yelled, "calling me out in front of Susan and Josiah is hostile enough!" He slammed the door.

Josiah, transfixed by the domestic drama, could barely wipe the smile off his face. Having avoided the pitfalls of marriage, he thoroughly enjoyed the show couples put on. Josiah never could understand why men and women wanted to marry. Sex he could understand, but marriage? To him it was the ball and chain.

Susan, not transfixed, was deeply sorry about the outburst, because she knew that Josiah would tell Mim and by sunset it would be all over town. The divorce was difficult enough without public displays. She also guessed that Fair, good passive-aggressive personality that he was, was playing "starve the wife." Husbands and their lawyers loved that game . . . and quite often it worked. The soon-to-be-ex wife would become dragged down by the subtle battering and give up. Emotionally the drain was too much for the women, and they would kiss off what they had earned in the marriage. This was made all the more difficult because men took housework and women's labor for granted. No dollar value was attached to it. When the wife withdrew that labor, men usually didn't perceive its value; instead they felt something had been done to them. The woman was a bitch.

After the sting wore off, Susan knew Fair would immediately set about to find another woman to love, and the by-product of this love would mean that the new wife would do the food shopping, juggle the social calendar, and keep the books. All for love.

Did Susan do this for Ned? In the beginning of the marriage, yes. After five years and two kids she had felt she was losing her mind. She balked. Ned was ripshot mad. Then they got to talking, really talking. She was fortunate. So was he. They found common ground. They learned to do with less so they could hire help. Susan took a part-time job to bring in some money and get out of the house. But Susan and Ned were meant for each other, and Harry and Fair were not. Sex brought them together and left them together for a while, but they weren't really connected emotionally and they certainly weren't connected intellectually. They were two reasonably good people who needed to free themselves to do what came next, and sadly, they weren't going to free themselves without anger, recrimination, and dragging their friends into it.

Susan's thoughts were abruptly short-circuited.

A siren echoed in the background, growing louder until the Crozet Rescue Squad ambulance flashed down the road, effectively ending the Harry versus Fair reverberation. They all ran out in front of the post office.

Harry, without thinking, touched Josiah's arm. "Not old Dr. Johnson." He had been her childhood physician and was becoming stooped and frail.

"He'll live to be one hundred. Don't worry." Josiah patted her hand.

The ambulance turned south on the Whitehall Road, also known as Route 240.

Big Marilyn Sanburne's Volvo sped to Shiflett's Market. She stopped and slammed the door of her car.

She thumped over to the group. "I damn near got run off the road by the Rescue Squad. They probably scare to death as many people as they save."

"Amen," Josiah agreed. He started to leave.

Harry called him back. "Josiah, you've got to sign and pay for a Turnbull and Asser package."

"It came." He beamed and then the glow went into remission. "How much?"

"One hundred and one dollars," Harry answered.

Josiah bore the blow. "Well, some things one cannot postpone from motives of economy. Consider the people I am compelled to meet."

"Di and Fergie," Harry solemnly intoned.

In fact, Josiah was in the vicinity of the Royals whilst in London buying up George III furniture before taking a hovercraft across the channel to acquire more of his beloved Louis XV.

Mim wheeled on Josiah, her constant escort whenever she could dump husband Jim. "Still dining out on that story."

"My dear Mim, I merely do business with royalty. You know them as friends." An allusion to the obscure Romanian countess much touted by Big Marilyn, who, when she was eighteen, paraded the European beauty about Crozet.

In the late fifties, Mim had looted Europe for Fabergé boxes and George III furnishings, her favorite period. Jim Sanburne didn't know what he was getting into when he married Mim—but then, who does? In Paris, Mim encountered a friend of the countess who told her the woman was a bakery assistant from Prague, albeit a beautiful one. Whoever she was, she was smart enough to outwit Mim, and Mrs. Sanburne did not take kindly to a reminder, nor did she appreciate the fact that the countess seduced Jim—but then, he was an easy lay. She made him pay for that indiscretion.

Pewter thundered out of the market as a customer opened the door. She was so fat that when she ran, her stomach wobbled from side to side.

Susan giggled. "Someone ought to put that cat on a diet." She diverted the topic of conversation but didn't mind Mim's moment of discomfort.

Pewter stood on her hind legs and scratched the post office door. "Let me in."

Harry opened the door for her as the humans kept talking outside. Pewter burst into the P.O., filled with importance. Even Mrs. Murphy paid attention to her.

"Guess what?" The gray whiskers swept forward and Pewter leaped onto the counter—not easy for her, but she was so excited she made it in one try.

Tucker craned her head upward. "I wish you'd come down here and tell your tale."

Pewter brushed aside the corgi's request. "Market got a call from Diana Farrell, of the Rescue Squad. You know Market does duty on weekends sometimes and they're friends."

"Get to the point, Pewter." Mrs. Murphy swished her tail.

"If that's your attitude, I'm leaving. You can find out from someone else."

"Don't go," Tucker pleaded.

"I am. I am most certainly going. I know when I'm not wanted." Pewter was in a real huff. She puffed her tail, and as Harry opened the door to come in she ran out.

"You're so rude," Tucker complained.

"She's a windbag." Mrs. Murphy did not feel like apologizing.

Josiah was paying out money and grumbling.

"She may be chatty," Tucker said, "but if she ran over here in this blistering heat, it had to be something big."

Mrs. Murphy knew Tucker was right, but she said nothing and curled up on the counter instead. Tucker, out of sorts, whined for Harry to open the door beside the counter. Harry did and Tucker lay down on her big pillow under the counter.

An hour passed with people coming and going. Maude Bly Modena opened her copy of Vogue and she and Harry read their horoscopes.

Maude declared that there were only twelve horoscope readings. Whatever the horoscope was for your sign, it would be moved to the next sign tomorrow. So if you were a Scorpio, your reading would move to Sagittarius the following day, and Libra's reading would then be yours. It took twelve days to complete the cycle. When Harry giggled with disbelief, Maude said people don't remember their horoscopes from one day to the next. They'd never remember twelve days' worth.

Maude said that instead of remembering an entire reading, remember the phrase "Opposite sex interested and shows it." That phrase will move through each sign in succession.

By the time Maude finished, Harry was laughing so hard she didn't care if Maude's theory was true or not. The important thing was that it was fun and Harry needed to know she could still have fun. Divorce was not the end of the world.

Harry's projection for August was "Revise routine. Rebuild for future. Important dates: 7th, 14th, and 29th." Important for what, this stellar prophecy declined to reveal. Harry swore she'd test Maude's theory after Maude left. She clipped the horoscope but within fifteen minutes it had gotten mixed up with postal patron notices.

Little Marilyn Sanburne came in and cooed about her wedding, sort of. With Little Marilyn a coo came from the more obscure regions of her throat. Harry pretended to be interested but personally felt Little Marilyn was making a huge mistake. She couldn't even get along with herself, much less anyone else.

A full hour passed before Market Shiflett pushed through the door.

"Harry, I would have come over sooner but it's been bedlam—sheer bedlam." He wiped his brow.

"Are you all right?" Harry noticed he looked peaked. "Can I get you something?"

He waved no, and then leaned up against the counter to steady himself. "Diana Farrell called me. Kelly Craycroft—at least they think it's Kelly Craycroft—was found dead about ten this morning."

Tucker jumped up. *"See, Mrs. Murphy? I told you she knew something big."*

Mrs. Murphy realized her mistake but couldn't do a damn thing about it now.

"My God, how?" Harry was stunned. She thought maybe a heart attack. Kelly was at that dangerous age for a man.

"Don't rightly know. The body's all tore up. Found him in one of the big cement grinders. He's not even in one piece. Diana said that if he was shot in the head or any other part of the body, they'd never know. Sheriff's Department has impounded the mixer. Guess they'll search for some lead in there. You know, Kelly was always climbing to the top of that mixer to show it to people."

"Murder—you're talking about murder." Harry's eyes widened.

"Well, hell, Harry, a big strong man like Kelly don't just fall into a cement mixer. Someone pushed him in."

"Maybe it isn't him. Maybe it's some drunk or—"

"It's him. Ferrari parked right there. Didn't show up at the office. Since his car was there, everyone figured he was on the grounds somewhere. They didn't really know until one of the men started up the grinder and it sounded funny."

Harry shuddered at the thought of what that poor fellow saw when he looked into the mixer.

"He wasn't a saint but who is? He couldn't have made anyone mad enough to kill him."

"Made someone mad enough." Market exhaled. He didn't like the news, but there was something special about being the messenger of such tidings and Market was not a man immune to those few moments of privileged status. "Thought you ought to know."

As he turned to leave, Harry called out, "Your mail."

"Oh, yeah." Market fished out the mail in his box and left.

Harry sat down on the stool behind the counter. She needed to order her mind. Then she went to the phone and rang up Appalachia Equine. Fair was out, so she left a message for him to call her pronto. Then she dialed Susan.

"Doodle, doodle, doodle." Susan answered the phone. She'd grown tired of "Hello."

"Susan!"

Susan knew from the sound of Harry's voice that something was amiss. "What's wrong?"

"Kelly Craycroft's body was found in a cement mixer. Market just told me, and he said it was murder."

"Murder?!"

3

Rick Shaw, Albemarle County sheriff, hitched up the broad Sam Browne belt. His gun felt even heavier in this stinking heat and it didn't help that he'd put on a pound or two in the last eighteen months. Before he became sheriff he had been more active but now he spent too much time behind his desk. His appetite did not diminish, however, and he began to think that the red tape he had to wade through actually increased his appetite through frustration. The sheriff who preceded him died fat as a tick. This was not a happy thought.

This was not a happy case. Rick had grown accustomed to the vileness of men. He'd seen shoot-outs, drunken knife fights, and corpses of people who had been bludgeoned to death. The traffic accidents weren't much better but at least they weren't premeditated. Albemarle County suffered about two murders a year, usually domestic. This was different, and he sensed it the minute he stepped out of the car.

Officer Cynthia Cooper had arrived on the scene first. A tall young woman with sense as well as experience, she had cordoned off the area. The fingerprint team was on the way but Rick didn't hope for much there. The staff at Craycroft Concrete stood in the sun, too hot to be standing around like that but they were dazed.

Someone was screaming somewhere, and according to Officer Cooper, Kelly's wife was at home, sedated. He regretted that and would have to have a word with Hayden McIntire, the doctor. Sedating should be done after the questioning, not before.

A BMW screeched through the entrance. Kelly Craycroft's wife vaulted from her seat and raced for the mixer.

"Boom Boom!" Rick hollered at her.

Boom Boom soared over the cordoning and roughly pushed her way past Diana Farrell of the Rescue Squad. Clai Cordle, another nurse and squad member, couldn't stop her either.

Cynthia Cooper made a flying tackle but it was a second too late and Boom Boom was climbing up the ladder to the opening of the mixer.

"He's my husband! You can't keep me from my husband!"

"You don't want to see that, girl." Rick moved his bulk as quickly as he could.

Cynthia scurried up the ladder and grabbed Boom Boom's ankle but not before the raven-haired woman lifted her head over the side of the mixer. Immobile for a second, she fell back into Cynthia Cooper's arms in a dead faint, nearly knocking the young policewoman off the ladder.

Rick reached up and held Cynthia around the waist as Diana ran over to help. They got Boom Boom to the ground.

Diana broke open the amyl nitrite.

Cynthia snatched it from her hand. "All she's got are these few moments before this hits her again. Let her have them."

Rick cleared his throat. He hated this. He also hated that Boom Boom might throw up when she came to and he fervently hoped she wouldn't. Blood and guts were one thing. Vomit was another.

Boom Boom moaned. She opened her eyes. Rick held his breath. She sat up and swallowed. He exhaled. She wasn't going to throw up. She wasn't even going to cry.

"He looks like something in the Cuisinart." Boom Boom's voice sounded flat.

"Don't think about it," Officer Cooper advised.

"I'll remember the sight for the rest of my natural life." Boom

Boom struggled to her feet. She swayed a bit and Rick steadied her. "I'm all right. Just . . . give me a minute."

"Why don't we go over to the office. The air conditioning will help."

Officer Cooper and Boom Boom walked over to the small office and Rick motioned to Diana and Clai to get the body pieces out of the mixer. "Don't let Boom Boom see the bag."

"Keep her inside," Diana requested.

"Do what I can but she's a wild one. Been that way since she was a kid." Rick took off his hat and entered the office.

Marie Williams, Craycroft Concrete's secretary, sobbed. At the sight of Boom Boom she emitted a wail.

Boom Boom stared at her in disgust. "Pull yourself together, Marie."

"I loved him. I just loved him. He was the best man in the world to work for. He'd bring me roses on Secretary's Day. He'd give me time off when Timmy was sick. Didn't dock my pay." A fresh outburst followed this.

Boom Boom hit the chair with a thump. Behind her a huge poster of a sitting duck slurping a drink, bullet holes in the wall behind him, gave the room a festive air. If Marie kept this up she'd throw her in the mixer. Boom Boom loathed displays of emotion. Circumstances did not alter her opinion on this.

"Mrs. Williams, why don't you come into Mr. Craycroft's office with me. Maybe you can explain his daily routine. We can't touch anything until the prints men come in."

"I understand." Marie shuffled off with Officer Cooper, shutting the door behind her.

"You don't really know if that's my husband in there." Boom Boom's voice didn't sound normal.

"No."

She leaned back in the chair. "It is, though."

"How do you know?" Rick's voice was gentle but probing.

"I feel it. Besides, his car is parked here and Kelly was never far from that car. Loved it more than anything, even me, his wife."

"Do you have any idea how this could have happened?"

"Apart from someone pushing him into the mixer, no." Her eyes glittered.

"Enemies?"

"Pharamond Haristeen—well, that's old. They aren't enemies anymore."

Rick knew the story of Fair making a pass at Boom Boom at last year's Hunt Club ball. Much liquor had been consumed but not enough for people to forget the overture. He'd need to question Fair. Emotions, like land mines, could explode when you least expected them to . . . years after an event. It wouldn't be impossible for Fair to be a murderer, only improbable. "What about business troubles?"

Boom Boom smiled a wan smile. "Kelly had the Midas touch."

Rick smiled back at her. "All of central Virginia knows that." He paused. "Perhaps he got into a disagreement over a bill or a paving bid. People get crazy about money. Anything, anything at all that comes to mind."

"Nothing."

Rick placed his hand on her shoulder. "I'll have Officer Cooper drive you home."

"I can drive."

"No, you can't. For once you'll do as I say."

Boom Boom didn't argue. She felt shakier than she wanted to admit. In fact, she'd never felt so terrible in her life. She loved Kelly, in her vague fashion, and he loved her in return.

Rick glanced up to see how the body removal was progressing. It wasn't easy. Even Clai Cordle, stomach of iron, was green around the gills.

Rick opened the door, blocking Boom Boom's view. "Clai, Diana, hold up a minute, will you? Officer Cooper's going to run Boom Boom home."

"Okay." Diana suspended her labors.

"Officer Cooper."

"Yo," Cynthia called out, then opened the door.

"Carry Boom Boom home, will you?"

"Sure."

"Find anything in there?"

Marie followed behind Officer Cooper. "Everything's filed and cross-filed, first alphabetically and then under subject matter. I did it myself."

As Boom Boom and Officer Cooper left, Rick went into the small, clean office with Marie.

"He believed in 'a place for everything and everything in its place,'" Marie whimpered.

Rick scanned the top of Kelly's desk. A silver-framed portrait of Boom Boom was on the right-hand corner. A Lamy pen, very bulky, was placed on a neat diagonal over Xeroxed papers.

Rick leaned over, careful not to touch anything, and read the top sheet.

> My Whig principles have been strengthened by the Mexican War. It broke out just as I was preparing to depart for Europe; my trunks were actually ready; that and the Oregon question, made me unpack them. Now my son is in it. Some pecuniary interest is at stake, the political horizon is clouded and I am forced to wait until all this ends. Since I have had my surfeit of war, I am for peace; but at this time I am still more so. Peace, peace rises at the top of all my thoughts and the feeling makes me twice a Whig. As soon as things are settled I cross the Atlantic. I might do it now, of course, but I do not wish to go for only a few months and my stay might now be curtailed by events.
>
> Very respectfully, Y'r most obed't.
> C. CROZET

"I don't recall Kelly being interested in history."

Marie shrugged. "Me neither, but he'd get these whims, you know."

Rick put his thumb under the heavy belt again, taking some of the weight off his shoulder and waist. "Crozet was an engineer. Maybe he wrote about paving or something. Built all our turnpikes, you know. Route 240, too, if I remember Miss Grindle's teachings in fourth grade."

"What a witch." Marie had had Miss Grindle too.

"Never had any disciplinary problems at Crozet Elementary when Miss Grindle was there."

"From the War Between the States until the Korean War." Marie half giggled, then caught herself. "How can I laugh at a time like this?"

"Need to. Your emotions will be a roller coaster for a while."

Tears welled up in Marie's eyes. "You'll catch him, won't you? Whoever did this?"

"I'm gonna try, Marie. I'm gonna try."

4

"Are you sure you want to do this?" Susan peered into Harry's face.

"You know I have to."

Not paying her condolences to Boom Boom would have been a breach of manners so flagrant it would be held against Harry forever. Not actively held against her, mind, just remembered, a black mark against her name in the book. Even if she had more good marks than bad, and she hoped that she did, it didn't pay to play social percentages in Crozet.

It wasn't just facing the jolt of a shocking death that caught Harry; it was having to face the entire social spectrum. Since asking Fair to leave, Harry had kept pretty much to herself. Of course, Fair would be at the Craycrofts'. Even if his big truck was not parked in the driveway she knew he'd be there. He was well brought up. He understood his function at a time like this.

The gathered Crozet residents would not only be able to judge how Boom Boom held up during the hideous crisis, but they'd also be able to judge the temperature of the divorce, a crisis of a different sort. Behaving bravely was tremendously important in Crozet. Stiff upper lip.

Harry often thought if she wanted a stiff upper lip she'd grow a moustache.

"*Are you going to leave me here?*" Tee Tucker asked.

"Yeah, what about me?" Mrs. Murphy wanted to know.

Harry looked down at her friends. "Susan, either we take the kids or you'll have to run me back home."

"I'll run you home. Really isn't proper to take the animals to the Craycrofts', I guess."

"You're right." Harry shooed Mrs. Murphy and Tucker out the post office door and locked it behind her.

Pewter, lounging in the front window of Market's store, yawned and then preened when she saw Mrs. Murphy. Pewter's countenance radiated satisfaction, importance, and power, however momentary.

Mrs. Murphy seethed. "A fat gray Buddha, that's what she thinks she is."

Tucker said, "You like her despite herself."

Mrs. Murphy and Tucker glanced at each other during the ride home.

Tucker rolled her eyes. "Humans are crazy. Humans and ants—kill their own kind."

"I've had a few thoughts along those lines myself," Mrs. Murphy replied.

"You have not. Stop being cynical. It isn't sophisticated. You'll never be sophisticated, Mrs. Murphy. You came from Sally Mead's SPCA."

"You can shut up any time now, Tucker. Don't take your bad mood out on me just because we have to go home."

Once in the house, Mrs. Murphy hopped on a chair to watch Susan and Harry drive off.

"You know what I found out at Pewter's?" Tucker asked.

"No."

"That it smelled like an amphibian over behind the cement mixer."

"How would she know? She wasn't there."

"Ozzie was," Tucker matter-of-factly replied.

"When did you find this out?" the cat demanded.

"When I went to the bathroom. I thought I'd go over and chat with Pewter to try and smooth over your damage." Tucker enjoyed chiding Mrs. Murphy. "Anyway, when Bob Berryman stopped by the store, Ozzie told me everything. Said it smelled like a big turtle."

"*That makes no sense.*" Mrs. Murphy paced on the back of the chair. "*And just what was Ozzie doing over there, anyway?*"

"*Didn't say. You know, Murph, a tortoise scent is very strong.*"

Not to people. The tiger thought.

"*Ozzie said Sheriff Rick Shaw and the others walked over the scent many times. Didn't wrinkle their noses. How they can miss that smell I'll never know. It's dark and nutty. I'd like to go over there and have a sniff myself.*" Tucker began trotting up and down the living room rug.

"*It probably has nothing to do with this . . . mess.*" Mrs. Murphy thought a minute. "*But on the other hand . . .*"

"*Want to go?*" Tucker wagged her tail.

"*Let's go tonight when Harry's asleep.*" Mrs. Murphy was excited. "*If there's a trace, we'll pick it up. We can't leave now. Harry's upset. If she comes back from the Craycrofts' and finds us gone it will make her even more upset.*"

"*You're right,*" the dog concurred. "*Let's wait until she's asleep.*"

Cars lined the long driveway into the imposing Craycroft residence.

Josiah and Ned parked people's cars for them. Susan and Harry pulled up.

Josiah opened Harry's door. "Hello, Harry. Terrible, terrible," was all the normally garrulous fellow could say.

When Harry walked into the house she found enough food to feed the Sandanistas, and was glad she'd brought flowers for the table. She was not glad to see Fair but damned if she'd show it.

Boom Boom sat in a huge damask wing chair by the fireplace. Drained and drawn, she was still beautiful, made more so, perhaps, by her distress.

Harry and Boom Boom, two years apart in school, were never close but they got along—until last year's Hunt Club ball. Harry put it out of her mind. She had heard the gossip that Boom Boom wanted to catch Fair, and the reverse. Were men rabbits? Did you snare them? Harry never could figure out the imagery many women used in discussing the opposite sex. She didn't treat her men friends any differently than her women friends and Susan swore that was the source of her marital difficulties. Harry would rather be a divorcée than a liar and that settled that.

Boom Boom raised her eyes from Big Marilyn Sanburne, who was sitting next to her, dispensing shallow compassion. Her eyelids flickered for a split second and then she composed herself and held out her hand to Fair, who had just walked up to her.

"I'm so sorry, Boom Boom. I . . . I don't know what to say." Fair stumbled verbally.

"You never liked him anyway." Boom Boom astonished the room, which was filled with most of Crozet.

Fair, befuddled, squeezed her hand, then released it. "I did like him. We had our differences but I did like him."

Boom Boom accepted this and said, "It was correct of you to come. Thank you." Not kind, not good, but correct.

Harry received better treatment. After extending her sympathy she went over to the bar for a ginger ale and to get away from Fair. What rotten timing that they had arrived so close together. The heat and the smoldering emotion made her mouth dry. Little Marilyn Sanburne poured a drink for her.

"Thanks, Marilyn."

"This is too awful for words."

Harry, ungenerously, thought that it might be too awful for a number of reasons, one being that Little Marilyn's impending wedding was eclipsed, temporarily at least, by this event. Little Marilyn, not having been in the limelight, just might learn to like it. Her marriage was the one occasion when her mother wouldn't be the star, or so she thought.

"Yes, it is."

"Mother's wretched." Little Marilyn sipped a stiff shot of Johnny Walker Black.

Mim's impeccable profile betrayed no outward sign of wretchedness, Harry thought to herself. "I'm sorry," she said to Little Marilyn.

Jim Sanburne blew into the living room. Mim joined him as he walked over to Boom Boom, whispered in her ear, and patted her hand.

Difficult as it was, he toned down his volume level. When finished with Boom Boom he hauled his huge frame around the room. Working a room, second nature to Jim, never came easily to his wife. Mim expected the rabble to pay court to her. It galled her that her husband sought out commoners. Commoners do vote, though, and Jim liked getting reelected. Being mayor was like a toy to him, a relaxation from the toils of expanding his considerable wealth. Since God rewarded Mim and Jim with money, it seemed to her that lower life forms should realize the Sanburnes were superior and vote accordingly.

Perhaps it was to Marilyn's credit that she grasped the fact that Crozet did not practice equality . . . but then, what community did? For Mim, money and social position meant power. That was all that mattered. Jim, absurdly, wanted people to like him, people who were not listed in the Social Register, people who didn't even know what it was, God forbid.

A tight smile split her face. An outsider like Maude Bly Modena would mistake that for concern for Kelly Craycroft's family. An insider knew Mim's major portion of sympathy was reserved for herself, for the trial of being married to a super-rich vulgarian.

Harry didn't know what possessed her. Maybe it was the suppressed suffering in the Craycroft house, or the sight of Mim grimly doing her duty. Wouldn't everyone be better off if they bellowed fury at God and tore their hair? This containment oddly frightened her. At any rate she stared Little Marilyn right in those deep blue eyes and said, "Marilyn, does Stafford know you're getting married?"

Little Marilyn, thrown, stuttered, "No."

"We aren't close, Marilyn. But if I never do anything else for you in your life let me do this one thing: Ask your brother to your wedding. You love him and he loves you." Harry put down her ginger ale and left.

Little Marilyn Sanburne, face burning, said nothing, then quickly sought out her mother and father.

*

Bob Berryman's hand rested on the doorknob of Maude's shop. She had turned the lights out. No one could see them, or so they thought.

"Does she suspect?" Maude whispered.

"No," Berryman told her to reassure her. "No one suspects anything."

He quietly slipped out the back door, keeping to the deep shadows. He had parked his truck blocks away.

Pewter, out for a midnight stroll, observed his exit. She made a mental note of it and of the fact that Maude waited a few moments before going upstairs to her apartment over the shop. The lights clicked on, giving Pewter a tantalizing view of the bats darting in and out of the high trees near Maude's window.

That night Mrs. Murphy and Tucker tried to distract Harry from her low mood. One of their favorite tricks was the Plains Indian game. Mrs. Murphy would lie on her back, reach around Tucker, and hang on like an Indian under a pony. Tucker would yell, "Yi, yi, yi," as though she were scared, then try to dump her passenger. Harry laughed when they did this. Tonight she just smiled.

The dog and cat followed her to bed and when they were sure she was sound asleep they bolted out the back door, which contained an animal door that opened into a dog run. Mrs. Murphy knew how to throw the latch, though, and the two of them loped across the meadows, fresh-smelling with new-mown hay.

There wasn't a car on the road.

About half a mile from the concrete plant Mrs. Murphy spied glittering eyes in the brush. "Coon up ahead."

"Think he'll fight?" Tucker stopped for a minute.

"If we have to make a detour, we might not get back by morning."

Tucker called out, "We won't chase you. We're on our way to the concrete plant."

"The hell you won't," the raccoon snarled.

"Honest, we won't." Mrs. Murphy sounded more convincing than Tucker.

"*Maybe you will and maybe you won't. Give me a head start. I might believe you then.*" With that the wily animal disappeared into the bushes.

"Let's go," Mrs. Murphy said.

"*And let's hope he keeps his promise. I'm not up for a fight with one of those guys tonight.*"

The raccoon kept his word, didn't jump out at them, and they arrived at the plant within fifteen minutes.

The dew held what scent there was on the ground. Much had evaporated. Gasoline fumes and rock dust pervaded. Human smells were everywhere, as was the scent of wet concrete and stale blood. Tucker, nose to the ground, kept at it. Mrs. Murphy checked out the office building. She couldn't get in. No windows were open; there were no holes in the foundation. She grumbled.

A tang exploded in Tucker's nostrils. "Here!"

Mrs. Murphy raced over and put her nose to the ground. "*Where's it go?*"

"It doesn't." Tucker couldn't fathom this. "*It's just a whiff, like a little dot. No line. Like something spilled.*"

"It does smell like a turtle." The cat scratched behind her ears.

"Kinda."

"*I've never smelled anything quite like it—have you?*"

"*Never.*"

5

Even Mrs. George Hogendobber's impassioned monologue on the evils of this world failed to rouse Mrs. Murphy and Tucker. Before Mrs. Hogendobber had both feet through the front door she had declared that Adam fell from grace over the apple, then man broke the covenant with God, a flood cleansed us by killing everyone but Noah and family, Moses couldn't prevent his flock from worshipping the golden calf, and Jezebel was on every street corner, to say nothing of record covers. These pronouncements were not necessarily in historical order but there was a clear thread woven throughout: We are by nature sinful and unclean. This, naturally, led to Kelly Craycroft's death. Mrs. H. sidestepped revealing exactly how Hebrew history as set down in the Old Testament culminated in the extinction of a paving contractor.

Harry figured if Mrs. Hogendobber could live with her logical lacunae, so could she.

Tossing her junk mail in the wastebasket, Mrs. Hogendobber spoke exhaustingly of Holofernes and Judith. Before reaching their gruesome biblical conclusion she paused, a rarity in itself, walked over to the counter, and glanced over. "Where are the animals?"

"Out cold. Lazy things," Harry answered. "In fact, they were so sluggish this morning that I drove them to work."

"You spoil those creatures, Harry, and you need a new truck."

"Guilty as charged."

Josiah entered as Harry uttered the word guilty.

"I knew it was you all along." He pointed at Harry. The soft pink of his Ralph Lauren polo shirt accented his tan.

"You shouldn't joke about a thing like that." Mrs. Hogendobber's nostrils flared.

"Oh, come now, Mrs. Hogendobber, I'm not joking about the Craycroft murder. You're oversensitive. We all are. It's been a terrible shock."

"Indeed it has. Indeed it has. Put not thy faith in worldly things, Mr. DeWitt."

Josiah beamed at her. "I'm afraid I do, ma'am. In a world of impermanence I take the best impermanence I can find."

A swirl of color rose on Mrs. Hogendobber's beautifully preserved cheeks. "You're witty and sought-after and too clever by half. People like you come to a bad end."

"Perhaps, but think of the fun I'll have getting there, and I really can't see that you're having any fun at all."

"I will not stand here and be insulted." Mrs. Hogendobber's color glowed crimson.

"Oh, come on, Mrs. H., you don't walk on water," Josiah coolly replied.

"Exactly! I can't swim." Her color deepened. She felt the insult keenly; she would never think of comparing herself to Jesus. She turned to Harry. "Good day, Harry." With forced dignity, Mrs. Hogendobber left the post office.

"Good day, Mrs. Hogendobber." Harry turned to the howling Josiah. "She has absolutely no sense of humor and you're too hard on her. She's quite upset. What seems a trifle to you is major to her."

"Oh, hell, Harry, she bores you every bit as much as she bores me. Truth?"

Harry wasn't looking for an argument. She was conversant with Mrs. Hogendobber's faults and the woman did bore her to tears, but Mrs. Hogendobber was fundamentally good. You couldn't say that about everybody.

"Josiah, her values are spiritual and yours aren't. She's overbearing and narrow-minded about religion but if I were sick and called her at three in the morning, she'd be there."

"Well"—his color was brighter now, too—"I hope you know I would come over too. You only have to ask. I value you highly, Harry."

"Thank you, Josiah." Harry wondered if he valued her at all.

"Did I tell you I am to be Mrs. Sanburne's walker for the funeral? It's not Newport but it's just as important."

Josiah often escorted Mim. They had their spats but Mim was not a woman to attend social gatherings without clinging to the arm of a male escort, and Jim would be in Richmond on the day of Kelly's funeral. Josiah adored escorting Mim; unlike Jim, he placed great store on status, and like Mim he needed much external proof of that status. They'd jet to parties in New York, Palm Beach, wherever the rich congregated. Mim and Josiah thought nothing of a weekend in London or Vienna if the guest list was right. What bored Jim about his wife thrilled Josiah.

"I dread the funeral." Harry did, too.

"Harry, try Ajax."

"What?"

Josiah pointed to her hands, still discolored from cleaning the stamps two days ago.

Harry held her hands up. She'd forgotten about it. Yesterday seemed years away. "Oh."

"If Ajax fails, try sulfuric acid."

"Then I won't have any hands at all."

"I'm teasing you."

"I know, but I have a sense of humor."

"Darn good one too."

The late afternoon sun slanted across the crepe myrtle behind the post office. Mrs. Murphy stopped to admire the deep-pink blossoms glowing in the hazy light. Harry locked the door as Pewter stuck her nose out from behind Market's store. Courtney could be heard calling her from inside.

"*Where are you going?*" the large cat wanted to know.

"Maude's," came Tucker's jaunty reply.

Pewter, dying to confide in someone, even a dog, that she had seen Bob Berryman sneak out of Maude's shop, switched her tail. Mrs. Murphy was such a bitch. Why give her the advantage of hot news, or at least warm news? She decided to drop a hint like a leaf of fragrant catnip. "*Maude's not telling all she knows.*"

Mrs. Murphy's head snapped around. "*What do you mean?*"

"Oh ... nothing." Pewter's delicious moment of torment was cut short by the appearance of Courtney Shiflett.

"There you are. You come inside." She scooped up the cat and took her back into the air-conditioned store.

Harry waved at Courtney and continued on her way to Maude Bly Modena's. She thought about going in the back door but decided to go through the front. That would give her the opportunity to see if anything new was in the window. Beautiful baskets spilling flowers covered the lorry in the front yard. Colorful cartons full of seed packets were in the window. Maude advertised that packing need not be boring and anything that would hold or wrap a present was her domain. She carried a good stock of greeting cards too.

Upon seeing Harry through the window, Maude waved her inside. Mrs. Murphy and Tucker trotted into the store.

"Harry, what can I do for you?"

"Well, I was cutting up the newspaper to send Lindsay a clipping about Kelly's death and then I decided to send her a CARE package."

"Where is she?"

"Heading toward Italy. I've got an address for her."

Mrs. Murphy nestled into a basket filled with crinkly paper. Tucker stuck her nose into the basket. Crinkly sounds pleased the cat, but Tucker thought, *Give me a good bone, any day.* She nudged Mrs. Murphy.

"*Tucker, this is my basket.*"

"*I know. What do you think Pewter meant?*"

"A bid for attention. She wanted me to beg her for news. And I'm glad that I didn't."

As the two animals were discussing the finer points of Pewter's personality, Harry and Maude had embarked on serious girl talk about divorce, a subject known to Maude, who endured one before moving to Crozet.

"It's a roller coaster." Maude sighed.

"Well, this would be a lot easier if I didn't have to see him all the time and if he'd take a little responsibility for what happened."

"Don't expect the crisis to change him, Harry. You may be changing. I think I can say that you are, even though we haven't known each other since B.C. But your growth isn't his growth. Anyway, my experience with men is that they'll do anything to avoid emotional growth, avoid looking deep inside. That's what mistresses, booze, and Porsches are all about." Maude removed her bright red-rimmed glasses and smiled.

"Hey, I don't know. This is all new to me." Harry sat down, suddenly tired.

"Divorce is a process of detachment, most especially detachment from his ability to affect you."

"He sure as hell can affect me when he doesn't send the check."

Maude's eyes rolled. "Playing that game, is he? Probably trying to weaken you or scare you so you'll accept less come judgment day. My ex tried it, too. I suppose they all do or their lawyers talk them into it and then when they have a moment to reflect on what a cheap shot it is—if they do—they can wring their hands and say, 'It wasn't my idea. My lawyer made me do it.' You hang tough, kiddo."

"Yeah." Harry would, too. "Not to change the subject, but are you still jogging along the C and O Railroad track? In this heat?"

"Sure. I try and go out at sunrise. It really is beastly hot. I passed Jim this morning."

"Jogging?" Harry was incredulous.

"No, I passed him as I ran back into town. He was out with the sheriff. Horrible as Kelly's death was, I do think Jim is getting some kind of thrill out of it."

"I doubt this town has had much excitement since Crozet dug the tunnels."

"Huh?" Maude's eyes brightened.

"When Claudius Crozet finished the last tunnel through the Blue Ridge. Well, actually, the town was named for him after that. Just a figure of speech. You have to realize that those of us who went to grade school here learned about Claudius Crozet."

"Oh. That and Jefferson, Madison, and Monroe, I guess. Virginia's glories seem to be in the past, as opposed to the present."

"I guess so. Well, let me take this big Jiffy bag and some colored paper and get out of your hair and get Mrs. Murphy out of your best basket."

"I love a good chat. How about some tea?"

"No thanks."

"Little Marilyn was in today, all atwitter. She needed tiny baskets for her mother's yacht party." Maude burst out laughing and so did Harry.

Big Marilyn's yacht was a pontoon boat that floated on the ten-acre lake behind the Sanburne mansion. She adored cruising around the lake and she especially liked terrorizing her neighbors on the other side. Between her pontoon boat and her bridge night with the girls, Mim kept herself emotionally afloat, forgive the pun.

She'd also gone quite wild when she redecorated the house for the umpteenth time and made over the bar so that it resembled a ship. There were little portholes behind the bar. Life preservers and colorful pennants graced the walls, as well as oars, life vests, and very large saltwater fish. Mim never caught a catfish, much less a sailfish, but she commissioned her decorators to find her imposing fish. Indeed they did. The first time Mrs. Murphy beheld the stuffed trophies she swooned. The idea of a fish that big was too good to be true.

Mim also had DRYDOCK painted over the bar. The big golden letters shone with dock lights she had cleverly installed. Throw a few fish-nets around, a bell, and a buoy, and the bar was complete. Well, it was really complete when Mim inaugurated it with a slosh of martinis for her bridge girls, the only other three women in Albemarle County she remotely considered her social equals. She'd even had matchbooks and little napkins made up with DRYDOCK printed on them, and she was hugely pleased when the girls noticed them as they smacked their martini glasses onto the polished bar.

Mim enjoyed more success in getting the girls to the bar than she did in getting them to her pontoon boat, which also had gold letters painted along the side: Mim's Vim. With the big wedding coming up, Mim knew she had the bargaining card to get her bridge buddies on the boat, where she could at last impress them with her abilities as captain. It wasn't satisfying to do something unless people saw you do it. If the bridge girls wanted good seats at the wedding, they would board Mim's Vim. Mim could barely wait.

Little Marilyn could happily wait, but being the dutiful drudge that she was, she appeared in Maude's shop to buy baskets as favors, baskets that would be filled with nautical party favors for the girls.

"Have you ever seen Mim piloting her yacht?" Harry howled.

"That captain's cap, it's too much." Maude was doubled over just thinking about it.

"Yeah, it's the only time she removes her tiara."

"Tiara?"

Harry giggled. "Sure, the Queen of Crozet."

"You are wicked." Maude wiped her eyes, tearing from laughter.

"If you'd grown up with these nitwits, you'd be wicked too. Oh, well, as my mother used to say, 'Better the devil you know than the devil you don't.' Since I know Mim, I know what to expect."

Maude's voice dropped. "I wonder. I wonder now if any of us know what to expect?"

6

The coroner's report lay opened on Rick Shaw's desk. The peculiarity in Kelly's body was a series of scars on the arteries into his heart. These indicated tiny heart attacks. Kelly, fit and forty, wasn't too young for heart attacks, but these would have been so small he might not have noticed when they occurred.

Rick reread the page. The skull, pulverized, yielded little. If there had been a bullet wound there'd be no trace of it. When the men combed through the mixer no bullets were found.

Much of the stomach was intact. Apart from a Big Mac, that yielded nothing.

There was a trace of cyanide in the hair samples. Well, that was what killed him but why would the killer mutilate the body? Finding the means of death only provoked more questions.

Rick smacked together the folder. This was not an accidental death but he didn't want to report it as a murder—not yet. His gut feeling was that whoever killed Kelly was smart—smart and extremely cool-headed.

Cynthia Cooper knocked.

"Come in."

"What do you think?"

"I'm playing my cards close to my chest for a bit." Rick slapped the report. He reached for a cigarette but stopped. Quitting was hell. "You got anything?"

"Everybody checks out. Marie Williams was right where she said she was on Monday night, and so was Boom Boom, if we can believe her servants. Boom Boom said she thought her husband was out of town on business and she was waiting for him to call. Maybe, maybe not. But was she alone? Fair Haristeen said he was operating late that evening, solo. Everyone else seems to have some kind of alibi."

"Funeral's tomorrow."

"The coroner was mighty quick about it."

"Powerful man. If the family wants the body buried by tomorrow, he'll get those tissue samples in a hurry. You don't rile the Craycrofts."

"Somebody did."

7

Boom Boom held together throughout the service at Saint Paul's Episcopal Church at the crossroads called Ivy. An exquisite veil covered her equally exquisite features.

Harry, Susan, and Ned discreetly sat in a middle pew. Fair sat on the other side of the church, in the middle. Josiah and Mim, both elegantly dressed in black, sat near the pulpit. Bob Berryman and his wife, Linda, were also in a middle pew. Old Larry Johnson, acting as an usher, spared Maude Bly Modena a social gaffe by keeping her from marching down the center aisle, which she was fixing to do. He firmly grabbed her by the elbow and guided her toward a rearward pew. Maude, a Crozet resident for five years, didn't merit a forward pew, but Maude was a Yankee and often missed such subtleties. Market and Courtney Shiflett were in back, as were Clai Cordle and Diana Farrell of the Rescue Squad.

The church was covered in flowers, signifying the hope of rebirth through Christ. Those who could, also gave donations to the Heart Fund. Rick had to tell Boom Boom about the tiny scars on the arteries and she chose to believe her husband had suffered a heart attack while inspecting equipment and fallen in. How the mixer could have been turned on was of no interest to her, not today anyway. She could absorb only so much. What she would do when she could really absorb events was anybody's guess. Better to bleed from the throat than to cross Boom Boom Craycroft.

8

Life must go on.

Josiah showed up at the post office with a gentleman from Atlanta who'd flown up to buy a pristine Louis XV bombé cabinet. Josiah liked to bring his customers down to the post office and then over to Shiflett's Market. Market smiled and Harry smiled. Customers exclaimed over the cat and dog in the post office and then Josiah would drive them back to his house, extolling the delights of small-town life, where everyone was a character. Why anyone would believe that human emotions were less complex in a small town than in a big city escaped Harry but urban dwellers seemed to buy it. This Atlanta fellow had "sucker" emblazoned across his forehead.

Rob came back at eleven. He'd forgotten a bag in the back of the mail truck and if she wouldn't tell, neither would he.

Harry sat down to sort the mail and read the postcards. Courtney Shiflett received one from one of her camp buddies who signed her name with a smiling face instead of a dot over the "i" in "Lisa." Lindsay Astrove was at Lake Geneva. The postcard, again brief, said that Switzerland, crammed with Americans, would be much nicer without them.

The mail was thin on postcards today.

Mim Sanburne marched in. Mrs. Murphy, playing with a rubber band on the counter, stopped. When Harry saw the look on Mim's face she stopped sorting the mail.

"Harry, I have a bone to pick with you and I didn't think that the funeral was the place to do it. You have no business whatsoever telling Little Marilyn whom to invite to her wedding. No business at all!"

Mim must have thought that Harry would bow down and say "Yes, Mistress." This didn't happen.

Harry steeled herself. "Under the First Amendment, I can say anything to anybody. I had something I wanted to say to your daughter and I did."

"You've upset her!"

"No, I've upset you. If she's upset she can come in here and tell me herself."

Suprised that Harry wasn't subservient, Big Marilyn switched gears. "I happen to know that you read postcards. That's a violation, you know, and if it continues I shall tell the postmaster at the head office on Seminole Trail. Have I made myself clear?"

"Quite." Harry compressed her lips.

Mim glided out, satisfied that she'd stung Harry. The satisfaction wouldn't last long, because the specter of her son would come back to haunt her. If Harry was brazen enough to speak to Little Marilyn, plenty of others were speaking about it too.

Harry turned the duffel bag upside down. One lone postcard slipped out. Defiantly she read it: "Wish you were here," written in computer script. She flipped it over and beheld a gorgeous photograph, misty and evocative, of the angel in an Asheville, North Carolina, cemetery. She turned it over and read the fine print. This was the angel that inspired Thomas Wolfe when he wrote *Look Homeward, Angel*.

She slipped it in Maude Bly Modena's box and didn't give it a second thought.

9

A pensive Pharamond Haristeen drove his truck back from Charlottesville. Seeing Boom Boom had rattled him. He couldn't decide if she was truly sorry that Kelly was dead. The zing had fled that marriage years ago.

No armor existed against her beauty. No armor existed against her icy blasts, either. Why wouldn't a woman like Boom Boom be sensible like Harry? Why couldn't a woman like Harry be electrifying like Boom Boom?

As far as Fair was concerned, Harry was sensible until it came to the divorce. She threw him out. Why should he pay support until the settlement was final?

It came as a profound shock to Fair when Harry handed him his hat. His vanity suffered more than his heart but Fair seized the opportunity to appear the injured party. The elderly widowed women in Crozet were only too happy to side with him, as were single women in general. He moped about and the flood of dinner invitations immediately followed. For the first time in his life, Fair was the center of attention. He rather liked it.

Deep in his heart he knew his marriage wasn't working. If he cared to look inward he would discover he was fifty percent responsible for the failure. Fair had no intention of looking inward, a quality that doomed his marriage and would undoubtedly doom future relationships as well.

Fair operated on the principle "If it ain't broke, don't fix it," but emotional relationships weren't machines. Emotional relationships didn't lend themselves to scientific analysis, a fact troubling to his scientifically trained mind. Women didn't lend themselves to scientific analysis.

Women were too damned much trouble, and Fair determined to live alone for the rest of his days. The fact that he was a healthy thirty-four did not deter him in this decision.

He passed Rob Collier on 240 heading east. They waved to each other.

If the sight of Boom Boom at her husband's funeral wasn't enough to unnerve Fair, Rick Shaw had zeroed in on him at the clinic, asking questions. Was he under suspicion? Just because two friends occasionally have a strained relationship doesn't mean that one will kill the other. He said that to Rick, and the sheriff replied with "People have killed over less." If that was so, then the world was totally insane. Even if it wasn't, it felt like it today.

Fair pulled up behind the post office. Little Tee Tucker stood on her hind legs, nose to the glass, when she heard his truck. He walked over to Market Shiflett's store for a Coca-Cola first. The blistering heat parched his throat, and castrating colts added to the discomfort somehow.

"Hello, Fair." Courtney's fresh face beamed.

"How are you?"

"I'm fine. What about you?"

"Hot. How about a Co-Cola?"

She reached into the old red bin, the kind of soft-drink refrigerator used at the time of World War II, and brought out a cold bottle. "Here, unless you want a bigger one."

"I'll take that and I'll buy a six-pack, too, because I am forever drinking Harry's sodas. Where's your dad?"

"The sheriff came by and Dad went off with him."

Fair smirked. "A new broom sweeps the place clean."

"Sir?" Courtney didn't understand.

"New sheriff, new anything. When someone takes over a job they have an excess of enthusiasm. This is Rick's first murder case since he was elected sheriff, so he's just busting his ... I mean, he's anxious to find the killer."

"Well, I hope he does."

"Me too. Say, is it true that you have a crush on Dan Tucker?" Fair's eyes crinkled. How he remembered this age.

Courtney replied quite seriously, "I wouldn't have Dan Tucker if he was the last man on earth."

"Is that so? He must be just awful." Fair picked up his Cokes and left. Pewter scooted out of the market with him.

Tucker ran around in circles when Fair stepped into the post office with Pewter on his heels. Maude Bly Modena rummaged around in her box, while Harry was in the back.

"Hi, Maudie."

"Hi, Fair." Maude thought Fair a divine-looking man. Most women did.

"Harry!"

"What?" The voice filtered out from the back door.

"I brought you some Cokes."

"Three hundred thirty-three"—the door opened—"because that's what you owe me." Harry appreciated his gesture more than she showed.

Fair shoved the six-pack across the counter.

Pewter hollered, "Mrs. Murphy, where are you?"

Tucker walked over and touched noses with Pewter, who liked dogs very much.

"I'm counting rubber bands. What do you want?" Mrs. Murphy replied.

Harry grabbed the Cokes off the counter. "Mrs. Murphy, what have you done?"

"I haven't done anything," the cat protested.

Harry appealed to Fair. "You're a veterinarian. You explain this." She pointed to the rubber bands tossed about the floor.

Maude leaned over the counter. "Isn't that cute? They get into everything. My mother once had a calico that played with toilet paper. She'd grab the end of the roll and run through the house with it."

"That's nothing." Pewter one-upped her: "*Cazenovia, the cat at Saint Paul's Church, eats communion wafers.*"

"Pewter wants on the counter." Fair thought the meow meant that. He lifted her onto the counter, where she rolled on her back and also rolled her eyes.

The humans thought this was adorable and fussed over her. Mrs. Murphy, boiling with disgust, jumped onto the counter and spat in Pewter's face.

"Jealousy's the same in any language." Fair laughed and continued to pet Pewter, who had no intention of relinquishing center stage.

Tucker moaned on the floor. "*I can't see anything down here.*"

Mrs. Murphy walked to the edge of the counter. "*What are you good for, Tee Tucker, with those short stubby legs?*"

"*I can dig up anything, even a badger.*" Tucker smiled.

"*We don't have any badgers.*" Pewter now rolled from side to side and purred so loudly the deaf could appreciate her vocal abilities. The humans were further enchanted.

"*Don't push your luck, Pewter,*" Tucker warned. "*Just because you've got the big head over knowing what happened before we did doesn't mean you can come in here and make fun of me.*"

"This is the most affectionate cat I've ever seen." Maude tickled Pewter's chin.

"*She's also the fattest cat you've ever seen,*" Mrs. Murphy growled.

"Don't be ugly," Harry warned the tiger.

"*Don't be ugly.*" Pewter mocked the human voice.

Mrs. Murphy paced the counter. A mail bin on casters rested seven feet from the counter top. She gathered herself and arched off the counter, smack into the middle of the mail bin, sending it rolling across the floor.

Maude squealed with delight and Fair clapped his hands together like a boy.

"She does that all the time. Watch." Harry trotted up behind the now-slowing cart and pushed Mrs. Murphy around the back of the post office. She made choo-choo sounds when she did it. Mrs. Murphy popped her head over the side, eyes big as eight balls, tail swishing.

"Now this is fun!" the cat declared.

Pewter, still being petted by Maude, was soured by Mrs. Murphy's audacious behavior. She put her head on the counter and closed her eyes. Mrs. Murphy might be bold as brass but at least Pewter behaved like a lady.

Maude leafed through her mail as she rubbed Pewter's ears. "I hate that!"

"Another bill? Or how about those appeals for money in envelopes that look like old Western Union telegrams? I really hate that." Harry continued to push Mrs. Murphy around.

"No." Maude shoved the postcard over to Fair, who read it and shrugged his shoulders. "What I hate is people who send postcards or letters and don't sign their names. For instance, I must know fourteen Carols and when I get a letter from one of them, if the return address isn't on the outside I haven't a clue. Not a clue. Every Carol I know has two-point-two children, drives a station wagon, and sends out Christmas cards with pictures of the family. The message usually reads 'Season's Greetings' in computer script, and little holly berries are entwined around the message. What's bizarre is that their families all look the same. Maybe there's one Carol married to fourteen men." She laughed.

Harry laughed with her and pretended to look at the postcard for the first time while she rocked Mrs. Murphy back and forth in the mail bin and the cat flopped on her back to play with her tail. Mrs. Murphy was putting on quite a show, doing what she accused Pewter of doing: wanting to be the center of attention.

Harry said, "Maybe they were in a hurry."

"Who do you know going to North Carolina?" Fair asked the logical question.

"Does anyone want to go to North Carolina?" Maude's voice dropped on "want."

"No," Harry said.

"Oh, North Carolina's all right." Fair finished his Coke. "It's just that they've got one foot in the nineteenth century and one in the twenty-first and nothing in between."

"You do have to give them credit for the way they've attracted clean industry." Maude thought about it. "The state of Virginia had that chance. You blew it about ten years ago, you know?"

"We know." Fair and Harry spoke in unison.

"I was reading about Claudius Crozet's struggle with the state of Virginia to finance railroads. He foresaw this at the end of the 1820's, before anything was happening with rail travel. He said Virginians should commit everything they had to this new form of travel. Instead they batted his ideas down and rewarded him with a pay cut. Naturally, he left, and you know what else? The state didn't do a thing about it until 1850! By that time New York State, which had thrown its weight behind railroads, had become the commercial center of the East Coast. If you think where Virginia is placed on the East Coast, we're the state that should have become the powerful one."

"I never knew that." Harry liked history.

"If there're any progressive projects, whether commercial or intellectual, you can depend on Virginia's legislature to vote 'em down." Maude shook her head. "It's as if the legislature doesn't want to take any chances at all. Vanilla pudding."

"Yeah, that's true." Fair agreed with her. "But on the other hand, we don't have the problems of those places that are progressive. Our crime rate is low except for Richmond. We've got full employment here in the county and we live a good life. We don't get rich quick but we keep what we've got. Maybe it isn't so bad. Anyway, you moved here, didn't you?"

Maude considered this. "Touché. But sometimes, Fair, it gets to me that this state is so backward. When North Carolina outsmarts us and enjoys the cornucopia, what can you think?"

"Where'd you learn about railroads?"

"Library. There's a book, a long monograph really, on Crozet's life. Not having the benefit of being educated in Crozet, I figured I'd better catch up, so to speak. Pity the railroad doesn't stop here anymore. Passenger service stopped in 1975."

"Occasionally it does. If you call up the president of the Chesapeake and Ohio Railroad and request a special stop—as a passenger and descendent of Claudius Crozet—they're supposed to stop for you right next to the post office here at the old depot."

"Has anyone tried it lately?" Maude was incredulous.

"Mim Sanburne last year. They stopped." Fair smiled.

"Think I'll try it," Maude said. "I'd better get back to my shop. Keep thy shop and thy shop keeps thee. 'Bye."

Pewter lolled on the counter as Harry put the Cokes in the small refrigerator in the back. Mrs. Murphy stayed in the mail bin hoping for another ride.

"Are these a peace offering?" Harry shut the refrigerator door.

"I don't know." And Fair didn't. He'd gotten in the habit, over the years, of picking up Cokes for Harry. "Look, Harry, can't we have a civil divorce?"

"Everything is civil until it gets down to money."

"You hired Ned Tucker first. Once lawyers get into it, everything turns to shit."

"In 1658 the Virginia legislature passed a law expelling all lawyers from the colony." Harry folded her arms across her chest.

"Only wise decision they ever made." Fair leaned against the counter.

"Well, they rescinded it in 1680." Harry breathed in. "Fair, divorce is a legal process. I had to hire a lawyer. Ned's an old friend."

"Hey, he was my friend too. Couldn't you have brought in a neutral party?"

"This is Crozet. There are no neutral parties."

"Well, I got a Richmond lawyer."

"You can afford Richmond prices."

"Don't start with money, goddammit." Fair sounded weary. "Divorce is the only human tragedy that reduces to money."

"It's not a tragedy. It's a process." Harry, at this point, would be bound to contradict or correct him. She half knew she was doing it but couldn't stop.

"It's ten years of my life, out the window."

"Not quite ten."

"Dammit, Harry, the point is, this isn't easy—and it wasn't my idea."

"Oh, don't pull the wounded dove with me. You were no happier in this marriage than I was!"

"But I thought everything was fine."

"As long as you got fed and fucked, you thought everything was fine!" Harry's voice sank lower. "Our house was a hotel to you. My God, if you ran the vacuum cleaner, angels would sing in the sky."

"We didn't have money for a maid," he growled.

"So it was me. Why is your time more valuable than my time? Jesus Christ, I even bought you your clothes, your jockey shorts." For some reason this was significant to Harry.

Fair, quiet for a moment to keep from losing his temper, said, "I make more money. If I had to be out on call, well, that's the way it had to be."

"You know, I don't even care anymore." Harry unfolded her arms and took a step toward him. "What I want to know is, were you, are you, sleeping with Boom Boom Craycroft?"

"No!" Fair looked wounded. "I told you before. I was drunk at the party. I—okay, I behaved as less than a gentleman . . . but that was a year ago."

"I know about that. I was there, remember? I'm asking about now, Fair."

He blinked, steadied his gaze. "No."

As the humans recriminated, Tucker, tired of being on the floor, out of the cat action, said, *"Pewter, we went over to Kelly Craycroft's concrete plant."*

Alert, Pewter sat up. *"Why?"*

"Wanted to sniff for ourselves."

"How can Mrs. Murphy smell anything? She's always got her nose up in the air."

"Shut up." Mrs. Murphy stuck her head over the mail bin.

"How uncouth." Pewter pulled back her whiskers.

"I was talking to Tucker, but you can shut up too. I'll kill two birds with one stone."

"Why were you telling me to shut up? I didn't do anything." Tucker was hurt.

"I'll tell you later," the tiger cat replied.

"It's no secret. Ozzie's probably blabbed it over three counties by now—ours, Orange, and Nelson. Maybe the whole state of Virginia knows, since Bob Berryman delivers those stock trailers everywhere and Ozzie goes with him," Tucker yipped.

"Nine states." Mrs. Murphy knew Tucker was going to tell.

"Tell me. What did Ozzie blab and why did you go to the concrete plant?" Pewter's pupils enlarged.

"Ozzie said there was a funny smell. And there was." Tucker liked this turnabout.

Pewter scoffed, "Of course, there was a funny smell, Tucker. A man was ground into hamburger meat and the day sweltered at ninety-seven degrees. Even humans can smell that."

"It wasn't that." Mrs. Murphy crawled out of the mail bin, disappointed that Harry had lost interest and was giving her full attention to Fair.

"Rescue Squad smells." Pewter was fishing.

"Smelled like a turtle."

"What?" The fat cat swept her whiskers forward.

Mrs. Murphy jumped up on the counter and sat next to Pewter. Since Tucker was going to yap she might as well be in the act. "It did. By the time we got there most of the scent was gone but there was this slight amphibian odor."

Pewter wrinkled her nose. "I did hear Ozzie say something about a turtle, but I didn't pay too much attention. There was so much going on." She sighed.

"Ever smell 'Best Fishes'?" Pewter's mind returned to food, her favorite topic. "Now that's a good smell. Mrs. Murphy, doesn't Harry have any treats left?"

"Yes."

"Think she'll give me one?"

"I'll give you one if you promise to tell us anything you hear about Kelly Craycroft. Anything at all. And I promise not to make fun of you."

"I promise." The fat chin wobbled solemnly.

Mrs. Murphy jumped off the counter and ran over to the desk. The lower drawer was open a crack. She squeezed her paw in it and hooked out a strip of dried beef jerky. She picked it up and gave it to Pewter, who devoured it instantly.

10

Bob Berryman laughed loudly during the movie *Field of Dreams*. He was alone. Apart from Bob, Harry and Susan didn't know anyone else in the theater. Charlottesville, jammed with new people, was becoming a new town to them. No longer could you drive into town and expect to see your friends. Not that the new people weren't nice—they were—but it was somewhat discomforting to be born and raised in a place and suddenly feel like a stranger.

The new residents flocked to the county in such numbers that they couldn't be absorbed quickly enough into the established clubs and routines. Naturally, the new people created their own clubs and routines. Formerly, the four great social centers—the hunt club, the country club, the black churches, and the university—provided stability to the community, like the four points of a square. Now young blacks drifted away from the churches, the country club had a six-year waiting list for membership, and the university was in the community but not of the community. As for the hunt club, most of the new people couldn't ride.

The road system couldn't handle the newcomers either. The state of Virginia was dickering about paving over much of the countryside with a bypass. The residents, old and new, were bitterly opposed to the destruction of their environment. The Highway Department people would be more comfortable in a room full of scorpions, because this was getting ugly. The obvious solution, of improving the central corridor road, Route 29, or even elevating a direct road over the existing route, did not occur to the powers-that-be in Richmond. They cried, "Expensive," while ignoring the outrageous sums they'd already squandered in hiring a research company to do their dirty work for them. They figured the populace would direct their wrath at the research company, and the Highway Department could hide behind the screen. The Republican party, quick to seize the opportunity to roast the reigning Democrats, turned the bypass into a political hot potato. The Highway Department remained obstinate. The Democrats, losing power, began to feel queasy. It was turning into an interesting drama, one in which political careers would be made and unmade.

Harry believed that whatever figure was published, you should double it. For some bizarre reason, government people could not hold the line on spending. She observed this in the post office. The regulations, created to help, just made things so much worse that she ran her post office as befitted the community, not as befitted some distant someone sitting on a fat ass in Washington, D.C. The same was true for the state government. They wouldn't travel the roads they'd build; they wouldn't have their hearts broken because beautiful farmland was destroyed and the watershed was endangered. They'd have a nice line on the map and talk to the governor about traffic flow. Every employee would justify his or her position by complicating the procedure as much as possible and then solving the complications.

Meanwhile the citizens of Albemarle County would be told to accept the rape of their land for the good of the counties south of them, counties that had contributed heavily to certain politicians' war chests. No one even considered the idea of letting people raise money themselves for improving the central corridor. Whatever the extra cost would be, compared to a bypass, Albemarle would pay for it. Self-government—why, the very thought was too revolutionary.

Harry, raised to believe the government was her friend, had learned by experience to believe it was her enemy. She softened her stance only with local officials whom she knew and to whom she could talk face-to-face.

One good thing about newcomers was, they were politically active. Good, Harry thought. They're going to need it.

She and Susan batted these ideas around at the Blue Ridge Brewery. Ice-cold beer on a sticky night tasted delicious.

"So?"

"So what, Susan?"

"You've been sitting here for ten minutes and you haven't said a thing."

"Oh. I'm sorry. Lost track of time, I guess."

"Apparently." Susan smiled. "Come on, what gives? Another bout with Fair?"

"You know, I can't decide who's the bigger asshole, him or me. What I do know is, we can't be in the same room together without an argument. Even if we start out on friendly terms . . . we end up accusing each other of . . ."

Susan waited. No completion of Harry's sentence was forthcoming. "Accusing each other of what?"

"I asked him if he'd slept with Boom Boom."

"What?" Susan's lower lip dropped.

"You heard me."

"And?"

"He said no. Oh, it went on from there. Every mistake I'd made since we dated got thrown in my face. God, I am so bored with him, with the situation"—she paused—"with myself. There's a whole world out there and right now all I can think of is this stupid divorce." Another pause. "And Kelly's murder."

"Fortunately the two are not connected." Susan took a long draft.

"I hope not."

"They aren't." Susan dismissed the thought. "You don't think they are either. He may not have been the husband you needed, but he's not a murderer."

"I know." Harry pushed the glass away. "But I don't know him anymore—and I don't trust him."

"Ever notice how friends love you for what you are? Lovers try to change you into what they want you to be." Susan drank the rest of Harry's beer.

Harry laughed. "Mom used to say, 'A woman marries a man hoping to change him and a man marries a woman hoping she'll never change.'"

"Your mother was a pistol." Susan remembered Grace's sharp wit. "But I think men try to change their partners, too, although in a different way. It's so confusing. I know less about human relationships the older I get. I thought it was supposed to be the other way around. I thought I was supposed to be getting wiser."

"Yeah. Now I'm full of distrust."

"Oh, Harry, men aren't so bad."

"No, no—I distrust myself. What was I doing married to Pharamond Haristeen? Am I that far away from myself?"

Back home, Mrs. Murphy prowled.

Tucker, in her wicker basket, lifted her head. *"Sit down."*

"Am I keeping you awake?"

"No," the dog grumbled. *"I can't sleep when Mommy's away. I've seen other people take their dogs to the movies. Muffin Barnes sticks her dog in her purse."* Muffin was a friend of Harry's.

"Muffin Barnes's dog is a chihuahua."

"Zat what he is?" Tucker, stiff-legged, got out of the basket. *"Wanna play?"*

"Ball?"

"No. How about tag? We can rip and tear while she isn't here. Actually, we should rip and tear. How dare she go away and leave us here. Let's make her pay."

"Yeah!" Mrs. Murphy's eyes lit up.

An hour later, when Harry flipped the lights on in the living room, she exclaimed, "Oh, my God!"

The ficus tree was tipped over, soil was thrown over the floor, and soiled kittyprints dotted the walls. Mrs. Murphy had danced in the moist dirt before hitting the walls with all four feet.

Harry, furious, searched for her darlings. Tucker hid under the bed in the back corner against the wall, and Mrs. Murphy lay flat on the top shelf of the pantry.

By the time Harry cleaned up the mess she was too tired to discipline them. To her credit, she understood that this was punishment for her leaving. She understood, but was loath to admit that the animals trained her far better than she trained them.

11

The prospect of the weekend lightened Harry's step as she walked along Railroad Avenue, shiny from last night's late thunderstorm, which had done nothing to lower the exalted temperature. Mrs. Murphy and Tucker, forgiven, scampered ahead.

The moment she caught sight of them, Pewter tore down the avenue to greet them.

"I didn't know she could move that fast." Harry whistled out loud.

When Pewter ran, the flab under her belly swayed from side to side. She started yelling half a block away from her friends. "I've been waiting outside the store for you!"

Panting, Pewter slid to a stop at Tucker's feet.

Harry, thinking that the animal had exhausted herself, stooped to pick her up. "Poor Fatty."

"Lemme go." Pewter wiggled free.

"What is it?" Mrs. Murphy rubbed against Harry's legs to make her feel better.

"Maude Bly Modena." The chartreuse eyes glittered. "Dead!"

"How?" Mrs. Murphy wanted details.

"Train ran over her."

"In her car, you mean?" Tucker was impatient waiting for Pewter to catch her breath as they continued walking toward the post office.

"No!" Pewter picked up the pace. "Worse than that."

"Pewter, I've never heard you so chatty." Harry beamed.

Pewter replied, "*If you'd pay attention you might learn something.*" She turned to Mrs. Murphy. "*They think they're so smart but they only pay attention to themselves. Humans only listen to humans and half the time they don't do that.*"

"Yes." Mrs. Murphy wanted to say "*Get on with it,*" but she prudently bit her lip.

"*As I was saying, it was worse than that. She was tied to the track, I don't know where exactly, but when the six o'clock came through this morning, the engineer couldn't stop in time. Cut her into three pieces.*"

"*How'd you find out?*" Tucker blinked at the thought of the grisly sight.

"*Unfortunately, Courtney heard about it first. Market let her come in and open up for the farm trade, the five A.M. crew. The Rescue Squad roared by—Rick Shaw too. Officer Cooper, in the second squad car, ran in for coffee. That's how we found out. Courtney phoned Market and he came right down. There's some weirdo out there killing people.*"

"*Like a serial killer, you mean?*" Tucker was very concerned for Harry's safety.

"*It's bad enough that humans kill once.*" Pewter sucked in her breath. "*But every now and then they throw one who wants to kill over and over.*"

Mrs. Murphy murmured, "*I liked Maude.*"

"*I did too.*" Tucker hung her head. "*Why don't people kill their sick young like we do? Why do they let them live and cause damage?*"

"*Well, as I understand it, these psychos*"—Pewter had an opinion on everything—"*can appear mentally normal.*"

"*That's no excuse for the ones they know are nuts from the beginning.*" Mrs. Murphy couldn't cover her distress.

"*They think it's wrong to weed out litters.*" Tucker's claws clicked on the pavement.

"*Yeah, they let the sickies grow up and kill them instead.*" Pewter laughed a harsh laugh. "*No one better come after Courtney or Market. I'll scratch their eyes out.*"

Harry noticed the three animals were attentive to one another.

"Whoever this is has something to cover up," Mrs. Murphy thought out loud.

"Yes, they have to cover up that they're demented and they'll kill again, during a full moon, I bet," Pewter said.

"No. I don't mean that." Mrs. Murphy's eyes became slits. Tucker had lived with Mrs. Murphy since she was a six-week-old puppy. She knew how the cat thought. "This person is after something—or has something to hide. It might not be a thrill killer."

"Don't you find it peculiar that he or she leaves the bodies about? Doesn't a killer try and bury the body?" Pewter figured that's what vultures were for, but then, people were different.

"That struck me about Kelly's body." Mrs. Murphy ignored a caterpillar, so intense was her concentration. "The killer is displaying the bodies . . ." Her voice drifted off because Market Shiflett emerged from his store and was waving at Harry.

"Harry, Harry!"

Harry heard the fear in his voice and ran down to the store. "What's the matter?"

"S'awful, just awful."

Harry put her arm around him. "Are you all right? Want me to call the Doc?" She meant Hayden McIntire.

Market nodded he was fine. "It's not me, Harry. It's another murder—Maude Bly Modena."

"What?!" Harry's color fled from her cheeks.

"I'm keeping my girl inside. There's a monster out there!"

"What happened, Market?" Harry, shocked, put her hand against the store window to steady herself.

"That poor woman was tied to the railroad tracks like in some silent movie. The fellow saw her—the brakeman, I guess, on the morning passenger train—but too late, too late. Oh, that poor woman." His lower lip trembled.

"Who else knows?" Harry's mind was moving at the speed of light.

"Why do you ask?" Market was surprised at the question.

"I'm not sure, Market, I . . . Woman's intuition."

"Do you know something?" His voice rose.

"No, I don't know a damn thing but I'm going to find out. This has to stop!"

"Well"—Market rubbed his chin—"Courtney knows, Rick Shaw and Officer Cooper, and Clai and Diana of the Rescue Squad, of course. Train people know, including the passengers. Train stopped. A lot of people know."

"Yes, yes." Her voice trailed off.

"What are you thinking?"

"That I wish so many people didn't know already. Controlling the information might have been a way to snag a clue."

"Yeah." The phone rang inside. "I've got to pick that up. Let's stick together, Harry."

"You bet."

Market opened the door and Pewter scooted in, calling her good-byes over her shoulder.

A miserable Harry unlocked the door to the post office, Mrs. Murphy and Tucker behind.

"Come on."

Mrs. Murphy looked at Tucker. *"You thinking what I'm thinking?"*

Tucker replied, *"Yes, but we don't know where."*

"Damn!" Mrs. Murphy fluffed her tail in fury and walked dramatically into the post office.

Tucker followed as Harry picked up the phone and started dialing. *"It could be miles and miles from here."*

"I know!" Mrs. Murphy crabbed. *"And we'll lose the scent—if it's there."*

"It held a little bit the other time. That day was stinky hot too."

Mrs. Murphy leaned up against the corgi. *"I hope so. Buddy-bud, we're going to have to use our powers to get to the bottom of this. Harry's smart but her nose is bad. Her ears aren't too good either. People can't move very fast. We've got to find out who's doing this so we can protect her."*

"I'll die before I let anyone hurt Harry!" Tucker barked loudly.

"Susan, there's been another murder."

"I'll be right there," Susan replied.

She started to dial Fair at the clinic but hung up the phone. It was a knee-jerk reaction to call him.

"Rick Shaw came by for Ned," Susan said as Harry unlocked the front door. It was 7:30 A.M.

"What's he want with Ned?"

"He wants him to organize a Citizen's Alert group. Harry, this is unbelievable. This is Crozet, Virginia, for Pete's sake, not New York City."

"Unbelievable or not, it's happening. Did Rick say anything about Maude?"

"What do you mean?"

"I mean, was she alive when she was run over?" Harry's entire body twitched at the thought and a wave of nausea engulfed her.

"I thought of that too. I asked him. He said they didn't know but they believed not. The coroner would know exactly when she died."

"If Rick said that, it means she was dead already. I mean, you'd have to be pretty stupid not to tell after a certain point. Did he say anything else?"

"Only that it happened out near the Greenwood tunnel, out on that first part of track."

Harry said, almost to herself, "What was she doing out that far?"

"God only knows." Susan sniffed. "What if this—this creature starts after our children?"

"That's not going to happen. I'm sure of it."

"How would you know?" A note of anger crept into Susan's voice.

"I'm sorry. I didn't mean to ignore your concern for the children, and you should keep the kids in at night. It's just that—well, I don't know. A feeling."

"There's a madman loose! Tell me what Kelly Craycroft and Maude Bly Modena had in common! Tell me that!"

"If we can figure that out, we might catch the killer." Command rang through Harry's voice. She was a born leader, although she never acknowledged it and even avoided groups.

Susan knew Harry had made up her mind. "You aren't trained in this sort of thing."

"Neither are you. Will you help me?"

"What do I have to do?"

"The police ask routine questions. That's fine, because they learn a lot. We need to ask different questions—not just 'Where were you on the night of . . . ?' but 'How did you feel about Kelly's Ferrari and how did you feel about Maude's big success with her store?' Emotions. Maybe emotions will get us closer to an answer."

"Count me in."

"I'll take Mrs. Hogendobber and Little Marilyn for starters. How about if you take Boom Boom and Mim. No, wait. Let me take Boom Boom. I have my reasons. You take Little Marilyn."

"Okay."

Rob sailed through the front door. He dropped the mail sacks like lead when Harry told him the news. He absolutely couldn't believe this was happening, but who could?

Tucker and Mrs. Murphy overheard Harry reveal the location of the murder.

"*We can't get there by ourselves unless we're willing to be gone an entire day.*"

"*Can't do that.*" Tucker pulled at her collar. The metal rabies tag tinkled.

"*So, how are we going to get out there? We need Harry to take us in the truck.*"

"*Half of Crozet will go out there. People have a morbid curiosity,*" Tucker observed.

"*When she gets in that truck, no matter when, we'd better pitch a fit.*"

"*Gotcha.*"

Mrs. Hogendobber was stopped by Market Shiflett as she ascended the post office steps. She emitted a piercing yell upon hearing the news.

Josiah, crossing the street, hesitated for a split second and then came over to see what was amiss.

"This is the work of the Devil!" Mrs. Hogendobber put her hand on the wall for support.

"It's shocking." Josiah tried to sound comforting but he never would like Mrs. Hogendobber. "Come on, Mrs. H., let me help you inside the post office." He swung open the door.

"When did you hear?" Mrs. Hogendobber's voice sounded even.

"On the radio this morning." Josiah fanned Mrs. H., now sitting by the stamp meter. "Would you like me to take you home?" Josiah offered.

"No, I came for my mail and I'm going to get it." Resolutely, Mrs. Hogendobber stood up and strode to her postal box.

Harry and Josiah followed her as Fair screeched up out front, killing the engine before turning off the key as his foot slipped off the clutch.

"You could have come right through the window," Mrs. Hogendobber admonished him.

Fair shut the door behind him. "I thought I'd give the taxpayers a break and not do that."

"This old building could use a rehab." Josiah turned the key in his box.

"Do you know about that sweet Maude Bly Modena? Murdered! In cold blood." Mrs. Hogendobber breathed heavily again.

"Now, now, don't get yourself overexcited," Josiah warned her.

"Quite right." Mrs. Hogendobber controlled herself. "So much evil in the land. Still, I never thought it would come home." She touched her eyebrow, trying to remember. "The last bad thing that happened here—apart from the drunken-driving accidents—why, that would be the robberies at the Farmington Country Club. Remember?"

"That was in 1978." Harry recalled the incident. "A gang of high-class thieves broke into the homes there and took the silver and the antiques."

"And left the silver plate." Mrs. Hogendobber didn't realize how funny that was and couldn't understand why, for a moment, Harry, Fair, and Josiah laughed.

"The theft wasn't funny, Mrs. H.," Harry explained. "But on top of being robbed, everyone would find out who had good stuff and who didn't. I mean, it added insult to injury."

Mrs. Hogendobber found no humor in it and made a harrumphf. "Well, this has been too much for one morning. I bid you adieu."

"Are you sure you don't want me to see you home?" Josiah offered again.

"No . . . thank you." And she was gone.

"Didn't they find that stuff stashed in a barn in Falling Water, West Virginia?" Fair asked.

"They did, and that was a stupid place to put it too." Josiah shut his mailbox.

"Why?" Harry asked.

"Putting exquisite pieces like that in a barn. Rodents could chew them or defecate on the furniture. The elements could expand and contract the woods. Just dumb. They knew good stuff from bad but they didn't know how to take care of it."

"Maybe they packed them up or crated them." Fair wasn't very knowledgeable about antiques.

"No, I remember the TV reports. They showed the inside of the barn." Josiah shook his head. "No matter, that's small beer compared to . . . this." He walked over to the counter where Fair was leaning. "What do you think?"

"I don't know."

"What about you, Harry?" Josiah's face registered concern.

"I think whoever did this was one of us. Someone we know and trust."

Josiah instinctively stepped back. "Why do you think that?"

"What's the killer doing? Flying in and out of Charlottesville to murder his victims? It has to be a local."

"Well, it doesn't have to be someone from Crozet." Josiah was offended at the idea.

"Why not? It's not so strange when you think about it." Fair ran his fingers through his thick hair. "Something goes wrong between friends or lovers; the hurt person blows. It can happen here. It has happened here."

Josiah slowly walked to the door and put his hand on the worn doorknob. "I don't like to think about it. Maybe it will stop now." He left and for good measure circled around the post office to Mrs. Hogendobber's house to make sure she arrived home safely.

"What can I do for you?" Harry, even-toned, asked Fair.

"Oh, nothing. I heard on the way to work and I thought I'd see if you were all right. You liked Maude."

Harry, touched, lowered her eyes. "Thanks, Fair. I did like Maude."

"We all did."

"That's it. That's what I need to find out. We all liked Maude. We mostly liked Kelly Craycroft. To the eye, everything looks normal. Underneath, something's horribly wrong."

"Find the motive and you find the killer," Fair said.

"Unless he or she finds you first."

12

Harry paused before knocking on Boom Boom Craycroft's dark-blue front door. She'd brought the cat and the dog along because when she left for her lunch break the animals carried on like dervishes. First the ficus tree, now this. Must be the heat. She glanced over her shoulder. Mrs. Murphy and Tucker, good as gold, sat in the front seat of the truck. The windows, wide open, gave them air but it was too hot to be in the truck. She turned around and opened the truck door.

"Now, you stay here."

The minute Harry disappeared through the front door of the Craycroft house, that order was forgotten.

Boom Boom's West Highland white shot around from behind the back of the house. *"Who's here? Who's here, and you'd better have a good reason to be here!"*

"It's us, Reggie," Tucker said.

"So it is." Reggie wagged his tail and touched noses with Tucker. He touched noses with Mrs. Murphy, too, even though she was a cat. Reggie had manners.

"How are you?"

"As good as can be expected."

"Bad, huh?" Tucker was sympathetic.

"She's just grim. Never smiles. I wish I could do something for her. I miss him too. He was a lot of fun, Kelly."

"*Do you have any idea what happened? Did he take you places that humans didn't know about?*" Mrs. Murphy asked.

"*No. I'm supposed to be a house dog. I've seen the concrete plant a few times but that's it.*"

"*Did he seem worried recently?*"

"*No, he was happy as a dog with a bone. Every time he made money he was happy and he made lots of it. Bones to them, I guess. He wasn't home much but when he was, he was happy.*"

Inside, Harry wasn't getting much from Boom Boom either.

"A nightmare." Boom Boom snapped open her platinum cigarette case. "And now Maude. Does anyone know if she has people?"

"No. Susan Tucker offered to put up the relatives but Rick Shaw told her that Maude had no siblings and her parents were dead."

"Who's going to claim the body?" Boom Boom, having undergone a funeral, was keenly aware of the technical responsibilities.

"I don't know but I'll be sure to mention that to Susan."

"I've gone over that last day a thousand times in my head, Harry. I've gone over the week before and the week before that and I can't think of a thing. Not a sign, not a hint, not anything. He kept me separate from the business but I had little interest in it anyway. Concrete and pouring foundations and roadbeds never was my idea of thrills." Boom Boom lit her dark Nat Sherman cigarette. "If he roughed a man up in business, I wouldn't know."

"Kelly might have crossed someone. He was very competitive." Harry picked up a crystal ashtray with a silver rim around it and felt its perfect proportions.

"He liked to win, I'll grant you that, but I don't think he was unfair. At least, he wasn't with me. Look, Harry, we've known each other since we were children. You know for the last few years Kelly and I were almost more like brother and sister than husband and wife, but he was a good friend to me. He was . . . good." Her voice got thick.

"I'm so sorry. I wish I could say or do something." Harry touched her hand.

"You've been kind to call on me. I never knew how many friends I had. He had. People have been wonderful—and I can be hard to be wonderful to . . . sometimes."

Harry thought to herself that someone was being anything but wonderful. Which one? Who? Why?

Boom Boom mused, "Kelly would have been amazed to see how many people did love him."

"Perhaps he knows. I'd like to think that."

"Yes, I'd like to think that too."

Harry put the ashtray back. She paused. "Have the cops gone over everything? His office?"

"Even his office here at home. The only thing on his desk the day he died was the day's mail."

"May I peek in the office? I don't want to be rude, but I think if there's anything that we can do to help Rick Shaw, we should. Perhaps if I poke around I'll find a clue. Even a blind pig finds an acorn sometimes."

"You've read too many mysteries sitting there in the post office." Boom Boom stood up and Harry did also.

"Spy thrillers this year."

"And for that you went to Smith College?" Boom Boom felt Harry should do more with her life, but who was she to judge? Boom Boom truly was the idle rich.

The walnut paneling glowed in the bright afternoon light. Neatly placed in the middle of an unblemished desk pad bound by red Moroccan leather was Kelly's mail.

"May I?" Harry didn't reach for the mail.

"Yes."

Harry picked it up and rifled through the letters, including the postcard, the beautiful postcard of Oscar Wilde's tombstone. She replaced the mail as she found it. At that moment she was more concerned with a certain evasiveness Boom Boom displayed toward her. She and Boom Boom got along well enough, but today there was something not right between them.

It wasn't until later, when she had left Boom Boom and was

rumbling past the tiny trailer park on Route 240, that she realized Maude had received a postcard of a beautiful tombstone as well. With the same inscription: "Wish you were here." My God, someone was telling them, I wish you were dead. It was a sick joke. She put her pedal to the metal.

"Hey, slow down," Mrs. Murphy said. "I don't like to drive fast."

Harry careened into Susan's manicured driveway, hit the brakes, and vaulted out of the truck. The cat and dog hit the turf too.

Susan stuck her head out the upstairs window. "You'll kill yourself driving that old truck like that."

"I found something."

Susan raced down the stairs and flung open the front door. Harry told Susan what she discovered, swore her to secrecy, and then they called Rick Shaw. He wasn't there, so Officer Cooper received the information.

Harry hung up the phone. "She didn't seem very excited about it."

"They shag so many leads. How's she to know if this is anything special?" Susan laced her sneakers. "Let's hope another one doesn't show up."

"Damn, I forgot to look."

"For what?"

"For the postmark on Kelly's card. Was it from Paris?"

"Let's go to Maude's shop and look at the postcard she received."

Maude's shop, closed, beckoned the passerby. The window boxes burst with pink and purple petunias. The sidewalk was swept clean.

Susan tried the door. "Locked."

Harry circled to the back and jimmied a window. The minute she got it open, Mrs. Murphy shot up on the windowsill and gracefully dropped into the shop. Harry followed and Susan handed Tucker to her and then followed herself.

The back room, an avalanche of packing materials, greeted them.

"I didn't know there were that many plastic peanuts in the world," Susan observed.

Harry made a beeline for Maude's rolltop desk in the front room.

"What if someone sees you there?"

"They can report me for breaking and entering." Harry snatched the mail, which was kept in boxes on the desk. "Found it!" She quickly flipped over the postcard. "Well, there goes that theory."

"What's it say?"

"Come here and read it. No one's going to arrest us."

Susan joined her. " 'Wish you were here.' " She then noticed the postmark. "Oh." It read Asheville, North Carolina.

Harry slid open the center drawer. A huge ledger book, pencils, erasers, and a ruler rattled. She reached for the ledger book. Sometimes accounting columns tell a story.

Footsteps on the sidewalk made her freeze. She closed the drawer.

"Let's get out of here," Susan whispered.

When Harry returned to the post office and relieved Dr. Johnson, she called Boom Boom and asked her to look at the postcard. It was marked PARIS, REPUBLIC OF FRANCE.

Baffled, Harry put down the receiver. Okay, the postmarks confused her. Still, she wasn't giving up. Those postcards were important. Whoever the killer was, he or she had a sense of humor, maybe even a sense of the absurd. Even the disposition of the corpses was macabre and trashy.

She racked her brain to think of who had a sharp sense of humor: everybody in Crozet except for Mrs. Hogendobber.

The shroud of mortality drew closer. Who could be next? Was she in danger? If only she could discover the link between Kelly and Maude, maybe she'd know that her friends would be safe. But if she discovered that link, she wouldn't be safe.

13

Harry was taken aback by the number of people milling about the railroad track. Getting there wasn't easy. People had to drive out to 691 and then cut right on 690. Bob Berryman, Josiah, Market, and Dr. Hayden McIntire glumly stared at the tracks.

When Mrs. Murphy and Tucker sped into the brush, Harry barely noticed.

Harry joined the men. She cast her eyes downward and saw blood spattered everywhere. Flies buzzed on the ground, feasting on what hadn't soaked up. Even the creosote odor of the railroad ties didn't blot out the sweltering odor of blood.

Josiah grimaced. "I had no idea that it could be so bad."

"Considering how many pints of blood are in the human body—" Hayden spoke like a physician.

Berryman, sweating profusely, cut him off. "I don't want to know." He backed away to his four-wheel-drive Jeep. Ozzie howled inside, furious that he couldn't get out. Berryman roared out of there, tearing hunks of earth as he went.

"I didn't mean to upset him," Hayden apologized.

"Don't worry about it." Market pinched his nose. "Damn, are we ghouls or what?"

"Of course not!" Josiah snapped. "Maybe we'll find something the police didn't. How much faith do you have in Rick Shaw? When he reads, his lips move."

"He's not that bad," Harry protested.

"Well, he's not that good." Hayden stuck up for Josiah.

Harry swept her eyes along the tracks. The cat and dog rummaged in the high weeds and then burst onto the tracks about one hundred yards west of where she was standing. At least they're happy, she thought.

"We know one thing," Harry stated.

"What?" Market pinched his nose again.

"She walked here."

"How do you know that?" Josiah peered intently at her features.

"Because there's no sign that the grasses are beaten down. If she'd been dragged there'd be a path even though it rained. A human's body is literally dead weight." The smell was getting to Harry and she moved away from the track.

"She could have been carried." Josiah joined her.

"Have to be a strong man." Hayden moved off the track too. "Don't know if the killer is male or female, although men commit over ninety percent of the murders in this country, statistically."

Josiah replied, "Not exactly. The women are too smart to get caught."

Market, the last to leave even though the stench turned his stomach, doubted that. "Maude was a good five feet ten inches. The road's back a stretch. The strongest among us was Kelly. The next strongest is Fair. No one else could have carried her, other than Jim Sanburne, and he has a bum back."

"A four-wheel-drive could have come up here." Josiah watched the animals as they moved closer.

"Cooper said no tire tracks," Market volunteered.

"She walked? So what?" Josiah thrust his hands into his pockets.

"Where was Fair last night?" Hayden asked, none too innocently.

"Ask him," Harry shot back.

"She walked out here in the middle of the night?" Market was thinking out loud. "Why?"

"She liked her jogging and usually ran along the track," Harry told them.

"Damn good jogger to get all the way out to Greenwood," Market said.

"In the middle of the night?" Hayden rubbed his chin.

"Beat the heat," Josiah offered. "Hey, how about Berryman getting squeamish like that?"

"He wasn't squeamish in school," Market recalled. "Hell, I saw the trainer stick a needle in his knee once during a football game. Took a bad hit, you know. Twisted his knee a bit. Anyway, Kooter Ashcomb—"

"I remember him!" Harry smiled.

Kooter was an old man by the time Harry attended Crozet High.

"Yeah, well, Kooter stuck a hypodermic needle right in his knee and drew out the fluid. Played the rest of the game, too."

"We win?" Harry wondered.

"You bet." Market folded his arms across his chest. Market liked remembering playing fullback a lot more than he liked the present.

"Back to Maude." One line of perspiration rolled down the side of Harry's face. "Did she come out here alone? Did she come out here to meet someone? Did she come out here with someone?"

"I had no idea you were so logical, Harry," Josiah observed.

"Obvious questions and I'm sure Rick Shaw and company have asked them too." Harry wiped away the sweat.

"Wish we could find some tracks." Hayden, not being a hunting man, wouldn't even know how to look.

In the distance, the finger of a dark thundercloud hooked over the Blue Ridge.

"No tracks if you walk on the train bed." Harry felt bad. The reality of Maude's death, the blood, began to press on her head. She felt a throbbing at her temples.

"There's nothing here"—Josiah's voice dropped—"except that." He pointed up to the stained site.

"But there is! There is!" Tucker barked.

Mrs. Murphy and Tucker swarmed over the site of the murder. Harry mistook this for attraction to the blood.

"Get out of there!" she shouted.

"Don't be mad at them, Harry. They're only animals," Market chided her.

"There's something here! That same smell is here!" Tucker barked.

Harry ran up to the dog and collared her. "You come with me right now!"

Mrs. Murphy ran alongside Harry. *"Don't do that! Come back. Come back and sniff!"*

Harry couldn't go back and it was just as well, because if she'd gotten down on her hands and knees to catch the scent she would also have seen a few strands of Maude's blood-soaked hair missed by the Sheriff's Department. That would have done her in.

Tucker and Mrs. Murphy had thoroughly investigated the area around the murder location. Not until they examined the exact site did they catch the faint amphibian odor. No track, no line. But again it was in one place, although this time there was more of it than a dot. There were a few dots, fading fast.

But no one would listen to them and they rode home in disgrace with Harry, who thought the worst of her best friends.

Later that evening the thunderstorm lashed Crozet. Marilyn Sanburne was put out because the power failed and she had a soufflé in the oven. Jim, just back from his business trip, said the hell with it. They could eat sandwiches. He was also being driven wild by the telephone ringing. As the mayor of murder hamlet, as one reporter called it, Jim was expected to say something. He did. He told them to "fuck off," and Mim screamed, "I hate the 'f' word." She would have left to go visit one of her cronies, but the storm was too intense. Instead, she flounced into her room and slammed the door.

Bob Berryman drove around aimlessly. A huge tree ripped out by the high winds crashed across the road. He avoided hitting it. Shaken, he turned the truck around and drove some more. Ozzie sat next to him wondering what was going on.

14

Boom Boom Craycroft thought the worst of everybody. Much as she tried to keep her emotions to herself they kept spilling over, and since she wouldn't express her sorrow, what she expressed was anger. Right now she was furious with Susan Tucker and she took a sabbatical on manners.

"I don't give a good goddam what you think. And I don't care if whoever killed Maude killed Kelly. I want whoever killed Kelly and I'm going to get him."

Susan hung her head. To a passerby it would appear she was addressing her golf ball with her five iron, an unusual choice off the tee. "Boom Boom, calm yourself. You were the one who wanted to play golf. You said sitting home would drive you crazy."

Boom Boom, warming up, swung her wood and dug up a clump of Farmington Country Club turf. If the greensman had been there he would have suffered a coronary. Susan, wordlessly, replaced Boom Boom's divot, then hit a beauty off the tee.

"Been a woody and you'd be on the green," Boom Boom advised. "I don't know why I kept this golf date with you. You do the screwiest things on a golf course."

"I still beat you."

"Not today you won't." Boom Boom stuck the tee in the ground, put the ball on it, and without a practice swing, socked away. The ball rose with a pleasing loft and then veered left, only to disappear in the rough.

"Shit!" Boom Boom threw her club on the ground. Not satisfied, she stamped on it. "Shit! Fuck! Damn!"

Susan held her breath during the indiscriminate rampage, which concluded with Boom Boom turning her expensive leather golf bag upside down. Balls and gloves fell out of the open zippers. Exhausted from her fury, Boom Boom sat on the ground.

"Honey, it's the pits." Susan sat next to her and put her arm around her. "Would you like to go home?"

"No. I hate it there more than I hate it here." Boom Boom shook when she inhaled. "Let's play. I feel better when I'm moving. I'm sorry I yelled at you when you were giving me the third degree. I didn't mind Rick Shaw so much but those grotesque newspeople ought to be horsewhipped. I slammed the door in their faces. I just didn't want to hear it from you."

"I am really sorry. Harry and I think if those of us who know one another as friends snoop around we might find something. It's a horrendous strain and I haven't helped."

"You have. I got to scream and holler and throw my bag on the ground. I feel better for it." She nimbly got up, righted her bag.

Susan picked up the balls. "Here." She noticed the brand name. "When did you buy these?"

"Last week. Ought to be gold-plated, the expensive buggers. See my initials on them." She pointed to a red B.B.C. carefully incised into the gleaming white surface.

"How'd you do that?"

"I didn't. Josiah did. He's got tools for everything. He cracks me up, buying this gilded junk, making repairs on it, and then selling it to some parvenu for a bundle."

"He is funny, though." Susan reached her ball.

Boom Boom waited until Susan was midway into her backswing. "Josiah said Mim has a purse with a lock on it. Isn't that perfect?" She laughed.

Naturally Susan's shot was ruined. "Damn you."

The ball plunked into the water, sending up a plume.

That made Boom Boom temporarily happy. She found her ball,

walked around it as though it were a snake, and finally hit it out of the rough. Not a bad shot.

"If you do think of anything, you will tell me?"

"Yes." Boom Boom picked up her bag. She wouldn't use golf carts because that defeated the purpose of golf for her. On weekends she'd use one because the club forced her to, and she complained plenty about it. She even pointed out one fat board member at the Nineteenth Hole and declared if he'd get out of his golf cart and walk, he might stop resembling the Michelin tire boy.

Susan peered into the water. The Canada geese peered back at her as they glided by. She carried a ball retriever for this very purpose and with some finesse she liberated her ball from the depths.

"I ought to get one of those."

"Especially when you're paying what you're paying for golf balls." Susan folded the retriever back and placed it in her bag. She then dropped her ball.

"Why do you think this is the work of one person?" Boom Boom had quieted enough to return to Susan's earlier question.

"Two gruesome murders—spectacularly gruesome—and within the same week."

"That's superficial evidence. The second murderer could be a copycat. The details of Kelly's murder covered the front page of the paper, the evening news, and God knows what else. A person wouldn't have to be too clever to figure out that the time is right to settle a score, and goodbye Maude Bly Modena."

"I never thought of that."

"I thought of something else too."

"What?"

"Susan, what if the police aren't telling us everything? What if they're holding something back?"

"I never thought of that either." Susan shuddered.

15

Rick Shaw hunched over another coroner's report. Normally, the office sank into a stupor on weekends except for the drunk-driving jobs. Not this weekend. People were tense. He was tense, and the damned newspaper was keeping a reporter on his tail. The bird perched in the parking lot after he threw him out of the office.

There was no evidence of sexual abuse. The victim had been dead for two hours before the train ran over her, which the coroner also reported. However, there were no bullet wounds, no bruises on the neck, and no contusions of any sort. Again, there was a tiny trace of cyanide in the hair. Whoever was killing these people with cyanide knew a great deal about chemistry. He or she wasn't wasting the cyanide. The killer took the victim's body weight into account.

Rick shook his head and closed the report, then sidled over to Officer Cooper's desk, where he filched a cigarette from an open pack. Illicit pleasure soon to be replaced by guilt, but not until the cigarette was smoked.

A deep draw soothed him. He'd have to remember to buy a pack of Tic Tacs on the way home or his wife would smell his breath. He studied a map of the county on the wall. The positions of the two bodies were in the same general vicinity, a few miles apart. The killer was most likely a local but not necessarily a Crozet resident. Albemarle County covered 743 square miles and anyone could drive in and out of Crozet fairly easily. Of course, they knew one another out there. A stranger would be reported. No such report. Even a resident of Charlottesville or a friend from out of town would be noticed. No such notice.

The postmistress and Market Shiflett were poised at the hub of social activity. Officer Cooper had mentioned that the postmistress had an idea about postcards. People usually think what they do is relevant, and Mary Minor Haristeen was no exception. He checked out the postcards within an hour of Harry's call and the postmarks were from different locales.

Still, he decided to call Harry. After a few pleasantries he thanked her for being alert, said he'd examined the postcards and they seemed okay to him.

"Could I have them—temporarily?" Harry asked him.

He considered this. "Why?"

"I want to match them with the inks that I have in the office—just in case."

"All right, if you promise not to harm them."

"I won't."

"I'll have Officer Cooper drop them by."

After Rick Shaw's call, Harry called Rob, and he agreed to "borrow" the first postcard from France that he came across at the main post office. She swore she'd give it back to him by the next day.

Then she remembered she was supposed to interrogate Mrs. Hogendobber. She called Mrs. H., who was surprised to hear from her but agreed on a tea-time get-together.

16

Mrs. Hogendobber served a suspiciously green tea. Little chocolate cupcakes oozing a tired marshmallow center reposed on a plate of Royal Doulton china. Mrs. Hogendobber snapped one up, devouring it at a gobble.

She reminded Harry of a human version of Pewter. Stifling a giggle, Harry reached for a leaking cupcake so as not to appear ungrateful for the sumptuous repast—well, repast.

"I stopped drinking caffeine. Made me testy." Mrs. H.'s little finger curled when she held her cup. "I purged soft drinks, coffee, even orange pekoe teas from my household."

Obviously, she had not purged refined sugar.

"I wish I had your willpower," Harry said.

"Stick to it, my girl, stick to it!" Another chocolate delight disappeared between the pink-lipsticked lips.

Mrs. Hogendobber's neat clapboard house was located on St. George Avenue, which ran roughly parallel to Railroad Avenue. A sweeping front porch with a swing afforded the large lady a vantage point. A trellis along the sides of the porch, choking with pink tea roses, allowed her to see everything while not being seen. The Good Lord said nothing about spying, so Mrs. Hogendobber spied with a vengeance. She chose to think of it as being curious about her fellow man.

"I'm so glad you agreed to see me," Harry began.

"Why wouldn't I?"

"Uh, well, come to think of it, why not?" Harry smiled, reminding Mrs. H. of when Harry was a cute seven-year-old.

"I'm here to, oh, root around for clues to the murders. The telling detail, thoughts—you're so observant."

"You have to get up early in the morning to put one over on me." Mrs. H. lapped up the compliment, and truthfully, she didn't miss much. "My late husband, God rest his soul, used to say, 'Miranda, you were born with eyes in the back of your head.' I could anticipate his wants and he thought I had special powers. No special powers. I was a good wife. I paid attention. It's the little things that make a marriage, my dear. I hope you have reviewed your marriage and will reconsider your acts. I doubt there are any men out there better than Fair—only different. They're all trouble in their unique ways." She poured herself more tea and opened her mouth but no sound escaped. "Where was I?"

". . . trouble in their unique ways." Harry hardly thought of herself in those terms.

"If you'd kick off those sneakers and buy some nice smocks instead of those jeans, I think he'd come to his senses."

"Love usually involves losing your senses, not coming to them."

Mrs. H. pondered this. "Yes . . . yes."

Before she could launch on to another tangent, Harry inquired, "What did you think of Maude Bly Modena?"

"I thought she was a Catholic. Italian-looking, you know. The shop proved how shrewd she was. Now I never socialized with her. My social life is the Church, and well, as I said, I think Maude was Catholic." Mrs. Hogendobber cleared her throat on "Catholic." "I, like yourself, only knew her for five years. Not a great deal of time but enough to get a feel for a person, I guess. She seemed quite fond of Josiah."

"What did you feel then?"

The bosom heaved. She was dying to be allowed to wander into the subjective. "I felt that she was hiding something—always, always."

"Like what?"

"I wish I knew. She didn't cheat anyone at the shop. I never heard of her shortchanging or overcharging but there was something, oh, not quite right. She spoke very little of her background." Unlike Mrs. Hogendobber, who fairly galloped down Memory Lane, given half a chance to speak of her past.

"She didn't tell me much either. I assumed she was discreet. After all, she was a Yankee."

"Not one of us, my dear, not one of us. Her manners were adequate. She missed the refinements, of course—they all do. But then there's Mim, who is overrefined, if you ask me."

"I liked her. I even grew accustomed to the accent." Uneasiness crept into Harry's heart. She felt that poor Maude wasn't here to defend herself and she was sorry for asking about her.

"I couldn't understand much of what she said. I relied on tone of voice, hand gestures, that sort of thing. I bet she's from a Mafia family."

"Why?"

"Well, she was Catholic and Italian."

"It doesn't follow that she was from a Mafia family."

"No, but you can't prove otherwise."

Driving home, Harry started to laugh. It was all so horrible and horribly funny. Did a person have to die before you discovered the truth about her? As long as someone is alive the chance exists that whatever you have said about her will get back to her. Therefore, Harry and most of Crozet measured their words. You thought twice before you spoke, especially if you intended to say what you thought.

The other thing Harry learned from Mrs. Hogendobber was the time, occupants, and license plate number of every car that had rolled down St. George Avenue in the last twenty-four hours. The Citizens' Alert was Mrs. Hogendobber's opportunity to be rewarded for her natural nosiness.

17

Ned Tucker dreamed of sleeping late on Sunday mornings but the alarm clanged at 6:30 A.M. He opened his eyes, cut off the offending noise, and sat up. The digital clock blinked the time in a turquoise-blue color. It occurred to Ned that a generation of American children wouldn't know how to tell time with a conventional clock. Then again, they couldn't add and subtract either. Calculators performed that labor for them.

Harry said she hated digital clocks. They reminded her of little amputees. No hands. Ned smiled, thinking about Harry. Susan turned over and he smiled even more. His wife could sleep through an earthquake, a thunderstorm, you name it. He'd give her an extra forty-five minutes and feed the kids. The chores of fatherhood comforted him. What worried him was the example he set. He didn't want to be a slave to his job but he didn't want to be too lazy either. He didn't want to be too stern but he didn't want to be too lax. He didn't want to treat his son any differently from his daughter but he knew he did. It was so much easier to love a daughter—but then, that was what Susan said about their son.

A shower and a shave brightened Ned; a cup of coffee popped him in gear. He'd need to awaken Brookie and Dan in twenty minutes to get them up for church. He decided to take what precious quiet time he had and peruse the bills. Everything was more expensive than it should have been and his heart dropped each time he wrote a check. First he scanned his bank statement. A five hundred dollar withdrawal last Monday really woke him up. He made no such withdrawal last Monday and neither did Susan. Anything over two hundred dollars had to be discussed between them. He wanted to crumple the statement but neatly put it aside. Couldn't contact the bank until tomorrow anyway.

The telephone rang at seven o'clock. Ned picked it up. "Hello."

"Ned, you're up as early as I am so I hope I'm not being rude in calling." Josiah DeWitt, mellow-voiced, sounded serious.

"What can I do for you?" Ned wondered.

"You are, were, Maudie's lawyer, am I right?"

"Yes." Ned hadn't thought of Maude since he got up. Being reminded brought back the uneasiness, the nagging suspicions.

"Since she has no living relatives I'd like to claim the body"—he sighed—"or what's left of it, and give her a decent burial. It's not right that she be left to a potter's field."

As Josiah was tight as the bark on a tree, Ned was astonished. "I think we can work this out, Josiah," he said, then added, "But if you'll allow me, I'll take up a collection for the interment. We should all pull our weight on this."

"I'd be most grateful." Josiah did sound relieved. "Do you know of anyone who might have a plot, who could help us out there?"

"I'll ask Herbie Jones. He'll know." Herbie Jones was the minister at Crozet Lutheran Church.

"Do we even know what denomination Maude was?" Josiah asked.

"No, but Herb has always had a wide embrace. I don't think he'd mind if she were a Muslim. Would you like me to inquire about a service also?"

"Yes—I think we should. And one more thing, Ned: I'd like to run her store and buy it when that's feasible. I don't know what paperwork will be involved but Maudie built a good business. It was her love, you know. I'll keep it up in her honor, and for the profit too. She'll come back to haunt me if I don't make a profit."

"She left her estate to the M.S. Foundation, so we will need to negotiate with them."

"Really?" Josiah was consumed with interest but refrained from boring in.

"She had a brother who died from the disease."

"You know more about Maude than any of us." Josiah was envious.

"Not really. But I'll do what I can. It would be wonderful to keep the shop going and I can't see that the M.S. Foundation has the personnel or the desire to come out here to Crozet and sell packing materials. I'll do my best."

"Thank you."

"No, Josiah, thank you. I wish Maude could know what good friends she had." And he thought to himself that good friend or not, Josiah was quick to see a way to make more money.

18

A persistent owl hooted in the distance. Mrs. Murphy and Tucker padded in the moonlight toward Maude Bly Modena's store. Tucker, restless, jauntily moved along, her tail wagging. They'd be back long before Harry woke up, so Tucker treated herself to small sniffs and explorations along the way.

As they approached the building Mrs. Murphy stiffened. Tucker stopped in her tracks.

"There's someone in there," Mrs. Murphy whispered. "Let me jump up on the window box. Maybe I can see who it is. You come sit by the front door. If he runs out, you can trip him."

Tucker quickly hopped up the steps and lay flat against the door. The only sound was the click-click of her claws and the tinkle of her rabies tag.

Mrs. Murphy tiptoed the length of the window box. She pressed her face against the glass panes. She couldn't see clearly because whoever it was had crawled under the desk.

Mrs. Murphy carefully dropped onto the earth. "S-s-st, come on."

They circled to the back as Mrs. Murphy explained why she couldn't see.

"I can't smell anything with the windows and door closed but we can pick up the scent by the back door or by a window."

Tucker, nose to the ground, needed no encouragement. She hit the trail by the back door. "I got him."

Before Mrs. Murphy could put her nose down to identify the scent the back door opened. Tucker crouched down and tripped the man coming out as Mrs. Murphy, claws at the ready, leaped onto his back. He stifled a shout, dropping his letters, which scattered in the light evening breeze.

He thrashed around but couldn't reach Mrs. Murphy, who was far more agile than he. Tucker sank her fangs clean into his ankle.

He yowled. A few houses down, a light clicked on in an upstairs bedroom. The man gathered up the letters as Mrs. Murphy jumped off and scurried up a tree. Tucker scooted around the corner of the house and they both watched Bob Berryman run with a limp down the back alleyway. In a few moments they heard the truck start up and peel out onto St. George Avenue.

Mrs. Murphy backed down the tree. She liked climbing up much more than she liked coming down. Tucker waited at the base.

"*Bob Berryman!*" Tucker couldn't believe it.

"*Let's go inside.*" Mrs. Murphy trotted to the back door, which Bob had left open in his haste to escape his attackers.

Tucker, head down, followed this trail. Berryman had entered through the back door. He passed through the storage room and went directly to and under the desk. He stopped at no other place. Tucker, intent on the scent, bumped her head into the back of the desk.

Mrs. Murphy, close behind her, laughed. "*Look where you're going.*"

"*Your eyes are better than mine,*" Tucker growled. "*But my nose is golden, cat. Remember that.*"

"*So, golden nose, what was he doing under the desk?*" Mrs. Murphy snuggled in next to Tucker.

"*His hands slid over the sides, the top, and the back.*" She followed the line.

Mrs. Murphy, pupils open to the maximum, stared. "*A secret compartment.*"

"*Yeah, but how'd he get it open?*"

"*I don't know, but he's a clumsy man. It can't be that hard.*" Mrs. Murphy stood on her hind legs and gently batted the sides of the desk.

A loud slam scared the bejesus out of both of them. They shot out from under the desk. Mrs. Murphy's tail looked like a bottlebrush. The hair on the back of Tucker's neck bristled. No other sound assailed their sensitive ears.

Mrs. Murphy, low to the ground, whiskers to the fore, slowly, one paw at a time, headed for the back room. Tucker, next to her, also crouched as low as she could, which was pretty low. When they reached the storage room they saw that the door was closed.

"Oh, no!" Tucker exclaimed. "Can you reach the doorknob?"

Mrs. Murphy stretched her full length. She could just get her paws on the old ceramic doorknob but she couldn't turn it the whole way. She exhausted herself trying.

Finally, Tucker said, "Give up. We're in for the night. Once people start moving about I'll set up a howl that will wake the dead."

"Harry will be frantic."

"I know but there's nothing we can do about it. We're already in her bad graces for our work at the railroad tracks. Boy, are we in for it now."

"No, she won't be mad."

"I hope not."

Mrs. Murphy leaned against the door catching her breath. "She loves us. We're all she's got, you know. I hate to think of Harry searching for us. It's been a terrible week."

"Yeah."

"If we're stuck here we might as well work."

"I'm game."

19

Pewter, hovering over the meat case, first heard Tucker howl. The sound was distant but she was sure it was Tucker. A huge roll of Lebanon baloney, her favorite, beckoned. Courtney lifted the scrumptious meat from the case. Sandwich duty occupied her morning. By 7:00 A.M. the farm crowd had wiped out the reserve she'd made up Sunday night.

"Gimme some! Gimme some! Gimme some!" Pewter hooked a corner of the roll with a claw.

"Stop that." Courtney smacked her paw.

"I'm hungry!" Pewter reached up again and Courtney cut her a hunk. Buying off Pewter was easier than disciplining her.

The cat seized the fragrant meat and hurried to the back door. Her hunger overwhelmed her curiosity but she figured she could eat, and listen at the same time. Another protracted howl convinced her the miserable dog was Tucker. She returned to Courtney, was severely tempted by the Lebanon baloney, summoned her willpower, and rubbed against Courtney's legs, then hustled to the back door. She needed to perform this identical routine three times before Courtney opened the back door for her. Pewter knew that humans learned by repetition, but even then you could never be sure they were going to do what you asked them. They were so easily distracted.

Once free from the store Pewter sat, waiting for another howl. Once she heard it she loped through the backyards, and came out into the alleyway. Another howl sent her directly to the back door of Maude Bly Modena's shop.

"Tucker!" Pewter yelled. "What are you doing in there?"

"Just get me out. I'll tell you everything later," Tucker pleaded.

Mrs. Murphy hollered behind the door: "Are there any humans around?"

"In cars. We need a walker."

"Pewter, if you run back to the store do you think you could get Courtney or Market to follow you?" Mrs. Murphy asked.

"Follow me? I can barely get them to open and close the door for me."

"What if you grabbed Mrs. Hogendobber on her way to the post office? She's around the corner." Tucker wanted out.

"She doesn't like cats. She wouldn't pay attention to me."

"She'll come down the alleyway. She walks it no matter what the weather. You could try," Mrs. Murphy said.

"All right. But while I'm waiting for that old windbag . . . What is it that Josiah calls her?"

"A ruthless monologist," Mrs. Murphy answered her, peeved that Pewter was insisting on a chat.

"Well, while I'm waiting why don't you tell me what you're doing in there?"

Mrs. Murphy and Tucker unfolded the adventure but only after swearing Pewter to secrecy. Under no circumstances was she to hint of any of this to Bob Berryman's dog, Ozzie.

"There she is!" Pewter called to them. "Let's try. Howl, Tucker."

Pewter thundered over to Mrs. Hogendobber. She circled her. She flopped on her back and rolled over. She meowed and pranced. Mrs. Hogendobber observed this with some amusement.

"Come on, Pruneface! Get the message," Pewter screeched. She moved toward Maude's shop and then returned to Mrs. Hogendobber.

Tucker emitted a piercing shriek. Mrs. Hogendobber halted her stately progress. Pewter ran around her legs and back toward Maude's shop, where Tucker let out another shriek. Mrs. Hogendobber started for the shop.

"I got her! I got her!" Pewter raced for the door. "Keep it up!"

Tucker barked. Mrs. Murphy meowed. Pewter ran in circles in front of the door.

Mrs. Hogendobber stood. She thought deeply. She put her hand on the doorknob, thought some more, and then opened the door.

"*Gangway!*" Tucker charged out of the door and hurried around the side of the house to relieve her bladder. Mrs. Murphy, with more bladder control, came out and rubbed Mrs. Hogendobber's legs in appreciation.

"Thank you, Mrs. H.," Mrs. Murphy purred.

"What were you doing in there?" Mrs. Hogendobber said out loud.

Tucker ran around and sat next to Pewter. She gave the gray cat a kiss. "*I love you, Pewter.*"

"*Okay, okay.*" Pewter appreciated the emotion but wasn't overfond of sloppy kisses.

"*Come on. Mom's got to be at work by now.*" Mrs. Murphy pricked up her ears.

The three small animals chased one another down the alleyway as Mrs. Hogendobber followed, deeply curious as to why Mary Minor Haristeen's cat and dog were trapped inside Maude's shop.

Harry hadn't sorted the mail. She hadn't properly thanked Rob for the French postcard he'd smuggled to her. She'd burned the telephone wires calling everyone she could think of who might have seen her animals.

The sight of Mrs. Murphy and Tucker along with Pewter and Mrs. Hogendobber puffing up the steps astonished her. Tears filled her eyes as she flung open the door.

Mrs. Murphy leaped into her arms and Tucker jumped up on her. Harry sat on the floor to hug her family. She hugged Pewter too. This enthusiasm was not extended to Mrs. Hogendobber, but Harry did get up and shake her hand.

"Thank you, Mrs. Hogendobber. I've been worried sick. Where'd you find them?"

"In Maude Bly Modena's store."

"What?" Harry was incredulous.

"We found a secret compartment! And Bob Berryman stole letters!" Tucker's excitement was so great that she wiggled from stem to stern.

"Tucker bit the shit out of his ankle," Mrs. Murphy added.

"Inside the store?"

"Yes. The door was shut and they couldn't get out. I was walking down the alleyway—my morning constitutional on my way to see you—and I heard a ruckus."

"You would have waddled right on by if it weren't for me," Pewter corrected her.

"What on earth were my girls doing in Maude Bly Modena's shop?" Harry put her hands to her temples. "Mrs. Hogendobber, do you mind going back there with me?"

Mrs. Hogendobber would like nothing better. "Well, if you think it's proper. Perhaps we should call the sheriff first."

"He could arrest Mrs. Murphy and Tucker for breaking and entering." Harry realized the instant the joke was out of her mouth that Mrs. Hogendobber wouldn't get it. "Let me call Market over to mind the office."

Market happily agreed and said he'd even sort the mail. He, too, wanted to read other people's mail. It was an irresistible temptation.

The crepe myrtle bloomed along the alleyway. Bumblebees laden with pollen buzzed around the two women.

"I was right here when I heard Tucker."

"Ha!" Pewter sarcastically remarked.

Harry followed Mrs. Hogendobber, who recounted in minute detail her every step to the door.

"... and I turned the knob—it wasn't locked—and out they came."

And in they ran too. *"Come on!"*

"Me, too." Pewter followed.

"Girls! Girls!" Harry vainly called.

Mrs. Hogendobber, thrilled at the possibility of entering, said, "We'll have to get them."

Harry entered first.

Mrs. Hogendobber, hot on her heels, stopped for a second in front of the huge bags of plastic peanuts piled to the ceiling. "My word."

Harry, already in the front room, exclaimed, "Where are they?"

Mrs. Murphy stuck her head out from under the desk. *"Here!"*

Mrs. Hogendobber, now in the room, saw this. "There." She pointed.

Harry got down on her hands and knees and crawled under the desk. Pewter, grumbling, had to get out, as there wasn't room for all of them.

Mrs. Murphy sat in front of the secret compartment that she had opened the night before. A small button alongside the thin molding on the seam was the key. *"Right here. Look!"*

Harry gasped, "There's a secret compartment here!"

"Let me see." Mrs. Hogendobber, negotiating gravity, hunkered down on her hands and knees. Tucker moved so she could see.

"Right here." Harry flattened against the side of the desk the best she could and pointed.

"I declare!" Mrs. Hogendobber, excited, gasped. "What's in there?"

Harry reached in and handed over a large ledger and a handful of Xeroxed papers. "Here."

Mrs. Hogendobber backed up on all fours and sat in the middle of the floor.

Harry backed out and joined her. "There's another ledger in the desk." She got up and opened the middle drawer. It was still there.

"A second set of books! I wonder who she was filching from."

"The IRS, most likely." Harry sat down next to Mrs. Hogendobber, who was flipping through the books.

"I used to keep Mr. H.'s books, you know." She laid the two ledgers side by side, her sharp eyes moving vertically down the columns. The hidden ledger was on her left. "My word, what a lot of merchandise. She was a better saleswoman than any of us knew." Mrs. Hogendobber pointed to the right-hand book. "See here, Harry, the volume—and the prices."

"I can't believe she would get fifteen thousand dollars for seventy bags of plastic peanuts."

This gave Mrs. Hogendobber pause. "It does seem unlikely."

Harry took a page off the large pile of Xeroxed papers. They were the letters of Claudius Crozet to the Blue Ridge Railroad. Scanning them, she realized they involved the building of the tunnels.

"What's that?" Mrs. Hogendobber couldn't tear her eyes away from the accounting books.

"Claudius Crozet's letter to the Blue Ridge Railroad."

"What are you talking about?" Mrs. Hogendobber looked up from her books.

"I don't know."

Harry had to get back to work. "Mrs. Hogendobber, would you do something if I asked you? It isn't dishonest but it's . . . tricky."

"Ask."

"Xerox these letters and the accounting books. Then we'll turn it all over to Rick Shaw but we won't tell him we have copies. I want to read these letters and I think, with your training, you may find something in the accounting books that the sheriff would miss. If he knows we're studying the information he might take that as a comment on his abilities."

Without hesitation, Mrs. Hogendobber agreed. "I'll call Rick after I've completed the job. I'll tell him about the animals. About us coming back here. And that's all I'll tell him. Where can I Xerox without drawing attention to myself? This is a great deal of work."

"In the back room at the post office. I can buy some extra paper and reset the meter. No one will know if you don't come out of the back room. As long as I put in the ink and the paper, I'm not cheating Uncle Sam."

"Maude Bly Modena sure was."

20

Ned Tucker was informed by Barbara Apperton at Citizen's National Bank that the withdrawal from his account was correct and had been made with his credit card after hours. Ned fulminated. Barbara said she'd get a copy of the videotape, since these transactions were recorded. That way they'd both find out who used the credit card. Mrs. Apperton asked if the credit card was missing and Ned said no. He said he'd be down at the bank tomorrow.

The missing five hundred dollars wouldn't break the Tucker family but it was unwelcome news when Ned was paying the bills.

Troubled by this small mystery on top of the grotesque ones, Susan entered the post office only to witness Rick Shaw grilling Harry.

"You can't prove where you were Friday night or in the wee hours Saturday morning?" The sheriff stuck his thumbs in his Sam Browne belt.

"No." Harry patted Mrs. Murphy, who watched Rick with her golden eyes.

Susan came alongside the counter. Rick kept at it. "No one was with you on the nights of the two murders?"

"No. Not after eleven P.M. on the night of Maude's murder. I live alone now."

"This doesn't look good, with your animals in Maude Bly Modena's shop. Just what are you up to and what are you hiding?"

"Nothing." This wasn't exactly true, because under the counter, neatly placed in a large manila envelope, were the Claudius Crozet letters. Mrs. Hogendobber had smuggled the copies of the accounting books to her home.

"You're telling me your cat and dog entered the shop without your opening the door?" Rick's voice dripped disbelief.

"Yes."

"*Bob Berryman let us in,*" Mrs. Murphy said but no one listened to her.

"*Buzz off, Shaw,*" Tucker growled.

"You don't leave town without telling me, Miz Haristeen." Rick slapped the counter with his right palm.

Susan intruded. "Rick, you can't possibly believe that Harry's a murderer. The only people who can prove where they were in the middle of the night are the married ones faithful to their spouses."

"That leaves out much of Crozet," Harry wryly noted.

"And the ones who are together can lie for each other. Maybe this isn't the work of one person. Maybe it's a team." Susan hoisted herself up on the counter.

"That possibility hasn't escaped me."

Harry put her mouth next to Mrs. Murphy's ear. "What were you doing in Maude's shop, you devil?"

"*I told you.*" Mrs. Murphy touched Harry's nose.

"She's telling you something," Susan observed.

"That she wants some kitty crunchies, I bet." Harry smiled.

"Don't take this so lightly," Rick warned.

"I'm not." Harry's face darkened. "But I don't know what to do about this, any more than you do. We're not stupid, Rick. We know the murderer is someone close to home, someone we know and trust. No one's sleeping soundly anymore in Crozet."

"Neither am I." Rick's voice softened. He rather liked Harry. "Look, I'm not paid to be nice. I'm paid to get results."

"We know." Susan crossed her legs under her. "We want you to and we'll help you in any way that we can."

"Thanks." Rick patted Mrs. Murphy. "What were you doing in there, kitty cat?"

"I told you," Mrs. Murphy moaned.

After Rick left, Susan whispered, "How did they get in the shop?"

Harry sighed. "I wish I knew."

That night, after a supper of cottage cheese on a bed of lettuce sprinkled with sunflower seeds, Harry pulled out the postcards and her mother's huge magnifying glass. She shone a bright light over the card to Kelly and placed the card Rob lent her next to it. The inks were different colors. The true Paris postmark was a slightly darker shade. Also, the lettering of the cancellation stamp on Kelly's postcard was not precisely flush. This was also the case for the lettering on Maude's postcard. The "A" in Asheville was out of line the tiniest bit. She switched off the light.

The postcards were a signal. She remembered when Maude received hers. She didn't act like a woman under the threat of death. She was irritated that the sender hadn't signed his or her name.

The floorboards creaked as Harry paced over them. What did she know? She knew the killer was close at hand. She knew the killer had a sense of humor and was perhaps even sporting, since he or she had fired a warning shot, so to speak. She knew the mangling of the bodies was designed to throw people off the scent. Just why, she wasn't sure. The mess might have been to disguise the method of murder or it might have been to keep people from looking elsewhere, but why and for what? Or worse, it could have been a sick joke.

The other thing she knew was that Claudius Crozet was important to Maude. Tomorrow she was determined to call Marie, the secretary at the concrete plant, to find out if Kelly ever mentioned the famous engineer. She fixed a stiff cup of coffee—a spoon could stand up in the liquid—and sat down at the kitchen table to read the letters.

By one in the morning she was ravenous and wished that someone would figure out a way to fax a pizza. She ate more cottage cheese and kept reading. Crozet wrote in detail about the process of cutting the tunnels. The boring for the tunnels proceeded around the clock in three eight-hour shifts for eight solid years. The Brooksville tunnel proved extremely dangerous. The rock, seemingly sound, was soft as the men bit deeper into the mountain. Cave-ins and rockslides dumped on their heads like hard rain.

The physical difficulties occasionally paled beside the human ones. The tunnel rats were men of Ireland, but from two different parts of the Emerald Isle. The men of Cork disdained the Fardowners, the men of Northern Ireland. One bitter night, on February 2, 1850, a riot shook Augusta County. The militia was called out to separate the warring factions and the jail burst at the seams with bloodied Irishmen. By the next morning both sides agreed that they'd only desired a little fight and the authorities accepted that explanation. After breaking a few bones and sitting out the night in jail, the men got along just fine.

The Blue Ridge Railroad Company ran out of money with alarming frequency. The state of Virginia wasn't much help. The general contractor, John Kelly, paid the men out of his own pocket and accepted paper from the state—a brave man indeed.

When Claudius Crozet described the mail train rolling through the last completed tunnel on April 13, 1858, Harry was almost as excited as he must have been.

She finished the letters, eyes burning, and hauled herself into bed. She sensed that the tunnels meant something, but why? And which one? The Greenwood and Brooksville had been sealed since after 1944. She was going to have to go out there. She finally fell into a troubled slumber.

21

A full moon radiated silvery light over the back meadows, making the cornflowers glow a deep purple. Bats darted in and out of the towering conifers and in and out of the eaves of Harry's house.

Mrs. Murphy sat on the back porch. Tucker's snoring could be heard in the background. The cat was restless but she knew in the morning she'd blame it on Tucker, telling her that she'd kept her awake. Tucker accused Mrs. Murphy of making up stories about her snoring.

What was really keeping Mrs. Murphy awake was Harry. She wished her friend lacked curiosity. Curiosity rarely killed the cat but it certainly got humans in trouble. She feared Harry might trigger a response in the killer if she got too close. Mrs. Murphy had great pride where Harry was concerned, and if any human was smart enough to put the pieces of this ragged puzzle together it would be her Harry. But putting together a puzzle and protecting yourself were two different things. Because Harry couldn't conceive of killing another human being, she couldn't believe anyone would want to kill her.

Humans fascinated Mrs. Murphy. Their time was squandered in pursuing nonessential objects. Food, clothing, and shelter weren't enough for them, and they drove themselves and everyone around them crazy, including animals, for their toys. Mrs. Murphy thought cars, a motor toy, absurd. That's why horses were born. What's the big hurry, anyway? But if people wanted speed she could accept that—after all, it was a physical pleasure. What she couldn't accept was that these creatures worked and worked and then didn't enjoy what they worked for; they were too busy paying for things they couldn't afford. By the time they paid for the toy it was worn out and they wanted another one. Worse, they weren't satisfied with themselves. They were always on some self-improvement jag. This astonished Mrs. Murphy. Why couldn't people just be? But they couldn't just be—they had to be the best. Poor sick things. No wonder they died from diseases they brought on themselves.

One of the reasons she loved Harry was that Harry was more animal-like than other people. She loved the outdoors. She wasn't driven to own a lot of toys. She was happy with what she had. She wished that Harry didn't have to go to the post office every day but it was fun to see the other people, so if the woman had to work, this wasn't so bad. However, people disregarded Harry because she wasn't driven. Mrs. Murphy thought they were foolish. Harry was better than any of them.

Good as Harry was, she displayed the weaknesses of her breed. Mating was complicated for her. Divorce, a human invention, further complicated the simplicity of biology. Also, Harry missed communication from Mrs. Murphy. Although Harry wasn't afraid of the night, she was vulnerable in it. Perhaps because their eyes are bad, humans feel like prey in the darkness.

Night animals are associated with evil by humans. Bats especially scared them, which Mrs. Murphy thought silly. Humans didn't know enough about the chain of life to go about killing animals that offended them. They killed bats, coyotes, foxes—the night hunters. Their fears and their inability to comprehend how animals are connected, including themselves, would bring everyone to a sorry state. Mrs. Murphy, semidomesticated and enjoying her closeness to Harry, had no desire to see the nondomesticated animals killed. She understood why the wild animals hated people. Sometimes she hated them, too, except for Harry.

A shadowy movement caught her eye. Her ears moved forward. She inhaled deeply. What was he doing here?

A sleek, handsome Paddy moved toward the back porch.

"Hello, Paddy."

"Hello, my sweet." Paddy's deep purr was hypnotic. "How are you on this fine, soft night?"

"Thinking long thoughts and watching the clouds swirl around the moon. Were you hunting?"

"A little of this and a little of that. I'm out for the medicinal powers of the velvety night air. And what were your long thoughts?" His whiskers sparkled against his black face.

"That the so-called bad animals like coyotes, bats, and snakes are more useful to earth than human drug addicts."

"I don't like snakes."

"But they are useful."

"Yes. They can be useful far away from me." He licked his paw and then rubbed his face. "Why don't you come out and play?"

He was tempting, even though she knew how worthless he was. He was still the best-looking tom in Crozet. "I've got to watch over Harry."

"It's the middle of the night and she's safe."

"I hope so, Paddy. I'm worried about this killer."

"Oh, that. What's that got to do with Harry?"

"She's sticking her nose where it doesn't belong. Miss Amateur Detective."

"Does the killer know?"

"That's just it, isn't it? We don't know who it is, only that it's someone we know."

"Summer's a strange time to kill anyone," Paddy reflected. "I can understand it in the winter when the food supply is low—not that I approve of it. But in the summer there's enough for everyone."

"They don't kill over food."

"True enough." Humans bored Paddy. "See those fireflies dancing? That's what I want to do: dance in the moonlight, sing to the stars, jump straight up at the moon." He turned a somersault.

"I'm staying inside."

"Oh, Mrs. Murphy, you've become much too serious. I remember you when you would chase sunbeams. You even chased me."

"I did not. You chased me." Her fur ruffled.

"Ha, all the girls chased me. I thought it was wonderful to be chased by a bright tiger lass whose name, of all things, was Mrs. Murphy. Humans give us the silliest names."

"Paddy, you're full of catnip and moonshine."

"Not Muffy or Skippy or Snowball or Scooter or even Rambette, but Mrs. Murphy." He shook his head.

"I was named for Harry's maternal grandmother and well you know it."

"I thought they named their children after their grandparents, not their cats. Oh, come on out here. For old times' sake."

"Fool me once, shame on you. Fool me twice, shame on me," Mrs. Murphy said with firmness but without rancor.

He sighed. "I'm faithful in my fashion. I'm here tonight, aren't I?"

"And you can keep on going."

"You're a hard girl, M.M." He was the only animal that called her M.M.

"No, just a wise one. But you can do me a favor."

"What?" He grinned.

"If you hear or see or smell anything that seems suspicious, tell me."

"I will. Now stop worrying about it. Time will do justice all around." He flicked his luxurious tail to the vertical and trotted off.

22

The dark-red doors of Crozet Lutheran Church reflected the intense heat of the morning. Outside the church, sweltering, shuffled the camera crews from television stations in Washington, D.C., Richmond, and Charlottesville. What little peace remained in the town was shattered by the news teams, whose producers decided to bump up the story. The second murder was God's gift to producers in the summer news doldrums.

Inside the simple church, people huddled together, unsure of who was friend and who was foe, although externally everyone acted the same: friendly.

The casket, adorned with a beautiful spray of white lilies, rested before the altar railing. Josiah forgot nothing. Two chaste floral displays stood on either side of the gold altar cross. Maude's Crozet friends filled the church with flowers. Few knew her well but only one among the congregation wanted her dead. The others truly mourned Maude, as much for her as for themselves. She added something to the town and she would be missed.

The organ music, Bach, filled the church with somber majesty.

Sitting at the rear of the church and to the side was Rick Shaw. He was impressed that Josiah DeWitt and Ned Tucker canvassed the townspeople for this funeral. Ned refused to divulge who gave what but Rick shrewdly allowed Josiah the opportunity to tell all, which he did.

People of modest means, like Mary Minor Haristeen, gave as generously as they could. Mim Sanburne gave a bit more and be-grudged every penny. Jim gave separately—a lot. The biggest sur-prise was Bob Berryman, who contributed $1,000. Apparently Bob's wife, a portly woman determined to wear miniskirts, was kept ignorant of this bequest until Josiah's judicious hints reached even her. Linda Berryman, glued to her husband's side, appeared more grim than sad.

After the mercifully short service, Reverend Jones, preceded by an acolyte, walked down the aisle to the front door. He stopped for a moment. Rick saw him wince. The good reverend did not want the camera crews to sully the sanctity of this moment. But the doors must open and news ratings meant more to producers than human decency. Reverend Jones nodded slightly and the acolyte opened the door.

Mim Sanburne discreetly fluffed her hair as she prepared to leave the church. Little Marilyn, less discreetly, checked her makeup and pointedly ignored Harry, who was immediately behind her. Josiah did not escort Mim, because he acted as next of kin to Maude and because Jim was there. Market Shiflett stood next to Harry, and Mim edged up even more lest someone (like a news reporter) think she would be accompanied by a—shudder—working man. Courtney Shiflett and Brookie and Danny Tucker quietly filed out the front door too. Susan and Ned stayed behind with Josiah to make certain nothing else needed to be done until the grave-site service.

A reporter rushed up to Mim. She stiffened and turned her back on him. He shoved his microphone under Little Marilyn's mouth. She started to open it when her mother clasped her wrist and yanked her away. Mrs. George Hogendobber waved her huge church fan in front of her face and made her escape.

Jim wheeled on the reporter. "I'm the mayor of this here town and I'll answer any questions you have, but right now leave these people alone."

As Jim was nearly a foot taller than the reporter, the squirt slunk off.

A woman reporter, straining to lower her voice to a more important register, buttonholed Harry, caught in the slow-moving mass of mourners.

"Were you a friend of the murdered woman?" the pert young thing asked.

Harry ignored her.

"Come on, girl." Market grabbed Harry's hand.

"Thanks, Market." Harry let him propel her toward his car.

Boom Boom Craycroft stayed away from Maude's funeral, which was appropriate. As she was still in deep mourning, no one expected her to make a public appearance anywhere but on the golf course, and everyone but Mrs. Hogendobber made allowances for that. As for Boom Boom, she would have taken apart the television crews, limb by limb.

The grave-site service progressed nicely until Reverend Jones tossed ashes on the casket. Bob Berryman began to sob. Linda was appalled. Bob moved away from the grave site and Linda didn't follow him. She sat like a stone in the tacky metal chair.

The moment the last syllable of the service was over, the "Amens" said, Josiah rushed to Bob's side. Harry and everyone else noticed him put his arm around Bob's shoulders, whispering earnestly in the shaken man's ear. Suddenly Bob pulled away from Josiah and slugged him square in the face. As the older man sank to his knees, Bob walked with deliberate control to his car. He turned to find his wife. She hurried to the car, opened the passenger door, and Bob drove off before she could even close it.

Ned reached Josiah first and found his face bloodied. Harry, Susan, and Mrs. Hogendobber got there next and Rick Shaw came more slowly. He was observing people's reactions to the outburst.

The cameras, zoom lenses intact, whirred away from a discreet distance. Jim Sanburne advanced on them, and the newspeople scurried like cockroaches. Susan pulled tissues from her bag but the gushing nosebleed poured through them.

Hayden McIntire took command. "Tilt your head back."

Josiah did as he was told. "What do you think? Broken?"

"I don't know. Come with me to the office and I'll do what I can. You're going to have two very black eyes tomorrow along with a fat nose."

Josiah wobbled to his feet with Hayden's assistance.

Mrs. Hogendobber, brimming with curiosity, blurted out what everyone else was thinking: "What did you say to him?"

"Well—I don't know." Josiah squinted. Everything hurt. "I told him this was a terrible thing, but for Maude's sake he should control himself. Those television vermin are across the road. What would people think?"

"That's all?" Harry asked, knowing perfectly well that what Josiah had just said would plant a fast-growing seed. Why would it look so bad? A nasty little emotional door had been opened and everyone would jam in front of it trying to peer inside.

Josiah nodded "yes" as Hayden led him off.

Rick silently watched this and then got in his squad car. He was going to tail Bob Berryman. He called to the dispatcher, gave a description of the car and the license plate number. He specified he didn't want Bob stopped unless he headed for the airport.

Rob Collier listened intently to the tale of Berryman's outburst. He lingered over his afternoon pickup.

". . . blood oozing onto his Turnbull and Asser shirt. I tell you, Rob, that must have hurt more than the blow."

Rob pulled his eyelashes, a nervous habit. "Something's not right."

"No shit, Sherlock."

Rob smiled good-naturedly. "Yeah, well, I'm not as dumb as you think. You're a woman and I'm a man. I know some things that you don't. Maybe a man cries because he killed someone and suddenly feels guilty."

Harry leaned over the counter, inadvertently touching Tucker, who was snoozing under it. The corgi awoke with a grunt.

"I don't know."

"See, what's going on here is, he's too full up to keep it to himself. Bob Berryman don't go 'round blubbering in public."

"Right."

Tucker yawned. Mrs. Murphy was sleeping with one eye open in a mail bin. Tucker could see the lump at the bottom of the canvas bin. She slunk over and very carefully, very gently bit the lump.

"Ah-h-h." Mrs. Murphy, startled, yelped. Tucker laughed and bit her again.

"Those two put on a real show, don't they?" Rob was diverted for a moment from his theory. "As I see it, Maude had something on Berryman. Bet your bottom dollar."

Harry drew in air between her teeth. "Well, something was going on."

"Maybe they were running drugs. Berryman travels nine states."

"I can't picture Maude as a drug dealer."

"Hey, sixty years ago booze was illegal. The son of one of the biggest bootleggers in the country became President. Business is business."

"Where does Kelly fit in?"

"Found out"—Rob shrugged—"or was in cahoots."

"Next you'll be telling me Mim Sanburne is a cocaine queen."

"Anything is possible."

"Let's don't talk about Mim, even though I brought her up. She's on my reserve shit list. She's mad at me. Oh, excuse me—ladies of Mim's quality don't get mad; they become agitated. She's agitated with me because I told Little Marilyn to invite her brother to the wedding."

Rob whistled. "Now there's an odd couple."

"Little Marilyn and Fitz-Gilbert Hamilton? He sure hasn't shown his face around here. Probably feels safe in Richmond."

"No, no—Stafford and Brenda Sanburne. She's about the prettiest thing I ever saw but . . . Well, I wish him happiness, but you can't go around breaking the rules and not expect to suffer for it."

"You're big on rules today." Harry thought, Love whomever you could. It was such a rare commodity in the world, you'd better take it where you could find it. No point arguing with Rob, who was a tender racist as opposed to the horrendous kind. Still, they did their damage, whether by trickle or by tidal wave.

Rob checked his watch. "Zip time."

He hopped into his mail truck as Mrs. Murphy hopped out of the mail bin. *"Tucker, I was sleepy. Your snoring kept me awake last night."*

"I don't snore."

"You do. Snort. Snort." Mrs. Murphy imitated a snore but she was far from it.

"What's with you two?" Harry walked over to the mail bin. "There's nothing in here." Mrs. Murphy rubbed against her leg. Harry gingerly stepped into the mail bin, pushed off with one leg, and then tucked that in the bin too. "Wheee!"

The door opened as she crashed into the wall.

"What are you doing, Miz Haristeen?" Rick Shaw stifled a laugh.

Harry stuck her head over the bin. "The cat has so much fun when she gets in here, I thought I'd try. Hell, anything to feel good these days."

Rick fished a cigarette out of his pocket, rolling it in his fingers. "I know what you mean."

"Thought you'd stopped."

"How'd you know?"

"Your eyes follow every lit cigarette."

"You're very observant, Harry." Rick appreciated that in a person. "Show me what you've got."

"I didn't think you'd answer my phone call today after the blowup at the funeral." She led him to the back room. "I'm impressed."

She shut the door behind them and brought out the two graveyard postcards. She handed him the magnifying glass and placed the legitimate French postcard on the table. He closed one eye and studied the cards, holding the unlit cigarette in his left hand.

"Uh-huh" was all he said.

"See the slight variation in the inks?"

"Yes."

"And the misalignment, very small, of the 'A' in 'Asheville.' "

"Yes." Rick twirled the magnifying glass. He handed the glass back to Harry. "Who else knows about this?"

"Susan Tucker. Rob knows I borrowed a postcard but he doesn't know why."

"Keep it to yourself. You and Susan."

"I will."

"Now, tell me what your cat and dog were doing in Maude's shop."

"I don't know."

"You were snooping in there, Harry. Don't lie to me."

"I wasn't. Somehow they got locked in there. I woke up in the morning. I couldn't find them. I drove around. I called around and just like I told you, Mrs. Hogendobber heard Tucker barking. She found them."

"I believe you. Thousands wouldn't." He dropped his bulk into a chair. "Gimme a Co-Cola, will you?" He lit up the cigarette as she brought him a soda from the little refrigerator. A long drag brought a smile to his lips. "It's a filthy habit but damn, it feels good. Next I'll try your mail bin." He inhaled. "I'm not really sorry I started up again. It's this or straight whiskey with a case like this, and with the whiskey I wouldn't be on the case long."

"What do you think—about the postcards, I mean."

"I think we've got someone so smart that he or she is laughing at us. I think we've got a fox that will lay a false trail."

Goose bumps dotted Harry's skin. "Scares me."

"Scares me too. If I only knew what the son of a bitch was after."

"Do you follow your hunches?"

"I do, but I do my homework first." Rick crossed his right leg over his left knee. "Okay, what's your hunch? You're itching to tell me."

"The old tunnels Claudius Crozet dug have something to do with this."

At the sound of the name Crozet, Rick sat up straight. "Why do you say that?"

"Because there was a letter from Crozet, a Xerox on Kelly's desk. Can you ride, Rick?"

"A little."

"Let's ride out to the closest tunnel, the Greenwood."

"In this heat, with the deer flies? No, ma'am. We're going in the squad car and we can walk up the rest of the way." He slapped her on the back. "I don't know why I'm doing this, but come on."

"You two stay here and be good now."

"No! No!" erupted the chorus of discontent.

Harry started to plead with Rick but he cut her off. "No way, Harry. They stay here."

Jungle vegetation couldn't have been much thicker than what Rick and Harry waded through.

"We should have taken horses," Harry grumbled.

"I haven't got two hours. This is quicker and you just be glad I'm including you."

"Including me? You wouldn't know about it if I hadn't told you. Hey, did you find Berryman?"

Rick slashed at pokeweed. "Yes. Was it that obvious after the funeral?"

"Where else would you go?"

"I found him at work. Selling a bronze stock trailer to the Beegles."

"Fireworks?"

"No, he was tired. Guess the excitement wore him out. He's got an alibi for the night Maude was killed. Home with his wife."

"She could lie for him."

"Do you honestly think, in your wildest dreams, Mary Minor Haristeen, that Linda Berryman would lie for Bob?"

"No." Harry stopped to catch her breath. The steamy heat sucked it right out of her.

Up ahead the outline of the tunnel loomed, covered and fantastic-looking with kudzu, honeysuckle, and a wealth of weeds unknown even to Harry. The old track, an offshoot of the newer line, ran up to the mouth of the tunnel.

"I've been keeping an eye out for broken grasses and tracks" —Rick wiped sweat off his forehead—"but with thick foliage like this, unless it's very recent, I don't have much hope. It's easier coming up the tracks but it takes twice as long."

As they reached the tunnel Harry cast her eyes upward. The chiseled remembrance of the men who built the tunnel, clear-cut and deep, was half covered by honeysuckle. The C. CROZET, CHIEF ENGINEER was visible. The rest was obscured except for A.D. 1852.

Harry pointed upward.

Kudzu grows about three feet a day, obscuring everything in its path.

"Treasure?" Harry said.

"The C and O searched the place top to bottom before they closed this off. And look at this rock. Nobody's getting through this stuff to hunt for treasure."

The mouth of the tunnel had been filled with debris, rock, and then sealed with concrete. The right side of the mouth was totally choked by vines.

Harry, crestfallen, reached out and touched the rock, warm from the sun. She withdrew her hand.

"There are three more tunnels to go."

"Brooksville is sealed off and Little Rock is still in use. I don't know if they shut off the Blue Ridge but it's so long and far away—"

"You're up on your tunnels." Harry smiled. She wasn't the only one sitting up at night reading.

"And so are you. Come on. There's nothing here."

As they trudged back Rick promised to send out a deputy to investigate the Brooksville, Little Rock, and Blue Ridge tunnels. They were outside his jurisdiction but he'd work that out with his counterparts in the other counties.

"What about calling the C and O?" Harry suggested.

"I did that. They got me the reports of closing the tunnels in 1944. Couldn't have been more helpful."

"And . . . ?"

"Just a dry recounting of shutting them up. There's no treasure, Harry. I don't know what the Crozet connection is. It's a dead end, kid."

He drove her back to the post office, where Tucker had chewed the corner of the door and Mrs. Murphy, with great violence, had thrown her Kitty Litter all over the floor.

23

Curving, sensuous, gilded pieces of Louis XV furniture dazzled Harry each time she entered Josiah's house. Gifted with a good eye and imagination, Josiah painted the walls stark white, which made the beautiful desks, bombé chests, and chairs stand out vividly. The floors, dark walnut, polished to perfection, reflected the glories of the furniture. The King Kong of pastel floral arrangements commanded the center of the coffee table. The flowers and the French pieces provided the only color in the room.

Josiah provided color of a different sort, valiantly sitting in a wing chair playing host to his callers, who had come as custom dictated. On a satinwood table next to the chair was a round cerise bowl that contained old marbles. Every now and then Josiah would reach into the bowl and run them through his fingers like worry beads. Another bowl contained old type bits; yet another contained doorknobs with mercury centers.

Susan rushed up to Harry to spill the rotten news about Danny's using his father's credit card to get money from the twenty-four-hour banking window. Ned had grounded him for the rest of the summer. Harry commiserated as Mrs. Hogendobber arrived with her famous potato salad. Mim, sleek in linen pants and a two-hundred-dollar T-shirt, glided over to assist Mrs. Hogendobber in carrying the heavy bowl. Hayden was just leaving as Fair came in. Little Marilyn served drinks out of a massive sterling-silver bowl.

Little Marilyn was spending a lot of time next to the liquor at these gatherings. Each time Harry looked her way, Little Marilyn found something fascinating to hold her attention. She wasn't going to acknowledge Harry with even a grimace, much less a smile.

"I've got to pay my respects to Josiah." Harry slipped her arm around Susan's waist. "The bank won't tell on Danny, so if you and Ned keep it quiet no one will know but me. I think a teenaged boy is allowed a few mistakes."

"A five-hundred-dollar one! And that's another thing. His father says he has to pay back every penny by Halloween."

"Halloween?"

"At first Ned said Labor Day but Danny cried and said he couldn't make enough from mowing lawns between the middle of July and Labor Day."

"This must be an up-to-date version of clipping a few bills from Mom's purse. Did you ever steal from your mother?"

"God, no." Susan's hand automatically covered her chest. "She would have beat me within an inch of my life. Still would, too."

Susan's mother was alive and extremely well in Montecito, California.

"My parents would not only have whopped me good," Harry said, "they would have told everyone they knew, to accent my humiliation, which would have made it ten times worse. Did I ever tell you about Mother not being able to get me up in the morning?"

"You mean when our classes started at six-thirty A.M.? I didn't want to get up either. Remember that? There were so many of us the schools couldn't handle it, so they staggered the times we'd arrive at school in the morning. If you missed your buddies at lunch hour, that was that."

"Poor Mom had to get up at five to try and get me up because I was on the 7:00 A.M. shift. I just wouldn't budge. Finally she threw water on me. She was not a woman to shy from a remedy once its potency was established."

Harry smiled. "I miss her. Odd, now I have no trouble getting up early. I even like it. It's too bad Mother didn't have more years to enjoy the fact that I've become an early bird." She collected herself. "I've got to say something cheery to Josiah."

Harry strolled over to Josiah, who was now being ministered to, literally, by Mrs. H., who was telling him about Lazarus. Josiah responded by saying that he, too, drew comfort from the thought of Lazarus waking from the dead but he, Josiah, was beat up, not dead. She needed to think of a better story. Then he reached for Harry.

"Dear Harry, you will forgive me for not rising."

"Josiah, this is the first time I've seen anyone's eyes match his shirt. Maroon."

"I prefer the descriptive burgundy." He leaned back in his chair.

"Now isn't that like you, making light of something terrible." Mrs. Hogendobber artlessly tried to pretend she liked Josiah and wished him well. Not that she disliked him, but she didn't feel he was exactly a man and she knew he wasn't a practicing Christian.

"It isn't so terrible. The man was distraught and lashed out. I don't know why Berryman's distraught, but if I were married to Our Lady of Cellulite perhaps I'd be distaught too."

Harry laughed. He was awful but he was on target.

"I had no idea that Linda Berryman evidenced an interest in film." Mrs. Hogendobber tentatively accepted a gin rickey—not that she was a drinker, mind you, but it had been an unusually difficult day and the sun was past the yardarm.

Fair, sitting across from Josiah, burst out laughing and then covered his mouth. Correcting Mrs. Hogendobber wasn't worth it.

"What's this I hear about the adorable Mrs. Murphy and the fierce Tee Tucker being caught red-handed, I mean red-pawed, in Maude's store—which I am buying, by the way?" Josiah asked Harry.

"I have no idea how they got in there."

"I found them, you know." Mrs. Hogendobber recounted, to the millisecond, the events leading to the discovery. She withheld the information about the desk but did give Harry a conspiratorial glance.

Josiah picked imaginary lint off his sleeve. "Don't you wish they could talk?"

"No." Harry smiled. "I don't want everyone to know my secrets."

"You have secrets?" Fair inclined his head toward Harry.

"Doesn't everyone?" Harry shot back.

The room quieted for a moment; then conversation hummed again.

"Not me," Mrs. Hogendobber said in a forthright voice, and then remembered that she had one now. She rather liked that.

"One teeny secret, Mrs. H., one momentary fall from grace, or at least a barstool," Josiah teased her. "I agree with Harry—we each have secrets."

"Well, someone's got a humdinger." Susan loathed the word humdinger, but it fit.

Harry exited the conversation on secrets as Mim joined it. She walked over to Little Marilyn, who couldn't weasel out of talking to her now.

"Marilyn."

"Harry."

"You're not talking to me and I don't much like it."

"Harry," Little Marilyn whispered, genuinely fearful, "not in front of my mother. I'm not mad at you. She is."

Harry also lowered her voice. "When are you going to cut the apron strings and be your own person? For chrissake, L.M., you're over thirty."

Little Marilyn flushed. She wasn't accustomed to honest conversation, since with Mim you glided around issues. Speaking directly about something was tactless. However, life in WASP nirvana was growing stale. "You have to understand"—she was now almost inaudible—"when I get married I can do what I want, when I want."

"How do you know you aren't exchanging one boss for another?"

"Not Fitz-Gilbert. He isn't remotely like Mother, which is why I like him." That admission popped out of Little Marilyn's mouth before she recognized what it meant.

"You can do what you want now."

"Why this sudden interest in me? You've never paid much attention to me before." A hint of belligerence crept into her voice. If she was going to rebel against Mama, why not practice on Harry?

"I love your brother. He's one of the most wonderful people I've ever known. He loves you and you'll hurt him if you keep him from your wedding. And I suppose if you'd stop hanging around with that vapid, phony chic set I could learn to like you. Why don't you motor out to the stables and get a little horse shit on your shoes? When we were kids you were a good rider. Go to New York for a weekend. Just . . . do something."

"Vapid? Phony? You're insulting my friends."

"Wrong. Those are friends your mother chose for you. You don't have any friends except for your brother." Tired, worried, and irritable underneath her public demeanor, Harry just blurted this out.

"And you're better off?" Little Marilyn began to enjoy this. "At least I'm getting the man I want. You're losing yours."

Harry blinked. This was a new Little Marilyn. She didn't like the old one. The new one was really a surprise.

"Harry?" Josiah's voice floated above the chatter. "Harry." He called a little louder. She turned. "It must be a glorious conversation. You haven't paid any attention to me and I've been calling."

Little Marilyn, defiantly, walked over to Josiah first. Harry brought up the rear.

"You two girls were jabbering like bluejays," Mim said with an edge. Then her husband, Jim, pushed open the front door with a booming greeting and Mim was truly on edge.

Harry eyed Little Marilyn's impeccable mother and thought that being in her company was like biting deeply into a lemon.

Fair saved the day, because Harry was teetering on the brink of letting everyone know exactly what she thought about them. He sensed that she was coiled, crabby. He knew he no longer loved his wife but after nearly a decade of being with someone, learning her habits, feeling responsible for her, it was a hard habit to break. So he rescued Harry from herself at that moment.

"What were you doing in Rick Shaw's squad car?" he asked.

A slow hush rolled over the room like a soft ground fog.

"We drove up to the Greenwood tunnel," Harry said, nonchalant.

"In this heat?" Josiah was incredulous.

"Maybe that was Rick's way of wearing her down for questioning," Susan said.

"I think the tunnels have something to do with the murders." Harry knew she should have shut her mouth.

"Ridiculous," Mim snapped. "They've been closed for over forty years."

Jim countered, "Right now no idea is ridiculous."

"What about the treasure stories?" Mrs. Hogendobber said. "After all, those stories must have some truth in them or they wouldn't have been circulated for over one hundred years. Maybe it's a treasure of a rare kind."

"Like my divine desk over there." Josiah swung his hand out like a casual auctioneer. "I've been meaning to tell you, Mim, that you need this desk. The satinwood glows with the light of the centuries."

"Now, now, Josiah." Mim smiled. "We're declaring a moratorium on selling until your eyes and your nose heal."

"If there were a treasure, the C and O would have found it." Fair fixed himself another drink. "People love stories about lost causes, ghosts, and buried treasure."

"Claudius Crozet was a genius. If he wanted to hide a treasure he could do it," Mrs. Hogendobber interjected. "It was Crozet who warned the state of Virginia that Joseph Carrington Cabell's canal company would never work. Cabell was a highly influential man in the decades before the War of Northern Aggression, and he deviled Crozet all his life. Cabell single-handedly held up the development of railroads, which Claudius Crozet believed heralded the future. And Crozet was right. The canal company expired, costing investors and the state millions upon millions of dollars."

"Mrs. Hogendobber, I'm quite impressed. I had no idea you were so knowledgeable about our ... namesake." Josiah sat up in his chair and then lapsed back again with a muffled moan.

"Here." Fair handed him a stiff Glenfiddich scotch.

"I—" Mrs. Hogendobber, unaccustomed to lying, couldn't think what to say next.

Harry jumped in. "I told you not to volunteer to head the 'Cele-brate Crozet' committee."

"Me?" Mrs. Hogendobber mumbled.

"Mrs. H., you've got *too much* on your mind. Recent events plus the committee . . . I'll come over tomorrow and help you, okay?"

Mrs. Hogendobber got the hidden message. She nodded in the affirmative.

"Well, Harry, what did you find at the Greenwood tunnel? Lots of florins and louis and golden Russian samovars?" Josiah smiled.

"Lots of pokeweed and honeysuckle and kudzu."

"Some treasure." Little Marilyn minced on "treasure."

"Well"—Josiah breathed the scotch fumes—"I give you credit for going up there in this beastly heat. We've got to find out who this . . . person is, and nothing is too far-fetched." He raised his glass to Harry in a toast and then proceeded to regale the group with his plans for Maude's store.

Later that night, Harry, who forgot to eat a decent dinner, got the munchies. She cranked up her mother's old blender, putting in whole milk, vanilla ice cream, wheat germ, and almonds. The al-monds clanked as the blades ground them. She drank the concoc-tion right out of the blender glass.

Tucker screeched into the kitchen, jumping on her hind legs. "*That's it! That's it!*"

"Tucker, get down. You can lick the glass when I'm finished."

Mrs. Murphy, hearing the fuss, roused herself from the living room sofa. "*What's going on, Tucker?*"

"*It's that smell.*" Tucker spun around in circles, her snow-white bib a blur. "*Close to the turtle smell, but much nicer, sweeter.*"

Mrs. Murphy jumped on the counter and sniffed the bits of wheat germ and almonds. The ice cream smell was strong. She sniffed with intensity and then vaulted from the counter onto Harry's shoulder.

"Hey, now, that's enough! You didn't learn these bad manners at home." Harry put the milkshake on the counter and lifted Mrs.

Murphy off her shoulder. Gently, Mrs. Murphy was placed on the floor.

Tucker touched noses with the cat. *"What did I tell you?"*

"Close. The almonds don't smell exactly like a turtle, but then a turtle doesn't smell exactly like whatever we smelled at the concrete plant and up at the railroad track. I wonder what it is?"

Mrs. Murphy and Tucker sat next to each other and stared up at Harry as she drained the last drop.

"Oh, all right." Harry grabbed dog biscuits and kitty treats out of the cupboard. She gave one to each animal. They ignored them.

"Not only bad manners, but picky too." Harry waved the kitty treat under Mrs. Murphy's nose. "One little nibble for Mommy."

"If she starts the Mommy routine she'll coo and croon next. You'd better eat it," Tucker advised.

"I'm trying to keep the smell of almonds. . . . Oh, well, you're probably right." Mrs. Murphy daintily removed the treat from Harry's fingers.

Tucker, with less restraint, gobbled up her biscuit with its gravylike coating.

"Good kitty. Good doggie."

"I wish she'd stop talking to us as if we were children," Mrs. Murphy grumbled.

24

Saturday sparkled, quite unusual for sticky July. The mountains glistened bright blue; the sky was a creamy robin's-egg blue. Mim Sanburne swaggered down to the little dock on the lake, which also gleamed in the pure light. Her pontoon boat, Mim's Vim, sides scrubbed, deck scrubbed, gently rocked in the lap of the tiny waves. The bar overflowed with liquid delight. A huge wicker basket filled with special treats like cream-cheese-stuffed snow peas sat next to the pilot's wheel. Everything was splendid, including Mim's attire. She wore bright-white clamdiggers, red espadrilles, a horizontally striped red-and-white T-shirt, and her captain's cap. Her lipstick, a glaring red smear, reflected the light.

Jim and Rick Shaw were huddled up at the house. She'd heard her husband say they ought to bring in the FBI, but Rick kept repeating that the case didn't qualify for the FBI's attention.

Little Marilyn followed a servant carrying the lovely baskets filled with party favors. Upon seeing the baskets, Mim entertained a fleeting thought of Maude Bly Modena. She quickly pushed it out of her mind. Her theory was that Maude must have surprised Kelly's killer and that was why she had been killed. She'd seen on many TV programs that a killer often has to kill again to cover his tracks.

After arranging the little favors on her boat, Mim languidly strolled up the terraces and walked around her house to the front. Day lilies shouted in yellow and burnt orange. Oddly, her wisteria still bloomed and the lavender was at full tide. She couldn't wait for her friends Port and Elliewood and Miranda Hogendobber. Not that Miranda was their social equal but she had distinctly heard Harry say to her last night at Josiah's that she was to head the newly formed "Celebrate Crozet" committee, and Big Marilyn meant to be a part of such a committee. Anyway, the lower orders were violently flattered at being included in little gatherings of the elite. Mim was confident that Miranda would fall all over herself when Mim suggested that she, too, help head the committee. The trick of the day would be to keep Miranda off religion, to keep Port off the grandchildren, and to keep Elliewood off the murders. No murder talk today—she absolutely forbade it.

As Mim waited for the various ladies of quality and one of lesser quality to drive down the two-mile approach to the house, she allowed herself to recall her "White Party." Decorated in silver and white by Josiah, this was to have been Mim's *Town and Country* party. She'd arranged to have a reporter there. Josiah contacted the press. It would never do for her to seek publicity openly.

Jim kept the Learjet busy zooming to New York and California to pick up people. Just two hundred of her nearest and dearest friends.

Josiah, using the bulldozing talents of Stuart Tapscott, created a thirty-foot oval pond at the end of the formal gardens. The tables were laid out among the garden paths and the very special guests were seated around the pond. Josiah lined the bottom of the pond so that it was really a swimming pool. He painted the bottom cobalt blue, and lights shone under the water. However, apart from the lighting, the pond appeared to fit the lay of the land. Marvelous water lilies enhanced the surface, as did heavily sedated swans, floating serenely. As the evening wore on the drugs wore off, and the swans underwent a personality change from serene to pugnacious. They stalked from the pond, dripping, flapping and pecking vigorously at one another, to assert their right to the brandy and bonbons. They honked and attacked guests, some of whom, having consumed too much brandy, fled into the pond. Mim herself was accosted by one of the larger swans. She was saved at the last minute by Jim, who lifted her off the ground while abandoning the table to the greedy bird.

Photos of the debacle splashed across *Town and Country*. The copy, lighthearted, did not declare the night a disaster, but Mim was stung nonetheless.

Miranda Hogendobber, punctual to a fault, came up the driveway in her ancient but impeccable Ford Falcon. She was soon followed by Elliewood and Port. After fulsome greetings, Little Marilyn helped her mother load the ladies. She pushed off the pontoon boat and waved from the shore. Then Little Marilyn sat on the dock, toes in the water.

The first round of drinks loosened everyone. Miranda allowed alcohol to scorch her lips. A nifty cure for the stomach ailment that had plagued her last night. She refused the second round but did take a tiny nip on the third.

Mim broke out a fresh deck of cards, still smelling of ink. Port and Elliewood played against Miranda and Mim. Mim just couldn't do enough for Miranda, which amused Port and Elliewood, who knew Mim was angling for something. Occasionally Mim would wave to a sunbathing Little Marilyn on the dock. It was perfect, really perfect, because Mim was winning.

After the first round of cards, Mim insisted on cranking the boat up and motoring on the lake. Speed was her downfall. She frightened Port, who continually asked her to slow down, but Mim, three sheets to the wind, told Port, in so many words, to shut up and live dangerously.

Finally, she stopped the boat for lunch. At first no one noticed anything wrong. The effects of the drink and the profound gratitude of not having Mim at the wheel dulled their senses.

Then Port felt something rather wet. She glanced down. "Mim, my feet are wet."

Everyone looked down. Everyone's feet were wet.

"Well, put your feet on the table." Mim cheerily poured another round.

"I get the distinct sensation that we are lower in the water," Mrs. Hogendobber said, even-voiced.

"Miranda, we *are* lower in the water," Port echoed, her face now white despite the sunburn.

Mim took off her soaking shoes and settled back for another swig. The group stared at her.

"Can you bail? I mean, Mim darling, do you have a pump?" Elliewood asked. Not a cursing woman, Elliewood had to exercise willpower to say "darling." She wanted to say "jerk," "asshole," anything to get Mim's attention.

By now the water was mid-calf. Port, unable to control herself any longer, emitted a heartrending shriek. "We're sinking! Help, my God, we're sinking."

She so startled the other women that Miranda put her hands to her ears and Elliewood fell out of her chair. She did not, however, spill her drink.

"I'll drown. I don't want to die," Port wailed.

"Shut up! Shut up this minute. You're embarrassing me." Mim spat the words. "Little Marilyn is there on the dock. I'll get her attention. There's not one thing to worry about."

Mim waved at her daughter. Little Marilyn didn't budge.

Elliewood and Miranda waved too.

"Little Marilyn," her mother called.

Little Marilyn sat still as a post.

"Little Marilyn! Little Marilyn!" the other three called.

"I can't swim! I'm going to drown," blubbered Port.

"Will you please be quiet," Mim demanded. "You can hold on to the boat."

"The goddamned boat is sinking, you bitch!" Port shouted.

Mim, outraged, pushed Port off her chair. Port sloshed in the water but bounced back up. She hauled off and caught Mim in the neighborhood of the left bosom.

Elliewood grabbed Mim, and Miranda grabbed Port.

"That's quite enough," Miranda ordered. "It won't settle anything."

"Who are you to tell me what to do?" Port got snotty.

"Bag it, Port." Mim, although in deep water, was not going to have her chances ruined. She returned her attentions to Little Marilyn.

She screamed. She hollered. She boldly took off her red-and-white T-shirt and waved it over her head, her lift-and-separate bra dazzling in the sun for all to see.

Little Marilyn, who was staring at them the entire time, finally rose to her feet and walked—not ran, but walked—up to the house.

"She's leaving us to die," Port sobbed.

"Can you swim?" Miranda matter-of-factly asked Elliewood. "I can't."

"I can't," howled Port.

"I can," replied Elliewood.

"Me too," said Mim.

"You'll leave me here. I just know you will. Mim, you're a cold-hearted, self-centered snake. You always were and you always will be. I curse you with my dying breath." Clearly, Port had once harbored secret dreams of being an actress.

"Shut the fuck up!" Mim shouted.

The use of the "f" word stunned the girls more than the fact that they were sinking.

Mim continued. "If help does not come in time, and I'm sure it will, we will nonetheless get you to shore, but you've got to lie on your back and shut up. I emphasize shut up."

Port put her head in her hands and cried.

Miranda, with calm resolution, prepared to meet her Maker.

Within minutes Jim, Rick Shaw, and Little Marilyn appeared on the shore. Little Marilyn pointed to the distressed band. Mim forgot she had taken her shirt off. Miranda did not. She covered Mim.

Jim and Rick ran in opposite directions. Jim hauled a canoe out of the dock house and Rick hopped in his squad car. He roared to the neighbor's on the other side of the lake. They really didn't want him to use their small motorboat. The sight of Mim's sinking was pleasing to their eyes but they gave in. The women were rescued as the water crept above their waistlines.

Later, Jim and Rick overturned the boat. One of the pontoons had been slashed and then covered with some manner of water-soluble pitch. Mim, fully recovered from her plight, stood next to the boat. Jim wished she hadn't seen this.

"Someone tried to kill me." Mim blinked.

"Well, it could have been ripped on the bottom," Jim lied.

"Don't tell me what I know. I never came near the bottom. Someone tried to kill me!" Mim was more angry than scared.

"Perhaps they only meant to give you a hard time." Rick hunkered down again to inspect the tear.

Mim, now in full hue and cry, whipped out her cellular phone to call the girls.

"Don't do that, Mrs. Sanburne." Rick pushed down the phone's aerial.

"Why not?"

"It might be prudent to keep this to ourselves for a while. If we withhold information, the guilty party might make a mistake, ask a leading question—you understand?"

"Quite." Mim pursed her lips.

"Now, Mim honey, don't you worry. I'll hire day and night bodyguards for you." Jim put his arm around his wife's shoulders.

"That's too obvious," Mim replied.

After further discussion Jim convinced her, saying he'd get female bodyguards and they'd pass them off as exchange students.

Later, when grilled by her mother concerning her inaction on the dock, Little Marilyn declared the sight of Mim sinking was so traumatic that she was temporarily paralyzed by the prospect of losing her mother.

25

Mondays made Harry feel as if she were shoveling a ton of paper with a toothpick. Susan's junk mail piled up like the Matterhorn. Harry couldn't fit it in her mailbox. Josiah received *Country Life* magazine from England and a letter from an antiques dealer in France. Fair's box was jammed with advertisements from drug companies: End Heartworms Now! Mrs. Hogendobber would be happy to receive her Christian mail-order catalogue. Jesus mugs were a hot item, or you could buy a T-shirt printed with the Sermon on the Mount.

Harry envied Christ. He was born before the credit card. Owning a credit card in the age of the mail-order catalogue was a dicey business. Bankruptcy, a phone call away, could be yours in less than two minutes.

Cranky, she upended the last duffel bag, and letters, postcards, and bills poured out like white confetti. Mrs. Murphy crouched, wiggled her behind, then pounced into the delicious pile.

"No claws. Citizens will know you're fooling with their mail and that's a federal offense." Harry scratched the base of her tail.

Tucker watched from her bed under the counter while Mrs. Murphy darted to the end of the room, rose up on her hind legs, pulled a 180, and charged back into the pile.

"Gangbusters!"

Tucker twitched her ears. *"You love paper. I don't know why. Bores me."*

"*The crinkle sounds wonderful.*" Mrs. Murphy rolled in the letters. "*And the texture of the different papers tickles my pads.*"

"*If you say so.*" Tucker sounded unconvinced.

By now Mrs. Murphy was skidding on the mail, much like kids skidding on ice without skates.

"That's enough now. You're going to tear something." Harry reached for the cat but she eluded her. Harry noticed a postcard on top of the latest pile Mrs. Murphy had assaulted. A pretty etching of a beetle was printed on the postcard. Harry picked it up and turned it over.

Written in computer script and addressed to her, it read: "Don't bug me."

Harry dropped the postcard as if it were on fire. Her heart raced.

"*What's the matter with Harry?*" Tucker called to Mrs. Murphy, still sliding on the letters.

The cat stopped. "*She's white as a sheet.*"

Harry sorted the mail slowly, as if in a trance, but her mind was moving so quickly she was nearly paralyzed by the speed. The killer had to be someone at Josiah's house, telling her to mind her own business. Her amateur sleuthing had struck a nerve. What the killer didn't know was that Harry knew the postcards were his or her signal. Nor did the killer realize that both Harry and Mrs. Hogendobber knew more about Maude than they were letting on. Harry sat down, put her head between her hands, and breathed deeply. If she put her head between her knees she'd pass out. Her hands would have to do. Her thoughts going back to Mrs. Hogendobber, Harry realized she would have to impress upon her the absolute necessity of not telling anyone about the second ledger. Even if Mrs. Hogendobber had a guardian angel, there was no point in testing him.

It flitted through her mind that Fair could have sent the bug postcard. This was his idea of sick humor. Really sick. The card might not have come from the killer. She clung to this hope for an instant. Fair had his faults but he wasn't this weird. Like a dying light bulb, her hope fizzled out. She knew.

Harry dialed Rick Shaw and gave him her latest report. He said he'd be right over. Then she finished sorting the mail, the one bright spot being another postcard from Lindsay Astrove, still in Europe.

Mrs. Hogendobber appeared on the doorstep. Tucker ran to the door and wagged her tail. Ever since Mrs. H. had released them from Maude's shop, Tucker harbored warm feelings for her.

Harry opened the door, reached for Mrs. Hogendobber, and yanked her into the post office. She shut the door behind her.

"Harry, I am capable of self-propulsion. You must have heard about my near-death experience on Mim's boat. I thank the Lord for my deliverance."

"No, I haven't heard a peep. I do want to hear about it but not right this instant. I want to remind you, to beseech you, not to tell anyone about those accounting books. You'll be in danger if you do."

"I know that," Mrs. Hogendobber replied. "And I know more than that, too. I've studied those books to the last penny, the last decimal point. That woman ordered enough packing to move every-one in Crozet. It makes no sense, and the money she was getting! Our Maude would never have been on food stamps."

"How much money?"

"She'd been here for five years—a rough average of one hundred and fifty thousand dollars per year on the left side of the ledger, if you know what I mean."

"That's a lot of plastic peanuts." Fear ebbed from Harry as her curiosity took over.

"I haven't a clue." Mrs. Hogendobber threw up her hands.

"I do—sort of." Harry peered out of the front window to make sure no one was coming in. "We have as our first victim a rich man who owned a concrete plant and heavy, heavy hauling trucks. The second victim was a woman who operated a packing shop. They were shipping something."

"Dope. Maude could fix up anything. She could pack a diamond or a boa constrictor. Remember the time she helped Donna Eicher ship ant farms?"

"That!" Harry recalled three years back, when Donna Eicher started her ant farms. Watching the insects create empires between two Plexiglas plates held an appeal for some people. It lost its appeal for Donna when her inventory escaped and devoured the contents of her pantry.

"If Maude could ship ants, she sure could ship cocaine."

"They've got dogs now that smell packages. I read it in the newspaper." Harry thought out loud. "She'd have to get it past them."

"We can smell anything. My nose detects a symphony of fragrance," Tucker yapped.

"Oh, Tucker, can it. You've got a good nose. Let's not get carried away with it." Mrs. Murphy wanted to hear what the women were saying.

"Piffle." Mrs. Hogendobber waved her hand. "She'd wrap the drugs with some odor to throw them off—Vicks VapoRub would do the job. A hundred fifty thousand a year, well, where else would one make profits like that?" Her back was to the door, which had just opened.

Harry winked at Mrs. Hogendobber, who stopped talking. Harry smiled. "Hi, Courtney. How's your summer going?"

"Fine, Mrs. Haristeen. Good morning, Mrs. Hogendobber." Courtney was down at the mouth but polite.

"How bad is it?" Harry asked.

"Danny Tucker is under house arrest for the rest of the summer. He even has a curfew! I can't believe Mr. and Mrs. Tucker are that cruel."

"Did he tell you why?" Harry inquired.

"No."

"Mr. and Mrs. Tucker aren't that cruel, so whatever he did, it was a doozy," Harry said.

"Doozy is such a funny word." Courtney wrinkled the mail by twisting it in her hands. She wasn't paying attention to it.

"Comes from Dusenberg," Mrs. Hogendobber boomed. "The Dusenberg was a beautiful, expensive car in the 1920's but to own one you also needed a mechanic. It broke down constantly. So a doozy is something spectacular and bad."

"Oh." Courtney was interested. "Did you own one?"

"That was a little before my time, but I saw a Dusenberg once and my father, who loved cars, told me about them."

Courtney thought the 1920's were as distant as the eleventh century. Age was something she didn't understand, and she wasn't sure if she'd just insulted Mrs. Hogendobber. She did know that her question would have insulted Mrs. Sanburne. Courtney left under this cloud of confusion.

"She's a dear child." Mrs. Hogendobber swung her purse to and fro. "No one ever forgets anything in this town. I know I never do."

"Yes?" Harry waited for the connective sentence.

"Oh, I don't know," Mrs. Hogendobber said. "Just crossed my mind. Now listen, Harry, I was due at the Ruth Circle five minutes ago but I'll be in constant touch and I want you to do the same."

"Agreed."

Mrs. Hogendobber rushed out for her women's church group meeting and Harry waited for the troops to march through, eagerly opening their mailboxes for a love letter and groaning when they found a bill instead. She waited for Rick Shaw too. She didn't know if he was a good sheriff or not. Too soon to tell, but she felt safer for having him around.

26

Fair Haristeen was washing his hands after performing surgery on an unborn ten-month-old fetus. Given the foal's bloodlines, he was worth a hundred thousand before he dropped. Fetal surgery was a new technique and Fair, a gifted surgeon, was in demand by Thoroughbred breeders in Virginia. His skill and the deference paid to him didn't go to his head. Fair still made the rounds to humble barns. He loved his work and when he allowed himself time to think about himself he knew it was his work that kept him alive.

Opening the door from the operating room, he found Boom Boom Craycroft sitting in his office. She smiled.

"Horse trouble?"

"No. Just ... trouble. I came to apologize for the way I treated you the day Kelly was killed. I took it out on you in my own bitchy way—you must be used to that by now."

Fair, unprepared for an apology, cleared his throat. "S'okay."

"It's not okay and I'm not okay and the whole town is crazy." Her voice cracked. "I've done some serious thinking. It's about time, you'll say. No, you wouldn't say anything. You're too much the gentleman, except for once in a blue moon when you lose your temper. But I have thought about myself and Kelly. He never grew up, you see. He was always the smart kid who puts one over on people, and I never grew up either. We didn't have to. Rich people don't."

"Some rich people do."

"Name three." Boom Boom's black eyes flashed.

"Stafford Sanburne, in our generation."

She smiled. "One. Well, I guess you're right. Maybe you have to suffer to grow up and usually we can pay someone to suffer for us. That didn't work this time. I can't run away from this one." She tilted her head back, exposing her graceful neck. "I also came to apologize for not understanding how important your work is to you. I don't think I will ever see how reaching into a horse's intestinal tract is wonderful, but—it's wonderful to you. Anyway, I'm sorry. I'm apologized out. That's what I came to say, and I'll go."

"Don't go." Fair felt like a beggar and he hated that feeling. "Give me a chance to say something. You weren't a spoiled rich brat each and every day and I wasn't a saint myself. We were kids when we married our spouses. Harry's a decent person. Kelly was a decent person. But what did we know in our early twenties? I thought love was sex and laughs. One big party. Hell, Boom Boom, I had no more idea of what I needed in a woman than ... uh, nuclear fusion."

"Fission."

"Fission's when they pop apart. Fusion's when they come together," Fair corrected her.

"I corrected you. That's a rude habit."

"Boom Boom, I can accept that you're thinking about your life but do you have to be so overpoweringly polite?"

"No."

"Anyway, I made mistakes, too, and I made them on Harry. I wonder if everyone learns by hurting other people."

"Isn't it odd? I feel that I know Kelly better now than when he was alive. I guess in some ways you feel you know Harry better now that you have some distance. You know, this is the first time we've had a heart-to-heart talk. God, is it like this for everyone? Does it take a crisis to get to the truth?"

"I don't know."

"Do we have to savage our marriages, give up the sex, before becoming friends? Why can't people be friends and lovers? I mean, are they mutually exclusive?"

"I don't know. What I know"—Fair lowered his eyes—"is that when we're together I feel something I've never felt before."

"Do you still love Harry?" Boom Boom held her breath.

"Not romantically. Right now I'm so mad at her I can't imagine being friends with her but people tell me that passes."

"She loves you."

"No, she doesn't. In her heart of hearts she knows. I hate lying to her. I know all the reasons why but when she finds out she'll hate me most for the lying."

Boom Boom sat quietly for a moment. Being female, there were many things she could say to Fair about his feelings for Harry but she'd taken enough of a risk by coming here to apologize. She wasn't going to take any more, not until she felt stronger, anyway. "I'm running the business, you know." She changed the subject.

"No, I didn't know. It will be good for you and good for the business."

"Isn't it a joke, Fair? I'm thirty-three years old and I've never had to report to work or be responsible to anyone or anything. I'm . . . I'm excited. I'm sorry it took this horror to wake me up. I wish I could have done something, made something out of myself while Kelly was alive but . . . I'm going to do it now."

"I'm happy for you."

She paused for a moment, and tears came to her eyes. "Fair"—she could barely speak—"I need you."

27

A swift afternoon thunderstorm darkened and drenched Crozet. It was a summer of storms. Harry couldn't see out to the railroad tracks during the downpour. Tucker cowered in her bed and Mrs. Murphy, herself not fond of thunder, stuck to Harry like a furry burr.

She heard a sizzle and a pop. The power had shut down, a not uncommon occurrence.

The sky was blackish green. It gave Harry the creeps. She felt under the counter for her ready supply of candles, found them, and lit a few. Then she stood by the front window and watched the deluge driven by stiff winds. Mrs. Murphy jumped onto her shoulder, so Harry reached up and brought the cat into her arms. She cuddled her like a baby, rocking her, and thought about Rick Shaw's response to the postcard—which was "Lay low."

Easier said than done. The death of two citizens must be accounted for somehow. And she felt that she had the end of a ragged thread. If she could follow that thread back, step by step, she would find the answer. She also knew she might find more than she bargained for—an answer in this case didn't mean satisfying her curiosity. Secrets are often ugly. She was peeling away the layers of the town. It might mean her own life. Rick forcefully impressed this upon her. She had been of help to him and he was grateful but she wasn't a professional so she should butt out. She wondered, too, if underneath his concern there might not be a hint of face-saving. The Sheriff's Department seemed to be running in circles. Better the citizens didn't know. She wondered, if Rick did solve the murders, whether he would get a gold star behind his name or at least a promotion. Maybe he didn't want to share the limelight.

Well, whatever, he was doing his job, and part of that job was protecting the citizens of Albemarle County and that meant her too.

A figure appeared in the swirling rain, oilskin flapping in the wind. It headed toward the post office. The hair on Harry's neck stood up. Mrs. Murphy sensed it, jumped down, and arched her back.

The door flew open and a bedraggled Bob Berryman swept in, leaves in his wake. He leaned against the door with his body close to it.

"Goddamn!" he roared. "Even nature's turned against us." He seemed unhinged.

Paralyzed by fear, Harry edged back by the counter. Bob followed her, dripping as he went. In this weather, if Harry screamed at the top of her lungs no one would hear her.

Tucker scurried out from under the counter. "She's scared of Bob Berryman?"

"Yes." Mrs. Murphy never took her eyes from Bob's glowering face.

"What can I do for you?" Harry squeaked.

Bob reached across the counter, pointing. "Gimme one of those registered slips. Harry, are you sick? You look . . . funny."

"Tucker, can you get out the door if I open it?" Mrs. Murphy asked. "He stole those letters. If he's the one and he makes a move for Harry, we can attack."

"Yeah." Tucker hurried to the door that separated the work area from the reception area.

Mrs. Murphy stretched her full length and began playing with the doorknob. This one was the right height for her. If she opened the door Harry would be on to one of her best tricks but Mrs. Murphy didn't think she had a choice. She strained and held the knob between her two paws. With a quick motion she forced the knob to the left and the door popped open.

"Smart cat," Berryman commented.

"So that's how she does it," Harry said weakly.

Tucker sauntered out, nonchalant, and sat three paces from Bob's juicy ankle. Mrs. Murphy leaped back up to the counter to watch and wait.

"The slip, Harry." Berryman's voice filled the room.

Harry pulled out a registered mail slip and filled it out as candle-light flickered and a sheet of rain lashed at the front window. She tore up the first copy and started another.

"I'll get it right," she mumbled.

Berryman reached across and held her hand. She froze. Tucker moved forward and Mrs. Murphy crept to the edge of the counter. Berryman observed the cat and looked down at the dog. Tucker's fangs were bared.

"Call off your dog."

"Let go of my hand first." Harry steadied herself.

He released her hand. Tucker sat down but continued to stare at Berryman.

"Don't be afraid of me. I didn't kill Maude. That's what you're thinking, isn't it?"

"Uh—"

"I didn't. I know it looks bad but I couldn't take any more at her funeral. Josiah's words of *wisdom*," he said bitterly, "were the straw that broke the camel's back. What does he know about men and women?!"

Harry, confused, said, "I expect he knows a great deal."

"You must be kidding. He uses Mim Sanburne to party in Palm Beach and Saratoga and New York and God knows where else."

"I didn't mean that. He's observant, and because he isn't married or involved he has more time than other people. I guess he—"

"You like him. All women like him. I can't for the life of me figure out why. Maude adored him. Said he made her laugh so hard her sides ached. He yapped about clothes and makeup and decorating. They always had their heads together. I used to tell her he was nothing but a high-class salesman but she told me to stop acting like

Joe Six-Pack—she wasn't going to give him up. She said he gave her what I couldn't and I gave her what he couldn't." Bob's lips compressed. "I hate that silly faggot."

"Don't call him a faggot," Harry admonished. "I don't care who he sleeps with or who he doesn't. You're mad at him because he was close to Maude. He made you jealous."

"So the cat's out of the bag." He sighed. "I don't care anymore. You want to know why I hit him? Really? He came over and told me to pull myself together. 'Think of your wife,' he said. I was afraid that Maude had told him about us, and then I knew she had. Damn him! Coming over and oozing concern. He didn't want Linda to go into a huff and ruin his orchestrated funeral. He didn't care about Maude."

"Of course he did. He paid for much of it."

"We all paid for the funeral. He wants to look good so he can take over her store. He and Maude talked business as much as they talked mascara. He knows what a moneymaker it is. I—well, I don't care about the business. Okay, it's out in the open. I loved Maude. She's dead and I'd give anything to have her back." He paused. "I'm leaving Linda. She can have the house, the car, everything. I'm keeping my business. I'm alone but at least I'm not living a lie." This admission calmed him. "I didn't kill Maude. I wouldn't have harmed a hair on her head."

"I'm so sorry, Bob."

"So am I." He handed over the envelope to be sent to the IRS. "Rain slacked off." Realizing what he'd said, he was embarrassed. He hesitated a minute before leaving.

Harry understood. "I'll keep my mouth shut."

"You can tell anyone you like. I apologize for fulminating. I'm not sorry for what I told you. I'm sorry for how I told you. You don't need to put up with that. I'm so up and down. I—I don't know myself. I mean, I go up and down." This was the only way he could describe his mood swings.

"Under the circumstances, I think that's natural."

"I don't know. I feel crazy sometimes."

"It will even out. Be easier on yourself."

He smiled a tight smile, said, "Yeah," and then left.

Harry, exhausted from the encounter, sat with a thud. Tucker walked back to her.

"*So the letters were love letters,*" Mrs. Murphy thought out loud.

"*Probably, but we don't know,*" Tucker replied. "*Anyway, he could have killed her in a lovers' quarrel. Humans do that. I overheard on the TV that four hundred and thirty-five Americans are killed each day. I think that's what the newscaster said. They'll kill over anything.*"

"*I know, but I don't think he killed her. I think he told Harry the truth.*"

"What are you meowing about, kitty cat? Now I'm on to your tricks. You've been opening doors all along, haven't you? You little sneak." Harry stroked Tucker's ears while Mrs. Murphy rubbed against her legs. Vitality seeped back into her limbs, which felt so heavy with fear when Bob first came into the post office. She hoped the rest of the day would pick up. But unfortunately, Harry's day went from bad to worse.

Mrs. Hogendobber drove up in her Falcon. She opened an umbrella against the rain. Mrs. H. saw no reason to trade in a useful automobile, and the interest rates on car loans were usury as far as she was concerned. Although once a month she drove over to Brady-Bushey Ford to allow Art Bushey the opportunity to sell her a new car, Art knew she had no intention of buying anything. She swooned over him, and being gallant, he took her to lunch each time she careened onto the lot.

"Harry! I made a mistake, a tiny mistake, but I thought you ought to know. I should have told you before now but I didn't think about it. I just . . . didn't. After you left the party or whatever you want to call it at Josiah's, I stayed on. Mim and I were commenting on the state of today's morals. Then Mim mentioned that you had encouraged Little Marilyn to contact Stafford in New York. I spoke about forgiveness and she haughtily told me she didn't need a sermon, she attended Saint Paul's for that, and I said that forgiveness extended through the other six days of the week as well."

"I'm sorry you got on the bad side of her." Harry leaned on the counter.

"No, no, that's not it. You see, then Josiah mentioned that the government, the federal government, has never forgiven the draft evaders, not really, and Ned, who arrived after you left—quite drawn-looking, too, I must say—well, Ned laughed and said the IRS never forgives anyone. The power to tax is the power to destroy, and I said maybe it was just as well that Maude was dead because they'd catch up with her sooner or later."

"Oh, no!" Harry exclaimed.

"Conversation ran to other topics and I didn't think about it until now."

"Why now?"

"I don't know exactly. The rain made me remember all that water in Mim's boat. What if—what if Mim wasn't the killer's target? After all, Mim can swim."

"I see." Harry rubbed her temples. This felt worse than a head-ache.

The entire town knew about Mim's slashed pontoon because the workers Jim used to lift the boat onto his truck saw the damage. By now everyone was jumping to conclusions, so the gossip all over town was that Mim was the intended victim.

Mrs. Hogendobber breathed in sharply. "What do I do now?"

"If anyone brings up your slip—you know, asks a leading question about Maude and the IRS—pick up the phone and call me. Better yet, call Rick Shaw."

"Oh, dear."

"Mrs. H., you must trust me. The killer gives a signal before he strikes—I can't tell you what it is. He gives warning, which makes me wonder if the slashed pontoon was really aimed at you."

"Do you think he'll kill me? Is that what you're saying?" Her voice was quite calm.

"I hope not."

"If I tell Rick Shaw he'll know what we've done."

"I think we'd better tell him. What's he going to do? Arrest us?

Listen to me. You have absolutely got to remember who was there after I left."

"Myself, Mim, Little Marilyn, Jim, old Dr. Johnson, and Ned. That reminds me, what is going on with Ned and Susan? Oh, Susan was there, of course."

"Just remember the names and I'll tell you about Ned."

This encouraged her. "U-m-m, Fair and Josiah—well, that's obvious."

"No, nothing is obvious. Are you certain there wasn't anyone else? What about Market? What about any of the kids?"

"No, Market wasn't there, nor Courtney."

"This isn't good."

Mrs. Hogendobber put her back to the wall for support. She wiped her brow. "I'm not used to not trusting people. I feel horrible."

Harry's voice softened. "None of us is used to that. You can't be expected to change a behavior overnight—and maybe it's better that you don't. Except until we catch this killer, well, we're going to have to be on our toes. Why don't you have Larry's wife stay with you tonight, or better yet, go over there."

"Do you think it's that bad?"

"No," Harry lied. "But why take chances?"

"You believe that Maude and Kelly were shipping out dope, don't you? I do. They had to be in business together. So who's the kingpin?"

"Some sweet Crozet person we play tennis with or go to church with. A woman or a man we've known for years."

"Why?" Mrs. Hogendobber might preach about evil, but when confronted with it she was at a loss. She expected the Devil with green horns or a human being with a snarling face. It had never once occurred to her in her long and relatively happy life that evil is ordinary.

Harry shrugged in answer to Mrs. Hogendobber's question. "Love or money."

After Mrs. Hogendobber drove off, Harry returned to work with renewed vigor. Since she felt helpless about Mrs. Hogendobber, she could feel purposeful in cleaning the office. She could get one thing to work right in her life.

Then Fair walked into the post office.

"I tried to be a good husband—you know that, don't you?" Fair cleared his throat.

"Yes." Harry held her breath.

"We never discussed what we expected from each other. Perhaps we should have."

"What's wrong? Come out and say it. Just come out with it, for chrissake." Harry reached out to touch him and stopped herself.

Fair stammered, "Nothing's wrong. We made our mistakes. I just wanted to say that."

He left. He wanted to tell her about Boom Boom. The truth. He tried. He couldn't.

Harry wondered, Was he mixed up in these murders? He was acting so strange. It couldn't be. No way.

28

Mrs. Hogendobber's fears were justified. Rick Shaw seethed when Harry and Mrs. Hogendobber confessed about Xeroxing the second ledger.

By the time Harry got home she decided if this wasn't the worst day in her life, it certainly qualified as so bad she didn't want it repeated.

She called Susan, telling her about Fair's peculiar behavior. Susan declared that Fair was in the grief stage of the divorce. Harry asked her to come to the post office in the morning for a long coffee break. After she hung up she decided she'd tell Susan about the bug postcard she had received. She needed Susan's response. Anyway, if she couldn't trust her best friend, life wasn't worth living.

29

Tucker chewed a big knucklebone behind the meat counter. Market Shiflett, in a generous mood, gave her a fresh one. Mrs. Murphy and Pewter received smaller beef bones. They happily gnawed away while catching up on recent events. Ozzie, Bob Berryman's Australian shepherd, had been down at the mouth. Pewter claimed he hardly wagged his tail and barked. Mim Sanburne's snotty Afghan hound had lost his testicles yesterday. The animal news, usually rich in the summer, lagged behind the human news this year.

Tucker recounted Rick Shaw's livid explosion. Poor Mrs. Hogendobber thought she was going to jail.

Courtney paid scant attention to these three animals cracking bones and talking among themselves. Her large hoop earrings clattered.

"When did Courtney start dressing like a gypsy?" Mrs. Murphy, conservative about attire, wanted to know.

"She's trying to attract Danny Tucker's attention. He'll be mowing Maude Bly Modena's lawn today. He'll hear her before he sees her." Pewter had eaten so much she lay down on one side and rested her head on her outstretched arm.

"Guess you heard what he did?"

"Mrs. Murphy told me yesterday while you were out doing potty, as Harry calls it." Pewter laughed. "I don't mind Harry's expressions so much except when she tells you to go potty her voice rises half an octave. Say, not only is

Courtney sticking big hoops in her ears but last night when Market was out she made herself a martini. She wants to be sophisticated and she thought drinking a martini would do it. Ha! Tastes like lighter fluid."

"She's young." Mrs. Murphy tore off a slender thread of red meat.

"Tell me about it. Human beings take forty years to grow up and half of them don't do it then. We're ready for the world at six months."

"We're not really grown up though, Pewter." Mrs. Murphy licked her chops. "I'd say we're fully adult at one year. I wonder, why does it take them so long?"

"Retarded," came Pewter's swift reply. "I mean, will you look at Courtney Shiflett. If she were a child of mine those earrings would be out of those ears so fast she wouldn't know what hit her."

"At least she works. Think of all those humans who don't even earn a living until their middle twenties. She works after school and she works in the summer. She's a good kid." Mrs. Murphy thought most humans lazy, the young ones especially.

"If you like her so much, you live with her. If I hear her George Michael tape one more time, I'm going to shred it with these very claws." She flashed her impressive talons. "Furthermore, the girl will make herself deaf—and me, too —if she doesn't turn down that boom box. Sometimes I think I'll walk out the door and never come back—live on field mice."

"You're too fat to catch mice," Mrs. Murphy taunted her.

"I'll have you know that I caught one last week. I gave it to Market and he went 'O-o-o.' He could have thanked me."

"They don't like mice." Tucker slurped at her bone.

"Try giving them a bird." Mrs. Murphy rolled her eyes. "The worst. Harry hollers and then buries the bird. She likes the moles and mice I bring her. I break their necks clean. No blood, no fuss. A neat job, if I do say so myself."

Pewter burped. "Excuse me. A neat job . . . Mrs. Murphy, the human murders were messy," she thought out loud.

"Why?" Tucker sat up but put her paw on her bone just in case. Pewter was known to steal food. "It's not efficient to kill a person that way. Throw one in a cement mixer and tie another one to the railroad track. Originally, it was a neat job. After they were dead the killer ground them into hamburger."

Pewter lifted her head. "The killer's not a vegetarian." Then she dropped her head back and laughed.

Mrs. Murphy pushed Pewter with her paw. "Very funny."

"I thought so."

Tucker said, "The police aren't revealing how Kelly and Maude died—if they know. The mess has to be to cover up something inside the bodies or to divert us from what the people were doing before they died."

"That's right, Tucker." Mrs. Murphy got excited. "What were they doing in the middle of the night? Kelly was at the concrete plant. Working? Maybe. And Maude willingly went out to the railroad tracks west of town. Humans sleep at night. If they were awake it had to be important, or"—she paused—"it had to be something they were used to doing."

30

"Mrs. Murphy and Tucker are at the back door." Susan interrupted Harry, who was sorting the mail and telling all simultaneously.

"Will you let them in?"

Susan opened the back door and the two friends raced through, meowing and barking. "They're glad to see you."

"And in a good mood too. Market handed out bones today."

"*We think we've got part of the puzzle,*" Mrs. Murphy announced.

"*They were in cahoots, Kelly and Maude, with something—*" Tucker shouted.

"*In the nighttime when no one could see,*" Mrs. Murphy interrupted.

"All right, girls, calm down." Harry smiled and petted them.

Mrs. Murphy, discouraged, hopped into the mail bin. "*I give up! She's so dense.*"

Tucker replied, "*Find another way to tell her.*"

Mrs. Murphy stuck her head over the bin. "*Let's go outside.*" She jumped out.

Tucker and the cat dashed to the back door. Tucker barked and whined a little.

"Don't tell me you have to go to the bathroom. You just came in," Harry chided.

Tucker barked some more. "*What are we going to do when we get out?*"

"*I don't know, yet.*"

Harry, exasperated, opened the door and Tucker nearly knocked her over.

"Corgis are a lot faster than you think," Susan observed.

After replaying yesterday's conversation with Fair one more time, both Susan and Harry were depressed. Harry shook out the last mailbag, three-quarters full. Susan made a beeline for the postcards. They both held their breath. A series of Italian postcards scared them but there were no graveyards on the front, and when turned over they revealed a number in the right-hand corner and the signature of their traveling friend, Lindsay Astrove. They exhaled simultaneously.

"I'll read you Lindsay's cards while you finish stuffing the mailboxes." Susan sat on a stool, crossed her legs, put the postcards in order, and began.

" 'Being abroad is not what it's cracked up to. be. I took a train across the Alps and when it pulled into Venice my heart stopped. It was beautiful. From there, everything went downhill.

" 'The Venetians are about as rude as anyone could imagine. They live to take the tourists for all they can. No one smiles, not even at each other. However, I was determined to transcend these mortal coils, so to speak, and drink in the beauty of the place. Blistered and exhausted, I tramped from place to place, seeing the Lord in painting after painting. I saw Jesus on the cross, off the cross, in a robe, in a loincloth, with nails, without nails, bleeding, not bleeding, hair up, hair down. You name it. I saw it. Along with the paintings were various other art forms of the Lord and his closest friends and family.

" 'Naturally, there were many, many, many pieces of the Virgin Mother. (A slight contradiction in terms.) In all of Venice, however, I was not able to find a snapshot of Joseph and the donkey. I could only conclude that they are ashamed of his stupidity for believing Mary's story about her and God and the conception thing and they only bring him out for Christmas.

" 'I did arrive at one possible conclusion. Since all of this artwork looks exactly alike, maybe one man is to blame. I find it plausible that one man did all of it and used many names. Or maybe all the little Italian boys born between 1300 and 1799, if their last name ended in "i" or "o," were given a paint-by-number kit. I am sure there is a logical explanation for all this.

" 'One closing thought and I will move on to my visit to Rome. I am grateful that Jesus was Italian and not Spanish. All of that art would have been Day-Glo on velvet instead of oil on canvas.

" 'On to Rome—the Infernal City.

" 'Rome combines the worst of New York and Los Angeles. The one thing the Romans do well is blow their horns. The noisiest city in the world. The Romans rival the Venetians for rudeness. The food in both cities is not nearly as good as the worst Italian restaurant in San Francisco.

" 'As you can probably guess, I got to go to the Vatican Museums. I also got to leave the Vatican Museums because I proclaimed in an audible voice that it is just disgusting to see the wealth the church is hoarding. On the interest alone, they could cure cancer, AIDS, hunger, and homelessness in less than a year. All of a sudden the people who did not speak English were fluent in the language. I was ushered out. I didn't even get to see the Pope in his satin dresses.

" 'The rest of Rome was no big deal either. The Colosseum was in shambles, the Spanish steps were littered with addicts and drunks, and the Trevi fountain was like any cruise bar.

" 'The designer shops were a delight. A designer outfit is one that does not fit, does not match, and does not cost less than your permanent residence. Did not shop in that city.

" 'I left Rome wondering why the Visigoths bothered to conquer it. However, Monaco was fabulous. The people, the food, the attitude, the absence of Renaissance culture!

" 'I'll see you all in September when I will have soaked up about as much of the Old World as I can possibly stand. I'm beginning to think that Mim, Little Marilyn, Josiah, and company are gilded sheep to rave on about Europe, furniture, and a face-lift in Switzerland. Oh, well, as you know, I think Mim impersonates the human condition. And don't show this to Mrs. Hogendobber! Do show Susan.

" 'Love, Lindsay' "

Susan and Harry laughed until tears rolled down their cheeks. Once they finally got hold of themselves they realized they hadn't laughed, true laughter, since Kelly's murder. Stress was exacting its toll.

"How many postcards did that take?"

Susan shuffled them like playing cards. "Twenty-one."

"Who are they addressed to?"

"You. You're the only one she could write this to."

Harry smiled and took the postcards. "I'll be glad when Lindsay comes home. Maybe this will be over by September."

"I hope so."

"Shred it up, like this." Mrs. Murphy ripped into the sparrow corpse, and feathers flew everywhere. A squeamish expression passed over Tucker's pretty face. "Oh, come on, Welsh corgis are supposed to be tough as nails. Tear that mole I caught into three pieces."

"She's going to hate this."

"So she hates it. Our message might sink in subliminally."

"She's smart for a person. She knows there's a connection between Kelly and Maude."

"Tucker, stop shilly-shallying. I want her to know we know. Maybe she'll start to listen to us for a change."

Tucker, with singular lack of enthusiam, tore the still-warm mole into three pieces. If that wasn't bad enough, Mrs. Murphy made her carry the hunks to the back door of the post office.

The cat reared up on her hind legs and beat on the door. A soft rattle echoed in the post office.

Harry opened the door. Neither animal budged. Instead they sat next to their kill, carefully placed together by Mrs. Murphy.

"How revolting," Harry exclaimed.

"I told you she'd hate it," Tucker snapped to the tiger cat.

"That's not the point."

"What?" Susan called out.

"The cat and dog brought back the remains of a mole and what must have been a bird only a short time ago." Harry peered for a closer look. "Ugh. The mole's in three pieces."

Susan stuck her head out the back door. "Like Maude."

"That's horrible. How could you say that?"

"Well—it's not hard to think of those things." Susan petted Tucker on the head. "Anyway, they're doing what comes naturally and they brought these pathetic corpses back to you as a present. You should be properly grateful."

"I'll be properly grateful after I clean them up."

Whether or not the bird and mole corpses inspired Harry, the animals couldn't say, but she did drive her blue truck to Kelly's concrete plant, leaving them outside while she went in for a chat.

After delicately dancing around the subject in Kelly's office, now taken over by his wife, Harry felt the time was right. She quietly leaned toward Boom Boom and asked, "Did Kelly ever do business with Maude?"

A wave of relief swept over the sultry woman's features. "Oh— sure. She packed up his Christmas business mailing for him. Is that what you mean?"

"No." Harry noticed the photos of Kelly with the county commissioners, the president of the University of Virginia, the state representatives. "What about business on a larger scale?"

"There's no record of it." Just to make certain, Boom Boom jangled Marie on the intercom and Marie confirmed the negative.

"What about a more intimate connection?" Harry whispered, and waited for the reaction.

Extramarital sex, shocking to many, barely dented Boom Boom's psyche. She expected it, even from her husband. "No. Maude wasn't Kelly's type, although she seems to have been Bob Berryman's."

"All over town?" Harry asked, knowing it was.

"Linda's given to fainting spells. Next come the faith healers, I guess. Hard to believe either Linda or Maude loved him, but then you really never know, do you?" Her long eyelashes, which reached into next week, fluttered for an instant.

"No."

Boom Boom's face flushed. "Kelly wasn't a saint and our marriage was far from perfect. If he strayed off the reservation, so to speak, he'd never have done it close to home. What do you think? You obviously believe something was going on between my husband and Maude."

"I don't know. My hunch is they were in business together. Illegal."

Boom Boom stiffened slightly. "He made tons of money legally."

"Kelly loved to screw the system. An enormous untaxable profit would have been a siren call to his rebellious self—if they were shipping drugs, I mean."

Realistic about Kelly, Boom Boom hesitated. It was not as if the thought hadn't occurred to her once or twice since his murder. "I don't know, but I sure hope you keep these thoughts to yourself. He's dead. Don't go about ruining his name."

"I won't, but I have to get to the bottom of this. Do you think Kelly's murder and Maude's murder are connected?"

"Well, at first I didn't think, period. The shock left me empty, and into the emptiness rushed anger. I just want to kill this son of a bitch. Barehanded." She put her hands together in a choking motion. "As the days have gone by—seems like years, in a funny way—I go over it and over it. I don't know why but yes, I believe they are connected."

"Shipping something—that's what I come up with no matter how I examine this."

"Contrary to what the public has been told by government types, drugs are easy to ship. It's possible. God knows they're also easy to hide. They don't take up that much space. You could cram two million dollars' worth of cocaine into these desk drawers."

"Whatever they did, they fell afoul of a partner or partners." Harry said this, realizing as the words were out of her mouth that Boom Boom could be one of those partners. She'd be committed to profit, but Harry couldn't imagine Boom Boom at her hardest doing business with Kelly's killer.

"If you find out, Mary Minor Haristeen, tell me twenty minutes before you tell Rick Shaw. I'll pay you ten thousand dollars for that information."

Harry choked. Ten thousand dollars. God, how she needed it.

A silence wrapped around them, an air of static antagonism. Boom Boom broke it: "Think it over."

Harry swallowed. "I will." She paused. "Why do I feel like you're holding out on me?"

Boom Boom's face became suddenly still. "I'm telling you everything I know about Kelly. If he had a secret, then he kept it from me too."

"What about Fair?" Harry's lips were white.

"I don't know what you mean." Boom Boom's eyes darted around the room. "Did you come here looking for clues about Kelly or clues about Fair? I mean, you threw him out, Harry. What do you care what he does?"

"I'll always care what he does. I just can't live with him." Harry's face flushed. "He just wasn't . . . there."

"What do you mean?"

"He wasn't there emotionally." She sighed. "It's one thing to lose your marriage, but it's just as bad to lose your friends. Everyone's taking sides."

"What did you expect?" No sympathy from Boom Boom.

That put the match to the tinderbox. "More of you!" Harry clenched her teeth. "He and Kelly were never the same after Fair made that pass at you, but we stayed friends."

"That was last year. Everyone was drunk! Look, Harry, people don't want to look at themselves. Let me give you some advice about Crozet."

Harry interrupted. "I've lived here all my life. What do you know that I don't?"

"That divorce frightens people. From the outside your marriage seemed fine. People want to accept appearances. Now you've gone and upset the apple cart. You might be looking inside yourself but no one in these parts will give you credit for it. This is Albemarle County. No change. Keep everything the same. You stay the same.

To change is viewed as an admission of guilt. Hell, people would rather live in their familiar misery than take a chance to change it."

Harry had never weathered blunt truth from Boom Boom before. She opened her mouth but nothing came out. Finally she found her voice. "I can see you've been doing a lot of thinking."

"Yes. I have."

The discussion had magnified tension instead of dispelling it.

As Harry drove home she noticed the late afternoon shadows seemed longer. A sense of menace began to haunt her.

She kept to her routine, as did everyone else. At first the routine cushioned the shock of the murders, as well as her separation, but now she felt off balance, the routine a charade. The macabre killings, the reality of them, began to sink in.

She touched down on the accelerator but she couldn't outrun the shadows of the setting sun.

31

" 'Wish you were here.' " Harry's hands shook as she read the post-card addressed to Mrs. George Hogendobber. The front of the postcard was a beautiful glossy photograph of Pushkin's grave. Another carefully faked postmark covered the upper right-hand corner.

Harry called Rick Shaw but he wasn't in the office. "Well, get him!" she yelled at the receptionist. Next she depressed the button and dialed Mrs. Hogendobber.

"Hello."

Harry never thought she would be thrilled to hear that hearty voice. "Mrs. Hogendobber, are you all right?"

"You call me first thing in the morning to see if I'm all right? I'll be over there in fifteen minutes."

"Let me walk over for you." Harry fought for a deep breath.

"What? Mary Minor Haristeen, I've been walking to the post office since before you were born."

"Please do as I say, Mrs. H. Go out on your front porch so that everyone can see you. I'll be there in one minute flat. Just do it, please." She hung up the phone and flew out the door, Tucker and Mrs. Murphy at her heels.

Mrs. Hogendobber was rocking in her swing, a perplexed Mrs. Hogendobber, an irritated Mrs. Hogendobber, but an alive Mrs. Hogendobber.

Harry burst into tears at the sight of her. "Thank God!"

"What in the world is wrong with you, girl? You need an Alka-Seltzer."

"You must get out of here. Get out of Crozet. What about your sister in Greenville, South Carolina?"

"It's just as hot there as it is here."

"What about your nephew in Atlanta?"

"Atlanta is worse than Greenville. I'm not going anywhere. Are you suffering from heat stroke? Maybe you're overworked. Why don't we go inside and pray together? You'll soon feel the hand of the Lord on your shoulder."

"I sincerely hope so but you're coming with me to the post office and you aren't leaving until Rick Shaw gets there."

Tucker licked Mrs. Hogendobber's ankles. Mrs. Hogendobber shooed her away, but Tucker returned. Finally, Mrs. Hogendobber let her lick. She was sweaty already on this blistering morning. What were wet ankles?

"Are you going to tell me what's going on here?"

"Yes. Each murder victim received an unsigned postcard. The handwriting was in computer script. It looks like real handwriting but it isn't. Anyway, on the face of each postcard was a photograph of a famous graveyard. The message read, 'Wish you were here.' You received one this morning."

Mrs. Hogendobber's hand fluttered to her ponderous bosom. "Me?"

Harry nodded. "You."

"What did I do? I've never even seen a marijuana cigarette, much less sold dope."

"Oh, Mrs. H. I don't know if this has anything to do with drugs or not but the killer knows you've seen the second set of books. At Josiah's gathering."

Mrs. Hogendobber's eyes narrowed. She might lack a sense of humor but she didn't lack a quick mind. "Ah, so it isn't just the IRS Maude was cheating. That ledger is an account of her turnover with whomever her partner was." She placed her hands on either side of the hanging swing. "Someone at Josiah's party. It's preposterous!"

"Yes—but it's real. You're in danger."

With great composure Mrs. Hogendobber rose and accompanied Harry back to the post office. She recovered sufficiently to say, "I always knew that you read the postcards, Harry."

When Rick Shaw arrived with Officer Cooper, he herded everyone into the back room.

"Harry, you act normal. If you hear anyone, go on out and talk to them." He studied the postcard.

"What about prints?" Officer Cooper asked.

"I'll send them to the lab. But the killer's smart. No prints. Not on the postcards. Not on the bodies. No nothing. This guy—or gal—must be invisible. We're checking with the computer companies in town to see if there's anything distinguishable in the script. Unfortunately, computers aren't like typewriters, which can be traced. A letter from a typewriter is almost like a fingerprint. Electronic printing is, well, homogenized. We're trying, but we're not hopeful on that front."

Officer Cooper watched Mrs. Murphy try to squeeze into a Kleenex box on the shelf.

"He's sporting, too. He gives us a warning even if the victims don't know it's a warning," Harry said.

"I hate the kind that put on finishing touches." Rick grimaced. "Give me a good old domestic murder any day." He swiveled his chair, facing Mrs. Hogendobber. "You're getting out of Dodge, ma'am."

"I'm prepared to accept what God has in store for me." Her chin jutted out. "I was prepared to drown on Mim's lake. This isn't any different."

"The Lord moves in mysterious ways, but I don't," Rick countered. "You can visit a relative and we'll make certain you arrive there safe and sound. We'll alert the authorities there to keep a close watch over your welfare and we won't inform anyone of your whereabouts. If you won't leave town, then we'll put you in jail. We'll treat you well, but, my dear Mrs. Hogendobber, you are not going to be the third victim of this cold, calculating murderer. Am I understood?"

"Yes." Mrs. Hogendobber's reply was not meek.

"Fine. You and Officer Cooper go home and pack. You can decide what you want to do, and tell no one but me."

"Not even Harry?"

"Not even Harry."

Mrs. Hogendobber reached over and squeezed Harry's hand. "Don't you worry about me. You'll be in my prayers."

"Thank you." Harry was touched. "You'll be in mine."

After Mrs. Hogendobber and Officer Cooper left through the back door, Harry crumpled a mailbag.

"He'll know that I know and that you know," the sheriff said. "He won't know if anyone else knows. Does anyone else know?"

"Susan Tucker."

Rick's eyebrows clashed together. "Oh, dammit to hell, Harry. Can't you keep your mouth shut about anything?!"

"She's my best friend. Besides, if anything happens to me I want someone to know at least as much as I did."

"How do you know Susan isn't the killer?"

"Never. Never. Never. She's my best friend."

"Your best friend. Harry, women who have been married to men for twenty years find out they've got another wife in another city. Or children grow up and find out that their sweet daddy was a Nazi war criminal who escaped to the United States. People are not what they seem and this killer appears normal, well-adjusted, and hey, one of the gang. He or she is one of the gang. Susan is under suspicion as much as anyone else. And what about Fair? He's got medical knowledge. Doctors make clever killers."

"Susan and Fair just wouldn't, that's all."

Rick exhaled through his nostrils. "I admire your faith in your friends. If it isn't justified you've got a good chance of meeting your Maker." He picked up a pencil and tapped it against his cheek. "Do you think Susan told Ned?"

"No."

"Wives usually talk to their husbands and vice versa."

"She gave me her word and I've known her far longer than Ned has. She won't tell."

"So it's only you and Susan and Mrs. Hogendobber who know the postcard signal?"

"Yes."

He kept tapping. "We're a small force but I'll assign Officer Cooper to guard you. She'll stay here in the post office and she'll go home with you too. For a couple of days, at least."

"Is that necessary?"

"Very necessary. Within twelve hours, max, the killer will know that Mrs. Hogendobber left town and he'll figure out the rest. She won't show up for her Ruth Circle at church. They'll ask questions. I'll have her make some calls from the station. She can say that her sister's taken ill and she's hurrying to Greenville. Whatever location she gives out won't be true, of course. But Mrs. Hogendobber's cover won't fool the killer, any more than Mim's exchange students are fooling anyone. Her departure is too abrupt and Mrs. Hogendobber talks for days if she's going into Charlottesville. For an emergency trip out of state, she'd take an ad out in the *Daily Progress*. See, that's what's tough about this one—he or she knows everyone's habits, foibles, routines. If he can't get to Mrs. H., I'm not sure what he'll do next. He might turn on you or he might get nervous and make a mistake. A tiny one but something we can use."

"I hope it's the latter and not the former."

"Me, too, but I'm not taking any chances."

Mrs. Murphy and Tucker drank in every word. If Harry was in danger, there was no time to lose.

32

Officer Cooper's presence at the post office electrified everyone. Mim, Little Marilyn, and the bodyguard stopped at the sight of her.

Little Marilyn hovered at her mother's elbow, as did the daytime female bodyguard, who could have used a shave.

"Uh, Harry, I've been meaning to talk to you about the Cancer Ball this year." Little Marilyn bit her lip as Mim watched.

Harry had served on the committee every year for the last six years. "Yes."

"Given that you're divorcing, well, it just won't do for you to be on the committee." Little Marilyn at least had the guts to tell her face-to-face.

"What?" Harry couldn't believe this—it was too silly and too painful.

Mim backed up her daughter. "We can't have you on the program. Think what it would do to dear, sweet Mignon Haristeen."

Mignon Haristeen, Fair's mother, was also in the Social Register and therefore important to Mim.

"She's living in Hobe Sound, for Christ's sake," Harry exploded. "I don't think she much cares what we do in Crozet."

"Really, have you no sense of propriety?" Mim sounded like a schoolmarm.

"Who the hell are you two to bump me off the Cancer Ball?" Harry seethed. "Mim, you're in a poisonous marriage. You sold out cheap. I don't care if Jim has umpteen million dollars. You can't stand him. What's umpteen million dollars compared to your emotional health, your soul?"

Mim roared back: "I came to the marriage with my own money."

In saying that, she said it all. Her life was about money. Love had nothing to do with it.

She slammed the door, leaving Little Marilyn and the bodyguard running to catch up.

Bad enough that Harry had lost her temper, she had criticized Mim in front of Officer Cooper.

Mim, entombed as she was in the white sepulcher of her impeccable lineage, was jarred by a person of low degree, Harry. Oh, she'd made allowances for Harry. After all, Fair had little money but the Haristeens had bloodlines. They'd once had money but lost it in the War Between the States. Never bounced back financially, but then that was the story of the South. It took vulgarians like Jim to make money again.

Mim about ripped the door off her Volvo. She was calling Mignon Haristeen the second she got home.

Courtney breezed in as Mim blew out. "Hey, what's the matter with her?"

"Change of life," Harry said.

Officer Cooper laughed. Courtney didn't get it. She banged open the postal box.

"Courtney, be careful. You'll twist the hinges if you keep that up."

"I'm sorry, Mrs. Haristeen. Officer Cooper, what are you doing here?"

"Guarding your post box from fraud and bent hinges."

Mrs. Murphy stuck her paw in the opened box from the inside. She could reach most of the boxes if the mail cart was underneath, which it was. Courtney touched her paw. Mrs. Murphy had performed this trick for Mrs. Hogendobber, who screamed when she saw the hairy little paw. Here she was, brave about her nasty postcard but scared of a cat's paw. Well, she wasn't used to animals. Mrs. Murphy thought about that as Courtney played with her.

Danny Tucker opened the door and carefully closed it, a change from his usual slam bang. Ever since the credit-card episode, he had walked on eggshells.

"Hello, Harry, Officer Cooper." He glanced at Courtney. "Hello, Courtney."

"Hello, Danny." Courtney shut the box, thereby depriving Mrs. Murphy of a great deal of satisfaction.

Danny leaned over the counter. "Mom says you should come over for supper tonight," he told Harry. "Dad's staying over in Richmond."

"Thank you. Officer Cooper will accompany me."

"You in trouble?" Danny half hoped Harry was, so he wouldn't be the only person with a black cloud hanging over his head.

"No."

"Terminal speeding tickets," Officer Cooper said laconically.

"You?" Danny exclaimed. "That old truck can't do but fifty full-out."

"The condition of my truck is much to be lamented but the condition of my bank account is even sorrier. Hence the truck. And I do not have a speeding ticket. Not even one."

"Why don't you drop a new engine in it or a rebuilt engine? My buddy Alex Baumgartner—he can do anything with an engine. Cheap, too."

"I'll give it my bright regard." Harry smiled. "And tell your mom we'll be over about six-thirty. Is that all right with you, Coop?"

"Great." Officer Cynthia Cooper lived alone. A home-cooked meal would be a little bit of heaven.

Danny's eyes twinkled. He wanted to appear suave but he still resembled the fourteen-year-old he in fact was. "Courtney, you come too."

"I thought you were grounded." Why seem eager?

"I am but you can visit me. It's only for supper, and Mom thinks you're a good influence." He laughed.

"You can ride in the squad car with us," Officer Cooper offered.

"Let me ask Daddy." She rushed out and was back within seconds. "He said it's okay."

Josiah came in. "I heard you were being watched, and I was nearly run over by Mim, Little Marilyn, and that bodyguard. Hello, kids." He noticed Courtney and Danny.

"Hello, Mr. DeWitt." They left the post office to talk outside.

Josiah's lower lip protruded; he pretended to be serious. "I vouch for the character of this woman. Pure as the driven snow. Clean as mountain water. Honest as Abe Lincoln. If only we could corrupt her."

"Try harder." Harry smiled.

He got his mail and yelled around the corner: "Is there anything I can do to relieve you of Officer Cooper's presence? Not that we don't think you're wonderful, Officer Cooper, but you'll ruin the poor girl's sex life."

"What sex life?" Harry said.

"My point exactly." Josiah returned to the counter. His tone was more serious. "Are you all right?"

"I'm fine."

"I'll take your word for it then." He hesitated, lowered his eyes, then raised them. "Any word from Stafford?"

"Not that I know of, and Mim let me know I wasn't winning any personality contest, but then she isn't winning one with me either, the stuck-up bitch."

Josiah's eyes opened wider. He'd rarely seen Harry angry. "She exhausted every adjective in describing to me her feelings about 'the Stafford episode,' as she calls it. Mim and I have an understanding of sorts. She doesn't meddle in my personal life and I don't meddle in hers, but she's quite wrong about this. Of course, just why Little Marilyn selected Fitz-Gilbert remains a mystery. Any quieter and the man would be in a coma."

"When's he going to show his face?" Harry inquired.

"Mama plans a small 'do' at Farmington Country Club but she keeps moving the date. She's more rattled than she lets on about . . . things."

"Aren't we all?" Harry pushed around the rubber-stamp holder.

He smoothed his salt-and-pepper hair. "Yes—but I prefer not to think about it. I can't do anything about it anyway."

33

Mrs. Murphy, ear cocked to catch mouse sounds, prowled in the barn. It had been a long day at the post office. When they arrived home Mrs. Murphy hurried toward the barn, accompanied by Tucker. High in the hayloft she caught sight of a black tail hanging over the side of a bale. She climbed up the ladder to the loft. "Paddy?"

He opened one golden eye. "You gorgeous thing. I've been waiting for you. It's a good thing you woke me up or I would have slept right through until tonight." He stretched. "I remembered our brief conversation under a full moon and a canopy of stars. . . ."

She twitched her tail. His flowery speech made her impatient. He continued.

"And spurned though I was, your words were engraved on my heart. I saw something odd. I didn't think about it at the time and I wish I had, because I would have investigated, but my blood was up and you know how that is."

"What?" Mrs. Murphy's ears pitched forward; her whiskers swept forward. Every muscle was on alert.

"I was hunting out near the old Greenwood tunnel. A rabbit shot out of the tunnel and I chased him clear down to the Purcell McCue estate. That damned golden retriever of theirs lumbered out, mouth running, and I lost my rabbit."

"Go up a tree?"

"Me? That toothless old hound. No, I dashed right in front of his nose and walked on home. Then I remembered what you said and I came here."

"The tunnel's sealed."

"But I saw the rabbit come out of it."

"Do you remember exactly where?"

"He moved pretty fast but I think it was near the bottom. It's covered with foliage. Hard to see."

"How do you know he wasn't hiding in the foliage and you flushed him out?"

"I don't, but I swear I saw him pop out of a hole at the very bottom. Can't be sure but, well—I thought you'd like to know."

"Thanks, Paddy. I don't know how I can make it up to you."

"I do."

"Not that way." Mrs. Murphy cuffed his ears. "Come on, let's tell Tucker."

The two cats joined Tucker. Conversation grew excited.

"We've got to get up there!" Tucker shouted above the voices. "That's the only way we'll ever know."

"I know we've got to get up there but it's a good day's journey, and we can't leave Harry now that she's in danger." Mrs. Murphy spat, she was so vehement.

"How are you going to convince her to go up there in the first place?" The human race didn't rank high in Paddy's book.

"Harry catches on if you keep after her." Tucker defended her friend.

"If we can just think of something—"

"More dead birds and moles?"

"No." Mrs. Murphy jumped on the water trough. "The Xeroxed papers. Let's try that when we get inside."

"Oh." Tucker's liquid brown eyes clouded. "That will fry her."

"Better mad than dead," Paddy said matter-of-factly.

34

"I'd better learn to quack, since I'm going to waddle for the next three days." Officer Cynthia Cooper rubbed her stomach as she entered Harry's house.

"Mim spends a fortune on her cook, and Susan Tucker's much better—for free, too." Harry dumped her satchel on the kitchen table, since they had come in through the back door. The last time Harry used the front door was for her father's funeral party. "Let me show you the guest bedroom."

"No, I'll sleep in your room and you sleep in the guest bedroom. If anyone sneaks around looking for you, he or she will come to your bedroom first."

"You don't really believe the killer is going to sneak around up here in the middle of the night just because he or she knows I've figured out the postcard signal?" Harry wanted to think she was safe.

"It seems unlikely, but then everything about this crime is unlikely."

"Follow me!" Mrs. Murphy shouted over her shoulder. She galloped into Harry's bedroom, knocked over a lamp, and threw the Xeroxed papers on the hooked rug.

"Yahoo!" Tucker pretended to chase Mrs. Murphy. "Should I chew the papers?"

"No, nitwit. Circle the bed," Mrs. Murphy ordered the dog. "When she gets here to spank us, hide under the bed with me."

Harry, followed by Officer Cooper, charged into the room. "All right, you two!"

Mrs. Murphy hopped on the bed, performed a perfect somersault, and then as Harry reached for her she scooted off and flattened herself under the bed. Tucker was already there.

The muslin material underneath the mattress hung invitingly. From time to time Mrs. Murphy would lie on her back and pull herself, paw over paw, from one end of the bed to the other. Shreds of material gave testimony to her lateral rappeling technique. She reached up and sank in her claws.

"Don't," Tucker warned. "She's furious enough as it is."

"That's enough, you two! I mean it. I really mean it this time. Damn, the lamp is broken."

"Was it valuable?" Officer Cooper knelt down to pick up the pieces. She could see a doggie, ears down, staring at her. "That dog is laughing at me, I swear it."

"A real comedienne." Harry hunkered down too. "Mrs. Murphy, what have you done to my bed?"

"If you'd clean under here more often you'd have noticed by now," Mrs. Murphy answered.

"The lamp not only wasn't valuable, it was the ugliest lamp in three counties. I never got around to buying a good one. Actually, I barely have time to brush my teeth and eat."

"H-m-m," said Cooper.

"Oh, jeeze," Mrs. Murphy moaned. "Here comes the lament of Father Time, gray hair and slowed reflexes. I wish she'd get over it! Dammit, Harry, the papers!"

"Don't yowl at me, pussycat. I can sit on this bed and wait a long time for you to come out," Harry threatened while still on her knees. "Might as well clean up this mess." She began picking up the papers.

Officer Cooper read one as she helped. "Where'd you find these?"

"You know perfectly well, or doesn't Rick Shaw tell you anything?"

"Oh, this and the ledger is what you filched from Maude's desk? That got his knickers in a twist." She giggled.

"Yeah." Harry put the papers on the bed. "Mrs. Hogendobber and I only copied them. It's not as if we obstructed justice."

"Our sheriff wants to know everything. He's a good sheriff." She began reading again.

"Which one is that?" Harry's knees cracked when she unbent to sit on the bed.

"November 4, 1851. Addressed to the President and Directors, Board of Public Works, from the Engineer's Office of the Blue Ridge Railroad."

"Too bad he couldn't start with 'Dear Honey'—think of the stationery it would have saved him," Harry remarked. "I think that letter is about the temporary bridge built at Waynesboro so the men could haul materials over the mountains."

"Yeah, that's the one. Wow. I can't believe this. The original price of labor when the tunnel was contracted was seventy-five cents per day, and it shot up to eighty-seven and a half cents for some workers and even one dollar for others. Men risked their lives for eighty-seven and a half cents!"

"A different world." Harry handed Officer Cooper another sheet, the overhead light casting a dim shadow on the policewoman's blond hair. "This one's interesting." She started to read.

"November 8, 1853. He wrote a lot in November, didn't he?" She read on. " '... we were suddenly taken by surprise by the eruption of a large vein of water, for which we were obliged to take hands from their work, and set them to pumping, until we could obtain machinery for the same purpose, working by horsepower. This circumstance has been repeated several times during the year, successive veins of water having been encountered, until the body of water we have now to keep down amounts to no less than one and a half hogshead per minute, ninety hogshead per hour.' " She whistled. "They could have drowned in there."

"Digging tunnels is dangerous work and this is before dynamite, remember. He created a siphon to evacuate the water and it was the longest siphon on record. Here's another one."

Mrs. Murphy grumbled under the bed. "*I don't feel like sleeping under the bed. Are they ever going to get it or not?*"

"*Beats me.*" Tucker yawned.

"H-m-m." Cooper squinted at the page. "December 9, 1855. Lot of technical stuff about the grades and curves and timbering the excavation." She selected a more dramatic passage. " ' ... some time in February, 1854, an immense slide from the mountain completely blocked up the western entrance, and, coming down as fast as removed, from a height of about one hundred feet, effectually prevented the construction of the arch at this end, until late in the fall of the same year.' " She turned to Harry. "How old was Claudius Crozet at this time?"

"He was born December 31, 1789, so he would have been just shy of his sixty-sixth birthday."

"Enduring this kind of physical labor? He must have been tough as nails."

"He was. He was a genius really. Politics cost him his job as First Engineer of the state, and twelve engineers couldn't do the work of one Crozet, so Richmond had to eat humble pie and ask him back in 1831. This was long before he built the tunnels. Know what else he did?"

"Not a clue."

"Brought the first blackboard to West Point. He taught there starting in 1816. Can you imagine teaching without a blackboard? America must have been primitive. The level of education was so low at West Point that he had to teach his class math before he could teach them engineering. It's a wonder we didn't lose the Mexican War."

"Guess he raised the standard of education. Lee was an engineer, you know."

"I know. Every good Southern kid knows that—that and Stonewall Jackson's Valley Campaign. And that 'you all' is plural, never singular, and that corn bread— How'd I get on this?"

"You're wound up. All that sugar in Susan's sauce on the veal."

"Maybe so. This is my favorite." Harry plucked a letter from the disorganized pile. "Crozet was being criticized in the newspapers both for the length of time the tunnels were taking and for their location, so he wrote to a friend: 'Strange things are now going on, of which you may have seen some notice. Most scurrilous and unfair attacks directed against me have appeared in some papers, especially the "Valley Star." Though few will notice such things, except with disgust, yet it is proper I should be informed of them, otherwise the seeds of slander may grow around me, without my having a chance to cut them off in time.' He then asks his friend to send him clippings he might come across. He gave as his address 'Brooksville, Albemarle.' " She kicked off her shoes and put down the letter. "The more things change, the more they stay the same. Try to do something new, something progressive, and you're crucified. I don't blame him for being touchy."

"Do you think there's treasure in one of the tunnels?"

"Oh—I'd like to think there is." Harry curled her toes.

"Car! Car! Car!" Tucker warned and ran from under the bed to the front door.

"Cut the lights," Officer Cooper commanded. "Get on the floor!"

Harry hit the floor so hard she knocked the wind out of herself and found herself nose to nose with Mrs. Murphy, who had started to wiggle out from under the bed.

Officer Cooper, pistol in hand, crept toward the front door. She waited. Whoever was in the car wasn't getting out, although the headlights had been turned off. The living room light gave evidence that someone was home and Tucker was hollering her head off.

"Shut up." Mrs. Murphy bumped the dog. "We know there's a car outside. Cover the back door. I'll take the front."

Tucker did as she was told. Officer Cooper flattened herself beside the front door.

The car door slammed. Footsteps clicked up to the front door. For a long agonizing moment nothing happened. Then a soft knock.

A harder knock, followed with "Harry, you in there?"

"Yes," Harry called out from the bedroom. "It's Boom Boom Craycroft," Harry told Officer Cooper.

"Stay on the floor!" Cooper yelled.

"Harry, what's wrong?" Boom Boom heard Cynthia Cooper's voice and didn't recognize it.

"Stay where you are. Put your hands behind your head." Officer Cooper flicked on the front porch light to behold a bewildered Boom Boom, hands clasped behind her head.

"I'm not armed," Boom Boom said. "But there's a thirty-eight in the glove compartment. It's registered."

Mrs. Murphy slunk behind Officer Cooper's heels. If anything went wrong she would climb up a leg—in Boom Boom's case a bare one—and dig as deeply as she could.

Officer Cooper slowly opened the door. "Stay right where you are." She frisked Boom Boom.

Harry, on all fours, peeked around the bedroom door. Sheepishly she stood up.

Boom Boom caught a glimpse of her. "Harry, are you all right?"

"I'm fine. What are you doing here?"

"Can I come inside?" Boom Boom's eyes implored Officer Cooper.

"Keep your hands behind your head and the answer is yes."

As Boom Boom entered the house, Cooper shut the door behind her, gun still cocked. Boom Boom had plenty she wanted to say to Harry but the presence of Officer Cooper inhibited her.

"Harry, I've ransacked Kelly's office. Ever since you dropped by I've just gone wild and—I found something."

35

Crumpled sheets of yellow legal paper, the penciled-in mileage numbers smeared, shone under the kitchen light. Harry, Boom Boom, Officer Cooper, Mrs. Murphy, and Tucker gathered around the old porcelain-topped table. Still leery, Coop kept her pistol in her hand.

"I checked the mileages of the trucks against the depreciation in Marie's ledger. They don't jibe," Boom Boom pointed out. "Nor is there any accounting for this bill." She produced a faded invoice for a huge amount of epoxy and paint resin. The bill was from North Carolina.

"Maybe the added mileage on the trucks reflects hauling the materials back here?" Harry said.

"It's three hours to Greensboro and three hours back. We're looking at thousands of miles." Boom Boom's misty-mocha fingernail pinned down the long number as though it were a butterfly. "Another thing. I asked around the plant if anyone had done extra hauling over the last four years. No one had. This isn't to say that someone might not be lying but my hunch is, whatever was being carried, Kelly drove it."

Officer Cooper flipped through the four years of mileage figures. "There's no way to tell if these were short hops or long ones. You only have the monthly figures."

"Right. But I subtracted them from Marie's figures, or rather I subtracted Marie's figures from these, and it averages out to one thousand miles per month for the big panel truck. The other trucks have less mileage on them."

"Jesus, that's a lot of resin." Harry pushed back her chair. "Anyone want a drink?"

"No, thanks," they both said.

"He wasn't transporting resin and epoxy. I found one bill for that. I mean, there could be others but that's all I found, so I think he was taking something else in the panel truck as well as occasionally using a smaller truck."

"Boom Boom, one thousand miles a month is a one-way trip to Miami, drug capital of the U.S.," Coop observed. "I take that back. Any city over five hundred thousand people is a drug capital these days."

"If Kelly was moving drugs he'd certainly be smart enough to disguise it as something else." Harry had always liked Kelly. "And he often drove the trucks. He liked being outside; he liked physical work. I suppose he and Maude linked up four years ago. She must have helped him package the stuff—if it was drugs."

"Don't get fixated on cocaine, or even heroin," Officer Cooper advised. "There's a big market in speed and steroids. He'd avoid the South Americans that way. Those boys play rough."

"He brought in drugs before, though, didn't he?" Harry asked.

Boom Boom closed her mouth.

"He's dead. There isn't anything I can do about crimes of the past," Coop said.

Boom Boom sighed. "He gave it up. He gave up using the stuff. He used to say that the drug lords and high government officials were in collusion over the drug trade. The congressmen and senators on the take, as well as the people under them, didn't want their nontaxable income removed. 'It's a damned sin,' he'd say. 'The American people are losing billions of dollars in taxes from drugs, taxes that could help people. Why is alcohol a state-supported drug to the exclusion of other drugs? You can't stop the trade. You can't legislate human behavior.' He was impassioned about it."

"Tobacco," Officer Cooper added laconically.

"What?" Boom Boom asked.

"It's a legal drug. Most addictive drug we've got. Ask Rick Shaw." The vision of Rick sneaking another cigarette made Coop laugh.

"Here in Virginia we know all about tobacco." Harry examined the yellow pages. "Where'd you find these?"

"Behind the frame of the poster he had on the wall. You know, the one where the duck is sitting in the lawn chair sipping a drink and there are bullet holes over his head. It was the last place I looked, and the corner of the backing was bent."

"I'm going to confiscate these." Cooper reached for the papers in Harry's hand.

"I don't want any of this in the paper. When you finally find out who the killer is you'll find out what they were really doing. The publicity has been grueling enough. No more!"

"I can't control the press, Boom Boom," Cooper truthfully replied.

"That's up to Rick, not Officer Cooper," Harry reminded Boom Boom.

"Do what you can, please," Boom Boom begged.

"I'll try."

Boom Boom left. Harry and the policewoman watched her pull out of the driveway.

Mrs. Murphy, who had politely listened to the coversation, emitted a loud shout. "*Go up to the tunnels. That's why I threw the papers on the floor. It's worth another look.*"

"What lungs." Cooper grinned.

"You ate leftovers from Susan's tonight." Harry used her Mother voice.

"*Listen to me!*" Mrs. Murphy bellowed.

Tucker sniffed at Mrs. Murphy's tail, hanging over the table. "*Save your breath.*"

"*Damn.*"

"All right." Harry got up and opened the big jar of Best Fishes. She placed four of the delicious tidbits under the cat's bright whiskers. Mrs. Murphy, in a fit, knocked the treats off the counter and stalked out of the room.

"So emotional," Officer Cooper said as Tucker scarfed down the treats.

"Like people," Harry said.

36

At seven forty-five the next morning, the phone rang in the Crozet post office.

"Hello," Harry answered.

"Did you catch the killer yet?" Mrs. Hogendobber's voice boomed.

"How are you?" Harry was surprised at how happy Mrs. Hogendobber's call made her.

"Bored. Bored. Bored. Being under threat of death isn't as much torture as being out of the swim. Did you catch him?"

"No."

"Any clues?"

"Yes."

"Tell me. I'm far away. I can't blab."

"Get thee behind me, Satan."

"Mary Minor Haristeen, how dare you quote the New Testament to me like that? Why, I'm appalled at the suggestion that I would tempt you. I'm not tempting you. I'm simply trying to help. Sometimes a person considering the same evidence will see something new. Many cases have been solved that way."

"If you're far away, Rick Shaw can't make your life miserable. He can sure muck up mine."

This idea dawned on Mrs. Hogendobber and set. "He'd be thrilled for an answer. Now, I've known you since the day you were born. Prettiest little baby I ever saw. Even prettier than Boom Boom Craycroft—"

"Don't stretch the truth," Harry interrupted.

"You were—upon my soul, you were. You know I won't breathe a word of this and I do have good ideas."

"Mrs. Hogendobber, I can't speak as freely as I would wish."

"Oh, I see." Mrs. Hogendobber's voice registered her thrill with the development. "Someone we know?"

"Yes, but not of the inner circle."

"Reverend Jones."

"Now why would you mention his name?"

"He's a lovely man but he's not of my denomination. I don't consider him of the inner circle."

"Hardly any of us attend your church. I'm an Episcopalian."

Mrs. Hogendobber, a self-confessed expert on Protestant churches, corrected Harry. "You are entirely too close to the Catholic church and so is Reverend Jones. The real Reformation came when churches such as mine, The Holy Light, freed The Word to the people. However, you don't even attend Saint Paul's, so you ought to stop claiming that you are an Episcopalian. You are a lapsed Episcopalian."

"Is that like fallen arches?"

"Harry, such subjects are not humorous and it grieves me that you don't see the light. That's why we're called The Holy Light."

"Yes, ma'am."

"Who's there? Will they be offended if you tell?"

"I don't think so. It's Officer Cooper."

"Really?" The husky voice shot upward.

"Really. Now I've got to get back to work. You take care of yourself."

"I want to come home." Mrs. Hogendobber sounded like a miserable child.

"We want you to come home." Harry thought to herself: Some of us do. Harry missed her.

"I'll call tomorrow. I can't give you my number. 'Bye."

" 'Bye." Harry hung up the phone. "She's a pip."

"There's another one at the door."

Harry smiled and kept silent as she unlocked the door for Mim

Sanburne, who was unusually early. She paused but did not say hello.

"Good morning, Mim." Harry decided a lesson in manners might be amusing.

Big Marilyn's expertly frosted hair caught the light. "Are you under house arrest?"

"We're rehashing the Stamp Act and how it led up to the Revolution," Officer Cooper retorted.

"Deference is greatly to be sought after in public servants. Our sheriff prides himself on his staff. But then—" Mim didn't finish what would have been a threat, for Josiah jauntily opened the door. Nor did she tell Harry that she had indeed called Mignon Haristeen, who told her to mind her own goddamned business and reinstate Harry on the Cancer Ball committee. Yes, Mignon deplored the divorce but Harry had worked hard for the charity and the charity should come first. That made Mim back down.

"Stop what you're doing and come on over to the shop," Josiah said. "I've worked a miracle."

"I'll come over when Larry gives me my lunch break."

"That's no fun. We should go now—the more the merrier." He swept his arm to include Mim and Officer Cooper.

"Thrilled," Mim said without conviction.

Susan pulled up at the same time as Rick Shaw.

Josiah watched them through the window. "I envy you, Harry. You're at the hub of Crozet—Grand Central."

"Hi," Susan called out.

Rick Shaw came in on her heels. "I need a buddy today when I ride," she said. "You're it, Harry."

"Okay—but I think we'll melt."

Rick ushered himself behind the counter and collected Boom Boom's papers from Officer Cooper. He made no attempt to hide this collection, but he didn't draw attention to it either. "Has she been a good girl?" He nodded in Harry's direction.

"Good as gold."

"Officer Cooper, how long are you going to shadow Harry? Will I

ever be able to have an intimate dinner with her?" Josiah empha-
sized the "intimate."

"Only if you do the cooking," came Cooper's swift reply.

"Where's Mrs. Murphy?" Susan inquired.

"Pouting in the mail bin," Harry said.

"Sheriff Shaw, would you like to see the shop before I open it?
You wouldn't know it was the same shop," Josiah persisted.

It wasn't. Harry dropped by after lunch. Well, after what started
out as lunch and ended up being an appetite killer. She zipped into
Crozet Pizza, only to behold Boom Boom and Fair in earnest conversation at a table. She was beginning to like Boom Boom more
and Fair less but she couldn't bear them together. She left without
even a slice of that famous pizza.

Maude's shop, transformed into a high-quality antiques show-
room, conveyed that sleek, urbane yet country mix that was Josiah's
forte. The packing materials were arranged in the back room and
even they looked inviting. Officer Cooper rummaged around. She
loved antiques.

"You're glum, sweetie. What's up?" Josiah sidled over to Harry.

"Oh, Fair and Boom Boom were at Crozet Pizza. It's silly for it to
hurt, but it does."

He curled his arm around her shoulders. "Harry, anyone who
ever died of love deserved it. There are other fish in the sea and
besides, you've wasted far too much time, far too much, on
Pharamond Haristeen."

"I guess."

Officer Cooper rested herself in a cushy wing chair to better
appreciate the discussion.

"It's a new day tomorrow, brighter and better." He turned to
Cooper. "You and I are going to be friends. You have exquisite taste,
I can see, but tell me, is my favorite postmistress really in danger?"

"I can't answer that."

Josiah pulled Harry even closer to him. "I wasn't born yesterday.
Mrs. Hogendobber certainly was packed off in great haste. If she's
on vacation, so to speak, and you've got a police dogsbody—pardon

me—that means the authorities are worried about her and you. Well, so am I."

Officer Cooper crossed her legs. "I know you've spoken to Rick but for my satisfaction, who do you think is the killer?"

"I don't know, which is so frustrating ... unless it was Mrs. Hogendobber and you've locked her up to keep the townies from lynching her. Mrs. H., a killer—unlikely, although she can kill a conversation faster than Limburger cheese."

"Any idea about motive?" Harry asked.

"Some sort of grudge, I should think."

"Why do you say that?" Officer Cooper shifted her position.

"He's humiliated the bodies, if you think about it. I think that bespeaks some kind of powerful emotion. Anger. Jealousy perhaps. Or he was spurned."

"You're such a romantic. I think it's over money, pure and simple." Harry folded her arms across her chest. "And the mutilation of the bodies is to keep us away from the real issue."

"Which is?" Josiah's eyebrows raised.

"Damned if I know." Harry threw up her hands.

"No. Damned if you do, because he would kill you—according to your analysis. According to my analysis you're perfectly safe."

"Let's hope you're right." Officer Cooper smiled up at Josiah.

37

Lolling under the crepe myrtle behind Maude's shop, Mrs. Murphy, Tucker, and Pewter waited for Harry to be released from her obligatory socializing.

Pewter batted at a red ant scooting through the grass. "Black ants are okay but these little red ones bite like blazes."

"Better than fleas." Mrs. Murphy lay on her back, her four legs in the air, tail straight out.

"Last year was the worst, the absolute worst." Tucker pricked her ears, then relaxed them. "Every week I was drenched with a bath, doused with flea killer, the worst."

"For me it was flea mousse. Harry doesn't like bathing me, for which I am grateful. But Pewter, this mousse smells like rancid raspberries and it's sticky. Rolling in dirt, grass, even rubbing against the bark of a tree does no good. This year I've been moussed once."

"Market embraces the concept of the flea collar. The first week the fumes were so intense my eyes watered. After that I figured out how to wriggle out of them. He's so slow it took four lost flea collars before he gave up."

"Do you like humans?" Tucker addressed Pewter.

"Not especially. A few I like. Most I don't" was her forthright reply.

"Why?" Mrs. Murphy twisted her head so she could better observe Pewter. She stayed on her back.

"You can't trust them. Hell's bells, they can't even trust each other. Take a cat, for instance. If you wander into another cat's territory, you know it right away. Unless there's an important reason to be there, you leave. The lines are clear. Nothing is clear with humans, not even mating. A human being will mate with another human being for social approval. They rarely sleep with the person who's right for them. But humans are much more like sheep than cats. They're easily led and they don't look where they're going until it's too late."

"They aren't all like sheep," Tucker responded.

"No, but I agree with Pewter—most of them are. Something terrible happened to the human race way back in time. They separated from nature. We live with a human who has some connection to the seasons, to other animals, but she's a country person. They're few and far between. And the further humans move from nature, the crazier they get. In the end it's what will destroy them."

"I don't give a damn if they die, every last one. I just don't want to go with them, if it's the bomb you're talking about." Pewter slashed her tail through the grass.

"The bomb's the least of it." Mrs. Murphy shook herself and sat up. "They'll kill the fish in the rivers and then the fish in the oceans. They'll wipe out more and more species of mammals. They won't have good water to drink after they kill the fish. They won't even have good air to breathe. If you don't have an adequate oxygen supply, how can you think clearly? Worse, they have no sense of when and how much to breed. Even a squirrel can read a bad acorn harvest and hold back breeding. A human can't read harvests. They keep reproducing. Do you know there are over five billion humans on the earth right now as I speak? They can't feed what they've got and they're breeding more."

"Plus they're breeding sick ones because they won't cull." Tucker's eyes were troubled. "Sick in body and sick in mind. If I have a weak puppy, I'll kill it. It's my obligation to the rest of the litter. They won't do that."

"Do it! My God, they scream murder, and when they have to raise taxes to pay for the criminal acts of the sick in mind, or pay for the increased care of the physically weak, they pitch a fit and fall in it. They just won't realize they're another animal and the laws of nature apply to them too." Pewter's pupils expanded.

"They think it's cruel. You know, Pewter, you are right. They are crazy. They won't kill a diseased newborn but they'll flock by the millions to kill one another in a war. Didn't *World War II* kill off about forty-five million of

them? *And World War I axed maybe ten million? It almost makes me laugh.*"
Mrs. Murphy watched Harry and Officer Cooper leave Maude's
shop by the back door. "*I don't much care if they die by the millions, truth
be told, but I don't want Harry to die.*"

Pewter trilled, a sound above a purr. "*Yeah, Harry's a brick. We
should make her an honorary cat.*"

"*Or an honorary dog,*" Tucker rejoined. "*She says that cats and dogs are
the lares and penates of a household, the protective household gods. Harry's big
on mythology but I fancy the comparison.*"

Harry and Officer Cooper walked over to the crepe myrtle.

"A kitty tea party." Harry scratched Pewter at the base of her tail.
Tucker licked her hand. "Excuse me, a kitty and doggie tea party.
Well, come on, troops. Back to work."

38

Bob Berryman prided himself on his physical prowess. Stronger in his early fifties than when he played football for Crozet High, he'd grown even more vain about his athletic abilities. Time's theft of speed made Berryman play smarter. He played softball and golf regularly. He was accustomed to dominating men and accepting deference from women. Maude Bly Modena didn't defer to him. If he thought about it, that was why he had fallen in love with her.

He thought about little else. He replayed every moment of their time together. He searched those recollections, fragments of conversation and laughter for clues. Far more painfully, he returned to the railroad tracks today. What was out here halfway between Crozet and Greenwood?

Immediately before her death, Maude had jogged this way. She took the railroad path once a week. She liked to vary her routes. Said it kept her fresh. She didn't run the railroad path more frequently than other jogging routes, though. He backtracked those also, with Ozzie at his heels.

Kelly and Maude had never seemed close to him. He drew a blank there. He reviewed every person in Crozet. Was she friendly to them? What did she truly think of them?

A searing wind whipped his thinning hair, a Serengeti wind, desert-like in its dryness. The creosote from the railroad tracks stank. Berryman shaded his eyes with his hand and scanned east toward town, then west toward the Greenwood tunnel.

She used to joke about Crozet's treasure, and given Maude's thoroughness, she'd read about Claudius Crozet. The engineer fascinated her. If she could only find the treasure she could retire. Retail was hard, she said, but then they shared that thought, since Berryman moved more stock trailers than anyone on the East Coast.

It wasn't until ten o'clock that evening, in the silence of his newly rented room, that Berryman realized the tunnel had something to do with Maude. Impulsively, driven by wild curiosity as well as grief, he hurried to his truck, flashlight in hand, Ozzie at his side, and drove out there.

The trek up to the tunnel, treacherous in the darkness on the overgrown tracks, had him panting. Ozzie, senses far sharper than his master's, smelled another human scent. He saw the dull glow at the lower edge of the tunnel where dappled light escaped through the foliage. Someone was inside the tunnel. He barked a warning to his master. Better he'd stayed silent. The light was immediately extinguished.

Berryman leaned against the sealed tunnel mouth to catch his breath. Ozzie heard the human slide through the heavy brush. He dashed after him. One shot put an end to Ozzie. The shepherd screamed and dropped.

Berryman, thinking of his dog before himself, ran to where Ozzie disappeared. He crashed through the brush and beheld the killer.

"You!"

Within one second he, too, was dead.

39

Rick Shaw, Dr. Hayden McIntire, and Clai Cordle and Diana Farrell of the Rescue Squad stared at Bob Berryman's body. He was seated upright behind the driver's wheel of his truck. Ozzie, also shot, lay beside him. Bob had been shot through the heart and once again through the head for good measure. In his breast pocket was a postcard of General Lee's tomb at Lexington, Virginia. It read, "Wish you were here." There was no postmark. His truck was parked at the intersection of Whitehall Road and Railroad Avenue, a stone's throw away from the post office, the train depot, and Market Shiflett's store. A farmer on his way to the acres he rented on the north side of town found the body at about quarter to five in the morning.

"Any idea?" Rick asked Hayden.

"Six hours. The coroner will be more exact but no more than six, perhaps a little less." Hayden thought his heart would break every time he looked at Ozzie. He and Bob had been inseparable in life and were now inseparable in death.

Rick nodded and reached into his squad car. Picking up the mobile phone, he commanded the switchboard to get him Officer Cooper.

A sleepy Cynthia Cooper soon greeted him.

"Coop. There's been another one. Bob Berryman. But this time the killer was in a hurry. He abandoned his usual *modus operandi*. No cyanide. He didn't have time to slice and dice the body either. He just left two bullet holes and a postcard. Stick to Harry. I'll talk to you later. Over and out."

40

Mrs. Murphy and Tucker learned the news from the town crier, Pewter. The fat gray cat, asleep in the store window, heard the truck in the near distance early that morning. Pewter was accustomed to hearing cars and trucks before dawn. After all, the drunks have to come home sometime; so do the lovers, and the farmers have to be up before dawn. Ozzie's death hit the animals like a bombshell. Was he killed protecting Berryman? Was he killed so he couldn't lead Rick Shaw to the murderer? Or was the murderer losing his marbles and going after animals too?

"*If only I'd known, I would have jumped on the ice cream case and seen who did this,*" Pewter moaned.

"*There was no way for you to know,*" Tucker comforted her.

"*Poor Ozzie.*" Mrs. Murphy sighed. The hyper dog had tried her patience but she didn't wish him dead.

Bedlam overtook the post office. Harry had time to adjust to this latest horror because Officer Cooper prepared her, but nobody was prepared for the onslaught of reporters. Even the *New York Times* sent down a reporter. Fortunately, Crozet had no hotels, so this swarm of media locusts had to nest in Charlottesville, rent cars, and drive west.

Rob Collier fought his way through a traffic jam to deliver his mail.

"Goddamn!" He chucked the bags on the floor, quickly shutting the door behind him as one reporter in a seersucker jacket tried to come through.

"Maybe we'd better bolt the windows," Harry remarked.

Mrs. Murphy, Tucker, and Pewter scratched at the back door. Officer Cooper let them in. "I think your children have relieved themselves. Pewter's in tow."

"*I refuse to stay in the market another minute!*" Pewter bitched loudly. "*You can't move in there.*"

Mrs. Murphy noted, "*You stayed long enough to push you mug in front of the TV cameras.*"

"*I did not! They chose to highlight me.*"

"Girls, girls, calm yourselves." Harry poured crunchies in a bowl for everyone and returned to the front.

Rob stared out the window. "I heard on the radio that the killer leaves a mark, a momento. That's how Rick knows it's the same fellow. Bob Berryman . . . well, ladies, at least he exited this life with speed."

Officer Cooper joined him at the window. "Strange country, isn't it?"

"We're more excited by bad news than by good news. Think these reporters would be here if you'd saved a child from drowning?"

"Locals, maybe. That's about it." He turned to Harry. "See you this afternoon. Might be late."

"Take care, Rob."

"Yeah. You too." He pushed open the front door and shut it quickly behind him, then sprinted for the truck.

The phone rang.

"Harry," the familiar voice rang out, "I just saw the *Today* show. Bob Berryman!"

"Mrs. Hogendobber, the world's gone mad," Harry said. "Don't come home. Whatever you do, stay put."

"The times. The morals. People have abandoned God, Harry—He hasn't abandoned us. It's time for a New Order."

"I always suspect that under a New Order, women will be kept in their old place."

"Feminism! You can think of feminism at a time like this?" Mrs. Hogendobber was both aghast and furious at being out of the center of events.

"I'm not talking about feminism but who runs your church. The women?" Harry would prefer to talk about anything but this latest murder. She was more frightened than she let on.

"No—but we contribute a great deal, Harry, a great deal."

"That's not the same thing as running the show or sharing in the power." Susan rapped on the window. Harry cradled the receiver between shoulder and ear and made a T for time sign with her hands. "Mrs. Hogendobber. I apologize. I'm so upset. The reporters have parachuted in. I'm taking it out on you. Forget everything I've said."

"Actually, I won't. You've given me something to think about," she uncharacteristically replied. Travel seemed to make Mrs. H. more liberal. "Now you watch out, hear?"

"I hear."

"I'll call tomorrow. Bye-bye."

Harry hung up the phone. Officer Cooper let Susan in.

"Jesus, Mary, and Joseph. If the killer has any heart maybe he'll fire on these reporters. What are we going to do? I had to walk over here. It's gridlock out there."

"You know"—Harry shoved a mail sack in Susan's direction; to hell with rules—"I think the killer is loving this."

Officer Cooper grabbed a mail bin. "I think so too."

"Well, I've got an idea." Harry motioned for Susan and Coop to get close. She whispered: "Let's give him a little zinger of our own. Let's put graveyard postcards in everyone's mailbox."

"You're kidding." Susan's hands involuntarily flew up to her chest as though to protect herself.

"No, I am not. No one knows about the postcards but me and you, and Rick and Coop. They know there's some telling sign, but they don't know what it is. Think Rick told anyone else?"

"Not yet," Coop answered.

"We won't scare anyone but the killer," Harry said. "He won't know who sent the postcard. But he'll know we're playing with him."

"You'd better damn well hope he doesn't figure out who we are." Susan folded her arms across her chest.

"If he does, I guess we'll fight it out," Harry replied.

"Harry, forget fighting. He'll blindside you." Coop's voice was low.

"Okay, okay, I shouldn't sound so cocky. He's killed three times. What's another one? But I think we can rattle his chain. Dammit, it's worth a try. Susan, will you buy the postcards? I know there are postcards of Jefferson's grave. Maybe you can find others."

"I'll do it, but I'm scared," Susan admitted.

41

Rick went through the roof. A third murder on his hands, the press tearing at him like horseflies, and Mary Minor Haristeen hit him with a crackbrained idea about postcards.

He screeched into Larry Johnson's driveway and slammed his squad car door so hard it was a wonder it didn't fall off. The retired doctor, tending his beloved pale yellow roses, calmly continued spraying. By the time Rick joined him he was somewhat calmed down.

"Larry."

"Sheriff. Bugs will take over the world, I swear it." The hand pump squished as the robust old man annihilated Japanese beetles. "What can I do for you? Tranquilizers?"

"God knows I need them." Rick exhaled. "Larry, I should have come to you before now. I hope I haven't offended you. It was natural to interview Hayden because he's practicing now, but you've known everybody and everything far longer than Hayden. I'm hoping you can help me."

"Hayden's a good man." Squish. Squish. "Ever hear that line about a new doctor means a bigger cemetery?"

"No, I can't say that I have."

"In Hayden's case it isn't true. He's catching on to our ways. Not like he's some Yankee. He was raised up in Maryland. Young man, bright future."

"Yes. We must be getting old, Larry, when thirty-eight seems young. Remember when it seemed ancient?"

Larry nodded and vigorously sprayed. "Banzai, you damned winged irritants! Go meet the Emperor." He had been a career Army physician in World War II and Korea before returning home to practice. His father, Lynton Johnson, practiced in Crozet before him.

"I'm going to ask you to break confidentiality. You don't have to, of course, but you're no longer practicing medicine, so perhaps it's not so bad."

"I'm listening."

"Did you ever see signs of anything unusual? Prescribe medications that might alter personality?"

"One time, I prescribed diet pills, back in the 1960's, to Miranda Hogendobber. My God, she talked nonstop for weeks. That was a mistake. Still only lost two pounds in two years. Mim suffers a nervous condition—"

"What kind of nervous condition?"

"This and that and who shot the cat. That woman had a list of complaints when she was still in the womb. Once through the vaginal portals, she was ready to proclaim them. What put her over the top was Stafford marrying that colored girl."

"Black, Larry."

"When I was a child that was a trash word. It's awful hard to change eighty years of training, you know, but all right, I stand corrected. That pretty thing was the best, the best thing that coulda happened to Stafford. She made a man out of him. Mim teetered perilously close to a nervous breakdown. I gave her Valium, of course."

"Could she be unstable enough to commit murder?" It occurred to Rick that Mim could have slashed her pontoon boat herself, so as to appear a target.

"Anyone could be if circumstances were right—or maybe I should say wrong—but no, I think not. Mim has settled down since then. Oh, she can be as mean as a snake shedding its skin but she's no longer dependent on Valium. Now the rest of us need it."

"Did you treat Kelly Craycroft?"

"I checked Kelly into the drug rehabilitation center."

"Well?"

"Kelly Craycroft was a fascinating son of a bitch. He recognized no law but his own, yet the man made sense. He had an addictive personality. Runs in the family."

"What about hereditary insanity? What family does that run in?"

" 'Bout ninety percent of the First Families of Virginia, I should say." A wicked grin crossed his face. The spraying slowed down.

"Gimme that. I'd like to knock off a couple." Rick attacked the beetles, their iridescent wings becoming wet with poison. A buzz, then a sputter, and then the bugs fell onto the ground, hard-backed shells making a light clinking noise. "What about Harry? Ever sick? Unstable?"

"Pulled out her back playing lacrosse in college. When it flared up I used to give her Motrin. I think Hayden still does. Harry's a bright girl who never found her profession. She seems happy enough. You don't think she's the killer, do you?"

"No." Rick rubbed his nose. The spray smelled disagreeable. "What do you think, Larry?"

"I don't think the person is insane."

"Fair Haristeen doesn't have an alibi for the nights of any of the killings . . . and he has a motive as regards Kelly. Since he lives alone now, he says there's no one to vouch for him."

Larry rubbed his brow. "I was afraid of that."

"What about cyanide? How hard is it to produce?" Rick pressed.

"Extremely hard, but a man with a medical background would have no trouble at all."

"Or a vet?"

"Or a vet. But any intelligent person who took a course in college chemistry can figure it out. Cyanide is a simple compound, cyanogen with a metal radical or an organic radical. Potassium cyanide shuts off your lights before you have time to blink. Painters, furniture strippers, even garage mechanics have access to chemicals that, properly distilled, could yield deadly results. You can do it in your kitchen sink." Larry watched the rain of dying beetles with satisfaction. "You know what this is all about, don't you?"

"No." Rick's voice rose high with curiosity.

"It's something right under our noses. Something we're used to seeing or passing every day, as well as someone we're used to seeing or passing. It's so much a part of our lives we no longer notice it. We've got to look at our community with new eyes. Not just the people, Rick, but the physical setup. Bob Berryman did. That's why he's dead."

42

Rick arrested Pharamond Haristeen III. He had no alibi. He was physically strong, highly intelligent, and possessed of expert medical knowledge. He bore a grudge against Kelly and vice versa. What he had against Maude Bly Modena, Rick wasn't sure, but if he did arrest him it would be an action soothing to the press and the public. It could also ruin Fair's life if he wasn't the killer. He weighed that fact but arrested him anyway. He had to play safe. He also said yes to Harry's plan. What did he have to lose, unless it was Harry? He issued her a revolver and no one except Cynthia Cooper knew Harry was now armed.

Mrs. Murphy sprawled on the butcher block in Harry's kitchen. Rhythmically, her tail flicked up and down. Tucker sat by Harry at the kitchen table. Harry, Susan, and Officer Cooper hunched over their postcards, writing again and again, "Wish you were here."

The phone rang. It was Danny for his mother. Susan grabbed the phone. "What is it this time?" She listened as he groaned that Dad had clicked off the TV in order to make him clean his room. Susan knew as she soaked up the litany of woes that having a teenaged child was aging her rapidly. Having a middle-aged husband sped up the process too. "Do as your father says." This was followed by a renewed outburst. "Danny, if I have to come home and negotiate between you and your father you are going to be grounded until Christmas!" Another howl. "I'll ground him, too, then. Go clean your room and don't bother me. I wouldn't be here if it wasn't important. Goodbye." Bang, she slammed the receiver down.

"Happy families," Harry said.

"Having a teenaged son isn't difficult. It's the combination of father and son that's difficult. Sometimes I think that Ned resents Danny growing stronger. He's already two inches taller than Ned."

"An old story." Cooper reached for another postcard. Dolley Madison's tombstone graced the front. "How many more of these to go?"

"About one hundred twenty-five. There are four hundred and two post boxes and we're on the home stretch."

"Why so few?" Susan asked.

"You want more?" Cooper was incredulous.

"No, I don't want more, but there are three thousand residents of Crozet, by my count."

"Rest of them didn't buy post boxes. Most of my people are right in town itself." Harry's index and middle fingers began to hurt.

As the three women continued to scribble Mrs. Murphy opened a cupboard and crawled in.

Tucker hated that she couldn't climb around like the cat. *"Don't go in there. I can't see you if you do."*

Mrs. Murphy stuck her head out. *"I like to smell the spices. There's an aromatic tea in here that reminds me of catnip."*

"Nothing up there that smells like a beef bone, I guess?"

"Bouillon cubes. They're in a package. I'll get them out." She examined the package. *"I'm sorry we couldn't sniff Bob Berryman. Wonder if that smell was on him?"*

"I doubt it. Bullet did him in. I've checked out everyone that comes into the post office just in case that smell would be on them—you know, like something in their work. Rob smells like gas and sweat. Market smells delicious. Mim drenches herself in that noxious perfume. Fair reeks of horses and medicine. Little Marilyn's hairspray makes my eyes water. Josiah smells like furniture wax plus his after-shave. Kelly smelled like concrete dust. Their smells are like their voices, individual."

"What does Harry smell like to you?"

"Us. Our scent covers her but she doesn't know it. I make sure to rub up against her and sit in her lap and so do you. Keeps other animals from getting ideas."

Harry glanced up and beheld Mrs. Murphy chewing the bouillon package. "Stop that." The cat jumped out of the cupboard before Harry reached her.

"Bet you get a bouillon cube." Mrs. Murphy winked.

"Well, this is useless," Harry fumed. She opened the package and gave Tucker one of the cubes Mrs. Murphy chewed. Brazenly, the tiger kitty sat on the counter. "Oh, here, dammit, you worked hard enough for it, but your manners are going to hell." Mrs. Murphy delicately took the cube from Harry's fingers.

"Last one!" Officer Cooper rejoiced.

"Now we'll see if the other shoe drops." Harry's eyes narrowed.

What dropped was Harry's jaw when she turned on the TV and saw Fair being led to jail. Damn Rick Shaw. He'd told nobody. Just let it come out on the eleven o'clock news.

She put on her shoes and dragged Cooper to the jail. Too late. Fair had been released. An alibi had been established, an alibi as upsetting to Harry as it was to Fair.

43

Ned puffed his pipe. At Harry's request, Officer Cooper waited in the living room with Susan. The murders were ghastly but this was painful.

Upon learning that Boom Boom freed Fair by confessing that he was with her on the night of Kelly's murder, as well as on the night of Maude's murder, Harry called Susan.

Logically, she knew it was absurd to be shaken. Her husband had been unfaithful. Millions of husbands are unfaithful. She knew, too, in her heart that this affair must have flourished before the separation. She would be divorcing him, affair or no affair, but when she learned the details at the jail she burst out crying. She couldn't help herself.

She called Ned. He told her to come right over.

"... irreconcilable differences. You can change that, of course, and now sue on grounds of adultery. You see, Harry, Virginia divorce law is, well, let's just say this isn't California. If you sue on grounds of adultery and the court finds in your favor, you won't have to divide up the monies you've acquired during the marriage."

"In other words, this is his punishment for fooling around." Harry's eyes got moist again.

"The law doesn't state punishment—"

"But that's what it is, isn't it? Suing on the grounds of adultery is an instrument of revenge." She sank back in the chair. Her head ached. Her heart ached.

Ned's words were measured. "In the hands of some lawyers and people, you might say it's an instrument of revenge."

After a long, deep pause Harry spoke with resolution and clarity. "Ned, it's bad enough that divorce in this town becomes public spectacle. This ... this adultery suit, well, that would turn spectacle into nightmare for me and a real three-ring circus for the Mim Sanburnes of the world. You know"—she glanced at the ceiling—"I can't even say that he's wrong. She has something I don't."

The friend in Ned overcame the lawyer. "She can't hold a candle to you, Harry. You're the best."

That made Harry cry again. "Thank you." When she'd regained her composure she continued. "What do I have to gain by hurting him because I'm hurt? I can't see anything in this but more money if I win, and my divorce isn't about money—it really is about irreconcilable differences. I'll stick with that. Sometimes, Ned, even with the best of intentions and the best people"—she smiled—"things just don't work out."

"You've got class, honey." Ned came over, sat on the edge of the chair, and patted her back.

"Maybe." She half laughed. "On the odd occasion, I'm capable of acting like a reasonable adult. I want to put this behind me. I want to go on with my life."

44

Like clockwork, Mrs. Hogendobber called for her gossip bulletin at seven forty-five the next morning. Pewter visited from next door. The post boxes, filled, awaited their owners, and when the door opened at 8:00 A.M., Harry and Officer Cooper acted normal. Well, they thought they were normal but Officer Cooper positioned herself so she could see the boxes. Harry burned off energy in giving Mrs. Murphy, Pewter, and even Tucker rides in the mail bin.

Danny Tucker arrived first, scooped out the mail, and didn't go through it. "Sorry I didn't get to see you last night. Mom said you had business with Dad."

"Yeah. We got things straightened out."

Just then Ned Tucker bounded up the steps. "Hello, everyone." He gave Harry a big smile, then noticed the mail in his son's hands. "I'll take that." He rapidly flipped through it, blinked when he saw the postcard, read it, and said aloud, "That's Susan's handwriting. What's she up to now?"

Harry hadn't thought of that. They should have assigned names. She wondered who else would recognize their handwriting.

"Dad, I've been really good and there's a party tonight—"

"The answer is no."

"Ah, come on. I could be dead by Halloween."

"That's not funny, Dan." Ned opened the door. "Harry, I will relieve you of our presence." Ned unceremoniously ushered his protesting son outside.

"Are you a regular letter writer?" Harry asked Coop.

"No. What about you?"

"Not much. We bombed that one."

"Let's hope he doesn't say anything except to Susan. Wonder what she'll tell him."

Market was next. He sorted out his mail and tossed the junk mail, including the postcard, into the trash. "Damn crap."

"Doesn't sound like you, Market." Harry forced her voice to be light.

"Business is booming but I'd rather make less and have peace of mind. If one more reporter or sadistic tourist tramps into my store, I think I'll paste them away. One newspaper creep leered at my daughter and had the gall to invite her to dinner. She's fourteen years old!"

"Remember *Lolita*," Harry said.

"I don't know anyone named Lolita and if I did I'd tell her to change her name." He stalked out.

"*I'm not going home until he's in a better mood*," Pewter remarked to her companions.

"*So far, Harry's idea has been a bust*." Mrs. Murphy licked her paw.

Fair sheepishly came in. "Ladies."

"Fair," they replied in tandem.

"Uh, Harry—"

"Later, Fair. I haven't got the strength to hear it now." Harry cut him off.

He went to his post box and yanked out the mail.

"What the hell is this?" He walked over to Harry and handed her the postcard.

"A pretty picture of Jefferson's marker."

" 'Wish you were here,' " Fair read aloud. "Maybe Tom thinks I should join him. Well, plenty of others do now; I guess I've made a mess of it." He skidded the card down the counter. "If T.J. returned to Albemarle County today, he'd die to get away from it."

"Why do you say that?" Officer Cooper asked.

"People come to worship at the shrine. I mean, the man stood for progressive thought, politically, architecturally. We haven't progressed since he died."

"You sound like Maude Bly Modena," Harry observed.

"Do I? I guess I do."

"Guess you'll be dating Boom Boom out in the open now."

Fair glared at Harry. "That was a low blow." He stormed out.

"Jesus, it isn't even ten in the morning. Wonder who else we can offend?" Officer Cooper laughed.

"It's the tension, and all those reporters keep rubbing the wound raw. And . . . I don't know. The air feels heavy, like before a storm."

Reverend Jones, Clai Cordle, Diana Farrell, and Donna Eicher picked up their mail. Nothing much came of that. Donna also got Linda Berryman's mail for her.

Once the post office was empty again, Harry remarked, "We were probably tasteless to put a card in Linda Berryman's box."

"In this case, the end justifies the means and the meanness."

Hayden McIntire dropped by. He, too, left without examining his mail.

Boom Boom Craycroft, however, caught the meaning immediately as she put her mail into three piles: personal, business, junk. "This is attractive." She handed the postcard to Harry. "Is this what you wish for me now?"

"I got one too," fibbed Harry.

"Sick humor." Boom Boom's lips curled. "These murders flush out every weirdo we've got. Sometimes I think all of Crozet is weird. What are we doing festering here like a pimple on the butt of the Blue Ridge Mountains? Poor Claudius Crozet. He deserved better." She paused and then said to Harry: "Well, I guess you deserve better, too, but I can't bring myself to apologize. I don't feel guilty."

As she walked out an astonished Harry noticed Mrs. Murphy heading for the stamp pads. Quickly she sped toward them and snapped them shut. Mrs. Murphy trotted right by them as though they were of no concern to her, and wasn't Harry silly? This upheaval over Boom Boom and Fair had upset the cat too. She hated seeing Harry suffer.

The name Crozet fired a nerve in Harry's brain. "Cooper, if I found the buried treasure would I have to pay income tax on it?"

"We even pay death duties in this country. Of course you'd have to pay."

"She may be getting it at last." Mrs. Murphy pranced.

"Getting what?" Pewter hated being left out of things, so Tucker filled her in.

"The profits in Maude's ledger. Maybe they involved selling the treasure in bits and pieces."

"You're soft as a grape." Cooper smiled. "But it's as good an explanation as any other. This doesn't address the small, trifling fact that the tunnels are sealed shut. Rock, debris, concrete. Poor Claudius. I'd be more worried about him returning than Thomas Jefferson. Imagine coming back and seeing your life's work, a world-class engineering feat, sealed up and forgotten."

"Let's go up there after work."

"Yeah—okay."

Just then Mim, Little Marilyn, and bodyguard entered the building. Josiah, like a well-groomed terrier, was at their heels.

Mother and daughter, strained with each other, cast a pall over the room. Josiah discreetly sorted his mail at the counter while the two women spoke in low tones.

The low tone erupted as Mim yanked the mail from Little Marilyn's hands. "I'll do it."

"I can sort the mail as easily as you can."

"You're too slow." Mim frantically flipped through the mail. The postcard barely dented her consciousness. She was looking for something else.

"Mother, give me my mail!"

Josiah read his postcard, Dolley Madison's tomb. He smiled at Harry. "Is this one of your jokes?"

"I'll give you your mail in a moment." The cords stood out on Mim's neck.

Little Marilyn, face empurpled, backhanded her mother's hands, and the mail flew everywhere. Mrs. Murphy leaped on the counter to watch, as did Pewter. Tucker, behind the counter, begged to go into the front and Harry opened the door for her. She sat by the stamp machine and watched.

"I know what you're looking for, Mother, and you won't find it."

Mim pretended to be in control and bent down to pick up wedding invitation replies. Josiah, leaving his mail on the counter, joined her. "Why don't you get some fresh air, Mim? I'll do this."

"I don't need fresh air. I need a new daughter."

"Fine. Then you won't have *any* children," Little Marilyn screamed at her. "You're looking for a letter from Stafford. You won't find one, Mother, because I didn't write him." Little Marilyn paused for breath and dramatic effect. "I called him."

"You what?" Mim leaped up so quickly the blood rushed from her head.

"Mim, darling—" Josiah attempted to calm her. She pushed him off.

"You heard me. I called him. He's my brother and I love him and if he's not coming to my wedding, then you aren't coming either. I'm the one getting married. Not you."

"Don't you dare speak to me like that."

"I'll speak to you any way I like. I've done everything you've ever asked of me. I attended the right schools. I played the appropriately feminine sports—you know, Mother, the ones where you don't sweat. Excuse me—glow. I made the right friends. I don't even like them! They're boring. But they're socially correct. I'm marrying the right man. We'll have two blond children and they'll go to the right schools, play the right sports *ad nauseam*. I am getting off the merry-go-round. Now. If you want to stay on, fine. You won't know you aren't going anywhere until you're dead." Little Marilyn shook with fury, which was slowly subsiding into relief and even happiness. She was doing it at long last. She was fighting back.

Harry, hardly breathing, wanted to cheer. Officer Cooper's eyes about popped out of her head. So this was the way the upper class behaved? The public display would eventually upset Mim more than the raw emotions.

"Darling, let's discuss this elsewhere. Please." Josiah gently cupped Mim's elbow. She allowed him to guide her this time.

"Little Marilyn, we'll talk about this later."

"No. There's nothing to talk about. I am marrying Fitz-Gilbert Hamilton. Excitement is not his middle name, but he's a good man and I honestly hope we make it, Mother. I would like to be happy, even if only for one day in my life. You are invited to my wedding. My brother's wife will be my matron of honor."

"Oh, my *Gawd!*" Mim fainted.

45

It wasn't until the diminishing hours of sunlight, the spreading of coppery-rich long shadows, about seven in the evening, that Harry understood what really happened in the post office.

Josiah and Officer Cooper revived Mim. Little Marilyn left. Whatever sorrow she might feel over her mother's acute distress was well hidden. Mim had caused her enough distress over the years. If she fainted in the post office and cracked her head, so be it.

When Mim came to, with the bodyguard shoving amyl nitrite under her nostrils, she said, "I don't fit here anymore. My life's like an old dress."

For a brief moment Harry pitied her.

Josiah tended to Mim, walking her to his shop.

People poured in and out of the post office for the rest of the day. Harry and Officer Cooper barely had time to go to the bathroom, much less think.

The thinking came later, in the oppressive heat redolent with the green odor of vegetation, as the two women, armed, climbed the grade on the old track up to the Greenwood tunnel. Mrs. Murphy and Tucker refused to stay in the parked car far below. They, too, panted.

"People hauled timbers up here. Even with mules, this was a bitch."

"The old tracks run to the tunnel. Crozet built serving roads and tracks before—" Harry stopped. A yellow swallowtail butterfly twirled before her and winged off.

"Is this one of your jokes? Coop . . . Coop! Josiah said that to me after reading his card."

"So what? Ned recognized Susan's handwriting. 'Wish you were here' fizzled."

"Don't you see? The killer knows that apart from the sheriff, I'm the one who recognized the postcard signal. I'm the one who ran to Mrs. Hogendobber even before your people got to her. I see the mail first. He slipped. It's him! Jesus Christ, Josiah DeWitt. I like him. How can you like a murderer?"

Officer Cooper's face, taut, registered the information. "Well, if there is someone in that tunnel, we're sitting ducks."

"Like Kelly Craycroft's poster." Harry's mind raced. "I don't know how long it will take him to realize what he's done."

"Not long. Our people are everywhere. He may not be able to leave his shop early. When he does he'll come for you."

"He doesn't know where I am."

"Then he'll come up here in the night if there really is anything here, or he'll slip away. I don't know what he'll do but he's not fearful."

The closed mouth of the tunnel, wreathed in kudzu, loomed before them.

"Let's go." Harry pressed on.

Cooper, mental radar scanning, cautiously stepped up to the mouth. Harry, paces behind, checked out the top of the tunnel. It would be rough going, coming up behind the tunnel. In fact, it would take hours, but it could be done.

The tunnel mouth was indeed sealed shut. Only dynamite would open it.

"Look for Paddy's rabbit hole." Mrs. Murphy and Tucker fanned out.

Nose to the ground, Tucker smelled the faintest remains of Bob and Ozzie. "Ozzie and Berryman were here."

Mrs. Murphy nodded. "Paddy's got to be right. If Berryman came up here, there is a treasure!" She raced ahead of the corgi while Harry and Coop tiptoed along the mouth of the tunnel.

Hidden behind the foliage, there was a small hole at the base of

the tunnel. A rabbit could easily go in and out of it. So could Mrs. Murphy.

"Don't go in there," Tucker warned. "We'll do it together."

"Okay. I'll go first. My eyes are better." Mrs. Murphy slipped through the hole. "Holy shit!"

"Are you all right?" Tucker, half in and half out of the hole, was digging for all she was worth.

"Yes." Mrs. Murphy ran back to her buddy. "Can you see yet?"

"Barely." Tucker blinked and blinked but she felt in a sea of India ink.

Slowly her eyes adjusted and she saw the treasure. It wasn't Claudius Crozet's treasure, but it was a king's ransom in paintings, Louis XV furniture, carpets painstakingly rolled in heavy protective covers. Mrs. Murphy soared onto a Louis XV desk. A golden casket rested atop it. She lifted up the lid with one paw. Old, expensive jewelry glistened inside. Near the mouth of the tunnel rested an old railroad handcart. A huge bombé cabinet was on it.

"Get Harry."

Tucker dashed to the rabbit hole and barked.

"Where's the dog?" Officer Cooper glanced around. "Sounds like she's inside the tunnel. That's impossible."

Harry pulled away brush, kudzu, and vine to reach the farthest right-hand corner of the tunnel. Tucker barked at her feet. "There's a rabbit hole. Tucker, come out of there."

Officer Cooper got down on her hands and knees. A black, wet nose twitched. "Come on, pooch."

"You come in here," Tucker replied.

"They won't fit." Mrs. Murphy joined her. "Let's go out. There has to be another way in."

Tucker grunted her way out and Mrs. Murphy danced out. Tucker jumped up at Harry. Mrs. Murphy circled her human friend. Harry understood. She crouched down, then lay flat on her belly as Cooper stepped out of the way. "There's something in there. I need a flashlight."

Cooper lay down. She cupped her hands around her eyes as

Harry moved so she could get a better look. "Antiques. I can't see how much but I see a big chest of drawers."

Harry leaped up and ran her hands along the tunnel mouth. Cooper joined her. Harry knocked on the right-hand side of the sealed mouth. It sounded hollow.

"Epoxy and resin. Makes sense now, doesn't it?" Harry said. "That furniture was not squeezed through the rabbit hole unless Josiah has Alice in Wonderland potions. Must be a trigger or a latch some- where. I bet Kelly loved making this. I wonder how long it took him?"

"Working nights, I don't know, a couple of months. A month. I've got it." Coop found a thick vine covering a latch. The vine, kudzu, was affixed to the false front. The natural foliage grew around it.

With a click the door opened, large enough to get a railroad lorry through. The two women entered the tunnel. Mrs. Murphy and Tucker scurried inside.

"There's a fortune in here," Harry whispered.

Tucker's ears went up. Mrs. Murphy froze.

"*Don't bark, Tucker. He knows the humans are here but he doesn't know we are. Whine. Give Harry a warning.*"

Tucker whined, softly. Harry leaned over to pat her. "*Mommy, please pay attention,*" the dog cried.

"*Hide, Tuck, hide.*" Mrs. Murphy jumped from a desk to the top of a wardrobe near the doorway. Tucker hid behind the lorry.

Harry felt their fear. "Cooper, Cooper," she whispered and grabbed Cynthia's arm. "Something's wrong."

Cooper pulled her pistol. Harry did too.

A light footfall played on their ears. Inside the tunnel, sounds were magnified and distorted in the 536 feet of rock. Harry crept to the right side of the opening. She stood on the other side of the lorry. Cooper remained in the deep shadows to the left.

A familiar, charming voice reached them. Josiah was too smart to appear in the opening. "I underestimated you, Harry. Never under- estimate a woman. Officer Cooper, I know you're armed. I suggest you toss out your weapon. No reason to defile Claudius Crozet's handiwork with bloodshed—especially mine." Cooper kept silent.

"If you don't toss out your weapon I'm going to throw in this gasoline-soaked rag and just the tiniest Molotov cocktail I happen to have with me for the evening's enjoyment. I also have a gun, as I guess you know. It's Kelly's. When ballistics files its report on Bob Berryman, it will frustrate that stellar public servant Rick Shaw, and tell him Bob was killed with a dead man's gun. It's nasty dying in a fire and if you run out I'll be forced to shoot you. If you throw out your weapon, Officer Cooper, perhaps we can make a deal. Something more lucrative than your vast public salaries—both of you."

"What was the deal you made with Kelly? Or Maude?" Harry's voice, sharp and hard, reverberated through the tunnel.

"Kelly enjoyed excellent terms, but after four years at twenty percent he got a little greedy. As you can see, there's enough stockpiled in the tunnel that I could dispense with his services for the future. When my inventory runs low I shall find another feckless fellow eager for profit."

"You used his paving enterprise."

"Of course."

"And his trucks."

"Harry, don't try my patience with the obvious. Officer Cooper, throw out your gun."

"First, I want to know why you killed Maude. It's obvious what she did, too."

"Maudie was a dear woman but her ovaries ruled her head, I fear. You see, she really was in love with Bob Berryman. When business reasons compelled me to remove Kelly Craycroft from our board of directors, she didn't want to be an accessory to murder."

"Was she?"

"No. But she became frightened. What if I were caught and what if our profitable venture were disclosed? Berryman, stringing her along, kept telling her he would leave Linda, and Maude loved that cretin. A shaky partner is worse than no partner at all. She could have given us away, or worse, she could have spilled the beans to Bob Berryman—pillow talk—who with his amusing sense of honor would have traipsed directly to the authorities. You see, poor Maude had to go. Now, darlings, I've indulged you long enough. Throw out the gun."

"Did you try to drown Mrs. Hogendobber?" Harry wanted to keep him talking. She had no plan, but it gave her time to think.

"No. Throw out your gun."

Harry dropped her voice to the gossip register, a tone she prayed would be irresistible to Josiah. "Well, if you didn't slash those pontoons, who did?"

He laughed. "I think it was Little Marilyn. A real passive-aggressive, our Little Marilyn. She didn't go for help until she realized that two of the ladies on Mim's yacht couldn't swim. She just wanted to ruin her mother's party. I can't prove it, but that's what I think." He laughed again. "I would have given anything to have seen that boat sink. Mim's face must have been fuchsia." He paused. "Okay, enough chat. Really, there's no point in anyone's being hurt. Just cooperate."

"Well, how did you get your victims to eat cyanide?"

"You are prolonging this." Josiah sighed. "I simply poured cyanide on a handkerchief, pretending it was cologne, and quickly put it over their mouths! Presto! An instant dead person. Now get with the program, girls."

Harry intoned. "You didn't have to mutilate them."

"An artist's touch." He sniggered.

"One more teeny-weeny question." Harry gulped for air. Her voice was steely calm in the suffocating atmosphere. "I know you brought the goods up here in a lorry, but where did you get them in the first place?"

Josiah hooted. "That's the best part, Harry. Mim Sanburne! I've been her 'walker' for years. The finest homes. New York, Newport, Palm Beach, Richmond, Charleston, Savannah, wherever there is an elegant party, a must gathering. I'd appraise the merchandise and then one or two years later, voilà—I'd return for an engagement of a different sort. No engraved invitations. That was the easy part. You bribe a servant—the rich are notoriously cheap, you know. Pay someone enough to live on for a year and a one-way ticket to Rio. How simple to get in when the master and mistress were gone. The hard part was lifting the lorry off the track and rolling it inside the tunnel each time we were finished—that and trying to stay awake the next day. We never had to work that hard, though. Perhaps three houses a year. Distribution is easy once the fuss dies down. A small load to Wilmington or Charlotte. A side trip to Memphis. Wouldn't snooty Mim just die? She looks down her long nose at thee and me, yet she's consorting with a criminal—an elegant criminal."

"Big profits, huh?"

"Ah, yes, sweet are the workings of capitalism—a lesson you've never learned, my girl. Now, time's up." His voice, hypnotic, promised all would be well. This was just a glorious lark.

Harry edged closer to the mouth and in pantomime to Coop said that she would throw out her gun. Cooper nodded. Mrs. Murphy fluffed her tail, ready to strike.

"You won't toss in that Molotov cocktail. The fire would ruin your inventory. The smoke and commotion would bring all of Crozet up here to the tunnel. Now that would spoil everything. If we're going into business, we'd better trust one another right now. You throw down your gun first and Officer Cooper will throw out hers."

"Don't take me for a fool, Harry. I'm not throwing down my gun first," he snapped.

"You're the creative one, Josiah. Think of something," Harry taunted him. "You can starve us out but Rick Shaw will notice you're missing. That won't do. We'd better reach an agreement now."

"You drive a hard bargain."

"Never underestimate the power of a woman," Harry mocked. "I'd hate for one of us to kill the other, because you couldn't remove the body until the middle of the night, and in this flaming heat the corpse will start to stink in two to three hours. That's disagreeable."

"Quite so," came Josiah's clipped response. "What would you do if you killed me?"

"What you did to Maude. Then I'd wait a year, and Coop and I would sell off your stash. Oh, we don't have your contacts, Josiah, but I'm sure we'd make some kind of profit." She lied through her teeth.

"Don't be an ass! With me you can make a fortune. By yourself, you'll get caught."

"I got this far, didn't I?"

A long silence followed. The unlit Molotov cocktail was placed at the opening. Josiah's hand quickly withdrew.

"Proof positive of what a saint I am. There's the Molotov cocktail."

"Josiah"—Harry hoped to keep him talking—"how did you fake the postmarks?"

"My latent artistic impulses surged to the fore." He smiled. "I've got waxes, inks, stains, bits of ormolu, you name it, to repair the furniture. I mixed up a color and then tapped the postmark letters with old typeface. The inscription came compliments of my computer. I thought the postcards a flourish. I rather relished the picture of poor Rick Shaw's face as he tried to make sense of it—once he realized the postcards were a signature. You realized quite quickly. I was terribly impressed."

"But not scared?"

"Me? Never."

"Your gun." Harry's voice made the demand sound like a social request.

"What about Coop? Is she really in there? I want to hear her voice. How do I know you haven't killed her?" Josiah made a demand of his own. What he wanted was to hear where she was.

"Here." Cooper nodded to Harry. She then swiftly moved to stand right beneath Mrs. Murphy. Tucker put her front paws on the lorry.

Harry, on Coop's signal, said, "On the count of three, you throw down your gun. She'll throw down hers. One ... two ... three." She tossed out her gun as Josiah threw his in the opening.

He had a second gun. He didn't waste time. He bolted into the tunnel, firing randomly. Mrs. Murphy jumped, claws at the ready, onto his head. Then slid to his back. Tucker, on her hind legs, pushed the lorry, which, despite its slow pace, knocked him off balance when it bumped into him. Tucker then bit his gun hand as he stumbled to the tunnel floor, his knee hitting a steel rail. Josiah lifted his gun hand, the dog still hanging on his wrist, and aimed straight for Harry, who dropped and rolled. Mrs. Murphy hung on his back, digging into him full force. Cooper, with deliberate precision and trained self-control, fired once. Josiah grunted as the bullet sank into his torso with a thud. He fired wildly. Cooper fired one more shot. Between the eyes. He twitched and was dead.

"Tucker!" Harry rushed to the dog, bruised but wagging her tail.

Cooper scooped up Mrs. Murphy as she walked over to Harry. She kissed the kitty, whose fur still stood straight up. "Bless you, Mrs. Murphy." She reached down and felt for Josiah's pulse. She dropped his arm as if it were rotten meat. "Harry, if these two hadn't thrown him off balance he would have hit one of us. His gun was on rapid fire. The tunnel isn't that wide. He was no dummy, except for his little slip in the post office."

Harry sat on the moist earth, Tucker licking the tears from her face. Mrs. Murphy stood on her hind legs, her front paws wrapped around Harry's neck. Harry rubbed her cheek against Mrs. Murphy's soft fur.

"It's a funny thing, Cooper. I didn't think about myself. I thought about these two. If he had hurt Mrs. Murphy or Tucker, I would have killed him with my bare hands if I could have. My mind was perfectly composed and crystal-clear."

"You've got guts, Harry. I was armed. You threw out your gun to sucker him in."

"He wouldn't have come in otherwise. I don't know—maybe he would have. God, it seems like a dream. What a cunning son of a bitch. He had two guns."

Cooper frisked the body. "And a stiletto."

46

Mrs. Hogendobber rapturously returned on the day following Harry's shoot-out with Josiah. The media had a field day with the heroic postmistress, her valiant cat and gallant dog, as well as stalwart Officer Cooper, so cool under fire. Harry found the hoopla almost as bad as being trapped in the tunnel.

Rick Shaw, fully briefed on the engagement with Josiah DeWitt, never mentioned in his prepared statement that Josiah's entry into wealthy homes was on Mim Sanburne's arm. Naturally, all of Crozet knew it, as well as Mim's rich friends, but at least that detail wasn't splashed across America. Jim secretly relished that his wife's snobbery had been her undoing, and he was thrilled to be rid of Josiah.

Pewter envied her friends terribly and ate twice as much to make up for being denied stardom.

Fair and Boom Boom dated. No promises were made yet. They struggled to find some equilibrium amid the torrid gossip concerning them. Harry went from being the tough wife who threw out her husband to the innocent victim—in public, but not Harry's, opinion.

Susan got Harry to take up golf for relaxation. Harry wasn't certain that it relaxed her, but it began to obsess her.

Little Marilyn and Mim made up, sort of. Mim had brains enough to know that she would never dominate her daughter again.

On schedule, Rob brought the mail and picked it up. Harry kept reading postcards. Lindsay Astrove returned from Europe, sorry to have missed the drama. Jim Sanburne and the town council of Crozet decided to make money from the scandal. They offered tours of the tunnel. Tourists rode up in handcarts. A nice booklet on the life of Claudius Crozet was printed and sold for $12.50.

Life returned to normal, whatever that is.

Crozet was an imperfect corner of the world with rare moments of perfection. Harry, Mrs. Murphy, and Tucker witnessed one of them on a crisp September day.

Harry looked out the post office window and saw Stafford Sanburne, with his beautiful wife, step off the train. He was greeted by Mim and Little Marilyn. He had a big smile on his face. So did Harry.

Afterword

I hope you enjoyed my first crime novel. Tell my publishers if you did. Maybe they'll give me an advance for another one.

Uh-oh, I hear footsteps in the hall.

"Sneaky Pie, what is this in my typewriter?"

Rest in Pieces

To the Beegles
and their dalmations

Cast of Characters

Mary Minor Haristeen (Harry), the young postmistress of Crozet, whose curiosity almost kills the cat and herself

Mrs. Murphy, Harry's gray tiger cat, who bears an uncanny resemblance to authoress Sneaky Pie and who is wonderfully intelligent!

Tee Tucker, Harry's Welsh corgi, Mrs. Murphy's friend and confidant; a buoyant soul

Pharamond Haristeen (Fair), veterinarian, formerly married to Harry

Boom Boom Craycroft, a high-society knockout

Blair Bainbridge, a handsome model and fugitive from the fast lane in Manhattan. He moves to Crozet for peace and quiet and gets anything but

Mrs. George Hogendobber (Miranda), a widow who thumps her own Bible!

Market Shiflett, owner of Shiflett's Market, next to the post office

Pewter, Market's fat gray cat, who, when need be, can be pulled away from the food bowl

Susan Tucker, Harry's best friend, who doesn't take life too seriously until her neighbors get murdered

Ned Tucker, a lawyer and Susan's husband

Jim Sanburne, mayor of Crozet

Big Marilyn Sanburne (Mim), queen of Crozet and an awful snob

Little Marilyn Sanburne, daughter of Mim, and not as dumb as she appears

Fitz-Gilbert Hamilton, Little Marilyn's husband, is rich by marriage and in his own right. His ambition sapped, he's content to live very well and be a "gentleman lawyer"

Cabell Hall, a trusted figure in Crozet, is preparing to retire from the bank where he is president

Ben Seifert, Cabell Hall's protégé, has come a long way from a callow teller to a bank officer. He was a year ahead of Harry in high school

Rick Shaw, Albemarle sheriff

Cynthia Cooper, police officer

Rob Collier, mail driver

Paddy, Mrs. Murphy's ex-husband, a saucy tom

Simon, an opossum with a low opinion of humanity. He slowly succumbs to Harry's kindness. He lives in the barn-loft along with a crabby owl and a hibernating black snake

Dear Reader:

Here's to catnip and champagne!

Thanks to you my mailbox overflows with letters, photos, mousie toys, and crunchy nibbles. Little did I think when I started the Mrs. Murphy series that there would be so many cats out there who are readers . . . a few humans, too.

Poor Mother, she's trying not to be a grouch. She slaves over "important themes" disguised as comedy and I dash along with a mystery series and am a hit. This only goes to prove that most cats and some dogs realize that a lighthearted approach is always the best. Maybe in a few decades Mom will figure this out for herself.

The best news is that I was able to afford my own typewriter. I found a used IBM Selectric III so I don't have to sneak into Mother's office in the middle of the night. I even have my own office. Do you think I should hire Pewter as a secretary?

Again, thank you, cats out there, and the dogs, too. Take care of your humans. And as for you humans, well, a fresh salmon steak would be a wonderful treat for the cat in your life.

All Best,

SNEAKY PIE

1

Golden light poured over the little town of Crozet, Virginia. Mary Minor Haristeen looked up from the envelopes she was sorting and then walked over to the large glass window to admire the view. It seemed to her as if the entire town had been drenched in butter. The rooftops shone; the simple clapboard buildings were lent a pleasing grace. Harry was so compelled by the quality of the light that she threw on her denim jacket and walked out the back door. Mrs. Murphy, Harry's tiger cat, and Tee Tucker, her corgi, roused themselves from a drowsy afternoon slumber to accompany her. The long October rays of the sun gilded the large trotting-horse weathervane on Miranda Hogendobber's house on St. George Avenue, seen from the alleyway behind the post office.

Brilliant fall days brought back memories of hotly contested football games, school crushes, and cool nights. Much as Harry loathed cold weather, she liked having to buy a new sweater or two.

At Crozet High she had worn a fuzzy red sweater one long-ago October day, in 1973 to be exact, and caught the eye of Fair Haristeen. Oak trees transformed into orange torches, the maples turned blood-red, and the beech trees became yellow, then as now. Autumn colors remained in her memory, and this would be that kind of fall. Her divorce from Fair had been final six months ago, or was it a year? She really couldn't remember, or perhaps she didn't want to remember. Her friends ransacked their address books for the names of eligible bachelors. There were two: Dr. Larry Johnson, the retired, widowed town doctor, who was two years older than God, and the other, of course, was Pharamond Haristeen. Even if she wanted Fair back, which she most certainly did not, he was embroiled in a romance with Boom Boom Craycroft, the beautiful thirty-wo-year-old widow of Kelly Craycroft.

Harry mused that everyone in town had nicknames. Olivia was Boom Boom, and Pharamond was Fair. She was Harry, and Peter Shiflett, who owned the market next door, was called Market. Cabell Hall, president of the Allied National Bank in Richmond, was Cab or Cabby; his wife of twenty-seven years, Florence, was dubbed Taxi. The Marilyn Sanburnes, senior and junior, were Big Marilyn, or Mim, and Little Marilyn respectively. How close it made everyone feel, these little monikers, these tokens of intimacy, nicknames. Crozet folks laughed at their neighbors' habits, predicting who would say what to whom and when. These were the joys of a small town, yet they masked the same problems and pain, the same cruelties, injustice, and self-destructive behavior found on a larger scale in Charlottesville, fourteen miles to the east, or Richmond, seventy miles beyond Charlottesville. The veneer of civilization, so essential to daily life, could easily be dissolved by crisis. Sometimes it didn't even take a crisis: Dad came home drunk and beat the living shit out of his wife and children, or a husband arrived home early from work to his heavily mortgaged abode and found his wife in bed with another man. Oh, it couldn't happen in Crozet but it did. Harry knew it did. After all, a post office is the nerve center of any community and she knew, usually before others, what went on when the doors were closed and the lights switched off. A flurry of legal letters might cram a box, or a strange medley of dental bills, and as Harry sorted the mail she would piece together the stories hidden from view.

If Harry understood her animals better, then she'd know even more, because her corgi, Tee Tucker, could scurry under porch steps, and Mrs. Murphy could leap into a hayloft, a feat the agile tiger cat performed both elegantly and with ease. The cat and dog carried a wealth of information, if only they could impart it to their relatively intelligent human companion. It was never easy, though. Mrs. Murphy sometimes had to roll over in front of her mother, or Tee Tucker might have to grab her pants leg.

Today the animals had no gossip about humans or their own kind. They sat next to Harry and observed Miranda Hogendobber— clad in a red plaid skirt, yellow sweater, and gardening gloves— hoe her small patch, which was producing a riot of squash and pumpkins. Harry waved to Mrs. Hogendobber, who returned the acknowledgment.

"Harry," Susan Tucker, Harry's best friend, called from inside the post office.

"I'm out back."

Susan opened the back door. "Postcard material. Picture perfect. Fall in central Virginia."

As she spoke the back door of the market opened and Pewter, the Shifletts' fat gray cat, streaked out, a chicken leg in her mouth.

Market shouted after the cat, "Damn you, Pewter, you'll get no supper tonight." He started after her as she headed toward the post office, glanced up, and beheld Harry and Susan. "Excuse me, ladies, had I known you were present I would not have used foul language."

Harry laughed. "Oh, Market, we use worse."

"*Are you going to share?*" Mrs. Murphy inquired of Pewter as she shot past them.

"*How can she answer? Her mouth is full,*" Tucker said. "*Besides, when have you known Pewter to give even a morsel of food to anybody else?*"

"That's a fact." Mrs. Murphy followed her gray friend, just in case.

Pewter stopped just out of reach of a subdued Market, now chatting up the ladies. She tore off a tantalizing hunk of chicken.

"How'd you get that away from Market?" Mrs. Murphy's golden eyes widened.

Ever ready to brag, Pewter chewed, yet kept a paw on the drumstick. "He put one of those barbecued chickens up on the counter. Little Marilyn asked him to cut it up and when his back was turned I made off with a drumstick." She chewed another savory piece.

"Aren't you a clever girl?" Tucker sniffed that delicious smell.

"As a matter of fact I am. Little Marilyn hollered and declared she wouldn't take a chicken that a cat had bitten into, and truthfully, I wouldn't eat anything Little Marilyn had touched. Turning into as big a snot as her mother."

With lightning speed Mrs. Murphy grabbed the chicken leg as Tucker knocked the fat kitty off balance. Mrs. Murphy raced down the alleyway into Miranda Hogendobber's garden, followed by a triumphant Tucker and a spitting Pewter.

"Give me that back, you striped asshole!"

"You never share, Pewter," Tucker said as Mrs. Murphy ran between the rows of cornstalks, moving toward the moonlike pumpkins.

"Harry," Mrs. Hogendobber bellowed, "these creatures will be the death of me yet."

She brandished her hoe in the direction of Tucker, who ran away. Now Pewter chased Mrs. Murphy up and down the rows of squash but Mrs. Murphy, nimble and fit, leapt over a wide, spreading squash plant with its creamy yellow bounty in the middle. She headed for the pumpkins.

Market laughed. "Think we could unleash Miranda on the Sanburnes?" He was referring to Little Marilyn and her equally distasteful maternal unit, Mim.

That made Susan and Harry laugh, which infuriated Mrs. Hogendobber because she thought they were laughing at her.

"It's not funny. They'll ruin my garden. My prize pumpkins. You know I'm going to win at the Harvest Fair with my pumpkins." Miranda's face turned puce.

"I've never seen that color on a human being before." Tucker stared up in wonderment.

"Tucker, watch out for the hoe," Mrs. Murphy yelled. She dropped the drumstick.

Pewter grabbed it. The fat swung under her belly as she shot back toward home, came within a whisker's length of Market and skidded sideways, evading him.

He laughed. "If they want it that bad I might as well bring over the rest of the chicken."

By the time he was back with the chicken, Mrs. Hogendobber, huffing and puffing, had plopped herself at the back door of the post office.

"Tucker could have broken my hip. What if she'd knocked me over?" Mrs. Hogendobber warmed to the scenario of damage and danger.

Market bit his tongue. He wanted to say that she was well padded enough not to worry. Instead he clucked sympathy while cutting meat off the chicken for the three animals, who hastily forgave one another any wrongdoing. Chicken was too important to let ego stand in the way.

"I'm sorry, Mrs. Hogendobber. Are you all right?" Harry asked politely.

"Of course I'm all right. I just wish you could control your charges."

"What you need is a corgi," Susan Tucker volunteered.

"No, I don't. I took care of my husband all my life and I don't need a dog to care for. At least George brought home a paycheck, bless his soul."

"They're very entertaining," Harry added.

"What about the fleas?" Mrs. Hogendobber was more interested than she cared to admit.

"You can have those without a dog," Harry answered.

"I do not have fleas."

"Miranda, when the weather's warm, everyone's got fleas," Market corrected her.

"Speak for yourself. And if I ran a food establishment I would make sure there wasn't a flea within fifty yards of the place. Fifty yards." Mrs. Hogendobber pursed her lips, outlined in a pearlized red that matched the red in her plaid skirt. "And I'd give more discounts."

"Now, Miranda." Market, having heard this *ad nauseam*, was prepared to launch into a passionate defense of his pricing practices.

An unfamiliar voice cut off this useless debate. "Anyone home?"

"Who's that?" Mrs. Hogendobber's eyebrows arched upward.

Harry and Susan shrugged. Miranda marched into the post office. As her husband, George, had been postmaster for over forty years before his death, she felt she could do whatever she wanted. Harry was on her heels, Susan and Market bringing up the rear. The animals, finished with the chicken, scooted in.

Standing on the other side of the counter was the handsomest man Mrs. Hogendobber had seen since Clark Gable. Susan and Harry might have chosen a more recent ideal of virility, but whatever the vintage of comparison, this guy was drop-dead gorgeous. Soft hazel eyes illuminated a chiseled face, rugged yet sensitive, and his hair was curly brown, perfectly cut. His hands were strong. Indeed, his entire impression was one of strength. On top of well-fitted jeans was a watermelon-colored sweater, the sleeves pushed up on tanned, muscular forearms.

For a moment no one said a word. Miranda quickly punctured the silence.

"Miranda Hogendobber." She held out her hand.

"Blair Bainbridge. Please call me Blair."

Miranda now had the upper hand and could introduce the others. "This is our postmistress, Mary Minor Haristeen. Susan Tucker, wife of Ned Tucker, a very fine lawyer should you ever need one, and Market Shiflett, who owns the store next door, which is very convenient and carries those sinful Dove bars."

"*Hey, hey, what about us?*" The chorus came from below.

Harry picked up Mrs. Murphy. "This is Mrs. Murphy, that's Tee Tucker, and the gray kitty is Pewter, Market's invaluable assistant, though she's often over here picking up the mail."

Blair smiled and shook Mrs. Murphy's paw, which delighted Harry. Mrs. Murphy didn't mind. The masculine vision then leaned over and patted Pewter's head. Tucker held up her paw to shake, which Blair did.

"I'm pleased to meet you."

"*Me, too,*" Tucker replied.

"May I help you?" Harry asked as the others leaned forward in anticipation.

"Yes. I'd like a post box if one is available."

"I have a few. Do you like odd numbers or even?" Harry smiled. She could be charming when she smiled. She was one of those fine-looking women who took few pains with herself. What you saw was what you got.

"Even."

"How does forty-four sound? Or thirteen—I almost forgot I had thirteen."

"Don't take thirteen." Miranda shook her head. "Bad luck."

"Forty-four then."

"Thirty-four ninety-five, please." Harry filled out the box slip and stamped it with pokeberry-colored ink, a kind of runny maroon.

He handed over the check and she handed over the key.

"Is there a Mrs. Bainbridge?" Mrs. Hogendobber brazenly asked. "The name sounds so familiar."

Market rolled his eyes heavenward.

"No, I haven't had the good fortune to find the right woman to—"

"Harry's single, you know. Divorced, actually." Mrs. Hogendobber nodded in Harry's direction.

At that moment Harry and Susan would have gladly slit her throat.

"Mrs. Hogendobber, I'm sure Mr. Bainbridge doesn't need my biography on his first visit to the post office."

"On my second, perhaps you'll supply it." He put the key in his pocket, smiled, and left, climbing into a jet-black Ford F350 du-ally pickup. Mr. Bainbridge was prepared to do some serious hauling in that baby.

"Miranda, how could you?" Susan exclaimed.

"How could I what?"

"You know what." Market took up the chorus.

Miranda paused. "Mention Harry's marital status? Listen, I'm older than any of you. First impressions are important. He might not have such a good first impression of me but I bet he'll have one of Harry, who handled the situation with her customary tact and humor. And when he goes home tonight he'll know there's one pretty unmarried woman in Crozet." With that astonishing justification she swept out the back door.

"Well, I'll be damned." Market's jaw hung slack.

"*That's what I say.*" Pewter cackled.

"Girls, I'm going back to work. This was all too much for me." Market laughed and opened the front door. He paused. "Oh, come on, you little crook."

Pewter meowed sweetly and followed her father out the door.

"*Can you believe Rotunda could run that fast?*" Tucker said to Mrs. Murphy.

"*That was a surprise.*" Mrs. Murphy rolled over on the floor, revealing her pretty buff underbelly.

"*This fall is going to be full of surprises. I feel it in my bones.*" Tucker smiled and wagged her stumpy tail.

Mrs. Murphy gave her a look. The cat was not in the mood for prophecy. Anyway, cats knew more of such things than dogs. She didn't feel like confirming that she thought Tucker was right. Something *was* in the air. But what?

Harry placed the check in the drawer under the counter. It was face up and she peered down at it again. "Yellow Mountain Farm."

"There is no Yellow Mountain Farm." Susan bent over to examine the check.

"Foxden."

"What? That place has been empty for over a year now. Who would buy it?"

"A Yankee." Harry closed the door. "Or someone from California."

"No." Susan's voice dropped.

"There is nothing else for sale around Yellow Mountain except Foxden."

"But, Harry, we know everything, and we haven't heard one word, one measly peep, about Foxden selling."

Harry was already dialing the phone as Susan was talking. "Jane Fogleman, please." There was a brief pause. "Jane, why didn't you tell me Foxden had sold?"

Jane, from the other end of the line, replied, "Because we were instructed to keep our mouths shut until the closing, which was at nine this morning at McGuire, Woods, Battle and Boothe."

"I can't believe you'd keep it from us. Susan and I just met him."

"Those were Mr. Bainbridge's wishes." Jane held her breath for a moment. "Did you ever see anything like him? I mean to tell you, girl."

Harry fudged and sounded unimpressed. "He's good-looking."

"Good-looking? He's to die for!" Jane exploded.

"Let's hope no one has to do that," Harry remarked drily. "Well, you told me what I wanted to know. Susan says hello and we'll be slow to forgive you."

"Right." Jane laughed and hung up.

"Foxden." Harry put the receiver in the cradle.

"God, we had some wonderful times at that old farm. The little six-stall barn and the gingerbread on the house and oh, don't forget, the cemetery. Remember the one really old tombstone with the little angel playing a harp?"

"Yeah. The MacGregors were such good people."

"Lived forever, too. No kids. Guess that's why they let us run all over the place." Susan felt old Elizabeth MacGregor's presence in the room. An odd sensation and not rational but pleasant, since Elizabeth and Mackie, her husband, were the salt of the earth.

"I hope Blair Bainbridge has as much happiness at Foxden as the MacGregors did."

"He ought to keep the name."

"Well, that's his business," Harry replied.

"Bet Miranda gets him to do it." Susan took a deep breath.

"You've got yourself a new neighbor, Sistergirl. Aren't you dying of curiosity?"

Harry shook her head. "No."

"Liar."

"I'm not."

"Oh, Harry, get over the divorce."

"I am over the divorce and I'm not majoring in longing and desire, despite all your hectoring for the last six months."

"You can't keep living like a nun." Susan's voice rose.

"I'll live the way I want to live."

"There they go again," Tucker observed.

Mrs. Murphy nodded. "Tucker, want to go over to Foxden tonight if we can get out of the house? Let's check out this Bainbridge guy. I mean, if everyone's going to be pushing Mom at him we'd better get the facts."

"Great idea."

2

By eleven that night Harry was sound asleep. Mrs. Murphy, dexterity itself, pulled open the back door. Harry rarely locked it and tonight she hadn't shut it tight. It required only patience for the cat, with her clever claws, to finally swing the door open. The screen door was a snap. Tucker pushed it open with her nose, popping the hook.

For October the night was unusually warm, the last flickering of Indian summer. Harry's old Superman-blue Ford pickup rested by the barn. Ran like a top. The animals trotted by the truck.

"*Wait a minute.*" Tucker sniffed.

Mrs. Murphy sat down and washed her face while Tucker, nose to the ground, headed for the barn. "*Simon again?*"

Simon, the opossum, enjoyed rummaging around the grounds. Harry often tossed out marshmallows and table scraps for him. Simon made every effort to get these goodies before the raccoons arrived. He didn't like the raccoons and they didn't like him.

Tucker didn't reply to Mrs. Murphy's question but ducked into the barn instead. The smell of timothy hay, sweet feed, and bran swirled around her delicate nostrils. The horses stayed out in the evenings and were brought inside during the heat of the day. That system would only continue for about another week because soon enough the deep frosts of fall would turn the meadows silver, and the horses would need to be in during the night, secure in their stalls and warmed by their Triple Crown blankets.

A sharp little nose stuck out from the feed room. "Tucker."

"Simon, you're not supposed to be in the feed room." Tucker's low growl was censorious.

"The raccoons came early, so I ran in here." The raccoons' litter proved Simon's truthfulness. "Hello, Mrs. Murphy." Simon greeted the sleek feline as she entered the barn.

"Hello. Say, have you been over to Foxden?" Mrs. Murphy swept her whiskers forward.

"Last night. No food over there yet." Simon focused on his main concern.

"We're going over for a look."

"Not much to see 'ceptin for the big truck that new fellow has. That and the gooseneck trailer. Looks like he means to buy some horses because there aren't any over there now." Simon laughed because he knew that within a matter of weeks the horse dealers would be trying to stick a vacuum cleaner hose in Blair Bainbridge's pockets. "Know what I miss? Old Mrs. MacGregor used to pour hot maple syrup in the snow to make candy and she'd always leave some for me. Can't you get Harry to do that when it snows?"

"Simon, you're lucky to get table scraps. Harry's not much of a cook. Well, we're going over to Foxden to see what's cooking." Tucker smiled at her little joke.

Mrs. Murphy stared at Tucker. She loved Tucker but sometimes she thought dogs were really dumb.

They left Simon munching away on a bread crust. As they crossed the twenty acres on the west side of Harry's farm they called out to Harry's horses, Tomahawk and Gin Fizz, who neighed in reply.

Harry had inherited her parents' farm when her father died years ago. Like her parents, she kept everything tiptop. Most of the fence lines were in good repair, although come spring she would need to replace the fence along the creek between her property and Foxden. Her barn had received a fresh coat of red paint with white trim this year. The hay crop flourished. The bales, rolled up like giant shredded wheat, were lined up against the eastern fence line. All totaled, Harry kept 120 acres. She never tired of the farm chores and probably was at her happiest on the ancient Ford tractor, some thirty-five years old, pulling along a harrow or a plow.

Getting up at five-thirty in the morning appealed to her except in darkest winter, when she did it anyway. The outdoor chores took so much of Harry's free time that she wasn't always able to keep up with the house. The outside needed some fresh paint. She and Susan had painted the inside last winter. Mrs. Hogendobber even came out to help for a day. Harry's sofa and chairs, oversized, needed to be reupholstered. They were pieces her mother and father had bought at an auction in 1949 shortly after they were married. They figured the furniture had been built in the 1930's. Harry didn't much care how old the furniture was but it was the most comfortable stuff she'd ever sat in. Mrs. Murphy and Tucker could lounge unrestricted on the sofa, so it had their approval.

A small, strong creek divided Harry's land from Foxden. Tucker scrambled down the bank and plunged in. The water was low. Mrs. Murphy, not overfond of water, circled around, revved her motors, and took a running leap, clearing the creek and Tucker as well.

From there they raced to the house, passing the small cemetery on its knoll. A light shone out from a second-story window into the darkness. Huge sweet gum trees, walnuts, and oaks sheltered the frame dwelling, built in 1837 with a 1904 addition. Mrs. Murphy climbed up the big walnut tree and casually walked out onto a branch to peer into the lighted room. Tucker bitched and moaned at the base of the tree.

"Shut up, Tucker. You'll get us both chased out of here."

"Tell me what you see."

"Once I crawl back down, I will. How do we know this human doesn't have good ears? Some do, you know."

Inside the lighted room Blair Bainbridge was engaged in the dirty job of steaming off wallpaper. Nasty strips of peony paper, the blossoms a startling pink, hung down. Every now and then Blair would put down the steamer and pull on the paper. He wore a T-shirt, and little bits of wallpaper stuck to his arms. A portable CD player, on the other side of the room, provided some solace with Bach's Brandenburg Concerto Number One. No furniture or boxes cluttered the room.

Mrs. Murphy backed down the tree and told Tucker that there wasn't much going on. They circled the house. The bushes had been trimmed back, the gardens mulched, the dead limbs pruned off trees. Mrs. Murphy opened the back screen door. The back porch had two director's chairs and an orange crate for a coffee table. The old cast-iron boot scraper shaped like a dashsund still stood just to the left of the door. Neither cat nor dog could get up to see in the back door window.

"Let's go to the barn," Tucker suggested.

The barn, a six-stall shed row with a little office in the middle, presented nothing unusual. The stall floors, looking like moon craters, needed to be filled in and evened out. Blair Bainbridge would sweat bullets with that task. Tamping down the stalls was worse than hauling wheelbarrows loaded with clay and rock dust. Cobwebs hung everywhere and a few spiders were finishing up their winter preparations. Mice cleaned out what grain remained in the feed room. Mrs. Murphy regretted that she didn't have more time to play catch.

They left the barn and inspected the dually truck and the gooseneck, both brand new. Who could afford a new truck and trailer at the same time? Mr. Bainbridge wasn't living on food stamps.

"We didn't find out very much," Tucker sighed. "Other than the fact that he has some money."

"We know more than that." Mrs. Murphy felt a bite on her shoulder. She dug ferociously. "He's independent and he's hard-working. He wants the place to look good and he wants horses. And there's no woman around, nor does there seem to be one in the picture."

"You don't know that." Tucker shook her head.

"There's no woman. We'd smell her."

"Yeah, but you don't know that one might not visit. Maybe he's fixing up the place to impress her."

"No. I can't prove it but I feel it. He wants to be alone. He listens to thoughtful music. I think he's getting away from somebody or something."

Tucker thought Mrs. Murphy was jumping to conclusions, but she kept her mouth shut or she'd have to endure a lecture about how cats are mysterious and how cats know things that dogs don't, ad nauseam.

As the two walked home they passed the cemetery, the wrought-iron fence topped with spearheads marking off the area. One side had fallen down.

"Let's go in." Tucker ran over.

The graveyard had been in use by Joneses and MacGregors for nearly two hundred years. The oldest tombstone read: CAPTAIN FRANCIS EGBERT JONES, BORN 1730, DIED 1802. A small log cabin once stood near the creek, but as the Jones family's fortunes increased they built the frame house. The foundation of the log cabin still stood by the creek. The various headstones, small ones for children, two of whom were carried off by scarlet fever right after the War Between the States, sported carvings and sayings. After that terrible war a Jones daughter, Estella Lynch Jones, married a MacGregor, which was how MacGregors came to be buried here, including the last occupants of Foxden.

The graveyard had been untended since Mrs. MacGregor's death. Ned Tucker, Susan's husband and the executor of the estate, rented out the acres to Mr. Stuart Tapscott for his own use. He had to maintain what he used, which he did. The cemetery, however, contained the remains of the Jones family and the MacGregor family, and the survivors, not Mr. Tapscott, were to care for the grounds. The lone descendant, the Reverend Herbert Jones, besieged by ecclesiastical duties and a bad back, was unable to keep up the plot.

It appeared things were going to change with Blair Bainbridge's arrival. The tombstones that had been overturned were righted, the grass was clipped, and a small camellia bush was planted next to Elizabeth MacGregor's headstone. The iron fence would take more than one person to right and repair.

"*Guess Mr. Bainbridge went to work in here too,*" Mrs. Murphy remarked.

"*Here's my favorite.*" Tucker stood by the marker of Colonel Ezekiel Abram Jones, born in 1812 and died in 1861, killed at First Manassas. The inscription read: BETTER TO DIE ON YOUR FEET THAN LIVE ON YOUR KNEES. A fitting sentiment for a fallen Confederate who paid for his conviction, yet ironic in its unintentional parallel to the injustice of slavery.

"*I like this one.*" Mrs. Murphy leapt on top of a square tombstone with an angel playing a harp carved on it. This belonged to Ezekiel's wife, Martha Selena, who lived thirty years beyond her husband's demise. The inscription read: SHE PLAYS WITH ANGELS.

The animals headed back home, neither one discussing the small graveyard at Harry's farm. Not that it wasn't lovely and well kept, containing her ancestors, but it also contained little tombstones for the beloved family pets. Mrs. Murphy and Tucker found that a sobering possibility on which they refused to dwell.

They slipped into the house as quietly as they had left it, with both animals doing their best to push shut the door. They were only partially successful, the result being that the kitchen was cold when Harry arose at five-thirty, and the cat and dog listened to a patch of blue language, which made them giggle. Discovering that the hook had been bent on the screen door called forth a new torrent of verbal abuse. Harry forgot all about it as the sun rose and the eastern sky glowed peach, gold, and pink.

Those extraordinarily beautiful October days and nights would come back to haunt Harry and her animal friends. Everything seemed so perfect. No one is ever prepared for evil in the face of beauty.

3

"He has not only the absence of fear but of all scruple." Mrs. Hogen-dobber's alto voice vibrated with the importance of her story. "Well, I was shocked completely when I discovered that Ben Seifert, branch manager of our local bank, indulges in sharp business practices. He tried to get me to take out a loan on my house, which is paid for, Mr. Bainbridge. He said he was sure I needed renovations. 'Renovate what?' I said, and he said wouldn't I be thrilled with a modern kitchen and a microwave? I don't want a microwave. They give people cancer. Then Cabby Hall, the president, walked into the bank and I made a beeline for him. Told him everything and he took Ben to task. I only tell you this so you'll be on your guard. This may be a small town but our bankers try to sell money just like those big city boys do, Mr. Bainbridge. Be on your toes!" Miranda had to stop and catch her breath.

"Please do call me Blair."

"Then to top it off, the choir director of my church walked into the bank to inform me that he thought Boom Boom Craycroft had asked Fair Haristeen to marry her, or perhaps it was vice versa."

"His vice was her versa." Blair smiled, his bright white teeth making him even more attractive.

"Yes, quite. As it turned out, no proposal had taken place." Mrs. Hogendobber folded her hands. She didn't cotton to having her stories interrupted but she was blossoming under the attention of Blair Bainbridge—doubly sweet, since Susan Tucker and Harry could see his black truck parked alongside Mrs. Hogendobber's house. Of course she was going to walk him through her garden, shower him with hints on how to achieve gargantuan pumpkins, and then bestow upon him the gifts of her green thumb. She might even find out something about him in the process. Some time ago Mrs. Hogendobber had borrowed some copies of New York magazine from Ned Tucker, for the crossword puzzles. After meeting Blair the other day, she had realized why his name was familiar: She had read about him in one of those magazines. There was an article about high-fashion romance. When he introduced himself, the name had seemed vaguely familiar. She was hoping to find out more today about his link to the article, his ill-fated relationship with a beautiful model named Robin Mangione.

The doorbell rang, destroying her plan. The Reverend Herbert Jones marched through the door when Mrs. Hogendobber opened it.

Now this curdled the milk in her excellent coffee. Mrs. Hogendobber felt competitive toward all rival prophets of Christianity. The Right Reverend Jones was minister of the Lutheran Church. His congregation, larger than hers at the Church of the Holy Light, served only to increase her efforts at conversion. The church used to be called The Holy Light Church, but two months ago Miranda had prevailed upon the preacher and the congregation to rename it the Church of the Holy Light. Her reasons, while serviceable, proved less convincing than her exhausting enthusiasm, hence the change.

A cup of coffee and fresh scones were served to Reverend Jones, and the three settled down for more conversation.

"Mr. Bainbridge, I want to welcome you to our small community and to thank you for fixing up my family's cemetery. Due to disc problems, I have been unable to discharge my obligations to my forebears as they deserve."

"It was my pleasure, Reverend."

"Now, Herbie"—Miranda lapsed into familiarity—"You can't lure Mr. Bainbridge into your fold until I've had a full opportunity to tell him about our Church of the Holy Light."

Blair stared at his scone. A whiff of brimstone emanated from Mrs. Hogendobber's sentence.

"This young man will find his own way. All paths lead to God, Miranda."

"Don't try to sidetrack me with tolerance," she snapped.

"I'd never do that." Reverend Jones slipped in that dig.

"I can appreciate your concern for my soul." Blair's baritone caressed Mrs. Hogendobber's ears. "But I'm sorry to disappoint you both. The fact is I'm a Catholic, and while I can't say I agree with or practice my faith as strictly as the Pope would wish, I occasionally go to Mass."

The Reverend laid down his scone, dripping with orange marmalade made by Mrs. Hogendobber's skilled hands. "A Lutheran is just a Catholic without the incense."

This made both Blair and his hostess laugh. The Reverend was never one to allow dogma to stand in the way of affection and often, in the dead of night, he himself found little solace in the rigors of doctrine. Reverend Jones was a true shepherd to his flock. Let the intellectuals worry about transubstantiation and the Virgin Birth—he had babies to baptize, couples to counsel, the sick to succor, and burials to perform. He hated that latter part of his calling but he prayed to himself that the souls of his flock would go to God, even the most miserable wretches.

"If you don't mind my asking, Reverend, how did you find out about the cemetery being mowed?" Blair wondered.

"Oh, Harry told me this morning as she walked in to work. Said her little doggie dashed over there as she was doing her chores and she caught her in the cemetery."

"She walks to work?" Blair was incredulous. "It has to be two miles at least, one way."

"Oh, yes. She likes the exercise. By the time she gets to the post office she's already put in a good two to three hours of farm chores. A born farmer, Harry. In the bones. She'll make a good neighbor."

"Which brings me to the subject of your renaming your place Yellow Mountain Farm." Mrs. Hogendobber composed herself for what she thought would be a siege of argument.

"It's at the base of Yellow Mountain and so I naturally—"

She interrupted him. "It's been Foxden since the beginning of the eighteenth century and I'm surprised Jane Fogleman did not inform you, as she is normally a fountain of information."

The Reverend shrewdly took a pass on this one, even though the land in question was part of his heritage. He hadn't the money to buy it nor the inclination to farm it, so he thought he had little right to tell the man what to call his purchase.

"That long?" Blair thought a moment. "Maybe Jane did mention it."

"Did you read your deed?" Mrs. Hogendobber demanded.

"No, I let the lawyers do that. I've tried to wrestle some order out of the place though."

"Pokeweeds," the Reverend calmly said as he downed another scone.

"Is that what you call them?"

"In polite company." Herbie laughed.

"Herbert, you are deliberately sidetracking this discussion, which, for the sake of the Historical Society of Greater Crozet, I must conduct."

"Mrs. Hogendobber, if it means that much to you and the Historical Society, I will of course keep the name of Foxden."

"Oh." Mrs. Hogendobber hadn't expected to win so easily. It rather disappointed her.

The Reverend Jones chuckled to himself that the Crozet Historical Society sometimes became the Crozet Hysterical Society but he was glad the old farm would keep its name.

Both gentlemen rose to go and she forgot to give Blair one of her pumpkins, a lesser specimen because she was saving the monster pumpkin for the Harvest Fair.

Blair walked with Reverend Jones to his church and then bade him goodbye, turning back to the post office. He passed a vagrant wearing old jeans and a baseball jacket and walking along the railroad track. The man appeared ageless; he could have been thirty or fifty. The sight startled him. Blair hadn't expected to see someone like that in Crozet.

As Blair pushed open the post office door Tucker rushed out to greet him. Mrs. Murphy withheld judgment. Dogs needed affection and attention so much that in Mrs. Murphy's estimation they could be fooled far more easily than a cat could be. If she'd given herself a minute to think, though, she would have had to admit she was being unfair to her best friend. Tucker's feelings about people hit the bull's-eye more often than not. Mrs. Murphy did allow herself a stretch on the counter and Blair came over to scratch her ears.

"Good afternoon, critters."

They replied, as did Harry from the back room. "Sounds like my new neighbor. Check your box. You've got a pink package slip."

As Blair slipped the key into the ornate post box he called out to Harry, "Is the package pink too?"

The sound of the package hitting the counter coincided with Blair's shutting his box. A slap and a click. He snapped his fingers to add to the rhythm.

Harry drawled, "Musical?"

"Happy."

"Good." She shoved the package toward him.

"Mind if I open this?"

"No, you'll satisfy my natural curiosity." She leaned over as Little Marilyn Sanburne flounced through the door accompanied by her husband, who sported new horn-rimmed glasses. Fitz-Gilbert Hamilton devoured Esquire and GQ. The results were as one saw.

"A bum on the streets of Crozet!" Little Marilyn complained.

"What?"

Little Marilyn pointed. Harry came out from behind the counter to observe the scraggly, bearded fellow, his face in profile. She returned to her counter.

Fitz-Gilbert said, "Some people have bad luck."

"Some people are lazy," declared Little Marilyn, who had never worked a day in her life.

She bumped into Blair when she whirled around to behold the wanderer one more time.

"Sorry. Let me get out of your way." Blair pushed his carton over to the side of the counter.

Harry began introductions.

Fitz-Gilbert stuck out his hand and heartily said, "Fitz-Gilbert Hamilton. Princeton, 1980."

Blair blinked and then shook his hand. "Blair Bainbridge. Yale, 1979."

That caught Fitz-Gilbert off guard for a moment. "Before that?"

"St. Paul's," came the even reply.

"Andover," Fitz-Gilbert said.

"I bet you boys have friends in common," Little Marilyn added—without interest, since the conversation was not about her.

"We'll have to sit down over a brew and find out." Fitz-Gilbert offered. He was genuinely friendly, while his wife was merely correct.

"Thank you. I'd enjoy that. I'm over at Foxden."

"We know." Little Marilyn added her two cents.

"Small town. Everybody knows everything." Fitz-Gilbert laughed.

The Hamiltons left laden with mail and mail-order catalogues.

"Crozet's finest." Blair looked to Harry.

"They think so." Harry saw no reason to disguise her assessment of Little Marilyn and her husband.

Mrs. Murphy hopped into Blair's package.

"Why don't you like them?" Blair inquired.

"It helps if you meet Momma. Big Marilyn—or Mim."

"Big Marilyn?"

"I kid you not. You've just had the pleasure of meeting Little Marilyn. Her father is the mayor of Crozet and they have more money than God. She married Fitz-Gilbert a year or so ago in a social extravaganza on a par with the wedding of Prince Charles and Lady Di. Didn't Mrs. Hogendobber fill you in?"

"She allowed as how everyone here has a history which she would be delighted to relate, but the Reverend Jones interrupted her plans, I think." Blair started to laugh. The townspeople were nothing if not amusing and he liked Harry. He had liked her right off the bat, a phrase that kept circling in his brain although he didn't know why.

Harry noticed Mrs. Murphy rustling in Blair's package. "Hey, hey, out of there, Miss Puss."

In reply Mrs. Murphy scrunched farther down in the box. Only the tips of her ears showed.

Harry leaned over the box. "Scram."

Mrs. Murphy meowed, a meow of consummate irritation.

Blair laughed. "What'd she say?"

"Don't rain on my parade," Harry replied, and to torment the cat she placed the box on the floor.

"No, she didn't," Tucker yelped. "She said, 'Eat shit and die.' "

"Shut up, Fuckface," Mrs. Murphy rumbled from the depths of the carton, the tissue paper crinkling in a manner most exciting to her ears.

Tucker, not one to be insulted, ran to the box and began pulling on the flap.

"Cut it out," came the voice from within.

Now Tucker stopped and stuck her head in the box, cold nose right in Mrs. Murphy's face. The cat jumped straight up out of the box, turned in midair, and grabbed on to the dog. Tucker stood still and Mrs. Murphy rolled under the dog's belly. Then Tucker raced around the post office, the cat dangling underneath like a Sioux on the warpath.

Blair Bainbridge bent over double, he was laughing so hard.

Harry laughed too. "Small pleasures."

"Not small—large indeed. I don't know when I've seen anything so funny."

Mrs. Murphy dropped off. Tucker raced back to the box. "I win."

"Do you have anything fragile in there?" Harry asked.

"No. Some gardening tools." He opened the box to show her. "I ordered this stuff for bulb planting. If I get right on it I think I can have a lovely spring."

"I've got a tractor. It's near to forty years old but it works just fine. Let me know when you need it."

"Uh, well, I wouldn't know what to do with it. I don't know how to drive one," Blair confessed.

"Where are you from, Mr. Bainbridge?"

"New York City."

Harry considered this. "Were you born there?"

"Yes, I was. I grew up on East Sixty-fourth."

A Yankee. Harry decided not to give it another minute's thought. "Well, I'll teach you how to drive the tractor."

"I'll pay you for it."

"Oh, Mr. Bainbridge." Harry's voice registered surprise. "This is Crozet. This is Virginia." She paused and lowered her voice. "This is the South. Someday, something will turn up that you can do for me. Don't say anything about money. Anyway, that's what's wrong with Little Marilyn and Fitz-Gilbert. Too much money."

Blair laughed. "You think people can have too much money?"

"I do. Truly, I do."

Blair Bainbridge spent the rest of the day and half the night thinking about that.

4

The doors of the Allied National Bank swung open and the vagrant breezed past Marion Molnar, past the tellers. Marion got up and followed this apparition as he strolled into Benjamin Seifert's office and shut the door.

Ben, a rising star in the Allied National system, a protégé of bank president Cabell Hall, opened his mouth to say something just as Marion charged in behind the visitor.

"I want to see Cabell Hall," he demanded.

"He's at the main branch," Marion said.

Protectively Ben rose and placed himself between the unwashed man and Marion. "I'll take care of this."

Marion hesitated, then returned to her desk as Ben closed the door. She couldn't hear what was being said but the voices had a civil tone.

Within a few minutes Ben emerged with the man in the baseball jacket.

"I'm giving the gentleman a lift." He winked at Marion and left.

5

The dew coated the grass as Harry, Mrs. Murphy, and Tucker walked along the railroad track. The night had been unusually warm again and the day promised to follow suit. The slanting rays of the morning drenched Crozet in bright hope—at least that's how Harry thought of the morning.

As she passed the railroad station she saw Mrs. Hogendobber, little hand weights clutched in her fists, approaching from the opposite direction.

"Morning, Harry."

"Morning, Mrs. H." Harry waved as the determined figure huffed by, wearing an old sweater and a skirt below the knee. Mrs. Hogendobber felt strongly that women should not wear pants but she did concede to sneakers. Even her sister in Greenville, South Carolina, said it was all right to wear pants but Miranda declared that their dear mother had spent a fortune on cotillion. The least she could do for that parental sacrifice was to maintain her dignity as a lady.

Harry arrived at the door of the post office just as Rob Collier lurched up in the big mail truck. He grunted and hauled off the mail bags, complaining bitterly that gossip was thin at the main post office in Charlottesville, hopped back in the truck, and sped off.

As Harry was sorting the mail Boom Boom Craycroft sauntered in, her arrival lacking only triumphant fanfare. Unlike Mrs. Hogendobber she did wear pants, tight jeans in particular, and she was keen to wear T-shirts, or any top that would call attention to her bosom. She had developed early, in the sixth grade. The boys used to say, "Baboom, Baboom," when she went sashaying past. Over the years this was abbreviated to Boom Boom. If her nickname bothered her no one could tell. She appeared delighted that her assets were now legend.

She did not appear delighted to see Harry.

"Good morning, Boom Boom."

"Good morning, Harry. Anything for me?"

"I put it in the box. What brings you to town so early?"

"I'm getting up earlier now to catch as much light as I can. I suffer from seasonal affect disorder, you know, and winter depresses me."

Harry, long accustomed to Boom Boom's endless array of physical ills, enough to fill many medical books, couldn't resist. "But Boom Boom, I thought you'd conquered that by removing dairy products from your diet."

"No, that was for my mucus difficulty."

"Oh." Harry thought to herself that if Boom Boom had even half of the vividly described maladies she complained of, she'd be dead. That would be okay with Harry.

"We"—and by this Boom Boom meant herself and Harry's ex-husband, Fair—"were at Mim's last night. Little Marilyn and Fitz-Gilbert were there and we played Pictionary. You should see Mim go at it. She has to win, you know."

"Did she?"

"We let her. Otherwise she wouldn't invite us to her table at the Harvest Fair Ball this year. You know how she gets. But say, Little Marilyn and Fitz-Gilbert mentioned that they'd met this new man—'divine looking' was how Little Marilyn put it—and he's your neighbor. A Yale man too. What would a Yale man do here? The South sends her sons to Princeton, so he must be a Yankee. I used to date a Yale man, Skull and Bones, which is ironic since I broke my ankle dancing with him."

Harry thought calling that an irony was stretching it. What Boom Boom really wanted Harry to appreciate was that not only did she know a Yale man, she knew a Skull and Bones man—not Wolf's Head or any of the other "lesser" secret societies, but Skull and Bones. Harry thought admission to Yale was enough of an honor; if one was tapped for a secret society, too, well, wonderful, but best to keep quiet about it. Then again, Boom Boom couldn't keep quiet about anything.

Tucker yawned behind the counter. "Murph, jump in the mail cart."

"Okay." Mrs. Murphy wiggled her haunches and took a flying leap from the counter where she was eavesdropping on the veiled combat between the humans. She hit the mail cart dead center and it rolled across the back room, a metallic rattle to its wheels. Tucker barked as she ran alongside.

"Hey, you two." Harry giggled.

"Well, I'll be late for my low-impact aerobics class. Have a good day." Boom Boom lied about the good day part and left.

Boom Boom attracted men. This only convinced Harry that the two sexes did not look at women in the same way. Maybe men and women came from different planets—at least that's what Harry thought on her bad days. Boom Boom had attractive features and the celebrated big tits but Harry also saw that she was a hypochondriac of the first water, managing to acquire some dread malady whenever she was in danger of performing any useful labor.

Susan Tucker used to growl that Boom Boom never fucked anyone poor. Well, she'd broken that pattern with Fair Haristeen, and Harry knew that sooner or later Boom Boom would weary of not getting earrings from Cartier's, vacations out of the country, and a

new car whenever the mood struck her. Of course she had plenty
of her own money to burn but that wasn't as much fun as burning
a hole in someone else's pocket. She'd wait until she had a rich
fellow lined up in her sights and then she'd dump Fair with lightning
speed. Harry wanted to be a good enough person not to gloat when
that moment occurred. However, she knew she wasn't.

This reverie of delayed revenge was interrupted when Mim
Sanburne strode into the post office. Sporting one of those boiled
Austrian jackets and a jaunty hunter-green hat with a pheasant
feather on her head, she might have come from the Tyrol. A pleasant thought if it meant she might blow back to the Tyrol.

"Harry." Mim's greeting was imperious.

"Mrs. Sanburne."

Mim had a box with a low number, another confirmation of
her status, since it had been in the family since the time postal
service was first offered to Crozet. Her arms full of mail and glossy
magazines, she dumped them on the counter. "Hear you've got a
handsome beau."

"I do?" came the surprised reply.

Mrs. Murphy jumped around in the mail bin as Tucker snapped
from underneath at the moving blob in the canvas.

"My son-in-law, Fitz-Gilbert, said he recognized him, this Blair
Bainbridge fellow. He's a model. Seen him in *Esquire*, *GQ*, that sort
of thing. Mind you, those models are a little funny, you know what
I mean?"

"No, Mrs. Sanburne, I really don't."

"Well, I'm trying to protect you, Harry. Those pretty boys marry
women but they prefer men, if I have to be blunt."

"First off, I'm not dating him."

This genuinely disappointed Mim. "Oh."

"Secondly, I have no idea as to his sexual preference but he
seems nice enough and for now I will take him at face value. Thirdly,
I'm taking a vacation from men."

Mim airily circled her hand over her head, a dramatic gesture
for her. "That's what every woman says until she meets the next

man, and there is a next man. They're like streetcars—there's always one coming around the corner."

"That's an interesting thought." Harry smiled.

Mim's voice hit the "important information" register. "You know, dear, Boom Boom will tire of Fair. When he comes to his senses, take him back."

As everyone had her nose in everyone else's business, this unsolicited, intimate advice from the mayor's wife didn't offend Harry. "I couldn't possibly do that."

A knowing smile spread across the carefully made-up face. "Better the devil you know than the devil you don't." With that sage advice Mim started for the door, stopped, turned, grabbed her mail and magazines off the counter, and left for good.

Harry folded her arms across her chest, a respectable chest, too, and looked at her animals. "Girls, people say the damnedest things."

Mrs. Murphy called out from the mail bin, "*Mim's a twit. Who cares? Gimmie a push.*"

"You look pretty comfortable in there." Harry grabbed the corner of the mail bin and merrily rolled Mrs. Murphy across the post office as Tucker yapped with excitement.

Susan dashed through the back door, beheld the fun, and put Tucker in another mail bin. "Race you!"

By the time they'd exhausted themselves they heard a scratching at the back door, opened it, and in strolled Pewter. So, with a grunt, Harry picked up the gray cat, placed her in Mrs. Murphy's cart, and rolled the two cats at the same time. She crashed into Susan and Tucker.

Pewter, miffed, reached up and grabbed the edge of the mail bin with her paws. She was going to leap out when Mrs. Murphy yelled, "*Stay in, wimp.*"

Pewter complied by jumping onto the tiger cat, and the two rolled all over each other, meowing with delight as the mail bin races resumed.

"Wheee!" Susan added sound effects.

"Hey, let's go out the back door and race up the alley," Harry challenged.

"*Yeah, yeah!*" came the animals' thrilled replies.

Harry opened the back door, she and Susan carefully lifted the mail bins over the steps, and soon they were ripping and tearing up and down the little alleyway. Market Shiflett saw them when he was taking out the garbage and encouraged them to run faster. Mrs. Hogendobber, shading her eyes, looked up from her pumpkins. Smiling, she shook her head and resumed her labors.

Finally, the humans pooped out. They slowly rolled the bins back to the post office.

"How come people forget stuff like this when they get older?" Susan asked.

"Who knows?" Harry laughed as she watched Mrs. Murphy and Pewter sitting together in the bin.

"Wonder why we still play?" Susan thought out loud.

"Because we discovered that the secret of youth is arrested development." Harry punched Susan in the shoulder. "Ha."

The entire day unfolded with laughter, sunshine, and high spirits. That afternoon, as Harry revved up the ancient tractor Blair Bainbridge drove up the driveway in his dually. Would she come over to his place and look at the old iron cemetery fence?

So Harry chugged down the road, Mrs. Murphy in her lap, and Tucker riding with Blair. Harry pulled up the fallen-down fence while Blair put concrete blocks around it to hold it until he could secure post corners. Working alongside Blair was fun. Harry felt closest to people when working with them or playing games. Blair wasn't afraid to get dirty, which she found surprising for a city boy. Guess she surprised him too. She advised him on how to rehabilitate his stable, how to pack the stalls, and how to hang subzero fluorescent lights.

"Why not use incandescent lights?" Blair asked. "It's prettier."

"And a whole lot more expensive. Why spend money when you don't have to?" She pushed her blue Giants cap back on her head.

"Well, I like things to look just so."

"Hang the subzeros high up in the spine of your roof and then put regular lighting along the shed row, with metal guards over it.

Otherwise you'll be picking glass out of your horses' heads. That's if you have to have, just have to have, incandescent lights."

Blair wiped his hands on his jeans. "Guess I look pretty stupid."

"No, you need to learn about the country. I wouldn't know what to do in New York City." She paused. "Fitz-Gilbert Hamilton says you're a model. Are you?"

"From time to time."

"Out of work?"

Harry's innocence about his field amused him and somehow made her endearing to him. "Not exactly. I can fly to a shoot. I just don't want to live in New York anymore and, well, I don't want to do that kind of work forever. The money is great but it's not . . . fitting."

Harry shrugged. "If a guy's as handsome as you are he might as well make money off of it."

Blair roared. He wasn't used to women being so direct with him. They were too busy flirting and wanting to be his date at the latest social event. "Harry, are you always so, uh, forthright?"

"I guess." Harry smiled. "But, hey, if you don't like that kind of work I hope you find something you do like."

"I'd like to breed horses."

"Mr. Bainbridge, three words of advice. Don't do it." His face just fell. She hastened to add, "It's a money suck. You'd do better buying yearlings or older horses and making them. Truly. Sometime we can sit down and talk this over. I've got to get back home before the light goes. I've got to run the manure spreader and pull out a fence post."

"You helped me—I'll help you." Blair didn't know that "making a horse" meant breaking and training the animal. He had asked so many questions he decided he'd give Harry a break. He'd ask someone else what the phrase meant.

They rode back to Harry's. This time Mrs. Murphy rode with Blair and Tucker rode with Harry.

As Mrs. Murphy sat quietly in the passenger seat she focused on Blair. An engaging odor from his body curled around her nostrils, a mixture of natural scent, a hint of cologne, and sweat. He smiled as he drove along. She could feel his happiness. What was even better, he spoke to her as though she were an intelligent creature. He told her she was a very pretty kitty. She purred. He said he knew she was a champion mouser, he could just tell, and that once he settled in he would ask her about finding a cat or two for him. Nothing sadder on this earth than a human being without a cat. She added trills to her purrs.

By the time they turned into Harry's driveway Mrs. Murphy felt certain that she had totally charmed Blair, although it was the other way around.

The fence post proved stubborn but they finally got it out. The manure spreading would wait until tomorrow because the sun had set and there was no moon to work by. Harry invited Blair into her kitchen and made a pot of Jamaican Blue coffee.

"Harry," he teased her, "I thought you were frugal. This stuff costs a fortune."

"I save my money for my pleasures," Harry replied.

As they drank the coffee and ate the few biscuits Harry had, she told him about the MacGregors and the Joneses, the history of Foxden as she knew it, and the history of Crozet, named for Claudius Crozet, also as she knew it.

"Tell me something else." He leaned forward, his warm hazel eyes lighting up. "Why does everyone's farm have fox in its name? Fox Covert, Foxden, Fox Hollow, Red Fox, Gray Fox, Wily Fox, Fox Haven, Fox Ridge, Fox Run"—he inhaled—"Foxcroft, Fox Hills, Foxfield, Fox—"

"How about Dead Fox Farm?" Harry filled in.

"No way. You're making that up."

"Yeah." Harry burst out laughing and Blair laughed along with her.

He left for home at nine-thirty, whistling as he drove. Harry washed up the dishes and tried to remember when she'd enjoyed a new person quite so much.

The cat and dog curled up together and wished humans could grasp the obvious. Harry and Blair were meant for each other. They wondered how long it would take them to figure it out and who, if anybody, would get in the way. People made such a mess of things.

6

The balmy weather held for another three days, much to the delight of everyone in Crozet. Mim lost no time in leaning on Little Marilyn to invite Blair Bainbridge to her house, during which time Mim just happened to stop by. She deeply regretted that Blair was too young for her and said so quite loudly, but this was a tack Mim usually took with handsome men. Her husband, Jim, laughed at her routine.

Fitz-Gilbert Hamilton's den struck Blair as a hymn to Princeton. How much orange and black could anyone stand? Fitz-Gilbert made a point of showing Blair his crew picture. He even showed him his squash picture from Andover Academy. Blair asked him what had happened to his hair, which Fitz-Gilbert took as a reference to his receding hairline. Blair hastily assured him that was not what he'd meant; he'd noticed that the young Fitz-Gilbert was blond. Little Marilyn giggled and said that in school her husband dyed his hair.

Fitz-Gilbert blustered and said that all the guys did it—it didn't mean anything.

The upshot of this conversation was that the following morning Fitz-Gilbert appeared in the post office with blond hair. Harry stared at the thatch of gold above his homely face and decided the best course would be to mention it.

"Determined to live life as a blond, Fitz? Big Marilyn must be wearing off on you."

Mim flew to New York City once every six weeks to have her hair done and God knows what else.

"Last night my wife decided, after looking through my year-books, that I look better as a blond. What do you think? Do blonds have more fun?"

Harry studied the effect. "You look very preppy. I think you'd have fun whatever your hair color."

"I could never have done this in Richmond. That law firm." He put his hands around his neck in a choking manner. "Now that I've opened my own firm I can do what I want. Feels great. I know I do better work now too."

"I don't know what I'd do if I had to dress up for work."

"Worse than that, you couldn't take the cat and dog to work with you," Fitz-Gilbert observed. "You know, I don't think people were meant to work in big corporations. Look at Cabell Hall, leaving Chase Manhattan for Allied National years ago. After a while the blandness of a huge corporation will diminish even the brightest ones. That's what I like so much about Crozet. It's small; the businesses are small; people are friendly. At first I didn't know how I'd take the move from Richmond. I thought it might be dull." He smiled. "Hard for life to be dull around the Sanburnes."

Harry smiled back but wisely kept her mouth shut. He left, squeezing his large frame into his Mercedes 560SL, and roared off. Fitz and Little Marilyn owned the pearlized black SL, a white Range Rover, a silver Mercedes 420SEL, and a shiny Chevy half-ton truck with four-wheel drive.

As the day unfurled the temperature dropped a good fifteen to twenty degrees. Roiling black clouds massed at the tips of the Blue Ridge Mountains. The rain started before Harry left work. Mrs. Hogendobber kindly ran Harry back home although she complained about having Mrs. Murphy and Tucker in her car, an ancient Ford Falcon. She also complained about the car. This familiar theme—Mrs. Hogendobber had been complaining about her car since George bought it new in 1963—lulled Harry into a sleepy trance.

"... soon time for four more tires and I ask myself, Miranda, is it worth it? I think, trade this thing in, and then I go over to the Brady-Bushey Ford car lot and peruse those prices and, well, Harry, I tell you, my heart fairly races. Who can afford a new car? So it's patch, patch, patch. Well, would you look at that!" she exclaimed. "Harry, are you awake? Have I been talking to myself? Look there, will you."

"Huh." Harry's eyes traveled in the direction of Mrs. Hogendobber's pointing finger.

A large sign swung on a new post. The background was hunter-green, the sign itself was edged in gold, and the lettering was gold. A fox peered out from its den. Above this realistic painting it read FOXDEN.

"That must have cost a pretty penny." Mrs. Hogendobber sounded disapproving.

"Wasn't there this morning."

"This Bainbridge fellow must have money to burn if he can put up a sign like that. Next thing you know he'll put up stone fences, and the cheapest, I mean the cheapest, you can get for that work is thirty dollars a cubic foot."

"Don't spend his money for him yet. A pretty sign doesn't mean he's going to go crazy and put all his goods in the front window, so to speak."

As they pulled into the long driveway leading to Harry's clapboard house, she asked Miranda Hogendobber in for a cup of tea. Mrs. Hogendobber refused. She had a church club meeting to attend and furthermore she knew Harry had chores. Given the continuing drop in the temperature and the pitch clouds sliding down the mountain as though on an inky toboggan ride, Harry was grateful.

Mrs. H. peeled down the driveway and Harry hurried into the barn, Mrs. Murphy and Tucker way in front of her.

Her heavy barn jacket hung on a tack hook. Harry threw it on, tugged off her sneakers and slipped on duck boots, and slapped her Giants cap on her head. Grabbing the halters and lead shanks, she walked out into the west pasture just in time to get hit in the face with slashing rain. Mrs. Murphy stayed in the barn but Tucker went along.

Tomahawk and Gin Fizz, glad to see their mother, trotted over. Soon the little family was back in the barn. Picking up the tempo, the rain pelted the tin roof. A stiff wind knifed down from the northeast.

As Harry mixed bran with hot water and measured out sweet feed, Mrs. Murphy prowled the hayloft. Since everyone had made so much noise getting into the barn, the mice were forewarned. The big old barn owl perched in the rafters. Mrs. Murphy disliked the owl and this was mutual, since they competed for the mice. However, harsh words were rarely spoken. They had adopted a live-and-let-live policy.

A little pink nose, whiskers bristling, stuck out from behind a bale of timothy. "Mrs. Murphy."

"Simon, what are you doing here?" Mrs. Murphy's tail went to the vertical.

"Storm came up fast. You know, I've been thinking, this would be a good place to spend the winter. I don't think your human would mind, do you?"

"As long as you stay out of the grain I doubt she'll care. Watch out for the blacksnake."

"She's already hibernating . . . or she's playing possum." Simon's whiskers twitched devilishly.

"Where?"

Simon indicated that the formidable four-foot-long blacksnake was curled up under the hay on the south side of the loft, the warmest place.

"God, I hope Harry doesn't pick up the bale and see her. Give her heart failure." Mrs. Murphy walked over. She could see the tip of a tail— that was it.

She came back and sat beside Simon.

"*The owl really hates the blacksnake,*" Simon observed.

"*Oh, she's cranky about everything.*"

"*Who?*"

"*You,*" Mrs. Murphy called up.

"*I am not cranky but you're always climbing up here and shooting off your big mouth. Scares the mice.*"

"*It's too early for you to hunt.*"

"*Doesn't change the fact that you have a big mouth.*" The owl ruffed her feathers, then simply turned her head away. She could swivel her gorgeous head around nearly 360 degrees, and that fascinated the other animals. Four-legged creatures had a narrow point of view as far as the owl was concerned.

Mrs. Murphy and Simon giggled and then the cat climbed back down the ladder.

By the time Harry was finished, Mrs. Murphy and Tucker eagerly scampered to the house.

Next door, Blair, cold and soaked to the skin, also ran into his house. He'd been caught by the rain a good half-mile away from shelter.

By the time he dried off, the sky was obsidian with flashes of pinkish-yellow lightning, an unusual fall thunderstorm. As he went into the kitchen to heat some soup, a deafening crack and blinding pink light knocked him back a foot. When he recovered he saw smoke coming out of the transformer box on the pole next to his house. The bolt had squarely hit the transformer. Electric crackles continued for a few moments and then died away.

Blair kept rubbing his eyes. They burned. The house was now black and he hadn't any candles. There was so much to do to settle in that he hadn't gotten around to buying candles or a lantern yet, much less furniture.

He thought about going over to Harry's but decided against it, because he was afraid he'd look like a wuss.

As he stared out his kitchen window another terrifying bolt of lightning hurtled toward the ground and struck a tree halfway between his house and the graveyard. For a brief moment he thought he saw a lone figure standing in the cemetery. Then the darkness again enshrouded everything and the wind howled like Satan.

Blair shivered, then laughed at himself. His stinging eyes were playing tricks on him. What was a thunderstorm but part of Nature's brass and percussion?

7

Tree limbs lay on the meadows like arms and legs torn from their sockets. As Harry prowled her fence lines she could smell the sap mixed in with the soggy earth odor. She hadn't time to inspect the fifty acres in hardwoods. She figured whole trees might have been uprooted, for as she had lain awake last night, mesmerized by the violence of the storm, she could hear, off in the distance like a moaning, the searing cracks and crashes of trees falling to their deaths. The good news was that no trees around the house had been uprooted and the barn and outbuildings remained intact.

"I hate getting wet," Mrs. Murphy complained, pulling her paws high up in the air and shaking them every few steps.

"Go back to the house then, fussbudget." This exaggerated fastidiousness of Mrs. Murphy's amused and irritated Tucker. There was nothing like a joyous splash in the creek, a romp in the mud, or if she was really lucky, a roll in something quite dead, to lift Tucker's corgi spirits. And as she was low to the ground, she felt justified in getting dirty. It would be different if she were a Great Dane. Many things would be different if she were a Great Dane. For one thing, she could just ignore Mrs. Murphy with magisterial dignity. As it was, trying to ignore Mrs. Murphy meant the cat would tiptoe around and whack her on the ears. Wouldn't it be fun to see Mrs. Murphy try that if she were a Great Dane?

"What if something important happens? I can't leave." Mrs. Murphy shook mud off her paw and onto Harry's pants leg. *"Anyway, three sets of eyes are better than one."*

"Jesus H. Christ on a raft."

The dog and cat stopped and looked in the direction of Harry's gaze. The creek between her farm and Foxden had jumped its banks, sweeping everything before it. Mud, grass, tree limbs, and an old tire that must have washed down from Yellow Mountain had crashed into the trees lining the banks. Some debris had become entangled; the rest was shooting downstream at a frightening rate of speed. Mrs. Murphy's eyes widened. The roar of the water scared her.

As Harry started toward the creek she sank up to her ankle in trappy ground. Thinking the better of it, she backed off.

The leaden sky overhead offered no hope of relief. Cursing, her foot cold and wet, Harry squished back to the barn. She thought of her mother, who used to say that we all live in a perpetual state of renewal. "You must realize there is renewal in destruction, too, Harry," she would say.

As a child Harry couldn't figure out what her mother was talking about. Grace Hepworth Minor was the town librarian, so Harry used to chalk it up to Mom's reading too many touchy-feely books. As the years wore on, her mother's wisdom often came back to her. A sight such as this, so dispiriting at first, gave one the opportunity to rebuild, to prune, to fortify.

How she regretted her mother's passing, for she would have liked to discuss emotional renewal in destruction. Her divorce was teaching her that.

Tucker, noticing the silence of her mother, the pensive air, said, *"Human beings think too much."*

"Or not at all" was the saucy feline reply.

8

The rain picked up again midmorning. Steady rather than torrential, it did little to lighten anyone's spirits. Mrs. Hogendobber's beautiful red silk umbrella was the bright spot of the day. That and her conversation. She felt it incumbent upon her to call up everyone in Crozet who had a phone still working and inquire as to their wellbeing. She learned of Blair's transformer's being blown apart. The windows of the Allied National Bank were smashed. The shingles of Herbie Jones's church littered the downtown street. Susan Tucker's car endured a tree branch on its roof, and horror of horrors, Mim's pontoon boat, her pride and joy, had been cast on its side. Worst of all, her personal lake was a muddy mess.

"Did I leave anything out?"

Harry cleaned out the letters and numbers in her postage meter with the sharp end of a safety pin. They'd gotten clogged with maroon ink. "Your prize pumpkin?"

"Oh, I brought her in last night." Mrs. Hogendobber grabbed the broom and started sweeping the dried mud out the front door.

"You don't have to do that."

"I know I don't have to but I used to do this for George. Makes me feel useful." The clods of earth soared out into the parking lot. "Weatherman says three more days of rain."

"If the animals go two by two, you know we're in trouble."

"Harry, don't make light of the Old Testament. The Lord doesn't shine on blasphemers."

"I'm not blaspheming."

"I thought maybe I'd scare you into going to church." A sly smile crossed Mrs. Hogendobber's lips, colored a bronzed orange today.

Fair Haristeen came in, wiped off his boots, and answered Mrs. Hogendobber. "Harry goes to church for weddings, christenings, and funerals. Says Nature is her church." He smiled at his former wife.

"Yes, it is." Harry was glad he was okay. No storm damage.

"Bridge washed out at Little Marilyn's and at Boom Boom's, too. Hard to believe the old creek can do that much damage."

"Guess they'll have to stay on their side of the water," Mrs. Hogendobber said.

"Guess so." Fair smiled. "Unless Moses returns."

"I know what I forgot to tell you," Mrs. Hogendobber exclaimed, ignoring the biblical reference. "The cat ate all the communion wafers!"

"Cazenovia at St. Paul's Episcopal Church?" Fair asked.

"Yes, do you know her?" Mrs. H. spoke as though the animal were a parishioner.

"Cleaned her teeth last year."

"Has she gotten in the wine?" Harry laughed.

Mrs. Hogendobber struggled not to join in the mirth—after all, the bread and wine were the body and blood of our Lord Jesus—but there was something funny about a cat taking communion.

"Harry, want to have lunch with me?" Fair asked.

"When?" She absent-mindedly picked up a ballpoint pen, which had been lying on the counter, and stuck it behind her ear.

"Now. It's noon."

"I barely noticed, it's so dark outside."

"Go on, Harry, I'll hold down the fort," Mrs. Hogendobber offered. Divorce troubled her and the Haristeen divorce especially, since both parties were decent people. She didn't understand growing apart because she and George had stayed close throughout their long marriage. Of course it helped that if she said, "Jump," George replied, "How high?"

"Want to bring the kids?" Fair nodded toward the animals.

"Do, Harry. Don't you leave me with that hoyden of a cat. She gets in the mail bins and when I walk by she jumps out at me and grabs my skirt. Then the dog barks. Harry, you've got to discipline those two."

"Oh, balls." Tucker sneezed.

"Why do people say 'balls'? Why don't they say 'ovaries'?" Mrs. Murphy asked out loud.

No one had an answer, so she allowed herself to be picked up and whisked to the deli.

The conversation between Fair and Harry proved desultory at best. Questions about his veterinary practice were dutifully answered. Harry spoke of the storm. They laughed about Fitz-Gilbert's blond hair and then truly laughed about Mim's pontoon boat taking a lick. Mim and that damned boat had caused more uproar over the years—from crashing into the neighbors' docks to nearly drowning Mim and the occupants. To be invited onto her "little yacht," as she mincingly called it, was surely a siren call to disaster. Yet to refuse meant banishment from the upper echelon of Crozet society.

As the laughter subsided, Fair, wearing his most earnest face, said, "I wish you and Boom Boom could be friends again. You all were friends once."

"I don't know as I'd say we were friends." Harry warily put down her plastic fork. "We socialized together when Kelly was alive. We got along, I guess."

"She understands why you wouldn't want to be friends with

her but it hurts her. She talks tough but she's very sensitive." He picked up the Styrofoam cup and swallowed some hot coffee.

Harry wanted to reply that she was very sensitive about herself and not others, and besides, what about her feelings? Maybe he should talk to Boom Boom about her sensitivities. She realized that Fair was snagged, hook, line, and sinker. Boom Boom was reeling him into her emotional demands, which, like her material demands, were endless. Maybe men needed women like Boom Boom to feel important. Until they dropped from exhaustion.

As Harry kept quiet, Fair haltingly continued: "I wish things had worked out differently and yet maybe I don't. It was time for us."

"Guess so." Harry twiddled with her ballpoint pen.

"I don't hold grudges. I hope you don't." His blond eyebrows shielded his blue eyes.

Harry'd been looking into those eyes since kindergarten. "Easier said than done. Whenever women want to discuss emotions men become more rational, or at least you do. I can't just wipe out our marriage and say let's be friends, and I'm not without ego. I wish we had parted differently, but done is done. I'd rather think good of you than ill."

"Well, what about Boom Boom then?"

"Where is she?" Harry deflected the question for a moment.

"Bridge washed out."

"Oh, yeah, I forgot. Once the water goes down she'll find a place to ford."

"Least the phone lines are good. I spoke to her this morning. She has a terrible migraine. You know how low pressure affects her."

"To say nothing of garlic."

"Right." Fair remembered when Boom Boom was rushed to the hospital once after ingesting the forbidden garlic.

"And then we can't forget the rheumatism in her spine on these cold, dank days. Or her tendency to heat prostration, especially when any form of work befalls her." Harry smiled broadly, the smile of victory.

"Don't make fun of her. You know what a tough family life she had. I mean with that alcoholic father and her mother just having affair after affair."

"Well, she comes by it honestly then." Harry reached over with her ballpoint pen, jabbed a hole in the Styrofoam cup, and turned it around so the liquid dribbled onto Fair's cords. She got up and walked out, Mrs. Murphy and Tucker hastily following.

Fair, fuming, sat there and wiped the coffee off his pants with his left hand while trying to stem the flow from the cup with his right.

9

The creek swirled around the larger rocks, small whirlpools forming, then dispersing. Tucker paced the bank, slick with mud deposits. The waters had subsided and were back within their boundaries but remained high with a fast current. A mist hung over the meadows and the trees, now bare, since the pounding rains had knocked off most of the brilliant fall foliage.

High in the hayloft Mrs. Murphy watched her friend through a crack in the boards. When she lost sight of Tucker she gave up her conversation with Simon to hurry backward down the ladder. Cursing under her breath, she surrendered hope of keeping dry and ran across the fields. Water splashed up on her creamy beige belly, exacerbating her bad mood. Tucker could do the dumbest things. By the time Mrs. Murphy reached the creek the corgi was right in the middle of it, teetering on the tip of a huge rock.

"Get back here," Mrs. Murphy demanded.

"No," Tucker refused. "Sniff."

Mrs. Murphy held her nose up in the air. "I smell mud, sap, and stale water."

"It's the faintest whiff. Sweet and then it disappears. I've got to find it."

"What do you mean, sweet?" Mrs. Murphy swished her tail.

"Damn, I lost it."

"Tucker, you've got short little legs—swimming in this current isn't a smart idea."

"I've got to find that odor." With that she pushed off the rock, hit the water, and pulled with all her might. The muddy water swept over her head. She popped up again, swimming on an angle toward the far shore.

Mrs. Murphy screeched and screamed but Tucker paid no heed. By the time the corgi reached the bank she was so tired she had to rest for a moment. But the scent was slightly stronger now. Standing up on wobbly legs, she shook herself and laboriously climbed the mudslide that was the creek bank.

"Are you all right?" the cat called.

"Yes."

"I'm staying right here until you come back."

"All right." Tucker scrambled over the bank and sniffed again. She got her bearings and trotted across Blair Bainbridge's land. The scent increased in power with each step. Tucker pulled up at the little cemetery.

The high winds had knocked over the tombstones Blair had righted, and the bad side of the wrought-iron fence had crashed down again. Carefully, the dog picked her way through the debris in the cemetery. The scent was now crystal clear and enticing, very enticing.

Nose to the ground, she walked over to the tombstone with the carved angel playing the harp. The fingers of a human hand pointed at the sky in front of the stone. The violence of the wind and rain had sheared off the loose topsoil; a section was rolled back like a tiny carpet. Tucker sniffed that too. When she and Mrs. Murphy passed the graveyard last week there was no enticing scent, no apparent change in the topsoil. The odor of decay, exhilarating to a dog, overcame her curiosity about the turf. She dug at the hand. Soon the whole hand was visible. She bit into the fleshy, swollen palm and tugged. The hand easily pulled out of the ground. Then she noticed that it had been severed at the wrist, a clean job of it, too, and the finger pads were missing.

Ecstatic with her booty, forgetting how tired she was, Tucker flew across the bog to the creek. She stopped because she was afraid to plunge into the creek. She didn't want to lose her pungent prize.

Mrs. Murphy, transfixed by the sight, was speechless.

Tucker delicately laid down the hand. "*I knew it! I knew I smelled something deliciously dead.*"

"*Tucker, don't chew on that.*" Mrs. Murphy was disgusted.

"*Why not? I found it. I did the work. It's mine!*" She barked, high-pitched because she was excited and upset.

"*I don't want the hand, Tucker, but it's a bad omen.*"

"*No, it's not. Remember the time Harry read to us about a dog bringing a hand to Vespasian when he was a general and the seers interpreting this to mean that he would be Emperor of Rome and he was? It's a good sign.*"

Mrs. Murphy dimly remembered Harry's reading aloud from one of her many history books but that was hardly her main concern. "*Listen to me. Humans put their dead in boxes. You know that if you found a hand it means the body wasn't packaged.*"

"*So what? It's my hand!*" Tucker hollered at the top of her lungs, although with a moment to reflect she knew that Mrs. Murphy was right. Humans didn't cut up their dead.

"*Tucker, if you destroy that hand then you've destroyed evidence. You're going to be in a shitload of trouble and you'll get Mother in trouble.*"

Dejected, Tucker squatted down next to the treasured hand, a gruesome sight. "*But it's mine.*"

"*I'm sorry. But something's wrong, don't you see?*"

"*No.*" Her voice was fainter now.

"*A dead human not in a box means either he or she was ill and died far away from others or that he or she was murdered. The other humans have to know this. You know how they are, Tucker. Some of them kill for pleasure. It's dangerous for the others.*"

Tucker sat up. "*Why are they like that?*"

"*I don't know and they don't know. It's some sickness in the species. You know, like dogs pass parvo. Please, Tucker, don't mess up that evidence. Let me go get Mother if I can. Promise me you'll wait.*"

"It might take her hours to figure out what you're telling her."

"I know. You've got to wait."

One miserable dog cocked her head and sighed. "All right, Murphy."

Mrs. Murphy skimmed across the pastures, her feet barely grazing the sodden earth. She found Harry in the bed of the truck. Nimbly Mrs. Murphy launched herself onto the truck bed. She meowed. She rubbed against Harry's leg. She meowed louder.

"Hey, little pussycat, I've got work to do."

The twilight was fading. Mrs. Murphy was getting desperate. "Follow me, Mom. Come on. Right now."

"What's gotten into you?" Harry was puzzled.

Mrs. Murphy hooted and hollered as much as she could. Finally she sprang up and dug her claws into Harry's jeans, climbing up her leg. Harry yelped and Mrs. Murphy jumped off her leg and ran a few paces. Harry rubbed her leg. Mrs. Murphy ran back and prepared to climb the other leg.

"Don't you dare!" Harry held out her hand.

"Then follow me, stupid." Mrs. Murphy moved away from her again.

Finally, Harry did. She didn't know what was going on but she'd lived with Mrs. Murphy for seven years, long enough and close enough to learn a little bit of cat ways.

The cat hurried across the meadow. When Harry slowed down, Mrs. Murphy would run back and then zip away again, encouraging her constantly. Harry picked up speed.

When Tucker saw them coming she started barking.

Breathing hard, Harry stopped at the bank. "Oh, damn, Tucker, how'd you get over there."

"Look!" the cat shouted.

"Mommy, I found it and it's mine. If I have to give this up I want a knuckle bone," Tucker bargained. She picked up the hand in her mouth.

It took Harry a minute to focus in the fading light. At first, she couldn't believe her eyes. Then she did.

"Oh, my God."

10

Albemarle County Sheriff Rick Shaw bent down with his flashlight. Officer Cynthia Cooper, already hunkered down, gingerly lifted the digits with her pocket knife.

"Never seen anything like this," Shaw muttered. He reached in his pocket and pulled out a cigarette.

The sheriff battled his smoking addiction with disappointing results. Worse, Cooper had begun to sneak cigarettes herself.

Tucker sat staring at the hand. Blair Bainbridge, feeling a little queasy, and Harry stood beside Tucker. Mrs. Murphy rested across Harry's neck. Her feet were cold and she was tired, so Harry had slung her around her neck like a stole.

"Harry, any idea where this came from?"

"I know," Tucker volunteered.

"Like I said, the dog was sitting on the creek bank with this hand. I ran back home and called, then hopped in the truck to meet you. I don't know any more than that."

"What about you, uh . . ."

"Blair Bainbridge."

"Mr. Bainbridge, notice anything unusual? Before this, I mean?"

"No."

Rick grunted when he stood up. Cynthia Cooper wrapped the hand in a plastic bag.

"*If you follow me, I can show you!*" Tucker yapped and ran toward the cemetery.

"She's got a lot to say." Cynthia smiled. She loved the little dog and the cat.

Shaw inhaled, then exhaled a long blue line of smoke, which didn't curl upward. Most likely meant more rain.

Tucker sat by the graveyard and howled.

"I, for one, am going to see what she's about." Harry followed her dog.

"Me too." Cynthia followed, carrying the hand in its bag.

Rick grumbled but his curiosity was up. Blair stayed with him. When the humans reached the iron fence Tucker barked again and walked over to the angel with the harp tombstone. Cooper flung her flashlight beam over toward Tucker.

"*Right here,*" Tucker instructed.

Harry squinted. "Coop, you'd better check this out."

Again Cynthia got down on her knees. Tucker dug in the dirt. She hit a pocket of air and the unmistakable odor of rotten flesh smacked Cynthia in the face. The young woman reeled backward and fought her gag reflex.

Rick Shaw, now beside her, turned his head aside. "Guess we've got work to do."

Blair, ashen-faced, said, "Would you like me to go back to the barn and get a spade?"

"No, thank you," the sheriff said. "I think we'll post a man out here tonight and start this in daylight. I don't want to take the chance of destroying evidence because we can't see."

As they walked back to the squad car Blair halted and turned to the sheriff, now on another cigarette. "I did see something. The night of the storm my transformer was hit by lightning. I didn't have any candles and I was standing by my kitchen window." He pointed to the window. "Another big bolt shot down and split that tree and for an instant I thought I saw someone standing up here in the cemetery. I dismissed it. It didn't seem possible."

Shaw wrote this down quickly in his small notebook as Coop called for a backup to watch the graveyard.

Harry wanted to make a crack about the graveyard shift but kept her mouth shut. Whenever things were grim her sense of humor kicked into high gear.

"Mr. Bainbridge, you're not planning on leaving anytime soon, are you?"

"No."

"Good. I might need to ask you more questions." Rick leaned against the car. "I'll call Herbie Jones. It's his cemetery. Harry, why don't you go home and eat something? It's past suppertime and you looked peaked."

"Lost my appetite," Harry replied.

"Yeah, me too. You never get used to this kind of thing, you know." The sheriff patted her on the back.

When Harry walked in the door she picked up the phone and called Susan. As soon as that conversation was finished she called Miranda Hogendobber. For Miranda, being the last to know would be almost as awful as finding the hand.

11

At first light a team of two men began carefully turning over the earth by the tombstone with the harp-playing angel. Larry Johnson, the retired elderly physician, acted as Crozet's coroner—an easy job, as there was generally precious little to do. He watched, as did Reverend Herbie Jones. Rick Shaw and Cynthia Cooper carefully sifted through the spadefuls of earth the men turned over. Harry and Blair stayed back at the fence. Miranda Hogendobber pulled up in her Falcon, bounded out of the car, and strode toward the graveyard.

"Harry, you called Miranda. Don't deny it, I know you did," Rick fussed.

"Well . . . she has an interesting turn of mind."

"Oh, please." Rick shook his head.

"Pay dirt." One of the diggers pulled his handkerchief up around his nose.

"I got it. I got it." The other digger reached down and gently extricated a leg.

Miranda Hogendobber reached the hill at that moment, took one look at the decaying leg, wearing torn pants and with the foot still in a sneaker, and passed out.

"She's your responsibility!" Rick pointed his forefinger at Harry.

Harry knew he was right. She hurried over to Mrs. Hogendobber and, assisted by Blair, hoisted her up. She began to come around. Not knowing what another look at the grisly specimen might do, they remonstrated with her. She resisted but then walked down to Blair's house supported by the two of them.

The police continued their work and discovered another hand, the fingertip pads also removed, and another leg, which, like its companion, had been cleaved where the thighbone joins the pelvis.

By noon, after sifting and digging for five hours, Rick called a halt to the proceedings.

"Want us to start in on these other graves?"

"As the ground is not disturbed I wish you wouldn't." Reverend Jones stepped in. "Let them rest in peace."

Rick wiped his forehead. "Reverend, I can appreciate the sentiment but if we need to come back up here ... well, you know."

"I know, but you're standing on my mother." A hint of reproach crept into Herb's resonant voice. He was more upset than he realized.

"I'm sorry." Rick quickly moved. "Go back to work, Reverend. I'll be in touch."

"Who would do that?" Herbie pointed to the stinking evidence.

"Murder?" Cynthia Cooper opened her hands, palms up, "Seemingly average people commit murder. Happens every day."

"No, who would cut up a human being like that?" The minister's eyes were moist.

"I don't know," Rick replied. "But whoever did it took great pains to remove identifying evidence."

After the good Reverend left, the four law enforcement officials walked a bit away from the smell and conferred among themselves. Where was the torso and where was the head?

They'd find out soon enough.

12

The starch in Tiffany Hayes's apron rattled as she approached the table. Little Marilyn, swathed in a full-length purple silk robe, sat across from Fitz-Gilbert, dressed for work. The pale-pink shirt and the suspenders completed a carefully thought-out ensemble.

Tiffany put down the eggs, bacon, grits, and various jams. "Will that be all, Miz Hamilton?"

Little Marilyn critically appraised the presentation. "Roberta forgot a sprig of parsley on the eggs."

Tiffany curtsied and repaired to the kitchen, where she informed Roberta of her heinous omission. At each meal there was some detail Little Marilyn found abrasive to her highly developed sense of decorum.

Hands on hips, Roberta replied to an appreciative Tiffany, "She can eat a pig's blister."

Back in the breakfast nook, husband and wife enjoyed a relaxing meal. The brief respite of sun was overtaken by clouds again.

"Isn't this the strangest weather?" Little Marilyn sighed.

"The changing seasons are full of surprises. And so are you." His voice dropped.

Little Marilyn smiled shyly. It had been her idea to attack her husband this morning during his shower. Those how-to-please sex books she devoured were paying off.

"Life is more exciting as a blond." He swept his hand across his forelock. His hair was meticulously cut with short sideburns, close cropped on the sides and back of the head, and longer on the top. "You really like it, don't you?"

"I do. And I like your suspenders too." She leaned across the table and snapped one.

"Braces, dear. Suspenders are for old men." He polished off his eggs. "Marilyn"—he paused—"would you love me if I weren't, well, if I weren't Andover-Princeton? A Hamilton? One of the Hamiltons?" He referred to his illustrious family, whose history in America reached back into the seventeenth century.

The Hamiltons, originally from England, first landed in the West Indies, where they amassed a fortune in sugar cane. A son, desirous of a larger theater for his talents, sailed to Philadelphia. From that ambitious sprig grew a long line of public servants, businessmen, and the occasional cad. Fitz-Gilbert's branch of the family, the New York branch, suffered many losses until only Fitz's immediate family remained. A fateful airplane crash carried away the New York Hamiltons the summer after Fitz's junior year in high school. At sixteen Fitz-Gilbert was an orphan.

Fitz appeared to withstand the shock and fight back. He spent the summer working in a brokerage house as a messenger, just as his father had planned. Despite his blue-blood connections, his only real friend in those days was another boy at the brokerage house, a bright kid from Brooklyn, Tommy Norton. They escaped Wall Street on weekends, usually to the Hamptons or Cape Cod.

Fitz's stoicism impressed everyone, but Cabell Hall, his guardian and trust officer at Chase Manhattan, was troubled. Cracks had begun to show in Fitz's facade. He totaled a car but escaped unharmed. Cabell didn't blow up. He agreed that "boys will be boys." But then Fitz got a girl pregnant, and Cabell found a reputable doctor to take care of that. Finally, the second summer of Fitz's Wall Street apprenticeship, he and Tommy Norton were in a car accident on Cape Cod. Both boys were so drunk that, luckily for them, they sustained only facial lacerations and bruises when they went through the windshield. Fitz, since he was driving, paid all the medical bills, which meant they got the very best care. But Fitz's recovery was only physical. He had tempted fate and nearly killed not only himself but his best friend. The result was a nervous breakdown. Cabel checked him into an expensive, quiet clinic in Connecticut.

Fitz had related this history to Little Marilyn before they got married, but he hadn't mentioned it since.

She looked at him now and wondered what he was talking about. Fitz was high-born, rich, and so much fun. She didn't remember anywhere in her books being instructed that men need reassurance of their worth. The books concentrated on sexual pleasure and helping a husband through a business crisis and then dreaded male menopause, but, oh, they were years and years away from that. Probably he was playing a game. Fitz was inventive.

"I would love you if you were"—she thought for something déclassé, off the board—"Iraqi."

He laughed. "That is a stretch. Ah, yes, the Middle East, that lavatory of the human race."

"Wonder what they call us?"

"The Devil's seed." His voice became more menacing and he spoke with what he imagined was an Iraqi accent.

One of the fourteen phones in the overlarge house twittered. The harsh ring of the telephone was too cacaphonous for Little Marilyn, who believed she had perfect pitch. So she paid bundles of money for phones that rang in bird calls. Consequently her house sounded like a metallic aviary.

Tiffany appeared. "I think it's your mother, Miz Mim, but I can't understand a word she's saying."

A flash of irritation crossed Marilyn Sanburne Hamilton's smooth white forehead. She reached over and picked up the phone, and her voice betrayed not a hint of it. "Mother, darling."

Mother darling ranted, raved, and emitted such strange noises that Fitz put down his napkin and rose to stand behind his wife, hands resting on her slender shoulders. She looked up at her husband and indicated that she also couldn't understand a word. Then her face changed; the voice through the earpiece had risen to raw hysteria.

"Mother, we'll be right over." The dutiful daughter hung up the receiver.

"What is it?"

"I don't know. She just screamed and hollered. Oh, Fitz, we'd better hurry."

"Where's your father?"

"In Richmond today, at a mayors' conference."

"Oh, Lord." If Mim's husband wasn't there it meant the burden of comfort and solution rested upon him. Small wonder that Jim Sanburne found so many opportunities to travel.

13

Those townspeople who weren't gathered in the post office were at Market Shiflett's. Harry frantically tried to sort the mail. She even called Susan Tucker to come down and help. Mrs. Hogendobber, positioned in front of the counter, told her gory tale to all, every putrid detail.

A hard scratching on the back door alerted Tucker, who barked. Susan rose and opened the door. Pewter walked in, tail to the vertical, whiskers swept forward.

"Hello, Pewter."

"Hello, Susan." She rubbed against Susan's leg and then against Tucker.

Mrs. Murphy was playing in the open post boxes.

Pewter looked up and spoke to the striped tail hanging out of Number 31. "Fit to be tied over at the store. What about here?"

"Same."

"I found the hand," Tucker bragged.

"Everybody knows, Tucker. You'll probably get your name in the newspaper—again." Green jealousy swept through the fat gray body. "Mrs. Murphy, turn around so I can talk to you."

"I can't." She backed out of the box, hung for a moment by her paws, and then dropped lightly to the ground.

Usually Susan and Harry were amused by the athletic displays of the agile tiger cat but today no one paid much attention.

Blair called Harry to tell her Rick Shaw had elected not to tear up the cemetery just yet, and to thank her for being a good neighbor.

Naturally, with Blair being an outsider, suspicion immediately fell on him. After all, the severed hands and legs were found in his—well, Herbie's really—graveyard. And no one would ever suspect Reverend Jones.

The ideas and fantasies swirled up like a cloud of grasshoppers and then dropped to earth again. Harry listened to the people jammed into the post office even as she attempted to complete her tasks. Theories ranged from old-fashioned revenge to demonology. Since no one had any idea of who those body parts belonged to, the theories lacked the authenticity of personal connection.

One odd observation crossed Harry's mind. So much of the conjecture focused on establishing a motive. Why? As the voices of her friends, neighbors, and even her few enemies, or temporary enemies, rose and fell, the thrust was that in some way the victim must have brought this wretched fate upon himself. The true question formulating in Harry's mind was not motive but, Why is it so important for humans to blame the victim? Do they hope to ward off evil? If a woman is raped she is accused of dressing to entice. If a man is robbed, he should have had better sense than to walk the streets on that side of town. Are people incapable of accepting the randomness of evil? Apparently so.

As Rick Shaw sped by, siren splitting the air, the group fell silent to watch. Rick was followed closely by Cynthia Cooper in her squad car.

Fair Haristeen opened the door and stepped outside. He knew

that Rick Shaw wasn't moving that fast just to dump off hands and legs; something else had happened. He walked over to Market's to see if anyone had fresher news. Being in Harry's presence wasn't that uncomfortable for him. Fair considered that women were irrational much of the time, a consideration reinforced by Boom Boom, who felt logic to be vulgar. He'd already forgiven Harry for punching a hole in his coffee cup. She chose to ignore him to his face, then watched him saunter next door. She breathed a sigh of relief. His presence rubbed like a pebble in her shoe.

"*You know, I want my knuckle bone.*" Tucker started to pout. "*That was the deal.*"

"Deal?" Pewter's long gray eyelashes fluttered.

Before Tucker could explain, the door flew open and Tiffany Hayes, still in her sparkling white apron, burst in. "Miz Sanburne's got a headless nekkid body in her boathouse!"

A split second of disbelief was followed by a roar of inquiry. How did she know? Who was it? Et cetera.

Tiffany cleared her throat and walked to the counter. Susan came up from the back. Mrs. Murphy and Pewter jumped on the counter and made circles to find papers to sit on, then did so. Tucker ran around front, ducking between legs to see Tiffany.

The Reverend Jones, a quick thinker, dashed next door to fetch the folks in the market. Soon the post office was over its fire code limit of people.

Once everyone was squeezed in, Tiffany gave the facts. "I was serving Little Marilyn and Mr. Fitz their eggs. She was complaining, naturally, but so what? I walked back into the kitchen and the phone rang. Roberta's hands were covered with flour, and Jack wasn't on duty yet so I picked it up. I recognized the voice as Miz Sanburne's, but lordy, I couldn't understand one word that woman was putting to me. She was crying and she was screaming and she was gasping and I just laid down that phone and left the kitchen to tell Little Marilyn her mother was on the phone and I couldn't understand her. I mean I couldn't say 'your mother is pitching a fit and falling in it,' now could I? So I waited while Little Marilyn picked up the phone and she couldn't understand her mother any better than I could. Well, the next thing I know she runs upstairs and starts to put on her makeup, and Mr. Fitz is waiting downstairs. He was so anxious he couldn't stand it no more so he bounded up those steps and told her in no uncertain terms that this was no time for makeup and to get a move on. So they left in that white Jeep thing of theirs. Not twenty minutes pass before the phone rings again and Jack, on duty now, picks up but Roberta and I couldn't help ourselves so we picked up too. It was Mr. Fitz. We could hear both Marilyns ascreaming in the background. Like banshees. Mr. Fitz, he was a little shaky, but he told Jack there was a headless corpse floating in Mim's boathouse. He told Jack to call and cancel all his business appointments for the day and all of Little Marilyn's social engagements. Then he told Jack to get hold of Mr. Sanburne in Richmond if in any way possible. The sheriff was on his way and not to worry. Nobody was in any danger. Jack asked a few questions and Mr. Fitz told him not to worry if he didn't get his chores done today. Thank God for Mr. Fitz."

She finished. This was possibly the only time in her life that Tiffany would be the center of attention. There was something touching about that.

What Tiffany didn't know was that the hands and legs had been dug up at Foxden. So now Miranda Hogendobber was able to tell her story again. Center stage was natural to Miranda.

Grateful to Mrs. Hogendobber for taking over the "entertainment" department, Harry returned to filling up the post boxes. She was glad she was behind the boxes because she was laughing silently, tears falling from her eyes. Susan came over, thinking she was upset.

Harry wiped her eyes and whispered, "Of all people, Mim! What will Town and Country think?"

Now Susan was laughing as hard as Harry. "Maybe whoever it was made the mistake of sailing in her pontoon boat."

This made them both break out in giggles again. Harry put her hand over her mouth to muffle her speech. "Mim has exhausted herself with accumulating possessions. Now she's got one that's a real original."

That did it. They nearly fell on the floor. Part of this explosion of mirth was from tension, of course. Yet part of it was directly attributable to Mim's character. Miranda said there was a good heart in there somewhere but no one wanted to find out. Maybe no one believed her. Mim had spent her life from the cradle onward tyrannizing people over bloodlines and money. The two are intertwined less frequently than Mim would wish. No matter what story you had, Mim could top it; if not, she would tip her head at an angle that made plain her distaste and social superiority.

Nobody would say it out loud but probably most people were delighted that a bloated corpse had found its way into her boathouse. More things stank over at the Sanburnes' than a rotten torso.

14

The deep glow from the firelit mahogany in Reverend Jones's library cast a youthful softening over his features. The light rain on the windowpane accentuated his mood, withdrawn and thoughtful, as well as exhausted. He had forgotten just how exhausting turmoil can be. His wife, Carol, her violet eyes sympathetic, entreated him to eat. When he refused she knew he was suffering.

"How about a cup of cocoa, then?"

"What? Oh, no, dear. You know I ran into Cabell at the bank and he thinks this is a nut case. Someone passing through, like a traveling serial killer. I don't think so, Carol. I think it's closer to home."

A loud crackle in the fireplace made him jump. He settled back down.

"Tell you what. I'll bring in the cocoa and if you don't want it, then the cat will drink it. It won't solve this horrible mess but it will make you feel better."

The doorbell rang and Carol answered it. Two cups of cocoa. She invited Blair Bainbridge into the library. He also appeared exhausted.

Reverend Jones lifted himself out of his armchair to greet his impromptu guest.

"Oh, please stay seated, Reverend."

"You have a seat then."

Ella, the cat, joined them. Her full name was Elocution and she lived up to her name. Eating communion wafers was not her style, like that naughty Episcopalian cat, but Ella did once shred a sermon of Herbie's on a Sunday morning. For the first time in his life he gave a spontaneous sermon. The topic, "living with all God's creatures," was prompted, of course, by Ella's wanton destructiveness. It was the best sermon of his life. Parishioners begged for copies. As he had not one note, he thought he couldn't reproduce his sermon but Carol came to the rescue. She, too, moved by her husband's loving invocation of all life, remembered it word for word. The sermon, reprinted in many church magazines beyond even his own Lutheran denomination, made the Reverend something of an ecclesiastical celebrity.

Ella stared intently at Blair, since he was new to her. Once satisfied, she rested on her side before the fire as the men chatted and Carol brought in a large pot of cocoa. Carol excused herself and went upstairs to continue her own work.

"I apologize for dropping in like this without calling."

"Blair, this is the country. If you called first, people would think you were putting on airs." He poured his guest and himself a steaming cup each, the rich aroma filling the room.

"Well, I wanted to tell you how sorry I am that this, this—I don't even know what to call it." Blair's eyebrows knitted together. "Well, that the awful discovery was made in your family plot. Since your back troubles you, I'm willing to make whatever repairs are necessary, once Sheriff Shaw allows me."

"Thank you." The Reverend meant it.

"How long before people start thinking that I've done it?" Blair blurted out.

"Oh, they've already gone through that possibility and most have dispensed with it, except for Rick, who never lets anyone off the hook and never rushes to judgment. Guess you have to be that way in his line of work."

"Dispensed . . . ?"

Herbie waved his right hand in the air, a friendly, dismissive gesture, while holding his cocoa cup and saucer in his left hand. "You haven't been here long enough to hate Marilyn Sanburne. You wouldn't have placed the body, or what was left of it, in her boathouse."

"I could have floated it in there."

"I spoke to Rick Shaw shortly after the discovery." Herb placed his cup on the table. Ella eyed it with interest. "From the condition of the body, he seriously doubted it could have floated into the boathouse without someone on the lake noticing its slow progress. Also, the boathouse doors were closed."

"It could have floated under them."

"The body was blown up to about three times normal size."

Blair fought an involuntary shudder. "That poor woman will have nightmares."

"She about had to be tranquilized with a dart gun. Little Marilyn was pretty shook up too. And I don't guess Fitz-Gilbert will have an appetite for some time either. For that matter, neither will I."

"Nor I." Blair watched as a log burned royal-blue from the bottom to crimson in the middle, releasing the bright-yellow flames to leap upward.

"What I dread are the reporters. The facts will be in the paper tomorrow. Cut and dried. But if this body is ever identified, those people will swarm over us like flies." Herb wished he hadn't said that because it reminded him of the legs and hands.

"Reverend Jones—"

"Herbie," came the interruption.

"Herbie. Why do people hate Marilyn Sanburne? I mean, I've only met her once and she carried on about pedigree but, well, everyone has a weakness."

"No one likes a snob, Blair. Not even another snob. Imagine living year in and year out being judged by Mim, being put in your place at her every opportunity. She works hard for her charities, undeniably, but she bullies others even in the performance of good works. Her son, Stafford, married a black woman and that brought out the worst in Mim and, I might add, the best in everyone else. She disowned him. He lives in New York with his wife. They made up, sort of, for Little Marilyn's wedding. I don't know, most people don't see below the surface when they look at others, and Mim's surface is cold and brittle."

"But you think otherwise, don't you?"

This young man was perceptive. Herb liked him more by the minute. "I do think otherwise." He pulled up a hassock for his feet, indicating to Blair that he should pull one up, too, then folded his hands across his chest. "You see, Marilyn Sanburne was born Marilyn Urquhart Conrad. The Urquharts, of Scottish origin, were one of the earliest families to reach this far west. Hard to believe, but even during the time of the Revolutionary War this was a rough place, a frontier. Before that, the 1720's, the 1730s, you took your life in your hands to come to the Blue Ridge Mountains. Marilyn's mother, Isabelle Urquhart Conrad, filled all three of her children's heads with silly ideas about how they were royalty. The American version. Jimp Conrad, her husband, not of as august lineage as the Urquharts, was too busy buying up land to worry overmuch about how his children were being raised. A male problem, I would say. Anyway, her two brothers took this aristocracy stuff to heart and decided they didn't have to do anything so common as work for a living. James, Jr., became a steeplechase jockey and died in a freak accident up in Culpeper. That was right after World War Two. Horse dragged him to his death. I saw it with my own eyes. The younger brother, Theodore, a good horseman himself, quite simply drank himself to death. The heartbreak killed Jimp and made Isabelle bitter. She thought she was the only woman who'd ever lost sons. She quite forgot that hundreds of thousands of American mothers had recently lost sons in the mud of Europe and the sands of the South Pacific. Her mother's bitterness rubbed off on Mim. As she was the remaining child, the care of her mother became her burden as Isabelle aged. Social superiority became her refuge perhaps."

He rested a moment, then continued: "You know, I see people in crisis often. And over the years I have found that one of two things happens. Either people open up and grow, the pain allowing them to have compassion for others, to gain perspective on themselves, to feel God's love, if you will, or they shut down either through drink, drugs, promiscuity, or bitterness. Bitterness is an affront to God, as is any form of self-destructive behavior. Life is a gift, to be enjoyed and shared." He fell into silence.

Ella purred as she listened. She loved Herbie's voice, its deep, manly rumble, but she loved what he said too. Humans had such difficulty figuring out that life is a frolic as long as you have enough to eat, a warm bed, and plenty of catnip. She was very happy that Herb realized life was mostly wonderful.

For a long time the two men sat side by side in the quiet of understanding.

Blair spoke at last. "Herbie, I'm trying to open up. I don't have much practice."

Sensing that Blair would get around to telling his story sometime in the future, when he felt secure, Herb wisely didn't probe. Instead he reassured him with what he himself truly believed. "Trust in God. He will show you the way."

15

Although the sheriff and Officer Cooper knew little about the pieces of body that had been found, they did know that a vagrant, not an old man either, had been in town not long ago.

Relentless legwork, telephone calls, and questioning led the two to the Allied National Bank.

Marion Molnar remembered the bearded fellow vividly. His baseball jacket, royal blue, had an orange METS embroidered on it. As a devout Orioles fan, this upset Marion as much as the man's behavior.

She led Rick and Cynthia into Ben Seifert's office.

Beaming, shaking hands, Ben bade them sit down.

"Oh, yes, walked into my office big as day. Had some cockamamie story about his investments. Said he wanted to meet Cabell Hall right then and there."

"Did you call your president?" Rick asked.

"No. I said I'd take him down to our branch office at the downtown mall in Charlottesville. It was the only way I knew to get him out of here." Ben cracked his knuckles.

"Then what happened?" Cynthia inquired.

"I drove him to the outskirts of town on the east side. Finally talked him out of this crazy idea and he got out willingly. Last I saw of him."

"Thanks, Ben. We'll call you if we need you," Rick said.

"Glad to help." Ben accompanied them to the front door.

Once the squad car drove out of sight he shut his office door and picked up his phone. "Listen, asshole, the cops were here about that bum. I don't like it!" Ben, a country boy, had transformed himself over time, smoothing off his rough edges. Now he was a sleek glad-hander and a big deal in the Chamber of Commerce. There was scarcely any of the old Ben left in his oily new incarnation, but worry was resurrecting it.

16

The Harvest Fair committee, under the command of Miranda Hogendobber, met hastily to discuss their plans for the fair and the ball that immediately followed it. The glorious events of the Harvest Fair and Ball, crammed into Halloween day and night, were eagerly awaited by young and old. Everybody went to the Harvest Fair. The children competed for having the best costume and scariest costume, as well as in bobbing for apples, running races in costume, and other events that unfolded over the early evening hours. The advantage of this was that it kept the children off the streets, sparing everyone the trick-or-treat candy syndrome that caused adults to eat as much as the kids did. The children, gorged on good food as well as their treats, fell asleep at the Harvest Ball while the adults danced. There were as many sleeping bags as pumpkins.

The crisis confronting Mrs. Hogendobber, Taxi Hall, and their charges involved Harry Haristeen and Susan Tucker. Oh, not that the two had done anything wrong, but each year they appeared as Ichabod Crane and the Headless Horseman, Harry being the Horseman. Harry's Tomahawk was seal brown but looked black at night, and his nostrils were always painted red. He was a fearsome sight. Harry struggled every year to see through the slits in her cape once the pumpkin head was hurled at the fleeing Ichabod. One year she lost her bearings and fell off, to the amusement of everyone but herself, although she did laugh about it later.

What could they do? This cherished tradition, ongoing in Crozet since Washington Irving first published his immortal tale, seemed in questionable taste this year. After all, a headless body had just been found.

After an agonizing debate the committee of worthies decided to cancel Ichabod Crane. As the ball was in a few days, they hadn't time to create another show. The librarian suggested she could find a story which could be read to the children. It wasn't perfect but it was something.

On her way to the post office, Miranda's steps dragged slower and slower. She reached the door. She stood there for a moment. She breathed deeply. She opened the front door.

"Harry!" she boomed.

"I'm right in front of you. You don't have to yell."

"So you are. I don't want to tell you this but the Harvest Ball committee has decided, wisely I think, to cancel the Headless Horseman reenactment."

Harry, obviously disppointed, saw the logic of it. "Don't feel bad, Mrs. H. We'll get back to it next year."

A sigh of relief escaped Miranda's red lips. "I'm so glad you see the point."

"I do and thank you for telling me. Would you like me to tell Susan?"

"No, I'll get over there. It's my responsibility."

As she left, Harry watched the squared shoulders, the straight back. Miranda could be a pain—couldn't we all—but she always knew the right thing to do and the manner in which to do it. Harry admired that.

17

Fitz-Gilbert could have used a secretary to make himself look like a functioning lawyer—which he wasn't.

It doesn't do for a man not to go to work, even a very wealthy man, so his office was mostly for show although it had developed into a welcome retreat from his mother-in-law and, occasionally, his wife.

He hadn't been to the office since the torso appeared in Mim's boathouse, two days ago.

He opened the door and beheld chaos. His chairs were over-turned; papers were scattered everywhere; his file cabinet drawers sat askew.

He picked up the phone and dialed Sheriff Shaw.

18

Finding the remains of a human body, while unpleasant, wasn't rare. Every year in the state of Virginia hunters stumble across bodies picked clean by birds and scavengers, a few tatters of clothing left clinging to the bones. Occasionally the deceased has been killed by mistake by other hunters; other times an elderly person who suffered from disease or loss of memory simply wandered off in winter and died from exposure. Then, too, there were those tortured souls who walked into the woods to end it all. Murder, however, was not that common.

In the case of this cut-up corpse, Rick Shaw figured it had to be murder. The life of a county sheriff is usually clogged with serving subpoenas, testifying in poaching cases and land disputes, chasing speeders, and hauling drunks into the pokey. Murder added excitement. Not that he thought of it that way, exactly, but as he sat at his cluttered desk his mind moved faster; he concentrated fiercely. It took an unjust death to give him life.

"All right, Cooper." He wheeled around in his chair, pushing with the balls of his feet. "Give."

"Give what?"

"You know what." He stretched out his hand.

Irritated, Cynthia opened her long desk drawer, retrieved a pack of unfiltered Lucky Strikes, and smacked them in his hand. "You could at least smoke filtered cigarettes."

"Then I'd smoke two packs a day instead of one. What's the difference? And don't think I don't know that you're sneaking some."

When it was put that way, Cooper couldn't think of a difference. The surface of her desk shone, the grain of the old oak lending solidity to the piece. Papers, neatly stacked in piles, paperweights on top, provided a contrast to Rick's desk. Their minds contrasted too. She was logical, organized, and reserved. Rick was intuitive, disorganized, and as direct as he could be in his position. She liked the politics of the job. He didn't. As he was a good twenty years older than she, he'd remain sheriff and she'd be deputy. In time, barring accident, Cynthia Cooper could look forward to being the first woman sheriff of Albemarle County. Rick never thought of himself as a feminist. He hadn't wanted her in the first place but as the years rolled by her performance won him over. After a while he forgot she was a woman or maybe it didn't matter. He saw her as his right hand, and turning the department over to her someday was as it should be, not that he was ready to retire. He was too young for that.

The cigarette calmed him. The phones jangled. The small office enjoyed a secretary and a few part-time deputies. The department needed to expand but so far the county officials had passed no funds for that to their overworked sheriff.

One reporter from the local paper had showed up yesterday, and Rick had refused to dwell on the grisly details of the case. His low-key comments had satisfied the reporter for the moment, but Rick knew he'd be back. Rick and Coop hoped they'd have enough answers to forestall a panic or a squadron of reporters showing up from other papers, not to mention the TV.

"You've got a feeling about this case, boss?"

"The obvious. Destroying the identity of the corpse was paramount in the killer's mind. No fingerprints. No clothes on the torso. No head. Whoever this poor guy was, he knew too much. And we'd know too much if we knew who he was."

"I can't figure out why the killer would take the trouble to divide up the body. Lot of work. Then he or she would have to bag it so it wouldn't bleed all over everything, and then drive the parts around to dump them."

"Could be an undertaker, or someone with mortuary experience. Could have drained the body and then chopped it."

"Or a doctor," Cynthia added.

"Even a vet."

"Not Fair Haristeen. Poor guy, he was a suspect for a bit in Kelly Craycroft's murder."

"Well, he did wind up with Boom Boom, didn't he?"

"Yeah, poor sod." Cynthia burst out laughing.

Rick laughed too. "That woman, she's like to run him crazy. Pretty though."

"Men always say that." Cynthia smiled.

"Well, I don't see how you women can swoon over Mel Gibson. What's so special about him?" Rick stubbed out his cigarette.

"If you knew, you and I would have a lot more to talk about," Cynthia cracked.

"Very funny." He reached in the pack to pull out another coffin nail.

"Come on, you just finished one!"

"Did I?" He picked up the ashtray and counted the butts. "Guess I did. This one's still smoking." He crushed it again.

"You're suffering one of your hunches. I know it. Come on, tell."

He lifted a shoulder and let it fall. He felt a little foolish when he had these hunches because he couldn't explain or defend them. Men are taught to back up what they say. He couldn't do that in this case but over time he had learned not to dismiss odd sensations or strange ideas. Often they led him to valuable evidence, valuable insights.

"Come on, boss. I can tell when you're catching the scent," Cynthia prodded.

He folded his hands on his desk. "Just this. Dividing up a body makes sense. That doesn't throw me. The hard rains worked against our killer. That and little Tucker. But really, the odds were that those legs and hands would never have been found. It's the boathouse that doesn't compute."

"He could have tossed the torso in the lake and, when it came up, gaffed it or something and dragged it into the boathouse." Cynthia stopped to think. "But everyone would have seen this person, male or female, unless it was the dead of night, and you can't schedule the appearance of waterlogged bodies, now can you?"

"Nope. That's why it doesn't compute. That piece of meat was put in the boathouse. No other explanation."

"Well, if the killer knows the community he would know or see Mim's pontoon boat at the dock. Nobody goes into the boathouse much unless she has one of her naval sorties planned. It's as good a place to hide a body as any other."

"Is it?"

They stared at each other. Then Cynthia spoke. "You think that head's going to show up?"

"I kinda hope it does and I kinda hope it doesn't." He couldn't fight temptation. He grabbed another cigarette but delayed lighting it. "See if there's a record for Blair Bainbridge in New York."

"Okay. Anyone else?"

"We know everyone else. Or we think we do."

19

The light frost crunched underfoot even though Mrs. Murphy trod lightly. The rain had finally stopped last night and she had risen early to hunt field mice. Tucker, flopped on her side on Harry's bed, was still sound asleep.

Although the cat's undercoat was thickening, the stiff wind sent a chill throughout her body. Another month and her coat would be more prepared for the cold. The prospect of running top speed after a rabbit or a mouse thrilled Mrs. Murphy, so what was a little cold? The mice ducked into their holes, which ended the chase, but the rabbits often ran across meadows and through woods. Occasionally she caught a rabbit, but more often a mouse. She'd come alongside and reach over to grab it at the base of the neck if she could. If not she'd bump and roll it. Mrs. Murphy dispatched her conquests rapidly; not for her the torture of batting her prey around until it was torn up and punch-drunk. A swift broken neck ended the business in a split second. Usually she brought the quarry back to Harry.

The frost held the scent. Even so it wasn't a good day for hunting. She growled once when she smelled a red vixen. Mrs. Murphy and fox competed for the same food, so the cat resented her rival. She also hotly resented that a fox had gotten into the henhouse years ago when she was a kitten and had killed every hen on the property. Feathers fluttered like snowflakes and the images of the pathetic bodies of ten hens and one rooster stayed in her mind. She couldn't have warned off the predator anyway, because of her youth, but Harry's dismay at the sight unnerved Mrs. Murphy. After that, Harry no longer kept chickens, which was a pity because, as a kitten, Mrs. Murphy had loved to flatten herself in the grass and watch the yellow chicks peep and run all over the place.

If Tucker wouldn't be so fussy, Harry could get a big dog, a dog that would live outside, to chase off foxes and those pesky raccoons. A puppy with big paws from the SPCA would grow up to fill the bill. The mere mention of it would send Tucker into a hissy fit.

"Would you tolerate another cat, I ask you?" Tucker would shriek.

"If we had a surplus of mice I guess I'd have to," Mrs. Murphy would usually reply.

Tucker declared that she could handle a fox. This was a patent lie. She could not. If a fox went to ground she might be able to dig it out but then what would she do with it? Tucker wasn't a good killer. Corgis were brave dogs—Mrs. Murphy had seen ample proof of that—but Tucker, at least, wasn't the hunter type. Corgis, bred to herd cattle, were low to the ground so that when a cow kicked, the small dog could easily duck the blow. Tough, resilient, and accustomed to animals much bigger than themselves, corgis could work with just about any large domesticated animal. But hunting wasn't in their blood, so Mrs. Murphy usually hunted alone.

A meow, deep and mellow in the distance, attracted Mrs. Murphy's attention. She tensed, and then relaxed when the splendidly handsome figure of her ex-husband slipped out of the woods. Paddy, as always, wore his black tuxedo; his white shirtfront was immaculate but the white spats were dirty. His gorgeous eyes glittered and he bounded up with unbridled enthusiasm to see his ex.

"Hunting, Sugar? Let's do it together."

"Thanks, Paddy. I'm better at it alone."

He sat down and flicked his tail. "That's what you always say. You know, Murph, you won't be young and beautiful forever."

"Neither will you," came the tart reply. "Still hanging around that silver slut?"

"Oh, her? She got very boring." Paddy referred to one of his many inamoratas, this one a silver Maine coon cat of extraordinary beauty. "I hate it when they want to know where you've been every moment, as well as what you're thinking at every turn. Give it a rest." His pink tongue accentuated his white fangs. "You never did that."

"I was too busy myself to worry about what you were doing." She changed the subject. "Find anything?"

"Hunting's not good. Let them get a little hungrier and then we'll catch a few. The field mice are fat and happy right now."

"Where'd you come from?"

"Yellow Mountain. I left home in the middle of the night. I've got that door, you know—don't know why Harry doesn't put one in for you. Anyway, I was going to head toward the first railroad tunnel but it was too far away and the promise of hunting was already dim, so I trotted up the mountain instead."

"Not much there either?"

"No," he replied.

"Did you hear, Paddy, about those body parts in the graveyard?"

"Who cares? Humans kill one another and then pretend it's awful. If it's so awful, then why do they do it so much?"

"I don't know."

"And think about it, Murphy. If the new guy is in his house, why would the killer drag those pieces of body down the driveway? Too risky."

"Maybe he didn't know the new man had moved in."

"In Crozet? You sneeze and your neighbor says God bless you. I think he, or she, parked somewhere within a mile—two legs and two hands aren't that heavy to carry. Came in off Yellow Mountain Road, up to the old logging road, and walked back through the woods into the pastures up to the cemetery. You wouldn't have seen the person from your place unless you were in the west meadows. You're usually out of the west meadows by sunset though, because the horses have been brought in, and this new guy, well, he was a risk but the cemetery is far enough away from the house that he might see someone up there but I doubt if he could have heard anything. Of course, the new guy could have done it himself."

Mrs. Murphy batted a soggy leaf. "Got a point there, Paddy."

"You know, people only kill for two reasons."

"What are they?"

"Love or money." His white whiskers shook with mirth. Both reasons seemed absurd to Paddy.

"Drugs."

"Still gets back to money," Paddy countered. "Whatever this is, it will come to love or money. Harry's safe, since it hasn't a thing to do with her. You get so worried about Harry. She's pretty tough, you know."

"You're right. I just wish her senses were sharper. She misses so much. You know, it takes her sometimes ten or twenty seconds longer to hear something and even then she can't recognize the difference in tire treads as they come down the driveway. She recognizes engine differences though. Her eyes are pretty good but I tell you she can't tell a field mouse five hundred yards away. Even though her eyes are better in daylight, she still misses the movement. It's so easy to hear if you just listen and let your eyes follow. At night, of course, she can't see that well and none of them can smell worth a damn. I just worry how she can function with such weak senses."

"If Harry were being stalked by a tiger, then I'd worry. Since one human's senses are about as bad as another's, they're equal. And since they seem to be their own worst enemies, they're well equipped to fight one another. Besides which, she has you and Tucker and you can give her the jump, if she'll listen."

"She listens to me—most of the time. She can be quite stubborn though. Selective hearing."

"They're all like that." Paddy nodded gravely. "Hey, want to race across the front pasture, climb up the walnut by the creek, run across the limb, and then jump out to the other side? We can be at your back door in no time. Bet I get there first."

"Deal!"

They ran like maniacs, arriving at the back porch door. Harry, coffeepot in hand and still sleepy, opened the back door. They both charged into the kitchen.

"Catting around?" She smiled and scratched Mrs. Murphy's head, and Paddy's too.

20

A crisp night dotted with bright stars like chunks of diamonds created the perfect Halloween. Each year the Harvest Fair was held at Crozet High. Before the high school was built in 1892, the fair was held in an open meadow across from the train station. The high school displayed the excesses of Victorian architecture. One either loved it or hated it. Since most everyone attending the Harvest Ball had graduated from Crozet High, they loved it.

Not Mim Sanburne, as she had graduated from Madeira, nor Little Marilyn, who had followed in her mother's spiked-heel steps. No, Crozet High smacked of the vulgate, the hoi polloi, the herd. Jim Sanburne, Mayor of Crozet, had graduated from CHS in 1939. He carefully walked up and down rows of tables placed on the football field. Corn, squash, potatoes, wheat sheaves, and enormous pumpkins crowded the tables.

The mayor and his son-in-law had been cataloguing contestant entries that morning. In order to be impartial, Fitz wrote down all the produce entries. Since Jim was judging that category, it wouldn't do for him to see them early.

The crafts filled the halls inside the school. Mrs. Hogendobber would take a step or two, stop, study, rub her hand on her chin, remove her glasses, put them back on, and say, "Hmmn." This process was repeated for each display. Miranda took judging the crafts to new levels of seriousness.

The gym, decorated as a witches' lair, would welcome everyone after the awards. The dance attracted even the lame and the halt. If you breathed you showed up. Rick Shaw and Cynthia Cooper sat in the gym judging costumes. Children scampered about as Ninja Turtles, angels, devils, cowboys, and one little girl whose parents were dairy farmers came as a milk carton. The teenagers, also in costume, tended to stick together, but as the task of decorating for the Harvest Ball fell upon CHS's students, they heaped glory upon themselves. Every senior class was determined to top the class preceding it. The freshman, sophomore, and junior classes were pledged to help, and on Halloween Day classes were suspended so the decorating could proceed.

As Harry, Susan, and Blair strolled through the displays they admired the little flying witches overhead. The electronics wizards at the school had built intricate systems of wires, operating the witches by remote control. Ghosts and goblins also flew. The excitement mounted because if this was the warm-up, what would the dance be like? That was always the payoff.

Harry and Susan, in charge of the Harvest Ball for their class of 1976, ruefully admitted that these were the best decorations they'd seen since their time. No crepe paper for these kids. The orange and black colors snaked along the walls and the outside tables with Art Deco severity and sensuality. Susan, bursting with pride, accepted congratulations from other parents. Her son Danny was the freshman representative to the decorations committee and it was his idea to make the demons fly. He was determined to outdo his mother and was already well on his way to a chairmanship as a senior. His younger sister had proved a help too. Brookie was already worried about what would happen two years from now when she had the opportunity to be a Harvest Ball class representative. Could she top this? Susan and Ned had sent the kids to private school in Charlottesville for a couple of years, the result being that both were turning into horrid snobs. They had yanked the kids out of the private school, to everyone's eventual relief.

Blair observed it all in wonder and amusement. These young people displayed spirit and community involvement, something which had been missing at his prep school. He almost envied the students, although he knew he had been given the gift of a superb education as well as impeccable social contacts.

Boom Boom and Fair judged the livestock competition. Boom Boom was formally introduced to Blair by Harry. She took one look at this Apollo and audibly sucked in her breath. Fair, enraptured by a solid Holstein calf, elected not to notice. Boom Boom, far too intelligent to flirt openly, simply exuded radiance.

As they walked away Susan commented, "Well, she spared you the Boom Boom brush."

"What's that?" Blair smiled.

"In high school—on these very grounds, mind you—Boom Boom would slide by a boy and gently brush him with her torpedoes. Naturally, the boy would die of embarrassment and joy."

"Yeah," Harry laughed. "Then she'd say, 'Damn the torpedoes and full speed ahead.' Boom Boom can be very funny when she puts her mind, or boobs, to it."

"You haven't told me what your theme was when you two co-chaired the Harvest Ball." Blair evidenced little curiosity about Boom Boom but plenty about Harry and Susan, which pleased them mightily.

"The Hound of the Baskervilles." Susan's voice lowered.

Harry's eyes lit up. "You wouldn't have believed it. I mean, we started working the day school started. The chair and co-chairs are elected the end of junior year. A really big deal—"

Susan interrupted. "Can you tell? I mean, we still remember everything. Sorry, Harry."

"That's okay. Well, Susan came up with the theme and we decorated the inside of the school like the inside of a Victorian mansion. Velvet drapes, old sofas—I mean, we hit up every junk shop in this state, I swear ... that and what parents lent us. We took rolls and rolls of old butcher paper—Market Shiflett's dad donated it—and the art kids turned it into stone and we made fake walls with that outside."

"Don't forget the light."

"Oh, yeah, we had one of the boys up in the windows that are dark on the second floor going from room to room swinging a lantern. Boy, did that scare the little kids when they looked up. Painted his face too. We even got Mr. MacGregor—"

"My Mr. MacGregor?" Blair asked.

"The very one," Susan said.

"We got him to lend us his bloodhound, Charles the First, who emitted the most sorrowful cry."

"We walked him up and down the halls that were not in use and asked him to howl, which he did, dear dog. We really scared the poop out of them when we took him up on the second floor, opened a window, and his piercing howl floated over the grounds." Susan shivered with delight.

"The senior class dressed like characters from the story. God, it was fun."

By now they were outside. The Reverend Herbie and Carol Jones waved from among the wheat sheaves. A few people remarked that they'd miss Harry on Tomahawk this year. The local reporter roved around. Everyone was in a good mood. Naturally people talked about the grim discoveries but since it didn't touch anyone personally—the victim wasn't someone they knew—the talk soon dissolved into delicious personal gossip. Mim, Little Marilyn, and Fitz-Gilbert paraded around. Mim accepted everyone's sympathy with a nod and then asked them not to mention it again. Her nerves were raw, she said.

One stalwart soul was missing this year: old Fats Domino, the huge feline who had played the Halloween cat every year for the last fifteen. Fats had finally succumbed to old age, and Pewter had been pressed into service. Her dark-gray coat could almost pass for black in the night and she hadn't a speck of white on her. She gleefully padded over the tables, stopping to accept pats from her admirers.

Pewter grew expansive in the limelight. The more attention she received, the more she purred. Many people snapped photos of her, and she gladly paused for them. The newspaper photographer grabbed a few shots too. Well, that pesky Tucker had got her name in the papers once, the last time there'd been a murder in Crozet, but Pewter knew she'd be in color on the front page because the Harvest Festival always made the front page. Nor could she refrain from a major gloat over the fact that Mrs. Murphy and Tucker had to stay home, while she was the star of the occasion.

The craft and livestock prizes had been awarded, and now the harvest prizes were being announced. Miranda hurried over to stand behind her pumpkin. The gargantuan pumpkin next to hers was larger, indisputably larger, but Miranda hoped the competition's imperfect shape would sway Jim Sanburne her way. With so much milling about and chatting she didn't notice Pewter heading for the pumpkins. Mrs. Hogendobber felt no need to share this moment with the cat.

Mim, Little Marilyn, and Fitz-Gilbert stood off to the side. Mim noticed Harry and Blair.

"I know this Bainbridge fellow attended Yale and St. Paul's but we don't really know who he is. Harry ought to be more careful."

"You never minded Fair as her husband and he's not a stockbroker." Little Marilyn was simply making an observation, not trying to start an argument.

"At the time," Mim snapped, "I was relieved that Harry married, period. I feared she would go the way of Mildred Yost."

Mildred Yost, a pretty girl in Mim's class at Madeira, spurned so many beaus she finally ran out of them and spent her life as an old maid, a condition Mim found fearful. Single women just don't make it to the top of society. If a woman was manless she had better be a widow.

"Mother"—Fitz-Gilbert called Mim "Mother"—"Harry doesn't care about climbing to the top of society."

"Whether she cares or not, she shouldn't marry a person of low degree ... I mean, once she's established the fact that she *can* get married."

Mim babbled on in this vein, making very little sense. Fitz-Gilbert heard her sniff that being a divorcée teetered on the brink of a shadowy status. Why was Mim so concerned with Harry and who she was dating? he wondered. No other reason than that she felt nothing could go on in Crozet without her express approval. As usual, Mim's conversation did not run a charitable course. She even complained that the little witches, ghosts, and goblins overhead whirred too much, giving her a headache. The shock of recent events was making her crabbier than usual. Fitz tuned her out.

Danny Tucker, as Hercule Poirot, scooted next to Mrs. Hogendobber. His was the enormous pumpkin.

"Danny, why didn't you inform me that you grew this ... fruit?" Mrs. Hogendobber demanded.

"Well, Mom didn't want to upset you. We all know you want that blue ribbon."

Pewter arrived to sit between the two huge orange pumpkins, the finalists. Mrs. Hogendobber, talking to Danny, still didn't notice her. Pewter was insulted.

Jim picked up Miranda's pumpkin. He quickly put it back down. "These damn things get heavier every year." Miranda shot him a look. "Sorry, Miranda."

Pewter smelled pumpkin goo, as though the insides had been removed for pumpkin pie. She sniffed Miranda's pumpkin.

"See, the cat likes my pumpkin." Miranda smiled to the crowd.

"I *don't like any pumpkins*," Pewter replied.

"Do I want to pick this one up? I might fall over from the size of it." Jim smiled but put his large hands around Danny's pumpkin anyway. The enormous pumpkin was much heavier than the other pumpkin, oddly heavy. He replaced it. Puzzled, he lifted it up again.

Pewter, never able to control her curiosity, inspected the back of the pumpkin. A very neat, very large circle had been cut out and then glued back into place. If one wasn't searching for it, the tampering could easily be missed.

"Look," she said with forcefulness.

Danny Tucker was the only human who paid attention to her. He picked up his pumpkin. "Mayor Sanburne, I know my pumpkin's heavy, but not this heavy. Something's wrong."

"That is your pumpkin," Miranda stated.

"Yes, but it's too heavy." Danny picked it up again.

Pewter reached up and swatted the back of the orange globe. This led Danny's eyes, much sharper than Jim's or Miranda's, to the patch job in the back.

"Jim, we're waiting. We want a winner," Mim called out impatiently.

"Yes, dear, in a minute," he replied and the crowd laughed.

Danny pushed the circle and it wiggled. He reached into his jacket, retrieved a pocketknife, and slid it along the cutting line. The glue dislodged easily and he pried out the big circle. "Oh, wow!" Danny saw the back of a head. He assumed one of his buddies had done this as a joke. He reached in, grabbed the head by the hair, and pulled it out. A wave of sweet stink alerted him. This was no joke, no rubber or plastic head. Not quite knowing what to do he held the head away from him, giving the crowd a fine view of the loathsome sight. What was left of the eyes stared straight at them.

Danny, now realizing what he held, dropped the head. It hit the table with a sickening splat.

Pewter jumped away. She ran down to the squashes. If this was what the job of playing Halloween cat entailed, she was resigning.

People screamed. Jim Sanburne, almost by reflex, handed the ribbon to Miranda.

"I don't want it!" Miranda screamed.

Boom Boom Craycroft fainted dead away. The next thud heard was Blair Bainbridge hitting the ground.

Then Little Marilyn screeched, "I've seen that face before!"

21

Therapists in the county agreed to work with the students at Crozet High to help them through the trauma of what they'd seen.

Rick Shaw wondered if they could help him. He disliked the sight of the decayed head himself but not enough to have nightmares over it. When he and Cynthia Cooper collected the head, the first thing they did, apart from holding their noses, was check the open mouth. Not one tooth remained in the head. No dental records.

Cynthia led Little Marilyn away from the sight and asked her to clarify her statement.

"I don't know him but I think that's the vagrant who was wandering around maybe ten days ago. I'm not certain as to the date. You see, he passed the post office and I walked to the window and got a good look at him. That's all I can tell you." She was shaking.

"Thank you. You've had more than your share of this." Cynthia patted Little Marilyn on the back.

Fitz-Gilbert put his arms around her. "Come on, honey, let's go home."

"What about Mother?"

"Your father's taking care of her."

Meekly, Little Marilyn allowed Fitz to shepherd her to their Range Rover.

Cynthia stuck her notebook back in her pocket. As Rick was talking to other observers, the press photographer fired off some shots.

Cynthia took statements from Harry, Susan, Herb, Carol, Market, just everyone she could find. She would have interviewed Pewter if she could have. Market held the cat in his arms, each of them grateful for the reassuring warmth of the other.

Holding his wife's hand, Cabell Hall mentioned to Cynthia that she and Rick might want to call the video stores and have them pull their more gruesome horror movies until things settled down.

"Actually, Mr. Hall, I have no authority to do that but as a prominent citizen you could, or your wife could. People listen to you all."

"I'll do it then," Taxi Hall promised.

It took Cynthia more than an hour to get everyone out of there. Finally, Cynthia and Rick had a moment to themselves.

"Worse than I imagined." Rick slapped his thighs, a nervous gesture.

"Yeah, I thought we'd find the head, if we found it at all, back in the woods somewhere. It would be something someone would stumble on."

"You know what we got, Coop?" Rick breathed in the cool night air. "We got us a killer with a sick sense of humor."

22

Firelight casts shadows, which, depending on one's mood, can either be friendly highlights on the wall or misshapen monsters. Susan, Harry, and Blair sat before Harry's fireplace. The best friends had decided that Blair needed some company before he returned to his empty house.

The Harvest Fair had rattled everyone and Harry found another surprise when she opened the door to her house. Tucker, in a fit of pique at being left behind, had demolished Harry's favorite slippers. Mrs. Murphy told her not to do it but Tucker, when furious, was not a reasonable creature. The dog's punishment was that she had to remain locked in the kitchen while the adults talked in the living room. To make matters worse, Mrs. Murphy was allowed in the living room with them. Tucker laid her head between her paws and howled.

"Come on, Harry, let her in," Susan chided.

"Easy for you to say—they weren't your slippers."

"Actually, you should have taken her. She finds more clues than anyone." Susan cast a glance at the alert Mrs. Murphy perched on Harry's armchair. "And Murphy, of course."

"Is anyone hungry?" Harry remembered to be a hostess.

"No." Blair shook his head.

"Me neither," Susan agreed. "Poor you." She indicated Blair. "You moved here for peace and quiet and you landed in the middle of murder."

The muscles in Blair's handsome face tightened. "There's no escaping human nature. Remember the men put off the H.M.S. *Bounty* on Pitcairn Island?"

"I remember the great movie with Charles Laughton as Captain Bligh," Susan said.

"Well, in real life those Englishmen stranded on that paradise soon created their own version of hell. The sickness was within. The natives—by then they were mostly women, since the whites had killed the men—slit the Englishmen's throats in the middle of the night while they slept. Or at least historians think they did. No one really knows how the mutineers died, except that years later, when a European ship stopped by, the 'civilized' men were gone."

"Is that by way of saying that Crozet is a smaller version of Manhattan?" Harry reached over and poked the fire with one of the brass utensils left her by her parents.

"Big Marilyn as Brooke Astor." Susan then added, "Actually, Brooke Astor is a great lady. Mim's a wannabe."

"In the main, Crozet is a kinder place than Manhattan, but whatever is wrong with us shows up wherever we may be—on a more reduced scale. Passions are passions, regardless of century and geography." Blair stared into the fire.

"True enough." Harry sank back into her seat. "How about Little Marilyn saying she recognized that head?" The memory of the head made Harry queasy.

"A hobo she saw walking down the tracks while she was inside the post office." Blair added, "I vaguely remember him too. He was wearing old jeans and a baseball jacket. I wasn't that interested. Did you get a look at him?"

Harry nodded. "I noticed the Mets jacket. That's about it. However, even if these body parts belong to the fellow, we still don't know who he is."

"A student at U.V.A.?"

"God, Susan, I hope not." Harry allowed Mrs. Murphy to crawl into her lap.

"Too old." Blair folded his hands.

"It's a little hard to tell." Susan also called up the grisly sight.

"Ladies, I think I'll go home. I'm exhausted and I'm embarrassed that I passed out. This is getting to me, I suppose."

Harry walked him to the door and bade him goodnight before returning to Susan. Mrs. Murphy had taken over her chair. She lifted up the cat, who protested and then settled down again.

"He was distant tonight," Susan observed. "Guess it has been right much of a shock. He doesn't have a stick of furniture in his house, he doesn't know any of us, and then they find pieces of a body on his land. Now this. There goes his bucolic dream."

"The only good thing about tonight was getting to see Boom Boom faint."

"Aren't you ugly?" Susan laughed at her.

"You have to admit it was funny."

"Kind of. Fair had the pleasure of reviving her, digging in her voluminous purse for her tranquilizers, and then taking her home. If she gets too difficult I guess he could hit her up with a cc of Ace."

The thought of Boom Boom dosed with a horse tranquilizer struck Susan as amusing. "I'd say that Boom Boom wasn't an easy keeper," she said, using an equine term—quite accurate, too, because Boom Boom was anything but an easy keeper.

"I suppose we have to laugh at something. This is so macabre, what else can we do?" Harry scratched Mrs. Murphy behind the ears.

"I don't know."

"Are you afraid?"

"Are you?" Susan shot back.

"I asked you first."

"Not for myself," Susan replied.

"Me neither, because I don't think it had anything to do with me, but what if I fall into it? For all I know the killer might have buried those body parts in my cemetery."

"I think we're all right if we don't get in the way," Susan said.

"But what's 'in the way'? What's this all about?"

Mrs. Murphy opened one eye and said, "*Love or money.*"

23

Sunday dawned frosty but clear. The day's high might reach into the low fifties but not much more. Harry loved Sundays. She could work from sunup to sundown without interruption. Today she was planning to strip stalls, put down lime, and then cover and bank the sides with wood shavings. Physical labor limbered up her mind. Out in the stable she popped a soothing tape into the boom box and proceeded to fill up the wheelbarrow. The manure spreader was pulled up under a small earthen bank. That way Harry could roll the wheelbarrow to the top of the bank and tip the contents over into the wagon. She and her father had built the ramp in the late sixties. Harry was twelve. She worked so hard and with so much enthusiasm that as a reward her father bought her a pair of fitted chaps. The ramp had lasted these many years and so did the memory of the chaps.

Both of Harry's parents thought that idle hands did the Devil's work. True to her roots, Harry couldn't sit still. She was happiest when working and found it a cure for most ills. After her divorce she couldn't sleep much, so she would work sometimes sixteen or eighteen hours a day. The farm reflected this intensity. So did Harry. Her weight dropped to 110, too low for a woman of five foot six. Finally, Susan and Mrs. Hogendobber tricked her into going to the doctor. Hayden McIntire, forewarned, slammed shut his office door as they dragged her through it. A shot of B_{12} and a severe tongue-lashing convinced her that she'd better eat more. He also prescribed a mild sedative so she could sleep. She took it for a week and then threw it out. Harry hated drugs of any sort but her body accepted sleep and food again, so whatever Hayden did worked.

Each year with the repetition of the seasons, the cycle of planting, weeding, harvesting, and winter repairs, it was brought home to Harry that life was finite. Perhaps LIFE in capital letters wasn't finite but her life was. There would be a beginning, a middle, and an end. She wasn't quite at the middle yet, but she endured hints that she wasn't fifteen either. Injuries took longer to heal. Actually, she enjoyed more energy than she'd had as a teenager but what had changed the most was her mind. She'd lived just long enough to be seeing events and human personality types for the second and third time. She wasn't easily impressed or fooled. Most movies bored her to death, for that reason as well. She'd seen versions of those plots long before. They enthralled a new generation of fifteen-year-olds but there wasn't anything for her. What enthralled Harry was a job well done, laughter with her friends, a quiet ride on one of the horses. She'd withdrawn from the social whirl after her divorce— no great loss, but she was shocked to find out how little a single woman was valued. A single man was a plus. A single woman, a liability. The married women, Susan excepted, feared you.

Although Fair lacked money he didn't lack prestige in his field and Harry had been dragged along to banquets, boring dinners at the homes of thoroughbred breeders, and even more boring dinners at Saratoga. It was the same old parade of excellent facelifts, good bourbon, and tired stories. She was glad to be out of it. Boom Boom could have it all. Boom Boom could have Fair too. Harry didn't know why she'd gotten so mad at Fair the other day. She didn't love him anymore but she liked him. How could you not like a man you've known since you were in grade school and liked at first sight? The sheer folly of his attachment to Boom Boom irritated her though. If he found a sensible woman like Susan she'd be relieved. Boom Boom would suck up so much of his energy and money that eventually his work would suffer. He'd spent years building his practice. Boom Boom could wreck it in one circle of the seasons if he didn't wake up.

The sweet smell of pine shavings caressed her senses. For an instant Harry picked up the wall-phone receiver. She was going to call Fair and tell him what she really thought. Then she hung it up. How could she? He wouldn't listen. No one ever does in that situation. They wake up when they can.

She spread fresh shavings in the stalls.

Mrs. Murphy checked out the hayloft. Simon, sound asleep, never heard her tiptoe around him. He'd dragged up an old T-shirt of Harry's and then hollowed out part of a hay bale. He was curled up in the hollow on the shirt. She then walked over to the south side of the loft. The snake was hibernating. Nothing would wake her up until spring. Overhead the owl also slept. Satisfied that everything was as it should be, Mrs. Murphy climbed back down the ladder.

"Tucker," she called.

"What?" Tucker lounged around in the tack room.

"Want to go for a walk?"

"Where?"

"Foxden pastures off Yellow Mountain Road."

"Why there?"

"Paddy gave me an idea the other day and this is the first time I've had a chance to look in the daylight."

"Okay." Tucker stood up, shook herself, and then trotted out into the brisk air with her companion.

Mrs. Murphy told Tucker Paddy's idea about someone parking off Yellow Mountain Road on the old logging road and carrying the body parts to the cemetery in a plastic bag or something.

Once in the pastures Tucker put her nose down. Too much rain and too much time had elapsed. She smelled field mice, deer, fox, lots of wild turkeys, raccoons, and even the faint scent of bobcat.

While Tucker kept her nose to the ground Mrs. Murphy cast her sharp eyes around for a glint of metal, a piece of flesh, but there was nothing, nothing at all.

"Find anything?"

"No, too late." Tucker lifted her head. "How else could the body get to the cemetery? If the murderer didn't walk through these pastures, then he or she had to go right down Blair's driveway in front of God and Blair, anyway. Paddy's right. He came through here. Unless it's Blair."

Mrs. Murphy jerked her head around to view her friend full in the face. "You don't think that, do you?"

"I hope not. Who knows?"

The cat fluffed out her fur and then let it settle down. She headed for home. "You know what I think?"

"No."

"I think tomorrow at work will be impossible. Lardguts will go on and on and on about the head in the pumpkin. She got her name and her picture in the paper. God help us." Mrs. Murphy laughed.

24

". . . and the maggots had a field day, I can tell you that." Pewter perched on the hood of Harry's truck, parked behind the post office.

Mrs. Murphy, seated next to her, listened to the unending paean of self-praise. Tucker sat on the ground.

"I heard you ran into the squashes," Tucker called up.

"Of course I did, nitwit. I didn't want to injure the evidence," Pewter bragged. "Boy, you should have heard people scream once they realized it was real. A few even puked. Now I watched everyone—everyone—from my vantage point. Mrs. Hogendobber was horrified but has a cast-iron stomach. Poor Danny, was he grossed out! Susan and Ned rushed up to him but he wanted to go to his friends instead. That age, you know. Oh, Big Marilyn, she wasn't grossed out at all. She was outraged. I thought she'd flip her lid after the corpse in the boathouse but no, she was mad, bullshit mad, I tell you. Fitz stood there with his mouth hanging open. Little Marilyn hollered that she recognized the face, what there was of it. Harry didn't move a muscle. Stood there like a stone taking it all in. You know how she gets when things are awful. Real quiet and still. Oh, Boom Boom dropped, tits into the sand, and Blair keeled over too. What a night. I knew something was wrong with that pumpkin. I sat next to it. It takes humans so long to see the obvious." Pewter sighed a superior sigh.

"You were a teeny weeny bit disgusted." Mrs. Murphy flicked her tail.

Pewter turned her head. She puffed out her chest, refusing to be baited by her dearest friend, who was also a source of torment. "Certainly not."

A door closed in the near distance. The animals turned, observing Mrs. Hogendobber striding up the alleyway. As she drew near the animals she opened her mouth to speak to them but closed it again. She felt vaguely foolish carrying on a conversation with animals. This didn't prevent her from talking to herself, however. She smiled at the creatures and walked into the post office.

"Why'd Harry bring the truck?" Pewter asked.

"Wore herself out yesterday," Tucker replied.

Mrs. Murphy licked the side of her right front paw and rubbed it over her ears. "Pewter, do you have any theories about this?"

"Yeah, we got a real nut case on the loose."

"I don't think so." Mrs. Murphy washed the other paw.

"What makes you so smart?" Pewter snapped.

Mrs. Murphy let that go by. "If a human being has the time to think about a murder he can often make it look like an accident or natural death. If one of them kills in the heat of passion it's a bullet wound or a knife wound. Right?"

"Right," Tucker echoed, while Pewter's eyes narrowed to slits.

"Murphy, we all know that."

"Then we know it was a hurry-up job and it wasn't passion. Someone in Crozet was surprised by the dead person."

"A nasty surprise." Tucker followed her friend's thinking. "But who? And what could be so terrible about the victim that he should have had to die for it?"

"When we know that, we'll know everything," the cat said in a low voice.

25

The coroner's conclusions, neatly typed, rested on Rick Shaw's desk. The deceased was a white male in his early thirties. Identity remained unknown but what was known was that this fellow, who should have been in the prime of life, was suffering from malnutrition and liver damage. Larry Johnson, meticulous in the performance of his duties, added in his bold vertical handwriting that while alcohol abuse might have contributed to the liver damage, the organ could have been diseased for reasons other than alcohol abuse. Then, too, certain medications taken over many years could also have caused liver damage.

Cooper charged into the office. She tossed more paperwork onto the sheriff's desk. "More reports from Saturday night."

Rick grunted and shoved them aside. "You haven't said anything about the coroner's report."

"Died of a blow to the head. A child can kill someone with a blow to the head if it's done right. We're still in the dark."

"What about a revenge motive?"

She was tired of kicking around ideas. Dead ends frustrated her. The fax machine hummed. She walked over to it almost absent-mindedly. "Boss, come over here."

Rick joined her and watched as the pages slowly rolled out of the machine. It was Blair Bainbridge's record.

He had been a suspect in the murder of his lover, an actress. However, he wasn't a suspect for long. The killer, an obsessed fan, was picked up by the police and confessed. The eerie thing was that the beautiful woman's corpse had been dismembered.

"Shit," was Cynthia's response.

"Let's go," was Rick's.

26

Heavy work gloves protected his hands as Blair righted tombstones, replaced the sod, and rolled it flat. The trees, now barren, surrounded the little cemetery like mournful sentinels. He stopped his labors when he saw the squad car roll down the driveway. He swung open the iron gate and headed down the hill to meet them.

A cool breeze eased off Yellow Mountain. Blair asked Rick Shaw and Cynthia Cooper inside. A couple of orange crates doubled as chairs.

"You know, there are wonderful auctions this time of year," Coop volunteered. "Check in the classifieds. I furnished my house, thanks to those auctions."

"I'll check it out."

Rick noticed that Blair was growing a thin military moustache. "Another modeling job coming up?"

"How'd you guess?" Blair smiled.

Rick rubbed under his nose. "Well, I'll get to the point. This isn't a social call, as I'm sure you've surmised. Your records indicate an actress with whom you were involved was brutally murdered and dismembered. What do you have to say?"

Blair blanched. "It was horrible. I thought when the police caught the murderer I'd feel some comfort. Well, I guess I did, in that I knew he wouldn't kill anyone else, but it didn't fill the ... void."

"Is there anyone in Crozet or Charlottesville who might know of this incident?"

"Not that I know of. I mean, a few people recognized my face from magazines but no one knows me here. Guess that doesn't look so good for me, huh?"

"Let's just say you're an unknown factor." Rick shifted his weight. The orange crate wasn't comfortable.

"I didn't kill anybody. I think I could kill in self-defense or to protect someone I love, but other than that, I don't think I could do it."

"What one person defines as self-defense another might define as murder." Cynthia watched Blair's handsome features.

"I am willing to cooperate with you in any way. And I've refused to talk to the press. They'll only muck it up."

"Why don't you tell me what happened in New York?" Rick's voice was steady, unemotional.

Blair ran his hands through his hair. "You know, Sheriff, I'd like to forget that. I came here to forget that. Can you imagine what it was like to see that head pulled out of a pumpkin?"

The sheriff softened. "Not pretty for any of us."

Blair took a deep breath. "I knew Robin Mangione from a shoot we did for Baker and Reeves, the big New York department store. I guess that was three years ago. One thing led to another and, well, we stopped dating other people and got involved. Our work schedules often took us out of town but whenever we were in New York we were together."

"You didn't live together?" Rick asked.

"No. It's a little different in New York than here. In a place like this people get married. In New York, people can be as good as married and yet live in separate apartments for their entire lives. Maybe because of the millions of people, one needs a sense of privacy, of separate space, more than you do here. Anyway, living together wasn't a goal."

"What about her goals?" Cooper was suspicious about this living-apart stuff.

"She was more independent than I was, truthfully. Anyway, Robin inspired devotion from men. She could stop traffic. Fame, any kind of fame really, brings good and bad. The flotsam and jetsam of fame is how I think of it, and Robin was sometimes hassled by male admirers. Usually a sharp word from her, or if needs be from me, took care of the problem. Except for the guy who killed her."

"Know anything about him?" Rick asked.

"What you know, except that I watched him at the trial. He's short, balding, one of those men you could pass on the street and never notice. He sent letters. He called. She changed her number. He'd wait for her outside the theater. I got in the habit of picking her up because he was such a nuisance. He began to threaten. We told the police. With predictable results." Rick dropped his gaze for a moment while Blair continued: "And one day when I was out of town on a shoot he broke the locks and got into her apartment. She was alone. The rest you know."

Indeed they did. Stanley Richards, the crazed fan, panicked after he killed Robin. Disposing of a body in New York City would try the imagination of a far more intelligent man than Stanley. So he put her in the bathtub, cut her throat and wrists and ankles, and tried to drain most of the blood out of the body. Then he dismembered her with the help of a meat cleaver. He fed pieces of the body to the disposal but it jammed up on the bone. Finally, desperate, he spent the rest of the night hauling out little bits of body and dumping her east, west, north, and south. The head he saved for the Sheep Meadow, in the middle of Central Park, where in exhaustion he put it down on the grass. A dawn jogger saw him and reported him as soon as he found a cop.

Neither Rick nor Cynthia felt the need to rehash those details.

"Don't you find it curious that—"

"Curious?!" Blair erupted, cutting off Rick. "It's sick!"

"Do you have any enemies?" Cynthia inquired.

Blair lapsed into silence. "My agent, occasionally."

"What's his name?" Rick had a pencil and pad out.

"Her name. Gwendolyn Blackwell. She's not my enemy but she broods if I don't take every job that comes down the pike. That woman would work me into an early grave if I let her."

"That's it? No irate husbands? No jilted ladies? No jealous competitor?"

"Sheriff, modeling isn't as glamorous as you might suppose."

"I thought all you guys were gay," Rick blurted out.

"Fifty-fifty, I'd say." Blair had heard this so many times it didn't rock his boat.

"Is there anyone you can think of—the wildest connection doesn't matter—anyone who would know enough to duplicate what happened to Robin?"

Blair cast his deep eyes on Cynthia. It made her heart flutter. "Not one person. I really do think this is a grim coincidence."

Rick and Cynthia left as baffled as they were when they arrived. They'd keep an eye on Blair, but then they'd keep an eye on everyone.

27

The western half of Albemarle County would soon feel the blade of the bulldozer. The great state of Virginia and its Department of Highways, a little fiefdom, decided to create a bypass through much of the best land in the county. Businesses would be obliterated, pastures uprooted, property values crunched, and dreams strangled. The western bypass, as it came to be known, had the distinction of being outmoded before it was even begun. That and the fact that it imperiled the watershed meant little to the highway department. They wanted the western bypass and they were going to have it no matter who they displaced and no matter how they scarred the environment.

The uproar caused by this high-handed tactic obscured the follow-up story about the head in the pumpkin. Since no one could identify the corpse, interest fizzled. It would remain a good story for Halloweens to come.

The respite was appreciated by Jim Sanburne, mayor, and the civic worthies of Crozet. Big Marilyn refused to discuss the subject, so it withered in her social circle, which was to say the six or seven ladies as snobbish as herself.

Little Marilyn recovered sufficiently to call her brother, Stafford, and invite him home for a weekend. This upset Mim more than the sum of the body parts. It meant she'd have to be sociable with his wife, Brenda.

This projected discomfort, awarded to Little Marilyn in lavish proportions by her mother, almost made the young woman back down and uninvite her brother and his wife. But it was opening hunt, such a pretty sight, and Stafford loved to photograph such events. She kept her nerve. Stafford would be home next weekend.

Weary of the swirl of tempestuous egos, Fitz-Gilbert decided to stay out late that night. First he stopped at Charley's, where he bumped into Ben Seifert on his way out. Fitz tossed back one beer and then hit the road again. He ran into Fair Haristeen at Sloan's and pulled up the barstool next to the vet.

"A night of freedom?"

Fair signaled for a beer for Fitz. "You might call it that. What about you?"

"It's been a hell of a week. You know my office was ransacked. Doesn't appear to have anything to do with the ... murder ... but it was upsetting on top of everything else. The sheriff and his deputy came out, took notes and so forth. Some money was missing, and a CD player, but obviously it's not at the top of their list. Then Cabell Hall called me to tell me to watch my stock market investments, since the market is on a one-way trip these days—down—and my mother-in-law—oh, well, why talk about her? Oh, I just ran into Ben Seifert at Charley's. He's an okay guy, but he's just burning to suc- ceed Cabell some day. The thought of Ben Seifert running Allied National gives me pause. And then of course there's my father-in- law. He wants to call out the National Guard."

"Those are my problems. What are yours?" Fitz asked.

"I don't know." Fair was puzzled. "Boom Boom's out with that model guy. She says he asked her to the Cancer Fund Ball but I don't know. He didn't seem that interested in her when I met him. I kind of thought he liked Harry."

"Here's to women." Fitz-Gilbert smiled. "I don't know anything about them but I've got one." He clinked glasses with Fair.

Fair laughed. "My daddy used to say, 'You can't live with them and you can't live without them.' I didn't know what he was talking about. I do now."

"Marilyn is great by herself. It's when she's in the company of her mother ..." Fitz-Gilbert wiped froth off his lips. "My mother-in-law can be a whistling bitch. I feel guilty just being here ... like I slipped my leash. But I'm glad I didn't get dragged to the Cancer Ball. Marilyn says she can only do but so many a year, and she wanted to get things ready for Stafford and Brenda. Thank God. I need the break."

Fair changed the subject. "Do you think this new guy likes Harry? I thought guys like that wanted leggy blondes or other guys."

"Can't speak for his preferences, but Harry's a good-looking woman. Natural. Outdoorsy. I'll never know why you guys broke up, buddy."

Fair, unaccustomed to exchanging much personal information, sat quietly and then signaled for another beer. "She's a good person. We grew up together. We dated in high school. We, well, she was more like my sister than my wife."

"Yeah, but you knew Boom Boom since you were yay-high," Fitz countered.

"Not the same."

"That's the truth."

"Just what do you mean by that?" Fair felt prickly anxiety creeping up his spine.

"Uh ... well, I mean that they are so totally different from one another. One's a quarter horse and the other's a racehorse." What he wanted to say was, "One's a quarter horse and the other's a jackass," but he didn't. "Boom Boom puts lead in your pencil. I've seen her start motors that have been stalled for years."

Fair smiled broadly. "She is attractive."

"Dynamite, buddy, dynamite." Fitz, less inhibited than usual, kept on. "But I'd take Harry any day of the week. She's funny. She's a partner. She's a friend. That other stuff—hey, Fair, it gets old."

"You're certainly forthcoming," came the dry reply.

"Nothing's preventing you from telling me to keep my mouth shut."

"While we're on the subject, tell me what you see in Little Marilyn. She's a miniature of her mother, on her way to being as cold as a wedge, and near as I can tell she's even slacking off on the charity work. What's the—"

"Attraction?" Fitz decided not to take offense. After all, he was handing it out so he'd better take it. "The truth? The truth is that I married her because it was the thing to do. Two respectable family fortunes. Two great family names. My parents, had they lived, would have been proud. Superficial stuff, when you get right down to it. And I was kind of wild as a kid. I was ready to settle down. I needed to settle down. What's strange is that I've come to love Marilyn. You don't know the real Marilyn. When she's not knocking herself out trying to be superior she's pretty wonderful. She's a shy little bug and underneath it there's a good heart. And what's so funny is that I think she likes me too. I don't think she married me for love, any more than I married her for it. She went along with the merger orchestrated by that *harridan*"—he sputtered the word—"of a mother. Maybe Mim knew more than we did. Whatever the reason, I have learned to love my wife. And someday I hope I can tear her away from this place. We'll go someplace where the names Sanburne and Hamilton don't mean diddly."

Fair stared at Fitz, and Fitz returned the stare. Then they burst out laughing.

"Another beer for my buddy." Fitz slapped money on the counter.

Fair eagerly grabbed the cold glass. "We might as well get shitfaced."

"My sentiments exactly."

By the time Fitz reached home, supper was cold and his wife was not amused. He cajoled her with the tidbit about Boom Boom and Blair attending the Cancer Fund Ball and then poured them each a delicious sherry for a nightcap, a ritual of theirs. By the time they crawled into bed, Little Marilyn had forgiven her husband.

28

Two men argued at the end of an old country road. Heavy cloud cover added to the tension and gloom. Way up in the distance beckoned the sealed cavern of Claudius Crozet's first tunnel through the Blue Ridge Mountains.

One man clenched his fists and shook them in the face of the other. "You goddamned bloodsucker. I'm not giving you another cent. How was I to know he'd show up? He's been locked away for years!"

Ben Seifert, being threatened, just laughed. "He showed up in my office, not yours, asshole, and I want something for my pains— a bonus!"

The next thing he knew a brightly colored climbing rope was flipped over his neck and the word *bonus* was choked right out of him. Strangulation took less than two minutes.

Still furious, the killer viciously kicked the body, breaking some ribs. Then he shook his head, collected his wits, and bent down to pick up the limp corpse. This was an unpleasant task, since the dead man had voided himself.

Cursing, he tossed the body over his shoulder, for he was a strong man, and carried him up to the tunnel. Although it had been sealed after World War II, there was an opening of loose stones which had been dug out by a former Crozet resident. The railroad had overlooked resealing the tunnel.

His brain worked clearly now. He removed the stones with care so as not to tear up his hands and then dragged the body into the tunnel. He could hear the click of little claws as he slammed his unwanted burden on the ground. He walked outside and replaced the stones. Then he picked his way down the hillside, composing himself, brushing off his clothes. People rarely hiked up to the tunnels. With luck it would be months before they found that bastard, if they found him at all.

The problem was Seifert's car. He searched the seats, trunk, and glove compartment to make certain no note existed, no clue to their meeting. Then he started the engine and drove to the outskirts of town, leaving the car at a gas station. He wiped off the steering wheel, the door handle, everything he'd touched. The car shone when he finished with it. Shrewdly, he'd left his own car three miles away, where the victim had picked him up on Three Chopt Road. That was at one o'clock this morning. It was now four-thirty and darkness would soon enough give way to light.

He jogged the three miles to his own car, parked behind one of the cement trucks at Craycroft Cement. Unless someone walked around the mixer they'd never have seen his car.

He had figured killing his unwanted partner was a possibility, hence the preparation. Not that he had wanted to kill the dumb son of a bitch, but he'd gotten so greedy. He kept bleeding him. That left little choice.

Blackmail rarely ended with both parties wreathed in smiles.

29

The mail slid into the boxes but the magazines had to be folded. Ned Tucker received more magazines than anyone in Crozet. What was even more amazing was that he read them. Susan said it was like living with an encyclopedia.

The morning temperature hovered at thirty-nine degrees Fahrenheit, so Harry, Mrs. Murphy, and Tucker hopped to work at a brisk pace. Harry brought the blue truck only when the weather was filthy or she had errands to run. As she'd done her grocery shopping yesterday, the blue bomb reposed by the barn.

Harry cherished the quiet of her walk and the early hour alone in the post office after Rob Collier dropped off the mail. The repetition of chores soothed her, like a labor's liturgy. There was comfort in consistency.

The back door opened and closed. Mrs. Murphy, Tucker, and even Harry could tell by the tread that it was Mrs. Hogendobber.

"Harry."

"Mrs. H."

"Missed you at the Cancer Ball."

"Wasn't invited."

"You could have gone alone. I do sometimes."

"Not at a hundred and fifty dollars a ticket I can't."

"I forgot about that part. Larry Johnson paid for my ticket. He's quite a good dancer."

"Who all was there?"

"Susan and Ned. She wore her peach organdy dress. Very becoming. Herbie and Carol. She wore the ice-blue gown with the ostrich feather ruff. You should have seen Mim. She had on one of those gowns Bob Mackie designs for *Dynasty*."

"Did she really?"

"I am here to tell you, girl, she did, and that dress must have cost her as much as a Toyota. There isn't a bugle bead left in Los Angeles, I am sure of it. Why, if you dropped her in that lake of hers she'd attract every fish in it."

Harry giggled. "Maybe she'd get along better with the fish than she does with people."

"Let's see, I said Ned and Susan. Fair wasn't there. Little Marilyn and Fitz weren't there either—must be taking a break from the black-tie circuit. Most of the Keswick and Farmington Hunt Clubs showed up, and the country club set too. Wall to wall." Mrs. Hogendobber picked up a handful of mail and helped to sort.

Mrs. Murphy sat in a mail bin. She had sat so long waiting for a push that she fell asleep. Mrs. Hogendobber's arrival woke her up.

"What did you wear?"

"You know that emerald-green satin dress I wear at Christmas?"

"Uh-huh."

"I had it copied in black with gold accents. I don't look so fat in black."

"You're not fat," Harry reassured her. It was true. She wasn't fat but she was, well, ample.

"Ha. If I eat any more I'm going to resemble a heifer."

"How come you haven't told me that Blair escorted Boom Boom to the ball?"

"If you know it why should I tell you?" Mrs. Hogendobber liked to stand behind the post boxes and shoot the letters in. "Well, he did. Actually, I think she asked him, because the tickets were in her name. The hussy."

"Did he have a good time?"

"He just looked so handsome in his tuxedo and I like his new moustache. Reminds me of Ronald Colman. Boom Boom dragged him to meet everyone. She was wearing her party face. I guess he had a good time."

"No dread disease?"

"No. She danced so much I doubt she even had time to tell him of the sorrows of her youth and how awful her parents were." Miranda didn't crack a smile when she relayed this observation but her eyes twinkled.

"My, my, doesn't he have something to look forward to: 'The Life and Times of Boom Boom Craycroft.' "

"Don't worry about her."

"I'm not."

"Harry, I've known you since you were born. Don't lie to me. I remember the day you insisted we call you Harry instead of Mary. Funny that you later married Fair Haristeen."

"You remember everything."

"I do indeed. You were four years old and you loved your kitty—now let me see, her name was Skippy. You wanted to be furry like Skippy, so you asked us to call you Hairy, which became Harry. You thought if we called you that, you'd get furry and turn into a kitty. Name stuck."

"What a great cat Skippy was."

This aroused Mrs. Murphy from her half-slumberous state. "Not as great as the Murphy!"

"Ha!" Tucker laughed.

"Shut up, Tucker. There was a dog before you, you know. A German shepherd. His photo is on the desk at home, for your information."

"Big deal."

"Playtime." Harry heard the meows and thought Mrs. Murphy

wanted a push in the mail bin. Although it wasn't what the cat was talking about, she happily rolled around in the canvas-bottomed cart.

Mrs. Hogendobber unlocked the front door. She no sooner turned the key than Blair appeared, wearing a heavy red Buffalo-checked jacket over a flannel shirt. He rubbed his boots over the scraper.

"Good morning, Mrs. Hogendobber. I enjoyed our dance last night. You float over the floor."

Mrs. Hogendobber blushed. "Why, what a sweet thing to say."

Blair stepped right up to the counter. "Harry."

"No packages."

"I don't want any packages. I want your attention."

He got Mrs. Hogendobber's too.

"Okay." Harry leaned over the other side of the counter. "My full attention."

"I've been told there are furniture and antique auctions on the weekends. Will you tell me which are the good ones and will you go along with me? I'm getting tired of sitting on the floor."

"Of course." Harry liked to help out.

Mrs. Murphy grumbled and then jumped out of the mail bin, sending it clattering across the floor. She hopped up on the counter.

"The other request I have is that you accompany me to a dinner party Little Marilyn is giving for Stafford and Brenda tomorrow night. I know it's short notice but she called this morning to ask me."

"What's the dress?" Harry couldn't believe her ears.

"I'm going to wear a yellow shirt, a teal tie, and a brown herringbone jacket. Does that help?"

"Yes." Mrs. Hogendobber answered because she knew Harry was hopeless in these matters.

"I've never seen you dressed up, Harry." Blair smiled. "I'll pick you up tomorrow night at seven." He paused. "I looked for you at the Cancer Ball last night."

Harry started to say that she wasn't invited but Mrs. Hogendobber leapt into this breach. "Harry had another engagement. She's kept so busy."

"Oh. Well, I wanted to dance with you." He jammed his hands in his pockets. "That Craycroft woman is a real motor-mouth. Never stopped talking about herself. I know it isn't gallant of me to criticize someone who made such an effort to have me meet people, but jeez"—he let out his breath—"she likes to party."

Both Harry and Mrs. Hogendobber tried to conceal their delight at this comment.

"*Boom Boom knows you're rich,*" Mrs. Murphy piped up. "*Plus you're single, good-looking, and she's not above driving Fair crazy with you, either.*"

"She has a lot to say this morning, doesn't she?" Blair patted Mrs. Murphy's head.

"*You bet, buster. Stick with me, I'll give you the scoop on everybody.*"

Blair laughed. "Now, Murphy—I mean, Mrs. Murphy; how rude of me—you promised to help me find a friend exactly like you."

"*I'm going to throw up,*" Tucker mumbled from the floor.

Blair picked up his mail, got to the door, and stopped. "Harry?"

"What?"

He held up his hands in entreaty. Mrs. Hogendobber kicked Harry behind the counter. Blair couldn't see this.

"Oh, yes, I'd love to go."

"Seven tomorrow." He left, whistling.

"That hurt. I'll have a bruised ankle tomorrow."

"You have no sense when it comes to men!" Miranda exclaimed.

"I wonder what got into him?" Harry's gaze followed him to his truck.

"Yours is not to reason why. Yours is but to do and die."

Just then Susan sauntered in through the back door. " 'Into the valley of Death rode the six hundred.' "

"Blair Bainbridge just asked her to a dinner party at the Hamiltons' tomorrow night and he wants her to take him to some auctions."

"Yahoo!" Susan clapped her hands together. "Good work, girl."

"I didn't do anything."

"Susan, help me with her. She nearly told him she didn't have a date for the Cancer Ball. She's going to iron her jeans for the dinner party and think she's dressed. This calls for action."

Miranda and Susan looked at each other and then both looked at Harry. Before she knew it, each one grabbed an arm and she was propelled out the back door and thrown into Susan's car.

"Hey, hey, I can't leave work."

"I'll take care of everything, dear." Miranda slammed shut the door as Susan cranked the motor.

30

The Allied National Bank overlooked Benjamin Seifert's tardiness. No one called Cabell Hall to report Ben's absence. If Ben had found out about such a call the perpetrator wouldn't have kept his job for long. Often on the run and not the most organized man in the office, Benjamin might have made morning appointments without notifying the secretary. Ben, a bright light at Allied, could look forward to taking over the huge new branch being built on Route 29N in Charlottesville, so no one wanted to get on his bad side. The more astute workers realized that his ambitions extended beyond the new branch at 29N.

When he didn't phone in after lunch the little group thought it odd. By three, Marion Molnar was worried enough to call his home. No answer. Benjamin, divorced, often stayed out into the wee hours. No hangover lasted this long.

By five, everyone expressed concern. They dialed Rick Shaw,

who said he'd check around. Just about the time Marion called, so did Yancey Mills, owner of the little gas station. He recognized Benjamin's car. He'd figured something was wrong with it and that Benjamin would call in. But it was near to closing time and he hadn't heard anything and there was no answer at Ben's house.

Rick sent Cynthia Cooper over to the gas station. She checked out the car. Seemed fine. Neither she nor Rick pressed the panic button but they routinely called around. Cynthia called Ben's parents. By now she was getting a bit alarmed. If they found no trace of him by morning they'd start looking for him. What if Ben had refused a loan, or the bank had foreclosed, and someone had it in for him? It seemed far-fetched, but then nothing was normal anymore.

31

It was her face reflecting back from the mirror, but Harry needed time to get used to it. The new haircut revealed those high cheekbones, full lips, and strong jaw so reminiscent of her mother's family, the Hepworths. The clear brown Minor eyes looked back at her too. Like everyone else in Crozet, Harry combined the traits of her parents, a genetic testimony to the roulette of human breeding. The luck held in her case. For others, some of them friends, this wasn't true. Multiple sclerosis haunted generation after generation of one Crozet family; others never escaped the snares of cancer; still others inherited a marked tendency to drink or drugs. The older she got the luckier she felt.

As she focused on the mirror she recalled her mother seated before this very mirror, paint pots out, lipsticks marshaled like stubby soldiers, powder puffs lurking like peach-colored land mines. Much as Grace Hepworth Minor had harassed, wheedled, and bribed her sole child, Harry steadfastly refused the lure of feminine artifice. She was too young then to articulate her steely rejection of the commercialization of womanness. All she knew was that she didn't want to do it, and no one could make her. As years sped by, this instinctual rejection was examined. Harry realized that she thought she was clean and neat in appearance, healthy, and outgoing. If a man needed that fake stuff, in her opinion he wasn't much of a man. She was determined to be loved for herself and not because she'd paid out good money to fit the current definition of femininity. Then again, Harry never felt the need to prove that she was feminine. She felt feminine and that was enough for her. It ought to be enough for him. In the case of Fair it turned out to be enough for a while.

In this respect Boom Boom and Harry represented the two poles of female philosophy. Maybe it was why they never could get along. Boom Boom averaged one thousand dollars each month on her upkeep. She was waxed, dyed, massaged. She was awash in nutrients which took into account her special hormonal needs. At least that's what the bottles said. She dieted constantly. She thought nothing of flying to New York to shop. Then the bills truly rolled in. One pair of crocodile shoes from Gucci was $1,200. Sleek, up-to-date, and careful to cover any flaws, real or imagined, Boom Boom represented a triumph of American cosmetics, fashion, and elective surgery. Her self-centeredness, fed by this culture, blossomed into solipsism of the highest degree. Boom Boom marketed herself as an ornament. In time she became one. Many men chased after that ornament.

When Harry inspected the new Harry, courtesy of the strong-arm tactics of Miranda and Susan, she was relieved to see a lot of the old Harry. Okay, blusher highlighted those cheeks, lipstick warmed her mouth, but nothing too extreme. No nasty eyeshadow covered her lids. The mascara only accentuated her already long black lashes. She looked like herself, only maybe more so. She was trying to make sense of it, trying to like the simple suede skirt and silk shirt that Susan had forced her to buy upon pain of death. Spending is worse than pain, she thought; it lasts longer.

Too late now. The check had been written, the merchandise carried home. No more time to fret over it anyway because Blair was knocking at the front door.

She opened it.

He studied Harry. "You're the only woman I know who looks as good in jeans as in a skirt. Come on."

Mrs. Murphy and Tucker stood on the back of the sofa and watched the humans motor down the driveway.

"*What do you think?*" Tucker asked the cat.

"*She looks hot.*" Mrs. Murphy batted Tucker. "*Aren't you glad we don't have to wear clothes? Wouldn't you look adorable in a little gingham dress?*"

"*And you'd have to wear four bras.*" Tucker nudged Mrs. Murphy in the ribs, nearly knocking her off the sofa.

That appealed to Mrs. Murphy's demented sense of humor. She rocketed off the back of the sofa, calling for the dog to chase her. She dashed straight for the wall, enticing Tucker to think that she was trapped, and then hit the wall with all fours, banking off it, sailing right over Tucker's head while the dog skidded into the wall with a hard bump. Mrs. Murphy performed this maneuver with a demonic sense of purpose. Enraged, Tucker's feet spun so fast under her that she shook like a speeded-up movie. Around and around they ripped and tore until finally, as Tucker charged under an end table and Mrs. Murphy pranced on top of it, the lamp on the table teetered and tottered, only to wobble on its base and smash onto the floor. The crash scared them and they flew into the kitchen. After a few moments of quiet they ventured out.

"Uh-oh," Tucker said.

"*Well, she needed a new lamp anyway. This one had gray hairs.*"

"She'll blame me for it." Tucker already felt persecuted.

"*As soon as we hear the truck, we'll hide under the bed. That way she can rant and rave and get it out of her system. She'll be over it by tomorrow morning.*"

"*Good idea.*"

32

"The meringue tarts." Little Marilyn triumphantly nodded to Tiffany to serve the dessert.

Little Marilyn practiced nouvelle cuisine. Big Marilyn followed suit, which was the first time mother had imitated daughter. Jim Sanburne complained that nouvelle cuisine was a way to feed people less. Bird food, he called it. Fortunately, Big Marilyn and Jim weren't invited to the small dinner tonight. Cabell Hall was, though. Fitz continually flattered the important banker, his justification being that three years ago Cabell had introduced him to Marilyn. Little Marilyn's septic personality had been somewhat sweetened by the absence of her maternal unit, so she, too, showered attention on Cabell and Taxi.

"Tell Blair how you were nicknamed Taxi." Little Marilyn beamed at the older woman.

"Oh, that. He doesn't want to hear that." Taxi smiled.

"Yes, I do." Blair encouraged her as Cabby watched with affection his wife of nearly three decades.

"Cabell is called Cabby. Fine and good but when the children were little I hauled them to school. I picked them up from school. I carried them to the doctor, the dentist, Little League, dance lessons, piano lessons, and tennis lessons. One day I came home dog tired and ready to bite. My husband, just home from his own hard day, wanted to know how I could be so worn out from doing my duties as a housewife. I explained in vivid terms what I'd been doing all day and he said I should start a local taxi service, as I already ran one for my own children. The name stuck. It's sexier than Florence."

"Honey, you'd be sexy if your name were Amanda," Cabby praised her.

"What's wrong with the name Amanda?" Brenda Sanburne asked.

"Miss Amanda Westover was the feared history teacher at my prep school," her husband told her. "She taught Cabell, me—she may have even taught Grandfather. *Mean*." Stafford Sanburne and Cabell Hall were both Choate graduates.

"Not as mean as my predecessor at the bank." Cabell winked.

"Artie Schubert." Little Marilyn tried to recall a face. "Wasn't it Artie Schubert?"

"You were too young to remember." Taxi patted Little Marilyn's bejeweled hand. "He made getting a loan a most unpleasant process, or so I heard. Cabby and I were still in Manhattan at the time and he was approached by a board member of Allied National to take over the bank. Well, Richmond seemed like the end of the earth—"

Cabby interrupted: "It wasn't that bad."

"What happened was that we fell in love with central Virginia, so we bought a house here and Cabby commuted to work every day."

"Still do. Mondays, Wednesdays, and Fridays. Tuesdays and Thursdays I'm at the branch in the downtown mall in Charlottesville. Do you know that in the last ten years or so our growth rate has exceeded that of every other bank in the state of Virginia—by percentage, of course. We're still a small bank when compared to Central Fidelity, or Crestar, or Nations Bank."

"Darling, this is a dinner party, not a stockholders' meeting." Taxi laughed. "Is it obvious how much my husband loves his job?"

As the guests agreed with Taxi and speculated on how people find the work that suits them, Fitz-Gilbert asked Blair, "Will you be attending opening hunt?"

Blair turned to Harry. "Will I be attending opening hunt?"

Stafford leaned toward Blair. "If she won't take you, I will. You see, Harry will probably be riding tomorrow."

"Why don't you help me get ready in the morning and then you can meet everyone there?" Harry's voice registered nothing but innocence.

This drew peals of laughter from the others, even Brenda Sanburne, who knew enough to realize that getting ready for a fox hunt can be a nerve-racking experience.

"Nice try, Harry." Fitz-Gilbert toasted in her direction.

"Now my curiosity's got the better of me. What time do I have to be at your barn?"

Harry twirled her fork. "Seven-thirty."

"That's not so bad," Blair rejoined.

"If you drink enough tonight it will be," Stafford promised.

"Don't even mention it." Fitz-Gilbert put his hand to his forehead.

"I'll say. You've been getting snookered lately. This morning when I woke up, what a sorry face I saw." Little Marilyn pursed her lips.

"Did you know, Blair, that Virginia is home to more fox-hunting clubs than any other state in the Union? Nineteen in all—two in Albemarle County," Cabell informed him. "Keswick on the east side and Farmington on the west side."

"No, I didn't know that. I guess there are a lot of foxes. What's the difference between the two clubs here? Why don't they have just one large club?"

Harry answered, a wicked smile on her face, "Well, you see,

Blair, Keswick Hunt Club is old, old, old Virginia money living in old, old, old Virginia homes. Farmington Hunt Club is old, old, old Virginia money that's subdivided."

This caused a whoop and a shout. Stafford nearly choked on his dessert.

Once recovered from this barb, the small group discussed New York, the demise of the theater, a topic creating lively debate, since Blair didn't think theater was pooping out and Brenda did. Blair told some funny modeling stories which were enlivened by his talent for mimicry. Everyone decided the stock market was dismal so they'd wait out the bad times.

After dessert, the women moved over to the window seat in the living room. Brenda liked Harry. Many white people were likable but you couldn't really trust them. Even though she knew her but slightly, Brenda felt she could trust Harry. In her odd way, the postmistress was color blind. What you saw with Harry was what you got and Brenda truly appreciated that. Whenever a white person said, "I'm not prejudiced myself . . . ," you knew you were in trouble.

The men retired to the library for brandy and Cuban cigars. Fitz-Gilbert prided himself on the contraband and wouldn't divulge his source. Once you smoked a Montecristo, well, there was no looking back.

"One day you'll spill the beans." Stafford passed the cigar under his nose, thrilling to the beguiling scent of the tobacco.

Cabell laughed. "When hell freezes over. Fitz can keep a secret."

"The only reason you guys are nice to me is because of my cigars."

"That and the fact that you were first oar for Andover." Stafford puffed away.

"You look more like a wrestler than a first oar." Blair, too, surrendered to the languor the cigar produced.

"I was skinny as a rail when I was a kid." Fitz patted his small potbelly. "Not anymore."

"Ever know Binky Colfax when you were at Andover? My class at Yale."

"Binky Colfax. Valedictorian." Fitz-Gilbert flipped through his yearbook and handed it to Blair.

"God, it's a good thing Binky was an academic." Blair laughed. "You know, he's in the administration now. An undersecretary in the State Department. When you remember what a wuss the guy was, it makes me fear for our government. I mean, think of it, all those guys we knew at Yale and Harvard and Princeton and . . ."

"Stanford," Stafford chipped in.

"Do I have to?" Blair asked.

"Uh-huh." Stafford nodded.

". . . Stanford. Well, the nerds went into government or research. In ten years' time those guys will be the bureaucracy serving the guys that will be elected." Blair shook his head.

"Do you think every generation goes through this? You pick up the paper one day or you watch the six o'clock news and there's one of the wieners." Fitz-Gilbert laughed.

"My father—he was Yale '49—said it used to scare him to death. Then he got used to it," Blair said.

Cabby chimed in: "Everyone muddles through. Think how I feel. The guys in my class at Dartmouth are starting to retire. Retire? I remember when all we thought about was getting . . ."

He stopped, as his hostess had stuck her head into the library, hand curled around the door frame. "Are you fellows finished yet? I mean, we've solved the problems of the world in the last forty-five minutes."

"Lonesome, honey?" Fitz called to her.

"Oh, an eensie-weensie bit."

"We'll be out in a minute."

"You know, Fitz, I think we must know a lot of people in common since so many of your schoolmates came to Yale. Someday we'll have to compare notes," Blair said.

"Yes, I'd like that." Fitz, distracted by Little Marilyn, wasn't paying much attention.

"Yale and Princeton. Yeck." Stafford made a thumbs-down sign.

"And you went to Stanford?" Blair quizzed him.

"Yes. Finance."

"Ah." Blair nodded. No wonder Stafford was making so much money as an investment banker, and no wonder Cabell shone smiles upon him. No doubt these two would talk business over the weekend.

"You were smart not to become a lawyer." Fitz twirled his cigar, the beautiful, understated band announcing MONTECRISTO. "A lawyer is a hired gun, even if it's tax law. I'll never know how I passed the bar, I was so bored."

"There are worse jobs." Cabell squinted his eyes from the smoke. "You could be a proctologist."

The men laughed.

The phone rang. Tiffany called out from the kitchen, "Mr. Hamilton."

"Excuse me."

As Fitz picked up the phone, Stafford, Cabell, and Blair joined the ladies in the living room. In a few minutes Fitz-Gilbert joined them too.

"Has anyone seen or heard from Benjamin Seifert?"

"No. Why?" Little Marilyn asked.

"He didn't go to work today. That was Cynthia Cooper. She's spent the evening calling his business associates and family. Now she's calling friends and acquaintances. I told them you were here, Cabby. They'd like to talk to you."

Cabell left the room to pick up the phone.

"He's out of the office as much as he's in it," Harry volunteered, now that Ben's boss was out of earshot.

"I told him just last week to watch his step, but you know Ben." Fitz pulled up a chair. "He'll show up and I bet the story will be a doozie."

Harry opened her mouth but closed it. She wanted to say "What if this has something to do with the vagrant's murder?" What if Ben was the killer and skipped town? Realizing Little Marilyn's sensitivity to the topic, she said nothing.

Harry had forgotten all about Ben Seifert when Blair dropped her at her door. He promised he'd be there at seven-thirty in the morning. She opened the door and turned on the lights. Only one came on. She walked over to the debris on the floor, the lamp cord yanked out of the wall.

"Tucker! Mrs. Murphy!"

The two animals giggled under the bed but they stayed put. Harry walked into the bedroom, knelt down and looked under the bed, and beheld two luminous pairs of eyes staring back at her.

"I know you two did this."

"*Prove it*," was all Mrs. Murphy would say, her tail swaying back and forth.

"I had a wonderful time tonight and I'm not going to let you spoil it."

It was good that Harry had that attitude. Events would spoil things soon enough.

33

The earth glittered silvery and beige under its cloak of frost. The sun, pale and low in the sky, turned the ground fog into champagne mist. Mrs. Murphy and Tucker curled up in a horse blanket in the tack room and watched Harry groom Tomahawk.

Blair arrived at seven forty-five. As Harry had already brushed and braided Tomahawk, painted his feet with hoof dressing, and brushed him again, she was ready for a clean-up.

"What time did you get up?" Blair admired her handiwork.

"Five-thirty. Same time I always get up. Wish I could sleep past it but I can't, even if I go to bed at one in the morning."

"What can I do?"

Harry shed her garage mechanic overalls to reveal her buff breeches. A heavy sweater covered her good white shirt. Her worn boots, polished, leaned against the tack room wall. Her derby, brushed, hung on a tack hook. Harry had earned her colors with the hunt while she was in high school and her ancient black melton coat with its Belgian-blue collar was carefully hung on the other side of the tack hook.

Harry placed a heavy wool cooler over Tomahawk and tied it at the front. Unhooking the crossties, she led him to his stall. "Don't even think about rubbing your braids, Tommy, and don't get tangled up in your cooler." She gave her horse a pat on the neck. "Tommy'll be good but I always remind him, just in case," she said to Blair. "Come on, everything's done. Let's get some coffee."

After a light breakfast, Blair watched Harry replace Tomahawk's square cooler with a fitted wool dress sheet, put on his leather shipping halter, and load him into her two-horse gooseneck, which, like the truck, was showing its age but still serviceable. He hopped in the cab, camera in his coat pocket, ready for the meet.

He was beginning to appreciate Harry's make-do attitude as he perceived how little money she really had. False pride about possessions wasn't one of her faults but pride about making her own way was. She wouldn't ask for help, and as the blue bomb chugged along he realized what a simple gift it would have been for him to offer the use of his dually to pull her rig. If he had asked politely she might even have let him. Harry was funny. She feared favors, maybe because she lacked the resources to return them, but by Blair's reckoning she kept her accounts even in her own way.

Opening meet of the hunt brought out everyone who had ever thrown a leg over a horse. Blair couldn't believe his eyes as Harry pulled into the flat pasture. Horse trailers littered the landscape. There were little tag-alongs, two-horse goosenecks, four-horse goosenecks. There were a few semis pulling rigs a family could live in, Imperatore vans with the box built onto the back of the truck, and there was even one of the new Mitsubishi vans, its snub nose exciting both admiration and derision.

Horses, unloaded and tied to the sides of these conveyances, provided splashes of color. Each stable sported its own colors and these were displayed both in the paint jobs of the rigs and on the horses themselves, blanketed in their own special uniforms, the sheets or blankets indicating their allegiances. Harry's colors were royal-blue and gold, so Tomahawk's blue wool dress sheet was trimmed in gold and had a braided gold tail cord on the hindquarters. There were coolers and blankets in a myriad of color combinations: hunter-green and red, red and gold, black and red, blue and green, tan and blue, tan and hunter-green, silver and green, sky-blue and white, white and every color, and one cooler was even purple and pink. The purple and pink one belonged to Mrs. Annabelle Milliken, who had ordered a purple and white cooler years ago but the clerk wrote down the wrong colors and Mrs. Milliken was too polite to correct her. After a time everyone became accustomed to the purple and pink combination. Even Mrs. Milliken.

Big Marilyn's colors were red and gold. Her horse, a shining seal-brown, could have galloped out of a Ben Marshall painting, just as Little Marilyn's bold chestnut might have trotted out of a George Stubbs.

Harry put on her stock tie, her canary vest, her coat, derby, and deerskin gloves. Using the trailer fender as a mounting block, she swung into the saddle. Blair asked her if she wanted a leg up but she said that she and Tomahawk were used to the do-it-yourself method. Good old Tommy, in a D-ring snaffle, stood quietly, ears pricked. He loved hunting. Blair handed Harry her hunting crop with its long thong and lash just as Jock Fiery rode by and wished her "good hunting."

As Harry trotted off to hear the words of wisdom from the Joint Masters, Jill Summers and Tim Bishop, Blair found Mrs. Hogendobber. Together they watched the tableau as the Huntsman, Jack Eicher, brought the hounds to the far side of the gathering. Horse, hounds, staff, and field glistened in the soft light. Susan joined the group. She was still struggling with her hairnet, which she dropped. Gloria Fennel, Master of the Hilltoppers, reached in her pocket and gave Susan another hairnet.

Blair turned to Mrs. Hogendobber. "Does everyone ride?"

"I don't, obviously." She nodded in the direction of Stafford and Brenda, both of them madly snapping photos. "He used to."

"Guess I'd better take some lessons."

"Lynne Beegle." Mrs. Hogendobber pointed out a petite young

lady on a gloriously built thoroughbred. "Whole family rides. She's a wonderful teacher."

Before Blair could ask more questions, the staff, which consisted of three Whippers-In, the Huntsman, and the Masters, moved the hounds down to where the pasture dropped off. The field followed.

"The Huntsman will cast the hounds."

Blair heard a high-pitched "Whooe, whoop whoop, whooe." The sounds made no sense to him but the hounds knew what to do. They fanned out, noses to the ground, sterns to heaven. Soon a deep-throated bitch named Streisand gave tongue. Another joined her and then another. The chorus sent a chill down Blair's spine. The animal in him overrode his overdeveloped brain. He wanted to hunt too.

So did Mrs. Hogendobber, as she motioned for him to follow on foot. Mrs. H. knew every inch of the western part of the county. An avid beagler, she could divine where the hounds would go and could often find the best place to watch. Mrs. H. explained to Blair that beagling was much like fox hunting except that the quarry was rabbits and the field followed on foot. Blair gained a new respect for Mrs. Hogendobber. Rough terrain barely slowed her down.

They reached a large hill from which they could see a long, low valley. The hounds, following the fox's line, streaked across the meadow. The Field Master, the staff member in charge of maintaining order and directing the field, led the hunt over the first of a series of coops—a two-sided, slanted panel, jumpable from both directions. It was a solidly imposing three feet three inches high.

"Is that Harry?" Blair pointed to a relaxed figure floating over the coop.

"Yes. Susan's in her pocket and Mim isn't far behind."

"Hard to believe Mim would endure the discomforts of fox hunting."

"For all her fussiness that woman is tough as nails. She can ride." Mrs. Hogendobber folded her arms in front of her. Big Marilyn's seal-brown gelding seemed to step over the coop. The obstacle presented no challenge.

As the pace increased, Harry smiled. She loved a good run but she was grateful for the first check. They held up and the Huntsman recast the hounds so they could regain the line. Joining her in the first flight were the Reverend Herbert Jones, dazzling in his scarlet frock coat, or "pinks"; Carol, looking like an enchantress in her black jacket with its Belgian-blue collar and hunt cap; Big Marilyn and Little Marilyn, both in shadbelly coats and top hats, the hunt's colors emblazoned on the collars of their tailed cutaways; and Fitz-Gilbert in his black frock coat and derby. Fitz had not yet earned his colors, so he did not have the privilege of festooning himself in pinks. The group behind them ran up and someone yelled, "Hold hard!" and the followers came to a halt. As Harry glanced around her she felt a surge of affection for these people. On foot she could have boxed Mim's ears but on a horse the social tyrant didn't have the time to tell everyone what to do.

Within moments the hounds had again found the line, and giving tongue, they soon trotted off toward the rough lands formerly owned by the first Joneses to settle in these parts.

A steep bank followed a bold creek. Harry heard the hounds splashing through the water. The Field Master located the best place to ford, which, although steep, provided good footing. It was either that or slide down rocks or get stuck in a bog. The horses picked their way down to the creek. Harry, one of the first to the creek, saw a staff member's horse suddenly plunge in up to his belly. She quickly pulled her feet up onto the skirts of her saddle, just in the nick of time. A few curses behind her indicated that Fitz-Gilbert hadn't been so quick and now suffered from wet feet.

No time to worry, for once on the other side the field tore after the hounds. Susan, right behind Harry, called out, "The fence ahead. Turn sharp right, Harry."

Harry had forgotten how evil that fence was. It was like an airplane landing strip but without the strip. You touched down and you turned, or else you crashed into the trees. Tomahawk easily soared over the fence. In the air and as she landed Harry pressed hard with her left leg and opened her right rein, holding her hand away from and to the side of Tommy's neck. He turned like a charm and so did Susan's horse right on her heels. Mim boldly took the fence at an angle so she didn't have to maneuver as much. Little Marilyn and Fitz made it. Harry didn't look over her shoulder to see who made it after that because she was moving so fast that tears were filling her eyes.

They thundered along the wood's edge and then found a deer path through the thick growth. Harry hated galloping through woods. She always feared losing a kneecap but the pace was too good and there wasn't time to worry about it. Also, Tomahawk was handy at weaving in and out through the trees and did a pretty good job keeping his sides, and Harry's legs, away from the trunks. The field wove its way through the oaks, sweet gums, and maples to emerge on a meadow, undulating toward the mountains. Harry dropped the reins on Tomahawk's neck and the old boy flew. His joy mingled with her joy. Susan drew alongside, her dappled gray running with his ears back. He always did that. Didn't mean much except it sometimes scared people who didn't know Susan or the horse.

A three-board fence, interrupted by a three-foot-six coop, hove into view. Before she knew it Harry had landed on the other side. The pace and the cold morning air burned her lungs. She could see Big Marilyn out of the corner of her left eye. Standing in her stirrup irons with her hands well up her gelding's neck, Mim urged on her steed. She was determined to overtake Harry. A horse race, and what a place for it! Harry glanced over at Mim, who glanced back. Clods of earth spewed into the air. Susan, not one to drop back, stayed right with them. A big jump with a drop on the other side beckoned ahead. The Field Master cleared it. Mim's horse inched in front of Tomahawk. Harry carefully dropped behind Mim's thoroughbred. It wouldn't do to take a jump in tandem unplanned. Mim soared over with plenty of daylight showing underneath her horse's belly. Harry let the weight sink into her heels, preparing to absorb the shock of the drop on the other side, and flew over it, though her heart was in her mouth. Those jumps with a drop on the other side made you feel as if you were airborne forever and the landing often came as a jarring surprise.

A steep hill rose before them and they rode up it, little stones clattering underneath. They pulled up at the crest. The hounds had lost the line again.

"Good run." Mim smiled. "Good run, Harry."

Mrs. Hogendobber and Blair drove in her Falcon to where she thought the run would go. The old car nosed into a turnaround. She sprang out of the vehicle. "Hurry up!"

Blair, breathing hard, followed her up another large hill, this one with a commanding view of the Blue Ridge Mountains. His eyes moved in the direction of her pointing finger.

"That's the first of Crozet's tunnels, way up there. This is the very edge of Farmington's territory."

"What do you mean by that?"

"Well, there's a national association that divides up the territory. No one can hunt up in the mountains, too rough really, but on the other side the territory belongs to another hunt, Glenmore, I think. To our north it's Rappahanock, then Old Dominion; to the east, Keswick and then Deep Run. Think of it like states."

"I don't know when I've ever seen anything so beautiful. Did the hounds lose the scent?"

"Yes. They've checked while the Huntsman casts the hounds. Think of it like casting a net with a nose for fox. Good pack too. As fleet as sound."

Far, far in the distance she heard the strange cry of a hound.

Down at the check, all heads turned.

Fitz, now winded, whispered to Little Marilyn, "Honey, can we go in soon?"

"You can."

"This terrain is really pretty rugged. I don't want to leave you alone."

"I'm not alone and I'm a better rider than you are," Little Marilyn informed him, somewhat haughtily but still in a whisper.

The Huntsman followed the cry of his lone hound. The pack moved toward the call. The Field Master waited for a moment, then motioned for the field to move off. The sweet roll of earth crunched up. More rock outcroppings challenged the sure-footedness of the horses.

"We're about out of real estate," Harry said to Susan. She kept her voice low. It was irritating to strain to hear the hounds and have someone chattering behind you. She didn't want to bother any of the others.

"Yeah, he'll have to pull the hounds back."

"We're heading toward the tunnel," Mim stated.

"Can't go there. And we shouldn't. Who knows what's up there? That's all we need, for a bear or something to jump out of the tunnel and scare the bejesus out of these horses." Little Marilyn wasn't thrilled at the prospect.

"Well, we can't go up there, that's for sure. Anyway, the Chesapeake and Ohio sealed up the tunnel," Fitz-Gilbert added.

"Yes, but Kelly Craycroft opened it up again." Susan referred to Kelly Craycroft's clever reopening and camouflaging of the tunnel. "Wonder if the railroad did seal it back up?"

"I don't want to find out." Fitz's horse was getting restive.

The cry of the lone hound soon found answers. The pack worked its way toward the tunnel. The Field Master held back the field. The Huntsman stopped. He blew his horn but only some of the hounds returned as they were bidden. The stray hound cried and cried. A few others now joined in this throaty song.

"Letting me down. Those hounds are letting me down," the Huntsman, shamed by their disobedience, moaned to a Whipper-In who rode along with him to get the hounds back in line.

The Whipper-In flicked the lash at the end of his whip after a straggler, who shuttled back to the pack. "Deer? But they haven't run deer. Except for Big Lou."

"That's not Big Lou up there though." The Huntsman moved toward the sound. "Well, come along with me and we'll see if we can't get those babies back down before they ruin a good day's hunting."

The two staff horses picked their way through the unforgiving terrain. They could now see the tunnel. The hounds sniffed and worried at the entrance. A huge turkey vulture flew above them, swooped down on an air current, bold as brass, and disappeared into the tunnel.

"Damn," the Whip exclaimed.

The Huntsman blew his horn. The Whipper-In made good use of his whip but the animals kept speaking. They weren't confused; they were upset.

As this had never happened before to the Huntsman in his more than thirty years of hunting, he dismounted and handed his reins to the Whip. He walked toward the entrance. The vulture emerged, another in its wake. The Huntsman noticed hunks of rancid meat dangling from their beaks. He caught a whiff of it too. As he neared the tunnel entrance he caught another blast, much stronger. The hounds whined now. One even rolled over and showed its belly. The Huntsman noticed that some stones had fallen away from the entrance. The odor of decay, one he knew well from life in the country, seeped out of the hole full bore. He kicked at the stones and a section rolled away. The railroad had neglected to reclose the entrance after all. He squinted, trying to see into the darkness, but his nose told him plenty. It was a second or two before he recognized that the dead creature was a human being. He involuntarily stepped back. The hounds whined pitifully. He called them away from the tunnel, swaying a bit as he came out into the light.

"It's Benjamin Seifert."

34

A sensuous Georgian tea service glowed on the long mahogany sideboard. Exquisite blue and white teacups, which had been brought over from England in the late seventeenth century, surrounded the service. A Hepplewhite table, loaded with ham biscuits, cheese omelettes, artichoke salad, hard cheeses, shepherd's pie, and fresh breads commanded the center of the dining room. Brownies and pound cake rounded out the offerings.

Susan had knocked herself out for the hunt breakfast. The excited hum of voices, ordinarily the sign of a successful hunt, meant something different today.

After the Huntsman identified Ben Seifert he rode with the Whip down to the Masters, the Field Master, and the other Whips. They decided to lift the hounds and return to the kennels. Not until everyone was safely away from the tunnel and had arrived at the breakfast did the Masters break the news.

After caring for the hounds, the Huntsman and the Whip who'd accompanied him to the grisly sight returned to the tunnel to help Rick Shaw and Cynthia Cooper.

Despite the dolorous news, appetites drove the riders and their audience to the table. The food disappeared and Susan filled up the plates and bowls again. Her husband, Ned, presided over the bar.

Big Marilyn, seated in an apricot-colored wing chair, balanced her plate on her knees. She hated buffets for that very reason. Mim wanted to sit at the table. Herbie and Carol sat on the floor along with Harry, Blair, and Boom Boom, who was making a point of being charming.

Cabell and Taxi arrived late and were told the news by a well-meaning person. They were so shocked they left for home.

Fair hung back at the food table. He noticed the gathering on the floor and brought desserts for everyone, including his ex-wife. Fitz-Gilbert and Little Marilyn joined Mim. Mrs. Hogendobber wouldn't sit on the floor in her skirt so she grabbed the other wing chair, a soothing mint-green.

"Miranda." Big Marilyn speared some omelette. "Your views."

"Shall we judge society by its malcontents?"

"And what do you mean by that?" Big Marilyn demanded before Mrs. Hogendobber could take another breath.

"I mean Crozet will be in the papers again. Our shortcomings will be trumpeted hither and yon. We'll be judged by these murders instead of by our good citizens."

"That's not what I was asking." Mim zeroed in. "Who do you think killed Ben Seifert?"

"We don't know that he was murdered yet." Fitz-Gilbert spoke up.

"Well, you don't think he walked up to that tunnel and killed himself, do you? He'd be the last person to commit suicide."

"What do you think, Mim?" Susan knew her guest was bursting to give her views.

"I think when money passes hands it sometimes sticks to fingers. We all know that Ben Seifert and the work ethic were unacquainted with one another. Yet he lived extremely well. Didn't he?"

Heads nodded in agreement. "The only person who would have wanted to kill him is his ex-wife and she's not that stupid. No, he fiddled in someone's trust. He was the type."

"Mother, that's a harsh judgment."

"I see no need to pussyfoot."

"He handled many of our trusts, or at least Allied did, so he knew who had what." Fitz gobbled a brownie. "But Cabell would have had his hide if he thought for an instant that Ben was dishonest."

"Maybe someone's trust was running out." Carol Jones thought out loud. "And maybe that person expected a favor from Ben. What if he didn't deliver?"

"Or someone caught him with his hand in the till." The Reverend Jones added his thoughts.

"I don't think this has anything to do with Ben and sticky fingers." Harry crossed her legs underneath her. "Ben's death is tied to that unidentified body."

"Oh, Harry, that's a stretch." Fitz reached for his Bloody Mary.

"It's a feeling. I can't explain it." Harry's quiet conviction was unsettling.

"You stick to your feelings. I'll stick to facts," Fitz-Gilbert jabbed.

Fair spoke up, defending Harry. "I used to think that way, too, but life with Harry taught me to listen to, well, feelings."

"Well, what do your deeper voices tell you now?" Mim said "deeper" with an impertinent edge.

"That we don't know much at all," Harry said firmly. "That now one of us has been killed and we can't feel so safe in our sleep anymore because we haven't one clue, one single idea as to motive. Is this a nut who comes out at the full moon? Is it someone with a grudge finally settling the score? Is this a cover-up for something else? Something we can't begin to imagine? My deeper voice tells me to keep eyes in the back of my head."

That shut up the room for a moment.

"You're right." Herbie placed his plate on the coffee table. "And I am not unconvinced that there may not be some satanic element to this. I've not spoken of it before because it's so disturbing. But certain cults do practice ritual killings and how they dispatch their victims is part of the ritual. We have one corpse dismembered, and, well, we don't know how Ben died."

"Do we know how the other fellow died?" Little Marilyn asked.

"Blow to the head," Ned Tucker informed them. "Larry Johnson performed the autopsy and I ran into him after that. I don't believe, Herbie, that satanic cults usually bash in heads."

"No, most don't."

"So, we're back to square one." Fitz got up for another dessert. "We're not in danger. I bet you when the authorities examine Ben's books they'll find discrepancies, or another set of books."

"Even if this is over misallocation of funds, that doesn't tell us who killed him or who killed that other man," Susan stated.

"These murders do have something to do with Satan." Mrs. Hogendobber's clear alto voice rang out. "The Devil has sunk his deep claws into someone, and forgive the old expression, but there will be hell to pay."

35

Long shadows spilled over the graves of Grace and Cliff Minor. The sun was setting, a golden oracle sending tongues of flame up from the Blue Ridge Mountains. The scarlet streaks climbed heavenward and then changed to gold, golden pink, lavender, deep purple, and finally deep Prussian-blue, Night's first kiss.

Harry wrapped her scarf around her neck as she watched the sun's last shout on this day. Mrs. Murphy and Tucker sat at her feet. The aching melancholy of the sunset ripped through her with needles of sorrow. She mourned the loss of the sun; she wanted to bathe in rivers of light. Each twilight she would suspend her chores for a moment, to trust that the sun would return tomorrow like a new birth. And this evening that same hope tugged but with a sharper pull. The future is ever blind. The sun would rise but would she?

No one believes she will die; neither her mother nor her father did. Like a game of tag, Death is "it," and around he chases, touching people who fall to earth. Surely she would get up at dawn; another day would unfold like an opening rose. But hadn't Ben Seifert believed that also? Losing a parent, wrenching and profound, felt very different to Harry than losing a peer. Benjamin Seifert graduated from Crozet High School one year ahead of Harry. This time Death had tagged someone close to her—at least close in age.

A terrible loneliness gnawed at Harry. Those tombstones covered the two people who gave her life. She remembered their teachings, she remembered their voices, and she remembered their laughter. Who would remember them when she was gone, and who would hold the memory of her life? Century after century the human race lurched two steps forward and one step back, but always there were good people, funny people, strong people, and their memories washed away with the ages. Kings and queens received a mention in the chronicles, but what about the horse trainers, the farmers, the seamstresses? What about the postmistresses and stagecoach drivers? Who would hold the memory of their lives?

The loneliness filled her. If she could have, she would have embraced every life and cherished it. As it was, she was struggling on with her own.

Harry began to fear the coming years. Formerly, time was her ally. Now she wasn't so sure. If death could snatch you in an instant, then life had better be lived to the fullest. The worst thing would be to go down in the grave without having lived.

The bite of the night's air made her fingertips tingle and her toes hurt. She whistled to Tucker and Mrs. Murphy and started back for the house.

Harry was not by nature an introspective person. She liked to work. She liked to see the results of her work. Deeper thoughts and philosophic worries were for other people. But after today's jolt Harry turned inward, if only for a brief moment, and was suffused with life's sadness and harmony.

36

A terrible rumpus outside awoke Mrs. Murphy and Tucker. Mrs. Murphy ran to the window.

"It's Simon and the raccoons."

Tucker barked to wake up Harry, because now that it was cold Harry made sure to shut the back door tight, and they couldn't get out to the screened-in porch. That door was easy to open, so if Harry would just open the back door they could get outside.

"Go away, Tucker," Harry groaned.

"Wake up, Mom. Come on."

"Goddammit." Harry's feet hit the cold floor. She thought the dog was barking at an animal or had to go to the bathroom. She tramped downstairs and opened the back door and both creatures zoomed out. "Go on out and freeze your asses. I'm not letting you back in."

The cat and dog didn't have time to reply. They streaked toward Simon, backed up against the barn by two masked raccoons.

"Beat it!" Tucker barked.

Mrs. Murphy, fur puffed up to the max, ears flat back, spit and howled, "I'll rip your eyes out!"

The raccoons decided they didn't want to fight, so they waddled off.

"Thanks," Simon puffed, his flanks heaving.

"What was all that about?" Mrs. Murphy asked.

"Marshmallows. Blair put out marshmallows and I love them. Unfortunately, so do those creeps. They chased me all the way back here." A trickle of blood oozed from Simon's pink nose. His left ear was also bleeding.

"You got the worst of the fight. Why don't we go up to the loft?" Mrs. Murphy suggested.

"I'm still hungry. Did Harry put out leftovers?"

"No. She had a bad day," Tucker answered. "The humans found another body today."

"In pieces?" Simon was curious.

"No, except that the vultures got at it." Mrs. Murphy quivered as the wind kicked up. It felt like zero degrees.

"I've always wondered why birds like the eyes. First thing they'll go for: the eyes and the head." Simon rubbed his ear, which had begun to sting.

"Let's go inside. Come on. It's vile out here."

They wiggled under the big barn doors. Simon paused to pick up bits of grain that Tomahawk and Gin Fizz had dropped. As the horses were sloppy eaters, Simon could enjoy the gleanings.

"That ought to hold me until tomorrow." The gray possum sat down and wrapped his pink tail around him. "If you come upstairs it's warm in the hay."

"I can't climb the ladder," Tucker whimpered.

"Oh, yeah, I forgot about that." Simon rubbed his nose.

"Let's go into the tack room. That old, heavy horse blanket is in there, the one Gin Fizz ripped up. The lining is fleecy and we could curl up in that."

"It's hanging over the saddle rack," Tucker called.

"So? I'll push it down." Mrs. Murphy was already hooking her claws under the door bottom. The door, old and warped, wavered a little and she wedged her paw behind it while Tucker stuck her nose down to see if she could help. In a minute the door squeaked open.

The cat leapt onto the saddle rack, dug her claws in the blanket, and leaned over with it. She came down with the blanket. The three snuggled next to one another in the fleece.

When Harry hurried into the barn the next morning she felt guilty for leaving her pets outside. She knew she'd find them in the barn but she was quite surprised to find them curled up with a possum in the tack room. Simon was surprised, too, so surprised that he pretended to be dead.

Tucker licked Harry's gloved hands while Mrs. Murphy rubbed against her legs.

"This little guy's been in the ring." Harry noticed Simon's torn ear and scratched nose.

"*Simon, wake up. We know you're not dead.*" Mrs. Murphy patted his rump.

Harry reached for a tube of ointment and while Simon squeezed his eyes more tightly shut she rubbed salve on his wounds. He couldn't stand it. He opened one eye.

Mrs. Murphy patted his rump again. "*See, she's not so bad. She's a good human.*"

Simon, who didn't trust humans, kept silent, but Tucker piped up, "*Look grateful, Simon, and maybe she'll give you some food. Let her pick you up. She'll love that.*"

Harry petted Simon's funny little head. "You'll be all right, fella. You stay here if you want and I'll do my chores."

She left the animals and climbed into the hayloft.

Simon panicked for a moment. "*She won't steal my treasures, will she? I think I'd better see.*" Simon walked out of the tack room and grabbed the lowest ladder rung. He moved quickly. Mrs. Murphy followed. Tucker stayed where she was and looked up. She could hear the hay moving around as Harry prepared to toss it through the holes in the loft floor over the stalls.

Harry turned around to see Simon and Mrs. Murphy hurrying toward the back. She put down her bale and followed them.

"You two certainly are chummy."

The T-shirt made Harry laugh. Simon's nest was much improved since Mrs. Murphy had last visited.

"Shut up, down there," the owl called out.

"Shut up, yourself, flatface," Mrs. Murphy snarled.

Harry knelt down as Simon darted into his half-cave. He'd brought up some excess yarn Harry had used to braid Tomahawk for opening hunt. He also had shredded the sweet feed bag and brought it up in strips. Simon's nest was now very cozy and the T-shirt had been lovingly placed over his homemade insulation. One ballpoint pen, two pennies, and the tassled end of an old longe line were artfully arranged in one corner.

"This is quite a house." Harry admired the possum's work.

A shiny glint caught Mrs. Murphy's sharp eye. "What's that?"

"Found it over at Foxden."

"I didn't think possums were pack rats." Harry smiled at the display.

"I operate on the principle that it is better to have something and not need it than need it and not have it. I am not a pack rat," Simon stated with dignity.

"Where at Foxden did you find this?" Mrs. Murphy reached out and grabbed the shiny object. As she drew it toward her she saw that it was a misshapen earring.

"I like pretty things." Simon watched with apprehension as Harry took the earring from her cat. "I found it on the old logging road in the woods—out in the middle of nowhere."

"Gold." Harry placed the earring in her palm. It seemed to her that she had seen this earring before. It was clearly expensive. She couldn't make out the goldstamp, as it appeared the earring had been run over or stepped on. She was able to make out the T-I-F of TIFFANY. She turned the earring over and over.

"She's going to give it back to me, isn't she?" Simon nervously asked. "I mean, she isn't a thief, is she?"

"No, she's not a thief, but if you found it over at Foxden she ought to take it. It might be a clue."

"Who cares? Humans kill one another all the time. You catch one, and somebody else starts killing."

"It's not as bad as that."

The owl called out again, "Keep it down!"

Harry loved the sound of an owl hooting but she detected the crabby note. She placed the earring back in Simon's nest. "Well, kiddo, it looks like you're part of the family. I'll set out the scraps."

Simon, visibly relieved, stuck his nose out of his nest and regarded Harry with his bright eyes. Then he spoke to Mrs. Murphy. "I'm glad she's not going to kill me."

"Harry doesn't kill animals."

"She goes fox hunting," came the stout reply.

As Harry returned to dropping the hay down to the horses, the cat and the possum discussed this.

"Simon, they only kill the old foxes or the sick ones. Healthy ones are too smart to get caught."

"What about that fox last year that ran into Posy Dent's garage? He was young."

"And that exception proves the rule. He was dumb." Mrs. Murphy laughed. "I feel about foxes the way you feel about raccoons. Well, Harry's going back down, so I'll follow her. Now that she knows where you live she'll probably want to talk to you. She's like that, so try and be nice to her. She's a good egg. She put stuff on your scratches."

Simon thought about it. "I'll try."

"Good." Mrs. Murphy scampered down the ladder.

As she and Tucker trotted back to the house for breakfast the cat told the dog about the earring. The more they talked, the more questions they raised. Neither animal was sure the earring was important to the case but if Simon found it in a suspicious place, its value couldn't be overlooked. All this time they'd assumed the killer was a man but it could be a woman. The body was cut up and stashed in different places. The parts weren't heavy by themselves. As to dragging Ben Seifert into the tunnel, that would be hard, but maybe the two deaths weren't connected.

Mrs. Murphy stopped. "Tucker, maybe we're barking up the wrong tree. Maybe the killer is a man but he's killing for a woman."

"Getting rid of competitors?"

"Could be. Or maybe she's directing him—maybe she's the brains behind the brawn. I wish we could get Mom to see how important that earring is, but she doesn't know where it came from and we can't tell her."

"Murphy, what if we took it from Simon and put it where he found it?"

"Even if he'd part with it, how are we going to get her over there?"

Inside now, they waited for their breakfasts.

Tucker thought of something: "What if a man is killing for a woman, killing to keep her? What if he knows something she doesn't?"

Mrs. Murphy leaned her head on Tucker's shoulder for a moment. "I hope we can find out, because I've got a bad feeling about this."

37

Not only had Larry Johnson taken the precaution of sending tissue samples to Richmond, he wisely kept the head of the unidentified corpse rather than turning it over to the sheriff. After contacting a forensics expert, the elderly doctor sent the head to a reconstruction team in Washington, D.C. Since Crozet did not have a potter's field, a burial ground for the indigent, the Reverend Jones secured a burial plot in a commercial cemetery on Route 29 in Charlottesville. When he asked his congregation for contributions they were forthcoming, and to his pleasant surprise, the Sanburnes, the Hamiltons, and Blair Bainbridge made up the balance. So the unknown man was put to rest under a nameless but numbered brass marker.

Larry never dreamed he would have a second corpse on his hands. Ben's family arranged for interment in the Seifert vault, but Cabell Hall handled all the funeral details, which was a tremendous help to the distraught couple. Larry's examination determined that

Ben had been strangled with a rope and that death had occurred approximately three days before discovery. The temperature fluctuated so much between day and night, he felt he could not pinpoint the exact time of death based on the condition of the corpse. Also, the animal damage added to the difficulty. Larry insisted on sparing Ben's mother and father the ordeal of identifying the corpse. He knew Ben; that was identification enough. For once, Rick Shaw agreed with him and relented.

Rick did put up a fight about shipping off the head of the original victim. He was loath to part with this one piece of evidence. Damaged as the head was, it was his only hope. Someone had to have known the victim. Larry patiently showed him the work of the reconstructive artists. Cynthia Cooper helped, too, as she was impressed with what could be done.

After carefully studying the head in its present condition, the team would strip the skull of the remaining flesh and then build a new face, teeth, hair, everything. Drawings would be made to assist in the rebuilding. Once complete, drawings and photographs of the head would be sent to Rick Shaw. They would also be sent to other police stations and sheriff's offices. Long shots do come in. Someone, somewhere, might identify the face.

Since a second murder had followed closely on the heels of the first, Larry Johnson called Washington and asked them to hurry.

This they did. Rick Shaw walked into the post office with a large white envelope in his hand.

"Sheriff, want me to weigh that?" Harry offered.

"No. This just arrived Federal Express." Rick pulled out the photograph and slid it over the counter to Harry. "This is a reconstruction of the head of the dismembered victim. Looks like an all right guy, wouldn't you say?"

Harry stared at the photograph. The face was pleasant, not handsome but attractive. Sandy hair, combed to one side, gave the face a clean-cut appearance. The man had a prominent, jutting chin. "He could be anybody."

"Put it on the wall. Let's hope somebody here recognizes him. Triggers a memory."

"Or a mistake."

"Harry, you'll know before I do." Rick tapped the counter twice. It was his way of saying "Be careful."

She pinned the photograph by the counter. No one could miss it. Mrs. Murphy stared at it. The man was no one she knew, and she saw people from a vastly different angle than did Harry.

Brookie and Danny Tucker stopped by after school. Harry explained to them who the photograph was. Danny couldn't believe that it was a likeness of the head he'd plucked out of his pumpkin. The photographed head lacked a beard, which made the man appear younger.

Mim came in later. She also studied the photograph. "Don't you think this will upset people?"

"Better upset than dead."

Those ice-blue eyes peered into Harry's own. "You think we've got a serial killer on the loose? That's jumping to conclusions. *Any-thing* could have happened to this man." A long, frosted fingernail pointed at the bland face. "How do we know he wasn't killed in some sort of bizarre sexual episode? A homeless person, no one to care, he's offered a meal and a shower. Who's to know?"

How interesting that a sliver of Mim's fantasies were showing. Harry replied, "I can't think of one woman who would go to bed with a man and then kill him and cut him up."

"Insects do it all the time."

"We're mammals."

"*And poor excuses at that.*" Tucker chuckled.

Mim went on. "Maybe it was a group of people."

"In my wildest imaginings I can't think of any group here in town that would do that. Wife swapping, yes. Sex murders, no."

Mim's eyes brightened. "Wife swapping? What do you know that I don't?"

"The postmistress knows everything in a small town," Harry teased.

"Not everything or you'd know who the killer is. I still think it's some group thing and Ben was in on it. Or it was about money. But I spoke with Cabell Hall today and he's had a team scouring the books, just going over them with a fine-tooth comb, and everything is in order. Very, very strange."

Boom Boom, Fair, Fitz-Gilbert, and Little Marilyn crowded in at once. They, too, examined the photo.

"Makes me nauseated to think about that." Boom Boom held her stomach. "I wasn't right for days. I thought I'd seen everything when my husband was killed."

Fair put his arm around her. "I wonder what Kelly would have made of this?"

"He would have found humor in it somewhere." Little Marilyn had liked Boom Boom's deceased husband.

Fitz-Gilbert nearly put his nose on the photograph. "Isn't it something what these guys can do? Imagine putting together a face, given the condition of that head. It's just amazing. He looks better than he did in life, I bet."

"The organization behind something like this is amazing, too," Harry said. "Rick told me that this photograph will be in every police station in the country. He's hoping it will pay off."

"So do we," Mim announced.

Mrs. Hogendobber let herself in through the back door. She bustled over to see what was going on and was drawn to the photograph. "He was young. Thirty, early thirties, I should say. What a shame. What a shame for a life to end so young and so violently and we don't even know who he was."

"He was a no-count. We do know that." Fitz-Gilbert referred to the man's vagabond existence.

"No one's a no-count. Something must have happened to him, perhaps something awful. Perhaps an illness." Mrs. Hogendobber folded her arms across her chest.

"I bet he was one of those people who used to live in halfway houses," Little Marilyn put in. "So many of these places have been shut down, now that the programs have been cut off. They say that flophouses in big cities are full of those people—low normals, you'd call them, or people who aren't a hundred percent functional. Anyway, the state pays hotels to give them lodging because they can't work. I bet he was one of those people. Just thrown out into a world where he couldn't cope." Little Marilyn's high-pitched voice lowered a trifle.

"Then what in the world was he doing in Crozet?" Mim never could give her daughter credit for anything.

"On his way to Miami?" Fitz-Gilbert posited. "The homeless who can leave the northern cities in winter try to get to the Sunbelt cities. He could have hopped on a freight at Penn Station."

"What could he have in common with Ben Seifert?" Boom Boom wondered.

"Bad luck." Fitz smiled.

"If these murders are connected, there is one interesting thing." Harry stroked Mrs. Murphy, lounging on the counter. "The killer didn't want us to know the dismembered victim, yet he or she didn't care at all if we recognized Ben Seifert."

"Identify the dismembered man and you'll identify the killer." Fair's clear voice seemed to echo in the room.

"We'd at least be halfway home," Mrs. Hogendobber added.

"That's what worries me," Mim confessed. "We are home. These murders are happening here."

38

Layers of sweaters, winter golf gloves, and heavy socks protected Cabby and Taxi Hall from the cold. Avid golfers, they tried to squeeze in nine holes after Cabell's work hours when the season permitted, and they never missed a weekend.

Taxi's relaxed swing off the tee placed her ball squarely in the fairway. "Good shot if I do say so myself."

She stepped aside as Cabell stuck his orange tee into the ground. He placed a bright-yellow ball on the tee, stepped back, shifted around a little, and fired. The ball soared into the air and then drifted right, into the woods. He said nothing, just climbed back into the cart. Taxi joined him. They reached the woods. As the ball was such a bright color they easily located it, even though it had plopped into the leaves.

Cabell studied his position. Then he pulled out a five iron. This was a risky shot, since he'd have to shoot through the trees or go over them. He planted his feet, took a deep breath, and blasted away.

"What a shot!" Taxi exclaimed as the ball miraculously cleared the trees.

Cabby smiled his first genuine smile since Ben was discovered dead. "Not bad for an old man."

They headed back to the cart. "Honey," Taxi said, "what's wrong, other than the obvious?"

"Nothing," he lied.

"Don't shut me out." Her voice carried both firmness and reproach.

"Florence, sugar, I'm plain tired. Between worried employees, the sheriff's investigation, and a constant stream of questions from our customers, I am beat, crabby—you name it."

"I will. You're preoccupied. I've seen you handle bank problems and people problems before. This is different. Are the books cooked? Was Ben a thief?"

"I told you as soon as we had that audit, around the clock— can't wait for the bill on that one—no. Ben's books look okay."

"Is someone running through his trust fund? Fitz-Gilbert spends like there's no tomorrow."

Cabby shook his head. "For him there is no tomorrow. He's got more money than God. I tried to instill some restraint in him when he was a boy but I obviously failed. Combine his fortune with the Sanburnes' and, well"—Cabell swung his club—"what's the purpose in restraint?"

"It's not right for a man not to work, no matter how much money he has. He could do charity work." Taxi got in the driver's seat of the cart. Cabell hopped in. "See"—she pointed—"you've got a good lie. I don't know how you made that shot."

"Neither do I."

"Cab . . . are we in trouble?"

"No, dear. Our investments are sound. I've put enough away. I'm just puzzled. I can't imagine what Ben got himself into. I mean, he was my anointed. I trusted him. How does this look to the board of directors?"

Taxi cast a sharp glance at her husband. "You never really liked Ben."

Cabell sighed. "No. He was a smarmy little bastard, impressed with money and bloodlines, but he worked harder than people gave him credit for, he had very good ideas, and I felt he could run Allied when I stepped down."

"In other words, you don't have to like the chicken to enjoy the omelette."

"I never said I didn't like Ben. Not once in his eight years at the bank have I said that."

Taxi pulled up by the bright-yellow ball. "We've been married twenty-seven years."

"Oh." Cabby sat for a moment, then got out and fussed over which iron to use.

"The seven," Taxi advised.

"Well"—he took a look at the green—"well, you might be right."

As they continued play, Cabell Hall thought about the differences between women and men, or perhaps between his wife and himself. Taxi always knew more about him than he realized. He wasn't sure that he knew his wife as well as she knew him: his likes, dislikes, hidden fears. True, he kept much of his business life from her, but then she didn't share every moment of her day either. He didn't care if the washer repairman came on time any more than she cared whether one of the tellers had a bad cold.

Still, it was a curious thing to be reminded that his life partner could see into him and possibly through him.

"Cabell," Taxi interrupted his reverie, "I'm serious about Fitz. A man needs a real life, real responsibilities. I know Fitz seems happy enough, but he's so aimless. I'm sure it all goes back to losing his parents when he was so young. You did all you could for him, but—"

"Honey, you aren't going to improve Fitz. Nobody is. He's going to drift through life surrounded by things. Besides, if he did something useful like, say, taking over the Easter Seal drive, it would mean he couldn't play with his wife. Work might conflict with deep-sea fishing in Florida and skiing in Aspen."

"Just an idea." Taxi chipped onto the green.

He waited, then spoke: "Do you have any idea who killed Ben?"

"Not one."

Cabell let out a long, low breath, shook his head, snatched what he thought was his putter out of a bag. "I swear I'm going to put all of this out of my mind and concentrate on golf."

"Then I suggest you replace my putter and use your own."

█████████████

39

Late that night Harry's telephone rang.

Susan's excited voice apologized. "I know you're asleep but I had to wake you."

"You okay?" came the foggy reply.

"I am. Ned got home from his office about fifteen minutes ago. He was Ben's lawyer, you know. Anyway, Rick Shaw was at the office asking him a lot of questions, none of which Ned could answer, since all he ever did for Ben was real estate closings. It turns out that after the sheriff and the bank inspected their books they checked over Ben's personal accounts. Spread among the bank, the brokerage house, and the commodities market, Ben Seifert had amassed seven hundred and fifty thousand dollars. Even Cabell Hall was amazed at how sophisticated Ben was."

That woke up Harry. "Seven hundred and fifty thousand dollars?

Susan, he couldn't have made more than forty-five thousand a year at the bank, if he made that. Banks are notoriously cheap."

"I know. They also called in his accountant and double-checked his IRS returns. He was clever as to how he declared the money. Mostly he identified the gains as stock market wins, I guess you'd say. Well, the accountant reported that Ben said he'd get his records to him but he never did. He figured he'd alerted Ben plenty of times. If the materials weren't there, it was Ben's problem come audit day. Assuming that day ever came."

"Funny."

"What's funny?"

"He didn't cheat on his income taxes but he must have been cheating somewhere. Actually, it doesn't sound like cheating. It sounds like payoffs or money-laundering."

"I never thought Ben was that smart."

"He wasn't," Harry agreed. "But whoever was in this with him was, or is."

"Smart people don't kill."

"They do when they're cornered."

"Why don't you come into town and stay with me?"

"Why?"

"You know what Cynthia Cooper told us about Blair. I mean, about his girlfriend."

"Yes."

"He seems awfully smart to me."

"Does your gut tell you he's a murderer?"

"I don't know what to think or feel anymore."

Harry sat up in the bed. "Susan, I just thought of something. Listen, will you come over here tomorrow morning before I go to work? This sounds crazy but I found a little possum—"

"No more of your charity cases, Harry! I took the squirrel with the broken leg, remember? She ate my dresses."

"No, no. This little guy had an earring in his nest. It's kind of bent up, but well, I don't know. It's a very expensive earring, and he could have picked it up anywhere. What if it has something to do with these deaths?"

"Okay, I'll see you in the morning. Lock your doors."

"I did." Harry hung up the phone.

Mrs. Murphy remarked to Tucker, also on the bed, *"Sometimes she's smarter than I think she is."*

40

Simon heard Harry climbing the ladder. He anticipated her arrival, since she'd put out delicious chicken bones, stale crackers, and Hershey's chocolate kisses last night.

Mrs. Murphy sank her claws into the wood alongside the ladder and pulled herself into the loft before the humans could get there. *"Don't fret, Simon. Harry's bringing a friend."*

"One human's all I can stand." Simon shuttled farther back in the timothy and alfalfa bales.

Harry and Susan sat down in front of Simon's nest.

"Do you charge him for all this?" Susan cracked.

"If it isn't nailed down, he takes it." Mrs. Murphy laughed.

"I only take the good stuff," the possum said under his breath.

"See." Harry reached in and retrieved the earring.

Susan held the object in her palm. "Good piece. Tiffany."

"That's what I thought." Harry took the earring, holding it to the light. "This isn't yours and it isn't mine. Nor is it Elizabeth MacGregor's."

"What's Mrs. MacGregor got to do with it?"

"The only women out here on this part of Yellow Mountain Road are me, you when you're visiting me, and formerly Elizabeth MacGregor. Oh, and Miranda drops by sometimes but this isn't her type of earring. It's more youthful."

"True, but we have no way of knowing where this came from."

"In a way we do. We know that this nest is home base. At the largest, a possum's territory is generally a rough circle about a mile and a half in diameter. If we walk north, east, south, and west to the limit of that perimeter, we'll have a pretty good idea of where this earring might have come from."

"*I can tell her,*" Simon called out from his hiding place.

"*She can't understand but she'll figure it out,*" Mrs. Murphy said.

"*Is that other one okay, really?*"

"*Yes,*" the cat reassured him.

Simon peeped his head up over the alfalfa bale and then cautiously walked toward the two women. Harry held out a big peanut butter cookie. He approached, sat down, and reached for the cookie. He put it in his nest.

"What a cute fellow," Susan whispered. "You've always had a way with animals."

" 'Cept for men."

"They don't count."

Simon shocked them. He reached up, grabbing the earring out of Harry's hand, and then dashed into his nest. "*Mine!*"

"*Maybe he's a drag queen.*" Harry laughed at Simon, then remembered one of those odd tidbits from reading history books. During Elizabeth I's reign in England only the most masculine men wore earrings.

They were still laughing as they climbed down the ladder.

"*Well?*" Tucker demanded.

"We're going to have to make a circle following the possum's territory." Harry thought out loud.

"*Let's run over to the graveyard and see if they follow,*" Tucker sensibly proposed.

"*You know Harry—she's going to be thorough.*" The cat walked out the barn door and Tucker followed.

The two women, accompanied by the animals, walked the limits of the possum's turf. By the time they swept by the cemetery, both considered that it was possible, just possible, that the earring came from there.

Susan stopped by the iron fence. "How do we know the earring doesn't belong to Blair? It could have been his girlfriend's. There could be a woman now that we don't know about."

"I'll ask him."

"That might not be wise."

Harry considered that. "Well, I don't agree but I'll do it your way." She paused. "What's your way?"

"To casually ask our women friends if anyone has lost an earring, and what does it look like?"

"Well, Jesus, Susan, if a woman is the killer or is in on this, that's going to get—"

Susan held up her hands. "You're right. You're right. Next plan. We get into the jewelry boxes of our friends."

"Easier said than done."

"But it can be done."

41

Frost coated the windowpanes, creating a crystalline kaleidoscope. The lamplight reflected off the silver swirls. Outside it was black as pitch.

Little Marilyn and Fitz-Gilbert, snug in Porthault sheets and a goose-down comforter, studied their Christmas lists.

Little Marilyn checked off Carol Jones's name.

Fitz looked over her list. "What did you get Carol?"

"This wonderful book of photographs which create a biography of a Montana woman. What a life, and it's pure serendipity that the old photos were saved."

Fitz pointed to a name on her list. "Scratch that."

Little Marilyn, Xeroxing last year's Christmas list as a guide, had forgotten to remove Ben Seifert's name. She grimaced.

They returned to their lists and after a bit she interrupted Fitz. "Ben had access to our records."

"Uh-huh." Fitz wasn't exactly paying attention.

"Did you check our investments?"

"Yes." Fitz remained uninterested.

She jabbed him with her elbow.

"Ow." He turned toward her. "What?"

"And? Our investments?!"

"First of all, Ben Seifert was a banker, not a stockbroker. There's little he could have done to our investments. Cabby doubled-checked our accounts just to make sure. Everything's okay."

"You never liked Ben, did you?"

"Did you?" Fitz's eyebrow rose.

"No."

"Then why are you asking me what you already know?"

"Well, it's curious how you get feelings about people. You didn't like him. I didn't like him. Yet we were nice to him."

"We're nice to everybody." Fitz thought that was true, although he knew his wife could sometimes be a pale imitation of her imperious mother.

They went back to work on their lists. Little Marilyn interrupted again. "What if it was Ben who ransacked your office?"

Surrendering to the interruption, Fitz put down his list. "Where on earth do you get these ideas?"

"I don't know. Just popped into my head. But then what would you have that he wanted? Unless he was siphoning off our accounts, but both you and Cabby say all is well."

"All is well. I don't know who violated my office. Rick Shaw doesn't have a clue and since the computer and Xerox machine were unmolested, he's treating it as an unrelated vandalism. Kid stuff, most likely."

"Like whoever is knocking over mailboxes with baseball bats in Earlysville?"

"When did that happen?" Fitz's eyes widened in curiosity.

"Don't you read the 'Crime Report' in the Sunday paper?" He shook his head, so Little Marilyn continued. "For the last six or seven months someone's been driving around in the late afternoon, smashing up mailboxes with baseball bats."

"You don't miss much, do you, honey?" Fitz put his arm around her.

She smiled back. "Once things settle down around here ..."

"You mean, once they downshift from chaos to a dull roar?"

"Yes ... let's go to the Homestead. I need a break from all this. And I need a break from Mother."

"Amen."

42

Weeks passed, and the frenzy of Christmas preparations clouded over the recent bizarre events until they were virtually obscured by holiday cheer. Virginia plunged into winter, skies alternating between steel-gray and brilliant blue. The mountains, moody with the weather, changed colors hourly. The spots of color remaining were the bright-red holly berries and the orange pyracantha berries. Fields lapsed into brown; the less well cared-for fields waved with bright broomstraw. The ground thawed and froze, thawed and froze, so fox hunting was never a sure thing. Harry called before each scheduled meet.

The post office, awash in tons of mail, provided Harry with a slant on Christmas different from other people's. Surely the Devil invented the Christmas card. Volume, staggering this year, caused her to call in Mrs. Hogendobber for the entire month of December, and she wangled good pay for her friend too.

So far, Susan had rummaged through Boom Boom's jewelry, an easy task, since Boom Boom loved showing off her goodies. Harry picked over Miranda's earrings, not such an easy task, since Miranda kept asking "Why?" and Harry lied by saying that it had to do with Christmas. The result was that she had to buy Miranda a pair of earrings to put under her Christmas tree. Biff McGuire and Pat Harlan found the perfect pair for Mrs. H., large ovals of beaten gold. They were a bit more than Harry could comfortably afford, but what the hell—Miranda had been a port in a storm at the post office. She also splurged and bought Susan a pair of big gold balls. That exhausted her budget except for presents for Mrs. Murphy and Tucker.

Fair and Boom Boom were holding and eroding. She asked Blair to accompany her to a Piedmont Environmental Council meeting under the guise of acquainting him with the area's progressive people. This she did but she also performed at her best and Blair began to revise somewhat his opinion of Boom Boom, enough, at least, to invite her to a gala fund-raiser in New York City.

Harry and Miranda were up to their knees in Christmas cards when Fair Haristeen pushed open the front door.

"Hi," Harry called to him. "Fair, we're behind. I know you've got more mail than is in your box but I don't know when I'll find it. As you can see, we're hard pressed."

"Didn't come in for that. Morning, Mrs. Hogendobber."

"Morning, Fair."

"Guess you know that Boom Boom left this morning for New York. Her Christmas shopping spree."

"Yes." Harry didn't know how much Fair knew, so she kept mum.

"Guess you know, too, that Blair Bainbridge is taking her to the Knickerbocker Christmas Ball at the Waldorf. I hear princes and dukes will be there."

So he did know. "Sounds very glamorous."

"Eurotrash," Mrs. Hogendobber pronounced.

"Miranda, you've been reading the tabloids again while you're in line at the supermarket."

Mrs. Hogendobber tossed another empty mail bag into the bin, just missing Mrs. Murphy. "What if I have? I have also become an expert on the marriage of Charles and Diana. In case anyone wants to know." She smiled.

"What I want to know"—Fair spoke to Mrs. Hogendobber—"is what is going on with Blair and Boom Boom."

"Now, how would I know that?"

"You know Boom Boom."

"Fair, forgive the pun but this isn't fair," Harry interjected.

"I bet you're just laughing up your sleeve, Harry. I've got egg all over my face."

"You think I'm that vindictive?"

"In a word, yes." He spun on his heel and stormed out.

Miranda came up next to Harry. "Overlook it. It will pass. And he does have egg on his face."

"Lots of yolk, I'd say." Harry started to giggle.

"Don't gloat, Mary Minor Haristeen. The Lord doesn't smile on gloaters. And as I recall, you like Blair Bainbridge."

That sobered Harry up in a jiffy. "Sure, I like him, but I'm not mooning about over him."

"Ha!" Tucker snorted.

"You do like him though." Miranda stuck to her guns.

"Okay, okay, so I like him. Why is it that a single person is an affront to everyone in Crozet? Just because I like my neighbor doesn't mean I want to go out with him, doesn't mean I want to go to bed with him, and doesn't mean I want to marry him. Everyone's got the cart before the horse. I actually like living alone. I don't have to pick up Fair's clothes, I don't have to wash and iron them, and I don't have to worry about what to make for supper. I don't have to pick up the phone at seven and hear that he's got a foaling mare in trouble and he won't be home. And I suspect some of those mares were Boom Boom Craycroft. My nightmare. I am not taking care of another man."

"Now, now, marriage is a fifty-fifty proposition."

"Oh, balls, Miranda. You show me any marriage in this town and I'll show you the wives doing seventy-five percent of the work, both physical and emotional. Hell, half of the men around here don't even mow their lawns. Their wives do it."

The grain of truth in this outburst caused Miranda to think it over. Once she took a position it was quite difficult for her to reverse it—modify it perhaps, but not reverse. "Well, dear, don't you think that the men are exhausted from their work?"

"Who's rich enough to keep a wife that doesn't work? The women are exhausted too. I'd come home and the housework would land in my lap. He wouldn't do it, and I think I worked pretty damn hard myself."

Little Marilyn came in. "Are you two having a fight?"

"No!" Harry yelled at her.

"Christmas." Miranda smiled as if to explain the tension.

"Take Valium. That's what mother does. Her shopping list contains close to three hundred names. You can imagine what a tizz she's in. Can't say that I enjoy this either. But you know we have a position to maintain, and we can't let down the little people."

That toasted Harry, pushed her right over the edge. "Well, Marilyn, allow me to relieve you and your mother of one little person!" Harry walked out the back door and slammed it hard.

"She never has liked me, even when we were children." Little Marilyn pouted.

Miranda, inviolate in her social position, spoke directly. "Marilyn, you don't make it easy."

"And what do you mean by that?"

"You've got your nose so far up in the air that if it rains, you'll drown. Stop imitating your mother and be yourself. Yes, be yourself. It's the one thing you can do better than anyone else. You'll be a lot happier and so will everyone around you."

This bracing breeze of honesty so stunned the younger woman that she blinked but didn't move. Mrs. Murphy, hanging out of the mail bin, observed the stricken Little Marilyn.

"Tucker, go on around the counter. Little Marilyn's either going to faint or pitch a hissy."

Tucker eagerly snuck around the door, her claws clicking on the wooden floorboards.

Little Marilyn caught her breath. "Mrs. Hogendobber, you have no right to speak to me like that."

"I have every right. I'm one of the few people who sees beneath your veneer and I'm one of the few people who actually likes you despite all."

"If this is your idea of friendship I find it most peculiar." The color returned to Little Marilyn's narrow face.

"Child, go home and think about it. Who tells you the truth? Who would you call at three in the morning if you were feeling low? Your mother? I think not. Are you doing anything with your life that makes you truly happy? How many bracelets and necklaces and cars can you buy? Do they make you happy? You know, Marilyn, life is like an aircraft carrier. If there's a mistake in navigation, it takes one mile just to turn the ship around."

"I am not an aircraft carrier." Little Marilyn recovered enough to turn and leave.

Miranda slapped letters on the counter. "It's going to be that kind of day." She said this to the cat and dog, then realized who she was talking to and shook her head. "What am I doing?"

"*Having an intelligent conversation,*" Mrs. Murphy purred.

Harry sheepishly opened the back door. "Sorry."

"I know." Miranda opened another sack of mail.

"I hate Christmas."

"Oh, don't let work get to you."

"It isn't just that. I can't wipe the murders out of my mind and I suppose I am more upset than I realized about Blair taking Boom Boom to that stupid ball. But why would he ask me? I can't afford to travel to New York and I don't have anything to wear. I'm not an impressive specimen on a man's arm. Still . . ." Her voice trailed off. "And I can't believe Fair can be taken in by that woman." She paused. "And I miss Mom and Dad the most at Christmas."

Tucker sat beside Harry's feet and Mrs. Murphy walked over to her too.

Miranda understood. She, too, lived with her losses. "I'm sorry,

Harry. Because you're young I sometimes think that everything's wonderful. But I know what it's like to hear the carols and wish those old familiar voices were singing with us. Nothing is ever quite the same again." She went over and patted Harry on the back, for Mrs. Hogendobber wasn't a physically demonstrative woman. "God never closes one door that he doesn't open another. You try and remember that."

43

Resplendent sashes swept across the men's chests; medals dangled over hearts. Those in military dress caused the women to breathe harder. Such handsome men, such beautiful women laden with jewelry, the aggregate sum of which was more than the gross national product of Bolivia.

Boom Boom's head spun. Blair, in white tie and tails, squired her around the dance floor, one of the best in America. What was Crozet compared to this? Boom Boom felt she had arrived. If she couldn't turn Blair's head, and he was attentive but not physically attracted to her—she could tell—she knew she'd snare someone else before the night surrendered to dawn.

A coral dress accentuated her dark coloring, the low-cut bodice calling attention to her glories. When she and Blair returned to their table after dancing, a college friend of his joined them. After the introductions, Orlando Heguay pulled up a chair.

"How's life in the boonies?"

"Interesting."

Orlando smiled at Boom Boom. "If this lovely lady is proof, I should say so."

Boom Boom smiled back. Her teeth glistened; she'd had them cleaned the day before. "You flatter me."

"Quite the contrary. My vocabulary fails me."

Blair smiled indulgently. "Come visit for New Year's. I might even have furniture by then."

"Blair, that's a deal."

"Orlando, refresh my memory. Were you at Exeter or Andover?"

"Andover. Carlos was Exeter. Mother and Dad thought we should go to separate schools, since we were so competitive. And now we're in business together. I suppose they were right."

"And what is your business, Mr. Heguay?"

"Oh, please call me Orlando." He smiled again. He was a fine-looking man. "Carlos and I own The Atlantic Company. We provide architects and interior designers to various clients, many of whom reside in South America as well as North America. I was the original architect and Carlos was the original interior designer, but now we have a team of fifteen employees."

"You sound as though you love it," Boom Boom cooed.

"I do."

Blair, amused by Boom Boom's obvious interest—an interest reflected by Orlando—asked, "Didn't you go to school with Fitz-Gilbert Hamilton?"

"Year behind me. Poor guy."

"What do you mean?"

"His parents were killed in a small plane crash one summer. Then he and a buddy were in a car wreck. Messed them up pretty badly. I heard he'd had kind of a breakdown. People were surprised when he made it to Princeton in the fall, 'cause there'd been so much talk about him his senior year. People thought he was definitely on the skids."

"He lives in Crozet, too ... seems to be perfectly fine."

"How about that. Remember Izzy Diamond?"

"I remember that he wanted to make Pen and Scroll so badly at Yale that I thought he'd die if he didn't. Didn't make it either."

"Just got arrested for an investment scam."

"Izzy Diamond?"

"Yes." Orlando's eyebrows darted upward, then he gazed at Boom Boom. "How rude of us to reminisce about college. Mademoiselle, may I have this dance?" He turned to Blair. "You're going to have to find yourself another girl."

Blair smiled and waved them off. He felt grateful to Boom Boom for easing his social passage into Central Virginia. In an odd way he liked her, although her need to be the center of attention bored him the more he was around her. Asking her to the Knickerbocker Ball was more of a payback than anything else. He couldn't have been happier that Orlando found her tremendously attractive. Many of the men there cast admiring glances at Boom Boom. Blair was off women for a while, although he found himself thinking of Harry at the oddest times. He wondered what she'd do at a ball. Not that she'd be awkward but he couldn't imagine her in a ball gown. Her natural element was boots, jeans, and a shirt. Given Harry's small rear end, her natural element illuminated her physical charms. She was so practical, so down to earth. Suddenly Blair wished she were with him. Wouldn't she find some funny things to say about this crowd?

44

"Who'll start at fifteen thousand? Do I hear fifteen thousand? Now you can't buy this new for under thirty-five. Who'll bid fifteen thousand?"

As the auctioneer sang, insulted, joked, and carried on, Harry and Blair stood at the edge of the auction ground. A light rain dampened the attendance, and as temperatures were dropping, the rain could quite possibly turn to snow. People stamped their feet and rubbed their hands together. Even though she wore silk long johns, a T-shirt, a heavy sweater, and her down jacket, the cold nipped at Harry's nose, hands, and feet. She could always keep her body warm but the extremities proved difficult.

Blair shifted from foot to foot. "Now you're sure I need a seventy-horsepower tractor?"

"You can get along with forty-five or so, but if you have seventy you can do everything you'll ever want to do. You want to turn up that back field of yours and fertilize it, right? You'll want to bush-hog. You've got a lot to do at Foxden. I know that John Deere is old but it's been well maintained and if you have a tiny bit of me-chanical ability you can keep it humming."

"Do I need a blade?"

"To scrape the driveway? You could get through the winter without one. It doesn't usually snow much in Virginia. Let's concen-trate on the essentials."

Life in the country was proving more complicated and expen-sive than Blair had imagined. Fortunately, he had resources, and fortunately, he had Harry. Otherwise he would have walked into a dealer and paid top dollar for a piece of new equipment, plus oodles of attachments he didn't need immediately and might never even use.

The green and yellow John Deere tractor beckoned to more folks than Blair. Bidding was lively but he finally prevailed at twenty-two thousand five hundred, which was a whopping good buy. Harry did the bidding.

Harry, thrilled with his purchase, crawled up into the tractor, started her up, and chugged over in first gear to her gooseneck, a step-up. She'd brought along a wooden ramp, which weighed a ton. She kept the tractor running, put it in neutral, and locked the brake.

"Blair, this might take another man."

He lifted one end. "How'd you get this thing on in the first place?"

"I keep it on the old hay wagon and when I need it I take it to the earthen ramp and then shove it off into the trailer, backed up to the ramp. I expand my vocabulary of abuse too." She noticed Mr. Tapscott, who had purchased a dump truck. "Hey, Stuart, give me a hand."

Mr. Tapscott ambled over, a tall man with gorgeous gray hair. " 'Bout time you replenished your tractor, and you got the best deal today."

"Blair bought it. I just did the bidding." Harry introduced them.

Mr. Tapscott eyed Blair. As he liked Harry his eye was critical.

He didn't want any man hanging around who didn't have some backbone.

"Harry showed me the roadwork you did out at Reverend Jones'. That was quite a job."

"Enjoyed it." Mr. Tapscott smiled. "Well, you feeling strong?"

To assist in this maneuver, Travis, Stuart's son, joined in. The men easily positioned the heavy ramp, and Harry, in the driver's seat, rolled the tractor into the gooseneck. Then the men slid the ramp into the trailer, leaning it against the tractor.

"Thank you, Mr. Tapscott." Blair held out his hand.

"Glad to help the friend of a friend." He smiled and wished them good day.

Once in her truck, Harry drove slowly because she wanted the ramp to bang up against the tractor only so much.

"I'm going to take this to my place, because we can drive the tractor straight off. Then you can help me slide off the wooden ramp. Wish they made an aluminum ramp that I could use, but no luck."

"At the hunt meets I've seen trailers with ramps."

"Sure, but those kinds of trailers cost so much—especially the aluminum ones, which are the best. My stock trailer is serviceable but nothing fancy like a ramp comes with it."

She backed up to the earthen ramp. Took two tries. They could hear Tucker barking in the house. They rolled off the tractor, after which they pushed and pulled on the wooden ramp.

"Well, how are we going to get it off the bank?" Blair was puzzled, as the heavy wooden ramp was precariously perched on the earthen rampart.

"Watch." Harry pulled the gooseneck away, hopped out of the truck, and unhitched it. Then she climbed back in the truck and backed it over to the old hay wagon. A chain hung from the wagon's long shaft, a leftover from the days when it was drawn by horses. She dropped the chain over the ball hitch on her bumper. Harry wisely had both hitches on her trailer: the steel plate and ball bolted into the bed of her truck for the gooseneck and another hitch welded onto the frame under the bed of the truck, with its adjustable ball mount. Then she drove the hay wagon alongside the embankment.

"Okay, now we push the ramp onto the wagon."

Blair, sweating now despite the temperature, pushed the heavy wooden ramp onto the beckoning platform. "Presto."

Harry cut the motor, rolled up her windows, and got out of the truck. "Blair, I spoke too soon. I think it's going to snow. We can put the tractor in my barn or you can drive it over to yours and I'll follow you in your truck."

As if on cue the first snowflake lazed out of the darkening sky.

"Let's leave it here. I don't know how to work one of these contraptions yet. You still gonna teach me?"

"Yeah, it's easy."

The heavens seemed to have opened a zipper then; snow poured out of the sky. The two of them walked into the house after Harry parked the tractor in the barn. The animals joyously greeted their mother. She put on coffee and dug out lunch meat to make sandwiches.

"Harry, your truck isn't four-wheel-drive, is it?"

"No."

"Hold those sandwiches for about twenty minutes. I'll run down to the market and get food, because this looks like a real snowstorm. Your pantry is low and I know mine is."

Before she could protest he was gone. An hour later he returned with eight bags of groceries. He'd bought a frying chicken, a pork roast, potatoes, potato chips, Cokes, lettuce, an assortment of cheese, vegetables, apples, and some for the horses too. Pancake mix, milk, real butter, brownie mix, a six-pack of Mexican beer, expensive coffee beans, a coffee grinder, and two whole bags of cat and dog food. He truly astounded Harry by putting the food away and making a fire in the kitchen fireplace, using a starter log and some of the split wood she had stacked on the porch. Her protests were ignored.

"Now we can eat."

"Blair, I don't know how to make a pork roast."

"You make a good sandwich. If this keeps up like the weather report says, there'll be two feet of snow on the ground by tomorrow noon. I'll come over and show you how to cook a pork roast. Can you make waffles?"

"I watched Mother do it. I bet I can."

"You make breakfast and I'll make dinner. In between we'll paint your tack room."

"You bought paint too?"

"It's in the back of the truck."

"Blair, it'll freeze." Harry jumped up and ran outside, followed by Blair. They laughed as they hauled the paint into the kitchen, their hair dotted with snowflakes, their feet wet. They finished eating, took off their shoes, and sat back down with their feet toward the fire.

Mrs. Murphy sprawled before the fire, as did Tucker.

"How come you haven't asked me about taking Boom Boom to the Knickerbocker Ball?"

"It's none of my business."

"I apologize for not asking you, but Boom Boom has been helpful and for two seconds there I found her intriguing, so I thought I'd take her to the Waldorf as sort of a thank you."

"Like buying the groceries?"

He pondered this. "Yes and no. I don't like to take advantage of people and you've both been helpful. She met someone there that I went to college with, Orlando Heguay. A big hit." He wiggled his toes.

"Rich?"

"Um, and handsome too."

Harry smiled. As the twilight deepened, a soft purple cast over the snow like a melancholy net. Blair told her about his continuing struggles with his father, who had wanted him either to be a doctor like himself or go into business. He talked about his two sisters, his mother, and finally he got to the story about his murdered girlfriend. Blair confessed that although it had happened about a year and a half ago he was just now beginning to feel human again.

Harry sympathized and when he asked her about her life she told him that she had studied art history at Smith, never quite found her career direction, and fell into the job at the post office which, truthfully, she enjoyed. Her marriage had been like a second job and when it ended she was amazed at the free time she had. She was casting about for something to do in addition to the post office. She was thinking of being an agent for equine art but she didn't know enough about the market. And she was in no hurry. She, too, was beginning to feel as if she was waking up.

She wondered whether to ask him to stay. His house was so barren, but it didn't seem right to ask him just yet. Harry was never one to rush things.

When he got up to go home, she hugged him goodbye, thanked him for the groceries, and said she'd see him in the morning.

She watched his lights as he drove down the curving driveway. Then she put on her jacket and took out scraps for the possum.

45

Tucked into bed with the latest Susan Isaacs novel, Harry was surprised when the phone rang.

Fair's voice crackled over the line. "Can you hear me?"

"Yes, kind of."

"The lines are icing up. You might lose your power and your phone. Are you alone?"

"What kind of question is that? Are you?"

"Yes. I'm worried about you, Harry. Who knows what will happen if you're cut off from the world?"

"I'm in no danger."

"You don't know that. Just because nothing has happened recently doesn't mean that you might not be in danger."

"Maybe you're in danger." Harry sighed. "Fair, is this your way of apologizing?"

"Uh . . . well, yes."

"Is the bloom off the rose with Boom Boom?"

A long silence filled with static was finally broken. "I don't know."

"Fair, I was your wife and before that I was one of your best friends. Maybe we'll get back to being best friends over time. So take that into consideration when I ask this next question. Have you spent a lot of money on her?"

This time the silence was agonizing. "I suppose I have, by my standards. Harry, it's never enough. I buy her something beautiful— you know, an English bridle, and those things aren't cheap. But anyway, for example, an English bridle, and she's all over me, she's so happy. Two hours later she's in a funk and I'm not sensitive to her needs. Does she ever run out of needs? Is she this way with women or is this something reserved for men?"

"She's that way with women. Remember her sob story to Mrs. MacGregor and how Mrs. MacGregor helped her out and lent her horses—this was way back before she married Kelly. Mrs. MacGregor wearied of it before long. She'd have to clean the tack and the horse for Boom Boom, who showed up late for their rides. She's just, oh, I don't know. She's just not reliable. The best thing that ever happened to her was marrying Kelly Craycroft. He could afford her."

"Well, that's just it, Harry. We know Kelly left a respectable estate and she's crying poor."

"Pity gets more money out of people than other emotions, I guess. Are you strapped? Did you spend . . . a lot?"

"Well . . . more than I could afford."

"Can you pay your rent on the house and the office?"

"That's about all I can pay for."

Harry thought awhile. "You know, if you owe on equipment you can ask for smaller payments until you're back on your feet. And if your hunt club dues are a problem, Jock couldn't be more understanding. He'll work with you."

"Harry"—Fair's words nearly choked him—"I was a fool. I wish I'd given the money to you."

Tears rolled down Harry's cheeks. "Honey, it's water over the dam. Just get back on your feet and take a break from women, a sabbatical."

"Do you hate me?"

"I did. I'm over that, I hope. I wish things had turned out differently. My ego took a sound beating, which I didn't appreciate, but who would? It's amazing how the most reasonable people become unreasonable and, well, not very bright, when love or sex appears. Does it even appear? I don't know what it is anymore."

"Me, neither." He swallowed. "But I know you loved me. You never lied to me. You worked alongside me and you didn't ask for things. How we lost the fire, I don't know. One day it was gone."

Now it was Harry's turn to be quiet. "Who knows, Fair, who knows? Can people get that feeling back? Maybe some can but I don't think we could have. It doesn't mean we're bad people. It slipped away somehow. Over time we'll come back to that place where we can appreciate—I guess that's the word—the good things about each other and the years we had. Most of Crozet doesn't believe that's possible between a man and a woman but I hope we prove them wrong."

"Me too."

After he hung up Harry dialed Susan and told all. By now she was working on a good cry. Susan consoled her and felt happy that perhaps she and Fair could be friends. Once Harry purged herself she returned to her primary focus these days, a focus she shared only with Susan: the murders.

"No leads on that money in Ben's portfolio?"

"Not that I know of, and I pumped Cynthia Cooper at the supermarket too," Susan replied. "And Ned has worked with Cabell, who's taking this hard."

"And nothing is missing from the bank?"

"No. And they've checked and double-checked. Everyone asks that same question. It's driving Cabell crazy."

"Did you get into any more jewel boxes?"

"Very funny. My idea wasn't so good after all."

"I felt positively guilty asking Miranda to go through her stuff.

She's in her Christmas mood. Even the mail doesn't stop her. Did you see her tree? I think it's bigger than the one at the White House."

"It's the Christmas-tree pin that kills me, all those little twinkling lights on her bosom. She must have a mile of wire under her blouse and skirt," Susan laughed.

"You going to Mim's party?"

"I didn't know we were allowed to miss it."

"I'm going to wear the earring. It's our only chance."

"Harry, don't do that."

"I'm doing it."

"Then I'm telling Rick Shaw."

"Tell him afterwards. Otherwise he'll come and take the earring. Which reminds me, do you have an earring without a mate . . . ?"

"Thanks a lot, pal!"

"No, no, I don't mean that. I have so few earrings I was hoping you'd have one I could have, preferably a big one."

"Why?"

"So I can trade with the possum."

"Harry, for heaven's sake, it's an animal. Take it some food."

"I do that. This little guy likes shiny things. I have to trade."

Susan sighed dramatically. "I'll find something. You're looney-tunes."

"What's that say about you? You're my best friend."

On this note they hung up.

Mrs. Murphy asked Tucker, *"Did you know that cats wore golden earrings in ancient Egypt?"*

"I don't care. Go to sleep." Tucker rolled over.

"What a crab," the cat thought to herself before she crawled under the covers. She liked to sleep with her head on the pillow next to Harry's.

46

All through the night heavy snow fell over Central Virginia. A slight
rise in the temperature at dawn changed the snow to freezing rain,
and soon the beautiful white blanket was encased in thick ice. By
seven the temperature plunged again, creating more snow. Driving
was treacherous because the ice was hidden. State police blared
warnings over the TV and radio for people to stay home.

Blair spun around in front of the barn when he tried to get his
dually down the driveway. He grabbed his skis and poles and slid
cross-country to the creek between his property and Harry's. The
edges of the creek were caked with ice; icicles hung down from
bushes, and tree branches sparkled even in the gray light and the
continued snow. Blair removed his skis, threw them to the other
side of the creek, and then used his poles to help him get across.
Any stepping stone he could find was slick as a cue ball. What normally took a minute or two took fifteen. By the time he arrived at

Harry's back door he was panting and red in the face. The waffles returned his vigor.

When Harry and Blair reached the tack room it was warm enough to paint, because Harry had set up a space heater in the middle of the room. They painted all day. Blair cooked his pork roast as promised. Over dessert they sat talking. He borrowed a strong flashlight, strapped on his skis, and left for home early, at 8:30 P.M. He called Harry at close to 9:00 P.M. to let her know he'd finally made it. They agreed it had been a great day and then they hung up.

47

The snow continued to fall off and on through Sunday. Monday morning Susan Tucker slowly chugged out to Harry's to pick her up for work. The ancient Jeep, sporting chains, was packed with Harry, Mrs. Murphy, and Tucker. As they drove back to town Harry was astonished at the number of vehicles left by the side of the road or that had slipped off and now reposed at the bottom of an embankment. She knew the owners of most of the cars too.

"What a boon to the body shop," Harry remarked.

"And what a boon to Art Bushey. Most of those people will be so furious they'll tow the car out as soon as possible and take it over to him for a trade. Four-wheel drive is more expensive to run but you gotta have it in these parts."

"I know." Harry sounded mournful.

Susan, well-acquainted with her best friend's impecunious state, smiled. "A friend with four-wheel drive is as good as owning it yourself."

Harry shifted Tucker's weight on her lap as the little dog's hind foot dug into her bladder. "I need to come up with a sideline. Really. I can't make it on the post office salary."

"Bad time to start a business."

"Do you think we're on the verge of a depression? Forget this recession garbage. Politicians create a euphemism for everything."

"You can always tell when a politician is lying. It's whenever his mouth is moving." Susan slowed down even more as they reached the outskirts of town. Although the roads had been plowed and plowed again, the ice underneath would not yield. "Yes, I think we're in for it. We're going to pay for the scandals on Wall Street, and even worse, we're going to pay for the savings and loan disaster for the rest of our natural lives. The party's over."

"Then I'd better come up with a party clean-up business." Harry was glum.

Susan slowly slid into the wooden guard rails in front of the post office when she applied her brakes. The Jeep was four-wheel drive but not four-wheel stop. She could see Miranda already at work. "I've got to get back home. Oh, here, I almost forgot." She reached into her purse and retrieved a large gold earring.

"This isn't real gold, is it? I can't take it if it is."

"Gold plate. And I go on record as being opposed to your plan."

"I hear you but I'm not listening." Harry opened the door. Tucker leapt out and sank into the snow over her head.

Mrs. Murphy laughed. "Swim, Tucker."

"Very funny." Tucker pushed through the snow, leaping upward every step to get her head above the white froth.

The cat remained on Harry's shoulder. Harry helped Tucker along and Mrs. Hogendobber opened the door.

"I've got something to show you." Mrs. Hogendobber shut the door and locked it again. "Come here."

As Harry removed her coat and extra layers, Miranda plunked a handful of cards on the counter. They appeared to be sale postcards sent out at regular intervals by businesses wanting to save the additional postage on a regular letter. Until Harry read one.

" 'Don't stick your nose where it don't belong,' " she read aloud. "What is this?"

"I don't know what it is, apart from incorrect grammar, but Herbie and Carol have received one. So have the Sanburnes, the Hamiltons, Fair Haristeen, Boom Boom, Cabby and Taxi—in fact, nearly everyone we know."

"Who hasn't received one?"

"Blair Bainbridge."

Harry held up the card to the light. "Nice print job. Did you call Sheriff Shaw?"

"Yes. And I called Charlottesville Press, Papercraft, Kaminer and Thompson, King Lindsay, every printer in Charlottesville. No one has any record of such an order."

"Could a computer with a graphics package do something like this?"

"You're asking me? That's what children are for, to play with computers." Mrs. Hogendobber put her hands on her hips.

"Well, here come Rick and Cynthia. Maybe they'll know."

The officers thought the postcards could have been printed with an expensive laser printer but they'd check with computer experts in town.

As they drove slowly away Cynthia watched new storm clouds approaching from the west. "Boss?"

"What?"

"Why would a killer do something like this? It's stupid."

"On the one hand, yes; on the other hand . . . well, I don't know." Rick gripped the wheel tighter and slowed to a crawl. "We have next to nothing. He or she knows that, but there's something inside this person, something that wants to show off. He doesn't want to get caught but he wants us and everyone else to know he's smarter than the rest of us put together. Kind of a classic conflict."

"He needs to reaffirm his power, yet stay hidden." She waved to Fair, stuck in the snow. "We'd better stop. I think we can get him out."

Rick rolled his eyes and stared at the ceiling. "Look, I know this is illegal so I won't ask you directly but wouldn't it be odd if these postcards were misplaced for a day—just a day?" He paused. "We got someone smart, incredibly smart, and someone who likes to play cat and mouse. Dammit. Christmas!"

"Huh?"

"I'm afraid for every Christmas present under every tree right now."

48

A stupendous Douglas fir scraped the high ceiling in Mim Sanburne's lovely mansion. The heart-pine floors glowed with the reflection of tree lights. Presents were piled under the tree, on the sideboard in the hall, everywhere—gaily colored packages in green, gold, red, and silver foil wrapping paper topped off with huge multicolored bows.

Approximately 150 guests filled the seven downstairs rooms of the old house. Zion Hill, as the house was named, originated as a chinked log cabin, one room, in 1769. Indians swooped down to kill whites, and Zion Hill had no neighbors until after the Revolutionary War. There were rifle slits in the wall where the pioneers retreated to shoot attacking Indians. The Urquharts, Mim's mother's family, prospered and added to the house in the Federal style. Boom times covered the United States in a glow in the 1820's. After all, the country had won another war against Great Britain, the West was opening up, and all things seemed possible. Captain Urquhart, the third generation to live at Zion Hill, invested in the pippin apple, which people said was brought into the county from New York State by Dr. Thomas Walker, physician to Thomas Jefferson. The Captain bought up mountain land dirt-cheap and created miles of orchards. Fortunately for the Captain, Americans loved apple pie, apple cider, applesauce, apple tarts, apple popovers, apples. Horses liked them too.

Before the War Between the States, the next generation of Urquharts bought into the railroad heading west and more good fortune was heaped upon their heads. Then the War Between the States ravaged them; three out of four sons were sacrificed. Two generations later, only one daughter and one son survived. The daughter had the good sense to marry a Yankee who, although locally despised, arrived with money and frugal New England values. The brother, never free of his war wounds, worked for his sister's husband, not a comfortable arrangement but better than starvation. The stigma of Yankee blood had slightly faded by World War II, faded enough so that Mim didn't mind using her paternal family name, Conrad, although she always used her mother's name first.

Architecture buffs liked an invitation to Zion Hill because the rooms had been measured by the distance from the foreman's elbow to the end of his middle finger. The measurements weren't exact, yet visually the rooms appeared perfect. Gardeners enjoyed the boxwoods and the perennial and annual gardens lovingly tended for over two centuries. Then, too, the food pleased everyone. The fact that the hostess lorded it over them pleased no one, but there were so many people to talk to at the Christmas party, you only had to say "Hello" to Mim and "Thank you for the wonderful time" as you left.

The lushes of Albemarle County, glued to the punch bowl as well as the bar, had noses as red as Santa's outfit. Santa appeared precisely at 8:00 P.M. for the children. He dispensed his gifts and then mommies and daddies could take home their cherubs for a good night's rest. Once the small fry were evacuated, folks kicked into high gear. Someone could be depended on to fall down dead drunk every year, someone else would start a fight, someone would cry, and someone would seduce a hapless or perhaps fortunate partygoer.

This year Mim hired the choir from the Lutheran Church. They would go on at 9:30 P.M. so the early risers could carol and go home.

The acid green of Mim's emeralds glittered on her neck. Her dress, white, was designed to show off the jewels. Dangling emerald earrings matched the necklace, the aggregate value of which, retail at Tiffany's, would have topped $200,000. Hot competition in the jewelry department came from Boom Boom Craycroft, who favored sapphires, and Miranda Hogendobber, who was partial to rubies. Miranda, not a wealthy woman, had inherited her sumptuous ruby and diamond necklace and earrings from her mother's sister. Susan Tucker wore modest diamond earrings and Harry wore no major stones at all. For a woman, Mim's Christmas party was like entering the lists. Who wore what counted for more than it should have and Harry couldn't compete. She wished she were above caring but she would have liked to have one stunning pair of earrings, necklace, and ring. As it was she was wearing the misshapen gold earring.

The men wore green, red, or plaid cummerbunds with their tuxedos. Jim Sanburne wore mistletoe as a boutonniere. It produced the desired effect. Fitz-Gilbert sported a kilt, which also produced the desired effect. Women noticed his legs.

Fair escorted Boom Boom. Harry couldn't figure out if this had been a longstanding date, if he was weakening, or if he was just a glutton for punishment. Blair accompanied Harry, which pleased her even if he did ask at the last minute.

Fitz-Gilbert passed out Macanudos. He kept his Cuban Monte-cristos for very special occasions or his personal whim, but a good Macanudo was as a Jaguar to the Montecristo Rolls-Royce. Blair gladly puffed on the gift cigar.

Susan and Ned joined them, as did Rick Shaw, in a tuxedo, and Cynthia Cooper wearing a velvet skirt and a festive red top. The little group chatted about the University of Virginia's women's basketball team, of which everyone was justly proud. Under the astute guid-ance of coach Debbie Ryan, the women had evolved into a national power.

Ned advised, "If only they'd lower the basket, though. I miss the dunking. Other than that it's great basketball and those ladies can shoot."

"Especially the three-pointers." Harry smiled. She loved that basketball team.

"I'm partial to the guards myself," Susan added. "Brookie's hero is Debbie Ryan. Most girls want to grow up to be movie stars or players. Brookie wants to be a coach."

"Shows sense." Blair noticed Susan's daughter in the middle of a group of eighth-graders. What an awkward age for everyone, the young person and the adults.

Market Shiflett joined them. "Some party. I wait for this each year. It's the only time Mim invites me here unless she wants a delivery." His face shone. He'd been downing Johnnie Walker Black, his special brand.

"She forgets," Harry diplomatically told him.

"The hell she does," Market rejoined. "How'd you like your last name to be Shiflett?"

"Market, if you're living proof I'd be honored to have Shiflett as my last name." Blair's baritone soothed.

"Hear, hear." Ned held up his glass.

The tinkle of shattered glass diverted their attention. Boom Boom had enraged Mrs. Drysdale by swinging her breasts under Patrick Drysdale's aquiline nose. Patrick, not immune to such bounty, forgot he was a married man, a condition epidemic at such a large party. Missy threw a glass at Boom Boom's head. Instead, it narrowly missed Dr. Chuck Beegle's head and smashed against the wall.

Mim observed this. She cocked her head in Little Marilyn's direction.

Little Marilyn glided over, "Now, Missy, honey, how about some coffee?"

"Did you see what that vixen did? Obviously, she has nothing to recommend her other than her ... her tits!"

Boom Boom, half in the bag, laughed, "Oh, Missy, get over it.

You've been jealous of me since sixth grade, when we were studying pirates and those boys called you a sunken chest."

Her remark inflamed Missy, who reached into a bowl of cheese dip. The gooey yellow handful immediately decorated Boom Boom's bosom.

"Damn you for getting that stuff on my sapphires!" Boom Boom pushed Missy.

"Is that what you call them ... sapphires?" Missy shrieked.

Harry nudged Susan. "Let's go."

"May I assist?" Blair volunteered.

"No, this is women's work," Susan said lightly.

Under her breath Harry whispered to her friend, "If she swings she'll take a roundhouse. Boom Boom can't throw a straight punch."

"Yeah, I know."

Susan swiftly wrapped an arm around Boom Boom's small waist, propelling her into the kitchen. The sputtering died away.

Harry, meanwhile, ducked a punch and came up behind Missy, putting both hands on Missy's shoulders, and steered her toward the powder room. Little Marilyn followed.

"God, I hate her. I really hate her," Missy seethed, her frosted hair bobbing with each step. "If I were really awful I'd wish her upon Patrick. She ruins every man she touches!" Missy realized who was shepherding her. "I'm sorry, Harry. I'm so mad I don't know what I'm saying."

"It's all right, Missy. You do know what you're saying and I agree."

This opened a new line of conversation and Missy calmed down considerably. Once in the immense bathroom, Little Marilyn ran a washcloth under cold water and applied it to Missy's forehead.

"I'm not drunk."

"I know," Little Marilyn replied. "But when I get rattled this works for me. Mother, of course, supports Upjohn Industries."

"What?" Missy didn't get the joke.

"Mummy has pills to calm her down, pills to pep her up, and pills to put her to sleep, forgive the expression."

"Marilyn"—Missy put her hand over Little Marilyn's—"That's serious."

"I know. She won't listen to her family and if Hayden McIntire won't prescribe them she simply goes to another doctor and pays him off. So Hayden goes on writing out the prescriptions. That way he has an idea of how much she's taking."

"Are you okay now?" Harry inquired of Missy.

"Yes. I lost my temper and I'll go apologize to your mother, Marilyn. Really, Patrick's not worth fussing over. He can look at anything he wants on the menu but he can't order, that's all."

This was an expression both Harry and Little Marilyn heard frequently from married couples. Little Marilyn smiled and Harry shrugged. Little Marilyn stared at Harry, bringing her face almost nose to nose.

"Harry!"

"What?" Harry stepped backward.

"I had earrings like that, except that one looks—"

"Squashed?"

"Squashed," Little Marilyn echoed. "And you only have one. Now that's peculiar because I lost one. I wore them all the time, my Tiffany disks. Anyway, I thought I lost it on the tennis court. I never did find it."

"I found this one."

"Where?"

"In a possum's nest." Harry studied Little Marilyn intently. "I traded the possum for it."

"Come on." Missy reapplied her lipstick.

"Scout's honor." Harry raised her right hand. "Did you keep the mate?" she asked Little Marilyn.

"I'll show you tomorrow. I'll bring it to the post office."

"I'd love to see what it looks like in pristine condition."

Little Marilyn took a deep breath. "Harry, why can't we be friends?"

Missy stopped applying her lipstick in mid-twirl. A Sanburne was being emotionally honest, sort of.

In the spirit of the season Harry smiled and replied, "We can try."

Three quarters of an hour later Harry, having spoken to everyone on her way back from the bathroom, managed to reach Susan. She whispered the news in Susan's ear.

"Impossible." Susan shook her head.

"Impossible or not, she seems to think it's hers."

"We'll see tomorrow."

Boom Boom swooped upon them. "Harry and Susan, thank you ever so much for relieving me of Missy Drysdale's tedious presence."

Before they could reply, and it would have been a tart reply, Boom Boom threw her arms around Blair, who was relieved to find his date finally sprung from the powder room. "Blair, darling, I need a favor—not a humongous favor but a teeny-weeny one."

"Uh . . ."

"Orlando Heguay says he'll come down for New Year's Eve and I can't put him up at my place—I hardly know the man. Would you?"

"Of course." Blair held out his hands as if in benediction. "It's what I meant to do all along."

Susan whispered to Harry, "Has Fair spent a lot on his Christmas present for Our Lady of the Sorrows?"

"He says he can't return it. He had a coat specially made from 'Out of the Blue.' "

"Ouch." Susan winced. Out of the Blue, an expensive but entertaining ladies' apparel store, couldn't take back a personalized item. Anyway, few women fit Boom Boom's specifications.

"Tim-ber!" Harry cupped her hands to her mouth at the exact moment Fitz-Gilbert Hamilton hit the floor, drunk as a skunk.

Everyone laughed except for the two Marilyns.

"I'd better make up for that." Harry wiggled through the crowd to Little Marilyn. "Hey, we're all under pressure," she whispered. "Too much party tonight. Don't get too mad at him."

"Before this night is out we'll have them stacked like cordwood."

"Where are you going to put them?"

"In the barn."

"Sensible." Harry nodded.

The Sanburnes thought of everything. The loaded guests could sleep it off in the barn and puke in the barn—no harm done to the Persian rugs. And no guilt over someone being in an accident after the party.

Before the night was over Danny Tucker's girlfriend cried because he didn't ask her to dance enough.

The juiciest gossip of all was that Missy Drysdale left Patrick, drunk and soon a stable candidate. She traipsed out of the party with Fair Haristeen, who dumped Boom Boom when he overheard her talking about Orlando Heguay's visit.

Boom Boom consoled herself by confiding to Jim Sanburne how misunderstood she was. She would have made real progress if Mim hadn't yanked him away.

Another Christmas party: Peace on Earth, Goodwill toward Men.

49

Harry sat in the middle of an avalanche of paper. Mrs. Murphy jumped from envelope pile to envelope pile while Tucker, head on paws, tail wagging, waited for the cat to dash through the room.

"You're it." Mrs. Murphy jumped over Tucker, who leapt up and chased her.

"Stay on the ground. It's not fair if you go to the second story." Tucker made up the rules as she ran.

"Says who?" Mrs. Murphy arced upward, landing on the counter.

Mrs. Hogendobber barely noticed the two animals, a sign that she had become accustomed to their antics.

"One more day of this, Harry. There's a bit of aftermath, as you well know, but the worst will be over tomorrow and then we can take off Christmas Eve and Christmas Day."

Harry, sorting out mail as fast as she could, replied, "Miranda, I barely recover from one Christmas before the next one is on the way."

Reverend Jones, Little Marilyn, and Fitz-Gilbert pushed through the door in a group, Market on their heels. Everyone plucked the offending postcards out of their boxes.

Mrs. Hogendobber headed off their protests. "We got them too. The sheriff knows all about it, and face it, we had to deliver them. We'd violate a federal law if we withheld your mail."

"Maybe we wouldn't mind so much if he were literate," Fitz joked.

"Christmas is almost upon us. Let's concentrate on the meaning of that," Herb counseled.

Pewter scratched at the front door. While the humans talked, Mrs. Murphy and Tucker told Pewter about Simon and the earring.

As if on cue, Little Marilyn reached into her pocket and pulled out the undamaged Tiffany earring. "See."

Harry placed the damaged earring next to the shiny gold one. "A pair. Well, so much for a Tiffany earring. It was the only way I was going to get one."

"Put not thy faith in worldly goods." The Reverend smiled. "Those are pretty worldly goods, though."

Fitz poked at the bent-up earring. "Honey, where did you lose this? They were your Valentine's present last year."

"Now, Fitz, I didn't want to upset you. I was hoping I'd find it and then you'd—"

"Never know." He shook his head. "Marilyn, you'd lose your head if it weren't fastened to your shoulders." After he said this he wished he could have retracted it, considering the Halloween horror. His wife didn't seem to notice.

"I don't know where I lost it."

"When's the last time you remember wearing them?" Miranda asked the logical question.

"The day before the hard rains—oh, October, I guess. I wore my magenta cashmere sweater, played tennis over at the club, changed there, and when I got back into the car I couldn't find one earring when I got home."

"Maybe it popped off when you pulled your sweater over your head. Mine do that sometimes," Harry mentioned.

"Well, I did take my sweater off in the car and I had a load of dry cleaning on the front seat. If the earring flew off, it might have landed in the clothing and I wouldn't have heard that tinkle, like when metal hits the ground."

"Which car were you in, honey?" Fitz asked.

"The Range Rover. Well, it doesn't matter. I thank you for finding this, Harry. I wonder if Tiffany's can repair it. Did you really find it in a possum's nest?"

"I did." Harry nodded.

"What are you doing ransacking possums' nests?" Fitz pinched Harry's elbow.

"I have this little guy who lives with me."

"You found my earring on your property?" Little Marilyn was astonished. "I was nowhere near your property."

"I found it but who knows where the possum found it? Maybe he's a member of Farmington Country Club."

This made everyone laugh, and after more chatter they left and the next wave of people came in, also upset when they pulled the "Don't stick your nose where it don't belong" postcards out of their boxes.

The animals observed the human reactions. Pewter washed behind her ears and asked Mrs. Murphy again. *"You believe that earring is connected to the first murder?"*

"I don't know. I only know it's very peculiar. I keep hoping someone will find the teeth. That would be a big help. If the earring was dropped, what about the teeth?"

"Since those would identify the first victim, you can bet the killer got rid of the teeth," Tucker said.

"Once the snow melts, let's go back to the graveyard. Can't hurt to look."

"I want to come." Pewter pouted.

"You'd be a big help," Mrs. Murphy flattered her, *"but I don't see how we can get Mother to bring you out. You can do one thing, though."*

"What?" Pewter's eyes enlarged, as did her chest. She was puffing up like a broody hen.

"Pay atttention to each human who comes to the store. Let me know if anyone seems stressed."

"Half of Crozet," Pewter grumbled but then she brightened. "I'll do my best."

Tucker cocked her head and stared at her friend. "What's wrong, Murphy?"

"What's wrong is the postcard. It's kind of smartass. I mean, if it is from the killer, which we don't know, but if it is, it's also a warning. It means, to me, that maybe this person thinks someone just might get too close."

50

Using the Sheaffer pen that had once been his father's, Cabell wrote his wife a note. The black ink scrawled boldly across the pale-blue paper.

My Dearest Florence,

Please forgive me. I've got to get away to sort out my thoughts. I've closed my personal checking account. Yours remains intact, as does our joint account and the investments. There's plenty of money, so don't worry.

I'll leave the car at the bank parking lot behind the downtown mall. Please don't call Rick Shaw. And don't worry about me.

Love,
Cabell

Taxi did just that. The letter was propped up against the coffee machine. She read it and reread it. In all the years she had known her husband, he had never done anything as drastic as this.

She dialed Miranda Hogendobber. She'd been friends with Miranda since kindergarten. It was seven-thirty in the morning.

"Miranda."

Mrs. H. heard the strain in her friend's voice immediately. "Florence, what's the matter?"

"Cabell has left me."

"What!"

"I said that wrong. Here. Let me read you the letter." As she finished, Florence sobbed, "He must be suffering some kind of breakdown."

"Well, you've got to call the sheriff."

"He forbids me to do that." Florence cried harder.

"He's wrong. If you don't call him I will."

By the time Rick and Cynthia arrived at the beautiful Hall residence, Miranda had been there for a half hour. Sitting next to her friend, she supplied support during the questioning.

Rick, who liked Taxi Hall, smoked half a pack of cigarettes while he gently asked questions. Cynthia prudently refrained from smoking, or the room would have been filled with blue fog.

"You said he's been preoccupied, withdrawn."

Taxi nodded, and Rick continued. "Was there any one subject that would set him off?"

"He was terribly upset about Ben Seifert. He calmed down once the books were audited but I know it still bothered him. Ben was his protégé."

"Was there resentment at the bank over Ben's being groomed to succeed your husband?"

She folded her arms across her chest and thought about this. "There's always grumbling but not enough for murder."

"Did your husband ever specifically name anyone?"

"He mentioned that Marion Molnar couldn't stand Ben but she

managed to work with him. Really, the politics of the bank are pretty benign."

Rick took a deep breath. "Have you any reason to suspect that your husband is seeing another woman?"

"Is that necessary?" Miranda bellowed.

"Under the circumstances, yes, it is." Rick softened his voice.

"I protest. I protest most vigorously. Can't you see she's worried sick?"

Taxi patted Miranda's hand. "It's all right, Miranda. Everything must be considered. To the best of my knowledge Cabell is not involved with another woman. If you knew Cabby like I do, you'd know he'd much rather play golf than make love."

Rick smiled weakly. "Thank you, Mrs. Hall. We will put out an all-points alert. We'll fax photos of Cabby to other police and sheriff's departments. And the first time he uses a credit card we'll know. Try to relax and know that we are doing everything we can."

Outside the door Rick dropped a cigarette, which sizzled in the snow.

Cooper observed the snow melting around the hot tip. "Well, looks like we know who killed Ben Seifert. Why else would he run?"

"Goddammit, we're going to find out." He stepped on the extinguished cigarette. "Coop, nothing makes sense. Nothing!"

51

Harry wondered where Mrs. Hogendobber was, for she was scrupulously punctual. Being a half hour late was quite out of line. The
mail bags clogged the post office and Harry was falling behind. If it
had been any time other than Christmas, Harry would have left her
post and gone to Miranda's house. As it was, she called around. No
one had seen Mrs. Hogendobber.

When the back door opened relief flooded through Harry.
Those emotional waters instantly dried up when Mrs. Hogendobber
told her the news.

Within fifteen minutes of Miranda's arrival—half an hour before
the doors opened to the public—Rick Shaw knocked on the back
door.

He walked through the mail bags and up to the counter, glanced
at the composite picture of the reconstructed head. "Lot of good

that's done. Not a peep! Not a clue! *Nada!*" He slammed his hand on the counter, causing Mrs. Murphy to jump and Tucker to bark.

"Hush, Tucker," Harry advised the dog.

Rick opened his notebook. "Mrs. Hogendobber, I wanted to ask you a few questions. No need to cause Mrs. Hall further upset."

"I'm glad to help."

Rick looked at Harry. "You might as well stay. She'll tell you everything anyway, the minute I leave." He poised his pencil. "Have you noticed anything unusual in Cabell Hall's behavior?"

"No. I think he's exhausted, but he hasn't been irritable or anything."

"Have you noticed a strain in the marriage?"

"See here, Rick, you know perfectly well that Florence and Cabby have a wonderful marriage. Now this line of questioning has got to stop."

Rick flipped shut his notebook, irritation, frustration, and exhaustion dragging down his features. He looked old this morning. "Dammit, Miranda, I'm doing all I can!" He caught himself. "I'm sorry. I'm tired. I haven't even bought one Christmas present for my wife or my kids."

"Come on, sit down." Harry directed the worn-out man to a little table in the back. "We've got Miranda's coffee and some Hotcakes muffins."

He hesistated, then pulled up a chair. Mrs. Hogendobber poured him coffee with cream and two sugars. A few sips restored him somewhat. "I don't want to be rude but I have to examine all the angles. You know that."

"Yeah, we do."

Rick said, "Well, you tell me how one partner in a marriage knows what the other's doing if she's asleep."

Miranda downed a cup of coffee herself. "You don't. My George could have driven to Richmond and back, I'm such a sound sleeper, but well, you know things about your mate and about other people. Cabell was faithful to Taxi. His disappearance has nothing to do with an affair. And how do we know he wrote that letter voluntarily?"

"We don't," Rick agreed. A long silence followed.

"I have a confession to make." Harry swallowed and told Rick about the misshapen earring.

"Harry, I could wring your neck! I'm out of here."

"Where are you going?" Harry innocently asked.

"Where do you think I'm going, nitwit? To Little Marilyn's. I hope I get there before she mails off that earring to New York. If you ever pull a stunt like this again I'll have your hide—your hide! Do you understand?"

"Yes," came the meek voice.

Rick charged out of the post office.

"Oh, boy, I'm in the shit can," Harry half-whispered.

Rick opened the door and yelled at both of them, "Almost forgot. Don't open any strange Christmas presents." He slammed the door again.

"Just what does that mean?" Mrs. Hogendobber kicked a bag of mail. She regretted that the instant she did it, because there was so much mail in the bag.

"Guess he's afraid presents will be booby-trapped or something."

"*Don't worry. We can sniff them first,*" Tucker advised.

Harry interpreted the soft bark to mean that Tucker wanted to go outside. She opened the back door but the dog sat down and wouldn't budge.

"What gets into her?" Harry wondered.

"She's trained you," Mrs. Hogendobber replied.

"*You guys are dumb,*" Tucker grumbled.

"*There goes our expedition,*" Mrs. Murphy said to her friend. "*Look.*"

Tucker saw the storm clouds rolling in from the mountains.

Harry pulled a mail bag over to the back of the boxes. She started to sort and then paused. "It's hard to concentrate."

"I know but let's do our best." Miranda glanced at the old wooden wall clock. "Folks will be here in about fifteen minutes. Maybe someone will have an idea about all this . . . crazy stuff."

As the day wore on, people trooped in and out of the post office but no one had any new ideas, any suspects. It took until noon for the news of Cabell's vanishing act to make the rounds. A few people thought he was the killer but others guessed he was having a nervous breakdown. Even the falling snow and the prospect of a white Christmas, a rarity in central Virginia, couldn't lift spirits. The worm of fear gnawed at people's nerve endings.

52

Christmas Eve morning dawned silver gray. The snow danced down, covering bushes, buildings, and cars, which were already blurred into soft, fantastic shapes. The radio stations interrupted their broadcasts for weather bulletins and then returned to "God Rest Ye Merry Gentlemen." A fantastic sense of quiet enshrouded everything.

When Harry turned out Tomahawk and Gin Fizz, the horses stood for a long time, staring at the snowfall. Then old Gin kicked up her heels and romped through the snow like a filly.

Chores followed. Harry picked up Tucker while Mrs. Murphy reclined around her neck. She waded through the snow. A snow shovel leaned against the back porch door. Harry put the animals, protesting, into the house and then turned to the odious task of shoveling. If she waited until the snow stopped she'd heave twice as much snow. Better to shovel at intervals than to tackle it later, because the weather report promised another two feet. The path to the barn seemed a mile long. In actuality it was about one hundred yards.

"*Let me out. Let me out,*" Tucker yapped.

Mrs. Murphy sat in the kitchen window. "*Come on, Mom, we can take the cold.*"

Harry relented and they scampered out onto the path she had cleared. When they tried to go beyond that, the results were comical. Mrs. Murphy would sink in way over her depth and then leap up and forward with a little cap of snow on her striped head. Tucker charged ahead like a snowplow. She soon tired of that and decided to stay behind Harry. The snow, shoveled and packed, crunched under her pads.

Mrs. Murphy, shooting upward, called out, "*Wiener, wiener! Tucker is a wiener!*"

"*You think you're so hot,*" Tucker grumbled.

Now the tiger cat turned somersaults, throwing up clots of snow. She'd bat at the little balls, then chase them. Leaping upward, she tossed them up between her paws. Her energy fatigued Tucker while making Harry laugh.

"*Yahoo!*" Mrs. Murphy called out, the sheer joy of the moment intoxicating.

"Miss Puss, you ought to be in the circus." Harry threw a little snowball up in the air for her to catch.

"*Yeah, the freak show,*" Tucker growled. She hated to be outdone.

Simon appeared, peeping under the barn door. "*You all are noisy today.*"

Harry, bent over her shovel, did not yet notice the bright eyes and the pink nose sticking out from under the door. As it was, she was only halfway to her goal, and the snow was getting heavier and heavier.

"*No work today.*" Mrs. Murphy landed head-deep in the snow after another gravity-defying leap.

"*Think Harry will make Christmas cookies or pour syrup in the snow?*" Simon wondered. "*Mrs. MacGregor was the best about the syrup, you know.*"

"*Don't count on it,*" Tucker yelled from behind Harry, "*but she got*

you a Christmas present. Bet she brings it out tomorrow morning, along with the presents for the horses."

"Those horses are so stupid. Think they'll even notice?" Simon criticized the grazing animals. He nourished similar prejudices against cattle and sheep. *"What'd she get me?"*

"Can't tell. That's cheating." Mrs. Murphy decided to sit in the snow for a moment to catch her breath.

"Where are you, Murph?" Tucker always became anxious if she couldn't see her best friend and constant tormentor.

"Hiding."

"She's off to your left, Tucker, and I bet she's going to bust through the snow and scare you," Simon warned.

Too late, because Mrs. Murphy did just that and both Tucker and Harry jumped.

"Gotcha!" The cat swirled and shot out of the path again.

"That girl's getting mental," Tucker told Harry, who wasn't listening.

Harry finally noticed Simon. "Merry Christmas Eve, little fellow."

Simon ducked away, then stuck his head out again. "Uh, Merry Christmas, Harry." He then said to Mrs. Murphy, who made it to the barn door, *"It unnerves me talking to humans. But it makes her so happy."*

A deep rumble alerted Simon. *"See you, Murphy."* He hurried back down the aisle, up the ladder, and across the loft to his nest. Murphy, curious, stuck her head out of the barn door. A shiny new Ford Explorer, metallic hunter-green with an accent stripe and, better yet, a snow blade on the front, pulled into the driveway. A neat path had been cleared.

Blair Bainbridge opened his window. "Hey, Harry, out of the way. I'll do that."

Before she could reply, he quickly plowed a walkway to the barn.

He cut the motor and stepped out. "Nifty, huh?"

"It's beautiful." Harry rubbed her hand over the hood, which was ornamented with a galloping horse. Very expensive.

"It's beautiful and it's your chariot for the day with me as your driver. I know you don't have four-wheel drive and I bet you've got presents to deliver, so go get them and let's do it."

Harry, Mrs. Murphy, and Tucker spent the rest of the morning dropping off presents for Susan Tucker and her family, Mrs. Hogendobber, Reverend Jones and Carol, Market and Pewter, and finally Cynthia Cooper. Harry was gratified to discover they all had gifts for her too. Every year the friends exchanged gifts and every year Harry was surprised that they remembered her.

Christmas agreed with Blair. He enjoyed the music, the decorations, the anticipation on children's faces. By tacit agreement Cabell would not be discussed until after Christmas. So as Blair accompanied Harry, the cat, and the dog into various houses, people marveled at the white Christmas, and at the holiday bow tied on Tucker's collar, compliments of Susan. Eggnog would be offered, whiskey sours, tea, and coffee. Cookies would be passed around in the shapes of trees and bells and angels, covered with red or green sparkles. This Christmas there were as many fruitcakes as Claxton, Georgia, could produce, plus the homemade variety drowning in rum. Cold turkey for sandwiches, cornbread, cranberry sauce, sweet potato pie, and mince pie would be safely stowed in Tupperware containers and given to Harry, since her culinary deficiencies were well known to her friends.

After dropping off Cynthia's present, they would drive through the snow to the SPCA, for Harry always left gifts there. The sheriff's office was gorged with presents but not for Rick or Cynthia. These were "suspicious" gifts. Cynthia was grateful for her nonsuspicious one.

Blair remarked, "You're a lucky woman, Harry."

"Why?"

"Because you have true friends. And not just because the back of the car is crammed with gifts." He slowed. "Is this the turn?"

"Yes. The hill's not much of a grade but in this weather nothing is easy."

They motored up the hill and took a right down the little lane leading to the SPCA. Fair's truck was parked there.

"Still want to go in?"

"Sure." She ignored the implication. "The doors are probably locked anyway."

Together they unloaded cases of cat and dog food. As they carted their burden to the door, Fair opened it and they stepped inside.

"Merry Christmas." He gave Harry a kiss on the cheek.

"Merry Christmas." She returned it.

"Where is everybody?" Blair inquired.

"Oh, they go home early on Christmas Eve. I stopped by to check a dog hit by a car. He didn't make it." Harry knew that Fair never could get used to losing an animal. Although he was an equine vet, he, like other veterinarians, donated his services to the SPCA. Every Christmas during their marriage, Harry brought food, so Fair naturally took those days to work at the shelter.

"Sorry." Harry meant it.

"Come here and look." He led them over to a carton. Inside were two little kittens. One was gray with a white bib and white paws and the other was a dark calico. The poor creatures were crying piteously. "Some jerk left them here. They were pretty cold and hungry by the time I arrived. I think they'll make it, though. I checked them over and gave them their shots, first series. No mites, which is a miracle, and no fleas. Too cold for that. Scared to death, of course."

"Will you fill out the paperwork?" Harry asked Fair.

"Sure."

She reached into the carton and picked up a kitten in each hand. Then she put them into Blair's arms. "Blair, this is the only love that money can buy. I can't think of anything I'd rather give you for Christmas."

The gray kitten had already closed her eyes and was purring. The calico, not yet won over, examined Blair's face.

"Say yes." Fair had his pen poised over the SPCA adoption forms. If he was surprised by Harry's gesture, he wasn't saying so.

"Yes." He smiled. "Now what am I going to call these companions?"

"Christmas names?" Fair suggested.

"Well, I guess I could call the gray one Noel, and the calico Jingle Bells. I'm not very good at naming things."

"That's perfect." Harry beamed.

On the way home Harry held the carton on her lap. The kittens fell asleep. Mrs. Murphy poked her head over the side and made an ungenerous comment. She soon went to sleep herself. The cat had eaten turkey at every stop. She must have gobbled up half a bird all totaled.

Tucker took advantage of Mrs. Murphy's food-induced slumber to give Blair the full benefit of her many opinions. *"A dog is more useful, Blair. You really ought to get a dog that can protect you and keep rats out of the barn too. After all, we're loyal and good-natured and easy to keep. You can housebreak a corgi puppy in a week or two,"* she lied.

Blair patted her head. Tucker chattered some more until she, too, fell asleep.

Harry could recall less stressful Christmases than this one. Christmases filled with youth and promise, parties and laughter, but she could not remember giving a gift that made her so blissfully happy.

53

Highly potent catnip sent Mrs. Murphy into orbit. Special dog chew-
ies pleased Tucker. She also received a new collar with corgis embroidered on it. Simon liked his little quilt, which Harry had placed
outside his nest. It was a small dog blanket she had bought at the
pet store. The horses enjoyed their carrots, apples, and molasses
treats. Gin Fizz received a new turn-out blanket and Tomahawk got
a new back-saver saddle pad.

After chores Harry opened her presents. Susan gave her a gift
certificate to Dominion Saddlery. If Harry added some money to it
she might be able to afford a new pair of much needed boots. When
she opened Mrs. Hogendobber's present she knew she would be
able to afford them, because Mrs. H. had also given her a certificate.
Susan and Miranda had obviously put their heads together on this
one and Harry felt a surge of affection wash over her. Herbie and
Carol Jones gave her a gorgeous pair of formal deerskin gloves, also

for hunting. Harry kept rubbing them between her fingers; the buttery texture felt cool and soft. Market had wrapped up a knuckle bone for Tucker, more turkey for Mrs. Murphy, and a tin of shortbread cookies for Harry. Cynthia Cooper's present was a surprise, a facial at an upscale salon in Barracks Road Shopping Center.

No sooner had she opened her packages than the phone rang. Miranda, another early riser, loved her earrings. She also promised Harry she'd bring all the food gifts she'd received to work so that whoever came to the post office could help themselves, thereby removing the temptation from Mrs. Hogendobber's lips. Hanging up the phone, Harry realized that she and Miranda would wipe out the food before anyone walked through the door.

As the day progressed the sun appeared. The icicles sparkled and the surface of the snow at times shone like a rainbow, the little crystals reflecting red, yellow, blue, and purple highlights. The Blue Ridge Mountains loomed baby-blue. Wind devils picked up snow in the meadows and swirled it around.

More friends called, including Blair Bainbridge, who said he'd never had so much fun in his life as he did watching the kittens. He said he'd take her to work tomorrow and promised to give her a Christmas present before tomorrow night. He enjoyed being mysterious about it.

Then Susan called. She also loved her earrings. Harry spent too much money on her, but that's what friends were for. The noise in the background tried Susan's patience. She gave up and said she'd see Harry tomorrow. She, Ned, and the kids were going outside to make syrup candy in the snow.

Harry thought that was a great idea, and armed with a tin of Vermont maple syrup, she plunged into the snow, now mid-thigh in depth. Mrs. Murphy shot down the path to the barn, covered from yesterday's snow but at least not over her head.

"Simon," the cat called out, "syrup in the snow."

The possum slid down the ladder. He hurried outside the barn and then stopped.

"Come on, Simon. It's okay," Tucker encouraged him.

Emboldened by the smell and halfway trusting Harry, the gray creature followed in Mrs. Murphy's footsteps. He sat near Harry and when she poured out the syrup he gleefully leapt toward it with such intensity that Harry took a step backward.

Watching him greedily eat the frozen syrup reminded Harry that life ought to be a feast of the senses. Living with the mountains and the meadows, the forest and the streams, Harry knew she could never leave this place, because the country nourished her senses. City people drew their energy from one another. Country people drew their energy, like Antaeus, from the earth herself. Small wonder that the two types of humans could not understand each other. This deep need for solitude, hard physical labor, and the cycle of the seasons removed Harry from the opportunity for material success. She'd never grace the cover of *Vogue* or *People*. She'd never be famous. Apart from her friends no one would even know she existed. Life would be a struggle to make ends meet and the older she got the harsher the struggle. She knew that. She accepted it. Standing in the snow, surrounded by the angelic tranquillity, guarded by the old mountains of the New World, watching Simon eat his syrup, cat and dog next to her, she was grateful that she knew where she belonged. Let others make a shout in the world and draw attention to themselves. She regarded them as conscripts of civilization. Her life was a silent rebuke to the grabbing and the getting, the buying and the selling, the greediness and lust for power that she felt infected her nation. Americans died in sordid martyrdom to money. Indeed, they were dying for it in Crozet.

She poured out more syrup into the snow, watching it form lacy shapes, and wished she had heated chocolate squares and mixed the two together. She reached down and scooped up a graceful tendril of hard syrup. It tasted delicious. She poured more for Simon and thought that Jesus was wise in being born in a stable.

54

"We need a pitchfork." Harry, using her broom, jabbed at the mail on the floor. "I don't remember there being this much late mail last year."

"That's how the mind protects itself—it forgets what's unpleasant." Mrs. Hogendobber was wearing her new earrings, which were very becoming. The radio crackled; Miranda walked over, tuned it, and turned up the volume. "Did you hear that?"

"No." Harry pushed the mail-order catalogues across the floor with her broom. Tucker chased the broom.

"Another storm to hit tomorrow. My lands, three snowstorms within—what's it been—ten days? I don't ever recall that. Well now, maybe I do. During the war we had a horrendous winter—'44, I think, or was it '45?" She sighed. "Too many memories. My brain needs to find more room."

Mim, swathed in chinchilla, swept through the front door. A

gust of wind blew in snow around her feet. "How was it?" She referred to Christmas.

"Wonderful. The service at the church, well, those children in the choir outshone themselves." Miranda glowed.

"And you, out there all alone?" Mim stamped the snow from her feet as she addressed Harry.

"Good. It was a good Christmas. My best friends gave me certificates to Dominion Saddlery."

"Oh." Mim's eyebrows shot upward. "Nice friends."

Mrs. Hogendobber tilted her head, earrings catching the light. "How about these goodies? Harry gave them to me."

"Very nice." Mim appraised them. "Well, Jim gave me a week at the Greenbrier. Guess I'll take it in February, the longest month of the year," she joked. "My daughter framed an old photo of my mother, and she gave me season's tickets to the Virginia Theater. Fitz gave me an auto emergency kit and a Fuzzbuster." She smiled. "A Fuzzbuster, can you imagine? He said I need it." Her face changed. "And someone gave me a dead rat."

"No." Mrs. Hogendobber stopped sorting mail.

"Yes. I am just plain sick of all this. I sat up last night by myself in Mother's old sewing room, the room I made my reading room. I've gone over everything so many times I'm dizzy. A man is killed. We don't know him or anything about him other than that he was a vagrant or a vagabond. Correct?"

"Correct."

Mim continued: "Then Benjamin Seifert is strangled and dumped in Crozet's first tunnel. I even thought about the supposed treasure in the tunnels, but that's too far-fetched." She was referring to the legend that Claudius Crozet had buried in the tunnels the wealth he received from his Russian captor. The young engineer, an officer in Napoleon's army, was seized during the horrendous retreat from Moscow and taken to the estate of a fabulously wealthy aristocrat. So useful was the personable engineer, building many devices for the Russian, that when prisoners were finally freed, he bestowed upon Crozet jewels, gold, and rubies. Or so they said.

Harry spoke. "And now Cabell has . . ." She clicked her fingers in the air to indicate disappearance.

Mim waved a dismissive hand. "Two members of the same bank. Suspicious. Maybe even obvious. What isn't so obvious is why am I a target? First the"—she grimaced—"torso in the boathouse. Followed by the head in the pumpkin when my husband was judging. And then the rat. Why me? I can't think of any reason why, other than petty spite and envy, but people aren't killed for that."

Harry weighed her words. "Did Ben or Cabell have access to your accounts?"

"Certainly not, even though Cabell is a dear friend. No check goes out without my signature. And of course I studied my accounts. As a precaution I'm having my accountant audit my own books. And then"—she threw up her hands—"that earring. Well, Sheriff Shaw acted as though my daughter was a criminal. Forgive me, Harry, but a possum with an earring doesn't add up to evidence."

"No, it doesn't," Harry concurred.

"So . . . why me?"

"Maybe you should review your will." Miranda was blunt.

This knocked Mim back. But she didn't lash out. She thought about it. "You don't mince words, do you?"

"Mim, if you think this is somehow directed at you, then you may be in danger," Mrs. Hogendobber counseled. "What would someone want of you? Money. Do you own land impeding a developer? Are you in the way of anything that converts to profit? Do you have business ventures we don't know about? Is your daughter your sole beneficiary?"

"When Marilyn married I settled a small sum upon her as a dowry and to help them with their house. She will, of course, inherit our house and the land when Jim and I die and I've created a trust that jumps a generation, so most of the money will go to her children should she have them. If not, then it will go to her and she'll have to pay oodles of taxes. My daughter isn't going to kill me for money, and she wouldn't bother with a banker." Mim was forthright.

"What about Fitz?" Harry blurted out.

"Fitz-Gilbert has more money than God. You don't think we let Marilyn marry him without a thorough investigation of his resources."

"No." Harry's reply was tinged with regret. She'd have hated for her parents to do that to the man she loved.

"A shirttail cousin?" Miranda posited.

"You know my relatives as well as I do. I have one surviving aunt in Seattle."

"Have you talked to the sheriff and Coop about this?" Harry asked.

"Yes, and my husband too. He's hiring a bodyguard to protect me. If one can ever get through the snow. And another storm is coming." Mim, not a woman easily frightened, was worried. She headed for the door.

"Mim, your mail." Miranda reached into her box and held it out to her.

"Oh." Mim took the mail in one Bottéga Veneta–gloved hand and left.

A bit later Fitz arrived. He and Little Marilyn had indulged in an orgy of spending. He listed the vast number of gifts with glee and no sense of shame. "But the best is, we're going to the Homestead for a few days starting tonight."

"I thought Mim was going to the Greenbrier." Miranda was getting confused.

"Yes, Mother is going, she says, in February, but we're going tonight. A second honeymoon maybe, or just getting away from all this. You heard that Mim received an ugly present." They nodded and he continued: "I think she ought to go to Tahiti. Oh, well, there's no talking to Mim. She'll do as she pleases."

Blair came in. "Hey, I've got good news for you. Orlando Heguay is coming down on the twenty-eighth and he can't wait to see you."

"Orlando Heguay." Fitz pondered the name. "Miami?"

"No. Andover."

Fitz clapped his hand to his face. "My God, I haven't seen him since school. What's he doing?" Fitz caught his breath. "And how do you know him?"

"We'll catch up on all that when he gets here. He's looking forward to seeing you."

"How about dinner at the club Saturday night?" Fitz smiled.

"I'm not a member."

"I'll take care of it." Fitz clapped him on the back. "Be fun. Six?"

"Six." Blair answered.

As Fitz left with an armful of mail, Blair looked after him. "Does that guy ever work?"

"He handled a real estate closing last year," Harry laughed.

"Are you going to be home after work?" Blair asked her.

"Yes."

"Good. I'll stop by." Blair waved goodbye and left.

Alone again, Miranda smiled. "He likes you."

"He's my neighbor. He has to like me."

55

Four bags of sweet feed, four bags of dog crunchies, and four bags of cat crunchies, plus two cases of canned cat food astounded Harry. Blair unloaded his Explorer to her protests that she couldn't accept such gifts. He told her she could stand there and complain or she could help unload and then make them cocoa. She chose the latter.

Inside, as they sipped their chocolate drinks, he reached into his pocket and pulled out a small light-blue box.

"Here, Harry, you deserve this."

She untied the white satin ribbon. TIFFANY & CO. in black letters jumped out at her from the middle of the blue box. "I'm afraid to open this."

"Go on."

She lifted the lid and found a dark-blue leather box with TIFFANY written in gold. She opened that to behold an exquisitely beautiful pair of gold and blue-enameled earrings nestled in the white lining. "Oh," was all she could say.

"Your colors are blue and gold, aren't they?"

She nodded yes and carefully removed the earrings. She put them in her ears and looked at herself in the mirror. "These are beautiful. I don't deserve this. Why do you say I deserve this? It's ... well, it's ..."

"Take them, Mom. You look great," Murphy advised.

"Yeah, it was bad enough you tried to give back our crunchies. You need something pretty," Tucker chimed in.

Blair admired the effect. "Terrific."

"Are you sure you want to give me these?"

"Of course I'm sure. Harry, I'd be lost out here without you. I thought I was hardworking and reasonably intelligent but I would have made a lot more mistakes without you and I would have spent a lot more money. You've been helpful to someone you hardly know, and given the circumstances, I'm grateful."

"What circumstances?"

"The body in the graveyard."

"Oh, that." Harry laughed. She'd thought he was talking about Boom Boom. "I don't mean that quite the way it sounds, Blair, but I'm not worried about you. You're not killer material."

"Under the right—or perhaps I should say wrong—circumstances I think anyone could be killer material, but I appreciate your kindness to a stranger. Wasn't it Blanche DuBois who said, 'I have always depended on the kindness of strangers'?"

"And it was my mother who said, 'Many hands make light work.' Neighbors help one another to make light work. I was glad to do it. It was good for me. I learned that I knew something."

"What do you mean?"

"I take bush-hogging, knowing when to plant, knowing how to worm a horse, those kinds of things, as a given. Helping you made me realize I'm not so dumb after all."

"Girls who go to Seven Sisters colleges are rarely dumb."

"Ha." Harry exploded with mirth and so did Blair.

"Okay, so there are some dumb Smithies and Holy Jokers but then, there are some abysmal Old Blues and Princeton men too."

"Have you ever tracked, after a snow?" Harry changed the subject, since she didn't like to talk about herself or emotions.

"No."

"I've got my father's old snowshoes. Want to go out?"

"Sure."

Within minutes the two suited up and left the house. Not much sunlight remained.

"These snowshoes take some getting used to." Blair picked up a foot.

They trekked into the woods where Harry showed him bobcat and deer tracks. The deer followed air currents. Seeing these things and smelling the air, feeling the difference in temperature along the creek and above it, Blair began to appreciate how intelligent animal life is. Each species evolved a way to survive. If humans humbled themselves to learn, they might be able to better their own lives.

They moved up into the foothills behind Blair's property. Harry was making a circle, keeping uppermost in her mind that light was limited. She put her hand on his forearm and pointed up. An enormous snowy owl sat in a walnut tree branch.

She whispered, "They rarely come this far south."

"My God, it's huge," he whispered back.

"Owls and blacksnakes are the best friends a farmer can have. Cats too. They kill the vermin."

Long pink shadows swept down from the hills, like the skirts of the day swirling in one last dance. Even with snowshoes, walking could be difficult. They both breathed harder as they moved out of the woods. At the edge of the woods Harry stopped. Her blood turned as cold as the temperature. She pointed them out to Blair. Snowshoe footprints. Not theirs.

"Hunters?" Blair said.

"No one hunts here without permission. The MacGregors and Mom and Dad were fierce about that. We used to run Angus, and

the MacGregors bred polled Herefords. You can't take the chance of some damn fool shooting your stock—and they do too."

"Well, maybe someone wanted to track, like we're doing."

"He wanted to track all right." The sharp cold air filled her lungs. "He wanted to track into the back of your property."

"Harry, what's wrong?"

"I think we're looking at the killer's tracks. Why he wants to come back here I don't know, but he dumped hands and legs in your cemetery. Maybe he forgot something."

"He wouldn't find it in the snow."

"I know. That's why I'm really worried." She knelt down and examined the tracks. "A man, I think, or a heavy woman." She stepped next to the track and then picked up her snowshoe. "See how much deeper his track is than mine?"

Blair knelt down also. "I do. If we follow these, maybe we'll find out where he came from."

"We're losing the light." She pointed to the massing clouds tethered to the peaks of the mountains. "And here comes the next snowstorm."

"Is there an old road back up in here?"

"Yes, there's an old logging road from 1937, which was the last time this was select-cut. It's grown over but he might know it. He could take a four-wheel drive off Yellow Mountain Road and hide it on the logging road. He couldn't take it far but he could get it out of sight, I reckon."

A dark shadow, like a blue finger, crept down toward them. The sun was setting. The mixture of clear sky and clouds was giving way to potbellied clouds.

"What would anyone want back up here?" Blair rubbed his nose, which was getting cold.

"I don't know. Come on, let's get back."

In the good weather the walk back to Harry's would have taken twenty minutes but pushing along through the snow they arrived at Harry's back door in the dark one hour later. Their eyes were running, their noses were running, but their bodies stayed warm because of the exercise. Harry made more cocoa and grilled cheese sandwiches. Blair gratefully accepted the supper and then left to take care of his kittens.

As soon as he left, Harry called Cynthia Cooper.

Cynthia and Harry knew each other well enough not to waste time. The officer came to the point. "You think someone is after Blair?"

"Why else would someone be up there scoping the place?"

"I don't know, Harry, but then nothing about these murders makes any sense except for the fact that Ben was up to no good. But just what kind of no good we still don't know. I think Cabell knows, though. We'll find him. Ben died a far richer man than he lived. Bet that took discipline."

"What?"

"Not spending the money."

"Oh, I never thought of that," Harry replied. "Look, Coop, is there any way you can put someone out in Blair's barn? Hide someone? Whoever this is doesn't intend to barge down his driveway. He'll sweep down from the mountainside."

"Harry, can you think of any reason, any reason at all, why someone would want to kill Blair Bainbridge?"

"No."

A long sigh came through the phone. "Me neither. And I like the guy, but liking someone doesn't mean they can't be mixed up in monkey business. We called his mother and father—routine, plus I wondered why he didn't go home for Christmas or why they didn't come here. His mother was very pleasant. His father wasn't rude but I could tell there's tension there. He disapproves of his son. Calls him a dilettante. No wonder Blair didn't go home. Anyway, there wasn't much from them. No red flags went up."

"Will you put a man out there?"

"I'll go out myself. Feel better?"

"Yes. I owe you one."

"No, you don't. Now sleep tight tonight. Oh, you heard about the dead rat present to Mim?"

"Yeah. That's odd."

"I can think of about one hundred people who would like to do that."

"But would they?"

"No."

"Are you nervous about this? It's not over yet. I can feel it in my bones."

A silence from Coop told Harry what she needed to know. Cynthia finally said, "One way or the other, we'll figure this out. You take care."

56

The wind lashed across the meadows in the early morning darkness. Even silk long johns, a cotton T-shirt, a long-sleeved Patagonia shirt, and a subzero down jacket couldn't stave off the bitter cold. Harry's fingers and toes ached by the time she reached the barn.

Simon was grateful for the food she brought him. He had stayed in last night. Harry even tossed out some raw hamburger for the owl. Given the mice that crept into the barn when the weather became cruel, Harry needn't have fed the owl. She dined heartily on what the barn itself could supply, a fact that greatly irritated Mrs. Murphy, who believed that every mouse had her name on it.

When the chores were finished and Harry ventured back out, the wind was blowing harder. She couldn't see halfway across the meadow, much less over to Blair's. She was glad she had kept the horses in this morning, even if it would mean more mucking chores.

Tucker and Mrs. Murphy followed on her heels, their heads low, their ears swept back.

"*If this ever stops I'm asking the owl to look where those prints were*," Tucker said.

"*They're covered now.*" Mrs. Murphy blinked to keep out the snow.

"*Who knows what she'll find? She can see two miles. Maybe more.*"

"*Oh, Tucker, don't believe everything she says. She's such a blowhard, and she probably won't cooperate.*"

Both animals scooted through the door when Harry opened it. The phone was ringing inside. It was seven o'clock.

Cynthia's voice greeted her "hello" with "Harry, all's well over here."

"Good. How was Blair?"

"At first he thought it was silly for me to sleep out in the barn but then he came around."

"Is he awake yet?"

"Don't see any lights on in the house. That boy's got to get himself some furniture."

"We're waiting for a good auction."

"Got enough to eat? I think the electricity might go out and the phone lines might come down if this keeps up."

"Yeah. Can you get out okay?" Harry asked.

"If not, I'll spend an interesting day with Blair Bainbridge, I guess." A distant rumble alerted the young policewoman. "Harry, I'll call you right back."

She ran outside and strained her ears. A motor, a deep rumble, cut through even the roar of the wind. The snow was blowing so hard and fast now that Cynthia could barely see. She'd parked her cruiser in front of the house. She heard nothing for a moment and then she heard that deep rumble again. She ran as fast as she could through the deep snow but it was no use. Whoever was rolling down the driveway finally saw the police car and backed out. She ran back into the barn and called Harry.

"Harry, if anyone comes down your driveway other than Susan or Mrs. Hogendobber, call me."

"What's the matter?"

"I don't know. Listen, I've got to get out on the driveway before all the tracks are covered. Do as I say. If I'm not back at the barn, call Blair. If he doesn't pick up, you call Rick. Hear?"

"I hear." Harry hung up the phone. She patted Tucker and Mrs. Murphy and was very glad for their sharp ears.

Meanwhile, Cynthia struggled through the blinding snow. She thought she knew where she was going until she bumped into an ancient oak. She'd veered to the right off the driveway. She got back on the driveway again and reached the backup tracks. The tread marks were being covered quickly. If only she had a plaster kit, but she didn't. By the time she got one this would be gone. She knelt on her hands and knees and puffed away a little snow. Wide tires. Deep snow treads. Tires like that could be on any regular-sized pickup truck or large, heavy, family four-wheel drive like a Wagoneer, a Land Cruiser, or a Range Rover. She hunkered down in the snow and smashed her fist into the powder. It flew up harmlessly. Half of the people in Crozet drove those types of vehicles and the other half drove big trucks.

"Damn, damn, damn!" she shouted out loud, the wind carrying away her curses.

On her way back to the barn she slammed into the corner of the house. There'd be no getting out of Foxden today. She hugged the side of the building and slowly made her way to the back porch. She opened the back door, stepped inside the porch, closed the door behind her, and leaned against it. It wasn't eight yet and she was exhausted. She could no longer see the barn.

She used the dachsund foot scraper and cleaned off her boots. She unzipped her heavy parka and shook off the snow. She hung it on the hook outside the door to the kitchen.

She stepped into the kitchen and dialed Harry. "You okay?"

"Yeah, no one's coming down my driveway."

"Okay, here's the plan. You can't get to work today. Mrs. Hogendobber will go in if she can even get down the alleyway. Call her."

"I've never missed a day because of weather."

"You're missing today," Cynthia ordered her. "Blair has that

Explorer. We'll pack up his kittens and him and we're coming over there. I don't want you alone, or him alone, for a while anyway."

"Nobody wants me."

"You don't know that. I can't take any chances. So, I'll get him up and we'll be over there within the hour."

57

"*What* pests." Mrs. Murphy flicked her tail away from Jingle Bells, the calico, who was madly chasing it.

"*Human babies are worse.*" Tucker ignored the gray kitty, Noel, who climbed up one side of her body only to slide down the other screaming "*Wheee!*"

Harry, Blair, and Cynthia busied themselves making drawings of each room of Blair's house. Then they drew furniture for each room, cut it out, and fiddled with different placements.

"Have you told us everything?" Cynthia asked again.

"Yes." Blair pushed a sofa with his forefinger. "Doesn't go there."

"What about this, and put a table behind it? Then put the lamps on that." Harry arranged the pieces.

"What about a soured business deal?" Cynthia asked.

"I told you, the only deal I made was to buy Foxden . . . and the tractor at the auction. If something is on my property that is valuable or germane to the case, don't you think whoever this is would have taken it?"

"I don't know," Cynthia said.

"Whoops," Harry yelled as the lights went out. She ran to the phone and put the receiver to her ear. "Still working."

The sky darkened and the wind screamed. The storm continued. Fortunately, Harry kept a large supply of candles. They wouldn't run out.

After supper they sat around the fireplace and told ghost stories. Although the storm slackened, a stiff wind still rattled the shutters on the house. It was perfect ghost story time.

"Well, I've heard that Peter Stuyvesant still walks the church down on Second Avenue in New York. You can hear his peg leg tap on the wood. That's it for me and ghost stories. I was always the kid who fell asleep around the campfire." Blair smiled.

"There's a ghost at Castle Hill." Cynthia mentioned a beautiful old house on Route 22 in Keswick. "A woman appears carrying a candle in one of the original bedrooms. She's dressed in eighteenth-century clothing and she tells a guest that they ought not to spend the night. Apparently she has appeared to many guests over the last two hundred years."

"What? Don't they meet her social approval?" Harry cracked.

"We know their manners won't be as good," Blair said. "Socializing has been in one long downward spiral since the French Revolution."

"Okay." Cynthia jabbed at Harry. "Your turn."

"When Thomas Jefferson was building Monticello, he brought over a Scotsman by the name of Dunkum. This highly skilled man bought land below Carter's Ridge and he built what is now Brookhill, owned by Dr. Charles Beegle and his family, wife Jean, son Brooks, and daughters Lynne and Christina. The Revolutionary War finally went our way and after that Mr. Dunkum built more homes along the foot of the ridge. You can see them along Route Twenty—simple, clean brick work and pleasing proportions. Anyway, as he prospered, less fortunate relatives came to stay with him, one being a widowed sister, Mary Carmichael. Mary loved to garden and she laid out the garden tended today by Jean Beegle. One hot summer day Jean thought she'd run the tractor down the brick path to the mess of vines at the end which had resisted her efforts with the clippers. Jean was determined to wipe them out with the tractor. To her consternation, no sooner did she plunge into the vines than she dropped into a cavity. The tractor didn't roll over—it just sat in the middle of a hole in the earth. When Jean looked down she beheld a coffin. Needless to say, Jean Beegle burnt the wind getting off that tractor.

"Well, Chuck borrowed a tractor from Johnny Haffner, the tractor man, and together the two men pulled out the Beegles' tractor. Curiosity got the better of them and they jumped back into the grave and opened the casket. The skeleton of a woman was inside and even a few tatters of what must have been a beautiful dress. A wave of guilt washed over both Chuck and Johnny as they closed up the coffin and returned the lady to her eternal slumbers. Then they filled in the cavity.

"That night a loud noise awakened Jean. She heard someone shout three times. Someone—a voice she didn't recognize—was calling her. 'Jean Ritenour Beegle, Jean, come to the garden.'"

"Well, Jean's bedroom didn't have a window on that side, so she went downstairs. She wasn't afraid, because it was a woman's voice. I would have been afraid, I think. Anyway, she walked out into her garden and there stood a tall well-figured woman.

"She said, 'My name is Mary Carmichael and I died here in 1791. As I loved the garden, my brother buried me out here and planted a rosebush over my grave. When he died the new owners forgot that I was buried here and didn't tend to my rosebush. I died in the kitchen, which used to be in the basement of the house. The fireplace was large and it was so cold. They kept me down there.'

"Jean asked if there was anything she could do to make Mary happy.

"The ghost replied, 'Plant a rosebush over my grave. I love pink roses. And you know, I built a trellis, which I put up between the two windows.' She pointed to the windows facing the garden, which would be the parlor. 'If it would please you and it does look pretty, put up a white trellis and train some yellow tearoses to climb it.'

"So Jean did that, and she says that in the summers on a moonlit night she sometimes sees Mary walking in the garden."

As the humans continued their ghost stories, Mrs. Murphy gathered the two kittens around her. "Now, Noel and Jingle, let me tell you about a dashing cat named Dragoon. Back in the days of our ancestors . . ."

"When's that?" the gray kitten mewed.

"Before we were a country, back when the British ruled. Way back then there was a big handsome cat who used to hang around with a British officer, so they called him Dragoon. Oh, his whiskers were silver and his paws were white, his eyes the brightest green, and his coat a lustrous red. The humans had a big ball one night and Dragoon came. He saw a young white Angora there, wearing a blue silk ribbon as a collar. He walked over to her as other cats surrounded her, so great was her beauty. And he talked to her and wooed her. She said her name was Silverkins. He volunteered to walk Silverkins home. They walked through the streets of the town and out into the countryside. The crickets chirped and the stars twinkled. As they neared a little stone cottage with a graveyard on the hill, the pretty cat stopped.

" 'I'll be leaving you here, Dragoon, for my old mother lives inside and I don't want to wake her.' Saying that, she scampered away.

"Dragoon called after her, 'I'll come for you tomorrow.'

"All the next day Dragoon couldn't keep his mind on his duties. He thought only of Silverkins. When night approached he walked through the town, ignoring the catcalls of his carousing friends. He walked out on the little country path and soon arrived at the stone cottage. He knocked at the door and an old cat answered.

" 'I've come to call on Silverkins,' he said to the old white cat.

" 'Don't jest with me, young tom,' the old lady cat snarled.

" 'I'm not jesting,' said he. 'I walked her home from the ball last evening.'

" 'You'll find my daughter up on the hill.' The old cat pointed toward the graveyard and then shut the door.

"Dragoon bounded up the hill but no Silverkins was in sight. He called her name. No answer. He leapt from tombstone to tombstone. Not a sign of her. He reached the end of a row of human markers and he jumped onto a small square tombstone. It read, 'Here lies my pretty pet, Silverkins. Born 1699. Died 1704.' And there on her grave was her blue silk ribbon."

The kittens screamed at the end of the story.

Harry glanced over at the scared babies. Mrs. Murphy was lying on her side in front of them, eyes half-closed.

"Mrs. Murphy, are you picking on those kittens?"

"*Hee hee*" was all Mrs. Murphy would say.

58

No goblins bumped in the night; no human horrors either. Harry, Cynthia, and Blair awoke to a crystal-clear day. Harry couldn't remember when a winter's day had sparkled like this one.

Perhaps Harry had overreacted. Maybe those tracks belonged to someone looking, illegally, for animals to trap. Maybe the truck or car Cynthia heard coming down Blair's driveway was simply someone who had lost his way in the snow.

By the time Harry arrived at work she felt a little sheepish about her concerns. Outside the windows she saw road crews maneuvering the big snowplows. One little compact car by the side of the road was being completely covered by snow.

Mrs. Hogendobber bustled around and the two gossiped as they worked. Boom Boom was the first person at the post office. She'd borrowed a big four-wheel-drive Wagoneer from the car dealer just before the storm. She hadn't bought it yet. "How fortunate to have such a long-term loan," was Mrs. Hogendobber's comment.

"Orlando arrives today. The ten-thirty. Blair said he'd pick him up and we'd get together for dinner. Wait until you meet him. He really is special."

"So's Fair," Harry defended her ex. If she'd thought about it she probably would have kept her mouth shut, but that was the trouble: She didn't think. She said what came into her head at that exact moment.

Boom Boom's long eyelashes fluttered. "Of course he is. He's a dear sweet man and he's been such a comfort to me since Kelly died. I'm very fond of him but well, he is provincial. All he really knows is his profession. Face it, Harry, he bored you too."

Harry threw the mail she was holding onto the floor. Mrs. Hogendobber wisely came alongside Harry . . . just in case.

"We all bore one another occasionally. No one is universally exciting." Harry's face reddened.

Mrs. Murphy and Tucker pricked their ears.

"Oh, come off it. He wasn't right for you." Boom Boom derived a sordid pleasure from upsetting others. Emotions were the only coin Boom Boom exchanged. Without real employment to absorb her, her thoughts revolved around herself and the emotions of others. Sometimes even her pleasures became fatiguing.

"He was for a good long time. Now why don't you pick up your mail and spare me your expertly made-up face." Harry gritted her teeth.

"This is a public building and I can do what I want."

Miranda's alto voice resonated with authority. "Boom Boom, for a woman who proclaims exaggerated sensitivity, you're remarkably insensitive to other people. You've created an uncomfortable situation. I suggest you think on it at your leisure, which is to say the rest of the day."

Boom Boom flounced off in a huff. Before the day reached noon she would call everyone she knew to inform them of her precarious emotional state due to the personally abusive behavior of Harry and Mrs. Hogendobber, who crudely ganged up on her.

She would also find it necessary to call her psychiatrist and then to find something to soothe her nerves.

Mrs. Hogendobber bent over with some stiffness, scooping up the mail Harry had tossed on the floor.

"Oh, Miranda, I'll do that. I was pretty silly."

"You still love him."

"No, I don't," Harry quietly replied, "but I love what we were to each other, and he's worth loving as a friend. He'll make some woman out there a good companion. Isn't that what marriage is about? Companionship? Shared goals?"

"Ideally. I don't know, Harry, young people today want so much more than we did. They want excitement, romance, good looks, lots of money, vacations all the time. When I married George we didn't expect that. We expected to work hard together and improve our lot. We scrimped and saved. The fires of romance burned brighter sometimes than others but we were a team."

Harry thought about what Mrs. Hogendobber said. She also listened as Miranda turned the conversation to church gossip. The best soprano in the choir and the best tenor had started a row over who got the most solos. Mrs. Hogendobber interspersed her pearls of wisdom throughout.

At one o'clock Blair brought in Orlando Heguay. The airplane was late, the terminal crowded, but all was well. Orlando charmed Mrs. Hogendobber. Harry thought he was exactly right for Boom Boom: urbane, wealthy, and incredibly attractive. Whether or not he was a man who needed to give a woman the kind of constant attention Boom Boom demanded would be known in time.

As Blair opened his post box a hairy paw reached out at him. He yanked back his hand.

"*Scared you*," Mrs. Murphy laughed.

"You little devil." Blair reached back into his box and grabbed her paw for a minute.

Orlando walked around and then paused before the photograph of the unidentified victim. Studying it intently, he let out a low whistle. "Good God."

"I beg your pardon," Mrs. Hogendobber said.

Harry walked over to explain why it was on the wall but before she could open her mouth Orlando said, "That's Tommy Norton."

Everyone turned to him, ashen-faced. Harry spoke first. "You know this man?"

"It's Tommy Norton. I mean, the hair is wrong and he looks thinner than when I knew him but yes, if it isn't Tommy Norton it's his aging double."

Miranda dialed Rick Shaw before Orlando finished his sentence.

59

After profuse apologies for disrupting Orlando's holiday, Rick and Cynthia closed the door to Rick's office. Blair waited outside and read the newspaper.

"Continue, Mr. Heguay."

"I met Fitz-Gilbert in 1971. We were not close at school. He had a good friend in New York, Tommy Norton. I met Tommy Norton in the summer of 1974. He worked as a gofer in the brokerage house of Kincaid, Foster and Kincaid. I was seventeen that summer and I guess he was fifteen or sixteen. I worked next door at Young and Fulton Brothers. That convinced me I never wanted to be a stockbroker." Orlando took a breath and continued. "Anyway, we'd have lunch once or twice a week. The rest of the time they'd work us through lunch."

"We?" Cynthia asked.

"Tommy, Fitz-Gilbert Hamilton, and myself."

"Go on." Rick's voice had a hypnotic quality.

"Well, there's not much to tell. He was a poor kid from Brooklyn but very bright and he wanted to be like Fitz and me. He imitated us. It was sad, really, that he couldn't go to prep school, because it would have made him so happy. They weren't giving out as many scholarships in those days."

"Did he ever come up to Andover to visit?"

"Well, Fitz's parents were killed in that awful plane crash that summer, and the next year, at school, Fitz was really out of control. Tommy and Fitz were close, though, and Tommy did come up at least once that fall. He fit right in. Since I was a year older than Tommy, I lost touch after graduating and going to Yale. Fitz went to Princeton, once he straightened out, and I don't know what happened to Tommy. Well, I do remember that he worked again at Kincaid, Foster and Kincaid the following summer and so did Fitz."

"Can you think of anyone else who might know Tommy Norton?" Rick asked.

"The head of personnel in those days was an officious toad named Leonard, uh, Leonard Imbry. Funny name. If he's still there he might remember Tommy."

"What makes you think the photograph reconstruction is Norton?" Cynthia thought Orlando, with his dark hair and eyes, was extremely handsome and she wished she were in anything but a police uniform.

"I wouldn't want to bet my life on it but the reconstruction had Tommy's chin, which was prominent. The nose was a little smaller maybe, and the haircut was wrong." He shrugged. "It looked like an older version of that boy I knew. What happened to him? Before I could get the story from the ladies in the post office you whisked me away."

Cynthia answered. "The man in the photograph was murdered, his face severely disfigured, and his body dismembered. The fingerprints were literally cut off the fingerpads and every tooth was knocked out of his head. Over a period of days people here kept finding body parts. The head turned up in a pumpkin at our Harvest

Festival. It was really unforgivable and there are children and adults who will have nightmares for a long time because of that."

"Why would anyone want to kill Tommy Norton?" Orlando was shocked at the news.

"That's what we want to know." Rick made more notes.

"When was the last time you saw Fitz-Gilbert Hamilton?" Cynthia wished she could think of enough questions to keep him there for hours.

"At my graduation from Andover Academy. His voice had deepened but he was still a little slow in developing. I don't know if I would recognize him today. I'd like to think that I would."

"You said he attended Princeton—after he straightened out."

"Fitz was a mess there for a while after his parents died. He was very withdrawn. None of us boys was particularly adept at handling a crisis like that. Maybe we wouldn't be adept today either. I don't know, but he stayed in his room playing Mozart's *Requiem*. Over and over."

"But he stayed in school?" Rick glanced up from his notes.

"Where else could they put him? There were no other relatives, and the executor of his parents' estate was a New York banker with a law degree who barely knew the boy. He got through the year and then I heard that summer of '75 that he started to come out of his shell, working back at Kincaid, Foster and Kincaid with Tommy. They were inseparable, those two. Then there was the accident, of course. I never heard of any trouble at Princeton but Fitz and I weren't that close, and anything I did hear would have been through the grapevine, since we'd all gone off to different colleges. He was a good kid, though, and we all felt so terrible for what happened to him. I look forward to seeing him."

They thanked Orlando, and Blair, too, for waiting. Then Cynthia got on the horn and called Kincaid, Foster and Kincaid. Leonard Imbry still ran personnel and he sounded two years older than God.

Yes, he remembered both boys. Hard to forget after what happened to Fitz. They were hard workers. Fitz was unstable but a good boy. He lost track of both of them when they went off to college. He thought Fitz went to Princeton and Tommy to City College.

Cynthia hung up the phone. "Chief."

"What?"

"When are Little Marilyn and Fitz returning from the Homestead?"

"What am I, social director of Crozet? Call Herself." *Herself* was Rick's term for Big Marilyn Sanburne.

This Cynthia did. The Hamiltons would be back tonight. She hung up the phone. "Don't you find it odd that Orlando recognized the photograph, if it is Tommy Norton, and Fitz-Gilbert didn't?"

"I'm one step ahead of you. We'll meet them at their door. In the meantime, Coop, get New York to see if anyone in the police department, registrar, anyone, has records on Tommy Norton or Fitz-Gilbert Hamilton. Don't forget City College."

"Where are you going?" she asked as he took his coat off the rack.

"Hunting."

60

In just a few days at the Homestead, Little Marilyn knew she'd gained five pounds. The waffles at breakfast, those large burnished golden squares, could put a pound on even the most dedicated dieter. Then there were the eggs, the rolls, the sweet rolls, the crisp Virginia bacon. And that was only breakfast.

When the telephone rang, Little Marilyn, languid and stuffed, lifted the receiver and said in a relaxed voice, "Hello."

"Baby."

"Mother." Little Marilyn's shoulder blades tensed.

"Are you having a good time?"

"Eating like piggies."

"You'll never guess what's happened here."

Little Marilyn tensed again. "Not another murder?"

"No, no, but Orlando Heguay—he knows Fitz from prep school—recognized the unidentified murdered man. He said it was someone called Tommy Norton. I hope this is the breakthrough we've been waiting for, but Sheriff Shaw, as usual, appears neither hopeful nor unhopeful."

The daughter smiled, and although her mother couldn't see it, it was a false smile, a knee-jerk social response. "Thank you for telling me. I know Fitz will be relieved when I tell him." She paused. "Why did Rick Shaw tell you who the victim was?"

"He didn't. You know him. He keeps his cards close to his chest."

"How did you find out?"

"I have my sources."

"Oh, come on, Mother. That's not fair. Tell me."

"This Orlando fellow walked into the post office and identified the photograph. Right there in front of Harry and Miranda. Not that anyone is one hundred percent sure that's the victim's true identity, but well, he seems to think it is."

"The whole town must know by now," Little Marilyn half-snorted. "Mrs. Hogendobber is not one to keep things to herself."

"She can when she has to, but no one instructed her not to tell and I expect that anyone would do the same in her place. Anyway, I think Rick Shaw went over there, slipping and sliding in the snow, and had a sitdown with both of them. I gave him the key to Fitz's office. Rick said he needed to get back in there too. He thought the fingerprint people might have missed something."

"Here comes Fitz back from his swim. I'll let you tell him everything." She handed the phone to her husband and mouthed the word "Mother."

He grimaced and took the phone. As Mim spun her story his face whitened. By the time he hung up, his hand was shaking.

"Darling, what's wrong?"

"They think that body was Tommy Norton. I knew Tommy Norton. I didn't think that photo looked like Tommy. Your mother wants me to come home and talk to Rick Shaw immediately. She says it doesn't look good for the family that I knew Tommy Norton."

Little Marilyn hugged him. "How awful for you."

He recovered himself. "Well, I hope there's been a mistake. Really. I'd hate to think that was . . . him."

"When was the last time you saw him?"

"I think it was 1976."

"People's appearances change a lot in those years."

"I ought to recognize him though. I didn't think that composite resembled him. Never crossed my mind.

"He had a prominent chin. I remember that. He was very good to me and then we lost track when we went to separate colleges. Anyway, I don't think boys are good at keeping up with one another the way girls are. You write letters to your sorority sisters. You're on the phone. Women are better at relationships. Anyway, I always wondered what happened to Tom. Listen, you stay here and enjoy yourself. I'll drive back to Crozet, if for no other reason than to calm Mother and look at the drawing with new eyes. I'll fetch you tomorrow. The major roads are plowed. I'll have no trouble getting through."

"I don't want to be here without you, and you shouldn't have to endure a blast from Mother alone. God forbid she should think our social position is compromised the tiniest bit—the eensiest."

He kissed her on the cheek. "You stay put, sweetie. I'll be back in no time. Eat a big dinner for me."

Little Marilyn knew she wouldn't change his mind. "I think I've already eaten enough."

"You look gorgeous."

He changed his clothes and kissed her goodbye. Before he could reach the door the phone rang. Little Marilyn picked up the receiver. Her eyes bugged out of her head.

"Yes, yes, he's right here." Little Marilyn, in a state of disbelief, handed the phone to Fitz.

"Hello." Fitz froze upon hearing Cabell Hall's voice. "Are you all right? Where are you?"

Little Marilyn started for the suite's other phone. Fitz grabbed her by the wrist and whispered, "If he hears the click he might hang up." He returned to Cabell. "Yes, the weather has been bad." He paused. "In a cabin in the George Washington National Forest? You must be frozen." Another pause. "Well, if you go through Rockfish Gap I could pick you up on the road there." Fitz waited. "Yes, it would be frigid to wait, I agree. You say it's warm in the cabin, plenty of firewood? What if I hiked up to the cabin?" He paused again. "You don't want to tell me where it is. Cabell, this is ridiculous. Your wife is worried to death. I'll come and get you and take you home." He held the receiver away from his ear. "He hung up. Damn!"

"What's he doing in the George Washington National Forest?" Marilyn asked.

"Says he'd been taking groceries up there for a week before he left. He's got plenty of food. Went up there because he wanted to think. About what I don't know. Sounds like his elevator doesn't go to the top anymore."

"I'll call Rick Shaw," she volunteered.

"No need. I'll see him after I visit Taxi. She needs to know Cabby's physically well, if not mentally."

"Do you know exactly where he is?"

"No. In a cabin not far from Crabtree Falls. The state police can find him though. You stay here. I'll take care of everything."

He kissed her again and left.

61

Sheriff Shaw had investigated the theft at Fitz-Gilbert's office when it was first reported. Now, alone in the office, he sat at the desk. He hoped for a false-bottomed drawer but there wasn't one. The drawers were filled with beautiful stationery, investment brochures, and company year-end reports. He also found a stack of *Playboy* magazines. He fought the urge to thumb through them.

Then he got down on his hands and knees. The rug, scrupulously clean, yielded nothing.

The kitchen, however, yielded a bottle of expensive port, wine and scotch, crackers, cheese, and sodas. The coffee maker appeared brand-new.

He again got down on his hands and knees, once he opened the closet door. Again it was clean, except for a tuft of blond hair stuck in the corner on the floor.

Rick placed the hair in a small envelope and slipped it into his jacket pocket.

As he closed the door to the office he knew more than when he walked in, but he still didn't know enough.

He needed to be methodical and cautious before some high-ticket lawyer smashed his case. Those guys could get Sherman's March reduced to trespassing.

62

Cynthia Cooper discovered that Tommy Norton had never matriculated at City College of New York. By two in the afternoon her ear hurt, she'd been on the phone so long. Finally she hit pay dirt. In the summer of 1976, a Thomas Norton was committed to Central Islip, one of the state's mental institutions. He was diagnosed as a hebephrenic schizophrenic. Unfortunately, the file was incomplete and the woman on the other end of the phone couldn't find the name of his next of kin. She didn't know who admitted him.

Cynthia was then transferred to one of the doctors, who remembered the patient. He was schizophrenic but with the help of drugs had made progress toward limited self-sufficiency in the last five years. Recently he was remitted to a halfway house and given employment as a clerical worker. He was quite bright but often disoriented. The doctor gave a full physical description of the man and also faxed one for Cynthia.

When the photo rolled out of the office fax she knew they'd found Tommy Norton.

She then called the halfway house and discovered that Tommy Norton had been missing since October. The staff had reported this to the police but in a city of nine million people Tommy Norton had simply disappeared.

She roused Rick on his radio. He was very interested in everything she knew. He told her to meet him at Fitz-Gilbert Hamilton's house with a search warrant.

63

The pale-orange sun set, plunging the temperature into the low twenties. As Venus rose over the horizon she seemed larger than ever in the biting night air. A violent orange outline ran across the top of the Blue Ridge Mountains, transforming the deep snows into golden waves. So deep was the snow that even the broomstraw was engulfed. A thin crust of ice covered the snow.

Giving Orlando the full tour of Crozet wasn't possible because many of the side roads remained snowed under. Blair asked his friend's indulgence as he turned down Harry's driveway at 5:10 P.M. He'd picked up a round black de-icer for her to try in the water trough and he thought tonight would be a good test. If it didn't work, Paul Summers at Southern States said he could bring it back and get his money refunded.

"I don't remember you being the country type." Orlando reached for a hand strap as the vehicle slowly rocked down the driveway. "In fact, I don't remember you getting up before eleven."

"Times change and people change with them." Blair smiled.

Orlando laughed. "Couldn't have anything to do with the post-mistress."

"Hmmn" was Blair's comment.

Orlando, serious for a moment, said, "It's none of my business but she seems like a good person and she's easy on the eyes. Fresh-looking. Anyway, after what you've been through you deserve all the happiness you can find."

"I loved Robin but I could keep a distance from her. You know, if we'd gotten married I don't think it would have lasted. We lived a pretty superficial life."

Orlando sighed. "I guess I do too. But look at the business I'm in. If you want the clients with deep pockets, you shmooze with them. I envy you."

"Why?"

"Because you had the guts to get out."

"I'll still go on shoots from time to time until I get too wrinkled or they don't want me anymore. See, you were smarter than I was. You picked a career where age is irrelevant."

Orlando smiled when the clapboard house and barn came into view. "Clean lines."

"She has little sense of decoration, so tread lightly, okay? I mean, she's not a blistering idiot but she hasn't a penny, really, so she can't do much."

"I read you loud and clear."

They pulled up in front of the barn and the two men got out. Harry was mucking the stalls. Her winter boots bore testament to the task. The doors to the stalls hung open as the used shavings were tossed into the wheelbarrow. At the end of the aisle another wheelbarrow, filled with sweet-smelling shavings, stood. The door to the tack room was open also. Tucker greeted everyone and Mrs. Murphy stuck her head out of the loft opening. An errant sliver of hay dangled on her whisker. When Harry saw the two men she waved and called out, "Hola!" This amused Orlando.

"*Who is it?*" Simon asked.

"*Blair and his friend Orlando.*"

"*She won't bring them up here, will she?*" The possum nervously paced. "*She brought Susan up once and I didn't think that was right.*"

"*Because of the earring. That was a special case. They won't climb up the ladder. The one guy's too well-dressed, anyway.*"

"*Shut up down there.*" The owl ruffled her feathers, turned around, and settled down while expanding on everyone's deficiencies.

Down below Orlando admired the barn and the beautiful construction work. The barn had been built in the late 1880's, the massive square beams prepared to bear weight for centuries to come.

Tucker barked, "*Someone's coming.*"

A white Range Rover pulled up next to Blair's Explorer. Fitz-Gilbert Hamilton opened the door and hurried into the barn.

"Orlando, I've been looking at Blair's for you, and then thought you might be here."

"Fitz . . . is it really you?" Orlando squinted. "You look different."

"Fatter, older. A little bald." Fitz laughed. "You look the same, only better. It's amazing what the years do to people—inside and outside."

As the two men shook hands, Harry noticed a bulge, chest-high, in Fitz's bomber jacket. This wasn't an ordinary bomber jacket—it was lined with goose down so Fitz could be both warm and dashing.

Tucker lifted her nose and sniffed. "*Murphy, Murphy.*"

The cat again stuck her head out the opening. "*What?*"

"*Fitz has the stench of fear on him.*"

Mrs. Murphy wiggled her nose. A frightened human being threw off a powerful, acrid scent. It was unmistakable, so strong that a human with a good nose—for a human—could even smell it once they had learned to identify it. "*You're right, Tucker.*"

"*Something's wrong,*" Tucker barked.

Harry leaned down to pat the corgi's head. "Pipe down, short stuff."

Mrs. Murphy called down, "*Maybe he found another body.*" She stopped herself. If he'd found another body he would have said that immediately. "Tucker, *get behind him.*"

The little dog slunk behind Fitz, who continued to chat merrily with Orlando, Blair, and Harry. Then he changed gears. "What made you think that picture was Tommy Norton?"

Orlando tipped his head. "Looked like him to me. How is it you didn't notice?"

Fitz unzipped his jacket and pulled out a lethal, shiny .45. "I did, as a matter of fact. You three get against the wall there. I don't have time for an extended farewell. I need to get to the bank and the airport before Rick Shaw finds out I'm here and I'll be damned if you're going to wreck things for me—so."

As Orlando stood there, puzzled, Tucker sank her teeth up to the gums into Fitz's leg. He screamed and whirled around, the tough dog hanging on. The humans scattered. Harry ran into one of the stalls, Orlando dove into the tack room, shutting the door, and Blair lunged for the wall phone in the aisle, but Fitz recovered enough to fire.

Blair grunted and rolled away into Gin's stall.

"You all right?" Harry called. She didn't see Blair get hit.

"Yeah," Blair, stunned, said through gritted teeth. The force of being struck by a bullet is as painful as the lead intruding into the flesh. Blair's shoulder throbbed and stung.

Tucker let go of Fitz's leg and scrambled to the barn doors, bullets flying after her. Once she wriggled out of the barn she slunk alongside the building. Tucker didn't know what to do.

Mrs. Murphy, who had been peering down from the loft, ran to the side and peeked through an opening in the boards. "*Tucker, Tucker, are you all right?*"

"*Yes.*" Tucker's voice was throaty and raw. "*We've got to save Mother.*"

"*See if you can get Tomahawk and Gin Fizz up to the barn.*"

"*I'll try.*" The corgi set out into the pastures. Fortunately, the cold had hardened the crust of the snow and she could travel on the surface. A few times she sank into the powder but she struggled out.

Simon, scared, shivered next to Mrs. Murphy.

Down below, Fitz slowly stalked toward the stalls. The cat again peered down. She realized that he would be under the ladder in a few moments.

Harry called out, "Fitz, why did you kill those people?" She played for time.

Mrs. Murphy hoped her mother could stall him, because she had a desperate idea.

"Ben got greedy, Harry. He wanted more and more."

As Fitz spoke, Orlando, flattened against the wall, moved nearer to the door of the tack room.

"Why did you pay him off in the first place?"

"Ah, well, that's a long story." He moved a step closer to the loft opening.

Tucker, panting, reached Tomahawk first. *"Come to the barn, Tommy. There's trouble inside. Fitz-Gilbert wants to kill Mom."*

Tomahawk snorted, called Gin, and they thundered toward the barn, leaving Tucker to follow as best she could.

Inside, the tiger cat heard the hoofbeats. Their pasture was on the west side of the barn. She vaulted over hay bales and called through a space in the siding. *"Can you jump the fence?"*

Gin answered, *"Not with our turn-out rugs in this much snow."*

Simon wrung his pink paws. *"Oh, this is awful."*

"Crash the fence then. Make as much noise as you can but count to ten." Tucker caught up to the horses. *"Tucker,"* Mrs. Murphy called, *"help them count to ten. Got it? Slow."* She spun around and called to Simon over her shoulder. *"Help me, Simon."*

The gray possum shuttled over the timothy and alfalfa as quickly as he could. He joined Mrs. Murphy at the south side of the barn. Hay flew everywhere as the cat clawed at a bale.

"What are you doing?"

"Getting the blacksnake. She's hibernating, so she won't curl around us and spit and bite."

"Well, she's going to wake up!" Simon's voice rose.

"Worry about that later. Come on, help me get her out of here."

"I'm not touching her!" Simon backed up.

At that moment Mrs. Murphy longed for her corgi friend. Much as Tucker griped and groaned at Mrs. Murphy, she had the heart of a warrior. Tucker would have picked up the snake in a heartbeat.

"*Harry has taken good care of you,*" the cat pleaded.

Simon grimaced. "*Ugh.*" He hated the snake.

"*Simon, there's not a moment to lose!*" Mrs. Murphy's pupils were so large Simon could barely see the gorgeous color of her iris.

A shadowy, muffled sound overhead startled them. The owl alighted on the hay bale. Outside, the horses could be heard making a wide circle. Within seconds they'd be smashing to bits the board fencing by the barn. In her deep, operatic voice the owl commanded, "*Go to the ladder, both of you. Hurry.*"

Bits of alfalfa wafted into the air as Mrs. Murphy sped toward the opening. Simon, less fleet of foot, followed. The owl hopped down and closed her mighty talons over the sleeping four-foot-long blacksnake. Then she spread her wings and rose upward. The snake, heavy, slowed her down more than she anticipated. Her powerful chest muscles lifted her up and she quietly glided to where the cat and the possum waited. She held her wings open for a landing, flapped once to guide her, and then softly touched down next to Mrs. Murphy. She left the snake, now groggy, at the cat's paws. She opened her wide wingspan and soared upward to her roost. Mrs. Murphy had no time to thank her. Outside, the sound of splintering wood, neighing, and muffled hoofbeats in the snow told her she had to act. Tucker barked at the top of her lungs.

"*Pick up your end,*" Mrs. Murphy firmly ordered Simon, who did as he was told. He was now more frightened of Mrs. Murphy than of the snake.

Fitz, distracted for a moment by the commotion outside, turned his head toward the noise. He was close to the loft opening. The cat, heavy snake in her jaws, Simon holding its tail, flung the snake onto Fitz's shoulders. By now the blacksnake was awake enough to curl around his neck for a moment. She was desperately trying to get her bearings and Fitz screamed to high heaven.

As he did so Mrs. Murphy launched herself from the loft opening and landed on Fitz's back.

"Don't do it!" Simon yelled.

The cat, no time to answer, scrambled with the snake underfoot as Fitz bellowed and attempted to rid himself of his tormentors. Mrs. Murphy mercilessly shredded his face with her claws. As she tore away at Fitz she saw, out of the corner of her eye, Blair come hurtling out of the stall.

"Orlando!" Blair called.

No sooner had he hollered for his friend than Harry, having shed her winter parka, moved from Tomahawk's stall like a streak.

Mrs. Murphy grabbed for Fitz's right eye.

He fired the gun in the air as the cat blinded him. Instinctively he covered the damaged eye with his right hand, the gun hand, and that fast, Harry hit him at the knees. He went down with an "oomph." The snake hit the ground with him. Mrs. Murphy gracefully jumped off. Tucker wiggled back into the barn.

"Get his gun hand!" Mrs. Murphy screeched.

Tucker raced for the flailing man. Fitz kicked Harry away and she lurched against the wall with a thud. Blair struggled to keep Fitz down but his one arm dangled uselessly. Orlando crept out of the tack room and, seeing the situation, swallowed hard, then joined the fight.

"Jesus!" Fitz bellowed as the dog bit clean through his wrist, pulverizing some of the tiny bones. His fingers opened and the gun was released.

"Get the gun!" Blair hit Fitz hard with his good fist, striking him squarely in the solar plexus. If he hadn't been wearing the down bomber jacket, Fitz would have been gasping.

Harry dove for the gun, skidding across the aisle on her stomach. She snatched it as Fitz kicked Blair in the groin. Orlando hung on his back like a tick. Fitz possessed the strength of a madman, or a cornered rat. He raced backward and squashed Orlando on the wall. Tucker kept nipping at his heels.

Fitz whirled around and beheld Harry pointing the gun at him. Blood and clear fluid coursed down from his sightless right eye. He moved toward Harry.

"You haven't got the guts, Mary Minor Haristeen."

Blair, panting from the effort and the pain, got between Fitz and Harry while Orlando, flat on his back, the wind knocked out of him, sucked wind like a fish out of water.

Her fur puffed out so she was double her size, Mrs. Murphy balanced herself on a stall door. If she had to, she'd launch another attack. Meanwhile, the blacksnake, half in a daze, managed to slither into Tomahawk's stall to bury herself in shavings. Simon stuck his head out of the loft opening. His lower jaw hung slack.

"You haven't got a prayer, Fitz. Give up." Blair held out his hand to stop the advancing man.

"Fuck off, faggot."

Blair had been called a faggot so many times it didn't faze him—that and the fact that the gay men he knew were good people. "Hold it right there."

Fitz swung at Blair, who ducked.

"Get out of the way, Blair." Harry held the gun steady and true.

"You'll never shoot. Not you, Harry." Fitz laughed, a weird, high-pitched sound.

"Get out of the way, Blair. I mean it." Harry sounded calm but determined.

Orlando struggled to his feet and ran to the phone. He dialed 911 and haltingly tried to explain.

"Just tell them Harry Haristeen, Yellow Mountain Road. Everybody knows everybody," she called to Orlando.

"But everybody doesn't know everybody, Harry. You don't know me. You didn't want to know me." Fitz kept stalking her.

"I liked you, Fitz. I think you've gone mad. Now stop." She didn't back up as he advanced.

"Fitz-Gilbert Hamilton is dead. He went to pieces." Fitz laughed shrilly.

Orlando hung up the phone. Blair's face froze. They couldn't believe their ears.

"What do you mean?" Orlando asked.

Fitz half-turned to see him with his good eye. "I'm Tommy Norton."

"But you can't be!" Orlando's lungs still ached.

"Oh, but I am. Fitz lost his mind, you know. Off and on, and then finally . . . off." Fitz, the man they knew as Fitz, waved his hand in the air at "off." "Half the time he didn't know his own name but he knew me. I was his only friend. He trusted me. After that car accident we both had to have plastic surgery. A little nose work for him, plus my chin was reduced while his was built up. He emerged looking more like Tommy Norton and I looked more like Fitz-Gilbert Hamilton. Once the swelling went down, anybody would have taken us for brothers. And as we were still young men, not fully matured, people would readily accept those little changes when I next met them: the deeper voice, the filled-out body. It was so easy. When he finally lost it completely, the executor and I put the new Tommy in Central Islip. As for my family—my father had left my mother when I was six. She was generally so damned drunk she was glad to be rid of me, assuming she even noticed."

"The executor! Wasn't Cabell the executor?" Harry asked.

"Yes. He was handsomely paid and was a good executor. We stayed close after he moved from New York to Virginia. Cabell even introduced me to my wife. He took his cut and all went well. Until 'Tommy' showed up."

A siren wailed in the distance.

"All you rich people. You don't know what it's like. Money is worth killing for. Believe me. I'd do it again. Fitz would still be alive if he hadn't wandered down here looking for me. I guess he was like England's George the Third—he would suffer years of insanity and then snap out of it. He'd be lucid again. I was easy to find. Little Marilyn and I regularly appear in society columns. Plus, all he would have to do was call his old bank and track down his executor. He was smart enough to do that. As pieces of his past came back to him he knew he was Fitz-Gilbert Hamilton. Well, I couldn't have that, could I? I was better at being Fitz-Gilbert than he was. He didn't need his money. He would have just faded out again and all that money would have been useless, untouchable."

The siren howled louder now and Tommy Norton, thinking Harry had grown less vigilant, leapt toward her. A spit of flame flashed from the muzzle of the gun. Tommy Norton let out a howl, deep and guttural, and clutching his knee, fell to the ground. Harry had blown apart his kneecap. Undaunted, he crawled toward her.

"Kill me. I'd rather be dead. Kill me, because if I get to you, I'll kill you."

Blair got behind him, putting his knee in Tommy's back while wrapping his good arm around the struggling man's neck. "Give it up, man."

The metal doors of the barn squeaked as they were rolled back. Rick Shaw and Cynthia Cooper, guns drawn, burst into the barn. Behind them stood Tomahawk and Gin Fizz, splinters of the fence scattered in the snow, the fronts of their blankets a mess.

"Did we do a good job?" they nickered.

"The best," Mrs. Murphy answered, her fur now returning to normal.

Cynthia attended to Blair. "I'll call an ambulance."

"I think I'd get there faster if I drove myself in the Explorer."

"I'll take you."

Tommy sat on the floor, blood spurting from his knee and his eye, yet he seemed beyond pain. Perhaps his mind couldn't accept what had just happened to him emotionally and physically.

"No, you won't. Both these men need care." Rick pointed for Orlando to call the hospital and he gave the number. "Tell them Sheriff Shaw is here. On the double."

As Harry and Blair filled in the officers, Tommy would laugh and correct little details.

"What was Ben Seifert's connection?" Rick wanted to know.

"Accidental. Stumbled on Cabell Hall's second set of books, the ones where he accounted for my payments. Cabell is somewhere up in the mountains, by the way. He ran away because he thought I'd kill him, I guess. He'll come down in good time. Anyway, Ben proved useful. He fed me information on who was near bankruptcy, and I'd buy their land or lend them money at a high interest rate. So I started to pay him off, too, but . . ." Tommy gasped as a jolt of pain finally reached his senses.

Harry walked over to Mrs. Murphy and picked her off the stall door. She buried her face in the cat's fur. Then she hunkered down to kiss Tucker. Tears rolled down Harry's cheeks.

Blair put his good arm around her. She could smell the blood soaking through his shirt and his jacket.

"Let's take this off." She helped him remove the jacket. He winced. Cynthia came over, while Rick kept his revolver trained on Tommy.

"Still in there." Cynthia referred to the bullet. "I hope it didn't shatter any bone."

"Me too." Blair was starting to feel woozy. "I think I better sit for a minute."

Harry helped him to a chair in the tack room.

Orlando stood next to Rick. He stared at this man whom he once knew. "Tom, you passed, you know."

Tiny bits of patella were scattered on the barn aisle. A faint smile crossed Tom's features as he fought back his agony. "Yeah, I fooled everybody. Even that insufferable snob, that bitch of a mother-in-law." A dark pain twisted his face. His features contorted and he fought for control. "I would never have been able to marry Little Marilyn. Fitz-Gilbert could marry her. Tommy Norton couldn't."

"Maybe you're selling her short." Orlando's voice was soothing.

"She's controlled by her mother" was the matter-of-fact reply. "But you know what's funny? I learned to love my wife. I never thought I could love anybody." He looked as if he would weep.

"How much was the Hamilton fortune worth?" Sheriff Shaw asked.

"When I inherited it, so to speak, it was worth twenty-one million. With Cabell's management and my own attention to it, once I came of age it had grown to sixty-four million. There are no heirs. No Hamiltons are left. Before I killed Fitz, I asked if he had children and he said no." Tommy deliberately did not look at his knee, as if not seeing it would control the pain.

"Who will get the money?" Orlando wanted to know. After all, money is fascinating.

"Little Marilyn. I made sure of that twice over. She's the recipient of my will and Fitz-Gilbert's, the one he signed in my office that October day. Trusting as a lamb. It might take a while but one way or the other my wife gets that money."

"Exactly how did you kill Fitz-Gilbert Hamilton?" Cynthia inquired.

"Ben panicked. Typical. Weak and greedy. I always told Cabell that Ben could never run Allied after Cabell retired. He didn't believe me. Anyway, Ben was smart enough to get Fitz in his car and out of the bank before he caused an even greater scene or blurted out who he was. He drove him to my office. Ben was prepared to hang around and become a nuisance. I told him to go back to the bank, that Fitz and I would reach some accord. I said this in front of Fitz. Ben left. Fitz was all right for a bit. Then he became angry when I told him about his money. I made so much more with it than he ever could have! I offered to split it with him. That seemed fair enough. He became enraged. One thing led to another and he swung at me. That's how my office was wrecked."

"And you stole the office money from yourself?" Cynthia added.

"Of course. What's two hundred dollars and a CD player, which is what I listed as missing?" Sweat drenched Tommy's face.

"So, how did you kill him?" She pressed on.

"With a paperweight. He wasn't very strong and the paperweight was heavy. I caught him just right, I suppose."

"Or just wrong," Harry said.

Tommy shrugged and continued. "No matter. He's dead now. The hard part was cutting up the body. Joints are hell to cut through."

Rick picked up the questioning. "Where'd you do that?"

"Back on the old logging trail off Yellow Mountain Road. I waited until night. I stored the body in the closet in my office, picked him up, and then took him out on the logging road. Burying the hands and legs was easy until the storm came up. I never expected it to be that bad, but then everything was unexpected."

"What about the clothes?" Rick scribbled in his notebook.

"Threw them in the dumpster behind Safeway—the teeth too. If it hadn't rained so hard and that damned dog hadn't found the hand, nobody would know anything. Everything would be just as it was . . . before."

"You think Ben and Cabell wouldn't have given you trouble?" Harry cynically interjected.

"Ben would have, most likely. Cabell stayed cool until Ben turned up dead." Tom leaned his head against the wall and shook with pain and fatigue. "Then he got squirrely. Take the money and run became his theme song. Crazy talk. It takes weeks to liquidate investments. Months. Although as a precaution I always kept a lot of cash in my checking account."

"Well, you might have gotten away with murder, and then again you might not have." Rick calmly kept writing. "But the torso and the head in the pumpkin—you were pushing it, Tommy. You were pushing it."

He laughed harshly. "The satisfaction of seeing Mim's face." He laughed again. "That was worth it. I knew I was safe. Sure, the torso in the boathouse pointed to obvious hostility against Marilyn San-burne but so what? The pieces of body in the old cemetery—considering what happened to Robin Mangione—was sure to throw you off the track at some point. I copied her murder to make Blair the prime suspect, just in case something should go wrong. I had backup plans to contend with people—not dogs." He sighed, then smiled. "But the head in the pumpkin—that was a stroke of genius."

"You ruined the Harvest Fair for the whole town," Harry accused him.

"Oh, bullshit, Harry. People will be telling that story for decades, centuries. Ruined it? I made it into a legend!"

"How'd you do it? In the morning?" Cynthia was curious.

"Sure. Jim Sanburne and I catalogued the crafts and the produce. Since he was judging the produce, we decided it wouldn't be fair for him to prejudge it in any way. I planned to put the head in a pumpkin anyway—another gift for Mim—but this was too good to pass up. Jim was in the auditorium and I was in the gym. We were alone after the people dropped off their entries. It was so easy."

"You were lucky," Harry said.

Tom shook his head as if trying to clear it. "No, I wasn't that lucky. People see what they want to see. Think of how much we miss every day because we discount evidence, because odd things don't add up to our vision of the world as it ought to be, not as it is. You were all easy to fool. It never occurred to Jim to tell Rick that I was alone with the pumpkins. Not once. People were looking for a homicidal maniac . . . not me."

The ambulance siren drew closer. "My wife saw what she wanted to see. That night I came home from Sloan's she thought I was drunk. I wasn't. We had our sherry nightcap and I took the precaution of putting a sleeping pill in hers. After she went to sleep I went out, got rid of that spineless wonder, Ben Seifert, and when I got back I crawled into bed for an hour and she was none the wiser. I pretended to wake up hungover, as opposed to absolutely exhausted, and she accepted it."

"Then what was the point of the postcards?" Harry felt anger rising in her face now that the adrenaline from the struggle was ebbing.

"Allied National has one of those fancy desk-top computers. So do most of the bigger businesses in Albemarle County, as I'm sure you found out, Sheriff, when you tried to hunt one down."

"I did," came the terse reply.

"They're not like typewriters, which are more individual. By now Cabell was getting nervous, so we cooked up the postcard idea. He thought it would cast more suspicion on Blair, since he didn't receive one. Although by that time few people really believed Blair had done it. Cabell wanted to play up the guilty newcomer angle and get you off the scent. Not that I worried about the scent. Everyone was so far away from the truth, but Cabell was worried. I did it for fun. It was enjoyable, jerking a string and watching you guys jump. And the gossip mill." He laughed again. "Unreal—you people are absolutely unreal. Someone thinks it's revenge. Someone else thinks it's demonology. I learned more about people through this than if I had been a psychiatrist."

"What did you learn?" Harry's right eyebrow arched upward.

"Maybe I reconfirmed what I always knew." The ambulance pulled into the driveway. "People are so damn self-centered they rarely see anybody or anything as it truly is because they're constantly relating everything back to themselves. That's why they're so easy to fool. Think about it." And with that his energy drained away. He could no longer hold his head up. Pain conquered even his remarkable willpower.

As the ambulance carried Tommy Norton away, Harry knew she'd be thinking about it for years to come.

64

The fire crackled, arching up the chimney. Outside the fourth storm of this remarkable winter crept to the top of the mountains' peaks.

Blair, his arm in a sling, Harry, Orlando, Mrs. Hogendobber, Susan and Ned, Cynthia Cooper, Market and Pewter, and the Reverend Jones and Carol gathered before the fire.

While Blair was in the hospital enduring the cold probe to find the bullet, Cynthia had called Susan and Miranda to tell them what happened and to suggest that they bring food to Harry's. Then she dispatched an officer to Florence Hall's to break the news to her of her husband's complicity as gently as possible. The state police might not find Cabell tonight but after the storm they'd flush him out of his cabin.

Orlando had stayed at the farm while Harry had followed the ambulance in the Explorer. He cooked pasta while the friends arrived. Tomorrow night would be time enough for him to see Boom Boom.

Rick organized guards for Norton while the doctors patched him up. He and Cynthia then enjoyed telling the reporters and TV crews how they apprehended this dangerous criminal. Then Rick let Cynthia join her friends.

While the women organized the food, Reverend Jones, after declaring himself a male chauvinist, went out and repaired the fence lines. His version of being a male chauvinist meant doing the chores he thought were hard and dirty. The result was that, behind his back, the women dubbed him the "male chauvinist pussycat." Market lent him a hand and within forty-five minutes they had replaced the panels and cleaned up the mess. Then they attended to the horses. Fortunately, the blankets had absorbed the damage. Both Tomahawk and Gin Fizz were none the worse for wear and they patiently waited in their stalls with the doors open—in the hurry to get Blair and Tommy to the hospital, no one had thought to put the horses in their stalls and close the doors.

Sitting on the floor, plates in their laps, the friends tried to fathom how something like this could happen. Mrs. Murphy, Pewter, and Tucker circled the seated people like sharks, should a morsel fall from a plate.

"What about the tracks behind my house?" Blair stabbed at his hot chicken salad.

Cynthia said, "We found snowshoes in Fitz's—I mean Tommy Norton's—Range Rover. He dropped the earring back there. There wasn't anything he could do about that mistake but it was the earring that rattled him. I mean, after the real Fitz initially shocked him. Anyway, he wanted to know how quickly he could get back here in the snow if he had to, if you or Orlando, most likely, proved difficult. He was performing a dry run, I think, or he was hoping to head you off before Orlando got here. He must have been getting pretty shaky knowing about Orlando's visit. Anything to prevent it would have been worth the risk."

"What would I have done?" Orlando asked.

"He wasn't sure. Remember, his whole life, the plan of many years, was jeopardized when the real Fitz showed up. Ben Seifert used the event to extort more money out of him. He was getting nervous. What if you noticed something, which, unlikely as it may have seemed to you, was not unlikely to him? You knew him before he was Fitz-Gilbert. The impossible was becoming possible," Cynthia pointed out. "And it turned out you did cause trouble. You recognized the face in the photograph. The face that must have cost a fortune in plastic surgery."

"What about the earring?" Carol was curious.

"We'll never really know," Harry answered. "But I remember Little Marilyn saying that she thought it must have popped off when she took her sweater off in the car, the Range Rover. Tommy had the body in a plastic bag on the front floor, and the sharp part of the earring, the part that pierces one's ear, probably got stuck on the bag or in a fold of the bag. Given his hurry he didn't notice. All we do know is that Little Marilyn's earring showed up in a possum's nest miles away from where she last remembered wearing it, and there's no way the animal would have traveled the four miles to her place."

"Does Little Marilyn know?" Mrs. Hogendobber felt sympathy for the woman.

"She does," Cynthia told her. "She still doesn't believe it. Mim does, of course, but then she'll believe bad about anybody."

This made everyone laugh.

"Did anyone in this room have a clue that it might be Fitz?" Mrs. Hogendobber asked. "Tommy. I can't get used to calling him Tommy. I certainly didn't."

Neither had anyone else.

"He was brilliant in his way." Orlando opened a delicate biscuit to butter it. "He knew very early that people respond to surfaces, just as he said. Once he realized that Fitz was losing it, he concocted a diabolically clever yet simple plan to become Fitz. When he showed up at Princeton as a freshman, he *was* Fitz-Gilbert Hamilton. He was more Fitz-Gilbert Hamilton than Fitz-Gilbert Hamilton. I remember when I left for Yale my brother said that now I could become a new person if I wanted to. It was a new beginning. In Tommy's case that was literal."

Blair took that in, then said, "I don't believe he ever thought he would have to kill anyone. I just don't."

"Not then," Cynthia said.

"Money changes people." Carol stated the obvious, except that to many the obvious is overlooked. "He'd become habituated to power, to material pleasures, and he loved Little Marilyn."

"Love or money," Harry half-whispered.

"What?" Mrs. Hogendobber wanted to know everything.

"Love or money. That's what people kill for. . . ." Harry's voice trailed off.

"Yes, we did have that discussion once." Mrs. Hogendobber reached for another helping of macaroni and cheese. It was sinfully tasty. "Maybe the road to Hell is paved with dollar bills."

"If that's the center of your life," Blair added. "You know, I read a lot of history. I like knowing other people have been here before me. It's a comfort. Well, anyway, Marie Antoinette and Louis the Sixteenth became better people once they fell from power, once the money was taken away. Perhaps somebody else would actually become a better person if he or she did have money. I don't know."

The Reverend considered this. "I suppose some wealthy people become philanthropists, but it's usually at the end of their lives when Heaven has not been secured as the next address."

As the group debated and wondered about this detail or that glimpse of the man they knew as Fitz, Harry got up and put on her parka. "You all, I'll be back in a minute. I forgot to feed the possum."

"In another life you were Noah," Herbie chuckled.

Mrs. Hogendobber cast the Lutheran minister a reproving glare. "Now, Reverend, you don't believe in past lives, do you?"

Before that subject could flare up, Harry was out the back door, Mrs. Murphy and Tucker tagging along. Pewter elected to stay in the kitchen.

She slid back the barn doors just enough for her to squeeze through to switch on the lights. It was hard to believe that a few hours ago she nearly met her death in this barn, the place that always made her happy.

She shook her head as if to clear the cobwebs. Mostly she wanted to reassure herself she was alive. Mrs. Murphy led the way, and Harry crawled up the ladder, Tucker under her arm, and handed the food to Simon, who was subdued.

Mrs. Murphy rubbed against the little fellow. "You done good, Simon."

"Mrs. Murphy, that was the worst thing I've ever seen. There's something wrong with people."

"Some of them," the cat replied.

Harry watched the two animals and wondered at their capacity to communicate and she wondered, too, at how little we really know of the animal world. We're so busy trying to break them, train them, get them to do our bidding, how can we truly know them? Did the masters on the plantation ever know the slaves, and does a man ever know his wife if he thinks of himself as superior—or vice versa? She sat in the hay, breathing in the scent, and a wave of such gratitude flushed through her body. She didn't know much but she was glad to be alive.

Mrs. Murphy crawled in her lap and purred. Tucker, solemnly, leaned against Harry's side.

The cat craned her head upward and called, "Thanks."

The owl hooted back, "Forget it."

Tucker observed, "I thought you didn't like humans."

"Don't. I happen to like the blacksnake less than I like humans." She spread her wings in triumph and laughed.

The cat laughed with her. "You like Harry—admit it."

"I'll never tell." The owl lifted off her perch in the cupola and swept down right in front of Harry, startling her. Then she gained loft and flew out the large fan opening at the end of the barn. A night's hunting awaited her, at least until the storm broke.

Harry backed down the ladder, Tucker under her arm. Harry stood in the center of the aisle for a moment. "I'll never know what got into you two," she addressed the horses, "but I'm awfully glad. Thank you."

They looked back with their gentle brown eyes. Tomahawk stayed in one corner of his stall while Gin, sociable, hung his head over the Dutch door.

"And Mrs. Murphy, I still don't know how the blacksnake came flying out of the loft, followed by you. I guess I'll never know. I guess I won't know a lot of things."

"*Put her back up in her place,*" Mrs. Murphy suggested, "*or she'll freeze to death.*"

"She doesn't know what you're talking about." Tucker scratched at Tomahawk's stall door and whined. "*Is this the one she hid in?*" the dog asked the cat.

"*Under the shavings in there somewhere.*" The tiger's whiskers swept forward as she joined Tucker in clawing at the door.

She knew the snake would be there but nonetheless it always made her jump when she saw one. Harry, curious, opened the door. Now she knew why Tomahawk was in one corner of his stall. He did not like snakes and he said so.

"*Here she is.*" Tucker stood over the snake.

Harry saw the snake, partially covered by shavings. "Is she alive?" She knelt down and placed her hand behind the animal's neck. Gently she lifted the snake and only then did she realize how big the reptile was. Harry suffered no special fear of snakes but it couldn't be said that she wanted to hold one, either. Nonetheless, she felt some responsiblity for this blacksnake. The animal moved a bit. Tomahawk complained, so they backed out of the stall.

Mrs. Murphy climbed up the ladder. "*I'll show you.*"

Harry racked her brain to think of a warm spot. Other than the pipes under her kitchen sink, only the loft came to mind, so she climbed back up.

The cat ran to her and ran away. Harry watched with amusement. Mrs. Murphy had to perform this act four times before Harry had enough sense to follow her.

Simon grumbled as they passed him, "*Don't you put that old bitch near me.*"

"*Don't be a fuss,*" the cat chided. She led Harry to the snake's nest.

"Look at that," Harry exclaimed. She carefully placed the snake in her hibernating quarters and covered her with loose hay. "The Lord moves in mysterious ways his wonders to perform," she said out loud. Her mother used to say that to her. The Lord performed His or Her wonders today with a snake, a cat, a dog, and two horses. Harry had no idea that she'd had more animal help than that, but she did know she was here by the grace of God. Tommy Norton would have shot her as full of holes as Swiss cheese.

As she closed up the barn and walked back to the house, a few snowflakes falling, she recognized that she had no remorse for shooting that man in the kneecap. She would have killed him if it had been necessary. In that respect she realized she belonged to the animal world. Human morality often seems at a variance with Nature.

Fair Haristeen's truck churned, sliding down the driveway. He hurriedly got out and grabbed Harry in his arms. "I just heard. Are you all right?"

"Yes." She nodded, suddenly quite exhausted.

"Thank God, Harry, I didn't know what you meant to me until I, until I . . ." He couldn't finish his sentence. He hugged her.

She hugged him hard, then released him. "Come on. Our friends are inside. They'll be glad to see you. Blair was shot, you know." She talked on and felt such love for Fair, although it was no longer romantic. She wasn't taking him back, but then he wasn't asking her to come back. They'd sort it out in good time.

When they walked into the kitchen, a guilty, fat gray cat looked at them from the butcher block, her mouth full. She had demolished an entire ham biscuit, the incriminating crumbs still on her long whiskers.

"Pewter," Harry said.

"*I eat when I'm nervous or unhappy.*" And indeed she was wretched for having missed all the action. "*Of course, I eat when I'm relaxed and happy too.*"

Harry petted her, put her down, and then thought her friends deserved better than canned food tonight. She put ham biscuits on the floor. Pewter stood on her hind legs and scratched Harry's pants.

"More?"

"More," the gray cat pleaded.

Harry grabbed another biscuit, plus some turkey Miranda had brought and placed it on the floor.

"*I don't see why you should get treats. You didn't do anything,*" Mrs. Murphy growled as she chewed her food.

The gray cat giggled. "*Who said life was fair?*"

Murder at Monticello

For Gordon Reistrup
because he makes us laugh.

Cast of Characters

Mary Minor Haristeen (Harry), the young postmistress of Crozet, whose curiosity almost kills the cat and herself

Mrs. Murphy, Harry's gray tiger cat, who bears an uncanny resemblance to authoress Sneaky Pie and who is wonderfully intelligent!

Tee Tucker, Harry's Welsh corgi, Mrs. Murphy's friend and confidant; a buoyant soul

Pharamond Haristeen (Fair), veterinarian, formerly married to Harry

Mrs. George Hogendobber (Miranda), a widow who thumps her own Bible!

Market Shiflett, owner of Shiflett's Market, next to the post office

Pewter, Market's fat gray cat, who, when need be, can be pulled away from the food bowl

Susan Tucker, Harry's best friend, who doesn't take life too seriously until her neighbors get murdered

Big Marilyn Sanburne (Mim), queen of Crozet

Oliver Zeve, the exuberant director of Monticello, to whom reputation means a lot

Kimball Haynes, energetic young head of archaeology at Monticello. He is a workaholic who believes in digging deeper

Wesley Randolph, owner of Eagle's Rest, a passionate Thoroughbred man

Warren Randolph, Wesley's son. He's trying to step into the old man's shoes

Ansley Randolph, Warren's pretty wife, who is smarter than people think

Samson Coles, a well-born realtor who has his eyes on more than property

Lucinda Payne Coles, Samson's bored wife

Heike Holtz, one of the assistant archaeologists at Monticello

Rick Shaw, Albemarle sheriff

Cynthia Cooper, police officer

Paddy, Mrs. Murphy's ex-husband, a saucy tom

Simon, an opossum with a low opinion of humanity

Author's Note

Monticello is a national treasure well served by its current executive director, Daniel P. Jordan. Some of you will recall Mr. Jordan and his wife, Lou, opening Thomas Jefferson's home to then–President-elect Clinton.

The architectural and landscape descriptions are as accurate as I could make them. The humans are made up, of course, and Oliver Zeve, Monticello's director in this novel, is not based on Mr. Jordan.

One eerie event took place while I was writing this mystery. In the book, a potsherd of good china is unearthed in a slave cabin. On October 18, 1992, four days after I sent off the first draft of this book to my publisher, an article appeared in *The Daily Progress*, the newspaper of Charlottesville, Virginia. This article described how William Kelso, Monticello's director of archaeology, found some fine china in the slave quarters believed to have been inhabited by Sally Hemings. These quarters were close to Jefferson's home. Often slave quarters were distant from the master's house, so the location of Miss Hemings's cabin is in itself worthy of note. Finding the china bits was life imitating fiction. Who knows, but it fluffed my fur.

My only quibble with Mr. Jordan and the wonderful staff at Monticello is that they aren't paying attention to the feline contributions to Mr. Jefferson's life. Who do you think kept the mice from eating all the parchment that Mr. Jefferson used? Then again, my ancestors drove the moles from the garden and the rodents from the stables too. No doubt when the great man wrote the Declaration of Independence he was inspired by a cat. Who is more independent than a cat?

Human Americans are having a fit and falling in it over multiculturalism. Well, how about multispecies-ism? You think the world centers around humans? When history is taught, Americans really ought to give full attention to the contributions of cats, dogs, horses, cattle, sheep, hens—why, just about any kind of domesticated animal and some of the wild too. Where would our Founding Fathers and Mothers be if they hadn't had wild turkeys to eat? So abandon that human-centric point of view.

For my part, my feline ancestors arrived on Tidewater shores in 1640. The first Americat was a tabby, one Tabitha Buckingham. I am, therefore, F.F.V.—First Felines of Virginia. Of course, I take pride in my heritage, but I believe any kitty who comes to this country is as much an Americat as I am. We're all lucky to be here.

As for the human concept of the past, let me just say that history is scandal hallowed by time. Fortunately, human beans (I think of you as beans) being what they are, every nation, every country, produces sufficient scandal. If you all ever behaved reasonably, what would I have to write about?

Always,
SNEAKY PIE

Thomas Jefferson (April 13, 1743 - July 4, 1826)
and
Martha Wayles Skelton (Oct. 19(?), 1748 - Sept. 6, 1782)

Children:

- **Martha ("Patsy")** (Sept. 27, 1772 - d. 1836)
  m. Feb. 23, 1790 **Thomas Mann Randolph**
- **Jane Randolph** (April 3, 1774 - Sept. 1775)
- **Son** (May 28, 1777 - June 14, 1777)
- **Maria ("Polly")** (Aug. 1, 1778 - April 17, 1804)
  m. Oct. 13, 1797 **John Wayles Eppes**
- **Lucy Elizabeth** (Nov. 30, 1780 - April 15, 1781)
- **Lucy Elizabeth** (May 8, 1782 - Oct. 13, 1784+)

Children of Martha ("Patsy") and Thomas Mann Randolph:

- **Anne Cary** (Jan. 23, 1791 - Feb. 11, 1826)
- **Thomas Jefferson** (Sept. 12, 1792 - Oct. 8, 1875)
- **Ellen Wayles** (Aug. 30, 1794 - July 26, 1795)
- **Ellen Wayles** (Oct. 13, 1796 - April 21, 1876)
- **Cornelia Jefferson** (July 26, 1799 - Feb. 24, 1871)
- **Virginia Jefferson** (Aug. 22, 1801 - April 26, 1882)
- **Mary Jefferson** (Nov. 2, 1803 - Mar. 29, 1876)
- **James Madison** (Jan. 17, 1806 - Jan. 23, 1834)
- **Benjamin Franklin** (July 14, 1808 - Feb. 18, 1871)
- **Meriwether Lewis** (Jan. 31, 1810 - Sept. 24, 1837)
- **Septimia Anne** (Jan. 3, 1814 - Sept. 14, 1887)
- **George Wythe** (March 10, 1818 - April 13, 1867)

Children of Maria ("Polly") and John Wayles Eppes:

- **Infant** (Dec. 31, 1799 - Jan. 25, 1800)
- **Francis** (Sept. 20, 1801 - May 30, 1881)
- **Maria** (Feb. 15, 1804 - July 1807)

1

Laughing, Mary Minor Haristeen studied the nickel in her up-turned palm. Over the likeness of Monticello was inscribed our nation's motto, E Pluribus Unum. She handed the nickel to her older friend, Mrs. Miranda Hogendobber. "What do you think?"

"That nickel isn't worth a red cent." Mrs. Hogendobber pursed her melon-tinted lips. "And the nickel makes Monticello appear so big and impersonal when it's quite the reverse, if you'll forgive the pun."

The two women, one in her mid-thirties and the other at an age she refused to disclose, glanced up from the coin to Monticello's west portico, its windows aglow with candlelight from the parlor behind as the last rays of the early spring sun dipped behind the Blue Ridge Mountains.

If the friends had strolled to the front door of Thomas Jefferson's house, centered in the east portico, and then walked to the edge of the lawn, they would have viewed a sea of green, the ever-flattening topography to Richmond and ultimately to the Atlantic Ocean.

Like most born residents of central Virginia's Albemarle County, Harry Haristeen, as she was known, and Miranda Hogendobber could provide a fascinating tour of Monticello. Miranda would admit to being familiar with the estate since before World War II, but that was all she would admit. Over the decades increasing restoration work on the house itself, the dependencies, and gardens, both food and flowering, had progressed to the point where Monticello was the pride of the entire United States. Over a million out-of-town visitors a year drove up the tricky mountain road to pay their eight dollars, board a jitney bus, and swirl around an even twistier road to the top of the hill and thence the red brick structure—each brick fashioned by hand, each hinge pounded out in a smithy, each pane of glass painstakingly blown by a glassmaker, sweating and puffing. Everything about the house suggested individual contribution, imagination, simplicity.

As the tulips braved the quickening western winds, Harry and Mrs. Hogendobber, shivering, walked around the south side of the grounds by the raised terrace. A graceful silver maple anchored the corner where they turned. When they reached the front they paused by the large doors.

"I'm not sure I can stand this." Harry took a deep breath.

"Oh, we have to give the devil his due, or should I say her due?" Mrs. Hogendobber smirked. "She's been preparing for this for six decades. She'll say four, but I've known Mim Sanburne since the earth was cooling."

"Isn't this supposed to be the advantage of living in a small town? We know everyone and everyone knows us?" Harry rubbed her tight shoulder muscles. The temperature had dropped dramatically. "Well, okay, let's brave Mim, the Jefferson expert."

They opened the door, slipping in just as the huge clock

perched over the entrance notched up seven P.M. The day, noted by a weight to the right as one faced the door, read Wednesday. The Great Clock was one of Jefferson's many clever innovations in the design of his home. Even great minds err, however. Jefferson miscalculated the weight and pulley system and ran out of room to register all the days of the week in the hall. Each Friday the day weight slipped through a hole in the floor to the basement, where it marked Friday afternoon and Saturday. The weight then reappeared in the hall on Sunday morning, when the clock was wound.

Harry and Mrs. Hogendobber had arrived for a small gathering of Albemarle's "best," which is to say those whose families had been in Virginia since before the Revolution, those who were glamorous and recently arrived from Hollywood, which Harry dubbed Hollyweird, and those who were rich. Harry fell into the first category, as did Mrs. Hogendobber. As the postmaster— Harry preferred the term postmistress—of the small town of Crozet, Mary Minor Haristeen would never be mistaken for rich.

Marilyn Sanburne, known as Mim or Big Marilyn, clasped and unclasped her perfectly manicured hands. The wife of Crozet's mayor and one of Albemarle's richer citizens, she should have been cool as a cucumber. But a slight case of nerves rattled her as she cast her eyes over the august audience, which included the director of Monticello, the exuberant and fun-loving Oliver Zeve. The head of archaeology, Kimball Haynes, at thirty quite young for such a post, stood at the back of the room.

"Ladies and gentlemen"—Mim cleared her throat while her daughter, Little Marilyn, thirty-two, viewed her mother with a skillful show of rapt attention—"thank you all for taking time out from your busy schedules to gather with us tonight on this important occasion for our beloved Monticello."

"So far so good," Mrs. Hogendobber whispered to Harry.

"With the help of each one of you, we have raised five hundred thousand dollars for the purpose of excavating and ultimately restoring the servant's quarters on Mulberry Row."

As Mim extolled the value of the new project, Harry reflected on the continued duplicity that existed in her part of the world. Servants. Ah, yes, servants—not slaves. Well, no doubt some of them were cherished, beloved even, but the term lent a nice gloss to an ugly reality—Mr. Jefferson's Achilles' heel. He was so tremendously advanced in most ways, perhaps it was churlish to wish he had been more advanced about his source of labor. Then again, Harry wondered what would happen if the shoe were on her foot: Would she be able to refuse a skilled labor force? She would need to house them, clothe them, feed them, and provide medical care. Not that any of that was cheap, and maybe in today's dollars it would add up to more than a living wage. Still, the moral dilemma if one was white, and Harry was white, nagged at her.

Nonetheless, Mim had provided the driving energy behind this project, and its progress was a great personal victory for her. She had also made the largest financial contribution to it. Her adored only son had sped away from Crozet to marry a sophisticated model, a flashy New York lady who happened to be the color of café au lait. For years Mim refused her son entry to the ancestral mansion, but two years ago, thanks to a family crisis and the soft words of people like Miranda Hogendobber, Big Marilyn had consented to let Stafford and Brenda come home for a visit. Confronting one's own prejudices is never easy, especially for a person as prideful as Mim, but she was trying, and her efforts to unearth this portion of Monticello's buried history were commendable.

Harry's eyes swept the room. A few Jefferson descendants were in attendance. His daughters, Martha and Maria, or Patsy and Polly as they were called within the family, had provided T.J. with fifteen grandchildren. Those surviving out of that generation in turn provided forty-eight great-grandchildren. The names of Cary, Coles, Randolph, Eppes, Wayles, Bankhead, Coolidge, Trist, Meikleham, and Carr were carrying various dilutions of Jefferson blood into the twentieth century and, soon, the twenty-first.

Tracing one's bloodlines back to the original red-haired resident of Monticello was a bit like tracing every Thoroughbred's history back to the great sires: Eclipse, 1764; Herod, 1758; and Matchem, 1748.

Nonetheless, people did it. Mim Sanburne herself adamantly believed she was related to the great man on her mother's side through the Wayles/Coolidge line. Given Mim's wealth and imperious temperament, no one challenged her slender claim in the great Virginia game of ancestor worship.

Harry's people had lurched onto Virginia's shores in 1640, but no intertwining with Mr. Jefferson's line was ever claimed. In fact, both her mother's family, the Hepworths, and her father's seemed content to emphasize hard work in the here and the now as opposed to dwelling on a glorious past.

Having fought in every conflict from the French and Indian War to the Gulf crisis, the family believed its contributions would speak for themselves. If anything, her people were guilty of reverse snobbery and Harry daily fought the urge to deflate Mim and her kind.

Once she had overcome her nerves, commanding the spotlight proved so intoxicating to Big Marilyn that she was loath to relinquish it. Finally, Oliver Zeve began the applause, which drowned out Mim's oratory, although she continued to speak until the noise overwhelmed her. She smiled a tight smile, nodded her appreciation—not a hair out of place—and sat down.

Mim's major fund-raising victims, Wesley Randolph and his son Warren, Samson Coles, and Center Berryman, applauded vigorously. Wesley, a direct descendant of Thomas Jefferson through Thomas's beloved older daughter, Martha, had been consistently generous over the decades. Samson Coles, related to Jefferson through his mother, Jane Randolph, gave intermittently, according to the fluctuations of his real estate business.

Wesley Randolph, fighting leukemia for the last year, felt a strong need for continuity, for bloodlines. Being a Thoroughbred breeder, this was probably natural for him. Although the cancer was in remission, the old man knew the sands in the hourglass were spinning through the tiny passage to the bottom. He wanted his nation's past, Jefferson's past, preserved. Perhaps this was Wesley's slender grasp on immortality.

After the ceremony Harry and Mrs. Hogendobber returned to Oliver Zeve's house, where Mrs. Murphy and Tee Tucker, Harry's tiger cat and Welsh corgi respectively, awaited her. Oliver owned a fluffy white Persian, one Archduke Ferdinand, who used to accompany him to Monticello to work. However, children visiting the shrine sometimes pestered Archduke Ferdinand until he spit and scratched them. Although the archduke was within his feline rights, Oliver thought it best to keep him home. This was a great pity, because a cat will see a national shrine with a sharper eye than a human.

Then, too, Archduke Ferdinand believed in a hereditary nobility that was quite at odds with Jefferson's point of view.

As of this moment the archduke was watching Mrs. Murphy from a vantage point at the top of the huge ficus tree in Oliver's living room.

Kimball, who accompanied them, exclaimed, "The female pursues the male. Now, I like that idea."

Mrs. Murphy turned her head. *"Oh, please. Archduke Ferdinand is not my type."*

The Archduke growled, *"Oh, and Paddy is your type? He's as worthless as tits on a boar hog."*

Mrs. Murphy, conversant with her ex-husband's faults, nonetheless defended him. *"We were very young. He's a different cat now."*

"Ha!" the Archduke exploded.

"Come on, Mrs. Murphy, I think you're wearing out your welcome." Harry leaned over and scooped up the reluctant tiger cat who was relishing the archduke's discomfort.

Oliver patted Harry on the back. "Glad you could attend the ceremony."

"*Well, I'm not. We didn't see a single thing!*" Harry's little dog grumbled.

Mrs. Hogendobber slung her ponderous purse over her left forearm and was already out the door.

"A lot of good will come from Mim's check." Kimball smiled as Harry and Mrs. H. climbed into the older woman's pristine Ford Falcon.

Kimball would have occasion to repent that remark.

2

One of the things that fascinated Harry about the four distinct seasons in central Virginia was the quality of the light. With the advent of spring the world glowed yet retained some of the softness of the extraordinary winter light. By the spring equinox the diffuse quality would disappear and brightness would take its place.

Harry often walked to the post office from her farm on Yellow Mountain Road. Her old Superman-blue pickup, nursed throughout the years, needed the rest. The early morning walk awakened her not just to the day but to the marvelous detail of everyday life, to what motorists only glimpse as they speed by, if they notice at all. The swelling of a maple bud, the dormant gray hornet's nest as big as a football, the brazen cries of the ravens, the sweet smell of the earth as the sun warmed her; these precious assaults on the senses kept Harry sane. She never could understand how people could walk with pavement under their feet, smog in their eyes, horns blaring, boom boxes blasting, their daily encounters with other human beings fraught with rudeness if not outright danger.

Considered a failure by her classmates at Smith College, Harry felt no need to judge herself or them by external standards. She had reached a crisis at twenty-seven when she heard her peers murmur incessantly about career moves, leveraged debt, and, if they were married, producing the firstborn. Well, at that time she was married to her high school sweetheart, Pharamond Haristeen, D.V.M., and it was good for a while. She never did figure out if the temptations of those rich, beautiful women on those huge Albemarle County farms had weakened her big blond husband's resolve, or if over time they would have grown apart anyway. They had divorced. The first year was painful, the second year less so, and now, moving into the third year of life without Fair, she felt they were becoming friends. Indeed, she confided to her best girlfriend, Susan Tucker, she liked him more now than when they were married.

Mrs. Hogendobber originally blew smoke rings around Harry's head over the divorce. She finally calmed down and took up the task of matchmaking, trying to set up Harry with Blair Bainbridge, a divinely handsome man who had moved next door to Harry's farm. Blair, however, was on a fashion shoot in Africa these days. As a model he was in hot demand. Blair's absence drew Fair back into Harry's orbit, not that he was ever far from it. Crozet, Virginia, provided her citizens with the never-ending spectacle of love found, love won, love lost, and love found again. Life was never dull.

Maybe that's why Harry didn't feel like a failure, no matter how many potentially embarrassing questions she was asked at those Smith College reunions. Lots of squealing around the daisy chain was how she thought of them. But she jumped out of bed every morning eager for another day, happy with her friends, and contented with her job at the post office. Small though the P.O. was, everybody dropped in to pick up their mail and have a chat, and she enjoyed being at the center of activity.

Mrs. Murphy and Tee Tucker worked there too. Harry couldn't imagine spending eight to ten hours each day away from her animals. They were too much fun.

As she walked down Railroad Avenue, she noticed that Reverend Herb Jones's truck was squatting in front of the Lutheran church with a flat. She walked over.

"No spare," she said to herself.

"*They don't pay him enough money,*" Mrs. Murphy stated with authority.

"*How do you know that, smarty-pants?*" Tucker replied.

"*I've got my ways.*"

"*Your ways? You've been gossiping with Lucy Fur, and all she does is eat communion wafers.*" Tucker said this gleefully, thrilled to prove that Herbie's new second cat desecrated the sacrament.

"*She does not. That's Cazenovia over at St. Paul's. You think every church cat eats communion wafers. Cats don't like bread.*"

"*Oh, yeah? What about Pewter? I've seen her eat a doughnut. 'Course, I've also seen her eat asparagus.*" Tucker marveled at the gargantuan appetite of Market Shiflett's cat. Since she worked in the grocery store next to the post office, the gray animal was constantly indulged. Pewter resembled a furry cannonball with legs.

Mrs. Murphy leapt on the running board of the old stepside truck as Harry continued to examine the flat. "*Doesn't count. That cat will eat anything.*"

"*Bet you she's munching away in the window when we pass the store.*"

"*You think I'm stupid?*" Mrs. Murphy refused the bet. "*But I will bet you that I can climb that tree faster than you can run to it.*" With that she was off and Tucker hesitated for a second, then tore toward the tree as Mrs. Murphy was already halfway up it. "*Told you I'd win.*"

"*You have to back down.*" Tucker waited underneath with her jaws open for full effect, her white fangs gleaming.

"*Oh.*" Mrs. Murphy's eyes widened. Her whiskers swept forward and back. She looked afraid, and the dog puffed up with victory. That fast Mrs. Murphy somersaulted off the tree over the back of the dog and raced to the truck, leaving a furious Tucker barking her head off.

"Tucker, enough." Harry reprimanded her as she continued toward the P.O. while making a mental note to call Herb at home.

"*Get me in trouble! You started it.*" The dog blamed the cat. "*Don't yell at me,*" Tucker whined to Harry.

"*Dogs are dumb. Dumb. Dumb. Dumb,*" the cat sang out, tail hoisted to the vertical, then ran in front of Tucker, who, of course, chased her.

Murphy flipped in the air to land behind Tucker. Harry laughed so hard, she had to stop walking. "You two are crazy."

"*She's crazy. I am perfectly sane.*" Tucker, put out, sat down.

"*Ha.*" Mrs. Murphy again sailed into the air. She was filled with spring, with the hope that always attends that season.

Harry wiped her feet off at the front door of the post office, took the brass keys out of her pocket, and unlocked the door just as Mrs. Hogendobber was performing the same ritual at the back door.

"Well, hello." They both called to each other as they heard the doors close in opposite ends of the small frame building.

"Seven-thirty on the dot," Miranda called out, pleased with her punctuality. Miranda's husband had run the Crozet post office for decades. Upon his death, Harry had won the job.

Never a government employee, Miranda nonetheless had helped George since his first day on the job, August 7, 1952. At first she mourned him, which was natural. Then she said she liked retirement. Finally she admitted she was bored stiff, so Harry politely invited her to drop in from time to time. Harry had no idea that Miranda would relentlessly drop in at seven-thirty each morning. The two discovered over time and a few grumbles that it was quite pleasant to have company.

The mail truck beeped outside. Rob Collier tipped his Orioles baseball cap and tossed the bags through the front door. He delivered mail from the main post office on Seminole Trail in Charlottesville. "Late" was all he said.

"Rob's hardly ever late," Miranda noted. "Well, let's get to it." She opened the canvas bag and began sorting the mail into the slots.

Harry also sifted through the morass of printed material, a tidal wave of temptations to spend money, since half of what she plucked out of her canvas bag were mail-order catalogues.

"Ahhh!" Miranda screamed, withdrawing her hand from a box.

Mrs. Murphy immediately rushed over to inspect the offending box. She placed her paw in and fished around.

"*Got anything?*" Tucker asked.

"*Yeah.*" Mrs. Murphy threw a large spider on the floor. Tucker jumped back as did the two humans, then barked, which the humans did not.

"*Rubber.*" Mrs. Murphy laughed.

"Whose box was that?" Harry wanted to know.

"Ned Tucker's." Mrs. Hogendobber frowned. "This is the work of Danny Tucker. I tell you, young people today have no respect. Why, I could have suffered a heart attack or hyperventilated at the very least. Wait until I get my hands on that boy."

"Boys will be boys." Harry picked up the spider and wiggled it in front of Tucker, who feigned indifference. "Oops, first customer and we're not halfway finished."

Mim Sanburne swept through the door. A pale yellow cashmere shawl completed her Bergdorf-Goodman ensemble.

"Mim, we're behind," Miranda informed her.

"Oh, I know," Mim airily said. "I passed Rob on the way into town. I wanted to know what you thought of the ceremony at Monticello. I know you told me you liked it, but among us girls, what did you really think?"

Harry and Miranda had no need to glance at each other. They knew that Mim needed both praise and gossip. Miranda, better at the latter than the former, was the lead batter. "You made a good speech. I think Oliver Zeve and Kimball Haynes were just thrilled, mind you, thrilled. I did think that Lucinda Coles had her nose out of joint, and I can't for the life of me figure out why."

Seizing the bait like a rockfish, or small-mouthed bass, Mim lowered her voice. "She flounced around. It's not as if I didn't ask her to be on my committee, Miranda. She was my second call. My first was Wesley Randolph. He's just too ancient, poor dear. But when I asked Lucinda, she said she was worn out by good causes even if it did involve sanitized ancestors. I didn't say anything to her husband, but I was tempted. You know how Samson Coles feels. The more times his name gets in the paper, the more people will be drawn to his real estate office, although not much is selling now, is it?"

"We've seen good times and we've seen bad times. This will pass," Miranda sagely advised.

"I'm not so sure," Harry piped up. "I think we'll pay for the eighties for a long, long time."

"Fiddlesticks." Mim dismissed her.

Harry prudently dropped the subject and switched to that of Lucinda Payne Coles, who could claim no special bloodlines other than being married to Samson Coles, descended from Jane Randolph, mother to Thomas Jefferson. "I'm sorry to hear that Lucinda backed off from your wonderful project. It truly is one of the best things you've ever done, Mrs. Sanburne, and you've done so much in our community." Despite Harry's mild antipathy toward the snobbish older woman, she was genuine in her praise.

"You think so? Oh, I am so glad." Big Marilyn clasped her hands together like a child at a birthday party excited over all those unwrapped presents. "I like to work, you know."

Mrs. Hogendobber recalled her Scripture. " 'Each man's work will become manifest; for the Day will disclose it, because it will be revealed with fire, and the fire will test what sort of work each one has done. If the work which any man has built on the foundation survives, he will receive a reward.' " She nodded wisely and then added, "First Corinthians, 3:13–14."

Mim liked the outward appearance of Christianity; the reality of it held far less appeal. She particularly disliked the passage about it being easier for a camel to pass through the eye of a needle than for a rich man to enter the kingdom of heaven. After all, Mim was as rich as Croesus.

"Miranda, your biblical knowledge never ceases to amaze me." Mim wanted to say, "to bore me," but she didn't. "And what an appropriate quotation, considering that Kimball will be digging up the foundations of the servants' quarters. I'm just so excited. There's so much to discover. Oh, I wish I had been alive during the eighteenth century and had known Mr. Jefferson."

"*I'd rather have known his cat,*" Mrs. Murphy chimed in.

"*Jefferson was a hound man,*" Tee Tucker hastened to add.

"*How do you know?*" The tiger cat swished her tail and tiptoed along the ledge under the boxes.

"*Rational. He was a rational man. Intuitive people prefer cats.*"

"*Tucker?*" Mrs. Murphy, astonished at the corgi's insight, could only exclaim her name.

The humans continued on, blithely unaware of the animal conversation which was more interesting than their own.

"Maybe you did know him. Maybe that's why you're so impassioned about Monticello." Harry almost tossed a clutch of mail-order catalogues in the trash, then caught herself.

"You don't believe that stuff," Mrs. Hogendobber pooh-poohed.

"Well, I do, for one." Mim's jaw was set.

"You?" Miranda appeared incredulous.

"Yes, haven't you ever known something without being told it, or walked into a room in Europe and felt sure you'd been there before?"

"I've never been to Europe," came the dry reply.

"Well, Miranda, it's high time. High time, indeed," Mim chided her.

"I backpacked over there my junior year in college." Harry smiled, remembering the kind people she had met in Germany and how excited she was at getting into what was then a communist country, Hungary. Everywhere she traveled, people proved kind and helpful. She used sign language and somehow everyone understood everyone else. She thought to herself that she wanted to return someday, to meet again old friends with whom she continued to correspond.

"How adventuresome," Big Marilyn said dryly. She couldn't imagine walking about, or, worse, sleeping in hostels. When she had sent her daughter to the old countries, Little Marilyn had gone on a grand tour, even though she would have given anything to have backpacked with Harry and her friend Susan Tucker.

"Will you be keeping an eye on the excavations?" Miranda inquired.

"If Kimball will tolerate me. Do you know how they do it? It's so meticulous. They lay out a grid and they photograph everything and also draw it on graph paper—just to be sure. Anyway, they painstakingly sift through these grids and anything, absolutely anything, that can be salvaged is. I mean, potsherds and belt buckles and rusted nails. Oh, I really can't believe I am part of this. You know, life was better then. I am convinced of it."

"Me too." Harry and Miranda sounded like a chorus.

"Ha!" Mrs. Murphy yowled. "Ever notice when humans drift back in history they imagine they were rich and healthy. Get a toothache in the eighteenth century and find out how much you like it." She glared down at Tucker. "How's that for rational?"

"You can be a real sourpuss sometimes. Just because I said that Jefferson preferred dogs to cats."

"But you don't know that."

"Well, have you read any references to cats? Everything that man ever wrote or said is known by rote around here. Not a peep about cats."

"*You think you're so smart. I suppose you happen to have a list of his favorite canines?*"

Tucker sheepishly hung her head. "*Well, no—but Thomas Jefferson liked big bay horses.*"

"*Fine, tell that to Tomahawk and Gin Fizz back home. They'll be overwhelmed with pride.*" Mrs. Murphy referred to Harry's horses, whom the tiger cat liked very much. She stoutly maintained that cats and horses had an affinity for one another.

"Do you think from time to time we might check out the dig?" Harry leaned over the counter.

"I don't see why not," Mim replied. "I'll call Oliver Zeve to make sure it's all right. You young people need to get involved."

"What I wouldn't give to be your age again, Harry." Miranda grew wistful. "My George would have still had hair."

"George had hair?" Harry giggled.

"Don't be smart," Miranda warned, but her voice carried affection.

"Want a man with a head full of hair? Take my husband." Mim drummed her fingers on the table. "Everyone else has."

"Now, Mim."

"Oh, Miranda, I don't even care anymore. All those years that I put a good face on my marriage—I just plain don't care. Takes too much effort. I've decided that I am living for me. Monticello!" With that she waved and left.

"I declare, I do declare." Miranda shook her head. "What got into her?"

"*Who* got into her?"

"Harry, that's rude."

"I know." Harry tried to keep her lip buttoned around Mrs. Hogendobber, but sometimes things slipped out. "Something's happened. Or maybe she was like this when she was a child."

"She was never a child." Miranda's voice dropped. "Her mother made her attend the public schools and Mim wanted to go away to Miss Porter's. She wore outfits every day that would have bankrupted an average man, and this was at the end of the Depression and the beginning of World War Two, remember. By the time we got to Crozet High, there were two classes of students. Marilyn, and the rest of us."

"Well—any ideas?"

"Not a one. Not a single one."

"*I've got an idea*," Tucker barked. The humans looked at her. "*Spring fever.*"

3

Fair Haristeen, a blond giant, studied the image on the small TV screen. He was taking an ultrasound of an unborn foal in the broodmare barn at Wesley Randolph's estate, Eagle's Rest. Using sound waves to scan the position and health of the fetus was becoming increasingly valuable to veterinarian and breeder alike. This practice, relatively new in human medicine, was even more recent in the equine world. Fair centered the image he wanted, pressed a small button, and the machine spat out the picture of the incubating foal.

"Here he is, Wesley." Fair handed the printout to the breeder.

Wesley Randolph, his son Warren, and Warren's diminutive but gorgeous wife, Ansley, hung on the veterinarian's every word.

"Well, this colt's healthy in the womb. Let's keep our fingers crossed."

Wesley handed the picture to Warren and folded his arms across his thin chest. "This mare's in foal to Mr. Prospector. I want this baby!"

"You can't do much better than to breed to Claiborne Farm's stock. It's hard to make a mistake when you work with such good people."

Warren, ever eager to please his domineering father, said, "Dad wants blinding speed married to endurance. I think this might be our best foal yet."

"Dark Windows—she was a great one," Wesley reminisced. "Damn filly put her leg over a divider when we were hauling her to Churchill Downs. Got a big knee and never raced after that. She was a special filly—like Ruffian."

"I'll never forget that day. When Ruffian took that moment's hesitation in her stride—it was a bird or something on the track that made her pause—and shattered the sesamoid bones in her fetlock. God, it was awful." Warren recalled the fateful day when Thoroughbred racing lost one of its greatest fillies to date, and perhaps one of the greatest runners ever seen, during her match race with Kentucky Derby–winner Foolish Pleasure at Belmont Park.

"Too game to stay down after her leg was set. Broke it a second time coming out of the anesthesia and only would have done it a third time if they'd tried to set the break again. It was the best thing to do, to save her any more pain, putting her down." Fair added his veterinary expertise to their memory of the black filly's trauma.

Wesley shook his head. "Damn shame. Damn shame. Would've made one hell of a brood mare. Her owners might even have tried to breed her to that colt she was racing against when it happened. Foolish Pleasure. Better racehorse than sire, though, now that we've seen his get."

"I'll never forget how the general public reacted to Ruffian's death. The beautiful black filly with the giant heart—she gave two hundred percent, every time. When they put her down, the whole country mourned, even people who had never paid attention to racing. It was a sad, sad day." Ansley was visibly moved by this recollection. She changed the subject.

"You got some wonderful stakes winners out of Dark Windows. She was a remarkable filly too." Ansley praised her father-in-law. He needed attention like a fish needs water.

"A few, a few." He smiled.

"I'll be back around next week. Call me if anything comes up." Fair headed for his truck and his next call.

Wesley followed him out of the barn while his son and daughter-in-law stayed inside. Behind the track, over a small knoll, was a lake. Wesley thought he'd go sit there later with his binoculars and bird-watch. Eased his mind, bird-watching. "Want some unsolicited advice?"

"Looks like I'm going to get it whether I want it or not." Fair opened the back of his customized truck-bed, which housed his veterinary supplies.

"Win back Mary Minor Haristeen."

Fair placed his equipment in the truck. "Since when are you playing Cupid?"

Wesley, gruff, bellowed, "Cupid? That little fat fellow with the quiver, bow, and arrows, and the little wings on his shoulders? Him? Give me some time and I'll be a real angel—unless I'm going downtown in the afterlife."

"Wesley, only the good die young. You'll be here forever." Fair liked teasing him.

"Ha! I believe you're right." Wesley appreciated references to his wild youth. "I'm old. I can say what I want when I want." He breathed in. " 'Course, I always did. The advantage of being stinking rich. So I'm telling you, go get that little girl you so foolishly, and I emphasize foolishly, cast aside. She's the winning ticket."

"Do I look that bad?" Fair wondered, the teasing fading out of him.

"You look like a ship without a rudder's what you look like. And running around with Boom Boom Craycroft. . . . big tits and not an easy keeper." Wesley likened Boom Boom to a horse that was expensive to feed, hard to put weight on, and often the victim of a breakdown of one sort or another. This couldn't have been a truer comparison, except in Boom Boom's case the weight referred to carats. She could gobble up more precious stones than a pasha. "Women like Boom Boom love to drive a man crazy. Harry's got some fire and some brains."

Fair rubbed the blond stubble on his cheek. He'd known Wesley all his life and liked the man. For all his arrogance and bluntness, Wesley was loyal, called it like he saw it, and was truly generous, a trait he passed on to Warren. "I think about it sometimes—and I think she'd have to be crazy to take me back."

Wesley put his arm around Fair's broad shoulders. "Listen to me. There's not a man out there who hasn't strayed off the reservation. And most of us feel rotten about it. Diana looked the other way when I did it. We were a team. The team came first, and once I grew up some I didn't need those—ah, adventures. I came clean. I told her what I'd done. I asked her to forgive me. Screwing around hurts a woman in ways we don't understand. Diana was in my corner two hundred percent. Heart like Ruffian. Always giving. Sometimes I wonder how a little poontang could get me off the track, make me hurt the person I loved most in this world." He paused. "Women are more forgiving than we are. Kinder too. Maybe we need them to civilize us, son. You think about what I'm saying."

Fair closed the lid over his equipment. "You aren't the first person to tell me to win back Harry. Mrs. Hogendobber works me over every now and then."

"Miranda. I can hear her now." Wesley laughed.

"I'm not saying you're wrong. Harry was a good wife and I was a fool, but how do you get over that guilt? I don't want to be with a woman and feel like a heel, even if I was."

"That's where love works its miracles. Love's not about sex, although that's where we all start. Diana taught me about love. It's as gossamer as a spiderweb and just as strong. Winds don't blow down a web. Ever watch 'em?" His hand moved back and forth. "That woman knew me, knew my every fault, and she loved me for me. And I learned to love her for her. The only thing that pleases me about my condition is when I get to the other side, I'm going to see my girl."

"Wesley, you look better than I've seen you look in the last eight months."

"Remission. Damn grateful for it. I do feel good. Only thing that gets me down is the stock market." He shivered to make his point. "And Warren. I don't know if he's strong enough to take over. He and Ansley don't pull together. Worries me."

"Maybe you ought to talk to them like you talked to me."

Wesley blinked beneath his bushy gray eyebrows. "I try. Warren evades me. Ansley's polite and listens, but it's in one ear, out t'other." He shook his head. "I've spent my whole life developing bloodlines, yet I can hardly talk to my own blood."

Fair leaned against the big truck. "I think a lot of people feel that way . . . and I don't have any answers." He checked his watch. "I'm due at Brookhill Farm. You call me about that mare and—and I promise to think about what you said."

Fair stepped into the truck, turned the ignition, and slowly traveled down the winding drive lined with linden trees. He waved, and Wesley waved back.

4

The old Ford truck chugged up Monticello Mountain. A light drizzle kept Harry alert at the wheel, for this road could be treacherous no matter what the weather. She wondered how the colonists had hauled up and down this mountain using wagons pulled by horses, or perhaps oxen, with no disc brakes. Unpaved during Thomas Jefferson's time, the road must have turned into a quagmire in the rains and a killer sheet of ice in the winter.

Susan Tucker fastened her seat belt.

"Think my driving's that bad?"

"No." Susan ran her thumb under the belt. "I should have done this when we left Crozet."

"Oh, I forgot to tell you. Mrs. H. pitched a major hissy when she reached into your mailbox and touched that rubber spider that Danny must have stuck in there. Mrs. Murphy pulled it out onto the floor finally."

"Did she throw her hands in the air?" Susan innocently inquired.

"You bet."

"A deep, throaty scream."

"Moderate, I'd say. The dog barked."

Susan smiled a Cheshire smile. "Wish I'd been there."

Harry turned to glance at her best friend. "Susan—"

"Keep your eyes on the road."

"Oh, yeah. Susan, did you put that spider in the mailbox?"

"Uh-huh."

"Now, why would you want to go and do a thing like that?"

"Devil made me do it."

Harry laughed. Every now and then Susan would do something, disrupt something, and you never knew when or where. She'd been that way since they first met in kindergarten. Harry hoped she'd never change.

The parking lot wasn't as full as usual for a weekend. Harry and Susan rode in the jitney up the mountain, which became more fog-enshrouded with every rising foot. By the time they reached the Big House, as locals called it, they could barely see their hands in front of their faces.

"Think Kimball will be out there?" Susan asked.

"One way to find out." Harry walked down to the south side of the house, picking up the straight road that was called Mulberry Row. Here the work of the plantation was carried out in a smithy as well as in eighteen other buildings dedicated to the various crafts: carpentry, nail making, weaving, and possibly even harness making and repair. Those buildings vanished over the decades after Jefferson's death when, a quarter of a million dollars in debt—roughly two and a half million dollars today—his heirs were forced to sell the place he loved.

Slave quarters also were located along Mulberry Row. Like

the other buildings, these were usually constructed of logs; sometimes even the chimneys were made of logs, which would occasionally catch fire, so that the whole building was engulfed in flames within minutes. The bucket brigade was the only means of firefighting.

As Harry and Susan walked through the fog, their feet squished in the moist earth.

"If you feel a descent, you know we've keeled over into the food garden." Harry stopped for a moment.

"We can stay on the path and go slow. Harry, Kimball isn't going to be out here in this muck."

But he was. Wearing a green oilskin Barbour coat, a necessity in this part of the world, big Wellies on his feet, and a water-repellent baseball hat on his head, Kimball resembled any other Virginia gentleman or gentlewoman on a misty day.

"Kimball!" Harry called out.

"A fine, soft day," he jubilantly replied. "Come closer, I can't see who's with you."

"Me," Susan answered.

"Ah, I'm in for a double treat." He walked up to greet them.

"How can you work in this?" Susan wondered.

"I can't, really, but I can walk around and think. This place had to function independently of the world, in a sense. I mean, it was its own little world, so I try to put myself back in time and imagine what was needed, when and why. It helps me understand why some of these buildings and the gardens were placed as they are. Of course, the people working under the boardwalks—that's what I call the terraces—had a better deal, I think. Would you two damsels like a stroll?"

"Love it." Harry beamed.

"Kimball, how did you come to archaeology?" Susan asked. Most men Kimball's age graduating from an Ivy League college were investment bankers, commodities brokers, stockbrokers, or numbers crunchers.

"I liked to play in the dirt as a child. This seemed a natural progression." He grinned.

"It wasn't one of those quirks of fate?" Harry wiped a raindrop off her nose.

"Actually, it was. I was studying history at Brown and I had this glorious professor, Del Kolve, and he kept saying, 'Go back to the physical reality, go back to the physical reality.' So I happened to notice a yellow sheet of paper on the department bulletin board —isn't it odd that I can still see the color of the flyer?—announcing a dig in Colonial Williamsburg. I never imagined that. You see, I always thought that archaeology meant you had to be digging up columns in Rome, that sort of thing. So I came down for the summer and I was hooked. Hooked on the period too. Come on, let me show you something."

He led them to his office at the back of the attractive gift shop. They shook off the water before entering and hung their coats on the wooden pegs on the wall.

"Cramped," Susan observed. "Is this temporary?"

He shook his head. "We can't go about building anything, you know, and some of what has been added over the years— well, the damage has been done. Anyway, I'm in the field most of the time, so this suffices, and I've also stashed some books in the second floor of the Big House, so I've a bit more room than it appears. Here, look at this." He reached into a pile of horseshoes on the floor and handed an enormous shoe to Harry.

She carefully turned the rusted artifact over in her hands. "A toe grab. I can't make out if there were any grabs on the back, but possibly. This horse had to do a lot of pulling. Draft horse, of course."

"Okay, look at this one." He handed her another.

Harry and Susan exclaimed at this shoe. Lighter, made for a smaller horse, it had a bar across the heel area, joining the two arms of the shoe.

"What do you think, Susan?" Harry placed the shoe in her friend's hands.

"We need Steve O'Grady." Susan referred to an equine vet in the county, an expert on hoof development and problems and strategies to overcome those problems. He was a colleague of Fair Haristeen, whose specialty was the equine reproductive system. "But I'd say this belonged to a fancy horse, a riding horse, anyway. It's a bar shoe . . ."

"Because the horse had a problem. Navicular maybe." Harry suggested a degenerative condition of the navicular bone, just behind the main bone of the foot, the coffin bone, often requiring special shoeing to alleviate the discomfort.

"Perhaps, but the blacksmith decided to give the animal more striking area in the back. He moved the point of contact behind the normal heel area." Kimball placed his hand on his desk, using his fingers as the front of the hoof and his palm as the back and showed how this particular shoe could alter the point of impact.

"I didn't know you rode horses." Harry admired his detective work on the horseshoe.

"I don't. They're too big for me." Kimball smiled.

"So how'd you know this? I mean, most of the people who do ride don't care that much about shoeing. They don't learn anything." Susan, a devout horsewoman, meaning she believed in knowing all phases of equine care and not just hopping on the animal's back, was intensely curious.

"I asked an expert." He held out his palms.

"Who?"

"Dr. O'Grady." Kimball laughed. "But still, I had to call around, dig in the libraries, and find out if horseshoeing has changed that much over the centuries. See, that's what I love about this kind of work. Well, it's not work, it's a magical kind of living in the past and the present at the same time. I mean, the past is ever informing the present, ever with us, for good or for ill. To work at what you love—a heaping up of joys."

"It is wonderful," Harry agreed. "I don't mean to imply that what I do is anything as exalted as your own profession, but I like my job, I like the people, and most of all, I love Crozet."

"We're the lucky ones." Susan understood only too well the toll unhappiness takes on people. She had watched her father drag himself to a job he hated. She had watched him dry up. He worried so much about providing for his family that he forgot to be with his family. She could have done with fewer things and more dad. "Being a housewife and mother may not seem like much, but it's what I wanted to do. I wouldn't trade a minute of those early years when the kids were tiny. Not one second."

"Then they're the lucky ones," Harry said.

Kimball, content in agreement, pulled open a drawer and plucked out a bit of china with a grayish background and a bit of faded blue design. "Found this last week in what I'm calling Cabin Four." He flipped it over, a light number showing on its reverse side. "I've been keeping it here to play with it. What was this bit of good china doing in a slave cabin? Was it already broken? Did the inhabitant of the little cabin break it herself—we know who lived in Cabin Four—and take it out of the Big House to cover up the misdeed? Or did the servants, forgive the euphemism, go straight to the master, confess the breakage, and get awarded the pieces? Then again, what if the slave just plain took it to have something pretty to look at, to own something that a rich white person would own, to feel for a moment part of the ruling class instead of the ruled? So many questions. So many questions."

"I've got one you can answer." Susan put her hand up.

"Shoot."

"Where's the bathroom?"

5

Larry Johnson intended to retire on his sixty-fifth birthday. He
even took in a partner, Hayden McIntire, M.D., three years before
his retirement age so Crozet's residents might become accustomed
to a new doctor. At seventy-one, Larry continued to see patients.
He said it was because he couldn't face the boredom of not working. Like most doctors trained in another era, he was one of the
community, not some highly trained outsider come to impose his
superior knowledge on the natives. Larry also knew the secrets:
who had abortions before they were legal, what upstanding citizens once had syphilis, who drank on the sly, what families carried a disposition to alcoholism, diabetes, insanity, even violence.
He'd seen so much over the years that he trusted his instincts. He
didn't much care if it made scientific sense, and one of the lessons
Larry learned is that there really is such a thing as bad blood.

"You ever read these magazines before you put them in our slot?" The good doctor perused the *New England Journal of Medicine* he'd just pulled out of his mailbox.

Harry laughed. "I'm tempted, but I haven't got the time."

"We need a thirty-six-hour day." He removed his porkpie hat and shook off the raindrops. "We're all trying to do too much in too little time. It's all about money. It'll kill us. It'll kill America."

"You know, I was up at Monticello yesterday with Susan—"

Larry interrupted her. "She's due for a checkup."

"I'll be sure to tell her."

"I'm sorry, I didn't mean to interrupt." He shrugged his shoulders in resignation. "But if I don't say what's on my mind when it pops into my head, I forget. Whoosh, it's gone." He paused. "I'm getting old."

"*Ha,*" Mrs. Murphy declared. "*Harry's not even thirty-five and she forgets stuff all the time. Like the truck keys.*"

"*She only did that once.*" Tucker defended her mother.

"You two are bright-eyed and bushy-tailed." Larry knelt down to pet Tucker while Mrs. Murphy prowled on the counter. "Now, what were you telling me about Monticello?"

"Oh, we drove up to see how the Mulberry Row dig is coming along. Well, you were talking about money and I guess I was thinking how Jefferson died in hideous debt and how an intense concern with money seems to be part of who and what we are as a nation. I mean, look at Light-Horse Harry Lee. Lost his shirt, poor fellow."

"Yes, yes, and being the hero, mind you, the beau ideal of the Revolutionary War. Left us a wonderful son."

"Yankees don't think so." The corner of Harry's mouth turned upward.

"I liken Yankees to hemorrhoids . . . they slip down and hang around. Once they see how good life is around here, they don't go back. Ah, well, different people, different ways. I'll have to think about what you said—about money—which I am spending at a rapid clip as Hayden and I expand the office. Since Jefferson never stopped building, I can't decide if he possessed great stamina or great foolishness. I find the whole process nerve-racking.''

Lucinda Payne Coles opened the door, stepped inside, then turned around and shook her umbrella out over the stoop. She closed the door and leaned the dripping object next to it. ''Low pressure. All up and down the East Coast. The Weather Channel says we've got two more days of this. Well, my tulips will be grateful but my floors will not.''

''Read where you and others''—Larry cocked his head in the direction of Harry—''attended Big Marilyn's do.''

''Which one? She has so many.'' Lucinda's frosted pageboy shimmied as she tossed her head. Little droplets spun off the blunt ends of her hair.

''Monticello.''

''Oh, yes. Samson was in Richmond, so he couldn't attend. Ansley and Warren Randolph were there. Wesley too. Carys, Eppes, oh, I can't remember.'' Lucinda displayed little enthusiasm for the topic.

Miranda puffed in the back door. ''I've got lunch.'' She saw Larry and Lucinda. ''Hello there. I'm buying water wings if this keeps up.''

''You've already got angel wings.'' Larry beamed.

''Hush, now.'' Mrs. H. blushed.

''What'd she do?'' Mrs. Murphy wanted to know.

''What'd she do?'' Lucinda echoed the cat.

''She's been visiting the terminally ill children down at the hospital and she's organized her church folks to join in.''

''Larry, I do it because I want to be useful. Don't fuss over me.'' Mrs. Hogendobber meant it, but being human, she also enjoyed the approval.

A loud meow at the back diverted the slightly overweight

lady's attention, and she opened the door. A wet, definitely over-weight Pewter straggled in. The cat and human oddly mirrored each other.

"*Fat mouse! Fat mouse!*" Mrs. Murphy taunted the gray cat.

"What does that man do over there? Force-feed her?" Lucinda stared at the cat.

"*It's all her own work.*" Mrs. Murphy's meow carried her dry wit.

"*Shut up. If I had as many acres to run around as you do, I'd be slender too,*" Pewter spat out.

"*You'd sit in a trance in front of the refrigerator door, waiting for it to open. Open Sesame.*" The tiger's voice was musical.

"*You two are being ugly.*" Tucker padded over to the front door and sniffed Lucinda's umbrella. She smelled the faint hint of oregano on the handle. Lucinda must have been cooking before she headed to the P.O.

Lucinda sauntered over to her postbox, opened it with the round brass key, and pulled out envelopes. She sorted them at the ledge along one side of the front room. The flutter of mail hitting the wastebasket drew Larry's attention.

Mrs. Hogendobber also observed Lucinda's filing system. "You're smart, Lucinda. Don't even open the envelopes."

"I have enough bills to pay. I'm not going to answer a form letter appealing for money. If a charity wants money, they can damn well ask me in person." She gathered up what was left of her mail, picked up her umbrella, and pushed open the door. She forgot to say good-bye.

"She's not doing too good, is she?" Harry blurted out.

Larry shook his head. "I can sometimes heal the body. Can't do much for the heart."

"She's not the first woman whose husband has had an affair. I ought to know." Harry watched Lucinda Coles open her car door, hop in while holding the umbrella out, then shake the umbrella, throw it over the back seat of the Grand Wagoneer, slam the door, and drive off.

"She's from another generation, Mary Minor Haristeen. 'Let marriage be held in honor among all, and let the marriage bed be undefiled; for God will judge the immoral and adulterous.' Hebrews 13:4.''

"I'm going to let you girls fight this one out." Larry slapped his porkpie hat back on his head and left. What he knew that he didn't tell them was with whom Samson Coles was carrying on his affair.

"Miranda, are you implying that my generation does not honor the vows of marriage? That just frosts me!" Harry shoved a mail cart. It clattered across the floor, the canvas swaying a bit.

"I said no such thing, Missy. Now, you just calm yourself. She's older than you by a good fifteen years. A woman in middle age has fears you can't understand but you will—you will. Lucinda Payne was raised to be an ornament. She lives in a world of charities, luncheons with the girls, and black-tie fund-raisers. You work. You expect to work, and if you marry again your life isn't going to change but so much. Of course you honored your marriage vows. The pity is that Fair Haristeen didn't."

"I kept remembering what Susan used to say about Ned. He'd make her so mad she'd say, 'Divorce, never. Murder, yes.' There were a few vile moments when I wonder how I managed not to kill Fair. They passed. I don't think he could help it. We married too young."

"Too young? You married Fair the summer he graduated from Auburn Veterinary College. In my day you would have been an old maid at that age. You were twenty-four, as I recall."

"Memory like a wizard." Harry smiled, then sighed. "I guess I know what you mean about Lucinda. It's sad really."

"For her it's a tragedy."

"*Humans take marriage too seriously.*" Pewter licked her paw and began smoothing down her fur. "*My mother used to say, 'Don't worry about tomcats. There's one coming around every corner like a streetcar.*' "

"*Your mother lived to a ripe old age, so she must have known something,*" Mrs. Murphy recalled.

"Maybe Lucinda should go to a therapist or something," Harry thought out loud.

"She ought to try her minister first." Mrs. Hogendobber walked over to the window and watched the huge raindrops splash on the brick walkway.

"You know what I can't figure?" Harry joined her.

"What?"

"Who in the world would want Samson Coles?"

6

The steady rain played havoc with Kimball's work. His staff stretched a bright blue plastic sheet onto four poles which helped keep off the worst of the rain, but it trickled down into the earthen pit as they had cut down a good five feet.

A young German woman, Heike Holtz, carefully brushed away the soil. Her knees were mud-soaked, her hands also, but she didn't care. She'd come to America specifically to work with Kimball Haynes. Her long-range goal was to return to Germany and begin similar excavations and reconstruction at Sans Souci. Since this beautiful palace was in Potsdam, in the former East Germany, she suffered few illusions about raising money or generating interest for the task. But she was sure that sooner or later her countrymen would try to save what they could before it fell down about their ears. As an archaeologist, she deplored the Russians' callous disregard for the majority of the fabulous architecture under their control. At least they had preserved the Kremlin. As to how they treated her people, she wisely kept silent. Americans, so fortunate for the most part, would never understand that kind of systematic oppression.

"Heike, go on and take a break. You've been in this chill since early this morning." Kimball's light blue eyes radiated sympathy.

She spoke in an engaging accent, musical and very seductive. She didn't need the accent. Heike was a knockout. "No, no, Professor Haynes. I'm learning too much to leave."

He patted her on the back. "You're going to be here for a year, and Heike, if the gods smile down upon me, I think I can get you an appointment at the university so you can stay longer than that. You're good."

She bent her head closer to her task, too shy to accept the praise by looking him in the eye. "Thank you."

"Go on, take a break."

"This will sound bizarre," she accented the bi heavily, "but I feel something."

"I'm sure you do," he laughed. "Chilblains."

He stepped out of the hearth where Heike was working. The fireplace had been one of the wooden fireplaces which caught fire. Charred bits studded one layer of earth, and they were just now getting below that. Whoever cleaned up after the fire removed as much ash as they could. Two other students worked also.

Heike pawed with her hands, carefully but with remarkable intensity. "Professor."

Kimball returned to her and quickly knelt down. He was working alongside her now. Each of them laboring with swift precision.

"Mein Gott!" Heike exclaimed.

"We got more than we bargained for, kiddo." Kimball wiped his hand across his jaw, forgetting the mud. He called to

Sylvia and Joe, his other two students working in this section.
"Joe, go on up and get Oliver Zeve."

Joe and Sylvia peered at the find.

"Joe?"

"Yes, Professor."

"Not a word to anyone, you hear? That's an order," he
remarked to the others as Joe ran toward the Big House.

"The last thing we want is for the papers to get hold of this
before we've had time to prepare a statement."

7

"Why wasn't I told first?" Mim jammed the receiver of the telephone back on the cradle. She put it back cockeyed so the device beeped. Furious, she smashed the receiver on correctly.

Her husband, Jim Sanburne, mayor of Crozet, six feet four and close to three hundred pounds, was possessed of an easygoing nature. He needed it with Mim. "Now, darlin', if you will reflect upon the delicate nature of Kimball Haynes's discovery, you will realize you had to be the second call, not the first."

Her voice lowered. "Think I was the second call?"

"Of course. You've been the driving force behind the Mulberry Row restorations."

"And I can tell you I'm enduring jealous huffs from Wesley Randolph, Samson Coles, and Center Berryman too. Wait until they find out about this—actually, I'd better call them all." She paced into the library, her soft suede slippers barely making any sound at all.

"Wesley Randolph? The only reason you and Wesley cross swords is that he wants to run the show. Just arrange a few photo opportunities for his son. Warren is running for state senate this fall."

"How do you know that?"

"I'm not the mayor of Crozet for nothing." His broad smile revealed huge square teeth. Despite his size and girth, Jim exuded a rough-and-tumble masculine appeal. "Now, sit down here by the fire and let's review the facts."

Mim dropped into the inviting wing chair covered in an expensive MacLeod tartan fabric. Her navy cashmere robe piped in camel harmonized perfectly. Mim's aesthetic sensibilities were highly developed. She was one hundred eighty degrees from Harry, who had little sense of interior design but could create a working farm environment in a heartbeat. It all came down to what was important to each of them.

Mim folded her hands. "As I understand it from Oliver, Kimball Haynes and his staff have found a skeleton in the plot he's calling Cabin Four. They've worked most of the day and into the night to uncover the remains. Sheriff Shaw is there too, although I can't see that it matters at this point."

Jim crossed his feet on the hassock. "Do they have any idea when the person died or even what sex the body is?"

"No. Well, yes, they're sure it's a man, and Oliver said an odd thing—he said the man must have been rich. I was so shocked, I didn't pursue it. We're to keep a tight lip. Guess I'd better wait to call the others but, oh, Jim, they'll be so put out, and I can't lie. This could cost contributions. You know how easy it is for that crew to get their noses out of joint."

"Loose lips sink ships." Jim, who had been a skinny eighteen-year-old fighting in Korea, remembered one of the phrases World War II veterans used to say. He tried to forget some of the other things he'd experienced in that conflict, but he vowed never to be so cold again in his entire life. As soon as the frosts came, Jim would break out his wired socks with the batteries attached.

"Jim, he's been dead for a hundred seventy-five to two hundred years. You're as bad as Oliver. Who cares if the press knows? It will bring more attention to the project and possibly even more money from new contributors. And if I can present this find to the Randolphs, Coleses, and Berrymans as an historic event, perhaps all will yet be well."

"Well, sugar, how he died might affect that."

8

Bright yellow tape cordoned off Cabin Four. Rick Shaw puffed on a cigarette. As sheriff of Albemarle County, he'd viewed more than his share of corpses: shotgun suicides, drownings, car accident after car accident, killings by knife, pistol, poison, ax—even a piano bench. People used whatever came to hand. However, this was the oldest body he'd studied.

His assistant, Cynthia Cooper, recently promoted to deputy, scribbled in her small notebook, her ball-point pen zipping over the blue lines. A photographer for the department snapped photos.

Rick, sensitive to the situation, arrived at six-thirty P.M., well after five P.M., when Monticello closed its doors for the night, allowing for the departure of straggling tourists. Oliver Zeve, arms folded across his chest, chatted with Heike Holtz. Kimball looked up with relief when Harry and Mrs. Hogendobber walked down Mulberry Row. Mrs. Murphy and Tucker trailed behind.

Oliver excused himself from Heike and walked over to Kimball. "What in the hell are they doing here?"

Kimball, nonplused, stuck his hands in his back pockets. "We're going to be here some time, people need to be fed."

"We're perfectly capable of calling a catering service." Oliver snapped.

"Yes," Kimball smoothly replied, "and they're perfectly capable of babbling this all over town as well as picking up the phone to The Washington Post or, God forbid, The Enquirer. Harry and Miranda can keep their mouths shut. Remember Donny Ensign?"

Kimball referred to an incident four years past when Mrs. Hogendobber served as secretary for the Friends of Restoration. She happened one night to check Donny Ensign's books. She always did George's books and she enjoyed the task. As treasurer, Donny was entrusted with the money, obviously. Mrs. H. had a hunch, she never did say what set her off, but she quickly realized that Mr. Ensign was cooking the books. She immediately notified Oliver and the situation was discreetly handled. Donny resigned and he continued to pay back a portion of what he had siphoned off until the sum, $4,559.12, was cleared. In exchange, no one reported him to Rick Shaw nor was his name destroyed in the community.

"Yes." Oliver drew out the word even as he smiled and trotted over to the two women. "Here, let me relieve you lovely ladies of this burden. I can't tell you how grateful I am that you're bringing us food. Kimball thinks of everything, doesn't he?"

Rick felt a rub against his leg. He beheld Mrs. Murphy. "What are you doing here?"

"Offering my services." She sat on the toe of the sheriff's shoe.

"Harry and Mrs. Hogendobber, what a surprise." A hint of sarcasm entered Rick's voice.

"Don't sound so enthusiastic, Sheriff." Miranda chided him.

"We aren't going to interfere in your case. We're merely offering nourishment."

Cynthia hopped out of the site. "Bless you." She scratched Tucker's head and motioned for Harry to follow her. Tucker followed also. "What do you make of this?"

Harry peered down at the skeleton lying facedown in the dirt. The back of his skull was crushed. Coins lay where his pockets must have been, and a heavy, crested ring still circled the bones of the third finger on his left hand. Tatters of fabric clung to the bones, a piece of heavily embroidered waistcoat. A bit more of the outer coat remained; the now-faded color must have once been a rich teal. The brass buttons were intact, as were the buckles on his shoes, again quite ornate.

"Mrs. H., come here," Harry called.

"I don't want to see it." Mrs. Hogendobber busily served sandwiches and cold chicken.

"It's not so bad. You've seen far worse at the butcher shop." Harry deviled her.

"That isn't funny."

Mrs. Murphy and Tucker shouldn't have been in the site, but so much was going on, no one really noticed.

"*Smell anything?*" The cat asked her companion.

"*Old smoke. A cold trail—this fellow's been dead too long for scenting.*" The corgi wrinkled her black nose.

Mrs. Murphy pawed a piece of the skull. "*Pretty weird.*"

"*What?*"

"*Well, the guy's had his head bashed, but someone put this big piece of skull back in place.*"

"Yeah." The dog was fascinated with the bones, but then, any bones fascinated Tucker.

"Hey, hey, you two, get out of here!" Harry commanded.

Tucker obediently left, but Mrs. Murphy didn't. She batted at the skull. "*Look, you dummies.*"

"She thinks everything is a toy." Harry scooped up the cat.

"I do not!" Mrs. Murphy puffed her tail in fury, squirmed out of Harry's arms, and jumped back to the ground to pat the skull piece again.

"I'm sorry, Cynthia, I'll put her back in the truck. Wonder if I could put her in Monticello? The truck's a ways off."

"She'll shred Mr. Jefferson's bedspread," Tucker warned. "If it has historic value, she can't wait to get her claws in it. Think what she'll say to Pewter, 'I tore up Thomas Jefferson's silk bedspread.' If it has tassles on it, forget it. There won't be any left."

"And you wouldn't chew the furniture legs?" the cat shot back.

"Not if they give me one of those bones, I won't." The corgi laughed.

"Stop being an ass, Tucker, and help me get these two nincompoops to really look at what they're seeing."

Tucker hopped into the dig and walked over to the skeleton. She sniffed the large skull fragment, a triangular-shaped piece perhaps four inches across at the base.

"What's going on here?" Harry, frustrated, tried to reach for the cat and the dog simultaneously. They both evaded her with ease.

Cynthia, trained as an observer, watched the cat jump sideways as though playing and return each time to repeatedly touch the same piece of the skull. Each time she would twist away from an exasperated Harry. "Wait a minute, Harry." She hunkered down in the earth, still soft from the rains. "Sheriff, come back here a minute, will you?" Cynthia stared at Mrs. Murphy, who sat opposite her and stared back, relieved that someone got the message.

"That Miranda makes mean chicken." He waved his drumstick like a baton. "What could tear me away from fried chicken, cold greens, potato salad, and did you see the apple pie?"

"There'd better be some left when I get out of here." Cynthia called up to Mrs. Hogendobber. "Mrs. H., save some for me."

"Of course I will, Cynthia. Even though you're our new deputy, you're still a growing girl." Miranda, who'd known

Cynthia since the day she was born, was delighted that she'd received the promotion.

"Okay, what is it?" Rick eyed the cat, who eyed him back.

For good measure, Mrs. Murphy stuck out one mighty claw and tapped the triangular skull piece.

He did notice. "Strange."

Mrs. Murphy sighed. *"No shit, Sherlock."*

Cynthia whispered, "Oliver's deflected us a bit, you know what I mean? We should have noticed the odd shape of this piece, but his mouth hasn't stopped running."

Rick grunted in affirmation. They'd confer about Oliver later. Rick took his index finger and nudged the piece of bone.

Harry, mesmerized, knelt down on the other side of the skeleton. "Are you surprised that there isn't more damage to the cranium?"

Rick blinked for a moment. He had been lost in thought. "Uh, no, actually. Harry, this man was killed with one whacking-good blow to the back of the head with perhaps an ax or a wedge or some heavy iron tool. The break is too clean for a blunt instrument—but the large piece here is strange. I wonder if the back of an ax could do that?"

"Do what?" Harry asked.

"The large, roughly triangular piece may have been placed back in the skull," Cynthia answered for him, "or at the time of death it could have been partially attached, but the shape of the break is what's unusual. Usually when someone takes a crack to the head, it's more of a mess—pulverized."

"Thank, you, thank you, thank you!" Mrs. Murphy crowed. *"Not that I'll get any credit."*

"I'd settle for some of Mrs. Hogendobber's chicken instead of thanks," Tucker admitted.

"How can you be sure, especially with a body—or what's left of it—this old, that one person killed him? Couldn't it have been two or three?" Harry's curiosity was rising with each moment.

"I can't be sure of anything, Harry." Rick was quizzical. "But I see what you're getting at. One person could have pinned him while the second struck the blow."

Tucker, now completely focused on Mrs. H.'s chicken, saucily yipped, *"So the killer scooped the brains out and fed them to the dog."*

"Gross, Tucker." Mrs. Murphy flattened her ears for an instant. *"You've come up with worse."*

"Tucker, go on up to Mrs. Hogendobber and beg. You're just making noise. I need to think," the cat complained.

"Mrs. Hogendobber has a heart of steel when it comes to handing out goodies."

"Bet Kimball doesn't."

"Good idea." The dog followed Mrs. Murphy's advice.

Harry grimaced slightly at the thought. "A neat killer. Those old fireplaces were big enough to stand in. One smash and that was it." Her mind raced. "But whoever did it had to dig deep into the fireplace, arrange the body, cover it up. It must have taken all night."

"Why night?" Cynthia questioned.

"These are slave quarters. Wouldn't the occupant be working during the day?"

"Harry, you have a point there." Rick stood up, his knees creaking. "Kimball, who lived here?"

"Before the fire it was Medley Orion. We don't know too much about her except that she was perhaps twenty at the time of the fire," came the swift reply.

"After the fire?" Rick continued his questioning.

"We're not sure if Medley came back to this site to live. We know she was still, uh, employed here because her name shows up in the records," Kimball said.

"Know what she did, her line of work?" Cynthia asked.

"Apparently a seamstress of some talent." Kimball joined them in the pit, but only after being suckered out of a tidbit by Tucker. "Ladies who came to visit often left behind fabrics for

Medley to transform. We have mention of her skills in letters visitors wrote back to Mr. Jefferson."

"Was Jefferson paid?" Rick innocently asked.

"Good heavens, no!" Oliver called from the food baskets. "Medley would have been paid directly either in coin or in kind."

"Slaves could earn money independently of their masters?" Cynthia inquired. This notion shed new light on the workings of a plantation.

"Yes, indeed, they could and that coin was coveted. A few very industrious or very fortunate slaves bought their way to freedom. Not Medley, I'm afraid, but she seems to have had quite a good life," Oliver said soothingly.

"Any idea when this fellow bit the dust, literally?" Harry couldn't resist.

Kimball leaned down and picked up a few of the coins. "Don't worry, we've photographed everything, from numerous different angles and heights, drawn the initial positions on our grids—everything is in order." Kimball reassured everyone that the investigation was not jeopardizing the progress of his archaeological work. "The nearest date we can come to is 1803. That's the date of a coin in the dead man's pocket."

"The Louisiana Purchase," Mrs. Hogendobber sang out.

"Maybe this guy was opposed to the purchase. A political enemy of T.J.'s," Rick jested.

"Don't even think that. Not for an instant. And especially not on hallowed ground." Oliver sucked in his breath. "Whatever happened here, I am certain that Mr. Jefferson had no idea, no idea whatsoever. Why else would the murderer have gone to such pains to dispose of the body?"

"Most murderers do," Cynthia explained.

"Sorry, Oliver, I didn't mean to imply . . ." Rick apologized.

"Quite all right, quite all right." Oliver smiled again. "We're just wrought up, you see, because this April thirteenth will be the two hundred fiftieth anniversary of Mr. Jefferson's birth, and we don't want anything to spoil it, to bleed attention away from his achievements and vision. Something like this could, well, imbalance the celebration, shall we say?"

"I understand." Rick did too. "But I am elected sheriff to keep the peace, if you will, and the peace was disturbed here, perhaps in 1803 or thereabouts. We'll carbon-date the body, of course. Oliver, it's my responsibility to solve this crime. When it was committed is irrelevant to me."

"Surely, no one is in danger today. They're all"—he swept his hand outward—"dead."

"I'd like to think the architect of this place would not find me remiss in my duties." Rick's jaw was set.

A chill shivered down Harry's spine. She knew the sheriff to be a strong man, a dedicated public servant, but when he said that, when he acknowledged his debt to the man who wrote the Declaration of Independence, the man who elevated America's sense of architecture and the living arts, the man who endured the presidency and advanced the nation, she recognized that she, too, all of them, in fact, even Heike, were tied to the redheaded man born in 1743. But if they really thought about it, they owed honor to all who came before them, all who tried to improve conditions.

As Oliver Zeve could concoct no glib reply, he returned to the food baskets. But he muttered under his breath, "Murder at Monticello. Good God."

9

Riding back to Crozet in Mrs. Hogendobber's Falcon, Mrs. Murphy asleep in her lap, Tucker zonked on the back seat, Harry's mind churned like an electric blender.

"I'm waiting."

"Huh?"

"Harry, I've known you since little on up. What's going on?" Mrs. Hogendobber tapped her temple.

"Oliver. He ought to work for a public relations firm. You know, the kind of people who can make Sherman's March look like trespassing."

"I can understand his position. I'm not sure it's as bad as he thinks, but then, I'm not responsible for making sure there's enough money to pay the bills for putting a new roof on Monticello either. He's got to think of image."

"Okay, a man was murdered on Mulberry Row. He had money in his pockets, I wonder how much by today's standards. . . ."

"Kimball will figure that out."

"He wore a big gold ring. Not too shabby. What in the hell was he doing in Medley Orion's cabin?"

"Picking up a dress for his wife."

"Or worse." Harry frowned. "That's why Oliver is so fussy. Another slave wouldn't have a brocaded vest or a gold ring on his finger. The victim was white and well-to-do. If I think of that, so will others when this gets reported. . . ."

"Soon, I should think."

"Mim will fry." Harry couldn't help smiling.

"She already knows," Mrs. Hogendobber informed her.

"Damn, you know everything."

"No. Everybody." Mrs. H. smiled. "Kimball mentioned it to me when I said, sotto voce, mind you, that Mim must be told."

"Oh." Harry's voice trailed off, then picked up steam. "Well, what I'm getting at is if I think about white men in slaves' cabins, so will other people. Not that the victim was carrying on with Medley, but who knows? People jump to conclusions. And that will bring up the whole Sally Hemings mess again. Poor Thomas Jefferson. They won't let that rest."

"His so-called affair with the beautiful slave, Sally, was invented by the Federalists. They loathed and feared him. The last thing they wanted was Jefferson as president. Not a word of truth in it."

Harry, not so sure, moved on. "Funny, isn't it? A man was killed one hundred ninety years ago, if 1803 was the year, and we're disturbed by it. It's like an echo from the past."

"Yes, it is." Miranda's brow furrowed. "It is because for one human being to murder another is a terrible, terrible thing. Whoever killed that man knew him. Was it hate, love, love turned to hate, fear of some punishment? What could have driven someone to kill this man, who must have been powerful? I can tell you one thing.''

"What?''

"The devil's deep claws tore at both of them, killer and killed.''

10

"I told Marilyn Sanburne no good would come of her Mulberry Row project." Disgusted, Wesley Randolph slapped the morning newspaper down on the dining table. The coffee rolled precariously in the Royal Doulton cup. He had just finished reading the account of the find, obviously influenced by Oliver Zeve's statement. "Let sleeping dogs lie," he growled.

"Don't exercise yourself," Ansley drawled. Her father-in-law's recitation of pedigree had amused her when Warren was courting her, but now, after eighteen years of marriage, she could recite them as well as Wesley could. Her two sons, Breton and Stuart, aged fourteen and sixteen, knew them also. She was tired of his addiction to the past.

Warren picked up the paper his father had slapped down and read the article.

"Big Daddy, a skeleton was unearthed in a slave's cabin. Probably more dust than bone. Oliver Zeve has issued what I think is a sensible report to the press. Interest will swell for a day or two and then subside. If you're so worked up about it, go see the mortal coil for yourself." Ansley half smiled when she stole the description from Hamlet.

Warren still responded to Ansley's beauty, but he detected her disaffection for him. Not that she overtly showed it. Far too discreet for that, Ansley had settled into the rigors of propriety as regarded her husband. "You take history too lightly, Ansley." This statement should please the old man, he thought.

"Dearest, I don't take it at all. History is dead. I'm alive today and I'd like to be alive tomorrow—and I think our family's contributions to Monticello are good for today. Let's keep Albemarle's greatest attraction growing."

Wesley shook his head. "This archaeology in the servants' quarters"—he puffed out his ruddy cheeks—"stirs up the pot. The next thing you know, some council of Negroes—"

"African Americans," Ansley purred.

"I don't give a damn what you call them!" Wesley raised his voice. "I still think 'colored' is the most polite term yet! Whatever you want to call them, they'll get themselves organized, they'll camp in a room underneath a terrace at Monticello, and before you know it, all of Jefferson's achievements will be nullified. They'll declare that they did them."

"Well, they certainly performed most of the work. Didn't he have something like close to two hundred slaves on his various properties?" Ansley challenged her father-in-law while Warren held his breath.

"Depends on the year," Wesley waffled. "And how do you know that?"

"Mim's lecture."

"Mim Sanburne is the biggest pain in the ass this county has suffered since the seventeenth century. Before this is all over, Jefferson will be besmirched, dragged in the dirt, made out to be a scoundrel. Mim and her Mulberry Row. Leave the servant question alone! Damn, I wish I'd never written her a check."

"But it's part of history." Ansley was positively enjoying this.

"Whose history?"

"America's history, Big Daddy."

"Oh, balls!" He glared at her, then laughed. She was the only person in his life who dared stand up to him—and he loved it.

Warren, worry turning to boredom, drank his orange juice and turned to the sports page.

"Have you any opinion?" Wesley's bushy eyebrows knitted together.

"Huh?"

"Warren, Big Daddy wants to know what you think about this body at Monticello stuff."

"I—uh—what can I say? Hopefully this discovery will lead us to a better understanding of life at Monticello, the rigors and pressures of the time."

"We aren't your constituency. I'm your father! Do you mean to tell me a corpse in the garden, or wherever the hell it was"— he grabbed at the front page to double-check—"in Cabin Four, can be anything but bad news?"

Warren, long accustomed to his father's fluctuating opinion of his abilities and behavior, drawled, "Well, Poppa, it sure was bad news for the corpse."

Ansley heard Warren's Porsche 911 roar out of the garage. She knew Big Daddy was at the stable. She picked up the phone and dialed.

"Lucinda," she said with surprise before continuing, "have you read the paper?"

"Yes. The queen of Crozet has her tit in the wringer this time," Lucinda pungently put it.

"Really, Lulu, it's not that bad."

"It's not that good."

"I never will understand why being related to T.J. by blood, no matter how thinned out, is so important," said Ansley, who understood only too well.

Lucinda drew deeply on her cheroot. "What else have our respective husbands got? I don't think Warren's half so besotted with the blood stuff, but I mean, Samson makes money from it. Look at his real estate ads in *The New York Times*. He wiggles in his relation to Jefferson every way he can. 'See Jefferson country from his umpty-ump descendant.' " She took another drag. "I suppose he has to make a living somehow. Samson isn't the brightest man God ever put on earth."

"One of the best-looking though," Ansley said. "You always did have the best taste in men, Lulu."

"Thank you—at this point it doesn't matter. I'm a golf widow."

"Count your blessings, sister. I wish I could get Warren interested in something besides his so-called practice. Big Daddy keeps him busy reading real estate contracts, lawsuits, syndication proposals—I'd go blind."

"Boom time for lawyers," Lulu said. "The economy is in the toilet, everybody's blaming everybody else, and the lawsuits are flying like confetti. Too bad we don't use that energy to work together."

"Well, right now, honey, we've got a tempest in a teapot. Every old biddy and crank scholar in central Virginia will pass out opinions like gas."

"Mim wanted attention for her project." Lulu didn't hide her sarcasm. She'd grown tired of taking orders from Mim over the years.

"She's got it now." Ansley walked over to the sink and began to run the water. "What papers did you read this morning?"

"Local and Richmond."

"Lulu, did the Richmond paper say anything about the cause of death?"

"No."

"Or who it is? The *Courier* was pretty sparse on the facts."

"Richmond too. They probably don't know anything, but we'll find out as soon as they do, I guess. You know, I've half a mind to call Mim and just bitch her out." Lucinda stubbed out her cheroot.

"You won't." An edge crept into Ansley's voice.

A long silence followed. "I know—but maybe someday I will."

"I want to be there. I'd pay good money to see the queen get her comeuppance."

"As she does a lot of business with both of our husbands, about all I can do is dream—you too." Lucinda bid Ansley good-bye, hung up the phone, and reflected for a moment on her precarious position.

Mim Sanburne firmly held the reins of Crozet social life. She paid back old scores, never forgot a slight, but by the same token, she never forgot a favor. Mim could use her wealth as a crowbar, a carrot, or even as a wreath to toss over settled differences—settled in her favor. Mim never minded spending money. What she minded was not getting her way.

11

The gray of dawn yielded to rose, which surrendered to the sun. The horses fed and turned out, the stalls mucked, and the opossum fed his treat of sweet feed and molasses, Harry happily trotted inside to make herself breakfast.

Harry started each morning with a cup of coffee, moved her great-grandmother's cast-iron iron away from the back door—her security measure—jogged to the barn, and got the morning chores out of the way. Then she usually indulged herself in hot oatmeal or fried eggs or sometimes even fluffy pancakes drenched in Lyon's Golden Syrup from England.

The possum, Simon, a bright and curious fellow, would sometimes venture close to the house, but she could never coax him inside. She marveled at how Mrs. Murphy and Tucker accepted the gray creature. Mrs. Murphy displayed an unusual tolerance for other animals. Often it took Tucker a bit longer.

"All right, you guys. You already had breakfast, but if you're real good to me, I might, I just might, fry an egg for you."

"*I'll be good, I'll be good.*" Tucker wagged her rear end since she had no tail.

"*If you'd learn to play hard to get, you'd have more dignity.*" Mrs. Murphy jumped onto a kitchen chair.

"*I don't want dignity, I want eggs.*"

Harry pulled out the number five skillet, old and heavy cast iron. She rubbed it with Crisco after every washing to help preserve its longevity. She dropped a chunk of butter into the middle of the pan, which she placed on low heat. She fetched a mixing bowl and cracked open four eggs, diced a bit of cheese, some olives, and even threw in a few capers. As the skillet reached the correct temperature, the butter beginning to sizzle, she placed the eggs in it. She folded them over once, turned it off, and quickly put the eggs on a big plate. Then she divided the booty.

Tucker ate out of her ceramic bowl, which Harry placed on the floor.

Mrs. Murphy's bowl, "Upholstery Destroyer" emblazoned on its side, sat on the table. She ate with Harry.

"*This is delicious.*" The cat licked her lips.

"*Yeah.*" Tucker could barely speak, she was eating so fast.

The tiger cat enjoyed the olives. Seeing her pick them out and eat them first made Harry laugh every time she did it.

"You're too much, Mrs. Murphy."

"*I like to savor my food,*" the cat rejoined.

"*Got any more?*" Tucker sat down beside her empty bowl, her neck craned upward, should any morsel fall off the table.

"*You're as bad as Pewter.*"

"*Thanks.*"

"You two are chatty this morning." Harry cheerfully drank her second cup of coffee as she thought out loud to the animals. "Guess being up at Monticello has made me think. What would

we be doing if this were 1803? I suppose, getting up at the same time and feeding the horses wouldn't have changed. Mucking stalls hasn't changed. But someone would have had to stoke a fire in an open hearth. If a person lived alone, it would have been a lot harder than today. How could anyone perform her chores, cook for herself, butcher meat—well, I guess you could have bought your meat, but only a day at a time unless you had a smokehouse or the meat was salted down. Think about it. And you two, no worm medicine or rabies shots, but then, no vaccines for me either. Clothing must have been itchy and heavy in the winter. Summer wouldn't have been too bad because the women could have worn linen dresses. Men could take off their shirts. And I resent that. If I can't take off my shirt, I don't see why they can." She carried on this conversation with her two friends as they hung on every word and every mouthful of egg that was shoveled into Harry's mouth. "You two aren't really listening, are you?"

"*We are!*"

"Here." Harry handed Mrs. Murphy an extra olive and gave Tucker a nibble of egg. "I don't know why I spoil you all. Look at how much you've had to eat this morning."

"*We love you, Mom.*" Mrs. Murphy emitted a major purr.

Harry scratched the tiger cat's ears with one hand and reached down to perform the same service for Tucker. "I don't know what I'd do without you two. It's so easy to love animals and so hard to love people. Men anyway. Your mom is striking out with the opposite sex."

"*No, you're not.*" Tucker consoled her and was very frustrated that Harry couldn't understand. "*You haven't met the right guy yet.*"

"*I still think Blair is the right guy.*" Mrs. Murphy put in her two cents.

"*Blair is off on some modeling job. Anyway, I don't think Mom needs a man who's that pretty.*"

"*What do you mean by that?*" the cat asked.

"*She needs the outdoor type. You know, a lineman or a farmer or a vet.*"

Mrs. Murphy thought about that as Harry rubbed her ears. *"You still miss Fair?"*

"Sometimes I do," the little dog replied honestly. *"He's big and strong, he could do a lot of farmwork, and he could protect Mom if something went wrong, you know."*

"She can protect herself." True as this was, the cat also worried occasionally about Harry being alone. No matter how you cut it, most men were stronger than most women. It was good to have a man around the farm.

"Yeah—but still," came the weak reply.

Harry stood up and took the dishes to the porcelain sink. She meticulously washed each one, dried them, and put them away. Coming home to dirty dishes in the sink drove Harry to despair. She turned off the coffeepot. "Looks like a Mary Minor Haristeen day." This meant it was sunny.

She paused for a moment to watch the horses groom one another. Then her mind drifted off for a moment and she spoke to her animal friends. "How could Medley Orion live with a body under her fireplace—if she knew? She may not have known a single thing, but if she did, how could she make her coffee, eat her breakfast, and go about her business—knowing? I don't think I could do it."

"If you were scared enough, you could," Mrs. Murphy wisely noted.

12

The old walnut countertop gleamed as Mrs. Hogendobber polished it with beeswax. Harry, using a stiff broom, swept out the back of the post office. The clock read two-thirty, a time for chores and a lull between people stopping in at lunchtime and on their way home from work. Mrs. Murphy, sound asleep in the mail cart, flicked her tail and cackled, dreaming of mice. Tucker lay on her side on the floor, made shiny from the decades of treading feet. She, too, was out cold.

"Hey, did I tell you that Fair asked me to the movies next week?" Harry attacked a corner.

"He wants you back."

"Mrs. H., you've been saying that since the day we separated. He sure didn't want me back when he was cavorting with Boom Boom Craycroft, she of the pontoon bosoms."

Mrs. Hogendobber waved her dust cloth over her head like a small flag. "A passing fancy. He had to get it out of his system."

"And so he did," came Harry's clipped reply.

"You must forgive and forget."

"Easy for you to say. It wasn't your husband."

"You've got me there."

Harry, surprised that Mrs. Hogendobber agreed with her so readily, paused a moment, her broom held off the ground. A knock at the back door brought the broom down again.

"Me," Market Shiflett called.

"Hi." Harry opened the door and Market, who owned the grocery store next door, came in, followed by Pewter.

"Haven't seen you today. What have you been up to?" Miranda kept polishing.

"This and that and who shot the cat." He smiled, looked down at Pewter, and apologized. "Sorry, Pewter."

Pewter, far too subtle to push the dog awake, flicked her fat little tail over Tucker's nose until the dog opened her eyes.

"I was dead to the world." Tucker blinked.

"Where's herself?" Pewter inquired.

"Mail cart, last time I saw her."

A gleam in her eye betrayed Pewter's intentions. She walked to the mail cart and halted. She scrunched down and wiggled her rear end, then with a mighty leap she catapulted herself into the mail cart. A holy howl attended this action. Had Mrs. Murphy not been a cat in the prime of her life, had she been, say, an older feline, she surely would have lost her bladder control at such a rude awakening. A great hissing and spitting filled the bin, which was beginning to roll just a bit.

"Now, that's enough." Market hurried over to the mail cart, where he beheld the spectacle of his beloved cat, claws out, rolling around the heavy canvas bag with Mrs. Murphy in the same posture. Tufts of fur floated in the air.

Harry dashed over. "I don't know what gets into these two.

They're either the best of friends or like Muslims versus Christians." Harry reached in to separate the two, receiving a scratch for her concern.

"*You fat pig!*" Mrs. Murphy bellowed.

"*Scaredy-cat, scaredy-cat,*" Pewter taunted.

"You ought not to make light of religious differences," Mrs. Hogendobber, faithful to the Church of the Holy Light, admonished Harry. "Cats aren't religious anyway."

"*Who says?*" Two little heads popped over the side of the cart.

This moment of peace lasted a millisecond before they dropped back in the cart and rolled over each other again.

Harry laughed. "I'm not reaching in there. They're bound to get tired of this sooner or later."

"Guess you're right." Market thought the hissing was awful. "I wanted to tell you I've got a special on cat food today. You want me to save you a case?"

"Oh, thanks. How about a nice, fresh chicken too."

"Harry, don't tell me you're going to cook a chicken?" Mrs. Hogendobber held her heart as though this was too much. "What's this world coming to?"

"Speaking of that, how about them finding a body up at Monticello?"

Before either woman could respond, Samson Coles blustered in the front door, so Market repeated his question.

Samson shook his leonine head. "Damn shame. I guarantee you that by tomorrow the television crews will be camped out at Mulberry Row and this unfortunate event will be blown out of all proportion."

"Well, I don't know. It does seem strange that a body would be buried under a cabin. If the death was, uh, legitimate, wouldn't the body be in a cemetery? Even slaves had cemeteries." Market said.

Both Harry and Mrs. H. knew the body didn't belong to a slave. So did Mrs. Murphy, who said so loudly to Pewter. They had exhausted themselves and lay together in the bottom of the cart.

"*How do you know that?*" the gray cat wondered.

"*Because I saw the corpse,*" Mrs. Murphy bragged. "*The back of the skull was caved in like a big triangle.*"

"*You aren't supposed to give out the details,*" Tucker chided.

"*Oh, bull, Tucker. The humans can't understand a word I'm saying. They think Pewter and I are in here meowing and you're over there whining at us.*"

"*Then get out of the cart so we can all talk,*" Tucker called up. "*I saw the body too, Pewter.*"

"*Did you now?*" Pewter grasped the edge of the cart with her chubby paws and peered over the side.

"*Don't listen to him. All he wanted was Mrs. Hogendobber's chicken.*"

"*I saw the body as plain as you did, bigmouth. It was lying facedown under the hearth, maybe two feet under where the floor must have been at the time of death. So there.*"

"*You don't say!*" Pewter's eyes widened into big black balls. "*A murder!*"

"Good point, Market." Samson cupped his chin in his hand for a moment. "Why would a body be buried—what did they say, under the fireplace?"

"*Hearth,*" the dog called out, but they didn't pay attention.

"Maybe the man died in the winter and they couldn't dig up the frozen ground. But the ground wouldn't be frozen under the hearth, would it?" Market threw this out. He didn't necessarily believe it.

"I thought the people at that time had mausoleums, or something like mausoleums anyway, dug into rock where they'd store bodies until the spring thaws. Then they'd dig the grave," Miranda added.

"Did they really?" Market shivered at the thought of bodies being stacked up somewhere like cordwood.

"Well, they were frozen, I suspect," Miranda answered.

"Gruesome." Samson grimaced. "Has Lucinda come in today?"

"No," Harry answered.

"I can't keep track of my own wife's schedule." His affable tone belied the truth—he didn't want Lucinda tailing him. He liked to know her whereabouts because he didn't want her to know his.

"What'd she think of the Monticello discovery?" Mrs. Hogendobber asked politely.

"Lucinda? Oh, she didn't think it would be positive publicity, but she can't see that it has anything to do with us today." Samson tapped the countertop, admiring Mrs. Hogendobber's handiwork. "I hear Wesley Randolph doesn't like this one bit. He's overreacting, but then, he always does. Lulu's interest in history isn't as deep as mine," he sighed, "but then, she doesn't have my connections to Mr. Jefferson. A direct line from his mother, Jane, you know, and then, of course, on my father's side I'm related to Dolley Madison. Naturally, my interest is keen and Lulu's people were new. I don't think they got over here until the 1780s." He stopped for a second, realized he was unrolling his pedigree to people who could recite it as well as he could. "I digress. Anyway, Lulu reads a good amount. Like me, she'll be glad when this episode is behind us. We don't want the wrong kind of attention here in Albemarle County."

"Samson, we're talking about almost two centuries between then and now." Market chuckled.

"The past lives on in Virginia, the mother of presidents." Samson beamed a Chamber of Commerce smile. He couldn't have known how true was that pronouncement, or how tragic.

As Samson left, Danny Tucker and Stuart and Breton Randolph boisterously rushed into the post office. Danny looked like his mother, Susan. Stuart and Breton also strongly resembled their mother, Ansley. Every mouth jabbered simultaneously as the teenage boys reached into the mailboxes.

"Eii—" Danny let out a yell and jerked back his hand.

"Mousetrap?" Stuart's sandy eyebrows shot upward.

"No such luck," Danny sarcastically replied.

Breton peeped in the mailbox. "Gross." He reached in and pulled out a fake eyeball.

Harry whispered to Mrs. Hogendobber. "Did you do that?"

"I won't say I did and I won't say I didn't."

"Harry, did you put this eyeball in the mailbox?" Danny, accompanied by his buddies, leaned on the counter.

"No."

"*Mother's not fond of rubber eyeballs,*" Mrs. Murphy disclosed.

Reverend Herb Jones walked into the hubbub. "A prayer meeting?"

"Hi, Rev." Stuart adored the pastor.

"Stuart, address Reverend Jones properly," Miranda ordered.

"I'm sorry. Hello, Reverend Jones."

"I always do what Mrs. H. tells me." Reverend Jones put his arm around Stuart's shoulders. "I'd be scared not to."

"Now, Herbie . . ." Miranda began to protest.

Breton, a sweet kid, chimed in. "Mrs. Hogendobber, we all do what you tell us because you're usually right."

"Well . . ." A long, breathless pause followed. "I'm glad you all realize that." She exploded in laughter and everyone joined in, including the animals.

"Harry." Herb put his hand on the counter as he laughed. "Thanks for calling me the other day about my flat tire. Fixed it— now just got another one."

"Oh, no," Harry responded.

"You need a new truck," Market Shiflett suggested.

"Yes, but I need the money, and so far—"

"No pennies from heaven." Harry couldn't resist. This set everyone off again.

"Reverend Jones, I'll help you change your tire," Danny volunteered.

"Me too." Breton jumped in.

"Me three." Stuart was already out the door.

As they bounded out, Danny flashed his rubber eye back at Harry, who made a cross with her fingers.

"Good kids. I miss Courtney. She's loving her first year at college. Still hard to let go." Market, a widower, sighed.

"You did a wonderful job with that girl," Miranda praised him.

"*Too bad you didn't do better with Lardguts,*" Mrs. Murphy called out.

"Thanks," Market replied.

"*I resent that,*" Pewter growled.

"Well, back to the salt mines." Market paused. "Pewter?"

"*I'm coming. I'm not staying here to be insulted by a—a string bean.*"

"*Oh, Pewter, where's your sense of humor?*" Tucker padded over to her and gave her a nudge.

"*How do you stand her?*" Pewter liked the corgi.

"*I tear up her catnip toys when she's not looking.*"

Pewter, at Market's heels, gaily sprang out the door as she thought of a catnip sock shredded to bits.

Harry and Miranda returned to their chores.

"You are the culprit. I know it." Harry giggled.

"An eye for an eye . . ." Mrs. H. quoted her Old Testament.

"Yeah, but it was Susan who put the rubber spider in the box, not Danny."

"Oh, darn." The older woman clapped her hands together. She thought, "Well, help me get even."

Harry tipped back her head and roared. Miranda laughed too, as did Mrs. Murphy and Tucker, whose laughter sounded like little snorts.

13

Samson Coles's bright red Grand Wagoneer stuck out like a sore thumb on the country roads. The big eight-cylinder engine harnessed to a four-wheel drive was essential to his business. He'd hauled prospective buyers through fields, forded rivers, and rumbled down old farm roads. The roominess inside pleased people, and he was disappointed when Jeep discontinued the boxy vehicle to replace it with a smaller, sleeker model, the Grand Cherokee. The Grand Cherokee suffered from a Roman nose and too much resemblance to the rest of the Jeep line, he thought. The wonderful thing about the old Wagoneer was that no other car looked like it. Samson craved standing apart from the crowd.

However, he didn't much crave it today. He parked behind a huge bank barn, pulled on his galoshes, and stomped through

624 RITA MAE BROWN & SNEAKY PIE BROWN

over a mile of slush to Blair Bainbridge's farm next to Harry's place.

He knew Harry was keeping an eye on the farm in Blair's absence. The great thing about a small town is that most people know your schedule. It was also the bad thing about a small town.

Harry usually sorted Blair's mail at work and put it in an international packet so he'd get it within a few days unless Blair happened to be on a shoot in a very remote area or in a political hot spot. She'd stop by Blair's Foxden Farm on her way home from work.

The squish of mud dragged him down. Hard to run in galoshes, and Samson was in a hurry. He had a two o'clock appointment at Midale. That listing, once the property sold, meant a healthy commission for Samson. He needed the money. He was listing the estate at $2.2 million. He thought Midale would sell between $1.5 and $1.8 million. He'd work that out with his client later. The important thing was to get the listing. He'd learned a long time ago that in the real estate business if you give the client a high price, you usually win the listing. Occasionally, he would sell a property for the listing price. More often than not, the place would sell for twenty to thirty percent less and he covered himself by elaborately explaining that the market had dipped, interest rates varied, whatever soothed the waters. After all, he didn't want a reputation for being an unrealistic agent.

He checked his watch. Eleven-fifteen. Damn, not much time. Two o'clock would roll around before he knew it.

The lovely symmetrical frame house came into view. He hurried on. At the back screen door he lifted the lid of the old milk box. The key dangled inside on a small brass hook.

He put the key in the door, but it was already unlocked. He opened and closed the door behind him.

Ansley rushed out from the living room, where she'd been waiting. "Darling." She threw her arms around his neck.

"Where'd you park your car?" Samson asked.

"In the barn, out of sight. Now, is that a romantic thing to say?"

He squeezed her tight. "I'll show you my romantic side in other ways, sweet thing."

14

The County of Albemarle wasted little money on the offices of the sheriff's department. Presumably they saw fit to waste the taxpayers' money in other ways. Rick Shaw felt fortunate that he and his field staff had bulletproof vests and new cars at regular intervals. The walls, once painted 1950s grade-school-green, had at least graduated to real-estate-white. So much for improvements. Spring hadn't really sprung. Rick was grateful. Every spring the incidence of drunkenness, domestic violence, and general silliness rose. Cynthia Cooper attributed it to spring fever. Rick attributed it to the inherent vile qualities of the human animal.

"Now, see here, Sheriff, is this really necessary?" Oliver Zeve's lips narrowed to a slit. A note of authority and class superiority slithered into his deep voice.

Rick, long accustomed to people of higher social position trying to browbeat him, politely but firmly said, "Yes."

During this discussion Deputy Cooper marched back and forth, occasionally catching Rick's eye. She knew her boss really wanted to pick up the director of Monticello by the seat of his tailored pants and toss him out the front door. Rick's expression changed when he spoke to Kimball Haynes. "Mr. Haynes, have you found anything else?"

"I'm pretty sure that the body was buried before the fire. There's no ash or cinder below the line where we discovered him —uh, the corpse."

"Couldn't the fire have been set to cover the evidence?" Rick doodled on his desk pad.

"Actually, Sheriff, that would have jeopardized the murderer if the murderer lived at Cabin Four or worked on the estate. You see, these fires were woefully common. Once the fire burned itself out and people could walk in the ruins, they would shovel up the cold ash and scrape the ground back down to the hard earth underneath."

"Why?" The sheriff stopped doodling and made notes.

"Courtesy more than anything. Every time it rained, who-ever had lived in the cabin would smell that smoke and ash. Also, what if after the fire they used the opportunity to enlarge the cabin or to make some improvement? You'd want to start on a good, flat surface. . . ."

"True."

"Burning the cabin would only have served the purpose of making it appear the victim had died in the fire. Given the obvi-ous status of the victim, that would be peculiar, wouldn't it? Why would a well-to-do white man be in a slave's cabin fire? Unless he was asleep and died of smoke inhalation, and you know what that would mean," Kimball offered.

Oliver's temper flared. "Kimball, I vigorously protest this specious line of reasoning. This is all conjecture. Very imaginative and certainly makes a good story but has little to do with the facts at hand. Namely, a skeleton, presumably almost two hundred years old, is found underneath the hearth. Spinning theories doesn't get us anywhere. We need facts."

Rick nodded gravely, then stung quickly. "That's exactly why the remains must go to the lab in Washington."

Caught, Oliver fought back. "As director of Monticello, I protest the removal of any object, animate or inanimate, human or otherwise, found on the grounds of Mr. Jefferson's home."

Kimball, exasperated, couldn't restrain his barbed humor. "Oliver, what are we going to do with a skeleton?"

"Give it a decent burial," Oliver replied through clenched teeth.

"Mr. Zeve, your protest is duly noted, but these remains are going to Washington and hopefully they'll be able to give us some boundaries concerning time, if nothing else, sex, and race," the sheriff stated flatly.

"We know it's a man." Oliver crossed his arms over his chest.

"What if it's a woman in a man's clothing? What if a slave had stolen an expensive vest—"

"Waistcoat," Oliver corrected him.

"Well, what if? What if she wanted to make a dress out of it or something? Now, I am not in the habit of theorizing, and I can't accept anything until I have a lab report. Do I think the skeleton is that of a male? Yes, I do. The pelvis in a male skeleton is smaller than that in a female. I've seen enough of them to know that. But as for the rest of it—I don't know much."

"Then may I ask you to please not theorize about the possibility of the victim's dying by smoke inhalation? Let's wait on that too."

"Oliver, that was my, uh, moment of imagination." Kimball

shouldered the blame since Oliver wanted to assign it. "Miscegenation is an old word and an ugly word, but it would have been the word and the law at the time. I understand your squeamishness."

"Squeamish?"

"Okay, wrong word. It's a delicate issue. But I return to my original scenario, and being an archaeologist, I have some authority here. In the process of preparing the burned cabin for a new building, the killer would run the very real risk that a spade would turn up the corpse. That is one strong reason against a fire having been set to cover up the evidence. The other, far more convincing data is that the layer of charred earth—again, scraped back as best they could—was roughly two feet above the corpse, allowing for the slight difference between the actual floor of the cabin and the floor of the hearth."

"Is there any record of this cabin burning?" Rick listened to the slow glide as the soft lead crossed the white page. He found it a consoling sound.

"If the murder occurred in 1803, as it would appear, Jefferson was in his first term as president. We have no record in his own hand of such an event, and he was a compulsive record-keeper. He'd even count out beans, nails—just compulsive. So, if he were home at the time, or visiting home from Washington, we can be certain he would have made a note of it. I'm sorry to say that the overseer lacked Mr. Jefferson's meticulous habits," Kimball replied.

"Unless the overseer was in on it and wanted no attention called to the cabin." Rick stopped writing.

An edge crept into Oliver's tone. "I guess after years on the job you would naturally think like that, Sheriff."

"Mr. Zeve, I understand that at this moment we seem to be in an adversarial position. In as plain a language as I can find: A man was murdered and it was covered up, forgive the pun, for nigh onto two hundred years. I am not the expert that you are on the end of the eighteenth century, the beginning of the nineteenth, but I would hazard a guess that our forefathers were more civilized and less prone to violence than we are today. I would especially think this is true of anyone who would have worked at Monticello, or visited the estate. So, whoever killed our victim had a powerful motive.''

15

In the parking lot the cool, clammy evening air caused Kimball to shudder. Oliver added to his discomfort.

"You weren't helpful in there." Oliver tried to sound more disappointed than angry.

"Usually you and I work easily together. Your position is far more political than mine, Oliver, and I appreciate that. It's not enough for you to be an outstanding scholar on Thomas Jefferson, you've got to play footsie with the people who write the checks, the National Historic Trust in D.C., and the descendants of the man. I'm sure I've left out other pressures."

"The people and artisans who work at Monticello." Oliver supplied this omission.

"Of course," Kimball agreed. "My one concern is discovering as much as we can about Mulberry Row and preserving the architectural and even landscaping integrity of Monticello at the time of Mr. Jefferson's peak. My interpretation of peak, naturally."

"Then don't offer up theories for the good sheriff. Let him find out whatever there is to find out. I don't want this turned into a three-ring circus and certainly not before the two hundred fiftieth birthday celebration. We need to make sure that celebration has the correct focus." He inhaled and whispered, "Money, Kimball, money. The media will turn somersaults on April thirteenth, and the attention will be a godsend to all our efforts to preserve, maintain, and extend Monticello."

"I know."

"Then, please, let's not give anyone ideas about white men sleeping in slave cabins, or with slave women. *Smoke inhalation.*" Oliver pronounced the two words as though they were a sentence of doom.

Kimball waited, turning this over in his mind. "All right, but I can't turn away the opportunity to help Sheriff Shaw."

"Of course not." Oliver intoned, "I know you well enough to know that. I'm in an optimistic frame of mind and I think whatever comes back from the lab will put this to rest. Then we can put the remains to rest in a Christian burial."

After saying good-night, Kimball hopped into his car. He watched Oliver's taillights as he backed out behind him and then sped away. A moment of darkness enveloped him, a premonition perhaps or a sense of sorrow over his disagreement with Oliver, who could bounce him right out of a job. Then again, maybe thinking about murder and death, no matter how far distant, casts a brooding spell over people. Evil knows no time. Kimball shuddered again and chalked it up to the cool, cloying dampness.

16

The biting wind on Monticello Mountain made the forty-five-degree temperature feel like thirty-five. Mim huddled in her down jacket. She wanted to wear her sable, but Oliver Zeve warned her that wouldn't look good for the Friends of Restoration. The antifur people would kick up a fuss. Made her spit. Furs had been keeping the human race warm for millennia. She did admit that the down jacket also kept her warm and was much lighter.

Montalto, the green spherical anchor at the northern end of Carter's Ridge, drifted in and out of view. Ground clouds snaked through the lowlands, and they were slowly rising with the advent of the sun.

Mim admired Thomas Jefferson. She read voraciously what he himself had written and what had been written about him by others. She knew that he had purchased Montalto on October 14,

1777. Jefferson drew several observatory designs, for he wished to build one on Montalto. There was no end to his ideas, his drawings. He would return to projects years later and complete them. He needed little sleep, so he could accomplish more than most people.

Mim, greedy for sleep, wondered how he managed with so little. Perhaps his schemes held loneliness at bay when he sat at his desk at five in the morning. Or perhaps his mind raced so fast he couldn't shut it off—might as well let it be productive. Another man might have gone on the prowl for trouble.

Not that Thomas Jefferson lacked his share of trouble or heartache. His father died when he was fourteen. His beloved tomboy older sister, Jane, died when he was twenty-two. His wife died on September 6, 1782, when he was thirty-nine, after he stayed home to nurse her for the last four painful months of her life. He sequestered himself in his room for three weeks following her death. After that he rode and rode and rode as if his horse could carry him away from death, from the burden of his crushing sorrow.

Mim felt she knew the man. Her sorrows, while not equal to Jefferson's, nonetheless provided her with a sense that she could understand his losses. She understood his passion for architecture and landscaping. Politics proved harder for her to grasp. As the wife of Crozet's mayor, she glad-handed, fed, and smiled at every soul in the community . . . and everybody wanted something.

How could this brilliant man participate in such a low profession?

A sound check in the background brought her out of her reverie. Little Marilyn pulled out a mirror for her mother. Mim scrutinized her appearance. Not bad. She cleared her throat. Then she stood up as she saw a production assistant walking her way.

Mim, Kimball, and Oliver would be discussing the corpse on *Wake-up Call*, the national network morning show.

She was to deflect any suggestions of miscegenation, as Samson Coles put it to her on the phone. Wesley Randolph, when she called on him, advised her to emphasize that Jefferson was probably in Washington at the time of the unfortunate man's demise. When Mim said that perhaps they'd have to wait for the pathology report from D.C., her rival and friend harrumphed. "Wait nothing. Don't be honest, Mim. This is politics even if centuries have passed. In politics your virtues will be used against you. There's private morality and public morality. I keep telling Warren that. Ansley understands, but my son sure doesn't. You get up there and say whatever you want so long as it sounds good—and remember, the best defense is a good offense."

Mim, poised at the edge of the lights behind the camera, watched as Kimball Haynes pointed to the site of the body.

Little Marilyn watched the monitor. A photo of the skeleton flashed on the screen. "Indecent." Mim fumed. "You shouldn't show a body until the next of kin are notified."

A hand gripped her elbow, guiding her to her mark. The sound technician placed a tiny microphone on the lapel of her cashmere sweater. She shed her jacket. Her perfect three strands of pearls gleamed against the hunter-green sweater.

The host glided over to her, flashed his famous smile, and held out his right hand, "Mrs. Sanburne, Kyle Kottner, so pleased you could be with us this morning."

He paused, listened to his earphone, and swiveled to face the camera with the red light. "I'm here now with Mrs. James Sanburne, president of the Friends of Restoration and the moving force behind the Mulberry Row project. Tell us, Mrs. Sanburne, about slave life during Thomas Jefferson's time."

"Mr. Jefferson would have called his people servants. Many of them were treasured as family members and many servants were highly skilled. His servants were devoted to him because he was devoted to them."

"But isn't it a contradiction, Mrs. Sanburne, that one of the fathers of liberty should own slaves?"

Mim, prepared, appeared grave and thoughtful. "Mr. Kottner, when Thomas Jefferson was a young man at the House of Burgesses before the Revolutionary War, he said that he made an effort at emancipation which failed. I think that the war diverted his attention from this subject, and as you know, he was sent to France, where his presence was crucial to our war efforts. France was the best friend we had." Kyle started to cut her off, but Mim smiled brightly. "And after the war Americans faced the herculean labor of forming a new kind of government. Had he been born later, I do believe he would have successfully tackled this thorny problem."

Amazed that a woman from a place he assumed was the Styx had gotten the better of him, Kyle shifted gears. "Have you any theories about the body found in Cabin Four?"

"Yes. I believe he was a violent opponent of Mr. Jefferson's. What we would call a stalker today. And I believe one of the servants killed him to protect the great man's life."

Pandemonium. Everyone started talking at once. Mim stifled a broad smile.

Harry, Mrs. Hogendobber, Susan, and Market were watching on the portable TV Susan had brought to the post office. Mrs. Murphy, Tucker, and Pewter stared at the tube as well.

"Slick as an eel." Harry clapped her hands in admiration.

"Stalker theory! Where does she come up with this stuff?" Market scratched his balding head.

"The newspapers," Susan answered. "You've got to hand it to her. She turned the issue of slavery on its head. She controlled the interviewer instead of vice versa. Until the real story surfaces, if it ever does, she's got the media chasing their tails."

"The real story will surface." Miranda spoke with conviction. "It always does."

Pewter flicked her whiskers fore and aft. "*Does anyone have a glazed doughnut? I'm hungry.*"

"No," Tucker replied. "*Pewter, you have no sense of mystery.*"

"*That's not true,*" she defended herself. "*But I see Mim on a daily* basis. *Watching her on television is no big deal.*" Pewter, waiting for a comeback from Mrs. Murphy, was disappointed when none was forthcoming. "*What planet are you on?*"

The gorgeous eyes widened, the tiger cat hunched forward and whispered, "*I've got a funny feeling about this. I can't put my paw on it.*"

"*Oh, you're hungry, that's all.*" Pewter dismissed Mrs. Murphy's premonition.

17

Harry and Warren Randolph grunted as they picked up the York rake and put it on the back of her truck.

"Either this thing is getting heavier or I'm getting weaker," Warren joked.

"It's getting heavier."

"Hey, come on for a minute. I want to show you something."

Harry opened the door to the truck so Tucker and Mrs. Murphy could leap out to freedom. They followed Harry to the Randolphs' beautiful racing barn, built in 1892. Behind the white frame structure with the green standing-seam tin roof lay the mile-long oval track. Warren bred Thoroughbreds. That, too, like this property, had been in the family since the eighteenth century. The Randolphs loved blooded horses. The impressive walnut-paneled foyer at the manor house, hung with equine paintings spanning the centuries, attested to that fact.

The generous twelve-by-twelve-foot stalls were back to back in the center line of the barn. The tack room, wash stalls, and feed room were located in the center of the stall block. Circling the outside of the stalls was a large covered aisle that doubled as an exercise track during inclement weather. Since many windows circled the outside wall, enough light shone on the track so that even on a blizzardy day a rider could work a horse.

Kentucky possessed more of these glorified shed-row barns than Virginia, so Warren naturally prized his barn, built by his paternal grandfather. Colonel Randolph had put his money in the Chesapeake and Ohio Railway as well as the Union Pacific.

"What do you think?" His hazel eyes danced.

"Beautiful!" Harry exclaimed.

"*What do you think?*" Mrs. Murphy asked Tucker.

Tucker tentatively put one paw on the Pavesafe rubber bricks. The dull reddish surface of interlocking bricks could expand and contract within itself, so no matter what the weather or temperature, the surface remained nonskid. The bricks were also specially treated to resist bacteria.

The tailless dog took a few gingery steps, then raced to the other curved end of the massive barn. *"Yahoo! This is like running on cushions."*

"Hey, hey, wait for me!" The cat bolted after her companion.

"Your cat and dog approve." Warren jammed his hands into his pockets like a proud father.

Harry knelt down and touched the surface. "This stuff is right out of paradise."

"No, right out of Lexington, Kentucky." He led her down the row of stalls. "Honey, they're so far ahead of us in Kentucky that it hurts my pride sometimes."

"I guess we have to expect that. It is the center of the Thoroughbred industry." Harry's toes tingled with the velvety feel underneath.

"Well, you know me, I think Virginia should lead the nation in every respect. We've provided more presidents than any other state. We provided the leadership to form this nation—"

Warren sang out the paean of Virginia's greatness, practicing perhaps for many speeches to follow. Harry, a native of the Old Dominion, didn't disagree, but she thought the other twelve colonies had assisted in the break from the mother country. Only New York approximated the original Virginia in size before the break from West Virginia, and it was natural that a territory that big would throw up something or someone important. Then, too, the perfect location of Virginia, in the center of the coastline, and its topography, created by three great rivers, formed an environment hospitable to agriculture and the civilizing arts. Good ports and the Chesapeake Bay completed the rich natural aspects of the state. Prideful as Harry felt, she thought bragging on it was a little shy of good manners or good sense. People not fortunate enough to have been born in Virginia nor wise enough to remove themselves to the Old Dominion hardly needed this dolorous truth pointed out to them. It made outsiders surly.

When Warren finished, Harry returned to the flooring. "Mind if I ask how much this stuff costs?"

"Eight dollars a square foot and nine fifty for the antistumble edge."

Harry calculated, roughly, the square footage before her and arrived at the staggering sum of forty-five thousand dollars. She gulped. "Oh" squeaked out of her.

"That's what I said, but I tell you, Harry, I haven't any worries about big knees or injuries of any sort on this stuff. Before, I used cedar shavings. Well, what a whistling bitch to keep hauling shavings in with the dump truck, plus there's the man-hours to fetch it, replenish the supply in the aisle, rake it out, and clean it three times a day. I about wore out myself and my boys. And the dust when we had to work the horses inside—not good for the horses in their stalls or the ones being exercised, so then you spend time sprinkling it down. Still use the cedar for the stalls though. I grind it up a bit, mix it in with regular shavings. I like a sweet-smelling barn."

"Most beautiful barn in Virginia." Harry admired the place.

"*Mouse alert!*" Mrs. Murphy screeched to a stop, fishtailed into the feed room, and pounced at a hole in the corner to which the offending rodent had repaired.

Tucker stuck her nose in the feed room. "*Where?*"

"*Here,*" called Mrs. Murphy from the corner.

Tucker crouched down, putting her head between her paws. She whispered, "*Should I stay motionless like you?*"

"*Nah, the little bugger knows we're here. He'll wait until we're gone. You know a mouse can eat a quart of grain a week? You'd think that Warren would have barn cats.*"

"*Probably does. They smelled you coming and took off.*" Tucker laughed as the tiger grumbled. "*Let's find Mom.*"

"*Not yet.*" Mrs. Murphy stuck her paw in the mouse hole and fished around. She withdrew a wad of fuzzy fabric, the result of eating a hole in a shirt hanging in the stable, no doubt. "*Ah, I feel something else.*"

A piece of paper stuck to Mrs. Murphy's left forefinger claw as she slid it out of the hole. "*Damn, if I could just grab him.*"

Tucker peered down at the high-quality vellum scrap. "*Goes through the garbage too.*"

"*So do you.*"

"*Not often.*" The dog sat down. "*Hey, there's a little bit of writing here.*"

Mrs. Murphy withdrew her paw from her third attempt at the mouse hole. "*So there is. 'Dearest darling.' Ugh. Love letters make me ill.*" The cat studied it again. "*Too chewed up. Looks like a man's writing, doesn't it?*"

Tucker looked closely at the shred. "*Well, it's not very pretty. Guess there are lovers at the barn. Come on.*"

"*Okay.*"

They joined Harry as she inspected a young mare Warren and his father had purchased at the January sale at Keeneland.

Since this was an auction for Thoroughbreds of any age, unlike the sales specifically for yearlings or two-year-olds, one could sometimes find a bargain. The yearling auctions were the ones where the gavel fell and people's pockets suddenly became lighter than air.

"I'm trying to breed in staying power. She's got the bloodlines." He thought for a moment, then continued. "Do you ever wonder, Harry, what it's like to be a person who has no blood? A person who shuffled through Ellis Island—one's ancestors, I mean. Would you ever feel that you belong, or would there be some vague romantic attachment, perhaps, to the old country? I mean, it must be dislocating to be a new American."

"Ever attend the citizenship ceremony at Monticello? They do it every Fourth of July."

"No, can't say that I have, but I'd better do it if I'm going to run for the state Senate."

"I have. Standing out there on the lawn are Vietnamese, Poles, Ecuadorians, Nigerians, Scots, you name it. They raise their hands, and this is after they've demonstrated a knowledge of the Constitution, mind you, and they swear allegiance to this nation. I figure after that they're as American as we are."

"You are a generous soul, Harry." Warren slapped her on the back. "Here, I've got something for you." He handed her a carton of the rubber paving bricks. It was heavy.

"Thank you, Warren, these will come in handy." She was thrilled with the gift.

"Oh, here. What kind of a gentleman am I? Let me carry this to the truck."

"We could carry it together," Harry offered. "And, by the bye, I think you should run for the state Senate."

Warren spied a wheelbarrow and placed the carton in it. "You do? Well, thank you." He picked up the arms of the wheelbarrow. "Might as well use the wheel. Just think if the guy who invented it got royalties!"

"How do you know a woman didn't invent the wheel?"

"You got me there." Warren enjoyed Harry. Unlike his wife, Ansley, Harry was relaxed. He couldn't imagine her wearing nail polish or fretting over clothes. He rather wished he weren't a married man when he was around Harry.

"Warren, why don't you let me come on out here and bush-hog a field or two? These bricks are so expensive, I feel guilty accepting them."

"Hey, I'm not on food stamps. Besides, these are an overflow and I've got nowhere else to use them. You love your horses, so I bet you could use them in your wash rack . . . put them in the center and then put rubber mats like you have in the trailer around that. Not a bad compromise."

"Great idea."

Ansley pulled into the driveway, her bronzed Jaguar as sleek and as sexy as herself. Stuart and Breton were with her. She saw Harry and Warren pushing the wheelbarrow and drove over to them instead of heading for the house.

"Harry," she called from inside the car, "how good to see you."

"Your husband is playing Santa Claus." Harry pointed to the carton.

"Hi, Harry." The boys called out. Harry returned their greeting with a wave.

Ansley parked and elegantly disembarked from the Jag. Stuart and Breton ran up to the house. "You know Warren. He has to have a new project. But I must admit the barn looks fabulous and the stuff couldn't be safer. Now, you come on up to the house and have a drink. Big Daddy's up there, and he loves a pretty lady."

"Thanks, I'd love to, but I'd better push on home."

"Oh, I ran into Mim," Ansley mentioned to her husband. "She now wants you on the Greater Crozet Committee."

Warren winced. "Poppa just gave her a bushel of money for her Mulberry Row project—she's working over our family one by one."

"She knows that, and she said to my face how 'responsible' the Randolphs are. Now she wants your stores of wisdom. Exact words. She'll ask you for money another time."

"Stores of wisdom." The left side of Harry's mouth twitched in a suppressed giggle as she looked at Warren. At forty-one, he remained a handsome man.

Warren grunted as he lifted the heavy carton onto the tailgate. "Is it possible for a woman to have a Napoleon complex?"

18

The human mouth is a wonderful creation, except that it can rarely remain shut. The jaw, hinged on each side of the face, opens and closes in a rhythm that allows the tongue to waggle in a staggering variety of languages. Gossip fuels all of them. Who did what to whom. Who said what to whom. Who didn't say a word. Who has how much money and who spends it or doesn't. Who sleeps with whom. Those topics form the foundation of human discourse. Occasionally the human can discuss work, profit and loss, and what's for supper. Sometimes a question or two regarding the arts will pass although sports as a subject is a better bet. Rare moments bring forth a meditation on spirituality, philosophy, and the meaning of life. But the backbeat, the pulse, the percussion of exchange, was, is, and ever shall be gossip.

Today gossip reached a crescendo.

Mrs. Hogendobber picked up her paper the minute the paperboy left it in the cylindrical plastic container. That was at six A.M. She knew that Harry's fading red mailbox, nailed to an old fence post, sat half a mile from her house. She usually scooped out the paper on her way to work, so she wouldn't have read it yet.

Mrs. H. grabbed the black telephone that had served her well since 1954. The click, click, click as the rotary dial turned would allow a sharp-eared person to identify the number being called.

"Harry, Wesley Randolph died last night."

"What? I thought Wesley was so much better."

"Heart attack." She sounded matter-of-fact. By this time she'd seen enough people leave this life to bear it with grace. One positive thing about Wesley's death was that he'd been fighting leukemia for years. At least he wouldn't die a lingering, painful death. "Someone from the farm must have given the information to the press the minute it happened."

"I just saw Warren Sunday afternoon. Thanks for telling me. I'll have to pay my respects after work. See you in a little bit."

Now, telling a friend of another friend's passing doesn't fall under the heading of gossip, but that day at work Harry sloshed around in it.

The first person to alert Harry and Mrs. Hogendobber to the real story was Lucinda Coles. Luckily Mim Sanburne was picking up her mail, so they could cross-fertilize, as it were.

"—everywhere." Lucinda gulped a breath in the middle of her story about Ansley Randolph. "Warren, in a state of great distress, naturally, was finally reduced to calling merchants to see if by chance Ansley had stopped by on her rounds. Well, he couldn't find her. He called me and I said I didn't know where she was. Of course, I had no idea the poor man's father had dropped dead in the library."

Mim laid a trump card on the table. "Yes, he called me too, and like you, Lulu, I hadn't a clue, but I had seen Ansley at about five that afternoon at Foods of All Nations. Buying a bottle of expensive red wine: Medoc, 1970, Château le Trelion. She seemed surprised to see me"—Mim paused—"almost as if I had caught her out . . . you know."

"Uh-huh." Lucinda nodded in the customary manner of a woman affirming whatever another woman has said. Of course, the other woman's comment usually has to do with emotions, which could never actually be qualified or quantified—that being the appeal of emotions. They both acknowledged a tyranny of correct feelings.

"She's running around on Warren."

"Uh-huh." Lucinda's voice grew in resonance, since she, as a victim of infidelity, was also an expert on its aftermath. "No good will come of it. No good ever does."

After those two left, Boom Boom Craycroft dashed in for her mail. Her comment, after a lengthy discussion of the slight fracture of her tibia, was that everybody screws around on everybody, and so what?

The men approached the subject differently. Mr. Randolph's demise was characterized by Market as a response to his dwindling finances and the leukemia. It was hard for Harry to believe a man would have a heart attack because his estate had diminished, thanks to his own efforts, from $250 million to $100 million, but anything was possible. Perhaps he felt poor.

Fair Haristeen lingered over the counter, chatting. His idea was that a life of trying to control everybody and everything had ruined Wesley Randolph's health. Sad, of course, because Randolph was an engaging man. Mostly, Fair wanted Harry to pick which movie they would see Friday night.

Ned Tucker, Susan's husband, took the view that we die when we want to, therefore Père Randolph was ready to go and nobody should feel too bad about it.

By the end of the workday speculation had run the gamut. The last word on Wesley Randolph's passing, from Rob Collier as he picked up the afternoon mail, was that the old man was fooling around with his son's wife. The new medication Larry Johnson had prescribed for his illness had revved up his sex drive.

Warren walked in on the tryst and his father died of a heart attack from the shock.

As Harry and Mrs. Hogendobber locked up, they reviewed the day's gossip. Mrs. Hogendobber dropped the key in her pocket, inhaled deeply, and said to Harry, "I wonder what they say about us?"

"Gossip lends to death a new terror." Harry smirked.

19

"You know, if I ever get tired of home, I'll come live in your barn," Paddy promised.

"No, you won't," Simon, the possum, called down from the hayloft. "You'll steal my treasures. You're no good, Paddy. You were born no good and you'll die no good."

"Quit flapping your gums, you overgrown rat. When I want your opinion, I'll ask for it." Paddy washed one of his white spats.

A large black cat permanently wearing a tuxedo and spats, Paddy was handsome and knew it. His white bib gleamed, and despite his propensity for fighting, he always cleaned himself up.

Mrs. Murphy sat on a director's chair in the tack room. Paddy sat in the chair opposite her while Tucker sprawled on the floor. Simon wouldn't come down. He hated strange animals.

The last light of day cast a peachy-pink glow through the outside window. The horses chatted to one another in their stalls.

"I wish Mom would come home," Tucker said.

"She'll be at Eagle's Rest a long time." Mrs. Murphy knew that calling upon the bereaved took time, plus everyone else in Crozet would be there.

"Funny how the old man dropped." Paddy started cleaning his other forepaw. "They're already digging his grave at the cemetery. I walked through there on my rounds. His plot's next to the Berrymans on one side and the Craigs on the other."

Tucker walked to the end of the barn, then returned. "The sky's bloodred over the mountains."

"Another deep frost tonight too," Paddy remarked. "Just when you think spring is here."

"Days are warming up," Mrs. Murphy noted. "Dr. Craig. Wasn't that Larry Johnson's partner?"

Paddy replied, "Long before any of us were born."

"Let me think."

"Murph." Tucker wistfully stood on her hind legs, putting her front paws on the chair. "Ask Herbie Jones, he remembers everything."

"If only humans could understand." Mrs. Murphy frowned, then brightened. "Dr. Jim Craig. Killed in 1948. He took Larry into his practice just like Larry took in Hayden McIntire."

Paddy stared at his former wife. When she got a bee in her bonnet, it was best to let her go on. She evidenced more interest in humans than he did.

"What set you off?"

The tiger cat glanced down at her canine companion. "Paddy said he walked through the cemetery. The Randolphs are buried between the Berrymans and the Craigs."

Tucker wandered around restlessly. "Another unsolved murder."

"Ah, one of those spook tales they tell you when you're a kitten to scare you," Paddy pooh-poohed. "Old Dr. Craig is found in his Pontiac, motor running. Found at the cemetery gates. Yeah, I remember now. His grandson, Jim Craig II, tried to reopen the case years back, but nothing came of it."

"*Shot between the eyes,*" Mrs. Murphy said. "*His medical bag stolen but no money.*"

"*Well, this town is filled with weirdos. Somebody really wanted to play doctor.*" Paddy giggled.

"In 1948." Mrs. Murphy triumphantly recalled the details told to her long ago by her own mother, Skippy. "*The town smothered in shock because everyone loved Dr. Craig.*"

"*Not everyone,*" Paddy said.

"*Hooray!*" Tucker jumped up as she heard the truck coming down the driveway. "*Mom's home.*"

"*Paddy, come on in. Harry likes you.*"

"*Yeah, get out of here, useless,*" Simon called down from the loft.

The owl poked her head out from under her wing, then stuck it back. She rarely joined in these discussions with the other animals since she worked the night shift.

The dog bounded ahead of them.

The tuxedo cat and the tiger strolled at a leisurely pace to the front door. It wouldn't do to appear too excited.

"*Ever wish we were still together?*" Paddy asked. "*I do.*"

"*Paddy, being in a relationship with you was like putting Miracle-Gro on my character defects.*" Her tail whisked to the vertical when Harry called her name.

"*Does that mean you don't like me?*"

"*No. It means I didn't like me in that situation. Now, come on, let's get some supper.*"

20

The upper two floors of Monticello, not open to the public, served as a haven and study for the long-legged Kimball Haynes. While most of the valuable materials relating to Mr. Jefferson and his homes reposed in the rare books section of the Alderman Library at the University of Virginia, the Library of Congress, or the Virginia State Library in Richmond, only a small library existed upstairs at Monticello.

One of Kimball's pleasures consisted of sitting in the rectangular room above the south piazza, or greenhouse, which connects the octagonal library to Jefferson's cabinet, the room he used as his private study. Kimball kept a comfortable wing chair there and a private library, which included copies of records that Jefferson or his white employees kept in their own hand. He pored over account books, visitors' logs, and weather reports for the year 1803. As Mr. Jefferson was serving his first term as president during that year, the records lacked the fullness of the great man's attention. Peas, tomatoes, and corn were planted as always. A coach broke an axle. The repairs were costly. The livestock demanded constant care. A visitor assigned to a third-floor room in November complained of being frightfully cold, a reasonable complaint, since there were no fireplaces up there.

As the night wore on, Kimball heard the first peepers of spring. He loved that sound better than Mozart. He thumbed the copies blackened by the soil on his hands. Ground-in dirt was an occupational hazard for an archaeologist. He had used these references for years, returning to the rare books collection at the University of Virginia only when he'd scrubbed his hands until they felt raw.

After absorbing those figures, Kimball dropped the pages on the floor and leaned back in the old chair. He flung one leg over a chair arm. Facts, facts, facts, and not a single clue. Whoever was buried in the dirt at Cabin Four wasn't a tradesman. A tinker or wheelwright or purveyor of fresh fish, even a jeweler, wouldn't have had such expensive clothing on his back.

The corpse belonged to a gentleman. Someone of the president's own class. 1803.

Now, Kimball knew that might not be the year of the man's death, but it couldn't have been far off. Whatever happened politically that year might have some bearing on the murder, but Kimball's understanding of human nature suggested that in America people rarely killed each other over politics. Murder was closer to the skin.

He recalled a scandal the year before, 1802, that cut Thomas Jefferson to the quick. His friend from childhood, John Walker, accused Jefferson of making improper advances to his wife. According to John Walker, this affair started in 1768, when Thomas Jefferson was not yet married, but Walker maintained that it continued until 1779, seven years after Jefferson had married Martha Wayles Skelton, on January 1, 1772. The curious aspect of this scandal was that Mrs. Walker saw fit to burden her husband with the disclosure of her infidelity only some time after 1784, when Jefferson was in France.

Kimball also remembered that upon Jefferson's return from France, he and John Walker began to move on separate political paths. Light-Horse Harry Lee, father of Robert E. Lee, later volunteered to mediate between the two former friends. As Light-Horse Harry loathed Thomas Jefferson, the result of this effort was a foregone conclusion. Things went from bad to worse with James Thomson Callender, a vicious tattletale, fanning the flames. It was at this time that the infamous allegations against Jefferson for sleeping with his slave, Sally Hemings, began to make the rounds.

By January of 1805 these stories gained enough currency to cause the *New-England Palladium* to castigate Mr. Jefferson's morals. Apparently, Mr. Jefferson did not stand for family values.

The fur flew. Few cocktails are more potent than politics mixed with sex. Drinks were on the house, literally. Congress wallowed in the gossip. Things haven't changed, Kimball thought to himself.

To make matters murkier, Jefferson admitted to making a pass at Mrs. Walker. Acting as a true gentleman, Jefferson shouldered all the blame for the affair, which he carefully noted as occurring before his marriage. In those days, the fellow accepted the stigma, no matter what had really happened. To blame the lady meant you weren't a man.

Thanks to Jefferson's virile stance, even his political enemies let the Walker affair go. Everyone let it go but John Walker. Only as Walker lay dying at his estate in Keswick, called Belvoir, did he acknowledge that Jefferson was as much sinned against as sinner. By then it was too late.

The Sally Hemings story, however, did damage the president. A white man sleeping with a black woman created a spectacular conundrum for everyone. A gentleman couldn't admit such a thing. It would destroy his wife and generate endless jokes at his expense. Let there be one red-haired African American at Monticello and the jig was up, literally. That little word-play ran from Maine to South Carolina in the early 1800s. Oh, how they must have laughed in the pubs. "The jig is up."

It did not help Mr. Jefferson's case that some fair-skinned African Americans did appear at Monticello bearing striking resemblance to the master. However, as Kimball recalled, Thomas wasn't the only male around with Jefferson blood.

So what if a cousin had had an affair with Sally? Bound by the aristocratic code of honor, Jefferson still must remain silent or he would cause tremendous suffering to the rake's wife. A gentleman always protects a lady regardless of her relation to him. A gentleman could also try to protect a woman of color by remaining silent and giving her money and other favors. Silence was the key.

One thing was certain about the master sleeping with a slave: The woman had no choice but to say yes. In that truth lay lyric heartache sung from generation to generation of black women. Broke the hearts of white women too.

Stars glittered in the sky, the Milky Way smeared in an arc over the buildings as it had centuries ago. Kimball realized this murder might or might not have something to do with Thomas Jefferson's personal life, but it surely had something to do with a violent and close relationship between a white man and a black woman.

He would go over the slave roster tomorrow. He was too sleepy tonight.

21

The Crozet Lutheran Church overflowed with people who had come to pay their last respects to Wesley Randolph. The deceased's family, Warren, Ansley, Stuart, and Breton, sat in the front pew. Kimball Haynes, his assistant Heike Holtz, Oliver Zeve and his wife, and the other staff at Monticello came to say good-bye to a man who had supported the cause for over fifty of his seventy-three years.

Marilyn and Jim Sanburne sat in the second pew on the right along with their daughter Marilyn Sanburne Hamilton, alluring in black and available thanks to a recent divorce. Big Mim would apply herself to arranging a more suitable match sometime in the future.

The entire town of Crozet must have been there, plus the

out-of-towners who had occasion to know Wesley from business dealings, as well as friends from all over the South.

The Reverend Herbert Jones, his deep voice filling the church, read the Scriptures.

Somber but impressive, the funeral would have been remembered in proportion to Wesley's services to the community. However, this funeral stuck in people's memories for another reason.

Right in the middle of Reverend Jones's fervent denial of death, "For if we believe we are risen in Christ," Lucinda Payne Coles whispered loud enough for those around her to hear, "You sorry son of a bitch." Red in the face, she slid out of the pew and walked down the aisle. The usher swung the door open for her. Samson, glued to his seat, didn't even swivel his head to follow his wife's glowering progress.

As the people filed out of the church, Mim cornered Samson in the vestibule. "What in the world was that all about?"

Samson shrugged, "She loved Wesley, and I think her emotions got the better of her."

"If she loved Wesley, she wouldn't have marred his funeral. I'm not stupid, Samson. What are you doing to her?" Mim took the position that men wronged women more often than women wronged men. In this particular case she was right.

Samson hissed, "Mim, this is none of your business." He stalked off, knowing full well she'd never refer a customer to him again. At that moment he didn't care. He was too confused to care.

Harry, Susan, and Ned observed this exchange, as did everyone else.

"You're going to get a call tonight." Susan squeezed her husband's forearm. "That's the price of being such a good divorce lawyer."

"Funny thing is, I hate divorce." Ned shook his head.

"Don't we all?" Harry agreed as the source of her former discontent, Fair, joined them.

"Damn."

"Fair, you always were a man of few words." Ned nodded a greeting.

"My patients don't talk," Fair replied. "You know, something's really wrong. That's not like Lulu. She knows her place."

"It's going to be a much poorer place now," Susan wryly noted.

"Mim will wreak vengeance on Samson. Bad enough he told her to bugger off, he did it in public. He'll have to crawl on his belly over hot coals—publicly—to atone for his sin." Ned knew how Mim worked. She used her money and her vast real estate holdings as leverage if she felt a pinch in the pocketbook would suffice. When her target was a woman, she generally preferred to cast her into social limbo. But the human is an animal nonetheless, and harsh lessons were learned faster than mild ones. Had Mim been a man, she would have been called a hard-ass, but she'd have been lauded as a good businessman. Since she was a woman, the term bitch seemed to cover it. Unfair, but that was life. Then again, had Mim been a man, she might not have had to teach people quite so many lessons. They would have feared her from the get-go.

Larry Johnson, physician to Wesley and the family, climbed into his car to follow the funeral procession to the family cemetery.

"Hear Warren wouldn't let anyone sign the death certificate but Larry," Fair mentioned. "Heard it over at Sharkey Loomis's stable."

"That must have been a sad task for Larry. They'd been friends for years." Harry wondered how it would feel to know someone for fifty, sixty years and then lose them.

"Come on, or we'll be last in line." Susan shepherded them to their cars.

22

A hard-driving rain assisted Kimball Haynes. The slashing of the drops against the windowpane helped him to concentrate. It was long past midnight, and he was still bent over the records of births and deaths from 1800 to 1812.

He cast wide his research net, then slowly drew it toward him. Medley Orion, born around 1785, was reported to be a beautiful woman. Her extraordinary color was noted twice in the records; her lovely cast of features must have been delicious. White people rarely noted the physiognomy of black people unless it was to make fun of them. But an early note in a lady's hand, quite possibly that of Martha, Jefferson's eldest daughter, stated these qualities.

Martha married when Medley was five or six. She would have seen the woman as a child and as she grew. Usually Martha kept good accounts, but this reference was on a scrap of paper on the reverse of a list penned in tiny, tiny handwriting about different types of grapes.

A flash of lightning seared across the night sky. A crackle, then a pop, sounded out in the yard. The electricity went off.

Kimball had no flashlight. He was wearing his down vest, since it was cold in the room. His hands fingered a square box of matches. He struck one. He hadn't placed any candles in the room, but then, why would he? He rarely worked late into the night at Monticello.

The rain pounded the windows and drummed on the roof, a hard spring storm. Even in this age of telephones and ambulances, this would be a hateful night in which to fall ill, give birth, or be caught outside on horseback.

The match fizzled. Kimball declined to strike another. He could have felt his way down the narrow stairway, a mere twenty-four inches wide, to the first floor, the public floor of Monticello. There were beeswax candles down there. But he decided to peer out the window. A rush of water and occasional glimpses of trees bending in the wind were all he could make out.

The house creaked and moaned. The day you see, the night you hear. Kimball heard the door hinges rasp in the slight air current sent up by the winds outside. The windows upstairs were not airtight, so a swish of wind snuck inside. The windows themselves rattled in protest at the driving rains. The winds howled, circled, then swept back up in the flues. Occasionally a raindrop or two would trickle down into the fireplace, bringing with it the memory of fires over two hundred years ago. Floorboards popped.

Perhaps in such a hard storm a wealthy person would light a candle to bring some cheer into the room. A fire would struggle in the fireplace because the downdraft was fierce, despite the flue. Still, a bit of light and good cheer would fill the room, and frightened children could be told stories of the Norse and Greek gods, Thor tossing his mighty hammer or Zeus hurtling a bolt of lightning to earth like a blue javelin.

"What would such a storm have been like in Cabin Four?" Kimball wondered. The door would be closed. Perhaps Medley might have had tallow candles. No evidence of such had been found in her cabin, but tallow candles had been found in other digs and certainly the smithy and joinery had them for people who worked after dark. A quilt wrapped around one's body would help. The fireplaces in the servants' quarters lacked the refinement of the fireplaces in the Big House, so more rain and wind would funnel down the chimneys, sending dust and debris over the room. At least Medley had a wooden floor. Some cabins had packed-earth floors, which meant on the cold mornings your bare feet would hit frost on the ground. Maybe Medley Orion would hop into bed and pull the covers up on such a night.

Kimball feverishly worked to piece together the bits of her life. This was archaeology of a different sort. The more he knew about the woman, the closer he would come to a solution, he thought. Then he'd double-think and wonder if she might be innocent. Someone was killed in her cabin, but maybe she knew nothing. No. Impossible. The body had to have been buried at night. She knew, all right.

The rain wrapped around Monticello like a swirling silver curtain. Kimball, grateful for the time to sit and cogitate, a man's word for dream, knew he'd have to keep pressing on. He did realize he needed advice from a woman friend or friends. Compared to men, women rarely killed. What would compel a slave woman to take a man's life, and a white man's at that?

23

Imbued with the seriousness of her task, Mim invited Lucinda Coles, Miranda Hogendobber, Port Haffner, Ellie Wood Baxter, and Susan Tucker and Mary Minor Haristeen for youth. Little Marilyn was also present in the capacity of acolyte to Mim in her own role as social priestess. Ansley Randolph would have been invited, but given that Wesley Randolph lay in the ground but a scant three days, that would never do.

When Kimball Haynes asked for assistance, he suffered an embarrassment of riches. Although not as politically canny as Oliver, Kimball possessed a scrap of shrewdness. One doesn't advance in this world without it. After his night at Monticello in the rainstorm, he thought the wisest policy would be to call Mim Sanburne. After all, she, too, felt some of the heat over what was happening at Monticello. She squeezed money out of turnips. She never turned down a hard job. She knew everybody, which was worth more than knowing everything. To top it off, Mim adored being at the center of activities.

Mim swooned when Kimball called saying that he wanted to get together with her because he thought she might have the key to the problem. He assured her that she had great insight into the female mind. That did it. Mim couldn't bear having great insight into the female mind without her friends knowing. Hence tonight.

Although furious at Samson, Mim bore no animosity toward Lulu other than that she should not have lost her temper in the middle of a funeral service. Then again, Mim felt some kinship with Lucinda since she was certain Samson was up to no good. Not that Mim wouldn't use Lucinda to bring Samson to heel if the occasion presented itself. She'd wait and see.

Caviar, chopped eggs and onions, fresh salmon, eleven different kinds of cheese and crackers, sliced carrots, snow peas stuffed with cream cheese, crisp cauliflower, and endive with bacon grease dribbled over it completed the warm-ups, as Mim called them. Lunch dazzled everyone. Mim found a divine recipe for lobster ravioli which proved so enticing, no one even mentioned her diet. Arugula salad and a sliver of melon balanced the palate. Those wishing megacalorie desserts gorged on a raspberry cobbler with a vanilla cream sauce or good old devil's food cake for the chocolate lovers.

Mim had the fruits flown down from New York City, as she kept an account there with a posh food emporium. Finally, everyone's mood elevated to the stratosphere. Should anyone require a revitalizing liquid after luncheon, a vast array of spirits awaited them.

Susan chose a dry sherry. She declared that the raw wind cut into her very bones. She knew perfectly well that someone had to stampede for the crystal decanters on the silver trays. Lucinda would die before she'd take the first drink, so Susan figured she'd be the one to save Lulu's life. Miranda declined alcohol, as did Harry and Ellie Wood, a septuagenarian in splendid health.

"I always feel prosperous on a full stomach." Mrs. Hogendobber accepted a cup of piping coffee from the maid dressed in black with a starched white apron and cap.

"Mim, you've outdone yourself. Hear! Hear!" Lulu held up her glass as the other ladies and Kimball did likewise or tapped their spoons to china cups from Cartier.

"A trifle." Mim acknowledged the praise. It might have been a trifle to her, but it damn near killed the cook. It wasn't a trifle to Mim either, but by making light of her accomplishments she added to her formidable reputation. She knew not one lady in the room could have pulled off a luncheon like that, much less at the last minute.

"You know Ansley is comatose with grief." Port, another dear friend of Mim's, paused as the maid handed her a brandy the color of dark topaz.

"Really?" Ellie Wood leaned forward. "I had no idea she was that fond of Wesley. I thought they were usually at sixes and sevens."

"They were," Port crisply agreed. "She's comatose with grief because she had to stay home. She made me swear that I would call her the instant we finished and tell her everything, including, of course, what we wore."

"Oh, dear," Harry blurted out honestly.

"You have youth, Harry, and youth needs no adornment." Miranda came to her rescue. Harry lacked all clothes sense. If she had an important date, Susan and Miranda would force her into something suitable. Harry's idea of dressing up was ironing a crease in her Levi 501s.

"I don't know." Susan kidded her schoolmate. "We're thirty-something, you know."

"Babies." Port kicked off one shoe.

"Time to have some." Mim glared at her daughter. Little Marilyn evaded her mother's demand.

Kimball rubbed his hands together. "Ladies, once again we are indebted to Mrs. Sanburne. I do believe she's the glue that holds us together. I knew we couldn't proceed at Mulberry Row without her leadership in the community."

"Hear. Hear." More toasts and teaspoons on china cups.

Kimball continued. "I'm not sure what Mim has told you. I called needing her wisdom once again and she has provided me with you. I must ask your indulgence as I review the facts. The body of a man was found facedown in Cabin Four. The back of his skull bore testimony to one mighty blow with a heavy, sharp object like an ax but probably not an ax, or else the bone fragment would have been differently smashed—or so Sheriff Shaw believes. The victim wore expensive clothes, a large gold ring, and his pockets were full of money. I counted out the coins and he had about fifty dollars in his pockets. In today's money that would be about five hundred. The remains are in Washington now. We will know when he died, his age, his race, and possibly even something about his health. It's amazing what they can tell these days. He was found under the hearth—two feet under. And that is all we know. Oh, yes, the cabin was inhabited by Medley Orion, a woman in her early twenties. Her birth year isn't clearly recorded. The first mention of her is as a child, so we can speculate. But she was young. A seamstress. Now, I want you to cast your minds back, back to 1803, since our victim was killed then or shortly thereafter. The most recent coin in his pocket was 1803. What happened?"

This stark question created a heavy silence.

Lucinda spoke first. "Kimball, we didn't know that a man was murdered. The papers said only a skeleton was unearthed. This is quite a shock. I mean, people speculated but . . ."

"He was killed by a ferocious blow to the head." Kimball directed his gaze toward Lucinda. "Naturally, Oliver didn't, and won't, want to attest to the fact that the person was murdered until the report comes back from Washington. It will give all of us at Monticello a bit more time to prepare."

"I see." Lucinda cupped her chin in her hand. In her late forties, she was handsome rather than beautiful, stately rather than sweet.

Ellie Wood, a logical soul, speculated. "If he was hit hard, the person would have had to be strong. Was the wound in the front of the skull or the back?"

"The back," Kimball replied.

"Then whoever did it wanted no struggle. No noise either." Ellie Wood quickly grasped the possibilities.

"Might this man have been killed by Medley's lover?" Port inquired. "Do you know if she had a lover?"

"No. I don't. I do know she bore a child in August of 1803, but that doesn't mean she had a lover as we understand the concept." Kimball crossed his arms over his chest.

"Surely you don't think Thomas Jefferson instituted a breeding program?" Lucinda was shocked.

"No, no." Kimball reached for the brandy. "He tried not to break up families, but I haven't found any records to indicate Medley ever had a permanent partner."

"Did she bear more children?" Little Marilyn finally joined in the conversation.

"Apparently not," he said.

"That's very odd." Puzzlement shone over Susan's face. "Birth control consisted of next to nothing."

"Sheepskin. A primitive form of condom." Kimball sipped the brandy, the best he had ever tasted. "However, the chance of a slave having access to anything that sophisticated is out of the question."

"Who said her partner was a slave?" Harry threw down the joker.

Mim, not wanting to appear old-fashioned, picked it up. "Was she beautiful, Kimball? If she was, then her partners may indeed have had access to sheep membrane." Mim implied that Medley therefore would have attracted the white men.

"By what few accounts I can find, yes, she was beautiful."

Lucinda scowled. "Oh, I hope we can just slide by this. I think we're opening a can of worms."

"We are, but somebody's got to open it." Mim stood her ground. "We've swept this sort of thing under the rug for centuries. Not that I enjoy the process, I don't, but miscegenation may be a motive for murder."

"I don't think a black woman would have killed a man merely because he was white," Ellie Wood said. "But if she had a black lover, he might be driven to it out of jealousy if nothing else."

"But what if it was Medley herself?" Kimball's voice rose with suppressed excitement. "What would drive a slave to kill a rich white man? What would drive a woman of any color to kill a man? I think you all know far better than I."

Catching his enthusiasm, Port jumped up. "Love. Love can run anyone crazy."

"Okay, say she loved the victim. Not that I think too many slaves loved the white men who snuck into their cabins." Harry grew bold. "Even at her most irrational, would she kill him because he walked out on her? How could she? White men walked out on black women every morning. They just turned their backs and poof, they were gone. Wouldn't she have been used to it? Wouldn't an older slave have prepared her and said something like, 'This is your lot in life'?"

"Probably would have said 'This is your cross to bear.'" Miranda furrowed her brow.

Unsettled as Lucinda was by Samson's infidelity, and she was getting closer and closer to the real truth, she recognized as the afternoon continued that her unhappiness at least had a front door. She could walk out. Medley Orion couldn't. "Perhaps he humiliated her in some secret place, some deep way, and she snapped."

"Not humiliated, threatened." Susan's eyes lit up. "She was a slave. She'd learned to mask her feelings. Don't we all, ladies?" This idea rippled across the room. "Whoever this was, he had a hold on her. He was going to do something terrible to her or to someone she loved, and she fought back. My God, where did she get the courage?"

"I don't know if I can agree." Miranda folded her hands together. "Does it take courage to kill? God forbids us to take another human life."

"That's it!" Mim spoke up. "He must have threatened to take someone else's life—or hers. What if he threatened to kill Mr. Jefferson—not my stalker theory, mind you, but an explosive rage on the dead man's part—something erratic?"

"I doubt she'd kill to save her master," Little Marilyn countered her mother. "Jefferson was an extraordinary human being, but he was still the master."

"Some slaves loved their masters." Lucinda backed up Mim.

"Not as many as white folks want to believe." Harry laughed. She couldn't help but laugh. While bonds of affection surely existed, it was difficult for her to grasp that the oppressed could love the oppressor.

"Well, then what?" Ellie Wood's patience, never her strong point, ebbed.

"She killed to protect her true lover." Port savored her brandy.

"Or her child," Susan quietly added.

An electric current shot around the room. Was there a mother anywhere in the world who wouldn't kill for her child?

"The child was born in August 1803." Kimball twirled the crystal glass. "If the victim were killed after August, he might have known the child."

"But he might have known the child even before it was born." Mim's eyes narrowed.

"What?" Kimball seemed temporarily befuddled.

"What if it were his?" Mim's voice rang out.

A silence followed this.

Harry then said, "Most men, or perhaps I should say some men, who have enjoyed the favors of a woman who becomes pregnant declare they don't know if the baby is theirs. Of course they can't get away with that now thanks to this DNA testing stuff. They sure could get away with it then."

"Good point, Harry. I say the child was born before he was killed." Susan held them spellbound. "The child was born and it looked like him."

"Good God, Susan, I hope you're wrong." Lucinda blinked. "How could a man kill his own child to—to save his face?"

"People do terrible things," Port flatly stated, for she didn't understand it either, but then, she didn't refute it.

"Well, he paid for his intentions, if that's what they were." Ellie Wood felt rough justice had been done. "If that's true, he paid for it, and done is done."

" 'Vengeance is mine, and recompense, for the time when their foot shall slip; for the day of their calamity is at hand and their doom comes swiftly.' Deuteronomy 32:35," Miranda intoned.

But done was not done. The past was coming undone, and the day of calamity was at hand.

24

"I thought it would take some of the burden off you. You don't need people at you right now." Ansley Randolph leaned on the white fence and watched the horses breeze through their morning workout around the track—the Fibar and sand mix kept the footing good year-round. "Not that anything will make you feel better, for a time."

Pain creased the lines around Warren's eyes. "Honey, I've no doubt that you thought you were doing the right thing, but number one, I am tired of being whipped into shape by Mim Sanburne. Number two, my family's diaries, maps, and genealogies stay right here at Eagle's Rest. Some are so old I keep them in the safe. Number three, I don't think anything of mine will interest Kimball Haynes, and number four, I'm exhausted. I don't want to argue with anyone. I don't even want to explain myself to anyone. No is no, and you'll have to tell Mim.''

Ansley, while not in love with Warren, liked him sometimes. This was one of those times. "You're right. I should have kept my mouth shut. I suppose I wanted to curry favor with Mim. She gives you business."

Warren clasped his hands over the top rail of the fence. "Mim keeps a small army of lawyers busy. If I lose her business, I don't think it will hurt either one of us, and it won't hurt you socially either. All you have to do is tell Mim that I'm down and I can't have anything on my mind right now. I need to rest and repair—that's no lie.''

"Warren, don't take this the wrong way, but I never knew you loved your father this much."

He sighed. "I didn't either." He studied his boot tips for a second. "It's not just Poppa. Now I'm the oldest living male of the line, a line that extends back to 1632. Until our sons are out of prep school and college, the burden of that falls entirely on me. Now I must manage the portfolio—''

"You have good help."

"Yes, but Poppa always checked over the results of our investments. Truth be told, darling, my law degree benefitted Poppa, not me. I read over those transactions that needed a legal check, but I never really paid attention to the investments and the land holdings in an aggressive sense. Poppa liked to keep his cards close to his chest. Well, I'd better learn fast. We've been losing money on the market."

"Who hasn't? Warren, don't worry so much."

"Well, I might have to delay running for the state Senate."

"Why?" Ansley wanted Warren in Richmond as much as possible. She intended to work nonstop for his election.

"Might look bad."

"No, it won't. You tell the voters you're dedicating this campaign to your father, a man who believed in self-determination."

Admiring her shrewdness, he said, "Poppa would have liked

that. You know, it's occurred to me these last few days that I'm raising my sons the way Poppa raised me. I was packed off to St. Clement's, worked here for the summers, and then it was off to Vanderbilt. Maybe the boys should be different—maybe something wild for them like"—he thought—"Berkeley. Now that I'm the head of this family, I want to give my sons more freedom."

"If they want to attend another college, fine, but let's not push them into it. Vanderbilt has served this family well for a long time." Ansley loved her sons although she despised the music they blasted throughout the house. No amount of yelling convinced them they'd go deaf. She was sure she was half deaf already.

"Did you really like my father?"

"Why do you ask me that now, after eighteen years of marriage?" She was genuinely surprised.

"Because I don't know you. Not really." He gazed at the horses on the far side of the track, for he couldn't look at her.

"I thought that's the way your people did things. I didn't think you wanted to be close."

"Maybe I don't know how."

Too late now, she thought to herself. "Well, Warren, one step at a time. I got along with Wesley, but it was his way or no way."

"Yep."

"I did like what he printed on his checks." She recited verbatim: "These funds were generated under the free enterprise system despite government's flagrant abuse of the income tax, bureaucratic hostilities, and irresponsible controls."

Warren's eyes misted. "He was tough duty, but he was clear about what he thought."

"We'll know even more about that at the reading of the will."

25

The reading of the will hit Warren like a two-by-four. Wesley had prepared his will through the old prestigious firm of Maki, Kleiser, and Maki. Not that Warren minded. It would be indelicate to have your son prepare your will. Still, he wasn't prepared for this.

A clause in his father's will read that no money could ever be inherited by any Randolph of any succeeding generation who married a person who was even one-twentieth African.

Ansley laughed. How absurd. Her sons weren't going to marry women from Uganda. Her sons weren't even going to marry African Americans, quadroons, octoroons, no way. Those boys weren't sent to St. Clements to be liberals and certainly not to mix with the races—the calendar be damned.

Warren, ashen when he heard the clause, sputtered, "That's illegal. Under today's laws that's illegal."

Old George Kleiser neatly stacked his papers. "Maybe. Maybe not. This will could be contested, but who would do that? Let it stand. Those were your father's express wishes." Apparently George thought the proviso prudent, or perhaps he subscribed to the let-sleeping-dogs-lie theory.

"Warren, you aren't going to do anything about this? I mean, why would you?"

As if in a trance, Warren shook his head. "No—but, Ansley, if this gets out, there go my chances for the state Senate."

George's stentorian voice filled the room. "Word of this, uh, consideration will never leave this room."

"What about the person who physically prepared the will?" Warren put his foot in it.

George, irritated, glided over that remark as he made allowances for Warren's recent loss. He'd known Warren since infancy, so he knew the middle-aged man in front of him was unprepared to take the helm of the family's great, though dwindling, fortune. "Our staff is accustomed to sensitive issues, Warren. Issues of life and death."

"Of course, of course, George—I'm just flabbergasted. Poppa never once spoke of anything like this to me."

"He was a genteel racist instead of an overt one." Ansley wanted to put the subject out of her mind and couldn't see why Warren was so upset.

"And aren't you?" Warren fired back.

"Not as long as we don't intermarry. I don't believe in mixing the races. Other than that, people are people." Ansley shook off Warren's barb.

"Ansley, you must promise me never, never, no matter how angry you may become with me or the boys—after all, people do rub one another's nerves—but you must never repeat what you've heard in this room today. I don't want to lose my chance because Poppa had this thing about racial purity."

Ansley promised never to tell.

26

But she did. She told Samson.

The early afternoon sun slanted across Blair Bainbridge's large oak kitchen table. Tulips swayed outside the long windows, and the hyacinths would open in a few days if this welcome warmth continued.

"I'm not surprised," Samson told Ansley. "The old man made a lifetime study of bloodlines, and to him it would be like crossing a donkey with a Thoroughbred." Then he smirked. "Of course, who is the donkey and who is the Thoroughbred?"

She held his hand as she sipped her hot chocolate. "It seems so—extreme."

Samson shrugged. The contents of Wesley's will held scant interest for him. Another twenty minutes and he would have to hit the road. His stomach knotted up each time he left Ansley.

"Say, I've got people coming in from California to look at Midale. Think I'll show them some properties in Orange County too. Awful pretty up there and not so developed. If I can sell Midale, I'll have some good money." He pressed his other hand on top of hers. "Then you can leave Warren."

Ansley stiffened. "Not while he's in mourning for his father."

"After that. Six months is a reasonable period of time. I can set my house in order and you can do the same."

"Honey"—she petted his hand—"let's leave well enough alone—for now. Lulu will skin you alive and in public. There's got to be a way around her, but I haven't found it yet. I keep hoping she'll find someone, she'll make life easier—but she has too much invested in being the wronged woman. And that scene at Big Daddy's funeral. My God."

Samson coughed. The knot in his stomach grew tighter. "Just one of those things. She leaned over to whisper in my ear and said she smelled another woman's perfume. I don't know what got into her."

"She knows my perfume, Diva. Anyway, when we're together I don't wear any perfume."

"Natural perfume." He kissed her hand in his.

She kissed him on the cheek. "Samson, you are the sweetest man."

"Not to hear my wife tell it." He sighed and bowed his head. "I don't know how much longer I can stand it. I'm living such a lie. I don't love Lulu. I'm tired of keeping up with the Joneses, who can't keep up with themselves. I'm tired of being trapped in my car all day with strangers and no matter what they tell you they want to buy, they really want the opposite. I swear it. Buyers are liars, as my first broker used to say. I don't know how long I can hold out."

"Just a little longer, precious." She nibbled on his ear. "*Was* there another woman's perfume on your neck?"

He sputtered, "Absolutely not. I don't even know where she

came up with that. You know I don't even look at other women, Ansley." He kissed her passionately.

As she drew back from the kiss she murmured, "Well, she knows, she just doesn't know it's me. Funny, I like Lulu. I call her most every morning. I guess she's my best friend, but I don't like her as your wife and I never did. I couldn't get it, know what I mean? You can sometimes see a couple and know why they're together. Like Harry and Fair when they were together. Or Susan and Ned—that's a good pair—but I never felt the heat, I guess you'd say, between Lulu and you. I don't really feel like I'm betraying her. I feel like I'm liberating her. She deserves the heat. She needs the right man for her—you're the right man for me."

He kissed her again and wished the clock weren't ticking so loudly. "Ansley, I can't live without you. You know that. I'll never be as rich as Warren, but I'm not poor. I work hard."

Her voice low, she brushed his cheek with her lips as she said, "And I want to make sure you don't join the ranks of the nouveau pauvre. I don't want your wife to take you to the cleaners. Give me a little time. I'll think of something or someone." She leapt out of her chair. "Oh, no!"

"What?" He hurried to her side.

Ansley pointed out the kitchen window. Mrs. Murphy and Tucker merrily raced to the stable. "Harry can't be far behind, and she's no dummy."

"Damn!" Samson ran his hands through his thick hair.

"If you slip out the front door I'll go out to the stable and head her off. Hurry!" She kissed him quickly. She could hear the heels of his shoes as he strode across the hardwood floors to the front door. Ansley headed for the back screen door.

Harry, much slower than her four-footed companions, had just reached the family cemetery on the hill. Ansley made it to the stable before Harry saw her.

"What's she doing in Blair's house?" Tucker asked.

Mrs. Murphy paused to observe Ansley. *"High color. She's het up about something and we know she's not stealing the silver. She's got too much of her own.''*

"*What if she's a kleptomaniac?*" Tucker cocked her head as Ansley walked toward them.

"*Nah. But give her a sniff anyway.*"

"Hi there, Mrs. Murphy. You too, Tucker," Ansley called to the animals.

"*Ansley, what are you up to?*" Tucker asked as she poked her nose toward Ansley's ankles.

Ansley waved at Harry, who waved back. She reached down to scratch Tucker's big ears.

"Hi, how nice to find you here." Harry diplomatically smiled.

"Warren sent me over to look at Blair's spider-wheel tedder. Says he wants one and maybe Blair will sell it."

A spider-wheel tedder turns hay for drying and can row up two swathes into one for baling. Three or four small metal wheels that resemble spiderwebs are pulled by a tractor.

"Thought you all rolled up your hay."

"Warren says he's tired of looking at huge rolls of shredded wheat in the fields and the middle of them is always wasted. He wants to go back to baling."

"Be a while." Harry noted the season.

Ansley lowered her voice. "He's already planning Thanksgiving dinner for the family. I think it's how the grief is taking him. You know, if he plans everything, then nothing can go wrong, he can control reality—although you'd think he would have had enough of that with his father."

"It will take time." Harry knew. She had lost both her parents some years before.

Mrs. Murphy, on her haunches, got up and trotted off toward the house. "*She's lying.*"

"*Got that right.*" The dog followed, her ears sweeping back for a moment. "*Let's nose around.*"

The two animals reached the back door. Tucker, nose straight to the ground, sniffed intently. Mrs. Murphy relied on her eyes as much as her nose.

Tucker picked up the scent easily. *"Samson Coles."*

"So that's it." Mrs. Murphy walked between the tulips. She loved feeling the stems brush against her fur. *"She must really be bored."*

27

The quiet at Eagle's Rest proved unnerving. Ansley regretted saying how much she loathed the loud music the boys played. Although cacophonous, it was preferable to silence.

Seven in the evening usually meant each son was in his room studying. How Breton and Stuart could study with that wall of reverberating sound fascinated her. They used to compete in decibel levels with the various bands. Finally she settled that by declaring that during the first hour of study time, from six to seven, Stuart could play his music. Breton's choice won out between seven and eight.

Both she and Warren policed what they called study hall. Breton and Stuart made good grades, but Ansley felt they needed to know how important their schoolwork was to their parents, hence the policing. She told them frequently, "We have our jobs to do, you have your schoolwork."

Unable, at last, to bear the silence, Ansley climbed the curving stairway to the upstairs hall. She peeked in Breton's room. She walked down to Stuart's. Her older son sat at his desk. Breton, cross-legged, perched on Stuart's bed. Breton's eyes were red. Ansley knew not to call attention to that.

"Hey, guys."

"Hi, Mom." They replied in unison.

"What's up?"

"Nothing." Again in unison.

"Oh." She paused. "Kind of funny not to have Big Daddy yelling about your music, huh?"

"Yeah," Stuart agreed.

"He's never coming back." Breton had a catch in his breath. "I can't believe he's never coming back. At first it was like he was on vacation, you know?"

"I know," Ansley commiserated.

Stuart sat upright, a change from his normal slouch. "Remember the times we used to recite our heritage?" He imitated his grandfather's voice. "The first Randolph to set foot in the New World was a crony of Sir Walter Raleigh's. He returned to the old country. His son, emboldened by stories of the New World, came over in 1632, and thus our line began on this side of the Atlantic. He brought his bride, Jemima Hessletine. Their firstborn, Nancy Randolph, died that winter of 1634, aged six months. The second born, Raleigh Randolph, survived. We descend from this son."

Ansley, amazed, gasped. "Word for word."

"Mom, we heard it, seems like every day." Stuart half smiled.

"Yeah. Wish I could hear him again and—and I hate all that genealogy stuff." Breton's eyes welled up again. "Who cares?"

Ansley sat next to Breton, putting her arm around his shoulders. He seemed bigger the last time she hugged him. "Honey, when you get older, you'll appreciate these things."

"Why is it so important to everyone?" Breton asked innocently.

"To be wellborn is an advantage in this life. It opens many doors. Life's hard enough as it is, Breton, so be thankful for the blessing."

"Go to Montana," Stuart advised. "No one cares there. Probably why Big Daddy never liked the West. He couldn't lord it over everybody."

Ansley sighed. "Wesley liked to be the biggest frog in the pond."

"Mom, do you care about that bloodline stuff?" Breton turned to face his mother.

"Let's just say I'd rather have it and not need it than need it and not have it."

They digested this, then Breton asked another question. "Mom, is it always like this when someone dies?"

"When it's someone you love, it is."

28

Medley Orion left Monticello in the dispersal after Thomas Jefferson's death in 1826. Kimball burned up tank after tank of gas as he drove down the winding county roads in search of genealogies, slave records, anything that might give him a clue. A few references to Medley's dressmaking skills surfaced in the well-preserved diaries of Tinton Venable.

Obsessed with the murder and with Medley herself, Kimball even drove to the Library of Congress to read through the notations of Dr. William Thornton and his French-born wife. Thornton imagined himself a Renaissance man like Jefferson. He raced blooded horses, designed the Capitol and the Octagon House in Washington, D.C., was a staunch Federalist, and survived the burning of Washington in 1814. His efforts to save the city during that conflagration created a bitter enmity between himself and the mayor of Washington. Thornton's wife, Anna Maria, rang out his praises on the hour like a well-timed church bell. When she visited Monticello in 1802 she wrote: "There is something more grand and awful than convenient in the whole place. A situation you would rather look at now and then than inhabit."

Mrs. Thornton, French, snob that she was, possessed some humor. What was odd was that Jefferson prided himself on convenience and efficiency.

Kimball's hunch paid off. He found a reference to Medley. Mrs. Thornton commented on a mint-green summer dress belonging to Martha Jefferson—Patsy. The dress, Mrs. Thornton noted, was sewn by Patsy's genie, as she put it, Medley Orion. She also mentioned that Medley's daughter, not quite a woman, was "bright," meaning fair-skinned, and extraordinarily beautiful like her mother, but even lighter. She further noted that Medley and Martha Jefferson Randolph got along quite well, "a miracle considering," but Mrs. Thornton chose not to explain that pregnant phrase.

Mrs. Thornton then went on to discuss thoroughly her feelings about slavery—she didn't like it—and her feelings about mixing the races, which she didn't like either. She felt that slavery promoted laziness. Her argument for this, although convoluted, contained a kernel of logic: Why should people work if they couldn't retain the fruits of their labors? A roof over one's head, food in the stomach, and clothes on one's back weren't sufficient motivation for industriousness, especially when one saw another party benefitting from one's own labor.

Kimball drove so fast down Route 29 on his way home that he received a speeding ticket for his excitement and still made it from downtown Washington to Charlottesville more than fifteen minutes faster than the usual two hours. He couldn't wait to tell Heike what he had discovered. He would have to decide what to tell Oliver, who grew more tense each day.

29

Kimball Haynes, Harry, Mrs. Hogendobber, Mim Sanburne, and Lucinda Coles crammed themselves into a booth at Metropolitain, a restaurant in Charlottesville's Downtown Mall. The Metropolitain combined lack of pretension with fantastic food. Lulu happened to be strolling in the mall when Kimball spotted her and asked her to lunch with the others.

Over salads he explained his findings about Medley Orion and Jefferson's oldest child, Martha.

"Well, Kimball, I can see that you're a born detective, but where is this leading?" Mim wanted to know. She was ready to get down to brass tacks.

"I wish I knew." Kimball cut into a grits patty.

"You all may be too young to have heard an old racist expression." Mim glanced at the ceiling, for she had learned to

despise these sayings. " 'There's a nigger in the woodpile somewhere.' Comes from the Underground Railway, of course, but
you get the drift."

Lulu Coles fidgeted. "No, I don't."

"Somebody's hiding something," Mim stated flatly.

"Of course somebody's hiding something. They've been
hiding it for two hundred years, and now Martha Jefferson Randolph is in on it." Lulu checked her anger. She knew Mim had
yanked properties away from Samson because of his outburst at
the funeral. Angry as she was at her husband, Lucinda was smart
enough not to wish for their net worth to drop. Actually, she was
angry, period. She'd peer in the mirror and see the corners of her
mouth turning down just as her mother's had—an embittered
woman she swore never to emulate. She was becoming her own
mother, to her horror.

Harry downed her Coke. "What Mim means is that somebody is hiding something today."

"Why?" Susan threw her hands in the air. The idea was
absurd. "So there's a murderer in the family tree. By this time we
have one of everything in all of our family trees. Really, who
cares?"

" 'Save me, Lord, from liars and deceivers.' Psalm 120:2."
Mrs. Hogendobber, as usual, recalled a pertinent scripture.

"Forgive me, Mrs. H., but there's a better one." Kimball
closed his eyes in order to remember. "Ah, yes, here it is, 'Every
one deceives his neighbor, and no one speaks the truth; they have
taught their tongue to speak lies; they commit iniquity and are
too weary to repent.' "

"Jeremiah 9:5. Yes, it is better," Mrs. Hogendobber agreed.
"I suppose letting the cat out of the bag these many years later
wouldn't seem upsetting, but if it's in the papers and on television, well—I can understand."

"Yeah, your great-great-great-great-grandfather was murdered. How do you feel about that?" Susan smirked.

"Or your great-great—how many greats?" Harry turned to

Susan, who held up two fingers. "Great-great-grandfather was a murderer. Should you pay the victim's descendants recompense? Obviously, our society has lost the concept of privacy, and you can't blame anyone for wanting to keep whatever they can away from prying eyes."

"Well, I for one would like a breath of fresh air. Kimball, you're welcome to go through the Coleses' papers. Maybe you'll find the murderer there." Lulu smiled.

"How generous of you. The Coleses' papers will be invaluable to me even if they don't yield the murderer." Kimball beamed.

Mim shifted on the hard bench. "I wonder that Samson has never donated his treasures to the Alderman Library. Or some other library he feels would do justice to the manuscripts and diaries. Naturally, I prefer the Alderman."

The olive branch was outstretched. Lulu grabbed it. "I'll work on him, Mim. Samson fears that his family's archives will be labeled, stuck in a carton, and never again see the light of day. Decades from now, someone will stumble upon them and they'll be decayed. He keeps all those materials in his temperature-controlled library. The Coleses lead the way when it comes to preservation," she breathed, "but perhaps this is the time to share."

"Yes." Mim appeared enlightened when her entrée, a lightly poached salmon in dill sauce, was placed in front of her. "What did you order, Lucinda? I've already forgotten."

"Sweetbreads."

"Me too." Harry's mouth watered as the dish's tempting aroma wafted under her nose.

"What a lunch." Kimball inclined his head toward the ladies. "Beautiful women, delicious food, and help with my research. What more is there to life?"

"A 16.1-hand Thoroughbred fox hunter that floats over a three-foot-six-inch coop." The rich sauce melted in Harry's mouth.

"Oh, Harry, you and your horses. You have Gin Fizz and Tomahawk." Susan elbowed her.

"Getting along in years," Mim informed Susan. Mim, an avid fox hunter, appreciated Harry's desire. She also appreciated Harry's emaciated budget and made a mental note to see if she could strong-arm someone into selling Harry a good horse at a low price.

Six months earlier the idea of helping the postmistress wouldn't have occurred to her. But Mim had turned over a new leaf. She wanted to be warmer, kinder, and more giving. It wasn't easy, overnight, to dump six decades of living a certain way. The cause of this volte-face Mim kept close to her chest, which was, indeed, where it began. She had visited Larry Johnson for a routine checkup. He found a lump. Larry, the soul of discretion, promised not to tell even Jim. Mim flew to New York City and checked into Columbia-Presbyterian. She told everyone she was on her semiannual shopping spree. Since she did repair to New York every spring and then again every fall, this explanation satisfied. The lump was removed and it was cancerous. However, they had caught the disease in time. Her body betrayed no other signs of the cancer. Procedures are so advanced that Mim returned home in a week, had indeed accomplished some shopping, and no one was the wiser. Until Jim walked in on her in the bathtub. She told him everything. He sobbed. That shocked her so badly that she sobbed. She still couldn't figure out how her husband could be chronically unfaithful and love her so deeply at the same time, but she knew now that he did. She decided to give up being angry at him. She even decided to stop pretending socially that he didn't have a weakness for women. He was what he was and she was what she was, but she could change and she was trying. If Jim wanted to change, that was his responsibility.

"Earth to Mrs. Sanburne," Harry called.

"What? I must have been roller-skating on Saturn's rings."

"We're going to help Kimball read through the correspondence and records of Jefferson's children and grandchildren," Harry told her.

"I can read with my eyes closed," Miranda said. "Oh, that doesn't sound right, does it?"

After lunch Lulu escorted Mim to her silver sand Bentley Turbo R, a new purchase and a sensational one. Lulu apologized profusely a second time for her outburst during Wesley's funeral. After Mim's luncheon she had smothered her hostess in "sorries." She had also confessed to Reverend Jones and he had told her it wasn't that bad. He forgave her and he was sure that the Randolphs would too, if she would apologize, which she did. Mim listened. Lulu continued. It was as though she'd pried the first olive out of the jar and the others tumbled out. She said she thought she'd smelled another woman's perfume on Samson's neck. She'd been on edge. Later she'd entered his bathroom and found a bottle, new, of Ralph Lauren's Safari.

"These days you can't tell the difference between men's colognes and women's perfumes," Mim said. "There is no difference. They put the unguents into different bottles, invent these manly names, and that's that. What would happen if a man used a woman's perfume? He'd grow breasts overnight, I guess." She laughed at her own joke.

Lulu laughed too. "It strikes me as odd that the worst thing you can call a man is a woman, yet they claim to love us."

Mim arched her right eyebrow. "I never thought of that."

"I think of a lot of things." Lulu sighed. "I'm a tangle of suspicions. I know he's cheating on me. I just don't know who."

Mim unlocked her car, paused, and then turned. "Lucinda, I don't know if that part matters. The whole town knows that Jim has enjoyed his little amours over the years."

"Mim, I didn't mean to open old wounds," Lulu stammered, genuinely distraught.

"Don't give it a second thought. I'm older than you. I don't care as much anymore, or I care in a new way. But heed my advice. Some men are swordsmen. That's the only word I can think of for it. They swash and they buckle. They need the chase and the conquest to feel alive. It's repetitive, but for some reason I can't fathom, the repetition doesn't bore them. Makes them feel young and powerful, I suppose. It doesn't mean Samson doesn't love you."

Tears glistened in Lucinda's green eyes. "Oh, Mim, if only that were true, but Samson isn't that kind of man. If he's having an affair, then he's in love with her."

Mim waited to reply. "My dear, the only thing you can do is to take care of yourself."

30

"If you light another cigarette, then I'll have to light one too," Deputy Cynthia Cooper joshed.

"Here." Sheriff Shaw tossed his pack of Chesterfields at her. She caught them left-handed. "Out at first," he said.

She tapped the pack with a long, graceful finger, and a slender white cigarette slid out. The deep tobacco fragrance made her eyelids flutter. That evil weed, that scourge of the lungs, that drug, nicotine, but oh, how it soothed the nerves and how it added to the coffers of the great state of Virginia. "Damn, I love these things."

"Think we'll die young?"

"Young?" Cynthia raised her eyebrows, which made Rick laugh, since he was already middle-aged.

"Hey, you want another promotion someday, don't you, Deputy?"

"Just a beardless boy, that Rick Shaw." She placed the cigarette in her mouth, lighting it with a match from a box of Redbuds.

They inhaled in sweet silence, the blue smoke swirling to the ceiling like a slow whirling dervish of delight.

"Coop, what do you think of Oliver Zeve?"

"He took the news as I expected. A nervous twitch."

Rick grunted. "His press statement was a model of restraint. But nothing, nothing, will beat Big Marilyn Sanburne advancing her stalker theory. She's good. She's really good." Rick appreciated Mim's skills even though he didn't like her. "I'd better call her."

"Good politics, boss."

Rick dialed the Sanburne residence. The butler fetched Mim. "Mrs. Sanburne, Rick Shaw here."

"Yes, Sheriff."

"I wanted to give you the report from Washington concerning the human remains found at Monticello." He heard a quick intake of breath. "The skeleton is that of a white male, aged between thirty-two and thirty-five. In good health. The left femur had been broken in childhood and healed. Possibly the victim suffered a slight limp. The victim was five ten in height, which although not nearly as tall as Jefferson's six foot four, would have been tall for the times, and given the density of bone, he was probably powerfully built. There were no signs of degenerative disease in the bones, and his teeth, also, were quite good. He was killed by one forceful blow to the back of the skull with an as yet undetermined weapon. Death, more than likely, was instantaneous."

Mim asked, "How do they know the man was white?"

"Well, Mrs. Sanburne, determining race from skeletal remains can actually be a little tricky sometimes. We're all much more alike than we are different. The races have more in common than they have dissimilarities. You could say that race has more to do with culture than physical attributes. However, forensics starts by considering the bone structure and skeletal proportions of a specimen. Specifically, the amount of projection of the cheekbones, the width of the nasal aperture, and the shape and distance between the eye sockets. Another factor is the amount of projection of the jaw. For instance, a white man's jaw is generally less prominent than a black man's is. Prognathism is the term for the way the jaw figures more prominently in the faces of those of African descent. There is also in many white skeletons the presence of an extra seam in the skull, which extends from the top of the nasal arch to the top of the head. Perhaps even more helpful is the amount of curvature in the long bones, especially the femur, of an individual. A white person's skeleton tends to have more twisting in the neck or head of the femur."

"Amazing."

"Yes, it is," the sheriff agreed.

"Thank you," Mim said politely, and hung up the phone.

"Well?" Cooper asked.

"She didn't succumb to the vapors." Rick referred to the Victorian ladies' habit of fainting upon hearing unwelcome news. "Let's run over to Kimball Haynes's. I want to see him away from Oliver Zeve. Oliver will shut him down if he can."

"Boss, the director of Monticello isn't going to obstruct justice. I know that Oliver walks a tightrope up there, but he's not a criminal."

"No, I don't think so either, but he's so supersensitive about this. He'll put the crimp on Kimball somehow, and I think Kimball is the one person who can lead us to the killer."

"I think it's Medley Orion."

"How often have I told you not to jump to conclusions?"

"Eleventy million times." She rolled her big blue eyes. "Still do it though."

"Still right most of the time too." He kicked at her as she

walked by to stub out her cigarette. "Well, I happen to agree. It was Medley or a boyfriend, father, somebody close to her. If we could just find the motive—Kimball knows the period inside and out and he's got a feel for the people."

"Got the bug."

"Huh?"

"Harry told me that Kimball eats and sleeps this case."

"Harry—next she'll have the cat and dog on it too."

31

The night air, cool and deep, carried stories to Tucker's nose. Deer followed the warm air currents, raccoons prowled around Monticello, a possum reposed on a branch of the Carolina silverbell near the terrace which Mrs. Murphy, like Kimball, thought of as a boardwalk. Overhead, bats flew in and out of the tulip poplar, the purple beech, and the eaves of the brick house.

"I'm glad Monticello has bats." Mrs. Murphy watched the small mammals dart at almost right angles when they wanted.

"Why?" Tucker sat down.

"Makes this place less august. After all, when Thomas Jefferson lived here, it probably didn't look like this. The trees couldn't have been this grand. The garbage had to go somewhere—know what I mean?—and it must have been filled with noises. Now there's a reverential silence except for the shuffling of human feet on the tours."

"It must have been fun, all the grandchildren, the slaves calling to one another, the clanging in the smithy, the neighing of the horses. I can imagine it, and I can envision a bright corgi accompanying Mr. Jefferson on his rides."

"Dream on. If he had dogs out with him, they would have been big dogs—coach dogs or hunting dogs."

"Like Dalmatians?" Tucker's ears dropped for a moment as she considered her spotted rival. "He wouldn't have owned Dalmatians. I think he had corgis. We're good herding dogs and we could have been useful."

"Then you would have been out with the cattle."

"Horses."

"Cattle."

"Oh, what do you know? Next you'll say a cat sat by Jefferson's elbow when he wrote the Declaration of Independence."

Mrs. Murphy's whiskers twitched. "No cat would ever have allowed the phrase 'All men are created equal' to pass. Not only are all men not created equal, cats aren't created equal. Some cats are more equal than others, if you know what I mean."

"He wrote it in Philadelphia. Maybe that affected his brain." Tucker giggled.

"Philadelphia was a beautiful city then. Parts of it are still beautiful, but it just got too big, you know. All of our cities got too big. Anyway, it's absurd to plunk an idea like that down on parchment. Men aren't equal. And we know for sure that women aren't equal. They weren't even considered at the time."

"Maybe he meant equal under the law."

"That's a farce. Ever see a rich man go to jail? I take that back. Every now and then a Mafia don gets marched to the slammer."

"Mrs. Murphy, how could Thomas Jefferson have dreamed of the Mafia? When he wrote the Declaration of Independence, only a million people lived in the thirteen colonies and they were mostly English, Irish, Scottish, and German, and, of course, African from the various tribes."

"Don't forget the French."

"Boy, were they stupid. Had the chance to grab the whole New World and blew it."

"Tucker, I didn't know you were a Francophobe."

"They don't like corgis. The Queen of England likes corgis, so I think the English are the best."

"Jefferson didn't." The cat's silken eyebrows bobbed up and down.

"Not fair. George III was mental. The whole history of the world might have been different if he'd been right in the head."

"Yeah, but you could pick out any moment in history and say that. What would have happened if Julius Caesar had listened to his wife, Calpurnia, on March fifteenth, when she begged him not to go to the Forum? Beware the Ides of March. What would have happened if Catherine the Great's attempt on her looney-tunes husband's life had failed and she was killed instead? Moments. Turning points. Every day there's a turning point somewhere with someone. I think the creation of the Society for the Prevention of Cruelty to Animals gets my vote as most important."

Tucker stood up and inhaled. "I pick the founding of the Westminster Dog Show. Say, do you smell that?"

Mrs. Murphy lifted her elegant head. "Skunk."

"Let's go back in the house. If I see her, then I'll chase her and you know what will happen. The odor of skunk in Monticello."

"I think it would be pretty funny myself. I wonder if Jefferson would like the idea of his home being a museum. I bet he'd rather have it filled with children and laughter, broken pottery and worn-out furniture."

"He would, but Americans need shrines. They need to see how their great people lived. They didn't have indoor plumbing. Fireplaces were the only source of heat in the winter. No washing machines, refrigerators, stoves, or televisions."

"The last would be a blessing." Mrs. Murphy's voice dripped disdain.

"No telephones, telegraphs, fax machines, automobiles, airplanes . . ."

"Sounds better and better." The cat brushed up against the dog. "Quiet except for natural sounds. Just think, people actually sat down and really talked to one another. They were under an obligation to entertain one another with their conversational abilities. You know what people do today? They sit in their living room or family room—isn't that a dumb word? Every room is a family room—they sit there with the television on and if they talk they talk over the sound of the boob tube."

"*Oh, Mrs. Murphy, they can't all be that crude.*"

"*Humph,*" the cat replied. She did not consider the human animal the crown of creation.

"*I'm surprised you know your history.*" Tucker scratched her ear.

"*I listen. I know human history and our history and no matter what, I am an Americat.*"

"*And there is an Ameriskunk.*" Tucker scurried to the front door, which was open just enough so she could squeeze in as a fat skunk at the edge of the lawn hastened in the opposite direction.

Mrs. Murphy followed. The two ran to the narrow staircase behind the North Square Room, turned left, and scampered up to Kimball's makeshift workroom.

Harry, Mrs. Hogendobber, and Kimball, now bleary-eyed, had sifted through as much correspondence as they could. Martha Jefferson, the future president's daughter, married Thomas Mann Randolph on February 23, 1790. Together they produced twelve children, eleven of whom gained maturity and most of whom lived to a ripe old age. The last died in 1882, and that was Virginia Jefferson Randolph, born in 1801. Martha's children in turn begat thirty-five children. Maria, her sister, had thirteen grandchildren through her son Francis Eppes, who married twice, which brings that generation's count to forty-eight. They, too, were fruitful and multiplied—not that everyone lived to breed. A few grew to adulthood and never married, but the descendants were plentiful even so.

Mrs. Hogendobber rubbed her nose. "This is like finding a needle in a haystack."

"But which needle?" Harry joined her chorus.

"Which haystack, Martha or Maria?" Kimball was also wearing down.

"You'd think someone would say something about Medley or her child." Harry noticed her friends enter the room. "What have you two been up to?"

"*Discussion of history,*" Mrs. Murphy answered.

"*Yeah, deep stuff.*" Tucker plopped at her mother's feet.

"The sad truth is that back then black lives weren't that important." Mrs. Hogendobber shook her head.

"There sure are enough references to Jupiter, Jefferson's body servant, and King and Sally and Betsey Hemings, and well, the list could go on and on. Medley gets a footnote." Kimball started pulling on his lower lip, an odd habit indicating intense thought.

"What about Madison Hemings? He sure caused a sensation. A dead ringer for Thomas Jefferson with a deep brown tan. He waited on the dinner guests. Bet he gave them a start." Harry wondered what the real effect must have been upon seeing a young mulatto man in livery who surely shared the president's blood.

"Born in 1805, and as an old man he said he was Jefferson's son. Said his mother, Sally, told him." Kimball abruptly leapt up. "But that could be a desire to be the center of attention. And Jefferson had a wealth of male relatives, each and every one capable of congress with Sally or her pretty sister, Betsey. And what about the other white employees of the plantation?"

"Well, Thomas Jefferson Randolph, Martha's oldest son, who was born in 1792 and lived to 1875, swore that Sally was Peter Carr's favorite mistress and Sally's sister, Betsey, was mistress to Sam Carr. Those were Jefferson's nephews, the sons of Dabney Carr and Martha Jefferson's younger sister. Wild as rats they were too." Kimball smiled, imagining the charms of a black purdah with one white sultan, or, in this case, two.

"Wonder if Sally and Betsey thought it was so great?" Harry couldn't resist.

"Huh"—he blinked—"well, maybe not, but Harry, you can't remove sexual fantasy from the life of the male. I mean, we all want to imagine ourselves in the arms of a beautiful woman."

"Yeah, yeah," Harry grumbled. "The imagining isn't so bad, it's the doing it when one is married. Oh, well, this is an ancient debate."

He softened. "I get your point."

"*And who slept with Medley?*" Mrs. Murphy flicked her tail. "*If she was as pretty as she is reputed to have been, she would have turned a white head or two.*"

"What a loud purr." Kimball admired Mrs. Murphy.

"*You should hear her burp.*" Tucker wagged her nontail, hoping to be noticed.

"Jealous." Mrs. Hogendobber said matter-of-factly.

"*She's got your number, stumpy.*" Mrs. Murphy teased her friend, who didn't reply because Kimball was petting her.

"Is it me or is there a conspiracy of silence surrounding Medley Orion and her child?" Harry, like a hound, struck a faint, very faint scent.

Both Kimball and Mrs. Hogendobber stared at her.

"Isn't that obvious?" Kimball said.

"The obvious is a deceitful temptation." Mrs. Hogendobber, by virtue of working with Harry, picked up the line now too. "We're overlooking something."

"The master of Monticello may not have known about whatever Medley was up to or whoever killed that man, but I bet you dollars to doughnuts that Martha did, and that's why she took Medley. She could easily have been sold off, you know. The family could have ditched this slave if she became an embarrassment."

"Harry, the Jeffersons did not sell their slaves." Kimball almost sounded like Mim. It wasn't true though. Jefferson did sell his slaves, but only if he knew they were going to a good home. Jefferson's policy demonstrated more concern than many slave owners evidenced, yet the disposal of other humans seemed both callous and mercenary to some of Jefferson's contemporaries.

"They could have given her away after Thomas died." Mrs. Hogendobber shifted in her seat, a surge of energy enlivening her thoughts. "One or both daughters protected Medley. Martha and Maria."

Kimball threw his hands in the air. "Why?"

"Well, why in the hell did not one family member suggest they pack off Sally and Betsey Hemings? My God, Jefferson was crucified over his alleged affair with Sally. Think about it, Kimball. It may have been two hundred years ago, but politics is still politics and people have changed remarkably little." Harry nearly shouted.

"A cover-up?" Kimball whispered.

"Ah"—Mrs. Hogendobber held up her forefinger like a schoolmarm—"not a cover-up but pride. If the Hemingses were 'dismissed,' shall we say, then it would have been an admission of guilt."

"But surely keeping them on this hill fed the gossipmongers too," Kimball exploded in frustration.

"Yes, but Jefferson didn't buy into it. So if he's mum, what can they do? They can make up stories. Any newspaper today is full of the same conjecture posing as fact. But if Jefferson levitated above them all in his serene way, then he stole some of their fire. He never sweated in front of the enemy is what I'm saying, and he made a conscious decision not to bag the Hemingses."

"Harry, those slaves came from his mother's estate."

"Kimball, so what?"

"He was a very loyal man. After all, when Dabney Carr, his best friend, died young, he created the family cemetery for him, and would lean on his grave and read to be close to him."

Harry held up her hands as if asking for a truce, "Okay. Okay, then try this. Sally and Betsey's mother, Betty Hemings, was half white. The skinny from the other slaves was that her father was an English sea captain. Thomas Jefferson freed Bob and James, Sally and Betsey's brothers, in 1790. Except for another daughter, Thenia, who was acquired by James Monroe, all the Hemingses stayed at Monticello. They had a reputation for being good workers and for being intelligent. Sally was never set free, but her daughter was, by Jefferson, in 1822. At least, that's what I'm getting out of all these papers."

"I know all that," Kimball fretted.

"I don't." Mrs. Hogendobber made a sign indicating for Harry to continue.

"Jefferson made provision for Sally's sons Madison and Eston to be freed upon reaching the age of twenty-one. Now, he wouldn't have done that if he didn't think these people could earn a living. It would be cruel to send them into the world otherwise. Right?"

"Right." Kimball paced.

"And the lovers of Sally and Betsey may not have been the Carr brothers. The slaves said that John Wayles took Sally as, what should I say, his common-law wife, after his third wife died, and that Sally had six children by him. John Wayles was Martha Jefferson's brother, T.J.'s brother-in-law. Jefferson took responsibility, always, for any member of his family. He loved Martha beyond reason. His solicitude makes sense in this light. Of course, others said that John Wayles was the lover of Betty Hemings, so that Sally and Betsey would have been Martha's cousins. Guess we'll never really know, but the point is, Sally and Betsey had some blood tie, or deep-heart tie, to T.J."

Kimball sat back down. He spoke slowly. "That does make sense. It would force him into silence, too, concerning the paternity slanders."

"John Wayles wasn't equipped to handle this kind of scrutiny. Jefferson was." Mrs. Hogendobber hit the nail on the head. "And even though they hurt Jefferson, the slandermongers, they couldn't really abridge his power."

"Why not?" Kimball was perplexed.

"And flush out all those white jackrabbits in the briar patch?" Mrs. Hogendobber laughed. "The question is not which southern gentlemen slept with slave women, the question is which ones did not."

"Oh, I do see." Kimball rubbed his chin. "The Yankees could fulminate properly, but the Southerners shut up and rolled right over, so to speak."

"Hell, yes, they wouldn't have nailed Jefferson to the cross for their own sins." Harry laughed. "The Northerners could do the nailing, but they never could quite catch him to do it. He was far too smart to talk and he always sheltered those weaker than himself."

"He had broad, broad wings." Mrs. Hogendobber smiled.

"And where does that leave Medley Orion?" Kimball stood up and paced again.

"She may or may not have been related to the Hemingses. Obviously, from the description of her as 'bright,' she was one quarter white if not half white. And her lover was white. The lover is the key. He was being protected," Harry said.

"I disagree. I think it's Medley who was being protected. I can't prove it, but my woman's intuition tells me the victim was Medley's white lover."

"What?" Kimball stopped in his tracks.

"The Jeffersons extended their grace to many people: to Wayles if he was the amour of Betty Hemings or her daughter, Sally; to the Carrs if they were involved. The corpse in Cabin Four wasn't a family member. His absence or death would have been noted somewhere. Someone had to make an explanation for that. Don't you see, whoever that man is—or was, I should say—once the Jeffersons found out, they didn't like him."

She paused for breath and Kimball butted in. "But to countenance murder?"

Mrs. Hogendobber dropped her head for a second and then looked up. "There may be worse sins than murder, Kimball Haynes."

32

Warren Randolph buttoned his shirt as Larry Johnson leaned against the small sink in the examining room. Larry was tempted to tell Warren it had taken his father's death to force him into this check-up, but he didn't.

"The blood work will be back within the week." Larry closed the file with the plastic color code on the outside. "You're in good health and I don't anticipate any problems, but"—he wagged his finger—"the last time you had blood drawn was when you left for college. You come in for a yearly check-up!"

Warren sheepishly said, "Lately I haven't felt well. I'm tired, but then I can't sleep. I drag around and forget things. I'd forget my head if it weren't pinned to my shoulders."

Larry put his hand on Warren's shoulder. "You've suffered a

major loss. Grief is exhausting and the things that pop into your mind—it'll surprise you."

Warren could let down his guard around the doctor. If you couldn't trust your lifelong physician, whom could you trust? "I don't remember feeling this bad when Mother died."

"You were twenty-four when Diana died. That's too young to understand what and whom you've lost, and don't be surprised if some of the grieving you've suppressed over your mother doesn't resurface now. Sooner or later, it comes out."

"I got worried, you know, about the listlessness. Thought it might be the beginning of leukemia. Runs in the family. Runs? Hell, it gallops."

"Like I said, the blood work will be back, but you don't have any other signs of the disease. You took a blow and it will take time to get back up."

"But what if I do have leukemia like Poppa?" Warren's brow furrowed, his voice grew taut. "It can take you down fast. . . ."

"Or you can live with it for years." Larry's voice soothed. "Don't yell 'ouch' until you're hurt. You know, memory and history are age-related. What you call up out of your mind at twenty may not be what you call up at forty. Even if what you remember is a very specific event in time, say, Christmas 1968, how you remember it will shift and deepen with age. Events are weighted emotionally. It's not the events we need to understand, it's the emotions they arouse. In some cases it takes twenty or thirty years to understand Christmas of 1968. You are now able to see your father's life as a whole: beginning, middle, and end. That changes your perception of Wesley, and I guarantee you will think a lot about your mother too. Just let it go through you. Don't block it. You'll be better off."

"You know everything about everybody, don't you, Doc?"

"No"—the old man smiled—"but I know people."

Warren glanced up at the ceiling, pushing back his tears. "Know what I thought about driving over here today? The damnedest thing. I remembered Poppa throwing the newspaper across the room when Reagan and his administration managed that Tax Reform Act of 1986. What a disaster. Anyway, Poppa was fussing and cussing and he said, 'The bedroom, Warren, the bedroom is the last place we're free until these sons of bitches figure out how to tax orgasms.' "

Larry laughed. "They broke the mold when they made Wesley."

33

The graceful three-sash windows, copied from Monticello, opened onto a formal garden in the manner of Inigo Jones. The library was paneled in a deep red mahogany and glowed as if with inner light. Kimball sat at a magnificent Louis XIV desk, black with polished ormolu, which Samson Coles's maternal great-great-great-grandmother was reputed to have had shipped over from France in 1700 when she lived in the Tidewater.

Handwritten diaries, the cursive script elegant and highly individualistic, strained the archaeologist's eyes. If he stepped away from the documents, the writing almost looked Arabic, another language of surpassing beauty in the written form.

Lucinda, the consummate hostess, placed a pot of hot tea, a true Brown Betty, on a silver tray along with scones and sinful jams and jellies. She pulled a chair alongside him and read too.

"The Coles family has a fascinating history. And the Randolphs, of course, Jefferson's mother's family. It's hard to remember how few people there were even at the beginning of the eighteenth century and how the families all knew one another. Married one another too."

"You know that America enjoyed a higher rate of literacy during the American Revolution than it does today? That's a dismal statistic. These early settlers, I mean, even going back to the early seventeenth century, were as a rule quite well educated. That common culture, high culture if you will, at least in the literary sense and the sense of the living arts"—he rubbed the desk to make his point—"must have given people remarkable stability."

"You could seize your quill and inkwell, scratch a letter to a friend in Charleston, South Carolina, and know that an entire subtext was understood." Lulu buttered a scone.

"Lulu, what was your major?"

"English. Wellesley."

"Ah." Kimball appreciated the rigors of Wellesley College.

"What was a girl to study in my day? Art history or English."

"Your day wasn't that long ago. Now, come on, you aren't even forty."

She shrugged and grinned. She certainly wasn't going to correct him.

Kimball, at thirty, hadn't begun to think about forty. "We're youth-obsessed. The people who wrote these diaries and letters and records valued experience."

"The people who wrote this stuff weren't assaulted on a daily basis with photographs and television shows parading beautiful young women, and men, for that matter. Your wife, hopefully the best woman you could find, did not necessarily have to be beautiful. Not that it hurt, mind you, Kimball, but I think our ancestors were much more concerned with sturdy health and strong character. The idea of a woman as ornament—that was off waiting to afflict us during Queen Victoria's reign."

"You're right. Women and men worked as a team regardless

of their level of society. They needed one another. I keep coming across that in my research, Lulu, the sheer need. A man without a woman was to be pitied and a woman without a man was on a dead-end street. Everyone pitched in. I mean, look at these accounts kept by Samson's great-grandmother—many greats, actually—Charlotte Graff. Nails, outrageously expensive, were counted, every one. Here, look at this account book from 1693.''

''Samson really should donate these to the Alderman's rare books collection. He won't part with them, and I guess in a way I can understand, but the public should have access to this information, or scholars at least, if not the public. Wesley Randolph was the same way. I ran into Warren coming out of Larry Johnson's office yesterday and asked him if he'd ever read the stuff. He said no, because his father kept a lot of it in the huge house safe in the basement. Wesley figured that if there were a fire, the papers would be protected in the safe.''

''Logical.''

Lulu read again. ''Whenever I read letters to and from Jefferson women I get totally confused. There are so many Marthas, Janes, and Marys. It seems like every generation has those names in it.''

''Look at it this way. They didn't know they were going to be famous. Otherwise maybe they would have varied the first names to help us out later.''

Lulu laughed. ''Think anyone will be reading about us one hundred years from now?''

''They won't even care about me twenty minutes after I'm gone—in an archival sense, I mean.''

''Who knows?'' She gingerly picked up Charlotte Graff's account book and read. ''Her accounts make sense. I picked up Samson's ledger the other day because he had laid it out on the desk and forgot to put it away. Couldn't make head or tails of it. I think the gene pool has degenerated, at least in the bookkeeping department.'' She rose and pulled a massive black book with a red spine out of the lower shelf of a closed cabinet. "You tell me, who does the better job?"

Good-naturedly, Kimball opened the book, the bright white paper with the vertical blue lines such a contrast from the aged papers he'd been reading. He squinted. He read a bit, then he paled, closed the book, and handed it back to Lulu. Not an accounting genius, he knew enough about double-entry bookkeeping to know that Samson Coles was lifting money out of clients' escrow funds. No broker or real estate agent is ever, ever to transfer money out of an escrow account even if he or she pays it back within the hour. Discovery of this abuse results in instant loss of license, and no real estate board in any county would do otherwise, even if the borrower were the president of the United States.

"Kimball, what's wrong?"

He stuttered, "Uh, nothing."

"You look pale as a ghost."

"Too much scones and jam." He smiled weakly and gathered the papers together just as Samson tooted down the driveway, his jolly red Wagoneer announcing his presence. "Lulu, put this book away before he gets here."

"Kimball, what's wrong with you?"

"Put the book back!" He spoke more sharply than he had intended.

Lulu, not a woman given to taking orders, did the exact reverse, she opened the account book and slowly and deliberately read the entries. Not knowing too much about bookkeeping or the concept of escrow even though she was married to a realtor, she was a bit wide of the mark. No matter, because Samson strode into the library looking the picture of the country squire.

"Kimball, my wife has enticed you with scones."

"Hello, dear." He leaned over and perfunctorily kissed her on the cheek. His gaze froze on the account book.

"If you two will excuse me, I must be going. Thank you so much for access to these materials." Kimball disappeared.

Samson, crimson-faced, tried to hide his shock. If he reacted, it would be far worse than if he didn't. Instead, he merely removed his ledger from Lulu's hands and replaced it on the lower shelf of the built-in cabinet. "Lulu, I was unaware that my ledger qualified as an archive."

Blithely she remarked, "Well, it doesn't, but I was reading over your umpteenth great-grandmother's accounts from 1693, and they made sense. So I told Kimball to see how the accounting gene had degenerated over the centuries."

"Amusing," Samson uttered through gritted teeth. "Methods have changed."

"I'll say."

"Did Kimball say anything?"

Lucinda paused. "No, not exactly, but he was eager to go after that. Samson, is there a problem?"

"No, but I don't think my ledger is anybody's business but my own."

Stung, Lulu realized he was right. "I'm sorry. I'd seen it when you left it out the other day, and I do say whatever pops into my head. The difference between the two ledgers just struck me. It isn't anybody else's business but it was—funny."

Samson left her gathering up the scones and the tea. He repaired to the kitchen for a bracing kick of Dalwhinnie scotch. What to do?

34

Mrs. Murphy, with special determination, squeezed her hindquarters into Mim Sanburne's post office box. From the postmistress's point of view, the wall of boxes was divided in half horizontally, an eight-inch ledge of oak being the divider. This proved handy when Harry needed to set aside stacks of mail or continue her refined sorting, as she called it.

As a kitten, Mrs. Murphy used to sleep in a large brandy snifter. She never acquired a taste for brandy, but she did learn to like odd shapes. For instance, she couldn't resist a new box of tissues. When she was small she could claw out the Kleenex and secrete herself into the box. This never failed to elicit a howl and laughter from Harry. As she grew, Mrs. Murphy discovered that less and less of her managed to fit into the box. Finally, she was reduced to sticking her hind leg in there. Hell on the Kleenex.

Usually the cat contented herself with the canvas mail bin. If Harry, or on rare occasion, Mrs. Hogendobber, wheeled her around, that was kitty heaven. But today she felt like squishing herself into something small. The scudding, frowning putty-colored clouds might have had something to do with it. Or the fact that Market Shiflett had brought over Pewter and three T-bones for the animals. Pewter had caused an unwelcome sensation in Market's store when she jumped into Ellie Wood Baxter's shopping cart and sunk her considerable fangs into a scrumptious pork roast.

Harry adored Pewter, so keeping her for the day was fine. The two cats and Tucker gnawed at their bones until weary. Everyone was knocked out asleep. Even Harry and Mrs. H. wanted to go to sleep.

Harry stopped in the middle of another massive catalogue sort. "Would you look at that?"

"Looks like a silver curtain. George and I loved to walk in the rain. You wouldn't think it to look at him, but George Hogendobber was a romantic. He knew how to treat a lady."

"He knew how to pick a good lady."

"Aren't you sweet?" Mrs. Hogendobber noticed Mrs. Murphy, front end on the ledge, back end jammed into Mim's box. She pointed.

Harry smiled. "She's too much. Dreaming of white mice or pink elephants, I guess. I do love that cat. Where's the culprit?" She bent down to see Pewter asleep under the desk, her right paw draped over the remains of her T-bone. The flesh had been stripped clean. "Boy, I bet Ellie Wood pitched a holy fit."

"Market wasn't too happy either. Maybe you ought to give him a vacation and take Pewter home tonight. She certainly could use a little outdoor exercise."

"Good idea. I can't keep my eyes open. I'm as bad as these guys."

"Low pressure system. The pollen ought to be a factor soon

too. I dread those two weeks when my eyes are red, my nose runs, and my head pounds.''

''Get Larry Johnson to give you an allergy shot.''

''The only person an allergy shot does any good for is Larry Johnson.'' She grumbled. ''He'll come by soon to give us a lunch hour today. He's back working full-time again. Remember when he first retired and he'd come in so you could take time for lunch? That lasted about six months. Then he was back working at his practice Monday, Wednesday, and Friday mornings. Soon it was every morning, and now he's back to a full schedule.''

''Do you think people should retire?''

''Absolutely not, I mean, unless they want to. I am convinced, convinced, Mary Minor, that retirement killed my George. His hobbies weren't the same as being responsible to people, being in the eye of the storm, as he used to say. He loved this job.''

''I'm trying to find a business I can do on the side. That way, when I retire, I can keep working. These government jobs are rigid. I'll have to retire.''

Miranda laughed. ''You aren't even thirty-five.''

''But it goes by so fast.''

''That it does. That it does.''

''Besides, I need money. I had to replace the carburetor in my tractor last week. Try finding a 1958 John Deere carburetor. What I've got in there is a hybrid of times. And I don't know how much longer the truck will hold up, she's a 1978. I need four-wheel drive—the inside of the house needs to be painted. Where am I going to get the money?''

''Things were easier when you were married. Anyone who doesn't think a man's salary helps isn't very realistic. Divorce and poverty seem to be the same word for most women.''

''Well, I lived just fine on my own before I was married.''

''You were younger then. You weren't maintaining a house. As you go along in life, creature comforts get mighty important. If

I didn't have my automatic coffee maker, my electric blanket, and my toaster oven, I'd be a crab and a half," she joked. "And what about my organ that George bought me for my fiftieth birthday? I couldn't live without that."

"I want a Toyota Land Cruiser. Never could afford it though."

"Does Mim have one of those?"

"Along with one of everything else. But yes, she's got the Land Cruiser and Jim's got the Range Rover. Little Marilyn has a Range Rover too. Speak of the devil."

Mim pulled up and sat in the car, trying to decide if the rain would let up. It didn't, so she made a dash for it. "Whoo," she said as she closed the door behind her. Neither Harry nor Mrs. Hogendobber informed her of Mrs. Murphy's slumber. She opened her post box. "A cat's tail. I have always wanted a cat's tail. And a cat's behind. Mrs. Murphy, what are you doing?" she asked as she gently squeezed the feline's tail.

Mrs. Murphy, tail tweaked, complained bitterly. *"Leave me alone. I don't pull your tail."*

Harry and Miranda laughed. Harry walked over to the cat, eyes now half open. "Come on, sweet pea, out of there."

"I'm comfortable."

Sensing deep resistance, Harry placed her hands under the cat's arms and gently removed her amid a torrent of abuse from the tiger. "I know you're comfy in there, but Mrs. Sanburne needs to retrieve her mail. You can get back in there later."

Tucker raised her head to observe the fuss, saw the situation, and put her head down on the floor again.

"You're a big goddamned help," the cat accused the dog.

Tucker closed her eyes. If she ignored Mrs. Murphy, the feline usually dropped it.

"Did she read my mail too?" Mim asked.

"Here it is." Miranda handed it over to Mim, whose engagement diamond, a marquise cut, caught the light and splashed a tiny rainbow on the wall.

"Bills, bills, bills. Oh, just what I always wanted, a catalogue from Victoria's Secret." She underhanded it into the trash, looked up, and beheld Harry and Miranda beholding her. "I love my cashmere robe. But this sexy stuff is for your age group, Harry."

"I sleep in the nude."

"True confessions." Mim leaned against the counter. "Heard you all have been helping Kimball Haynes. I guess he told you about the pathology report, or whatever they call those things."

"Yes, he did," Miranda said.

"All we have to do is find a thirty-two-year-old white male who may have walked with a slight limp in his left leg—in 1803."

"That, or find out more about Medley Orion."

"It is a puzzle." Mim crossed her arms over her chest. "I spoke to Lulu this morning and she said Kimball spent all of yesterday over there and Samson's mad at her."

"Why?" asked Harry innocently.

"Oh, she said he got out of sorts. And she admitted that maybe she should have waited until Samson was home. I don't know. Those two." She shook her head.

As if on cue, Samson stamped into the post office with customers from Los Angeles. "Hello there. What luck, finding you here, Mim. I'd like you to meet Jeremy and Tiffany Diamond. This is Marilyn Sanburne."

Mim extended her hand. "How do you do?"

"Fine, thank you." Jeremy's smile revealed a good cap job. His wife was on her second face-lift, and her smile no longer exactly corresponded to her lips.

"The Diamonds are looking at Midale."

"Ah," cooed Mim. "One of the most remarkable houses in central Virginia. The first to have a flying staircase, I believe."

Samson introduced the Diamonds to Harry and Miranda.

"Isn't this quaint?" Tiffany's voice hit the phony register. "And look, you have pets here too. How cozy."

"They sort the mail." Harry didn't have the knee-jerk re-

sponse to these kinds of people that Mim did, but she marveled at
big city people's assumption of superiority. If you lived in a small
town or the country, they thought, then you must be unambitious
or stupid or both.

"How cute."

Jeremy brushed a few raindrops off his pigskin blazer, teal
yet. "Samson's been telling us about his ancestor, Thomas Jefferson's mother."

I bet he has, Harry thought to herself. "Samson and Mrs.
Sanburne—Mrs. Sanburne is the chair, actually—have raised
money for the current restorations at Monticello."

"Ah, and say, what about the body in the slave quarters? I
know why you look familiar." He stared at Mim. "You were the
lady on *Wake-up Call* with Kyle Kottner. Do you really think the
victim was a stalker?"

"Whoever he was, he posed some danger," she replied.

"Wouldn't it be ironic, Samson, if he were one of your
relatives." Tiffany sank a small fishhook into Samson's ego. Her
unfortunate obsession with looking young and cute, and her faint
hint of superiority, hadn't dimmed her mind. She'd endured
enough of Samson's genealogical bragging.

Harry stifled a giggle. Mim relished Samson's discomfort,
especially since she hadn't fully forgiven him for his behavior at
Wesley's funeral.

"Well," he gulped, "who knows? Instead of living up to the
past, I might have to live it down."

"I'd rather live in the present," Tiffany replied, although her
penchant for attempting to keep her face in the twenty-year distant past stated otherwise.

After they vacated the premises, Mim walked back over and
leaned against the counter. "Sharp lady."

"She's got Samson's number, that's for sure."

"Harry"—Mim turned to Miranda—"Miranda, have you
found anything at all?"

"Just that Medley Orion lived with Martha Jefferson Randolph after 1826. She continued her trade. She had a daughter, but we don't know her name."

"What about searching for the victim? Surely the possibility of a limp could give him away. Someone somewhere knew a lame man visited Medley Orion. And he wasn't a tradesman."

"It's baffling." Miranda leaned on the opposite side of the counter. "But I've turned this over and over in my mind and I believe this has something to do with us now. Someone knows this story."

Mim tapped the counter with her mail. "And if we know, it will upset the applecart." She grabbed a letter opener off the counter and opened her personal mail. Her eyes widened as a letter fell out of a plain envelope postmarked Charlottesville. Letters were pasted on the paper: "Let the dead bury the dead." Mim blanched, then read it aloud.

"Already has," Harry said. "Yeah, the applecart's upset."

"I resent this cheap theatric!" Mim vehemently slapped the letter on the counter.

"Cheap or not, we'd better all be careful," Miranda quietly commented.

35

Ansley, in defiance of Warren, allowed Kimball Haynes to read the family papers. She even opened the safe. After she heard about Lulu's trouble with Samson, she figured the girls ought to stick together, especially since she didn't see anything particularly wrong with allowing it.

Reflecting on that later, she realized that she felt a kinship with Lulu since they shared Samson. Ansley knew she got the better part of him. Samson, a vain but handsome man, evidenced a streak of fun and true creativity in bed. As a young man, he was always in one scrape or another. The one told most often was how he got drunk and ran his motorcycle through a rail fence. Stumbling out of the wreckage, he cursed, "Damn mare refused the fence." Warren had been riding with him that day on his sleek Triumph 750cc.

They must have been wild young bucks, outrageous, still courteous, but capable of anything. Warren lost the wildness once out of law school. Samson retained vestiges of it but seemed subdued in the company of his wife.

Ansley wondered what would happen if and when Lucinda ever found out. She thought of Lucinda as a sister. Conventional emotion dictated that she should hate Lucinda as a rival. Why? She didn't want Samson permanently. Temporary use of his body was quite sufficient.

The more she thought about why she allowed Kimball access to the papers, the more she realized that Wesley's death had opened a Pandora's box. She had lived under that old man's thumb. So had Warren, and over the years she lost respect for her husband, watching him knuckle under to his father. Wesley had displayed virtues, to be sure, but he was harsh toward his son.

Worse, both men shut her out of the business. She wasn't an idiot. She could have learned about farming or Thoroughbred breeding, if nothing else. She might have even offered some new ideas, but no, she was trotted out to prospective customers, pretty bait. She served drinks. She kept the wives entertained. She stood on high heels for cocktail party after cocktail party. Her Achilles' tendon was permanently shortened. She bought a new gown for every black-tie fund-raiser on the East Coast and in Kentucky. She played her part and was never told she did a good job. The men took her for granted, and they had no idea how hard it was to be set aside, yet still be expected to behave graciously to people so hideously boring they should never have been born. Ansley was too young for that kind of life. The women in their sixties and seventies bowed to it. Perhaps some enjoyed being a working ornament, the unsung part of the proverbial marital team. She did not.

She wanted more. If she left Warren, he'd be hurt initially, then he'd hire the meanest divorce lawyer in the state of Virginia with the express purpose of starving her out. Rich men in divorce proceedings were rarely generous unless they were the ones caught with their pants down.

Ansley awoke to her fury. Wesley Randolph had crowed about his ancestors, notably Thomas Jefferson, one time too many. Warren, while not as bad, sang the refrain also. Was it because they couldn't accomplish much today? Did they need those ancestors? If Warren Randolph hadn't been born with a silver spoon in his mouth, he'd probably be on welfare. Her husband had no get-up-and-go. He couldn't think for himself. And now that Poppa wasn't there to tell him how and when to wipe his ass, Warren was in a panic. She'd never seen her husband so distressed.

It didn't occur to her that he might be distressed because she was cheating on him. She thought that she and Samson were too smart for him.

Nor did it occur to Ansley that a rich man's life was not necessarily better than a poor man's, except in creature comforts.

Warren, denied self-sufficiency, was like a baby learning to walk. He was going to fall down many times. But at least he was trying. He pored over the family papers, he studied the account books, he endured meetings with lawyers and accountants concerning his portfolio, estate taxes, death duties, and what have you. Ansley had waited so long for him to be his own man that she couldn't recognize that he was trying.

She took a sour delight from the look on his face when she told him that Kimball had read through the family papers from the years 1790 to 1820.

"Why would you do a thing like that when I asked you to keep him and everyone else out—at least until I could make a sound decision. I'm still—rocky." He was more shocked than angry.

"Because I think you and your father have been selfish. Anyway, it doesn't amount to a hill of beans."

He folded his hands as if in prayer and rested his chin on his fingertips. "I'm not as dumb as you think, Ansley."

"I never said you were dumb," came the hot retort.

"You didn't have to."

Since the boys were in their bedrooms, both parents kept their voices low. Warren turned on his heel and walked off to the stable. Ansley sat down and decided to read the family papers. Once she started, she couldn't stop.

36

The dim light filtering through the rain clouds slowly faded as the sun, invisible behind the mountains, set. The darkness gathered quickly and Kimball was glad he had driven straight home after leaving the Randolphs'. He wanted to put the finishing touches on his successful research before presenting it to Sheriff Shaw and Mim Sanburne. He was hopeful that he could present it on television too, for surely the media would return to Monticello. Oliver would not be pleased, of course, but this story was too good to suppress.

A knock on the door drew him away from his desk.

He opened the door, surprised. "Hello. Come on in and—"

He never finished his sentence. That fast, a snub-nosed .38 was pulled out of a deep coat pocket and Kimball was shot once in the chest and once in the head for good measure.

37

The much-awaited movie date with Fair turned into an evening work date at Harry's barn. The rain pattered on the standing-seam tin roof as Fair and Harry, on their knees, laid down the rubberized bricks Warren had given her. She did as her benefactor suggested, putting the expensive flooring in the center of the wash stall, checking the grade down to the drain as she did so. Fair snagged the gut-busting task of cutting down old black rubber trailer mats and placing them around the brick square. They weighed a ton.

"*This is Mother's idea of a hot date.*" Mrs. Murphy laughed from the hayloft. She was visiting Simon as well as irritating the owl, but then, everyone and everything irritated the owl.

Tucker, ground-bound since she couldn't climb the ladder and never happy about it, sat by the wash stall. Next to her was

Pewter, on her sleepover visit as suggested by Mrs. Hogendobber. Pewter could climb the ladder into the hayloft, but why exert herself?

"*Don't you think the horses get more attention than we do?*" Pewter asked.

"*They're bigger,*" Tucker replied.

"*What's that got to do with it?*" Mrs. Murphy called down.

"*They aren't as independent as we are and their hooves need constant attention,*" Tucker said.

"*Is it true that Mrs. Murphy rides the horses?*"

"*Of course it's true.*" Mrs. Murphy flashed her tail from side to side. "*You ought to try it.*"

Pewter craned her neck to observe the two horses munching away in their stalls. "*I'm not the athletic type.*"

"You're awfully good to help me." Harry thanked her ex-husband as he groaned, pulling a rubber mat closer to the wall. "Want a hand?"

"I've got it," he replied. "The only reason I'm doing this, Skeezits"—he used her high school nickname—"is that you'd do it yourself and strain something. For better or for worse, I'm stronger." He paused. "But you have more endurance."

"Same as mares, I guess."

"I wonder if the differences between human males and females are as profound as we think they are. Mares made me think of it. The equine spread is narrow, very narrow. But for whatever reason, humans have created this elaborate code of sexual differences."

"We'll never know the answer. You know, I'm so out of it, I don't even care. I'm going to do what I want to do and I don't much care if it's feminine or masculine."

"You always were that way, Harry. I think that's why I liked you so much."

"You liked me so much because we were in kindergarten together."

"I was in kindergarten with Susan, and I didn't marry her," he replied with humor.

"Touché."

"I happened to think you were special once I synchronized my testosterone level with my brain. For a time there, the gonads took over."

She laughed. "It's a miracle anyone survives adolescence. Everything is so magnified and so new. My poor parents." She smiled, thinking of her tolerant mother and father.

"You were lucky. Remember when I totaled my dad's new Saab? One of the first Saabs in Crozet too. I thought he was gonna kill me."

"You had help. Center Berryman is not my idea of a stable companion."

"Have you seen him since he got out of the treatment center?"

"Yeah. Seems okay."

"If I was ever tempted by cocaine, Center certainly cured me of that."

"He came to Mim's Mulberry Row ceremony at Monticello. One of his first appearances since he got back. He did okay. I mean, what must it have been like to have everyone staring at you and wondering if you're going to make it? There are those who wish you well, those who are too self-centered to care, those that are sweet but will blunder and say the wrong thing, and those— and these are my absolute faves—those who hope you'll fall flat on your face. That's the only way they can be superior—to have the next guy fail. Jerks." Harry grimaced.

"We became well acquainted with that variety of jerks during our divorce."

"Oh, Fair, come on. Every single woman between the ages of twenty and eighty fawned over you, invited you to dinner—the poor-man-alone routine. I got it both barrels. How could I toss out my errant husband? All boys stray. That's the way they're made. What a load of shit I heard from other women. The men, at least, had the sense to shut up."

He stopped cutting through the heavy rubber, sweat pouring off him despite the temperature in the low fifties. "That's what makes life interesting."

"What"—she was feeling angry just remembering—"dealing with jerks?"

"No—how we each see a slice of life, a degree or two of the circle but not the whole circle. What I was getting while you were getting that was older men like Herbie Jones or Larry Johnson on my case."

"Herbie and Larry?" Harry's interest shot into the stratosphere. "What did they say?"

"Basically that we all fall from grace and I should beg your forgiveness. Know who else invited me over for a powwow? Jim Sanburne."

"I don't believe it." She felt oddly warmed by this male solicitude.

"Harry, he's an unusual man. He said his life was no model but that infidelity was his fatal flaw and he knew it. He really blew me away because he's much more self-aware than I reckoned. He said he thought he started having affairs when he was young because he felt Mim lorded it over him, his being a poor boy, so to speak."

"He learned how to make money in a hurry." Harry always admired self-made people.

"Yeah, he did, and he didn't use a penny of her inheritance either. Fooling around was not just his way to get even but a way to restore his confidence." Fair sat down for a minute. Tucker immediately came over and sat in his lap.

"*Oh, Tucker, you're always sucking up to people,*" accused Pewter, who was the original brown-noser the minute the refrigerator door opened.

"*Pewter, you're jealous,*" Mrs. Murphy teased.

"No, I'm not," came the defensive reply. "But Tucker is so—so obvious. *Dogs have no subtlety.*"

"Pewter, you're just a chatty Cathy." Harry reached over and stroked her chin.

"*Gag me*," Tucker said.

"Why do you think you fooled around?" Harry thought the question would shake her, but it didn't. She was glad it was finally out there even if it did take three years.

"Stupidity."

"That's a fulsome reply."

"Don't get testy. I was stupid. I was immature. I was afraid I was missing something. The rose not smelled, the road not taken. That kind of crap. I do know, though, that I still had a lot of growing-up to do even after we were married—I spent so much of my real youth with my nose in a textbook that I missed a lot of the life experiences from which a person grows. What I was missing was me."

Harry stopped putting in the brick and sat down, facing him.

He continued. "With a few exceptions like wrecking the Saab, I did what was expected of me. Most of us in Crozet do, I guess. I don't think I knew myself very well, or maybe I didn't want to know myself. I was afraid of what I'd find out."

"Like what? What could possibly be wrong with you? You're handsome, the best in your field, and you get along with people."

"I ought to come over here more often." He blushed. "Ah, Harry, haven't you ever caught yourself driving down Garth Road or waking up in the middle of the night, haven't you ever wondered what the hell you were doing and why you were doing it?"

"Yes."

"Scared me. I wondered if I was as smart as everyone tells me I am. I'm not. I'm good in my field, but I can sure be dumb as a sack of hammers about other things. I kept running into limitations, and since I was raised to believe I shouldn't have any, I ran away from them—you, me. That solved nothing. Boom Boom was an exercise in terrible judgment. And the one before her—"

Harry interrupted. "She was pretty."

"Pretty is as pretty does. Anyway, I woke up one morning and realized that I'd smashed my marriage, I'd hurt the one person I loved most, I'd disappointed my parents and myself, and I'd made a fool of myself to others. Thank God I'm in a business where my patients are animals. I don't think any people would have come to me. I was a mess. I even thought about killing myself."

"You?" Harry was stunned.

He nodded. "And I was too proud to ask for help. Hey, I'm Fair Haristeen and I'm in control. Six-foot-four men don't break down. We might kill ourselves working, but we don't break down."

"What did you do?"

"Found myself at the good reverend's house on Christmas Eve. Christmas with Mom and Dad, oh, boy. Grim, resentful." He shook his head. "I flew out of that house. I don't know. I showed up at Herb's and he sat down and talked to me. He told me that no one's a perfect person and I should go slow, take a day at a time. He didn't preach at me either. He told me to reach out to people and not to hide myself behind this exterior, behind a mask, you know?"

"I do." And she did.

"Then I did something so out of character for me." He played with the edge of the rubber matting. "I found a therapist."

"No way."

"Yeah, I really did, and you're the only person who knows. I've been working with this guy for two years now and I'm making progress. I'm becoming, uh, human."

The phone cut into whatever Fair would have said next. Harry jumped up and walked into the tack room. She heard Mrs. Hogendobber almost before she picked up the phone. Mrs. H. told her that Kimball Haynes had just been found by Heike Holtz.

Shot twice. When he didn't show up for a date or answer his phone, she became worried and drove out to his place.

Harry, ashen-faced, paused for a moment. "Fair, Kimball Haynes has been murdered." She returned to Mrs. H. "We'll be right over."

38

A tea table filled with tarts and a crisp apple pie aroused the interest of Tucker, Mrs. Murphy, and Pewter. The humans at that moment were too upset to eat. Mrs. Hogendobber, a first-rate baker, liked to experiment with recipes before taking them to the Church of the Holy Light for suppers and benefits. The major benefit was to Harry, who was used as the guinea pig. If Harry ever stopped doing her high-calorie-burning farm chores, she'd be fat as a tick. Mrs. H. had planned to bring the treats to work tomorrow, but everything was up in the air.

"That bright young man. He had everything to live for." Miranda wiped her eyes. "Why would anyone kill Kimball?"

Fair sat next to her on one side of the sofa, Harry on the other.

Harry patted her hand. An awkward gesture, but it suited Mrs. Hogendobber, who was not a woman given to hugs or much public display of affection. "I don't know, but I think he stuck his nose too far in somebody's business."

Mrs. Hogendobber lifted her head. "You mean over this Monticello murder?"

"Not exactly. I don't know what I mean." Harry sighed.

Fair's baritone filled the room. "Crozet is a town filled with secrets, generations deep."

"Isn't every town full of secrets? The precepts for living don't seem to take into account true human nature." Harry smelled the apple pie. Pewter crouched, making ready to spring onto the teacart. "Pewter, no."

"*Nobody else is going to eat it,*" the cat sassed her. "*Why waste good food?*"

Her anger rising because Pewter not only refused to budge but wiggled her haunches again for the leap, Harry rose and chased the cat away from the cart. Pewter ran a few steps away and then sat down defiantly.

"*You're pushing it,*" Mrs. Murphy warned her.

"*What's she going to do? Smack pie in my face?*" Pewter wickedly crept closer to the sweet-laden cart.

"Listen, let's eat some of this before Pewter wears me out." Harry sliced three portions of pie, the rich apple aroma deliciously filling the room as the knife opened up the heart of the pie.

"Oh, Miranda, this is beautiful." Harry handed out three plates. She sat down to eat, but Pewter's creeping along toward the cart disturbed the peacefulness, which had been disturbed enough. Giving up, she cut a small slice for the two cats and a separate one for Tucker.

"You spoil those animals," said Mrs. Hogendobber.

"They're great testers. If they won't eat something, you know it's bad—not that your pastries could ever fall into that category."

"Many times I wished I weren't such a baker." She patted her stomach.

They enjoyed the pie until their thoughts returned to Kimball. As they talked, Harry got up and poured coffee for everyone. She often felt better if she could move around. Harry's mother used to say she had ants in her pants, which wasn't true, but she thought better if she walked about.

"Super. The best, Mrs. H.," Fair congratulated her.

"Thank you," she replied listlessly, then a tear fell again. "I hate crying. I keep thinking that he never had the chance to be married or to have children." She placed her cup on the coffee table. "I'm calling Mim. Surely she's heard."

Harry, Fair, and the animals watched as she dialed and Mim came on the line. A long conversation followed, but as Mim did most of the talking, Miranda's audience could only guess.

"She's right here. Let me ask her." Mrs. Hogendobber put her hand over the mouthpiece. "Mim wants us to meet with the sheriff tomorrow. Oliver Zeve has already been questioned. Noon?"

Harry nodded in the affirmative.

Miranda continued. "That's fine. We'll see you at your place, then. Can we bring anything? All right. Bye."

"Take her some of this pie," Fair suggested.

"I think I will." She remained by the phone. "Sheriff Shaw is doing a what-do-you-call-it, ballistics check? They're hoping to trace the gun."

"Fat chance." Harry put her face in her hands.

"Maybe not." Fair thought out loud. "What if the killer acted in haste?"

"Even if he acted in haste, I bet he's not that stupid—or she," Harry countered. "And to make matters worse, the rains washed out any chance of making a mold from tire tracks."

"*And washed out the scent too*," Tucker mourned.

"This is so peculiar." Mrs. Hogendobber joined them on the davenport.

"We need to go through the papers that Kimball read. I'm sure that Rick Shaw has already thought of that, but since we're somewhat familiar with the period and the players of that day, maybe we could help."

"And expose yourselves to risk? I won't have it," Fair said flatly.

"Fair, you didn't give me orders when we were married. Don't start now."

"When we were married, Mary Minor, your life was not in danger. If you don't have the sense to see where this is leading, I do! There's a man dead because he uprooted something. If he found it, chances are you'll find it, especially given your disposition toward investigation."

"Unless the killer removes the evidence."

"If that's possible," Mrs. Hogendobber said to Harry. "This may be a matter of going over those records and diaries and putting two and two together. It may not be one document—then again, it may."

"And I am telling you two nitwits"—Fair's voice rose, making Tucker prick up her ears—"what Kimball Haynes found may be something of current interest. In his research he might have stumbled over something that's dangerous to someone right now. It's very hard to believe that Kimball would have been killed over a murder in 1803."

"You've got a point there," Mrs. Hogendobber agreed, but she felt uneasy, deeply uneasy.

"I'm going through those papers." Harry was as defiant as Pewter had been. The gray cat watched in astonishment. Mrs. Murphy, privy to a few Mr.-and-Mrs. scenes, was less astonished.

"Harry, I forbid it!" He slammed his hand on the coffee table.

"*Don't do that,*" Tucker barked, but she didn't want her mother in danger either.

"Settle down, you two, just settle down." Mrs. Hogendobber leaned back on the sofa. "We know for certain that Kimball read through Mim's family histories, and the Coleses'. Don't know if he got the Randolphs' yet. Anyone else?"

"He kept a list. We'd better get that list or get Rick to let us photocopy it." Harry, mad at Fair, was still glad he cared, although she was confused as to why that should make her so happy. Harry was slow that way.

Fair crossed his arms over his chest. "You aren't listening to a word I'm saying. Let the police handle it."

"I am listening, but I liked Kimball. We were also helping him piece together the facts on this thing. If I can help catch whoever did him in, I will."

"I liked him too, but not enough to die for him, and that won't bring him back." Fair spoke the truth.

"You can't stop me." Harry's chin jutted out.

"No, but I can go along and help."

Mrs. Hogendobber clapped. "Bully for you!"

"*What do you think, Tucker?*" Mrs. Murphy picked up her tail with a front paw.

"*He's still in love with her.*"

"*That's obvious.*" Pewter lay down, far more interested in the pastries than human emotions.

"*Yeah, but will he win her back?*" the tiger asked.

39

"No." Sheriff Shaw shook his balding head for emphasis.

"Rick, they have a sound argument." Mim defended Harry and Mrs. Hogendobber. "You and your staff aren't familiar with the descendants of Thomas Jefferson or the personal histories of certain of his slaves. They are."

"The department will hire an expert."

"The expert is dead." Mim's lips pressed tightly together.

"I'll hire Oliver Zeve," the frustrated sheriff stated.

"Oh, and how long do you think that will last? Furthermore, he wasn't exactly interested in pursuing this case, nor was he as interested in the genealogies as Kimball. Harry and Mrs. Hogendobber were working with Kimball already."

"Fair Haristeen called me this morning and said you both ought to be locked up. I'll make that three." He cast his eyes at

Mim, who didn't budge. "He also said that whatever Kimball discovered must be threatening to somebody right now. And you all are obsessed with this Monticello thing."

"And you aren't?" Harry fired back.

"Well—well—" Rick Shaw stuck his hands in his Sam Browne belt. "Focused but not obsessed. Anyway, this is my job and I am mindful of the danger to you ladies."

"I'll work with them," Cynthia Cooper gleefully volunteered.

"You women sure stick together." He slapped his hat against his thigh.

"And men don't?" Mim laughed.

"Yeah, I bet Fair chewed your ears off because he thinks we're in danger. He's being a worrywart."

"He's being sensible and responsible." Rick fought the urge to enjoy another piece of Mrs. Hogendobber's pie. The urge won out. "Miranda, you ought to go into business."

"Why, thank you."

"Does anyone know if there will be a service for Kimball?" Harry inquired.

"His parents removed the body to Hartford, Connecticut, where they live. They'll bury him there. But that reminds me, Mrs. Sanburne, Oliver wants you to help him plan a memorial service for Kimball here. I doubt anyone will journey to Hartford, and he said he'd like some kind of remembrance."

"Of course. I'm sure Reverend Jones will assist in this matter also."

"Well?" Harry had her mind on business.

"Well, what?"

"Sheriff. Please." She sounded like a clever, pleading child at that moment.

Rick quietly looked at Harry and Mrs. Hogendobber, then at Cynthia, who was grinning in high hopes. "Women." They'd won. "The Coleses have agreed to allow us access to their libraries. The Berrymans, Foglemans, and Venables too, and I've got a list here of names that Kimball drew up. Mim, you're first on the list."

"When would you like to start?"

"How about after work today? Oh, and Mim, I need to bring Mrs. Murphy and Tucker along, otherwise I'd have to run them home. Churchill won't mind, will he?"

Churchill was Mim's superb English setter, a champion many times over. "No."

"Pewter too." Miranda reminded Harry of her visitor.

"Ellie Wood still hasn't recovered from the pork roast incident. Which reminds me, I think she is distantly related to one of the Eppes of Poplar Forest. Francis, Polly's son."

Polly was the family nickname for Maria, Thomas Jefferson's youngest daughter, who died April 17, 1804, an event which caused her father dreadful grief. Fortunately her son Francis, born in 1801, survived until 1881, but he, along with Jefferson's other grandchildren, bore the consequences of the president's posthumous financial disaster.

"We'll leave not a stone unturned," Mrs. Hogendobber vowed.

40

That evening, as Harry, Mrs. Hogendobber, and Deputy Cooper worked in Mim's breathtaking cherrywood library, Fair worked out in the stables. Book work soured him. He'd do it diligently if he had to, but he wondered how he'd gotten through Auburn Veterinary College with high honors. Maybe it was easier to read then, but he sure hated it now.

He was floating the teeth of Mim's six Thoroughbreds, filing down the sharp edges. Because a horse's upper jaw is slightly wider than the lower one, its teeth wear unevenly, requiring regular maintenance, or at least inspection. If the teeth are allowed to become sharp and jagged, they can cause discomfort to the animal when it has a bit in its mouth, sometimes making it more difficult to ride, and often this situation can cause digestive or nutrition problems because of the animal's restricted ability to chew and break down its food.

Mim's stable manager held the horses as Mim sat in a camp chair and chatted. "You made a believer out of me, Fair. I don't know how I lived without Strongid C. The horses eat less and get more nutrition from their food." Strongid C was a new wormer that came in pellet form and was added to a horse's daily ration. This saved the owner those monthly paste-worming tasks that more often than not proved disagreeable to both parties.

"Good. Took me a while to convince some of my clients, but I'm getting good results with it."

"Horse people are remarkably resistant to change. I don't know why, but we are." She pulled a pretty leather crop out of an umbrella stand. "How are the Wheelers doing?"

"Winning at the hunter shows and the Saddlebred shows, as always. You ought to get over there to Cismont Manor, Mim, and see the latest crop. Good. Really good." He finished with her bright bay. "Now, I happen to think you've got one of the best fox hunters in the country."

She beamed. "I do too. So much for modesty. Warren's cornered the market on racing Thoroughbreds."

"What market?" Fair shook his head. The depression, laughingly called a recession, coupled with changes in the tax laws, was in the process of devastating the Thoroughbred business, along with many other aspects of the equine industry. As most congressmen were no longer landowners, they hadn't a clue as to what they had done to livestock breeders and farmers with their stupid "reforms."

Mim spun the whip handle around in her hands. "I tell Jim he ought to run for Congress. At least then there'd be one logical voice in the bedlam. Won't do it. Won't even hear of it. Says he'd rather bleed from the throat. Fair, have you seen a reasonably priced fox hunter in your travels?"

"Mim, what's reasonable to you may not be reasonable to me."

"Quite so." She appreciated that insight. "I'll come directly to the point. Gin Fizz and Tomahawk are long in the tooth and you know Harry doesn't have two nickels to rub together—now."

He sighed. "I know. She absolutely refused alimony. My lawyer said I was crazy to want to pay. I do her vet work for free and it's a struggle to get her to go along with that."

"The Hepworths as well as the Minors have always been prickly proud about money. I don't know who was worse, Harry's mother or her father."

"Mim, I'm—touched that you'd be thinking of Harry."

"Touched, or amazed?"

He smiled. "Both. You've changed."

"For the better?"

He held up his hands for mercy. "Now, that's a loaded question. You seem happier and you seem to want to be friendlier. How's that sound?"

"I wearied of being a bitch. But what's funny, or not so funny, about Crozet is that once people get an idea about you in their heads, they're loath to surrender it. Not that I won't step on toes, I'll always do that, but I figured out, thanks to a little scare in my life, that life is indeed short. My being so superior made me feel in charge, I guess, but I wasn't happy, I wasn't making my husband happy, and the truth is, my daughter detests me underneath all her politeness. I wasn't a good mother."

"Good horsewoman though."

"Thank you. What is there about a stable that pulls the truth out of us?"

"It's real. Society isn't real." He studied Mim, her perfectly coiffed hair, her long fingernails, her beautiful clothes perfect even in the stable. The human animal could grow at any time in its life that it chooses to grow. On the outside she looked the same, but on the inside she was transforming. He felt the same way about himself. "You know, there's a solid $16.1^{1}/_{2}$-hand Percheron cross that Evelyn Kerr has. The mare is green and only six, but Harry can bring her along. Good bone, Mim. Good hooves too. Of course, it's got a biggish, draft-type head, but not roman-nosed, and no feathers on the fetlocks. Smooth gaits.''

"Why is Evelyn selling the horse?''

"She's got Handyman, and when she retired she thought she'd have more time, so she bought this young horse. But Evelyn's like Larry Johnson. She's working harder in retirement than before.''

"Why don't you talk to her? Sound her out for me? I'd like to buy the mare if she suits and then let Harry pay me off over time.''

"Uh—let me buy the mare. In fact, I wish I'd thought of this myself.''

"We can share the expense. Who's to know?'' Mim swung her legs under the chair.

41

The night turned unseasonably cool. The Reverend Jones built a fire in his study, his favorite room. The dark green leather chairs bore testimony to years of use; knitted afghans were tossed over the arms to hide the wear. Herb Jones usually wrapped one around his legs as he sat reading a book accompanied by Lucy Fur, the young Maine coon cat he'd brought home to enliven Elocution, or Ella, his older first cat.

Tonight Ansley and Warren Randolph and Mim Sanburne joined him. They were finishing up planning Kimball's memorial service.

"Miranda's taking care of the music." Mim checked that off her list. "Little Marilyn's hired the caterer. You've got the flowers under control."

"Right." Ansley nodded.

"And I'm getting a program printed up." Warren scratched his chin. "What do you call it? It's not really a program."

"In Memoriam," Ansley volunteered. "Actually, whatever you call it, you've done a beautiful job. I had no idea you knew so much about Kimball."

"Didn't. Asked Oliver Zeve for Kimball's résumé."

Mim, without looking up from her list, continued checking off jobs. "Parking."

"Monticello, or should I say Oliver, is taking care of that?"

"Well, that's it, then." Mim put down her pencil. She could have afforded any kind of expensive pencil, but she preferred a wooden one, an Eagle Mirado Number 1. She carried a dozen in a cardboard container, the sale carton, wherever she journeyed. Carried a pencil trimmer too.

The little group stared into the fire.

Herb roused himself from its hypnotic powers. "Can I fetch anyone another drink? Coffee?"

"No thanks," everyone replied.

"Herb, you know people's secrets. You and Larry Johnson." Ansley folded her hands together. "Do you have any idea, any hunch, no matter how wild?"

Herb glanced up at the ceiling, then back at the group. "No. I've gone over the facts, or what we know as the facts, in my mind so many times I make myself dizzy. Nothing jumps out at me. But even if Kimball or the sheriff uncover the secret of the corpse at Monticello, I don't know if that will have anything to do with Kimball's murder. It's tempting to connect the two, but I can't find any link."

Mim stood up. "Well, I'd better be going. We've pulled a lot together on very short notice. I thank you all." She hesitated. "I'm sorry about the circumstances, much as I like working with everyone."

•   •   •

Warren and Ansley left about ten minutes later. Driving the dark, winding roads kept Warren alert.

"Honey . . ." Ansley watched for deer along the sides of the road—the light would bounce off their eyes. "Did you tell anyone that Kimball read the Randolph papers?"

"No, did you?"

"Of course not—make you look like a suspect."

"Why me?"

"Because women rarely kill." She squinted into the inky night. "Slow down."

"Do you think I killed Kimball?"

"Well, I know you sent that letter with the cut-out message to Mim."

He decelerated for a nasty curve. "What makes you think that, Ansley?"

"Saw *The New Yorker* in the trash in the library. I hadn't read it yet, so I plucked it out and discovered where your scissors had done their work."

He glowered the rest of the way home, which was only two miles. As they pulled into the garage he shut off the motor, reached over, and grabbed her wrist. "You're not as smart as you think you are. Leave it alone."

"I'd like to know if I'm living with a killer." She baited him. "What if I get in your way?"

He raised his voice. "Goddammit, I played a joke on Marilyn Sanburne. It wasn't the most mature thing to do, but it was fun considering how she's cracked the whip over my head and everyone else's since year one. Just keep your mouth shut."

"I will." Her lips clamped tight, making them thinner than they already were.

Without letting go of her wrist he asked, "Did you read the papers? The blue diary?"

"Yes."

He released her wrist. "Ansley, every old Virginia family has its fair share of horse thieves, mental cases, and just plain bad eggs. What's the difference if they were crooked or crazy in 1776 or today? One doesn't air one's dirty laundry in public."

"Agreed." She opened the door to get out, and he did the same on the driver's side.

"Ansley."

"What?" She turned from her path to the door.

"Did you really think, for one minute, that I killed Kimball Haynes?"

"I don't know what to think anymore." Wearily she reached the door, opened it, and without checking behind her, let it slam, practically crunching Warren's nose in the process.

42

Harry, Mrs. Hogendobber, and Deputy Cooper exhausted themselves reading. Mim's connection to Thomas Jefferson was through the Wayles/Coolidge line. Ellen Wayles Randolph, his granddaughter, married Joseph Coolidge, Jr., on May 27, 1825. They had six children, and Mim's mother was related to a cousin of one of those offspring.

Slender though it was, it was a connection to the Sage of Monticello. Ellen maintained a lively correspondence with her husband's family. Ellen, the spark plug of Maria's—or Polly's—children, inherited her grandfather's way with words just as her older brother, called Jeff, inherited his great-grandfather's, Peter Jefferson's, enormous frame and incredible strength.

One of the letters casually mentioned that Ellen's younger

brother, James Madison Randolph, had fallen violently in love with a great beauty and seemed intent upon a hasty marriage.

Harry read and reread the letter, instantly conceiving an affection for the effervescent author. "Miranda, I don't remember James Madison Randolph marrying."

"I'm not sure. Died young though. Just twenty-eight, I think."

"These people had such big families." Deputy Cooper wailed as the task had begun to overwhelm her. "Thomas Jefferson's mother and father had ten children. Seven made it to adulthood."

Miranda pushed back her half-spectacles. When they slid down her nose again she took them off and laid them on the diary before her. "Jane, his favorite sister, died at twenty-five. Elizabeth, the one with the disordered mind, also died without marrying. The remainder of Thomas's brothers and sisters bequeathed to Virginia and points beyond quite a lot of nieces and nephews for Mr. Jefferson. And he was devoted to them. He really raised his sister Martha's children, Peter and Sam Carr. Dabney Carr, who married Martha, was his best friend, as you know."

"*Another* Martha?" Cynthia groaned. "His wife, sister, and daughter were all named Martha?"

"Well, Dabney died young, before thirty, and Thomas saw to the upbringing of the boys," Miranda went on, absorbed. "I am convinced it was Peter who sired four children on Sally Hemings. A stir was caused when Mr. Jefferson freed, or manumitted, one of Sally's daughters, Harriet, quite the smashing beauty. That was in 1822. You can understand why the Jefferson family closed ranks."

Officer Cooper rubbed her temples. "Genealogies drive me bats."

"Our answer rests somewhere with Jefferson's sisters and brother Randolph, or with one of his grandchildren," Harry posited. "Do you believe Randolph was simple-minded? Maybe not as bad as Elizabeth."

"Well, now, she wasn't simple-minded. Her mind would wander and then she'd physically ramble about aimlessly. She wandered off in February and probably died of the cold. Poor thing. No, Randolph probably wasn't terribly bright, but he seems to have enjoyed his faculties. Lived in Buckingham County and liked to play the fiddle. That's about all I know."

"Miranda, how would you like to be Thomas Jefferson's younger brother?" Harry laughed.

"Probably not much. Not much. I think we're done in. Samson's tomorrow night?"

43

Pewter grumbled incessantly as she walked with Harry, Mrs. Murphy, and Tucker to work. The fat cat's idea of exercise was walking from Market's back door to the back door of the post office.

"*Are we there yet?*"

"*Will you shut up!*" Mrs. Murphy advised.

"*Hey, look,*" Tucker told everyone as she caught sight of Paddy running top-speed toward them. His ears were flat back, his tail was straight out, and his paws barely touched the ground. He was scorching toward them from town.

"*Murph,*" Paddy called, "*follow me!*"

"*You're not going to, are you?*" Pewter swept her whiskers forward in anticipation of trouble.

"*What's wrong?*" Mrs. Murphy called out.

"I've found something—something important." He skidded to a stop at Harry's feet.

Harry reached down to scratch Paddy's ears. Not wanting to be rude, he rubbed against her leg. "Come on, Murph. You too, Tucker."

"Will you tell me what this is all about?" the little dog prudently asked.

"Well spoken." Pewter sniffed.

"Larry Johnson and Hayden McIntire's office." Paddy caught his breath. "I've found something."

"What were you doing over there?" Tucker needed to be convinced it really was important.

"Passing by. Look, I'll explain on the way. We need to get there before the workmen do."

"Let's go." Mrs. Murphy hiked up her tail and dug into the turf.

"Hey—hey," Tucker called, then added after a second's reflection, "Wait for me!"

Pewter, furious, sat down and bawled. "I will not run. I will not take another step. My paws are sore and I hate everybody. You can't leave me here!"

Perplexed at the animals' wild dash toward downtown Crozet, Harry called after them once but then remembered that most people were just waking up. She cursed under her breath. Harry wasn't surprised, though, by Pewter's staunch resistance to walk another step, having been quickly deserted by her fitter friends. She knelt down and scooped up the rotund kitty. "I'll carry you, you lazy sod."

"You're the only person I like in this whole wide world," Pewter cooed. "Mrs. Murphy is a selfish shit. Really. You should spend more time with me. She's running off with her no-account ex-husband, and that silly dog is going along like a fifth wheel." The cat laughed. "Why, I wouldn't even give that two-timing tom the time of day."

"Pewter, you have a lot on your mind." Harry marveled that the smallish cat could weigh so much.

• • •

As the three animals raced across the neat square town plots,
Paddy filled them in.

"*Larry and Hayden McIntire are expanding the office wing of the house. I
like to go hunting there. Lots of shrews.*"

"*You've got to catch them just right because they can really bite,*" Mrs.
Murphy interrupted.

"*It's easy to get in and out of the addition,*" he continued.

The tidy house appeared up ahead, with its curved brick
entranceway splitting to the front door and the office door. The
sign, DR. LAWRENCE JOHNSON & DR. HAYDEN MCINTIRE, swung, creaking, in
the slight breeze. "*No workmen yet,*" Paddy triumphantly meowed.
He ducked under the heavy plastic covering on the outside wall
and leapt into the widened window placement. The window had
not yet been installed. The newest addition utilized the fireplace as
its center point of construction. A balancing, new fireplace was
built on the other end of the new room. It matched the old
one.

"*Hey! What about me?*"

"*We'll open the door, Tucker.*" Mrs. Murphy gracefully sailed
through the window after Paddy and landed on a sawdust-covered
floor. She hurried to the door of the addition, which as yet had no
lock, although the fancy brass Baldwin apparatus, still boxed,
rested on the floor next to it. Mrs. Murphy pushed against the
two-by-four propped up against the door. It clattered to the floor
and the door easily swung open. The corgi hurried inside.

"*Where are you?*" Mrs. Murphy couldn't see Paddy.

"*In here,*" came the muffled reply.

"*He's crazier than hell.*" Tucker reacted to the sound emanating
from the large stone fireplace.

"*Crazy or not, I'm going in.*" Mrs. Murphy trotted to the cavern-
ous opening, the firebrick a cascade of silky and satiny blacks and
browns from decades of use. The house was originally constructed in 1824; the addition had been built in 1852.

Tucker stood in the hearth. "*The last time we stood in a fireplace there was a body in it.*"

"*Up here,*" Paddy called, his deep voice ricocheting off the flue.

Mrs. Murphy's pupils enlarged, and she saw a narrow opening to the left of the large flue. In the process of remodeling, a few loose bricks had become dislodged—just enough room for an athletic cat to squeeze through. "*Here I come.*" She sprang off her powerful haunches but miscalculated the depth of the landing. "*Damn.*" The tiger hung on to the opening, her rear end dangling over the side. She scratched with her hind claws and clambered up the rest of the way.

"*Tricky.*" Paddy laughed.

"*You could have warned me,*" she complained.

"*And miss the fun?*"

"*What's so important up here?*" she challenged him, then, as her eyes became accustomed to the diminished light, she saw he was sitting on it. A heavy waxed oilskin much like the covering of an expensive foul-weather coat, like a Barbour or Dri-as-a-Bone, covered what appeared to be books or boxes. "*Can we open this up?*"

"*Tried. Needs human hands,*" Paddy casually remarked although he was ecstatic that his find had produced the desired thrill in Mrs. Murphy.

"*What's going on up there?*" Tucker yelped.

Mrs. Murphy stuck her head out of the opening. "*Some kind of stash, Tucker. Might be books or boxes of jewelry. We can't open it up.*"

"*Think the humans will find it?*"

"*Maybe yes and maybe no.*" Paddy's fine features now came alongside Mrs. Murphy's.

"*If workmen repoint the fireplace, which they're sure to do, it's anyone's guess whether they'll look inside here or just pop bricks in and mortar them up.*" Mrs. Murphy thought out loud. "*This is too good a find to be lost again.*"

"*Maybe it's treasure.*" Tucker grinned. "*Claudius Crozet's lost treasure!*"

"*That's in the tunnel; one of the tunnels,*" Paddy said, knowing that

Crozet had cut four tunnels through the Blue Ridge Mountains in what was one of the engineering feats of the nineteenth century —or any century. He accomplished his feat without the help of dynamite, which hadn't yet been invented.

"*How long do you think this has been in here?*" Paddy asked.

Mrs. Murphy turned to pat the oilskin. "*Well, if someone hid this, say, in the last ten or twenty years, they'd probably have used heavy plastic. Oilskin is expensive and hard to come by. Mom wanted one of those Australian raincoats to ride in and the thing was priced about $225, I think.*"

"*Too bad humans don't have fur. Think of the money they'd save,*" Paddy said.

"*Yeah, and they'd get over worrying about what color they were because with fur you can be all colors. Look at me,*" Tucker remarked. "*Or Mrs. Murphy. Can you imagine a striped human?*"

"*It would greatly improve their appearance,*" Paddy purred.

Mrs. Murphy, mind spinning as the fur discussion flew on, said, "*We've got to get Larry over here.*"

"*Fat chance.*" Paddy harbored little hope for human intelligence.

"*You stay here with your head sticking out of the hole. Tucker and I will get him over here. If we can't budge him, then we'll be back, but don't you leave. Okay?*"

"*You were always good at giving orders.*" He smiled devilishly.

Mrs. Murphy landed in the hearth and took off for the door, Tucker close behind. They crossed the lawn, stopping under the kitchen window, where a light glowed. Larry was fixing his cup of morning coffee.

"*You bark, I'll jump up on the windowsill.*"

"*Not much of a windowsill,*" Tucker observed.

"*I can bank off it, if nothing else.*" And Mrs. Murphy did just that as Tucker yapped furiously. The sight of this striped animal, four feet planted on a windowpane and then pushing off, jolted Larry wide awake. The second thud from Mrs. Murphy positively sent him into orbit. He opened his back door and, seeing the culprits, thought they wanted to join him.

"Mrs. Murphy, Tucker, come on in."

"*You come out,*" Tucker barked.

"*I'll run in and right out.*" Mrs. Murphy flew past Larry, brushing his legs in the process, turned on a dime, and ran back out through his legs.

"What's the matter with you two?" The old man enjoyed the spectacle but was perplexed.

Again Mrs. Murphy raced in and raced out as Tucker ran forward, barked, and then ran a few steps away. "*Come on, Doc. We need you!*"

Larry, an intelligent man as humans go, deduced that the two animals, whom he knew and valued, were highly agitated. He grabbed his old jacket, slapped his porkpie hat on his head, and followed them, fearing that some harm had come to another animal or even a person. He'd heard about animals leading people to the site of an injured loved one, and a flash of fear ran through him. What if Harry'd been hurt on her way in to work?

He followed them into the addition. He stopped after walking through the door as Mrs. Murphy and Tucker dashed to the fireplace.

"*Howl, Paddy. He'll think you're trapped or something.*"

Paddy sang at his loudest, " '*Roll me over in the clover/Roll me over/ Lay me down and do it again.*' "

Tucker giggled as Mrs. Murphy leapt up to join Paddy, although she refrained from singing the song. Larry walked into the fireplace and beheld Paddy, his head thrown back and warbling for all he was worth.

"Got stuck up in there?" Larry looked around for a ladder. Not finding one, he did spy a large spackling compound bucket. He lifted it by the handle, discovering how heavy it was. He lugged it over to the hearth, positioned it under the opening, where both cats now meowed piteously, and carefully stood on it. He could just see inside.

He reached for Paddy, who shrank back. "Now, now, Paddy, I won't hurt you."

"I know that, you silly twit. Look."

"His eyes aren't good in the dark, plus he's old. They're worse than most," Mrs. Murphy told her ex. "Scratch on the oilskin."

Paddy furiously scratched away, his claws making tiny popping noises as he pulled at the sturdy cloth.

"Squint, Larry, and look real hard," Mrs. Murphy instructed.

As if he understood, Larry shielded his eyes and peered inside. "What the Sam Hill?"

"Reach in." Mrs. Murphy encouraged him by back-stepping, toward the treasure.

Larry braced against the fireplace with his left hand, now besmirched with soot, and reached in with his right. Mrs. Murphy licked his fingers for good measure. He touched the oilskin. Paddy jumped off and came to the opening. Mrs. Murphy tried to nudge the package, but it was too heavy. Larry tugged and pulled, succeeding in inching the weighty burden forward until it wedged into the opening. Forgetting the cats for a moment, he tried to pull out the oilskin-covered bundle, but it wouldn't fit. He poked at the bricks around the hole and they gave a bit. Cautiously he removed one, then two and three. These bricks had been left that way on purpose. The two kitty heads popped out of the new opening. Larry squeezed the package through and almost fell off the bucket because it was so heavy. He tottered and jumped off backward.

"Not bad for an old man," Tucker commented.

"Let's see what he's got." Mrs. Murphy sailed down. Paddy came after her.

Larry, on his knees, worked at the knot on the back side of the package. The three animals sat silent, watching with intent interest. Finally, victorious, Larry opened the oilskin covering. Inside lay three huge, heavy volumes, leather-bound. With a trembling hand Larry opened the first volume.

The bold, black cursive writing hit Larry like a medicine ball to the chest. He recognized the handwriting and in that instant the man he had admired and worked with came alive again. He was reminded of the fragrance of Jim's pipe tobacco, his habit of running his thumbs up and down under his braces, and his fervent belief that if he could cure human baldness, he'd be the richest doctor on the face of the earth. Larry whispered aloud, " 'The Secret Diaries of a Country Doctor, Volume I, 1912, by James C. Craig, M.D., Crozet, Virginia.' "

Seeing his distress, Mrs. Murphy and Tucker sat next to him, pressing their small bodies against his own. There are moments in every human life when the harpoon of fate rips into the mind and a person has the opportunity to perceive the world afresh through his own pain. This was such a moment for Larry, and through his tears he saw the two furry heads and reached out to pet them, wondering just how many times in this life we are surrounded by love and understanding and are too self-centered, too human-centered to know what the gods have given us.

44

A warm southerly breeze filled breasts with the hope that spring had truly arrived. Snowstorms could hit central Virginia in April, and once a snowstorm had blanketed the fields in May, but that was rare. The last frost generally disappeared mid-April, although days warmed before that. Then the wisteria would bloom, drenching the sides of buildings, barns, and pergolas with lavender and white. This was Mrs. Murphy's favorite time of the year.

She basked in the sun by the back door of the post office along with Pewter and Tucker. She was also basking in the delicious satisfaction of delivering to Pewter the news about the books in the hiding place. Pewter was livid, but one good thing was that her brief absence had allowed Market to overcome his temper and to make peace with Ellie Wood Baxter. The gray cat was now back

in his good graces, but if she had to hear the words "pork roast" one more time, she would scratch and bite.

The alleyway behind the buildings filled up with cars since the parking spaces in the front were taken. On one of the first really balmy days of spring, people always seem motivated to buy bulbs, bouquets, and sweaters in pastel colors.

Driving down the east end of the alleyway was Samson Coles. Turning in on the west end was Warren Randolph. They parked next to each other behind Market Shiflett's store.

Tucker lifted her head, then dropped it back on her paws. Mrs. Murphy watched through eyes that were slits. Pewter could not have cared less.

"How are you doing with the Diamonds?" Warren asked as he shut his car door.

"Hanging between Midale and Fox Haven."

Warren whistled, "Some kind of commission, buddy."

"How you been doing?"

Warren shrugged. "Okay. It's hard sometimes. And Ansley— I asked her for some peace and quiet, and what does she do but let Kimball Haynes go through the family papers. 'Course he was a nice guy, but that's not the point."

"I didn't like him," Samson said. "Lucinda pulled the same stunt on me that Ansley pulled on you. He should have come to me, not my wife. Smarmy—not that I wished him dead."

"Somebody did."

"Made your mind up about the campaign yet?" Samson abruptly changed the subject.

"I'm still debating, although I'm feeling stronger. I just might do it."

Samson slapped him on the back. "Don't let the press get hold of Poppa's will. Well, you let me know. I'll be your ardent supporter, your campaign manager, you name it."

"Sure. I'll let you know as soon as I do." Warren headed for the post office as Samson entered Market's by the back door. With remarkable self-control Warren acted as though not a thing was wrong, but he knew in that instant that Ansley had betrayed his trust and was betraying him in other respects too.

It never crossed Samson's mind that he had spilled the beans, but then, he was already spending the commission money from the Diamond deal in his mind before he'd even closed the sale. Then again, perhaps the trysting and hiding were wearing thin. Maybe subconsciously he wanted Warren to know. Then they could get the pretense over with and Ansley would be his.

45

Since Kimball had kept most of his private papers in his study room on the second floor of Monticello, the sheriff insisted that nothing be disturbed. But Harry and Mrs. Hogendobber knew the material and had been there recently with Kimball, so he allowed them, along with Deputy Cooper, to make certain nothing had been moved or removed.

Oliver Zeve, agitated, complained to Sheriff Shaw that lovely though the three ladies might be, they were not scholars and really had no place being there.

Shaw, patience ebbing, told Oliver to be grateful that Harry and Mrs. Hogendobber knew Kimball's papers and could decipher his odd shorthand. With a curt inclination of the head Oliver indicated that he was trumped, although he asked that Mrs. Murphy and Tucker stay home. He got his way on that one.

Shaw also had to pacify Fair, who wanted to accompany "the girls," as he called them. The sheriff figured that would put Oliver over the edge, and since Cynthia Cooper attended them, they were safe, he assured Fair.

Oliver's frazzled state could be explained by the fact that for the last two days he had endured network television interviews, local television interviews, and encampment by members of the press. He was not a happy man. In his discomfort he almost lost sight of the death of a valued colleague.

"Nothing appears to have been disturbed." Mrs. Hogendobber swept her eyes over the room.

Standing over his yellow legal pad, Harry noticed some new notes jotted in Kimball's tight scribble. She picked up the pad. "He wrote down a quote from Martha Randolph to her fourth child, Ellen Wayles Coolidge." Harry mused. "It's curious that Martha and her husband named their fourth child Ellen Wayles even though their third child was also Ellen Wayles—she died at eleven months. You'd think it'd be bad luck."

Mrs. Hogendobber interjected, "Wasn't. Ellen Coolidge lived a good life. Now, poor Anne Cary, that child suffered."

"You talk as though you know these people." Cynthia smiled.

"In a way we do. All the while we worked with Kimball, he filled us in, saving us years of reading, literally. Lacking telephones, people wrote to one another religiously when they were apart. Kind of wish we did that today. They left behind invaluable records, observations, opinions in their letters. They also cherished accurate judgments of one another—I think they knew one another better than we know each other today."

"The answer to that is simple, Harry." Mrs. H. peeked over her shoulder to examine the legal pad. "They missed the deforming experience of psychology."

"Why don't you read what he copied down?" Cooper whipped out her notebook and pencil.

"This is what Martha Randolph said: 'The discomfort of slavery I have borne all my life, but its sorrows in all their bitterness I never before perceived.' He wrote below that this was a letter dated August 2, 1825, from the Coolidge papers at U.V.A."

"Who is Coolidge?" Cooper wrote on her pad.

"Sorry, Ellen Wayles married a Coolidge—"

Cooper interrupted. "That's right, you told me that. I'll get the names straight eventually. Does Kimball make any notation about why that was significant?"

"Here he wrote, 'After sale of Colonel Randolph's slaves to pay debts. Sale included one Susan, who was Virginia's maid,' " Harry informed Cynthia. "Virginia was the sixth child of Thomas Mann Randolph and Martha Jefferson Randolph, the one we call Patsy because that's what she was called within the family."

"Can you give me an abbreviated history course here? Why did the colonel sell slaves, obviously against other family members' wishes?"

"We forgot to tell you that Colonel Randolph was Patsy's husband."

"Oh." She wrote that down. "Didn't Patsy have any say in the matter?"

"Coop, until a few decades ago, as in our lifetime, women were still chattel in the state of Virginia." Harry jammed her right hand in her pocket. "Thomas Mann Randolph could do as he damn well pleased. He started out with advantages in this life but proved a poor businessman. He became so estranged from his family toward the end that he would leave Monticello at dawn and return only at night."

"He was the victim of his own generosity." Mrs. Hogendobber put in a good word for the man. "Always standing notes for friends and then, pfft." She flipped her hand upside down like a fish that bellied up. "Wound up in legal proceedings against his own son, Jeff, who had become the anchor of the family and upon whom even his grandfather relied."

"Know the old horse expression 'He broke bad'?" Harry asked Cooper. "That was Thomas Mann Randolph."

"He wasn't the only one now. Look what happened to Jefferson's two nephews Lilburne and Isham Lewis." Mrs. Hogendobber adored the news, or gossip, no matter the vintage. "They killed a slave named George on December 15, 1811. Fortunately their mother, Lucy, Thomas Jefferson's sister, had already passed away, on May 26, 1810, or she would have perished of the shame. Anyway, they killed this unfortunate dependent and Lilburne was indicted on March 18, 1812. He killed himself on April tenth and his brother Isham ran away. Oh, it was awful."

"Did that happen here?" Cooper's pencil flew across the page.

"Frontier. Kentucky." Mrs. Hogendobber took the tablet from Harry. "May I?" She read. "Here's another quote from Patsy, still about the slave sale. 'Nothing can prosper under such a system of injustice.' Don't you wonder what the history of this nation would be like if the women had been included in the government from the beginning?—Women like Abigail Adams and Dolley Madison and Martha Jefferson Randolph."

"We got the vote in 1920 and we still aren't fifty percent of the government," Harry bitterly said. "Actually, our government is such a tangled mess of contradictions, maybe a person is smart to stay out of it."

"Oh, Harry, it was a mess when Jefferson waded in too. Politics is like a fight between banty roosters," Mrs. Hogendobber noted.

"Could you two summarize Jefferson's attitude about slavery? His daughter surely seems to have hated it." Cooper started to chew on her eraser, caught herself, and stopped.

"The best place to start is to read his *Notes on Virginia*. Now, that was first printed in 1785 in Paris, but he started writing before that."

"Mrs. Hogendobber, with all due respect, I haven't the time

to read that stuff. I've got a killer to find with a secret to hide and we're still working on the stiff from 1803, excuse me, the remains."

"The corpse of love," Harry blurted out.

"That's how we think of him," Miranda added.

"You mean because he was Medley's lover, or you think he was?" Cooper questioned her.

"Yes, but if she loved him, she had stopped."

"Because she loved someone else?" Cynthia, accustomed to grilling, fell into it naturally.

"It was some form of love. It may not have been romantic."

Cynthia sighed. Another dead end for now. "Okay. Someone tell me about Jefferson and slavery. Mrs. Hogendobber, you have a head for dates and stuff."

"Bookkeeping gives one a head for figures. All right, Thomas Jefferson was born April 13, 1743, new style calendar. Remember, everyone but the Russians moved up to the Gregorian calendar from the Julian. By the old style he was born on April 2. Must have been fun for all those people all over Europe and the New World to get two birthdays, so to speak. Well, Cynthia, he was born into a world of slavery. If you read history at all, you realize that every great civilization undergoes a protracted period of slavery. It's the only way the work can get done and capital can be accumulated. Imagine if the pharaohs had had to pay labor for the construction of the pyramids."

"I never thought of it that way." Cynthia raised her eyebrows.

"Slaves have typically been those who were conquered in battle. In the case of the Romans, many of their slaves were Greeks, most of whom were far better educated than their captors, and the Romans expected their Greek slaves to tutor them. And the Greeks themselves often had Greek slaves, those captured from battles with other poleis, or city-states. Well, our slaves were no different in that they were the losers in war, but the twist for America came in this fashion: The slaves that came to America were the losers in tribal wars in Africa and were sold to the Portuguese by the leaders of the victorious tribes. See, by that time the world had shrunk, so to speak. Lower Africa had contact with Europe, and the products of Europe enticed people everywhere. After a while other Europeans elbowed in on the trade and sailed to South America, the Caribbean, and North America with their human cargo. They even began to bag some trophies themselves—you know, if the wars slowed down. Demand for labor was heavy in the New World."

"Mrs. Hogendobber, what does this have to do with Thomas Jefferson?"

"Two things. He grew up in a society where most people considered slavery normal. And two—and this still plagues us today—the conquered, the slaves, were not Europeans, they were Africans. They couldn't pass. You see?"

Cynthia bit her pencil eraser again. "I'm beginning to get the picture."

"Even if a slave bought his or her way to freedom or was granted freedom, or even if the African started as a free person, he or she never looked like a Caucasian. Unlike the Romans and the Greeks, whose slaves were other European tribes or usually other indigenous Caucasian peoples, a stigma attached to slavery in America because it was automatically attached to the color of the skin—with terrible consequences."

Harry jumped in. "But he believed in liberty. He thought slavery cruel, yet he couldn't live without his own slaves. Oh, sure, he treated them handsomely and they were loyal to him because he looked after them so well compared to many other slave owners of the period. So he was trapped. He couldn't imagine scaling down. Virginians then and today still conceive of themselves as English lords and ladies. That translates into a high, high standard of living."

"One that bankrupted him." Mrs. Hogendobber nodded her head in sadness. "And saddled his heirs."

"Yeah, but what was most interesting about Jefferson, to me anyway, was his insight into what slavery does to people. He said it destroyed the industry of the masters while degrading the victim. It sapped the foundation of liberty. He absolutely believed that freedom was a gift from God and the right of all men. So he favored a plan of gradual emancipation. Nobody listened, of course."

"Did other people have to bankrupt themselves?"

"You have to remember that the generation that fought the Revolutionary War, for all practical purposes, saw their currency devalued and finally destroyed. The only real security was land, I guess." Mrs. Hogendobber thought out loud. "Jefferson lost a lot. James Madison struggled with heavy debt as well as with the contradictions of slavery his whole life, and Dolley was forced to sell Montpelier, his mother's and later their home, after his death. Speaking of slavery, one of James's slaves, who loved Dolley like a mother, gave her his life savings and continued to live with her and work for her. As you can see, the emotions between the master or the mistress and the slave were highly complex. People loved one another across a chasm of injustice. I fear we've lost that."

"We'll have to learn to love one another as equals," Harry solemnly said. " 'We hold these truths to be self-evident, that all men are created equal, that they are endowed by their Creator with inherent and unalienable rights, that among these are Life, Liberty, and the Pursuit of Happiness.' "

"History. I hated history when I was in college. You two bring it to life." Cynthia praised them and their short course on Jefferson.

"It is alive. These walls breathe. Everything that everyone did or did not do throughout the course of human life on earth impacts us. Everything!" Mrs. Hogendobber was impassioned.

Harry, spellbound by Mrs. Hogendobber, heard an owl hoot outside, the low, mournful sound breaking the spell and reminding her of Athena, goddess of wisdom, to whom the owl was sacred. Wisdom was born of the night, of solitary and deep thought. It was so obvious, so clearly obvious to the Greeks and those who used mythological metaphors for thousands of years. She just got it. She started to share her revelation when she spied a copy of Dumas Malone's magisterial series on the life of Thomas Jefferson. It was the final volume, the sixth, The Sage of Monticello.

"I don't remember this book being here."

Mrs. Hogendobber noticed the book on the chair. The other five volumes rested in the milk crates that served as bookcases. "It wasn't."

"Here." Harry opened to a page which Kimball had marked by using the little heavy gray paper divider found in boxes of teabags. "Look at this."

Cynthia and Mrs. Hogendobber crowded around the book, where on page 513 Kimball had underlined with a pink highlighter, "All five of the slaves freed under Jefferson's will were members of this family; others of them previously had been freed or, if able to pass as white, allowed to run away."

" 'Allowed to run away'!" Mrs. Hogendobber read aloud.

"It's complicated, Cynthia, but this refers to the Hemings family. Thomas Jefferson had been accused by his political enemies, the Federalists, of having an affair of many years' duration with Sally Hemings. We don't think he did, but the slaves declared that Sally was the mistress of Peter Carr, Thomas's favorite nephew, whom he raised as a son."

"But the key here is that Sally's mother, also a beautiful woman, was half white to begin with. Her name was Betty, and her lover, again according to oral slave tradition as well as what Thomas Jefferson Randolph said, was John Wayles, Jefferson's wife's brother. You see the bind Jefferson was in. For fifty years that man lived with this abuse heaped on his head."

"Allowed to run away," Harry whispered. "Miranda, we're on second base."

"Yeah, but who's going to come to bat?" Cooper scratched her head.

46

The Coleses' library yielded little that they didn't already know. Mrs. Hogendobber came across a puzzling reference to Edward Coles, secretary to James Madison and then the first governor of the Illinois Territory. Edward, called Ned, never married or sired children. Other Coleses carried on that task. But a letter dated 1823 made reference to a great kindness he performed for Patsy. Jefferson's daughter? The kindness was not clarified.

When the little band of researchers left, Samson merrily waved them off after offering them generous liquid excitements. Lucinda, too, waved.

After the squad car disappeared, Lucinda walked back into the library. She noticed the account book was not on the bottom shelf. She had not helped Harry, Miranda, and Cynthia go over the records because she had an appointment in Charlottesville, and Samson had seemed almost overeager to perform the niceties.

She scanned the library for the ledger.

Samson, carrying a glass with four ice cubes and his favorite Dalwhinnie, wandered in, opened a cabinet door, and sat down in a leather chair. He clicked on the television, which was concealed in the cabinet. Neither he nor Lulu could stand to see a television sitting out. Too middle class.

"Samson, where's your ledger?"

"Has nothing to do with Jefferson or his descendants, my dear."

"No, but it has a lot to do with Kimball Haynes."

He turned up the sound, and she grabbed the remote out of his hand and shut off the television.

"What the hell's the matter with you?" His face reddened.

"I might ask the same of you. I hardly ever reach you on your mobile phone anymore. When I call places where you tell me you're going to be, you aren't there. I may not be the brightest woman in the world, Samson, but I'm not the dumbest either."

"Oh, don't start the perfume accusation again. We settled that."

"What is in that ledger?"

"Nothing that concerns you. You've never been interested in my business before, why now?"

"I entertain your customers often enough."

"That's not the same as being interested in my business. You don't care how I make the money so long as you can spend it."

"You're clever, Samson, much more clever than I am, but I'm not fooled. You aren't going to sidetrack me about money. What is in that ledger?"

"Nothing."

"Then why didn't you let those women go through it? Kimball read it. That makes it part of the evidence."

He shot out of his chair and in an instant towered over her, his bulk an assault against her frailty without his even lifting a hand. He shouted. "You keep your mouth shut about that ledger, or so help me God, I'll—"

For the first time in their marriage Lucinda did not back down. "Kill me?" she screamed in his face. "You're in some kind of trouble, Samson, or you're doing something illegal."

"Keep out of my life!"

"You mean get out of your life," she snarled. "Wouldn't that make it easier for you to carry on with your mistress, whoever she is?"

Menace oozed from his every pore. "Lucinda, if you ever mention that ledger to anyone, you will regret it far more than you can possibly understand. Now leave me alone."

Lucinda replied with an icy calm, frightening in itself. "You killed Kimball Haynes."

47

The squad car, Deputy Cooper at the wheel, picked up an urgent dispatch. She swerved hard right, slammed the car into reverse, and shot toward Whitehall Road. "Hang on, Mrs. H."

Mrs. Hogendobber, eyes open wide, could only suck in her breath as the car picked up speed, siren wailing and lights flashing.

"Yehaw!" Harry braced herself against the dash.

Vehicles in front of them pulled quickly to the side of the road. One ancient Plymouth puttered along. Its driver also had a lot of miles on him. Coop sucked up right behind him and blasted the horn as well. She so astonished the man that he jumped up in his seat and cut hard right. His Plymouth rocked from side to side but remained upright.

"That was Loomis McReady." Mrs. Hogendobber pressed

her nose against the car window, only to be sent toward the other side of the car when Cynthia tore around a curve. "Thank God for seat belts."

"Old Loomis ought not to be on the road." Harry thought elderly people ought to take a yearly driver's test.

"Up ahead," Deputy Cooper said.

Mrs. Hogendobber grasped the back of the front seat to steady herself while she looked between Harry's and Cynthia's heads. "It's Samson Coles."

"Going like a bat out of hell, and in his Wagoneer too. Those things can't corner and hold the road." Harry felt her shoulders tense.

"Look!" Mrs. Hogendobber could now see, once they were out of another snaky turn, that a car in front of Samson's sped even faster than his own.

"Holy shit, it's Lucinda! Excuse me, Miranda, I didn't mean to swear."

"Under the circumstances—" Miranda never finished that sentence because a second set of sirens screeched from the opposite end of the road.

"You've got them now," Harry gloated.

As soon as Lucinda saw Sheriff Rick Shaw's car coming toward her, she flashed her lights and stopped. Cooper, hot on Samson's tail, slowed since she thought he'd brake, but he didn't. He swerved around Lulu's big brown Wagoneer on the right-hand side, one set of wheels grinding into a runoff ditch. Beaver Dam Road lay just ahead, and he meant to hang a hard right.

Sheriff Shaw stopped for Lucinda, who was crying, sobbing, screaming, "He'll kill me! He'll kill me!"

"Ladies, this is dicey," Cooper warned as she, too, plowed into the runoff ditch to the right of Lucinda. The squad car tore out huge hunks of earth and bluestone before reaching the road again.

Samson gunned the red Wagoneer toward Beaver Dam, which wasn't a ninety-degree right but a sharp, sharp reverse thirty-degree angle heading northeast off Whitehall Road. It was a punishing turn under the best of circumstances. Just as Samson reached the turn, Carolyn Maki, in her black Ford dually, braked for the stop sign. Samson hit the brakes and sent his rear end skidding out from underneath him. He overcorrected by turning hard right. The Wagoneer flipped over twice, finally coming to rest on its side. Miraculously, the dually remained untouched.

Carolyn Maki opened her door to assist Samson.

Cooper screeched to a stop next to the truck and leapt out of the squad car, gun in hand. "Get back in the truck," she yelled at Carolyn.

Harry started to open her door, but the strong hand of Mrs. Hogendobber grasped her neck from behind. "Stay put."

This did not prevent either one of them from hitting the automatic buttons to open the windows so they could hear. They stuck their heads out.

Cooper sprinted to the car where Samson clawed at the driver's door, pointing skyward as the car rested on its right side. Oblivious of the minor cuts on his face and hands, he thrust open the door and crawled out head first, only to stare into the barrel of Cynthia Cooper's pistol.

"Samson, put your hands behind your head."

"I can explain everything."

"Behind your head!"

He did as he was told. A third squad car pulled in from Beaver Dam Road, and Deputy Cooper was glad for the assistance. "Carolyn, are you okay?"

"Yes," a wide-eyed Carolyn Maki called from her truck.

"We'll need a statement from you, and one of us will try to get it in a few minutes so you can go home."

"Fine. Can I get out of the truck now?"

Cooper nodded yes as the third officer frisked Samson Coles. The wheels of his Jeep were still spinning.

Carolyn walked over to Mrs. Hogendobber and Harry, now waiting outside the squad car.

Harry heard Sheriff Shaw's voice on the special radio. She picked up the receiver, the coiled cord swinging underneath. "Sheriff, it's Harry."

"Where's Cooper?" came his gruff response.

"She's holding Samson Coles with his hands behind his head."

"Any injuries?"

"No—unless you count the Wagoneer."

"I'll be right there."

The sheriff left Lucinda Coles with one of his deputies. He was less than half a mile away, so he arrived in an instant. He strode purposefully over to Samson. "Read him his rights."

"Yes, sir," Cooper said.

"All right, handcuff him."

"Is that necessary?" Samson complained.

The sheriff didn't bother to respond. He sauntered over to the Wagoneer and stood on his tiptoes to look inside. Lying on the passenger side window next to the earth was a snub-nosed .38.

48

"Copious in his indignation, he was." Miranda held the attention of her rapt audience. She had reached the point in her story where Samson Coles, being led away to the sheriff's car, hands cuffed behind his back, started shouting. He didn't want to go to jail. He hadn't done anything wrong other than chase his wife down the road with his car, and hasn't every man wanted to bash his wife's head in once in a while? "Wasn't it Noel Coward who wrote, 'Women are like gongs, they should be struck regularly'?"

"He said that?" Susan Tucker asked.

"*Private Lives*," Mim filled in. Mim was sitting on the school chair that Miranda had brought around for her from the back of the post office. Larry Johnson, who hadn't told anyone about the diaries, Fair Haristeen, and Ned Tucker stood while Market Shiflett, Pewter next to him, sat on the counter. Mrs. Hogendobber paced the room, enacting the details to give emphasis to her story. Tucker paced with her as Mrs. Murphy sat on the postage scale. When Miranda wanted verification she would turn to Harry, also sitting on the counter, and Harry would nod or say a sentence or two to add color.

The Reverend Jones pushed open the door, come to collect his mail. "How much did I miss?"

"Almost the whole thing, Herbie, but I'll give you a private audience."

Herb was followed by Ansley and Warren Randolph. Mrs. Hogendobber was radiant because this meant she could repeat the adventure anew with theatrics. Three was better than one.

"*Oscar performance,*" Mrs. Murphy laconically commented to her two pals.

"*Wish we'd been there.*" Tucker hated to miss excitement.

"*I'd have thrown up. Did I tell you about the time I threw up when Market was taking me to the vet?*" Pewter remarked.

"*Not now,*" Mrs. Murphy implored the gray cat.

When Mrs. Hogendobber finished her tale for the second time, everyone began talking at once.

"Did they ever find the murder weapon? The gun that killed Kimball Haynes?" Warren asked.

"Coop says the ballistics proved it was a snub-nosed .38-caliber pistol. It was unregistered. Frightening how easy it is to purchase a gun illegally. The bullets matched the bore of the .38 they found in Samson's car. It had smashed the passenger window to bits. Must have had it on the seat next to him. Looks like he really was going to do in Lulu. Looks like he's the one that did in Kimball Haynes." Miranda shook her head at such violence.

"I hope not." Dr. Johnson's calm voice rang out. "Everyone has marital problems, and Samson's may be larger than most, but we still don't know what happened to set this off. And we don't know if he killed Kimball. Innocent until proven guilty. Remember, we're talking about one of Crozet's own here. We'd better wait and see before stringing him up."

"I didn't say anything about stringing him up," Miranda huffed. "But it's mighty peculiar."

"This spring has been mighty peculiar." Fair edged his toes together and then apart, a nervous habit.

"Much as I like Samson, I hope this settles the case. Why would he kill Kimball Haynes? I don't know." Ned Tucker put his arm around his wife's shoulders. "But we would sleep better at night if we knew the case was closed."

"Let the dead bury the dead." The little group murmured their assent to Ned's hopes.

No one noticed that Ansley had turned ghostly white.

49

Samson Coles denied ever having seen the snub-nosed .38. His lawyer, John Lowe, having argued many cases for the defense in his career, could spot a liar a mile away. He knew Samson was lying. Samson refused to give the sheriff any information other than his name and address and, in a funny reversion to his youth, his army ID number. By the time John Lowe reached his client, Samson was the picture of sullen hostility.

"Now, Samson, one more time. Why did you threaten to kill your wife?"

"And for the last time, we'd been having problems, real problems."

"That doesn't mean you kill your wife or threaten her. You're paying me lots of money, Samson. Right now it looks pretty bad for you. The report came back on the gun. It was the gun that killed Kimball Haynes." John, not averse to theatrics himself, used this last stunner, which was totally untrue—the ballistics results hadn't come back yet—in hopes of blasting his client into some kind of cooperation. It worked.

"No!" Samson shook. "I never saw that gun before in my life. I swear it, John, I swear it on the Holy Bible! When I said I was going to kill her, I didn't mean I really would, I wouldn't shoot her. She just pushed all my buttons."

"Buddy, you could get the chair. This is a capital-punishment state, and I wasn't born yesterday. You'd better tell me what happened."

Tears welled up in Samson's eyes. His voice wavered. "John, I'm in love with Ansley Randolph. I spent money trying to impress her, and to make a long story short, I've been dipping into escrow funds which I hold as the principal broker. Lucinda saw the ledger—" He stopped because his whole body was shaking. "Actually, she showed it to Kimball Haynes when he was over to read the family histories and diaries, you know, to see if there was anything that could fit into the murder at Monticello. There wasn't, of course, but I have accounts beginning in the last decades of the seventeenth century, kept by my maternal grandmother of many greats, Charlotte Graff. Kimball read those accounts, meticulously detailed, and Lucinda laughed that she couldn't make sense out of my books but how crystal clear Granny Graff's were. So Lucinda gave Kimball my ledger to prove her point. He immediately saw what I'd been doing. I kept two columns, you know how it's done. That's the truth."

"Samson, you have a high standing in Crozet. To many people's minds that would be more than sufficient motive to kill Kimball—to protect that standing as well as your livelihood. Answer me. Did you kill Kimball Haynes?"

Tears gushing down his ruddy cheeks, Samson implored John, "I'd rather lose my license than my life."

John believed him.

50

Obsessed by his former partner's diaries, Dr. Larry Johnson read at breakfast, between patients, at dinner, and late into the night. He finished volume one, which was surprisingly well written, especially considering he'd never thought Jim a literary man.

References to the grandparents and great-grandparents of many Albemarle County citizens enlivened the documents. Much of volume one centered on the effects of World War I on the returning servicemen and their wives. Jim Craig was then fairly new to the practice of medicine.

Z. Calvin Coles, grandfather to Samson Coles, returned from the war carrying a wicked dose of syphilis. Mim's paternal line, the Urquharts, flourished during the war, as they invested heavily in armaments, and Mim's father's brother, Douglas Urquhart, lost his arm in a threshing accident.

All the patients treated, from measles to bone cancer, were meticulously mentioned as well as their character, background, and the history of specific diseases.

The Minors, Harry's paternal ancestors, were prone to sinus infections, while on her mother's side, the Hepworths, they either died very young or made it into their seventies and beyond— good long innings then. Wesley Randolph's family often suffered a wasting disease of the blood which killed them slowly. The Hogendobbers leaned toward coronary disorders, and the Sanburnes to gout.

Jim's keen powers of observation again won Larry's admiration. Being young when he joined Jim Craig's practice, Larry had looked up to his partner, but now, as an old man, he could measure Jim in the fullness of his own experience. Jim was a fine doctor and his death at sixty-one was a loss for the town and for other doctors.

With eager hands Larry opened volume two, dated February 22, 1928.

51

Jails are not decorated in designer colors. Nor is the privacy of one's person much honored. Poor Samson Coles listened to stinking men with the DTs hollering and screaming, bottom-rung drug sellers protesting their innocence, and one child molester declaring that an eight-year-old had led him on. If Samson ever doubted his sanity, this "vacation" in the cooler reaffirmed that he was sane—stupid perhaps, but sane.

He wasn't so sure about the men in the other cells. Their delusions both fascinated and repelled him.

His only delusion was that Ansley Randolph loved him when in fact she did not. He knew that now. Not one attempt to contact him, not that he expected her to show her face at the correctional institute, as it was euphemistically called. She could have smuggled him a note though—something.

Like most men, Samson had been used by women, especially when he was younger. One of the good things about Lucinda was that she didn't use him. She had loved him once. He felt the searing pain of guilt each time he thought of his wife, the wife he'd betrayed, his once good name which he had destroyed, and the fact that he would lose his real estate license in the bargain. He'd wrecked everything: home, career, community standing. For what?

And now he stood accused of murder. Fleeting thoughts of suicide, accomplished with a bedsheet, occurred to him. He fought them back. Somehow he would have to learn to live with what he'd done. Maybe he'd been stupid, but he wasn't a coward.

As for Ansley, he knew she'd fall right back into her routine. She didn't love Warren a bit, but she'd never risk losing the wealth and prestige of being a Randolph. Not that being a Coles was shabby, but megamillions versus comfort and a good name—no contest. Then, too, she had her boys to consider, and life would be far more advantageous for them if she stayed put.

In retrospect he could see that Ansley's ambitions centered more on the boys than on herself, although she had the sense to be low-key about them. If she was going to endure the Randolph clan, then, by God, she would have successful and loving sons. Blood, money, and power—what a combination.

He swung his legs over the side of his bunk. He'd turn to pure fat in this place if he didn't do leg raises and push-ups. One good thing about being in the slammer, no social drinking. He wanted to cry sometimes, but he didn't know how. Just as well. Wimps get buggered in places like this.

How long he sat there, dangling his legs just to feel some circulation, he didn't know. He jerked his legs up with a start when he realized he was aptly named.

52

The buds on the trees swelled, changing in color from dark red to light green. Spring, in triumph, had arrived.

Harry endured a spring-cleaning fit each year when the first blush of green swept over the meadows and the mountains. The creeks and rivers soared near their banks from the high melting snow and ice, and the air carried the scent of earth again.

Piles of newspapers and magazines, waiting to be read, were stacked on the back porch. Harry succumbed to the knowledge that she would never read them, so out they went. Clothes, neatly folded, rested near the periodicals. Harry hadn't much in the way of clothing, but she finally broke down and threw out those articles too often patched and repatched.

She decided, too, to toss out the end table with three legs instead of four. She'd find one of those unfinished-furniture stores and paint a new end table. As she carried it out she stubbed her toe on the old cast-iron doorstop. This had been her great-grandmother's iron, heated on top of the stove.

"Goddammit!"

"*If you'd look where you were going, you wouldn't run into things.*" Tucker sounded like a schoolteacher.

Harry rubbed her toe, took off her shoe, and rubbed some more. Then she picked up the offending iron, ready to hurl it outside. "That's it!" She joyously called to Mrs. Murphy and Tucker. "The murder weapon. Medley Orion was a seamstress!"

53

Holding the iron aloft, Harry demonstrated to Mim Sanburne, Fair, Larry Thompson, Susan, and Deputy Cooper how the blow would have been struck.

"It certainly could account for the triangular indentation." Larry examined the iron.

Mrs. Murphy and Pewter sat tight against each other on the kitchen table. Although Mrs. Murphy would rather lose fur than admit it—she liked having a feline companion. Pewter did, too, but then, Pewter camped out on the kitchen table, since that's where the food was placed.

Tucker circled the table. *"Smart of Mom to call Big Marilyn."*

"Mim is head of the restoration project." Mrs. Murphy glanced down at her little friend. *"This way, too, Mim can tell Oliver Zeve and Coop can tell Sheriff Shaw. It's a pretty good theory."*

"I believe you've got it." Larry handed the iron to Mim, who felt its weight.

"One solid blow pushing straight out or slightly upward. People performed so much physical labor back then, she was no doubt strong enough to inflict a fatal blow. We know she was young." Mim gave the iron to Miranda.

"The shape of this iron would help when pressing lace or all the fripperies and fancies those folks wore."

"May I borrow the iron to show Rick? If he doesn't see it with his own eyes, he'll be skeptical." Cynthia Cooper held out her hands for the iron.

"Sure."

"We hear that Samson categorically denies killing Kimball even though that gun was in his car." Mim hated that Sheriff Shaw didn't tell her everything. But then, Mim wanted to know everything about everybody, as did Miranda, though for different reasons.

"He's sticking to his story."

"Has anyone visited Lulu?" Susan Tucker asked. "I thought about going there this evening."

"I've paid a call." Mim spoke first, as the first citizen of Crozet, which in essence she was. "She's terribly shaken. Her sister has flown up from Mobile to attend to her. She wonders how people will treat her now, and I've assured her that no blame attaches itself to her. Why don't you give her a day or two, Susan, and then go over."

"She loves shortbread," Mrs. Hogendobber remembered. "I'll bake some."

The rest of the group raised their hands and Miranda laughed. "I'll be in the kitchen till Easter!"

"I'm still not giving up on finding out the real story behind the corpse in Cabin Four." Harry walked over to the counter to make coffee.

"And I was thinking that I'd read through Dr. Thomas Walker's papers. He attended Peter Jefferson on his deathbed.

Quite a man of many parts, Thomas Walker of Castle Hill. Maybe, just maybe, I can find a reference to treating a broken leg. There was another physician also, but I can't think of his name off the top of my head,'' Larry said.

"We owe it to Kimball." Harry ground the beans, releasing the intoxicating scent.

"Harry, you never give up." Fair joined her, setting out cups and saucers. "I hope you all do get to the bottom of the story just so it's over, but more than anything, I'm glad Kimball's murderer is behind bars. That had me worried."

"Does it seem possible that Samson Coles could kill a man in cold blood?" Mim poured half-and-half into her cup.

"Mrs. Sanburne, the most normal-looking persons can commit the most heinous crimes," stated Deputy Cooper, who ought to know.

"I guess." Mim sighed.

"*Do you think Samson did it?*" Pewter asked.

Mrs. Murphy flicked her tail. "*No. But someone wants us to think he did.*"

"*The gun was in his car.*" Tucker wanted to believe the mess was over.

The tiger cat's pink tongue hung out of her mouth for a second. "*It's not over—feline intuition.*"

Miranda asked, "Did Kimball ever get to the Randolph papers?"

"Gee, I don't know." Harry paused, then walked over to the phone and dialed.

"Hello, Ansley. Excuse me for bothering you. Did Kimball ever get to read your family papers?" She listened. "Well, thanks again. I'm sorry to bother you." She hung up the phone receiver. "No."

"We still have a few more stops in duplicating Kimball's research. Something will turn up." Mrs. H. tried to sound helpful.

54

"*What a wuss,*" Mrs. Murphy groaned about Pewter. "*It's too far. It's too cold. I'll be so tired tomorrow.*"

Tucker's dog trot ate up the miles. "*Be glad she stayed home. She would have sat down and cried before we'd gone two miles. This way we can get our work done.*"

Mrs. Murphy, following feline instincts, felt the whole story was not out, not by a long shot. She convinced Tucker to head out to Samson Coles's estate late at night. The game little dog needed no convincing. Besides, the thrill of finding the books in the fireplace hadn't worn off. Right now they thought they could do anything.

They cut across fields, jumped creeks, ducked under fences. They passed herds of deer, the does with newborn fawns by their sides. And once, Mrs. Murphy growled when she smelled a dog

fox. Cats and foxes are natural enemies because they compete for
the same food.

As Lucinda and Samson's place was four miles by the path
they took, they arrived around eleven o'clock. Lights were on
upstairs as well as in the living room.

Massive walnut trees guarded the house. Mrs. Murphy
climbed up one and walked out a branch. She saw Lucinda Coles
and Warren Randolph through the living room window. She
backed down the tree and jumped onto the broad windowsill so
she could hear their conversation, since the window was open to
allow the cool spring air through the house, a welcome change
from the stuffy winter air trapped inside. The cat scarcely breathed
as she listened.

Tucker, knowing Mrs. Murphy to be impeccable in these
matters, decided to pick up whatever she could by scent.

Lucinda, handkerchief dabbing her eyes, nodded more than
she spoke.

"You had no idea?"

"I knew he was fooling around, but I didn't know it was
Ansley. My best friend, God, it's so typical." She groaned.

"Look, I know you've got enough troubles, and I don't want
you to worry about money. If you'll allow me, I can organize the
estate and do what must be done, along with your regular lawyers, of course. Just don't act precipitously. Even if Samson is
convicted, it doesn't mean you have to lose everything."

"Oh, Warren, I don't know how to thank you."

He sighed deeply. "I still can't believe it myself. You think
you know someone and then—I guess if the truth be told, I'm
more upset about the, uh, affair than the murder."

"When did you know?"

"Behind the post office. Tuesday. He slipped, made a comment about something only my wife could have known." He
hesitated. "I drove over here one night and cut the lights off. I was
going to come in and tell you, and then I chickened out in the
middle of it. Well, I saw his car in the driveway. So, like I said, I

backed out. I don't know if it would have made any difference if you'd known a few days ago instead of today."

"It wouldn't have saved the marriage." She cried anew.

"Did he really threaten to kill you?"

She nodded and sobbed.

Warren wrung his hands. "That should make the divorce go faster." He glanced to the window. "Your cat wants in."

Mrs. Murphy froze. Lucinda looked up. "That's not my cat." That fast Mrs. Murphy shot off the windowsill. "Funny, that looked like Mrs. Murphy."

"*Tucker, vamoose!*"

Mrs. Murphy streaked across the front lawn as Tucker, who could run like blazes, caught up with her. The front door opened and Lucinda, curious as well as wanting to forget the pain for a moment, saw the pair. "Those are Harry's animals. What in the world are they doing all the way over here?"

Warren stood beside her and watched the two figures silhouetted against silver moonlight. "Hunting. You'd be amazed at how large hunting territories are. Bears prowl a hundred-mile radius."

"You'd think there'd be enough mice at Harry's."

55

The crowd had gathered along the garden level at Monticello. Kimball Haynes's memorial service was held in the land he loved and understood. Monticello, shorn as she is of home life, makes up for it by casting an emotional net over all who work there.

At first Oliver Zeve balked at holding a memorial at Monticello. Enough negative attention, in his mind, had been drawn to the shrine. He brought it before the board of directors, each of whom had ample opportunity to know and care for Kimball. He was an easy man to like. The board decided without much argument to allow the ceremony to take place after public hours. Somehow it was fitting that Kimball should be remembered

where he was happiest and where he served to further understanding of one of the greatest men this nation or any other has
ever produced.

The Reverend Jones, Montalto looming behind him, cleared
his throat. Mim and Jim Sanburne sat in the front row along with
Warren and Ansley Randolph, as those two couples had made the
financial arrangements for the service. Mrs. Hogendobber, in her
pale gold robes with the garnet satin inside the sleeves and around
the collar, stood beside the reverend with the choir of the Church
of the Holy Light. Although an Evangelical Lutheran, Reverend
Jones had a gift for bringing together the various Christian groups
in Crozet.

Harry, Susan and Ned Tucker, Fair Haristeen, and Heike
Holtz sat in the second row along with Leah and Nick Nichols,
social friends of Kimball's. Lucinda Coles, after much self-torture,
joined them. Mim, in a long, agonizing phone conversation, told
Lulu that no one blamed her for Kimball's death and her presence
would be a tribute to the departed.

Members of the history and architecture departments from
the University of Virginia were in attendance, along with all of the
Monticello staff including the wonderful docents who conduct
the tours for the public.

The Reverend Jones opened his well-worn Bible and in his
resonant, hypnotic voice read the Twenty-seventh Psalm:

> The Lord is my light and my salvation;
>   whom shall I fear?
> The Lord is the stronghold of my life;
>   of whom shall I be afraid?

> When evildoers assail me,
>   uttering slanders against me,
> My adversaries and foes,
>   they shall stumble and fall.

Though a host encamp against me,
    my heart shall not fear;
Though war rise up against me,
    yet I will be confident.

One thing have I asked of the Lord,
    that will I seek after;
That I may dwell in the house of the Lord
    all the days of my life—

The service continued and the reverend spoke directly of sufferings needlessly afflicted, of promising life untimely cut down, of the evils that men do to one another, and of the workings of faith. Reverend Jones reminded them of how one life, Kimball Haynes's, had touched so many others and how Kimball sought to help us touch those lives lived long ago. By the time the good man finished, there wasn't a dry eye left.

As the people filed out to leave, Fair considerately placed his hand under Lulu's elbow, for she was much affected. After all, apart from her liking for Kimball and her feelings of responsibility, it was her husband who stood accused of his murder. And Samson sure had a motive. Kimball could have blown the whistle on his escrow theft. Worse, Samson had bellowed that he would kill her.

Ansley stumbled up ahead. High-heeled shoes implanted her in the grass like spikes. Lucinda pulled Fair along with her and hissed at Ansley. "I thought you were my best friend."

"I am," Ansley stoutly insisted.

Warren, high color in his cheeks, watched as if waiting for another car wreck to happen.

"What a novel definition of a best friend: one who sleeps with your husband." Lucinda raised her voice.

"Not here," Ansley begged through clenched teeth.

"Why not? Sooner or later everyone here will know the

story. Crozet is the only town where sound travels faster than light."

Before a rip-roaring shouting match could erupt, Harry slid alongside Lucinda on the right. Susan ran interference.

"Lulu, you are making a career of disrupting funerals," Harry chided her.

It was enough.

56

Dr. Larry Johnson, carrying his black Gladstone bag of medical gear, buoyantly swung into the post office. Tucker rushed up to greet him. Mrs. Murphy, splayed on the counter on her right side, tail slowly flicking back and forth, raised her head, then put it back down again.

"I think I know who the Monticello victim is."

Mrs. Murphy sat up, alert. Harry and Miranda hurried around the counter.

Larry straightened his hand-tied bow tie before addressing his small but eager audience. "Now, ladies, I apologize for not telling you first, but that honor belonged to Sheriff Shaw, and you will, of course, understand why I had to place the next call to Mim Sanburne. She in turn called Warren and Ansley and the other major contributors. I also called Oliver Zeve, but the minute the political calls were accounted for, I zoomed over here."

"We can't stand it. Tell!" Harry clapped her hands together.

"Thomas Walker, like any good medical man, kept a record of his patients. All I did was start at the beginning and read. In 1778 he set the leg of a five-year-old child, Braxton Fleming, the eighth child of Rebecca and Isaiah Fleming, who owned a large tract along the Rivanna River. The boy broke his leg wrestling with his older brother in a tree." He laughed. "Don't kids do the damnedest things? In a tree! Well, anyway, Dr. Walker noted that it was a compound fracture and he doubted that it would heal in such a manner as to afford the patient full facility with the limb, as he put it. He duly noted the break was in the left femur. He also noted that the boy was the most beautiful child he had ever seen. That aroused my curiosity, and I called down to the Albemarle County Historical Society and asked for help. Those folks down there are just terrific—volunteer labor. I asked them if they'd comb their sources for any information about Braxton Fleming. Seems he trod the course a wellborn young fellow typically trod in those days. He was tutored in Richmond, but then instead of going to the College of William and Mary he enrolled in the College of New Jersey, as did Aaron Burr and James Madison. We know it as Princeton. The Flemings were intelligent. All the surviving sons completed their studies and entered the professions, but Braxton was the only one to go north of the Mason-Dixon line to study. He spent some time in Philadelphia after graduating and apparently evidenced some gift for painting. Well, it was as hard then as now to make a living in the arts, so finally Braxton slunk home. He tried his hand at farming and did enough to survive, but his heart wasn't in it. He married well but not happily and he turned to drink. He was reputed to have been the handsomest man in central Virginia."

"What a story!" Mrs. Hogendobber exclaimed.

Larry held up his hands as if to squelch applause. "But we

don't know why he was killed. We only know how, and we have a strong suspect."

"Dr. J., does anyone know what happened to him? You know, some kind of mention about him not coming home or something?"

"Yes." He tilted his head and stared at the ceiling. "His wife declared that he took a gallon of whiskey and set out for Kentucky to make his fortune. May 1803. No more was ever heard from Braxton Fleming."

Harry whistled. "He's our man."

Larry stroked Mrs. Murphy under her chin. She rewarded him with important purrs. "You know, Fair and I were talking the other day, and he was telling me about retroviruses in cats and horses. He also mentioned a feline respiratory infection that can pass from mother to child and may erupt ten years later. Feline leukemia is rampant too. Well, Mrs. Murphy, you look healthy enough and I'm glad of it. I hadn't realized life was so precarious for cats."

"*Thank you,*" the cat responded.

"Larry, you must let us know if you find out anything else. What a detective you are." Praise from Mrs. Hogendobber was high praise indeed.

"Oh, heck, the folks down at the historical society did most of the work."

He picked up his mail, blew them a kiss, and left, eager to return to Jim Craig's diaries.

57

Diseases, like rivers, course through human history. What might have happened if Pericles had survived the plague in fifth-century B.C. Athens, or if the Europeans nearly two thousand years later had discovered that the bubonic plague was transmitted to humans by rat fleas?

Mrs. Murphy's ancestors saved medieval Europe, only to be condemned in a later century as accessories to witchcraft, then hunted and killed.

And what might have been Russia's fate had Alexei, the heir to the throne, not been born with hemophilia, a blood disease passed on by Queen Victoria's offspring?

One never realizes the blessings of health until they are snatched away.

Medical science, since opening up a cadaver to prove there

was such a thing as a circulatory system, became better at identifying diseases. The various forms of cancer no longer were lumped together as a wasting disease but categorized and named as cancer of the colon, leukemia, skin cancer, and so forth.

The great breakthrough came in 1796, when Sir William Jenner created the vaccine for smallpox.

After that, human hygiene improved, preventative medicine improved, and many could look forward to reaching their fourscore and ten years. Yet some diseases resisted human efforts, cancer being the outstanding example.

As Larry read his deceased partner's diagnoses and prognoses late into each night, he felt like a young man again.

He was pleased to read that Dr. Craig gruffly wrote down, "Young pup's damned good," and he was excited as he delved again into the 1940s cases he'd seen himself.

Vividly he recalled the autopsy they performed on Z. Calvin Coles, Samson's grandfather, in which the old man's liver was grotesquely enlarged and fragile as tissue paper.

When he prepared to write alcoholism on the death certificate as the cause of death, Jim stayed his hand.

"Larry, put down heart failure."

"But that's not what killed him."

"In the end we all die because our hearts stop beating. Write down alcoholism and you break his wife's heart and his children's too.

Through his mentor, Larry had learned how to diplomatically handle unsavory problems such as venereal disease. A physician had to report this to the state health department. This both Dr. Craig and Dr. Johnson did. The individual was to warn former sexual partners of his or her infectious state. Many people couldn't do it, so Dr. Craig performed the service. Larry specialized in scaring the hell out of the victims in the hope that they would repair their ways.

From Dr. Craig Larry learned how to tell a patient he was dying, a chore that tore him to pieces. But Dr. Craig always said,

"Larry, people die as they live. You must speak to each one in his or her own language." Over the years he marveled at the courage and dignity of seemingly ordinary people as they faced death.

. Dr. Craig never aspired to being other than what he was, a small-town practitioner. He was much like a parish priest who loves his flock and harbors no ambition to become a bishop or cardinal.

As Larry read on, he was surprised to learn of the termination of a pregnancy for a young Sweet Briar College junior, Marilyn Urquhart. Dr. Craig wrote: "Given the nervous excitability of the patient, I fear having a child out of wedlock would unhinge this young woman."

There were secrets Dr. Craig kept even from his young partner. It was part of the old man's character to protect a lady, no matter what.

The clock read two thirty-five A.M. Larry's head had begun to nod. He forced his eyes open to read just a bit more, and then they popped wide open.

March 3, 1948. Wesley Randolph came in today with his father. Colonel Randolph seems to be suffering from the habitual ailment of his clan. He hates needles. The son does also, but the old man shamed Wesley into getting blood pulled.

My suspicion, quite strong, is that the colonel has developed leukemia. I sent the blood to U.V.A. for analysis, requesting that they use the new electron microscope.

March 5, 1948. Dr. Harvey Fenton asked me to meet him at the U.V.A. Hospital. When I arrived he asked me of my relation to Colonel Randolph and his son. I replied that relations were cordial.

Dr. Fenton didn't say anything to my reply. He merely

pointed to the electron microscope. A blood sample, underneath, showed an avalanche of white cells.

"Leukemia," I said. "Colonel Randolph or Wesley?"

"No," Fenton replied. He slid another sample under
the microscope. "Look here."

I did, and a peculiar shape of cell was prominent. "I'm
not familiar with this cell deformation," I said.

"We're learning to identify this. It's a hereditary blood
disease called sickle cell anemia. The red blood cells lack
normal hemoglobin. Instead, they contain hemoglobin S and
the cells become deformed—they look like a sickle. Because
of the awkward shape, the hemoglobin S blood cells can't
flow like normal cells and they clog up capillaries and blood
vessels. Those traffic jams are extremely painful to the suf-
ferer.

"But there's a less serious condition in which red blood
cells have half normal hemoglobin and half hemoglobin S.
Someone with this condition has the sickle cell trait, but he
won't develop the disease.

"However, if he marries someone else with the trait,
their children stand a twenty-five percent chance of inherit-
ing the disease. The risk is very high.

"We don't know why, but sickle cells occur among
blacks. Occasionally, but rarely, someone of Greek, Arab, or
Indian descent will display the trait. The whole thing is baffling.

"You know all those jokes about Negroes being either
lazy or having hookworm?—well, in many cases we're realizing they had sickle cell anemia."

I didn't know what to say, as I have observed since
childhood that the white race delights in casting harsh judgments on the black race. So, I looked at the blood sample
again.

"Did the Negro from whom you obtained this blood
die?"

"The man this blood was drawn from is alive but failing from cancer. He has the trait but not the disease." Dr. Fenton paused. "This is Colonel Randolph's blood sample."

Stunned, I blurted out, "What about Wesley?"

"He's safe, but he carries the trait."

As I drove back home I knew I'd have to tell Colonel Randolph and Wesley the truth. The happy portion of the news was that the colonel was in no immediate danger. The unhappy portion of the news is obvious. I wonder what Larry will make of this? I want to take him down to Dr. Fenton to see for himself.

Larry pushed the book away.

Jim Craig was murdered March 6, 1948. He never got to tell Larry anything.

Legs wobbly and eyes bleary from so much reading, Larry Johnson stood up from his desk. He put on his hat and his Sherlock Holmes coat, as he called it. He hadn't paced the streets of Crozet like this since he tried to walk off a broken heart when Mim Urquhart spurned him for Big Jim Sanburne back in 1950.

As the sun rose, Larry felt his first obligation was to Warren Randolph. He called. Ansley answered, then put Warren on the phone. All the Randolphs were early risers. Larry offered to drive over to see Warren, but Warren said he'd come over to Larry's later that morning. It was no inconvenience.

What was inconvenient was that Larry Johnson was shot at 7:44 Saturday morning.

58

Harry, Miranda, Mim, Fair, Susan, Ned, Mrs. Murphy, and Tucker watched with mounting grief as their dear friend's body was rolled away under a sheet on a gurney. Deputy Cooper said Larry's maid, Charmalene, had found him at nine, when she came to work. He was lying in the front hall. He must have opened the door to let in the killer and taken a few steps toward the kitchen, when he was shot in the back. Probably the man never knew what hit him, but this was cold comfort to his friends. The maid said the coffee he'd made was fresh. He'd made more than usual, so maybe he expected company. He was probably awaiting the arrival of his killer, who then ransacked his office. Sheriff Shaw climbed in the back of the ambulance and they sped away.

Tucker, nose to the ground, picked up the scent easily enough, but the killer wore crepe-soled shoes which left such a distinct rubber smell that the dog couldn't catch a clear human signature. Unfortunately, the ambulance workers trudged over the footprints, for the killer, no fool, tiptoed on the sidewalk and put a foot down hard only in the driveway, probably when disembarking from the car.

"*What have you got, Tucker?*" Mrs. Murphy, worried, asked.

"*Not enough. Not enough.*"

"*A trace of cologne?*"

"*No, just this damned crepe-sole smell. And a wet smell—sand.*"

The tiger bent her own nose to the task. "*Is anyone else doing construction work? There's always sand involved in construction.*"

"*Sand on a lot of driveways too.*"

"*Tucker, we've got to stick close to Mom. She's done enough research to get her in trouble. Whoever the killer is, he's losing it. Humans don't kill one another in broad daylight unless it's passion or war. This was cold-blooded.*"

"*And hasty,*" Tucker added, still straining to place the rubber smell. She decided then and there to hate crepe-soled shoes.

Fair Haristeen read Larry's notes on a piece of blue-lined white paper as Cynthia Cooper held the paper with tweezers.

"Can you make some sense of this, Fair? You're a medical man."

"Yes, it's a kind of medical shorthand for sickle cell anemia."

"Don't only African Americans get that?"

"Mostly blacks are affected, but I don't think there's a hundred percent correspondence. It passes from generation to generation."

Cooper asked, "How many generations back?"

Fair shrugged, "That I can't tell you, Coop. I'm just a vet, remember."

"Thanks, Fair."

"Is there a nut case on the loose in Crozet?"

"That depends on how you define nut case, but it's safe to say that if the killer feels anyone is closing in on the truth, he's going to strike."

59

Diana Robb swept aside the ambulance curtains as Rick Shaw pulled the sheet off Larry Johnson.

The bullet had narrowly missed the right side of the good doctor's heart. It passed clearly through his body. The force of the blow, the shock, temporarily knocked him unconscious. When Charmalene discovered him, he was awakening.

Rick Shaw, the instant he knew Larry would live, bent over the older man who, just like a doctor, was giving orders as to how to handle him. "I need your help."

"Yes." Larry assented through a tight jaw.

"Who shot you?"

"That's just it. I left the front door open. I was expecting Warren Randolph sometime late morning. I walked out of the living room into the front hall. Whoever shot me—maybe Warren

—must have tiptoed in, but I never saw him." These five sentences took Larry a long time to utter, and his brow was drenched in sweat.

"Help me, Larry." The doctor nodded yes as Rick fervently whispered, "I need you to pretend you're dead for twenty-four hours."

"I nearly was."

Rick swore Charmalene to secrecy as well as the ambulance staff. When he crawled into the back of the vehicle he had but one thought, how to bait and trap Warren Randolph.

60

Back in the office Rick Shaw banged his fists against the wall. The staff outside his office jumped. No one moved. Rarely did the man they obeyed and had learned to admire show this much emotion.

Deputy Cooper, in the office with him, said nothing, but she did open a fresh pack of cigarettes and made a drinking sign when a fresh-faced patrolman snuck by. That meant a cold Coca-Cola.

"I let my guard down! I know better. How many years have I been an officer of the law? How many?"

"Twenty-two, Sheriff."

"Well, you'd think I would have goddamned learned something in twenty-two years. I relaxed. I allowed myself to think because of circumstantial evidence, because the bullet matched the thirty-eight that killed Kimball, that we had an open-and-shut

case. Sure, Samson protested his innocence. My God, ninety percent of the worst criminals in America whine and lie and say
they're innocent. I didn't listen to my gut."

"Don't be so hard on yourself. The case against Samson
looked airtight. I was sure a confession would be a matter of time,
once he figured out he couldn't outsmart us. It takes time for
reality to set in."

"Oh, Coop." Rick slumped heavily into his chair. "I blame
myself for Larry Johnson's shooting."

The patrolman held up the cold Coke at the glass window.
Cynthia rose, opened the door, took the Coke, and thanked the
young officer. She winked at him too, then gave the can to Rick,
whose outburst had parched him.

"You couldn't have known."

The sheriff's voice dropped. "When Larry called me about
Braxton Fleming, I should have known the other shoe hadn't
dropped. Kimball Haynes wasn't killed over Samson's stealing escrow money. I know that now."

"Hey, the state Samson Coles was in when we arrested him, I
would have believed he could have killed anybody."

"Oh, yeah, he was hot." Rick gulped down some more soda,
the carbonation fizzing down his throat. "He had a lot to lose, to
say nothing of his affair with Ansley blowing out the window."

"Lucinda Coles took care of that at Kimball's memorial service."

"Can't blame her. Imagine how she felt, being put in a social
situation with the woman who's playing around with her husband."

They sat and stared at each other.

"We've got twenty-four hours. If an obit notice doesn't appear in the papers after that, it's going to look awfully peculiar."

"And we've got to hold off the reporters without actually
lying." He rubbed his chin. Larry Johnson's wife had died some
years before, and his only son was killed in Vietnam. "Coop, who
would place the obituary notice?"

"Probably Mrs. Hogendobber, with Harry's help."

"You go over there and enlist their cooperation. See if they can stall a little."

"Oh, brother. They'll want to know why."

"Don't—don't even think about it." He twiddled the can. "I'm going to the hospital. I'm pretty sure we can trust Dr. Ylvisaker and the nurses. I'll set up a twenty-four-hour vigil, just in case." He stood up. "I've got to go get the rest of the story."

"I thought he never saw his attacker."

"He didn't. Before he passed out he told me this had to do with his partner, Dr. Jim Craig."

Cooper inhaled sharply. "Dr. Craig was found shot in the cemetery one icy March morning. I remember, when I first came on the force, reading through the files on the unsolved crimes. I wonder how it all fits?"

"We aren't home yet, but we're rounding second toward third."

61

Sunday morning at six-thirty, the air carried little tiny teeth of rain, not a whopping big rain, but a steady one that might lead to harder rain later.

Harry usually greeted the day with a bounce in her step, but this morning she dragged out to the barn. Larry's murder weighed heavily upon her heart.

She mixed up a warm bran mash which was Sunday's treat for the horses, plus a bit of insurance against colic, she believed. She took a scoop of sweet feed per horse, a half-scoop of bran, and mushed it up with hot water and a big handful of molasses. She stirred her porridge together and for an extra treat threw in two quartered apples. That along with as much timothy hay as Gin and Tommy would eat made them happy, and her too. Except for today.

She finished with the horses, climbed the loft ladder, and put out a bag of marshmallows for Simon, the possum. Then she clambered down and decided she might as well oil some tack since she'd fallen behind in her barn chores over these last few crazy weeks. She threw a bridle up on the tack hook, ran a small bucket full of hot water, grabbed a small natural sponge and her Murphy's Oil Soap, and started cleaning.

Tucker and Mrs. Murphy, feeling her sorrow, quietly sat beside her. Tucker finally laid down, her head between her paws.

She jerked her head up. *"That's the smell."*

"What?" Mrs. Murphy's eyes widened to eight balls.

"Yes! It's not a crepe sole, it's this stuff. I swear it."

"Eagle's Rest." The cat's long white whiskers swept forward then back as her ears flattened. *"But why?"*

"Warren must be in on the escrow theft," Tucker said.

"Or connected to the murder at Monticello." Mrs. Murphy blinked her eyes. *"But how?"*

"What are we going to do?"

"I don't know." The tiger's voice trembled with fear, not for herself, but for Harry.

62

" 'No laborious person was ever yet hysterical,' " Harry read aloud. Thomas Jefferson wrote this to his teenage daughter, Patsy, while she studied at the Abbaye Royale de Panthemont in the France of Louis XVI and Marie Antoinette.

"Sensible but not really what a young girl is inclined to wish to hear." Mrs. Hogendobber, fussy today and low over the loss of her old friend, reset the stakes for her sweet peas one more time as the Sunday sunshine bathed over her. The early morning rains had given way to clear skies.

Mrs. Murphy, Pewter, who had escaped Market one more time, and Tucker watched as the squarely built woman walked first to one side of the garden outline, then to the other. She performed this march every spring, and she turned her corners with all the precision of a Virginia Military Institute cadet on drill.

"The garden will be like last year's and the year's before that. The sweet peas go along the alleyway side of her yard." Pewter licked her paws and washed her pretty face.

"Don't deny her the pleasure of worrying about it," Mrs. Murphy advised the gray cat.

"We know who the killer is." Tucker shadowed Mrs. Hogendobber's every move, but from the other side of the garden.

"Why didn't you tell me the instant you got here? You're hateful." Pewter pouted.

Mrs. Murphy relished Pewter's distress for a moment. After all, Pewter lorded it over everybody if she knew something first. *"I thought you weren't interested in human affairs unless food was involved."*

"That's not true," the cat yowled.

"Harsh words are being spoken, and on the Sabbath." Mrs. Hogendobber chastized the two cats. "Harry, what is the matter with your dog? If I walk, she walks. If I stop, she stops. If I stand, she stands and watches me."

"Tucker, what are you doing?" Harry inquired of her corgi.

"Being vigilant," the dog responded.

"Against Mrs. Hogendobber?" Mrs. Murphy laughed.

"Practice makes perfect." The dog turned her back on the cats. Tucker believed that the good Lord made cats first, as an experiment. Then He created the dog, having learned from His mistake.

"Who?" Pewter cuffed Mrs. Murphy, who sat on her haunches and cuffed the gray cat right back. Within seconds a fierce boxing match exploded, causing both humans to focus their attention on the contenders.

"My money's on Pewter." Mrs. Hogendobber reached into her voluminous skirt pocket and pulled out a wrinkled dollar bill.

"Mrs. Murphy." Harry fished an equally wrinkled bill out of her Levi's.

"Pewter's bigger. She'll have more pow to her punch."

"Murphy's faster."

The two cats circled, boxed, then Pewter leapt on the tiger cat, threw her to the ground, and they wrestled. Mrs. Murphy wriggled free of the lard case on top of her and tore across the middle of the garden plot then up a black gum tree. Pewter, close behind, raced to the bottom of the trunk and decided to wait her out as opposed to climbing in pursuit.

"*She'll back down the tree and then shove off over your head,*" Tucker told Pewter.

"*Whose side are you on?*" Mrs. Murphy spat out.

"*Entertainment's.*"

Mrs. Murphy backed down just as Tucker had predicted, but then she dropped right on top of the chubby gray and rolled her over. A fulsome hissing and huffing emanated from the competitors. This time it was Pewter who broke and ran straight to Mrs. Hogendobber. Mrs. Murphy chased up to the lady's legs and then reached around Mrs. H.'s heavy English brogues to swat Pewter. Pewter replied in kind.

"They're going to scratch me and I've got on a new pair of nylons."

"*Shut up, Mrs. Hogendobber, we aren't going to touch your nylons,*" Pewter crabbed at her, though relishing the attention too.

" '*Fraidy-cat,*" Mrs. Murphy taunted.

"*Of what, a skinny alley cat? Dream on.*" Another left jab.

"*Fatty, fatty, two by four, can't get through the bathroom door!*" Mrs. Murphy cat-called.

"*That is so childish and gross.*" Pewter twirled on her rear end and stalked off.

"*Hey, you started it, bungbutt,*" Mrs. Murphy yelled at her.

"*Only because you had to get high and mighty about who the killer is. Why should I care? It's human versus human. I'm not a candidate for the graveyard.*"

"*You don't know,*" Mrs. Murphy sang out. "*It's Warren Randolph.*"

"*No!*" The gray cat spun around and ran right up to Mrs. Murphy.

"*We're pretty sure.*" She nodded toward Tucker.

As Tucker padded over to fully inform Pewter, Mrs. Hogendobber and Harry laughed at the animals.

"Spring, wondrous spring—not a season associated with

sorrows, but we've had plenty of them." Miranda blinked hard, then consulted her garden blueprint. "Now, Harry, what were you telling me about Patsy Jefferson Randolph before these little scamps put on such an adorable show?"

"Oh, just that her father might not have known how to talk to young women. But she was said to be a lot like him, so I guess it wasn't so bad. The younger sister never was as close, although she loved him, of course."

"Must have been quite an education for Patsy, being in an expensive French school. When was that now? Refresh my memory."

"You've been studying Patsy's and Polly's children. I've been studying Thomas Jefferson's brothers and sister and his own children. Otherwise you'd have these dates cold. Let's see. I think she enrolled at Panthemont in 1784. Apparently there were three princesses there also and they wore royal blue sashes. Called the American among them 'Jeffy.' "

"How fortunate Patsy was."

"She didn't feel that way when she had to read Livy. Of course, I didn't either. Livy and Tacitus just put me into vapor lock." Harry made a twisting motion at her temple, as though locking something.

"I stopped at Virgil. I didn't go to college or I would have continued. What else about Patsy?"

"Mrs. Hogendobber, you know I'd help you. I feel silly sitting here while you figure out your garden."

"I'm the only one who can figure it out. I'd like to stop those Japanese beetles before they start."

"Don't plant roses, then."

"Don't be absurd, Harry, one simply cannot have a garden without roses. The beetles be damned. If you'll pardon my French." She smiled a sly smile.

Harry nodded. "Okay, back to Panthemont. Patsy conceived a desire to be a nun. It was a Catholic school. That put her father's knickers in a twist and he paid the bill for both Patsy and her sister in full on April 20, 1789, and yanked those kids out of there. Pretty funny. Oh, yeah, something I forgot. Sally Hemings, who was about Patsy's age, traveled to France with her as her batman, you might say. What do you call a batman for a lady?"

"A lady's maid."

"Oh, that's easy enough. Anyway, I've been thinking that the experience of freedom, the culture of France, and being close to Patsy like that in a foreign country must have drawn the two together. Kind of like how Jefferson loved Jupiter, his man, who was also his age. They'd been together since they were boys."

"The self on the other side of the mirror," Miranda said with a dreamy look in her eye.

"Huh?"

"Their slaves who were their ladies' maids and batmen. They must have been alter egos. I never realized how complex, how deep and tangled the emotions on both sides of that mirror must have been. And now the races have drifted apart."

"Ripped apart is more like it."

"Whatever it is, it isn't right. We're all Americans."

"Tell that to the Ku Klux Klan."

"I'd be more inclined to tell them to buy a better brand of bedsheet." Miranda was in fine fettle today. "You know, if you listen to the arguments of these extremist groups or the militant right wing, there's a kernel of truth in what they say. They have correctly pinpointed many of our society's ills, and I must give them credit for that. At least they're thinking about the society in which they live, Harry, they aren't indulging in mindless pleasures, but their solutions—fanatical and absurd."

"But simple. That's why their propaganda is so effective and then I think, too, that it's always easier to be against something than to be for something new. I mean, we never have lived in a community of true racial equality. That's new and it's hard to sell something new."

"I never thought of that." Mrs. H. cupped her chin in her

hand and decided at that instant to shift the sweet peas to the other side of the garden.

"That's what makes Jefferson and Washington and Franklin and Adams and all those people so remarkable. They were willing to try something brand new. They were willing to risk their lives for it. What courage. We've lost it, I think. Americans have lost their vision and their appetite for struggle."

"I don't know. I remember World War Two clearly. We didn't lack courage then."

"Miranda, that was fifty years ago. Look at us now."

"Maybe we're storing up energy for the next push toward the future."

"I'm glad one of us is an optimist." Harry, by virtue of her age, had never lived through an American epoch in which people pulled together for the common good. "There's another thing, by the way. Sally and Betsey Hemings were like sisters to Medley Orion, although she was younger than they were. Apparently they were three beautiful women. It must have been fun to sit outside in the twilight, crickets chirping, and listen to Sally's tales of France before the Revolution."

Pewter meanwhile disagreed with Mrs. Murphy and Tucker over Warren Randolph as murderer. She countered that a man with that much money doesn't have to kill anyone. He can hire someone to do it for him.

Mrs. Murphy rejoined that Warren must have slipped a stitch somewhere along the line.

Pewter's only response was "Gross."

"Regardless of what you think, I don't want Mother to get in trouble."

"She's not going to do anything. She doesn't know that Warren's the killer," Pewter said.

The sweet purr of the Bentley Turbo R caught their attention. Mim got out of the car. "Miranda, have you spoken to Sheriff Shaw about Larry's obituary notice and funeral?"

Miranda, stake in hand poised midair, looked as though she

were ready to dispatch a vampire. "Yes, and I find it mighty peculiar."

Mim's crocodile loafers fascinated Mrs. Murphy as she crossed the lawn to join Harry and Mrs. Hogendobber.

"*Those are beautiful,*" the tiger cat admired.

"*Piddle. It's a big skink, that's all.*" Pewter compared the exotic crocodile skin to that of a sleek lizard indigenous to Virginia.

As the three women consulted, worried, and wondered about Rick Shaw's request, Harry noticed that Mrs. Murphy was stalking Mim's shoes. She bent down to scoop up her cat, but Mrs. Murphy scooted just out of reach.

"*Slowpoke,*" the cat taunted.

Harry did not answer but gave the cat a stern look.

"*Don't get her in a bad mood, Murph,*" Tucker pleaded.

In reply, Mrs. Murphy flattened her ears and turned her back on Tucker as Mim strode over to her Bentley to retrieve her portable phone. Miranda walked into her house. After ten minutes of phone calls, which left Harry reduced to putting in the garden stakes, Miranda reappeared.

"No, no, and no."

Mim's head jerked up. "Impossible."

Miranda's rich alto boomed. "Hill and Woods does not have the body. Thacker Funeral Home, ditto, and I even called places in western Orange County. Not a trace of Larry Johnson, and I don't mind telling you that I think this is awful. How can the rescue squad lose a body?"

Harry reached for Mim's mobile phone. "May I?"

"Be my guest." Mim handed over the small, heavy phone.

"Diana"—Harry reached Diana Robb—"do you know what funeral parlor has Larry Johnson's body?"

"No—we just dropped him off at the hospital." Diana's evasive tone alerted Harry, who'd known the nurse since their schooldays.

"Do you know the name of the hospital admissions clerk?"

"Harry, Rick Shaw will take care of everything. Don't worry."

Acidly Harry replied, "Since when do sheriffs arrange funerals? Diana, I need your help. We've got a lot of work to do here."

"Look, you talk to Rick." Diana hung up.

"She hung up on me!" Harry's face turned beet red. "Something is as queer as a three-dollar bill. I'm going down to the hospital."

"Don't do that—just yet." Mim smiled. She reached out for the phone, her frosted mauve fingernails complementing her plum-colored sweater. She dialed. "Is Sheriff Shaw there? All right, then. What about Deputy Cooper? I see." Mim paused. "Try and get her out of her meeting, if only for an instant."

A long pause ensued, during which Mim tapped her foot in the grass and Mrs. Murphy resumed stalking those crocodile loafers. "Ah, Deputy Cooper. I need your assistance. Neither Mrs. Hogendobber, Mrs. Haristeen, nor I can locate Larry Johnson's body at any of the funeral parlors in either Albemarle or Orange County. There are many arrangements to be made. I'm sure you appreciate that and—"

"Mrs. Sanburne, the body is still at the hospital. Sheriff Shaw wanted more tests run, and until he's satisfied that Pathology has everything they need, the body won't be released. You'll have to wait until tomorrow, I'm afraid."

"I see. Thank you." Mim pushed down the aerial and clicked the power to off. She related Cynthia's explanation.

"I don't buy it." Harry crossed her arms over her chest.

"I suppose once the blood is drained out of the body, the samples won't be as, uh, fresh." Mim grimaced.

Now Miranda grabbed the phone. She winked. "Hello, this is Mrs. Johnson and I'd like an update on my husband, Dr. Larry Johnson."

"Larry Johnson, Room 504?"

"That's right."

"He's resting comfortably."

Mrs. Hogendobber repeated the answer. "He's resting comfortably—he ought to be, he's dead."

A sputter and confusion on the other end of the phone convinced Miranda that something was really amiss. The line was disconnected. Miranda's eyebrows shot into her coiffure. "Come on, girls."

As Mrs. Hogendobber climbed into the front seat of the Bentley, Harry unlocked the back door of the post office, shushing the two cats and crestfallen dog inside.

"No fair!" was the animal chorus.

Harry hopped in the back seat as Mim floored it.

"By God, we'll get to the bottom of this!"

63

The front desk clerk at the Martha Jefferson Hospital tried to way-lay Mim, but Harry and Miranda outflanked her. Then Mim, taking advantage of the young woman's distress, slipped away too.

The three women dashed to the elevator. They reached the fifth floor and were met, as the doors opened, by a red-haired officer from the sheriff's department.

"I'm sorry, ladies, you aren't permitted up here."

"Oh, you've taken over the whole floor?" Mim imperiously criticized the young officer, who cringed because he knew more was coming. "I pay taxes, which means I pay your salary and . . ."

Harry used the opportunity to blast down the corridor. She reached Room 504 and opened the door. She screamed so loud, she scared herself.

64

"What a dirty, rotten trick." Mim lit into the sheriff, who was standing at Larry's bedside. This was after Harry, Miranda, and Mim cried tears of joy upon seeing their beloved friend again. They even made Larry cry. He had no idea how much he was loved.

"Mrs. Sanburne, it had to be done and I'm running out of time as it is."

Mim sat on the uncomfortable chair as Harry and Miranda stood on the other side of Larry's bed. Miranda would not release the older gentleman's hand until a sharp glance from Mim made her do so. She then remembered that Larry and Mim were once an item.

"Still jealous," Miranda thought to herself.

Larry, propped up on pillows, reached for a sip of juice.

Mim instantly supplied it to him. "Now, Larry, if we fatigue you, we can leave and the sheriff can fill us in. However, if you can talk . . ."

He slurped and handed the drink back to Mim, as unlikely a nurse as ever was born. "Thank you, dear. I can talk if Sheriff Shaw allows me."

A defeated Rick rubbed his receding hairline. "It's fine with me, because I think if these girls"—he came down heavy on "girls"—"hear from your own lips what happened, then maybe they'll behave."

"We will," came the unconvincing chorus.

"Harry, I have Mrs. Murphy, Tucker, and that funny Paddy to thank for this."

"Mrs. Murphy again?" Rick shook his head.

"They led me to where Jim Craig, who was killed before you were born, had hidden his diaries. He was my partner, as you may know. Actually, he took me into his practice and I would have purchased part of it in time—with a considerable discount, as Jim was a generous, generous man—but he died and, in effect, I inherited the practice, which afforded me the opportunity to become somewhat comfortable." He looked at Mim.

Mim couldn't meet his gaze, so she fiddled with the juice glass and the fat, bendable straw.

He continued. "Jim's diaries commenced in 1912 and went through to the day he died, March 5, 1948. I believe that either Colonel Randolph killed him, or Wesley, who was right out of the Army Air Corps at the time."

"But why?" Miranda exclaimed.

Larry leaned his white head back on the pillows and took a deep breath. "Ah, for reasons both sad and interesting. As detection advanced with the electron microscope, it was Jim who discovered that Wesley and his father carried the sickle cell trait. Now, that didn't give them leukemia—you can develop that disease quite apart from carrying the sickle cells—but what it meant was that no descendant of the colonel or Wesley could, uh, marry

someone of color—not without fear of passing on the trait. You
see, if the spouse also carried the trait, the children could very
well contract the full-blown disease, which has painful episodes,
and there's no cure. The accumulated damage of those episodes
can kill you."

"Oh, God." Mim's jaw dropped. "Wesley was, well, you
know . . ."

"A racist." Harry said it for her.

"That's a harsh way of putting it." Mim smoothed out the
bed sheet. "He was raised a certain way and couldn't cope with
the changes. But if he knew about the sickle cell anemia, you'd
think he would soften."

"Or become worse. Who is more anti-Semitic than another
Jew? Who is more antigay than another homosexual? More an-
tifeminist than another woman? The oppressed contain reservoirs
of viciousness reserved entirely for their own kind."

"Harry, you surprise me," Mim primly stated.

"She's right though." The sheriff spoke up. "Tell people
they're"—he paused because he was going to say "shit"—
"worthless, and strange behaviors occur. Let's face it. Nobody
wants to ape the poor. They want to ape the rich, and how many
rich black folks do you know?"

"Not in Albemarle County." Miranda began to walk around
the small room. "But the Randolphs don't appear to be black in
any fashion."

"No, but it's in the blood. With rare exceptions, sickle cell
anemia affects only people with African blood. It must be inherited. It can't be caught as a contagion, so to speak. This disease
seems to be the only remaining vestige of Wesley Randolph's
black heritage," Larry informed them.

"And Kimball Haynes found this out somehow." Harry's
mind was spinning.

"But how?" Larry wondered.

"Ansley said Kimball never read the Randolph papers,"
Harry chipped in.

"Absurd! It's absurd to kill over something like this!" Miranda exploded.

"Mrs. Hogendobber, I've seen a fourteen-year-old boy knifed for the five-dollar-bill in his pocket. I've seen rednecks blow each other away because one got drunk and accused the other of sleeping with his wife or called him a faggot. Absurd?" Rick shrugged.

"Did you know?" Harry, ever direct, asked Larry.

"No. Wesley came in for his physical occasionally through the years but always refused to have his blood taken. Being rich, he would fly out to one of those expensive drying-out or treatment clinics, they would take a blood test, and he'd have them read me the white cell count. I accepted that he had leukemia. He wouldn't let me treat him for it and I assumed it was because I am, after all, a country doctor. Oh, he'd come in for a flu shot, stuff like that, and we'd discuss his condition. I'd push and he'd retreat and then he'd check into the Mayo Clinic. He was out of reach, but Warren wasn't. He hated needles and I could do a complete physical on him only about once every fifteen years."

"Who do you think killed Jim Craig?" Mim spoke.

"Wesley, most likely. The colonel would have hated it, but I don't think he would have killed over the news. Jim wouldn't have made it public, after all. I could be wrong, but I just don't think Colonel Randolph would have murdered Jim. Wesley was a hothead when he was young."

"Do you think the Randolphs have always known?" Harry pointed to Mrs. Hogendobber, busily pacing back and forth, indicating that she sit down. She was making Harry dizzy.

"No, because it wouldn't have been picked up in blood tests until the last fifty years or so," said Larry. "All I'm saying is that in medical terms earlier generations would not have known about the sickle cell trait. What else they knew is anybody's guess."

"Never thought of that," Sheriff Shaw said.

"I don't care who knew what. You don't kill over something like that." Miranda couldn't accept the horror of it.

"Warren lived under the shadow of his father. His only outlet has been Ansley. Let's face it, she's the only person who regarded Warren as a man. When he found out she was carrying on with another man, right after his father's death, I think it was too much. Warren's not very strong, you know," Harry said.

"I thought Samson Coles was the one carrying on. Not Ansley too?" Miranda put her foot in it.

"Look no further." Mim pursed her lips.

"No." Harry, like Miranda, found the scandal, well, odd.

"Why don't you arrest Warren?" Mim drilled the sheriff.

"First off, Dr. Johnson didn't see his would-be killer, although we both believe it was Warren. Second, if I can trap Warren into giving himself away, it will make the prosecution's task much easier. Warren is so rich that if I don't nail him down, he'll get off. He'll shell out one or two million for the best defense lawyers in America and he'll find a way out, I can guarantee it. I had hoped that keeping Larry's survival under wraps for twenty-four hours might give me just the edge I need, but I can't go much further than that. The reporters will bribe someone, and it's cruel to have everyone mourning Larry's death. I mean, look at your response."

"Most gratified, ladies." Tears again welled up in Larry's eyes.

"Why can't you just go up to Warren and say Larry's alive and watch his response?" Mim wanted to know.

"I could, but he'd be on guard."

"He won't be on guard with me. He likes me," Harry said.

"No." Rick's voice rose.

"Well, do you have a better idea?" Mim stuck it to the sheriff.

65

As the Superman-blue Ford toodled down the long, winding, tree-lined road, Mrs. Murphy and Tucker plotted. Harry had been talking out loud, going back and forth over the plan, so they knew what she'd found out at the hospital. She was wired, and Sheriff Shaw and Deputy Cooper were positioned on a back road near the entrance to Eagle's Rest. They would hear every word she and Warren said.

"We could bite Warren's leg and put him out of commission from the get-go."

"Tucker, all that will happen is you'll be accused of having rabies." The cat batted the dog's upright ears with her paw.

"I've had my rabies shots." Tucker sighed. *"Well, do you have any better ideas?"*

"*I could pretend I'm choking to death.*"

"*Try it.*"

Mrs. Murphy coughed and wheezed. Her eyes watered. She flopped on her side and coughed some more. Harry pulled the truck to the side of the driveway. She picked up the cat and put her fingers down her throat to remove the offending obstacle. Finding no obstacle, she placed Mrs. Murphy over her left shoulder, patting her with her right hand as though burping a baby. "There, there, pussywillow. You're all right."

"*I know I'm all right. It's you I'm worried about.*"

Harry put Mrs. Murphy back on the seat and continued up to the house. Ansley, sitting on the side veranda under the towering Corinthian columns, waved desultorily as Harry, unannounced, came in sight.

Harry hopped out of the truck along with her critters. "Hey, Ansley, I apologize for not calling first, but I have some wonderful news. Where's Warren?"

"Down at the stable. Mare's ready to foal," Ansley laconically informed her. "You're flushed. Must be something big."

"Well, yes. Uh, come on down with me. That way I don't have to tell the story twice."

As they sauntered to the imposing stables, Ansley breathed deeply. "Isn't this the best weather? The spring of springs."

"I always get spring fever," Harry confessed. "Can't keep my mind on anything, and everyone has a glow—especially handsome men."

"Heck, don't need spring for that." Ansley laughed as they walked into the stable.

Fair, Warren, and the Randolphs' stable manager, Vanderhoef, crouched in the foaling stall. The mare was doing just fine.

"Hi." Fair greeted them, then returned to his task.

"I have the best news of the year." Harry beamed.

"*I wish she wouldn't do this.*" Mrs. Murphy shook her head.

"*Me too*," Tucker, heartsick, agreed.

"Well, out with it." Warren stood up and walked out of the stall.

"Larry Johnson's alive!"

"Thank God!" Fair exploded, then caught himself and lowered his voice. "I can't believe it." Luckily his crescendo hadn't startled the mare.

"Me neither." Warren appeared dazed for a moment. "Why anyone would want to kill him in the first place mystifies me. What a great guy. This is good news."

"Is he conscious?" Ansley inquired.

"Yeah, he's sitting up in bed and Miranda's with him. That's why I tore over here without calling. I knew you'd be happy to hear it."

"Did he see who shot him?" Warren asked, edging farther away from the stall door.

"Yes, he did."

"*Watch out!*" Tucker barked as Ansley knocked over Harry while running for her car.

"What in the hell?" Warren bolted down the aisle after her. "Ansley, Ansley, what's going on?"

She hopped into Warren's 911, parked in the courtyard of the barn, cranked it over, and spun out of the driveway. Warren ran after her. In a malicious curve she spun around—and baby, that car could handle—to bear down on her husband.

"Warren, zigzag!" Harry shouted from the end of the barn aisle.

"Get him back in here," Fair commanded just as the foal arrived.

Warren did zig and zag. The car was so nimble, Ansley almost caught him, but he darted behind a tree and she whirled around again and gunned down the driveway.

"Warren, Warren, get in here!" Harry called out. "In case she comes back."

Warren, sickly white, ran back into the stable. He sagged against the stall door. "My God, she did it."

Fair came out of the stall and put his arm around Warren's shoulder. "I'm gonna call the sheriff, Warren, for your own safety if nothing else."

"No, no, please. I can handle her. I'll take care of it and see she's put in a good home. Please, please," Warren pleaded.

"*Poor sucker.*" Mrs. Murphy brushed against Harry's legs.

"It's too late. Rick Shaw and Coop are at the end of the driveway," Harry told him.

Just then they heard the roar of the Porsche's engine, the peal of the siren and squealing tires. Ansley, a good driver, had easily eluded the sheriff and his deputy, who hadn't set up a roadblock but instead were prepared to roar into Eagle's Rest to assist Harry. They thought Harry could pull it off—and she did. The sirens faded away.

"She'll give them a good run for their money." Warren grinned even as the tears rolled down his cheeks.

"Yep." Harry felt like crying too.

Warren rubbed his eyes, then turned to admire the new baby.

"Boss, he's something special." Warren's stable manager hoped this foal would be something good for a man he had learned to like.

"Yes." Warren put his forehead on his hands, resting on the lower dutch door of the foaling stall, and sobbed. "How did you know?"

Harry, choking up, said, "We didn't—actually."

"*We had our wires crossed,*" Mrs. Murphy meowed.

"Suspicion was that it was you." Fair coughed. He was hugely embarrassed to admit this.

"Why?" Warren was dumbfounded. He turned and walked to the aisle doors. He stood looking out over the front fields.

"Uh, well," Harry stammered, then got it out. "Your daddy and well, uh, all the Randolphs put such a store by blood, pedigree, well, you know, that I thought because—I can't speak for anyone but me—I thought you'd be undone, just go ballistic about the African American blood. I mean about people knowing."

"Did you always know?" Fair joined them in front of the barn and handed Warren his handkerchief.

"No. Not until last year. Before Poppa's cancer went into remission he got scared he was going to die, so he told me. He insisted Ansley should never know—he'd never told Mother. I'm not making that mistake with my boys. All this secretiveness eats people alive."

The sirens were heading back toward Eagle's Rest.

"*Damn. We'd better get someplace safe—just in case,*" Tucker wisely noted.

"*Come on, Mom. Let's move it.*" Mrs. Murphy, no time to be subtle, sank her claws into Harry's leg, then ran away.

"Damn you, Murphy!" Harry cursed.

"*Run!*" Tucker barked.

Too late, the whine of the Porsche drowned out the animals' worries.

"Jesus H. Christ!" Harry beheld the Porsche heading straight for them.

Warren started to wave his wife off, but Fair, much stronger, picked Warren up and threw him back so she couldn't see him. Ansley swerved, nearly clipping the end of the barn, and headed down a farm road. Seconds behind her, Rick and Cooper, in their squad cars, threw gravel everywhere. In the distance more sirens could be heard.

"Can she get out that way?" Harry asked as she peered around the door.

"If she can corner the tight turn and take the tractor road around the lake, she can." Warren was shaking.

Harry stared at the dust, the noise. "Warren, Warren." She called his name louder. "How did she find out?"

"She read the diaries after Kimball did. She opened up the

safe and gave him the papers to defy me, and then sat down and read them herself.''

"You didn't hide them?''

"I kept them in the safe, but Ansley didn't have much interest in the family tree. I knew she'd never read them, but I never figured on—''

He didn't finish his sentence as the support cars drowned out his words.

Harry started to run down the farm road.

"Don't, Mom, she might come back again," the cat sensibly warned.

The sirens stopped. The cat and dog, much faster than their human counterparts, flew down the lane and rounded the curve.

"Oh—'' Tucker's voice trailed off.

Mrs. Murphy shuddered as she watched Ansley drowning in the Porsche which had skidded into the lake. Rick Shaw and Cooper had yanked off their bulletproof vests, their shoes, and dived in, but it was too late. By the time the others reached the lake, only the rear end of the expensive 911 was in view.

66

The grand library of Eagle's Rest smelled like old fires and fresh tobacco. Harry, Mrs. Hogendobber, Mim, Fair, Deputy Cooper, and a composed but subdued Warren had gathered around the fireplace.

"I have already read this to my boys. I've tried to explain to them that their mother's desire to protect them from this—news" —he blinked hard—"was a mistake. Times are different now, but no matter how wrong she was about race, no matter how wrong we all were and are, she acted out of love. It's important for them to have their mother's love." He couldn't continue, but slid the dark blue book over to Harry.

She opened the pages to where a ribbon, spotted and foxed with age, marked the place. Mrs. Murphy and Tucker, curled up at her feet, were as still as the humans.

Warren waved her on and excused himself. At the doorway
he stopped. "People talk. I know some folks will be glad to see the
Randolphs humbled. Some will even call my boys niggers just to
be hateful. I want you all to know the real story, especially since
you've worked with Kimball. And—and I thank you for your
help." He put his hand over his eyes and walked down the
hall.

A long, long moment of silence followed. Harry looked
down at the bold, clear handwriting with the cursive flourishes of
another age, an age when one's handwriting was a skill to be
cultivated and shared.

The diary and papers wedged into it, other people's letters,
belonged to Septimia Anne, the eleventh child of Patsy Jefferson
and Thomas Randolph. Septimia's letter to her mother was either
lost or in someone else's possession, but Patsy's response, written
in 1834, was interesting so Harry started there. In the letter she
recalled a terrific scandal in 1793, three years after she married
Thomas Mann Randolph, the same year in which they acquired
Edgehill for $2,000. At the time the farm was 1500 acres. Slaves
were also acquired in this lengthy transaction.

Thomas Mann Randolph's sister, Nancy, embarked on an
affair with yet another sister's husband, who was also their
cousin. This monkey in the middle was Richard Randolph. At
Glynlyvar in Cumberland County, Nancy, visiting at the time,
suffered a miscarriage. Richard removed the evidence. He was
charged with infanticide. Patrick Henry and George Mason defended Richard and he was found not guilty. The law had spoken
and so had everyone who lived in the thirteen colonies. This was
gossip too good to be true.

Patsy counseled Septimia that scandals, misfortunes, and
"commerce" with slave women were woven into the fabric of
society. "People are no better than they ought to be." She
quoted her own mother, whom she vividly remembered, as she
was three weeks short of her tenth birthday when her mother
died.

She made a reference to James Madison Randolph, her eighth child and Septimia's older brother by eight years.

"The more things change the more they stay the same," Harry said out loud. She turned pages wrapped up in notations about the weather harvests, floods and droughts, births and deaths. The death of Medley Orion riveted them to their chairs.

Harry read aloud:

Dear Septimia—

Today in the year of our Lord, Eighteen Hundred and Thirty-Five, my faithful servant and longtime companion, Medley Orion, departed this life, surrendering her soul gladly to a Higher Power, for she had devoted her earthly days to good works, kind words, and laughter. The Graces fitted her with physical beauty of a remarkable degree and this proved a harder burden to bear than one might imagine. As a young woman, shooting up like a weed and resembling my beloved father, not necessarily a benefit for a daughter, I resented Medley, for it seemed cruel to me that a slave woman should have been given such beauty, whereas I was given only some small wit.

Sally Hemings and I played together until such time as our race is separated from theirs and we are taught that we are the master. This happened shortly after my dearest mother died, and I felt I was twice removed from those I loved. No doubt many Southerners harbor these same feelings about their sable playmates. As Medley was younger than Sally and me, I began to watch over her almost as I watched over our dear Polly.

Medley remained at Monticello while I journeyed to France with my father and Sally, who for a year or two was no help at all, being too dazzled by the enticements of the Old Order. How Sally managed to find enticements at Abbaye Royale de Panthemont, I still do not know. When I would visit my father at the Hotel de Langeac on Sundays, I did notice that Sally, a beauty herself, seemed to be learning quite quickly how to subdue men.

Upon our return to our sylvan state, our free and majestic Virginia, I again became acquainted with Medley. If ever a woman was Venus on earth, it was she, and curious to note, she evidenced no interest in men. I married. Medley appeared chaste in this regard until that New World Apollo, Braxton Fleming, the boldest rider, the most outrageous liar, the incarnation of idle charm and indolent wit, arrived one day on the mountaintop to seek my father's assistance in a land matter. The sight of Medley as she walked along Mulberry Row unstrung his reason, and Braxton had precious little in the first place.

He laid siege to Medley, encouraged no doubt by the all too evident fact that Peter Carr had made Sally his mistress and Sam Carr enjoyed the favors of Betsey, her sister. And he could not have been ignorant of the condition of my uncle, John Wayles, a good man in most respects, who took Betty Hemings, Sally and Betsey's mother, as his mistress. The Federalists accused my father of being the sultan of a seraglio. Far from it, but politics seems to attract the coarsest forms of intelligence with a few luminous exceptions.

Medley eventually succumbed to Braxton's flambouyant infatuation. He dropped gold coins in her apron as though they were acorns. He bought her brocades, satins, and the sheerest silks from China. I believe he truly loved her, but two years passed, and his wife could no longer bear the whisperings. He was good with horses and bad with women and money. He drank, grew quarrelsome, and would occasionally take a strap to Medley.

At this time I was domiciled at Edgehill with my husband, but the servants would come and go between Edgehill and Monticello and I heard the tales. Father was president at this time. He was spared much of it, although I do fear his overseer at the time, Edmund Bacon, a trusted and able man, may have burdened him with it.

Braxton decayed daily in a manner we were later to see in the husband of Anne Cary. But I will greet the Almighty in the firm conviction that Charles Lewis Bankhead should have been placed in the care of an institution for dypsomaniacs. Braxton was a horse of a different color. He had not much mental power, as I have noted, but he was a sane man. However, circumstance and the crushing weight of impending financial ruin sapped whatever reserve and resolve he possessed. Upon learning that Medley was to bear his child, he—and this was reported to me by King, one of your grandfather's most loved servants—appeared to collapse in on himself. He was reputed to have gone to his wife and spurned her before their children. He declared the intention to divorce her and marry Medley. She told her father, who conducted a meeting with his son-in-law, which must have been incendiary. The man, now deranged, arrived at Monticello and plainly stated to Medley that since they could not live together they must die together. She should prepare to meet her Maker with a clean breast, for he was going to murder her. He, as the suicide, would bear the stigma for this deed. "Even in death I will protect you," he said.

Despite her love for Braxton, Medley felt she could not save him. She once said to me years later, "Miss Patsy, we were like two bright things caught in a spider's great web."

More, Medley wished for the unborn child to live. When Braxton turned from her, she seized her iron and smote him as hard as she could upon the back of the head. He perished immediately, and while it may be wicked to wish death upon another, I can only believe that the man was thereby released from his torments.

King, Big Roger, and Gideon buried his body underneath her hearth. That was May 1803.

The fruit of that union is the woman you know as Elizabeth Goorley Randolph. You are charged with protecting her children and never revealing to any her odyssey.

After the crisis Medley came to me, and when the baby was born, I recognized the child, even more beautiful than her mother, and a child who bore no trace of her African blood.

I believe no good can come from a system wherein one race enslaves another. I believe that all men are created equal, and I believe that God intended for us to live as brothers and sisters and I believe the South will pay in a manner horrible and vast for clinging to the sin of slavery. You know my mind upon this subject, so you will not be surprised that I raised Elizabeth as a distant cousin on the Wayles side.

Father knew of this deception. When Elizabeth turned seventeen I gave her seventy-five dollars and secured for her a seat on the coach to Philadelphia, where she would be joining Sally Hemings's brother, who made his life in that city after Father freed him. What I did not know was that James Madison Randolph wished to honor the lady with his heart and his life. He followed her to Philadelphia, and the rest you know. James, never strong, surely hoped to live longer than the scant twenty-eight years allotted to him, but he has left behind two children and Elizabeth. I am too old to raise more children, my dear, and I have heard death's heavy footfall more and more often in the twilight of my years.

I will not live to see an end to slavery, but I can die knowing I was an agent of sabotage and knowing, too, that I have honored my father's truest intentions on this issue.

I no longer fear death. I will rejoice to see my father in the bloom of youth, to see my husband before his misfortunes corrupted his judgment. I will embrace my mother and seek my friend Medley. The years that God bequeaths us are as moths to the flame, Septimia, but with whatever time

we own we must endeavor to make the United States of
America a land of life, liberty, and happiness for all her sons
and daughters.

Yours,

M.J.R.

"God bless her soul." Mrs. Hogendobber prayed. The little
group bowed their heads in prayer and out of respect.

67

Mrs. Murphy sat beside Pewter in Mrs. Hogendobber's garden. The stakes for the peas and tomatoes all had been driven into place at last.

"*I guess you all are lucky to be alive.*"

"*I guess so. She was crazy behind the wheel of that car.*" Mrs. Murphy knocked a small clod of earth over one of the rows. "*You know, humans believe in things that aren't real. We don't. That's why it's better to be an animal.*"

"*Like a social position?*" Pewter followed Mrs. Murphy's train of thought.

"*Money, clothes, jewelry. Foolish things. At least Harry doesn't do that.*"

"*Um. Might be better if she did believe in money a little bit.*"

Mrs. Murphy shrugged. "*Ah, well, can't have everything. And this color thing. It doesn't matter if a cat is black or white as long as it catches mice.*"

Tucker nosed out of the back door of the post office. "Hey, hey, you all. Come around to the front of the post office."

The cats trotted down the tiny path between the post office and the market. They screeched to a halt out front. Fair Haristeen, bestride a large gray mare and wearing his hunting clothes, rode into the post office parking lot. Mim Sanburne stood out front.

Harry opened the front door. Mrs. Hogendobber was right on her heels. "What are you doing? Vetting a horse on Main Street?"

"No. I'm giving you your new fox hunter and I'm doing it in front of your friends. If I took her to the farm, you'd turn me down because you don't like to take anything from anybody. You're going to have to learn how, Harry."

"Hear. Hear." Mim seconded the appeal.

"She's big—and what bone." Harry liked her on sight.

"Take the horse, Mom," Tucker barked.

"May I pet him?" Miranda tentatively reached out.

"Her. Poptart by name and she's got three floating gaits and jumps smooth as silk." Fair grinned.

"I can arrange to pay you over time." Harry folded her arms over her chest.

"No. She's a gift from Mim and me to you."

That really surprised Harry.

"I like her color," said the gray cat.

"Think Mom will take her?" Tucker asked.

Mrs. Murphy nodded. "Oh, it will take a while, but she will. Mother can love. It's letting someone love her. That's what's hard. That's what this is all about."

"How'd you get so smart?" Tucker came over and sat next to the tiger cat.

"Feline intuition."

Dear Highly Intelligent Feline:

Tired of the same old ball of string? Well, I've developed my own line of catnip toys, all tested by Pewter and me. Not that I love for Pewter to play with my little sockies, but if I don't, she shreds my manuscripts. You see how that is!

Just so the humans won't feel left out, I've designed a T-shirt for them.

If you'd like to see how creative I am, write to me and I'll send you a brochure.

Sneaky Pie Brown
c/o American Artists, Inc.
P.O. Box 4671
Charlottesville, VA 22905

In felinity,

SNEAKY PIE BROWN

P.S. Dogs, get a cat to write for you!